TUCSON

*Four Romances
in the Old Southwest*

NANCY J. FARRIER

BARBOUR
PUBLISHING

Sonoran Sunrise ©2000 by Barbour Publishing, Inc.
Sonoran Star ©2002 by Nancy J. Farrier
Sonoran Sweetheart ©2002 by Nancy J. Farrier
Sonoran Secret ©2002 by Nancy J. Farrier

Cover image © GettyOne

ISBN 1-58660-964-5

All Scripture quotations are taken from the King James Version of the Bible.

Published by Barbour Publishing, Inc., P.O. Box 719, Uhrichsville, Ohio 44683, www.barbourbooks.com.

ȅȼȖɅ Member of the
Evangelical Christian
Publishers Association

Printed in the United States of America.
5 4 3 2 1

TUCSON

NANCY J. FARRIER resides in Arizona. She is married and the mother of one son and four daughters. She is the author of numerous articles and short stories. She homeschools her three youngest daughters and writes in the evenings. Nancy enjoys sharing her faith through her writing.

Sonoran
Sunrise

To my Savior, Jesus Christ,
Who has blessed me so richly.
To my parents, John and Ruth,
who took the time to read to me
and passed on their love of books.

Chapter 1

Camp MacDowell, Arizona Territory—1870s

Daddy, how could you do this to me?" The petite young woman stalked through the open door, her rust-colored dress and parasol leaving a trail of travel dust.

Lieutenant Conlon Sullivan watched in amusement as the normally stern Captain Richard Wilton lost his military composure in the face of the fiery redhead's anger. Conlon knew this must be Glorianna Wilton, the captain's daughter, newly arrived at Camp MacDowell, Arizona Territory.

"I'm sorry, Sir." A red-faced orderly stood behind the young woman wringing his hands. "I tried to stop her."

Captain Wilton's mouth snapped closed and he waved a hand at the orderly, who stumbled over his feet as he backed from the room and pulled the door shut behind him.

"Daddy, I can't believe you would make me come to this horrible country to live. Do you hate me this much?" Jewel green eyes sparkled with fire. "There isn't even a decent road for miles. I've been bumped and jolted for days. Not to mention the abysmal boat trip up the Colorado River to get to Arizona Territory."

Captain Wilton stood and rounded the desk in record time. "Kitten, I didn't want to upset you, but I needed to see you." He tried to draw her into his arms, but the girl withdrew a step and stiffened her slender back.

Conlon watched in silence as Captain Wilton regained his composure. *Hmm. Anger doesn't appear to be working. I wonder if she'll try pleading now—or tears.*

"I'm sorry. I know the trip out here is strenuous. I thought it best, after your mother died, to bring you here to be with me."

Biting his lower lip to stifle his laughter, Conlon watched the rigidity melt from the girl. Her face took on a lost puppy look. *She's good. I'll bet she's used to wrapping him around her finger. Still, her wiles may not work now that she's grown.*

Taking advantage of the momentary lull, Conlon studied the captain's daughter. Her once shining dress, now travel-stained and dusty, covered a willowy figure. A crumpled, yet stylish hat sat askew on a head of the brightest red hair he had seen since leaving home. She reminded him of his mother with her fiery hair and temper. His fingers twitched as he longed to reach out and brush a strand of hair from her silky white cheek, wanting to know if her skin and hair were as soft as they appeared.

"I'm sorry, Daddy." Her apology broke the silence. "I wanted to see you, too. I just didn't realize the trip here would be so gruesome."

"Hey, Kitten." Richard Wilton lifted his daughter's chin with a gentle finger. "I didn't consider how difficult the journey would be for you. Now that you're here, I'm sure you'll love Arizona."

Shoulders slumped, she gazed up at her father. "Daddy, I must return home. Please. This was the worst time for me to come. You don't understand."

Captain Wilton's brows drew together in a puzzled frown as he looked down at his beautiful daughter. "Why do you want to go back to Boston?"

"Oh, Daddy, I have to get back to Kendrick. You remember Kendrick Hanford, don't you?" She reached out to brush a piece of lint from her father's cavalry jacket.

Captain Wilton's frown deepened. "Of course, I remember the Hanford boy. If I recall, he's the one who tipped over outhouses and threw rotten eggs at any likely target—including me. What about him?"

The young woman's cheeks reddened and her green eyes twinkled. "Oh, Daddy, he was just a boy when he did those things. Now he's a responsible young man, and I intend to marry him."

I suspect the tears will appear any second now. Conlon struggled to suppress a smile. *She's just like my sister Maria.*

"Marry him?" Captain Wilton questioned. "Has he declared his intentions?"

"Well, not exactly," she said as she twirled her dainty parasol, sending a dust shower to the floor. "But, I know he will, Daddy." She laid a slender hand on his shirtfront, her eyes bright with unshed tears. Like a drop of honey, a single tear traced a path down her cheek. "Daddy, I'm almost an old maid. In four months I'll be eighteen. I have to get married now."

Conlon almost laughed aloud at the thought of this vision's being an old maid. The slender beauty certainly didn't look the part. *Lord, I do believe she's an answer to my prayers.* At that moment, Conlon Sullivan knew without a doubt he would marry the captain's daughter. Softly, he cleared his throat.

Cat green eyes locked on his, and a soft rose blush crept up her apple blossom cheeks. Captain Wilton looked momentarily confused before his commanding demeanor returned. "Pardon me, Sullivan. I seem to have forgotten my manners." He gestured at his daughter. "Allow me to introduce you to my daughter, Glorianna. Glorianna, this is Lieutenant Conlon Sullivan."

She brushed the stray strands of hair out of her face and back into place, her eyes never leaving Conlon's face. "I'm pleased to meet you." Her lilting voice turned soft with almost a musical quality to it.

Conlon didn't think he would ever breathe again. This enchanting woman stole his every thought. Her heart-shaped face, like that of the angel on his mother's Christmas tree, captivated him. Moments passed. Suddenly, he realized they were staring at him. "Pleased," he stammered like an untried boy. Then, regaining a measure of his usual confidence, he continued. "I'm pleased to meet you, Miss Wilton. We don't usually have the privilege of such pleasant company in the middle of the desert."

Glorianna inspected the handsome cavalry lieutenant facing her. Laughing blue eyes, deep set beside a slightly crooked nose, started her heart tripping faster than normal. Even, white teeth lit up a face tanned from hours in the sun. Neatly combed coal black hair lay straight, except for one wayward shock hanging down on his forehead.

What would it be like to tuck that lock of hair back into place? she wondered. The thought of being that close to such a commanding, strong-muscled man took her breath away. *What is wrong with me? I want to marry Kendrick, yet here I am attracted to the first man I meet in Arizona.*

"I'm sure it would be okay for you to wait outside, Lieutenant, while I finish talking with my father." Glorianna knew she had to get this man out of here. "Isn't that right, Daddy?"

Captain Wilton frowned, then turned to Conlon. "Please excuse us, Lieutenant. Wait outside, though. I'll have you escort Glorianna to our quarters in a moment."

"But, Daddy, I thought you would show me around."

"I'd love to, Kitten, but I have a lot of work to finish here. Lieutenant Sullivan is perfectly capable."

Conlon flashed a smile at her as he walked out of the office. Glorianna tried hard to be angry at his obvious pleasure in being assigned to escort her. *He just doesn't know how much I love Kendrick. He'll give up soon.*

"Daddy," she said, turning to see her father once again standing behind his desk.

"Now, Glorianna, don't start. You just arrived. Give Arizona a chance. You might like it better than Boston."

"Daddy, it has nothing to do with Boston or Arizona. I have to marry Kendrick. Every girl in Boston wants to be his wife. If I don't get back right away, he might just agree to marry one of them."

"Well, if that's the case, then perhaps he isn't the right man for you anyway," Richard Wilton suggested.

Twirling her parasol again, Glorianna noted the cloud of dust drifting from its folds, and she shook free the rest of the travel dirt. "Daddy, it isn't just Kendrick."

"Then have a seat and tell me what it is."

Glorianna sank into the chair vacated by Conlon as her father dropped heavily into his desk chair. "Oh, Daddy, I've dreamed of marrying Kendrick and living in a cottage, just the two of us. I want a little cottage with a white picket fence. The neighbor ladies could open the little gate when they come to visit. We could sit outside and drink tea among the rose bushes while we listen to the birds sing." Glorianna heard the wistful note in her voice and shook herself back to reality. "Now do you understand?"

Richard Wilton's eyes shone with tears, and he watched his daughter a moment before speaking. "You look and sound so much like your mother, Kitten. I could almost believe she was sitting across from me." He stopped to clear the huskiness from his throat. "I believe I understand, but I just can't let you leave yet. You'll have to at least wait until a company is traveling across to the Colorado River. Right now, I can't spare the men necessary to escort you. Besides, I expect to receive new orders by Christmas. It's possible I'll be sent back east."

"Christmas!" Glorianna stiffened in anger. "Christmas is months away, and by then it could be too late."

"I'm sorry, Glorianna, but that's the way it is." Captain Wilton rose from his desk, stepped around, and took her arm. "Now come on. I'll have Lieutenant Sullivan show you to our quarters, and he can introduce you to some of our neighbors."

Smiling at his daughter, he continued. "Maybe it won't be so bad as you think. After all, you have no competition here, and I'm sure you could find plenty of suitors."

"That's the last thing I want," Glorianna shot back. "I don't want to be married to an army man who will be traipsing off who knows where just when I need him."

As the words left her mouth, Glorianna wished she could draw them back. She knew from the look on her father's face that she'd hurt him deeply. He couldn't help leaving her and her mother. The army was his job. You couldn't simply quit that kind of a job. He hadn't wanted to leave a sick wife and a young daughter, but he had had no choice.

"I'm sorry, Daddy," Glorianna said softly, gently touching his cheek. "You always did the best you could. Mother loved you so much."

Richard Wilton pulled her close, then said gruffly, "It's time for you to go. Lieutenant Sullivan!"

&

"These are the parade grounds," Conlon said, gesturing toward a large area of brown sand dotted with scraggly, unrecognizable plants. "Every morning we have our drills here and most everybody comes to watch." He grinned down at her, his bright smile lighting his face. "Here in the desert you take any excitement you can get."

Glorianna tried hard to contain her anger as Conlon Sullivan insisted on strolling slowly around the camp and pointing out the various sights before taking her by the officers' quarters. She simply had to get away from this man. His presence bothered her more than she cared to admit. She constantly found her gaze drifting to his arms. Even through the sleeves of his cavalry tunic, she could tell they were well muscled, and she kept wondering what it would feel like to be held by them.

12

"Would you please show me to my father's house, Lieutenant Sullivan?" She stiffened her resolve and tried hard to recall Kendrick's face, but only a pair of sparkling blue eyes set above a once-broken nose appeared. "I've had a long day, and I really need to refresh myself before the dinner hour." Glorianna knew she sounded like some haughty city girl, but she couldn't help herself. She needed to escape his presence.

"Oh, but Miss Wilton," Conlon took her hand and firmly tucked it in the crook of his elbow, "you'll want to meet your neighbors, and we haven't even seen John Smith's store." When she looked up, his azure eyes bore into hers. "Then, too, I'm sure you'll want to know where to find the dining hall. You don't want to run all over the camp hunting for your dinner, do you?"

Morning glory blue, she decided. *His eyes look just like the morning glory climbing Mother's fence. The only difference is, his eyes still have the sparkle of the dew in them.* Shaking herself, she tugged, gently at first, then harder, trying to free her captive hand. "If we're going to finish this tour, Lieutenant, could we do it at a faster pace? And would you please release my hand?"

"I didn't realize you might be willing to run a race in this heat," Conlon said, barely holding his laughter in check. "I guess we can trot along, but I insist that I hold on to your hand. On this uneven ground, you could fall. I don't want to have to explain such an unfortunate accident to your father. Come then, let's step lively." Conlon started off once again, this time at a pace that took her breath away.

Much later, breathless and flushed, Glorianna marched past a row of officers' houses. The line of identical clapboard and adobe houses stood in formation, one after the other. She wanted to breathe a sigh of relief as Conlon paused before one of the copycat houses and knocked on a door.

"This is the home of Timothy and Fayth Holwell," Conlon stated, as he straightened his already erect military bearing "I think you will like Fayth, and since you're next-door neighbors, you should meet her first."

The door opened and a slender, dark-haired young woman peered out at them from the dim, cool interior of her house. "Conlon." Her face lit up with a sweet smile of welcome. "Do come in." She stepped to one side, and Conlon slowly released Glorianna's hand so that she could precede him through the door.

Glorianna blinked her eyes to adjust after the brilliant sunshine outside. The inside of the house, surprisingly cool, exuded a homey atmosphere that put her at ease. A young girl toddled on unsteady legs across the uneven floor and hid her face in Fayth's skirt, peeking out to look at the visitors.

"Please sit down," Fayth said as she gestured to the few chairs grouped together at one side of the sparsely furnished room. "Conlon, what have you been doing to this young lady? Her face is as red as the sunset." Fayth called to someone in another room to bring drinks for them.

Conlon made the introductions. "She insisted we hurry our tour, Mrs. Holwell. I believe these Bostonians don't know how to move at the easier pace we Westerners are accustomed to."

"I certainly didn't intend to run a race, Lieutenant." Glorianna wished she could move her chair, for it sat much too close to Conlon's, and she could feel the heat of his gaze. She fought to avert her gaze lest she be captured once more by those eyes and find herself completely drawn to him.

Although she enjoyed the visit, Glorianna was relieved when she, at last, stood outside her door. "Thank you for the tour, Lieutenant Sullivan. I'm certain we shall cross paths again. It seems this is a rather small post."

An easy, heart-stopping smile swept over Conlon's face. "I'd say we'll cross paths again, Miss Wilton. After all, I heard you tell the captain about your dilemma. Since I'd hate to see such a beautiful woman become an old maid, I intend to ask your father's permission to court you."

Chapter 2

Shock rendered her speechless. Glorianna stared at Conlon open-mouthed. Gently he placed one finger on her chin and pushed upward, closing her mouth. Then, with a cocky grin and a mock salute, he turned and strode toward the parade grounds.

"Never in my life have I been so insulted." Glorianna's words were spoken too late to reach the retreating Conlon. "I'll have a thing or two to say about this, Lieutenant Sullivan. You just wait and see."

Glorianna turned and stormed into the small house that she would share with her father. She ignored the crude furniture and the naked, hard-baked beige adobe walls. Instead, her thoughts were filled with Conlon's tanned and handsome face, which sported that arrogant smile and wayward lock of ebony hair.

Throughout the evening she found herself thinking of him. She tried to concentrate on Kendrick and how much she missed him. Strangely enough, she couldn't vividly recall his face. Her memory of him, already fading from the long trip to Arizona Territory, slipped even farther away, as if pushed by a certain rugged cavalry officer.

"Lieutenant Sullivan asked my permission to court you." Her father's voice jolted her out of her reverie. He looked at her over the top of a newspaper.

"I will not have him courting me," snapped Glorianna. "I plan to marry Kendrick when I go back east. There's no need of my being courted by anyone here."

Richard Wilton frowned. "You said the Hanford boy hasn't declared his intentions yet. Why is that?"

"Well," Glorianna shifted in her chair, "he's busy learning his trade and probably wants to buy a house first."

"Exactly what is his trade? I seem to remember him as being rather shiftless."

"He is not shiftless." Glorianna's eyes flashed fire. "He's just trying out different positions to find the one that suits him best."

"Shiftless," Richard Wilton murmured, rustling his paper as he turned the page. From the depths of the wagon-train–carried, outdated newspaper, he stated, "I gave Sullivan my permission. He's smart, hardworking, and will make some woman a good husband. I think you'd do well to consider him."

Glorianna stood up stiffly, knowing when her father spoke in that tone there would be no changing his mind. "I believe I'll go on to bed. It's been a long day."

Tears of anger raced down her cheeks as she closed the door behind her. She threw herself on the bed, not caring about her already rumpled dress, nor about getting dirt on the bedclothes.

God, I know it's right for me to marry Kendrick. This is what I wanted so much. Why am I here when he's back there? I don't want to be courted by some cavalryman who will always be riding off to one battle or another. Glorianna buried her face in her covers and sobbed. She wondered if she would ever survive her father's edict.

❧

Conlon rose early, after a restless night filled with dreams of a red-haired girl with a freckled gumdrop nose. Walking through the predawn quiet, he left the camp to sit on a low rock. Every morning he liked to wait for the dawn and talk to God about the approaching day. This was his time to prepare and listen.

Thank You, God, for sending Glorianna here. He smiled, remembering the fiery beauty, longing to see her with that glorious chestnut hair hanging loose. Her flashing green eyes sparked with intelligence and a zest for life that he'd rarely seen in a woman.

Lord, I've waited a long time for a woman to share my dreams with, and here she is. I want to marry her now. So, please help me to quickly convince her that I'm the one You've chosen for her.

As if in answer to his prayer, the sun peeked over the horizon at that moment. A dazzling array of pinks, yellows, and blues swept across the sky, taking Conlon's breath away with its beauty. *This must be God saying yes to me,* he thought as he pushed off the rock and headed back into the fort, determined to win Glorianna's love.

❧

"Glorianna, can you come out here?" Her father's voice cut through the fog of deep sleep.

Dragging herself slowly out of bed, Glorianna noted the sun, barely awake itself, was already warming the day. She hadn't slept well during the night, and her eyes felt scratchy and heavy.

"I'll be right out."

Within minutes, Glorianna stepped out of her bedroom, wearing a fresh but travel-wrinkled dress, her hair neatly combed. "Good morning, Father," she said as she stretched up to kiss his newly shaven cheek.

"Sorry to wake you, Kitten." Her father smiled. "This is an army post and we rise early. If you want breakfast, you have to get up on time. Besides, I want you to meet someone." He turned toward his room and called, "Dirk, come here."

A man sidled into the room, his rounded shoulders hunching farther as he faced the captain. His pockmarked face split into a wide grin at the sight of Glorianna.

In a flashing thought, she compared his blackened stubby teeth with a certain lieutenant's brilliant white smile. Dirk's hair, wet and dark from hair tonic, lay slicked back from a narrow face and hooked nose. Glorianna did her best to repress a shudder.

"Glorianna, this is Dirk Smith. He keeps house for us." Richard Wilton turned to his daughter. "I know it would be better for you to have a woman here. I've inquired, but so far I haven't found one. Until I do, Dirk will be taking care of us. This morning you'll eat in the dining hall, but after this, Dirk will cook for us, too."

Dirk's dark gaze swept across Glorianna, making her squirm uncomfortably. She suppressed a shudder as his oily stare traveled over her. "It's nice to meet you, Mr. Smith," she said, trying to keep disgust from her voice. "I appreciate the help you give my father."

"Well, we'd better be off." Captain Wilton tugged his cap over his head. "We don't want to miss our breakfast."

Glorianna snapped open her parasol, shading herself from the sun even on the short walk to the mess hall. She hated the thought of more freckles popping out on her nose. They were such an embarrassment and impossible to get rid of once they appeared.

After breakfast, Glorianna's father headed to his office as she assured him that she would be fine unaccompanied on the short walk back to the house. Before she had gone two yards, Conlon Sullivan fell into step beside her, adjusting his long strides to match her shorter ones.

"Good morning, Miss Wilton."

Her cheeks warmed as his dazzling smile started her heart racing. "Good morning, Lieutenant Sullivan." She tried to take deep, slow breaths. "I'm sure you have other duties. I can find my way home just fine."

"Oh, but it's such a pleasure walking with you." His deep voice warmed her. She struggled between annoyance at his intrusion and her desire to hear him talk. "I guess your father told you that I spoke with him."

"Yes, he did." Glorianna stopped and faced Conlon. "I have to tell you, I intend to marry another man. Your attempts to court me will prove fruitless."

Conlon threw back his head and laughed aloud. Glorianna looked around furtively, hoping no one was watching them. "Please, Lieutenant Sullivan, I think you should give this up."

Tucking her hand in the crook of his arm, Conlon continued walking toward her house. "I don't intend to be turned away that easily, Miss Wilton. I believe God brought us together, and I intend to marry you."

Glorianna stopped suddenly and jerked her hand from Conlon's grasp. "Don't I have a say in this?" she asked as he turned to face her. "How dare you talk about our marriage as if you and God have already decided what's best for me."

Glorianna brushed past Conlon. Marching up to the nearest house, she knocked on the door.

Please be home. I have to get away from him.

A sigh of relief rushed from Glorianna's lips as Fayth Holwell opened the door. "Why, good morning, Glorianna." Fayth's face lit with a delighted smile.

"I'm so glad you stopped by. Won't you come in?"

Fighting tears of anger, she brushed by Fayth to enter the cool house. "Good morning, Fayth. I hope you don't mind my visiting so early." Her voice trembled with a huskiness that belied her emotion. She could almost feel Conlon's lingering gaze as he watched her enter the house, but she refused to turn and look at him.

"Are you okay?" Fayth's sympathetic voice broke the dam that held Glorianna's tears at bay.

"I'm sorry, I didn't mean to come here and fall apart like this. I just had to get away from him."

"Away from Conlon Sullivan?" Fayth's voice registered her surprise. "Why, he's always such a gentleman."

"Maybe that's because you're a married woman." Glorianna didn't mean to sound so bitter.

"Did he do something improper?" Fayth eyes widened.

"No," Glorianna sighed. "He wasn't improper." For the next hour, Fayth listened as Glorianna explained how her father left her in charge of her invalid mother when he returned to his post out West. She told about seeing the other girls her age having fun when she couldn't and of feeling left out because she had to care for her mother. She spoke of her longing to belong to the group and how she wanted to be courted by the handsome and much-sought-after Kendrick Hanford. Her voice softened as she described her longing to be married and live in a cottage surrounded by flowers and a picket fence.

"After Mother died, Father insisted I come out here. I tried to explain to him that I wanted to return to Boston right away, but he wouldn't listen." Glorianna shook her head and absently twirled her parasol. "Now he's given Lieutenant Sullivan permission to court me, despite my protests. Lieutenant Sullivan even had the audacity to tell me that he and God are in agreement that we should marry."

Fayth smiled and reached for Glorianna's hand. "Conlon is a good man. He's a little impatient, but if you give him a chance, you might find yourself attracted to him. As for God. . .well. . .He knows the plans He has for us. So, ask Him. I'm sure you'll find out in time what God wants for your life. Maybe you should even ask God what to look for in a husband."

"I guess you're right. I'll pray about the matter. But I'm sure God wants me to marry Kendrick." Glorianna lifted her head and looked around the neat room. "Meanwhile, is there something I can do to help you? I seem to have a lot of time on my hands, and I'm at a loss as to how to spend it."

Fayth gave a little laugh. "Have you any skill at sewing? I'm afraid I'm hopeless, and I'm trying to make a new dress for my daughter, Alyce."

"It just so happens I love to sew." Glorianna smiled in relief. "Let's get started."

❦

The flames leaping out of the forge served to remind Conlon of the fiery hair and sparkling green eyes of Glorianna Wilton. The smooth rhythmic clanging of the blacksmith's hammer lulled him temporarily. Conlon recalled the gentle weight of her hand on his arm, and he longed to see her again. But, Glorianna didn't want to see him. He shook his head and sighed as he focused his attentions on his friend, Josiah Washington, the company's blacksmith.

"Mornin', Conlon," Josiah said as he dunked the red-hot horseshoe in a pail of water. The water hissed and a cloud of steam enveloped Josiah's sweating body.

"Good morning, Josiah. I came to see if you have Champ's shoes ready."

"I'm just finishing them." Josiah gestured to the horseshoe dripping water. "I'll fit him right away. Are you in a hurry?"

"No hurry." Conlon shook his head, trying to concentrate on his reason for being here.

"The boys said the captain's daughter arrived yesterday. Did you meet her yet?" Josiah's brows drew together as he watched Conlon. "What is the matter with you, anyway?"

Conlon couldn't hold back a grin. "You won't believe her, Josiah. God answered my prayers and sent me an angel to marry."

"You mean you're going to marry the captain's daughter?" Josiah looked incredulous. "Did you know her before?"

"I met her for the first time yesterday," Conlon admitted. "But, I know she's the one for me."

"And how does this angel feel about your marriage?"

Conlon frowned. "Well she is still a little wary of the idea."

"Uh-huh." Josiah nodded. "I've seen you do some things on the spur of the moment, but this might be too much. Don't you think you should get to know her a little first?"

"I already have the captain's permission to court her. We'll get to know each other faster that way. Besides, she wants to go back east and marry some man who isn't even interested in her. She just needs a little convincing to understand that I'm the right one for her."

Josiah shook his head and picked up the horseshoe. He examined it, frowned, and stuck it back in the coals of the forge. "Well, I'll pray for you, Conlon. Try not to get too pushy, though. You'll scare her off if you do."

❦

Glorianna smiled as she opened the door and slipped into her house. She'd had a wonderful morning with Fayth and her young daughter, Alyce. The dress, well on its way to being complete, would look darling on the little girl. It felt so nice to have another woman to talk to. Fayth loved God and talked of Him as if He were her best friend. She reminded Glorianna of her mother.

Crossing the living room to her bedroom, Glorianna intended to lie down for awhile. The rapidly warming day, coupled with the fact that she hadn't slept much last night, made her drowsy.

Stepping through the open door into her room, Glorianna paused and drew in a sharp breath. Dirk, hunched over her trunk, was pawing through her dresses and underthings.

"What are you doing?" Glorianna's sharp tone brought the man to his feet, his eyes darting around the room as if looking for a way to escape. "I asked what you're doing! Why are you going through my clothing?"

Dirk's pockmarked face split into a lecherous grin as his inky eyes traveled slowly over her. "Why, I'm just taking care of you like your father ordered, Miss Wilton. I thought I could put away some of your things for you."

"I can take care of my own clothes, Mr. Smith. You may leave now."

Glorianna tried not to cringe as he approached. When he paused beside her, she closed her eyes and clenched her teeth. *Please, God, get him out of here.*

A sigh of relief escaped her lips as he passed out of the room.

Chapter 3

Summer arrived with a vengeance. The days lengthened, and the sun beat down unmercifully. Glorianna groaned as she dragged herself from bed after another sleepless night in her oven-hot room. Seated on the edge of her bed, she shook her head as she looked over her dresses. She couldn't bear the thought of putting on one of those snug-fitting dresses. The heavy material and tight bodices made her sweat, and her constricted breathing threatened to induce fainting spells.

"Glorianna?" her father called from outside the door. "I need to talk to you before breakfast."

"I'll be right out." Glorianna reached for her amber-colored dress. This one wasn't so formfitting. Perhaps she wouldn't be quite so miserable today.

"Good morning, Father." Glorianna gave him a quick kiss, trying to ignore Dirk as he worked at cleaning the room. He always followed her with his eyes, which repulsed her. He made excuses to be near her. His foul breath made her stomach churn.

She spent most of her days out of the house, helping the few wives in the fort with their sewing and mending. Only in the afternoon, when she knew Dirk had returned to the barracks, did she dare venture home.

"Good morning, Kitten. I wanted to tell you that I have to leave for a few days."

"What! Where are you going?" Glorianna tried to keep the rising note of panic from her voice as she noted the satisfied sneer that crossed Dirk's face.

"I have to go to Fort Lowell in Tucson on an inspection tour." Her father gently patted her cheek. "I'll be gone less than two weeks, and I've asked Lieutenant Sullivan to keep an eye on you. Show him a little more respect and don't try so hard to avoid him." He frowned down at her. Glorianna lowered her eyes, willing away the tears.

"I'll be okay," she said. She looked up at her father. "Why can't you ask Timothy and Fayth Holwell to look after me? They live right next door, and I know they wouldn't mind."

Richard Wilton smiled at her. "I have asked them to help keep an eye on you, but I think it's possible you'll need more than Fayth and Timothy."

"Oh, Fayth," Glorianna moaned, tugging at her sweat-soaked dress and fanning her hot face. "I don't know how anyone can live through this heat. Sometimes I think I'd be better able to bear it if I could wear my nightgown all the time."

"Why, that's it, Glorianna," Fayth said as a smile lit up her face.

"That's what?"

"The reason I bear the heat better than you do," Fayth informed her. "I still have to wear the dresses I used before I birthed Alyce."

Glorianna shook her head and grinned at her friend's enthusiasm. "I don't think I understand."

Fayth's voice took on the same tone as when she explained something to her young daughter. "My dresses are loose and yours are tight. Also, mine are light-weight calico and yours are heavier. Why don't we go over to Mr. Smith's store? I think he has some calico cloth. We can make you some dresses that will give you room to breathe and allow the air to flow through."

"What a wonderful idea, Fayth. Let's go right now."

By early afternoon, they had the first dress cut out and the stitching begun. Glorianna had two more lengths of material ready to start on as soon as she completed this dress.

"How are you and Conlon getting along these days?"

Glorianna bit her lip, trying to make it look like her sewing needed all her concentration. She waited until her feelings were more in control, then answered casually, "He follows me everywhere, but I've let him know I'm still waiting for Kendrick."

"You aren't beginning to like him, are you?" Fayth's penetrating gaze rested softly on Glorianna.

"I. . .uh, he is nice, but I know God wants me to marry Kendrick. That's what I want. Ouch!" Glorianna stuck her pinpricked finger into her mouth.

Fayth lifted Alyce to her lap. "I think perhaps you're spending more time thinking of Conlon than Kendrick. Don't you think it's possible that God brought you out here for a reason? Maybe He didn't think Kendrick would be the right husband for you."

"Are you on Conlon's side now?" Glorianna began to fold the material with jerky movements. "You know I might not mind him so much if he would quit pushing. He sticks closer to me than my shadow."

Fayth laughed. "He is a little presumptuous. But his heart is right, and I believe he's quite taken with you. I've watched the way he looks at you. Don't be too hasty to be rid of him."

"I'll try to be patient with him." Glorianna stood. "Now, I have to get home. I'll take the dress with me and work on it a bit more when the afternoon heat lets up. Thank you for the help."

Fayth walked to the door with Glorianna. "After all the help you've given everyone, I'm glad to finally be of some service to you."

Glorianna waded through the waves of heat, feeling the air pressing in on her. Oh, to get these tight clothes off and lie down for awhile. Her lack of sleep, combined with the close needlework, made her drowsy.

The interior of the house, though quiet, was only slightly cooler than the outside. The doors and windows were open, ready to draw in even the slightest afternoon breeze. She crossed to her room and put away her sewing. Taking the pins out of her hair, she shook it free and began to unbutton her dress.

"Now that's what I like to see." Glorianna froze as Dirk's whiskey-slurred words oozed across the room. She jerked her dress closed and turned her back to him.

"Mr. Smith, you will leave now or I'll speak to my father. If you have something you need to say to me, I'll be out in a moment."

In the quiet that followed, she could hear his shuffling footsteps getting nearer not farther away. Her heart began to pound. Her trembling hands fumbled madly at the undone buttons of her dress.

"It's okay, Missy, you don't need to fix up those buttons. You can open the rest if you want." A waft of whiskey-laden, rotten-toothed breath made her gag.

"Get out of here, Mr. Smith. Get out now, before my father comes."

A low chuckle turned her blood to ice. "Well, now, isn't it too bad the captain's gone? I guess he won't be here to see, will he?" One of his hands grasped her by the arm, pulling her back against him, while the other hand covered her mouth. Glorianna's scream of terror welled up too late to escape.

As quickly as he grabbed her, he let go. A strangled yelp echoed in her ear. "Perhaps the captain won't be here to see you, Dirk, but I will."

Glorianna nearly cried with relief at the sound of Conlon's voice. She turned around to see Conlon, his eyes hard and angry, holding Dirk in a grip of iron. Dirk's feet fought to touch the floor, and his eyes bulged almost out of their sockets as Conlon twisted his collar tighter.

"I'd like to beat you senseless." Conlon's cold voice drained what little color was left in the pockmarked face. "Get back to the barracks. I'll deal with you later." Setting the shorter man back on his feet, Conlon watched with Glorianna as Dirk sidled out the door. "Don't even think of trying to get away," Conlon called after him.

As Dirk disappeared through the door, Glorianna began to shake. She bit her lip, trying to hold back the sobs that welled up within. Suddenly, she felt herself engulfed in Conlon's strong arms. Without thinking, she leaned against his muscular chest and began to sob. For a long time she cried and trembled. He spoke soothing words and held her tight. His hand smoothed her long hair.

After awhile Glorianna's tears stopped. She rested against Conlon, noticing for the first time how wonderful it felt to be held within his strong embrace. She could hear the steady beating of his heart and feel the coarseness of his uniform tunic on her cheek.

Remembering where they were, Glorianna pushed away from Conlon. Her cheeks warmed in embarrassment. "Thank you, Lieutenant Sullivan," she said. "I'd appreciate it if you didn't say anything about this to anyone."

"Why didn't you report Dirk?" Conlon frowned. "I assume he's been making inappropriate gestures for awhile."

"He's my father's servant. It wasn't my place to question. Besides, I thought Mr. Smith to be harmless. Now, please go."

A slow smile spread across Conlon's face, lighting up the room and making Glorianna's heart beat faster. "Do you want me to leave because you don't think I'm harmless?" He lifted a hand as if to touch her, then paused. "I'll go, but I'll tell your father. He can pick someone else to help around the house." His tone turned more serious. "Don't worry, we'll keep this quiet."

✤

"Josiah." Conlon tried to make himself heard over the banging of the blacksmith's hammer. Josiah looked up and grinned, then thrust the piece of metal into the water to cool.

"Afternoon, Conlon. What are you doing out in this heat?"

"I guess I could ask the same of you. You're not only out in it, you're making more."

Josiah laughed, a hearty chuckle from deep inside. "This weather only reminds me how much I'll enjoy heaven when it's my turn to go. I don't want to lose sight of that."

Conlon grinned. "I can't imagine your losing sight of the Lord."

"So, what are you doing? I have the feeling you didn't come by here just to talk."

Looking around the blacksmith stall, Conlon paused a moment, rubbing his chin in thought. "I need to ask something of you, Josiah, and I need it kept quiet."

"You know me, Conlon. I'll not say anything."

"I know." Conlon smiled at his friend. "I need a pair of shackles I can fasten to a wall."

Josiah's eyebrows shot up as he looked at Conlon. "Why would you need those?" Then he hastily added, "Not that it's any of my business. You're in charge here with the captain away."

Conlon gazed out over the deserted parade ground before turning to Josiah. "One of the men tried to take liberties with the captain's daughter. I want to lock him up until the captain returns."

Black eyes flashed in anger as Josiah strode into the hot stall. He rummaged around in a box and soon returned with a set of cuffs. "These should do the trick. You can fasten them to the wall through here. Just don't tell me who the dirty dog is, or I might make these unnecessary."

Conlon nodded and hefted the heavy shackles. "I'll post a guard, too, but I don't plan to tell why the soldier's confined. Thanks."

"Say, Josiah." Conlon turned back as his friend picked up the lump of metal from the pail of water. "Can I ask you something?"

"Now what words of wisdom can I give you?" Josiah gave a mock bow.

"I'm a little stumped," Conlon hesitated. "You see, it's about Glorianna. I've tried to be patient with her, but she's just not coming around."

Josiah grinned. "You've been patient with her? That might be something to see." He chuckled. "Just how have you been courting her?"

"I try to be there all the time." Conlon frowned in thought. "I walk her to breakfast and dinner. I check on her during the day and stop in of an evening to talk."

"Maybe you're suffocating the poor girl," Josiah suggested. "Why don't you back off a little and see if she comes around. Remember how you win a horse's affection. Sometimes you have to ignore the animal, then before you know it, that horse is nudging you on the shoulder."

"Are you suggesting Miss Wilton is like a horse?" Conlon grinned at Josiah's look of discomfort. "Thanks, Josiah. I'd better go before you start asking me what size shoes you should make for her."

🌱

"Glorianna, are you there?" Fayth stepped through the open doorway.

"In here, Fayth." Glorianna splashed more water on her face, trying to erase the tearstains and puffiness.

"Guess what?" Fayth's eyes sparkled. "Timothy had the greatest idea."

"What is it?" Glorianna couldn't help but smile at her friend's obvious excitement.

"You know how the soldiers have taken to sleeping outside on their cots?" Glorianna nodded and Fayth continued. "Well, Timothy thinks we should do the same. That way, when there's a breeze, it won't be so hot and stuffy and we'll be able to rest."

"What a great idea." Relief flooded through Glorianna at the thought of more sleep. "In the middle of the night, the air cools off outdoors. I can't wait to try this."

For the next hour, they carried out cots and situated them under trees so they wouldn't be too hot to lie upon. "Here, Glorianna, let's put your cot under this paloverde tree. It should shade you from the morning sun a bit and provide you some privacy."

"Are you bringing out a cot for Alyce, too?"

"Yes," Fayth said. "And, Lord willing, she'll be quiet through the night. She's been tossing and turning as much as the rest of us."

After supper, Glorianna, Fayth, and Timothy sat outside and talked until dark. Glorianna found herself watching for Conlon. He always showed up this time of night. It irritated her that, although she wanted him to leave her alone, the first time he did, all she could think about was his absence.

Later, when all was quiet, Glorianna crept out to her cot, praying no one would notice her in the dark. As she lay on the cot with the light breeze caressing her, she remembered the feel of Conlon's strong arms surrounding her. *His embrace felt so good.* But she quickly pushed the thought away and struggled to think about Kendrick.

Slowly, her body gave in to the demands of the day, and weariness made her eyes drift shut. "Ouch!" Glorianna spluttered as she sat up in bed wondering what happened. At her movement, another pain shot up her leg and fire flared on her arm.

"Glorianna, what's wrong?" Fayth called.

"Owww!" Glorianna brushed wildly at her arms and legs. She hopped off the cot, grabbed the sheet, and shook it out. "Bugs, Fayth. There are bugs all over my bed." With that she made a dash for the house before a certain lieutenant came running. It wouldn't do to have him catch her in her nightclothes.

Chapter 4

A re you sick, Miss Wilton?" Conlon stared at her as he pulled out a chair and sat down. Glorianna, already seated at the Holwells' breakfast table, felt the warmth of a blush in her cheeks.

"No, Mr. Sullivan, I don't have the measles or any other dread disease. I'm perfectly healthy." Glorianna slowly and carefully unfolded the cloth napkin and arranged it in her lap. She hoped Conlon would drop the embarrassing subject.

Conlon reached across the table and grabbed one of her hands. She winced as he rubbed his thumb across the swollen, red bumps on the back of her hand. "So, what caused these?"

"That's none of your business." Glorianna tugged at her hand. She glanced toward the other room where Fayth and Timothy were getting Alyce dressed.

"I have to disagree." Conlon grinned at her, holding her hand tightly despite her attempts to free it. "Your father asked me to look after you. What will he think when he returns and finds you covered with spots while I know nothing about their cause?"

"He also asked Fayth and Timothy to watch over me. They know exactly what happened, so you needn't worry yourself over it." With a jerk that rocked her in her chair, Glorianna pulled her hand free.

✤

"Good morning, Conlon." He stood as Fayth walked into the room. Timothy followed carrying a still-sleepy Alyce. "Have you seen the nasty bites on Glorianna's hands?"

Conlon widened his eyes in mock surprise. "Bites? Now, who would be biting such a sweet young lady?"

Glorianna's face looked like a thundercloud as Fayth rose to the bait and began to tell of their humiliating trial the night before. "When the bugs began to bite Glorianna, we all came inside, knowing we would be next. Timothy's idea to sleep outside was good, but now we have to figure out how to get rid of the insects."

Conlon could feel his chest tighten as he tried to hold back the laughter. Poor Glorianna, or maybe that should be poor bugs. The thought was too much, and a deep chuckle broke loose. Soon everyone but Glorianna was laughing. Even little Alyce chortled happily, waving a spoon in the air as if directing their laughter.

"Well, I don't see what's so funny about being chewed up by bugs." The red spots in Glorianna's cheeks burned bright.

"I'm sorry." Conlon stifled his laughter. "I just thought of those poor bugs not knowing what they were getting into when they bit you." Taking a deep breath, he calmed himself. "I have an idea, Timothy. What do you think about putting the legs of the cots in cans of water? Then, if we keep the cots out from under the trees, the crawling bugs won't get on them anyway."

"That sounds good." Timothy nodded. "I know Alyce is happy this morning, but she fussed all night because of the heat and the couple of ant bites she got. I don't want to go through that again."

Conlon ate quickly, noticing how often Glorianna rubbed at her hands. He knew how nasty those ant bites could be. Excusing himself, he followed Fayth into the kitchen. A few minutes later, he knelt beside Glorianna. Before she could object, he plucked her hand off her lap.

"Has God told you this is the time to ask me to marry you, Lieutenant? I'll tell you right now the answer is 'no.' "

Conlon grinned. "I hadn't thought of asking you quite yet, Miss Wilton. I'll be sure to let you know when it's time. Right now, I have something to help take the itch out of those bug bites." With that, he began to smear a white paste over the swollen bites.

"What are you putting on her?" Fayth moved around the table to watch. "Can I use it on Alyce?"

"It's just a mixture of baking soda and water. Doc Clark told me about it when I ran into a bunch of ants awhile back. If you put it on wet and let it dry, it helps. If Alyce eats it, it won't hurt her. She probably won't like the taste, though."

Conlon handed the bowl of paste to Glorianna. "I'm sure you have other bites you would rather tend yourself." He smiled as pink stained her cheeks. He didn't want to let her know how hard it was to hold her hand and act like it didn't affect him. He remembered well the feel of holding her in his arms yesterday. He could still smell the faint scent of roses and feel the silkiness of her hair. *God, please help me to be patient,* he pleaded. *Help me find a common ground, something we both enjoy.*

"You know, Conlon," Fayth smiled sweetly at him, "Glorianna mentioned that she loves horses. Perhaps you could give her a quick tour of the stables."

"You like horses, too?" Conlon turned to Glorianna, astonished at the immediate answer to his prayer. "We have plenty of time before the nine o'clock guard-mount and roll calls begin. Would you like to see our horses?"

Glorianna, the bowl of paste gripped in her hands, looked like she couldn't decide whether to stay mad or succumb to her desire to visit the stables. "I'd love to see the horses," she said finally. "Do you think I could have a minute to finish putting on some of this paste?" She grimaced. "I know I'll be more comfortable."

✣

"This is my horse, Champ." Conlon's pride in the beautiful buckskin couldn't be hidden.

Glorianna slipped her hand over the stall door. Champ gently nudged her, his soft muzzle tickling her palm. "He's beautiful. Is he your own, or does he belong to the cavalry?"

"He's mine." Conlon reached up to tug on the horse's black forelock. "I brought him with me when I came out here from Kentucky. Come on, I'll show you the other horses. Fayth's favorite is right down here. She enjoys riding when someone has the time to go with her."

"Why does someone have to go with her?"

Conlon frowned. "Out here, there's danger everywhere. Between the Indians, rattlers, and cougars, it's best not to go out alone. And, in these wide-open spaces you can get lost pretty quickly. You need to remember that."

Glorianna followed Conlon down the aisle of stalls. "I couldn't see any danger when we came across the desert from Yuma. We didn't see a single rattlesnake. I don't think there's much to worry about."

"Glorianna, as long as I'm in charge of your safety, I want you to promise me you'll always have someone with you when you go riding." Conlon paused, his stern expression firming Glorianna's resolve to ride by herself as soon as she had the chance. "If I can't accompany you, then one of the other men will. Promise?"

"Oh, all right. I suppose I have to or you'll give orders that I can't have a horse to ride." *But, as soon as my father returns and you aren't in charge of my welfare, we'll see what happens.*

"Good." Conlon's grin set her heart pounding. "Now, let's see which horse you take a liking to."

"Oh, this one." Glorianna peered over the stall at a beautiful sorrel with a flaxen mane and tail. His head arched proudly, and his white socks flashed as he turned and pranced toward her.

"I must say you have excellent taste in horses, but I'm afraid this one is off limits, even to the captain's daughter."

"And why is that?"

"Because this is a man's horse, Miss Wilton. He's too high-spirited for a lady. We'll find you something a little calmer."

Conlon started off down the row of stalls. Glorianna stood by the sorrel's stall, hands clenched at her sides, waiting for Conlon to realize she wasn't following.

"Aren't you coming?" Conlon turned back to face her.

"Lieutenant Sullivan, I have always ridden spirited horses. I can easily control this horse, and you haven't given me a single reason why I shouldn't be allowed to ride him. You'll have to come up with something better than his being a man's horse."

Conlon slowly traced his steps back to her side, the soft dirt of the stable floor silencing his footsteps. He stopped in front of her, his blue eyes twinkling as if he was laughing at her. "Miss Wilton, this horse belongs to Josiah Washington, our blacksmith. To my knowledge no one else even feeds the horse, let alone rides him.

Now, if you want to take on Josiah, you may do so, but I'll warn you, he's quite a bit stronger than you."

Glorianna tried to step back, wanting to distance herself from Conlon. The stable wall stopped her. Why did his nearness always affect her this way? Rather than pursuing her desire to ride this horse, she found herself wanting to look at Conlon. She wanted to watch the way his blue eyes sparkled with humor. To brush that stray lock of hair off his forehead. To touch his handsome, chiseled face.

With a mental shake, Glorianna brought herself around. "I will talk with Mr. Washington at the first available moment, Lieutenant. Right now, I believe it's time to return home."

Conlon stepped back, bowed low, sweeping his arm toward the door. "Allow me to escort you, Miss Wilton."

Glorianna lifted her chin and swept past him, heading down the passage between the stalls. She studiously ignored the arm Conlon offered her. "I can find my own way back, Lieutenant. I'm sure you have other matters to attend. The morning inspection is fast approaching."

A sudden influx of soldiers proved Glorianna's point. Loud, raucous laughter filled the stables as the troops headed for their tack and horses to get ready for the drills and calls. She halted, unsure how to proceed with so many men in the way. The firm pressure of Conlon's hand on her elbow was a welcome relief, although she determined he would never know it.

"I'll get you to where the ladies will be gathering. Then I'm afraid I'll have to get Champ ready." Conlon's soft words spoken close to her ear sent a shiver down her spine.

※

Although her parasol blocked the sun's rays, it did little to cool the rising heat of the morning. Despite the warmth, Glorianna stared at the parade of horses and men, captivated with the beauty and symmetry of their movements. The proud horses' bowed necks complemented their riders' straight backs and oneness with their mounts.

"There's Timothy." Fayth's pride in her husband shone on her face. Glorianna glanced at her, then followed the direction she looked, and managed to spot Timothy Holwell riding a bay. The horse's dark brown coat gleamed in the sun.

"I still have some trouble knowing who's who," Glorianna admitted. "When they're in uniform and have their caps on, they all look alike." She sent an apologetic smile in Fayth's direction.

Fayth laughed and bounced Alyce higher on her hip. "Don't worry, we've all been through that. Imagine how I felt when I couldn't even recognize my own husband. You'll do better in no time."

Glorianna didn't know how she would ever tell one soldier from another. Even the horses were starting to blend together.

"Look, there's Conlon riding out on Champ."

Glorianna looked across the parade ground. Conlon's shining buckskin pranced to the center of the parade ground. His black-socked legs pistoned up and down in precision movements. Champ's black mane and tail perfectly complemented his gleaming tan hide. Conlon sat ramrod stiff, every inch the cavalry officer. The stable call began, each rider rigid in the saddle as he paraded in front of his commanding officer.

As they rode past, Glorianna found herself comparing each rider to Conlon. Every man in the cavalry lacked something. He was either too short, too slouchy, or too thin; not one of them could compare in looks.

"Didn't you love the call-to-arms?" Fayth whispered as the last of the horses high-stepped past. "I've seen it more times than I can count, and I still get a thrill from it."

"I don't know which I liked best," Glorianna admitted as they ambled toward their houses. Each of them held one of Alyce's small hands as she toddled between them. "Watching the soldiers leap for their rifles and the officers buckle on their swords in the call-to-arms could take your breath away. Then again, the sight of all those mounted soldiers sitting so perfectly on their glistening horses reminded me of knights in shining armor. I couldn't help but wonder what it would be like to be swept off my feet and ride off into the sunset with one of them."

Fayth stopped and stared open-mouthed at Glorianna "Are you telling me you're falling for Lieutenant Sullivan? I just knew you wouldn't be able to resist him."

"I did not say I was falling for anyone." Glorianna felt a blush heat her cheeks. "Remember Kendrick? He would make a wonderful knight in shining armor. Perhaps I'll go write a letter and tell him. Maybe I need to let him know exactly what my feelings are."

Quickly, Glorianna left her new friend and rushed across the parade ground toward her quarters. She tried to forget the small lie she'd told Fayth about picturing Kendrick as a knight. Instead, she began to plan how to word a letter to him. But, for some reason, she couldn't shut out the image of all those cavalrymen and horses. The vibrant picture of Conlon Sullivan sitting so straight and tall left little room to remember a passing acquaintance she hadn't seen for months.

※

As darkness fell, Glorianna, wrapped in a light blanket, made her way to the cot prepared for her. She sank down exhausted from so many nights of fitful sleep. As the cool night breeze washed over her, she drifted into a night of peaceful, much-needed sleep. She didn't even consider whether the cans of water would do their work, she simply slept.

Chapter 5

Towering maple and oak trees shaded them as Glorianna and her cousin, Kathleen O'Connor, strolled down the street. The quiet afternoon muted their conversation. Carriages rolled soundlessly down the rain-washed street. Other than the faint buzz of bees busy about their work, they were the only two in this world of silence.

Glorianna stopped, placing a restraining hand on her cousin's arm. "Look, Kathleen, it's him."

Kathleen turned her freckled pixie face toward Glorianna. "Who?" she asked, her hazel eyes darkening in question as she reached to pull her veil over her face.

"It's Kendrick. Can't you see him?"

Glorianna watched as Kathleen shook her head, her mahogany curls swinging with the motion. "I don't want to see him, Glory. I don't want you to see him, either. I've told you before he isn't worth your time."

"But, he's so handsome. I know you don't think he's a Christian, but he goes to church."

"Oh, Glory." Kathleen frowned at her. "You know the only time he attends church is when he can get a free meal or some entertainment. Besides, a man who loved God wouldn't get himself into as many scrapes as Kendrick does."

"He leads an interesting life." Glorianna twirled the handle of her parasol. "It would be so exciting to be married to him. Think of all the adventures you would have."

"I refuse to think of them," Kathleen said. "I wouldn't even allow him to call on me. If you know what's good for you, you'll discourage him, too."

"But, God wants me to marry Kendrick. I'm sure of it."

"How do you know such a thing, Glory? Doesn't the Bible say we shouldn't be unequally yoked? Have you stopped to look at Kendrick through God's eyes?"

"And what would God look for that I haven't?"

"I believe God would look for a man that will pray and read the Bible regularly with his family. Will Kendrick do that?" Kathleen's honest assessment made Glorianna fidget. "God wants a man for you who will take you to church every week. Will Kendrick do that?"

"He will." Glorianna tipped her parasol to the side so she could get a better look at her cousin. She hoped her doubts weren't reflected in her eyes. "He just needs some encouragement. He hasn't come from a Christian home. That makes it hard for him. A good wife will bring out the best in him."

"Glorianna." She turned as the deep voice called her name. Kendrick stood there,

32

his face set in its customary haughty smile. The persistent buzzing of bees near her head grew louder, but she ignored it. As she watched, his pale blue eyes deepened to a morning glory blue and filled with kindness. His blond hair darkened to black and his haughty expression changed to one of love. But he wasn't Kendrick anymore. What was happening?

"Don't move," he warned. "Please stay still."

She looked in confusion to see him raising a gun. Before she could even cry out, smoke belched from the gun's barrel and a loud bang reverberated through the air. Glorianna screamed and leapt from her cot.

"It's okay, Sweetheart." Suddenly, Conlon's arms were around her. Once again, she found herself sobbing into his shoulder, completely disoriented.

"I'm sorry, I thought you were awake. I didn't mean to scare you."

Glorianna pushed herself back from him. "You shot at me." Fear made her want to scream at him. "And I am not your sweetheart!"

"Glorianna, look." Conlon grabbed her by the shoulders and turned her around. There, on the ground beneath her cot, a headless rattlesnake writhed in its death throes. Glorianna's knees buckled. If he hadn't been behind her, she would have collapsed on the ground.

"I tried to warn you to lie still. I didn't want you to get off your cot with the snake under there." The sound of running footsteps startled her, and Glorianna realized she had nothing on but her nightdress.

"Oh!" She grabbed for her thin blanket, still crumpled on the cot. Running for her house, she could feel the heat of embarrassment burning her cheeks. What had Conlon been doing by her cot anyway? Did he spy on her while she slept? Maybe it wasn't worth the comfort of sleeping outside if it tempted him to watch her. She would question him about this later.

🜍

"Hello?" Fayth's light knock and query echoed through the silent house. Glorianna's trembling fingers fumbled at the final button of her dress.

"I'll be out in a moment." Glorianna hated the shreds of fear in her voice. She could still hear the buzzing from her dream and see the twitching body of the snake. The buzz hadn't been from bees as she dreamed. If she had gotten off her cot, the snake would have bitten her in an instant, before she was fully awake. She shuddered and took a deep breath to calm her queasy stomach.

"Are you okay?" Fayth's concern showed in the paleness of her face.

Glorianna forced a tentative smile. "I'm fine, I think. I'm just a little shaky. It isn't every morning I wake up to such excitement."

Fayth hugged her tight. "Timothy and I were so scared when we heard the shot. Thank God, Conlon happened along when he did."

"That's something that has me a little upset, too." Glorianna stiffened at the reminder of Conlon's seeing her in her nightdress. "What was he doing by my bed?"

Fayth smiled and grabbed Glorianna's hands, holding them tight. "I believe

God sent him. You see, we invited him for breakfast again. For some reason, you slept late. When he rounded the corner and saw you still asleep, he planned to walk on by."

"Then why didn't he?" Glorianna tried hard to hold on to her anger.

"Why? Because he heard the rattler. He couldn't very well leave you defenseless, could he?"

"I suppose not." A chill raced through her, raising bumps on her arms. "I don't know why I slept so late, anyway. I never do."

"But, don't you see?" Fayth continued, the excitement in her voice demanding Glorianna's attention. "God planned that. If you had awakened earlier, no one would have been there to kill the snake. It might have struck at you."

"I could have died."

"Yes, that's possible, but sometimes a person only gets sick from rattlesnake bites. If the venom gets drawn out right away, there's a good chance they will live."

Glorianna nodded, hoping she would never need to recall that information. She didn't ever want to see another snake again, especially one with rattles on its tail.

"Now, how about coming to our house for some breakfast? You look a little pale and I'm sure you're hungry. Emily should have the food ready to set on the table."

"I'd love to. Let me run a brush through my hair first. I don't want to scare Alyce." She attempted a smile, not sure her stomach would welcome any food. Still, she didn't want to upset Fayth, who was so thoughtfully trying to help.

⚜

Heat from the blacksmith's forge washed over Glorianna in waves, overwhelming the warmth of even the desert sun. Sweat beaded on her brow and threatened to trickle down her face. She sopped it with her handkerchief and pulled her parasol forward to block the hotter waves that radiated in front of her.

The smell of burning wood and the steady bang of the hammer against the anvil shut out the world around her. Mesmerized, Glorianna watched the blacksmith rhythmically pound a piece of red-hot metal, molding it into the U-shape of a horseshoe.

She hadn't seen the blacksmith before. If he was standing straight and not bent over his forge, he would tower over her. His muscles rippled and bulged, sweat covering his bare, ebony arms in a mirrored sheen. His huge hands looked as though one of them would wrap quite easily around her neck. A tremor of fear swept through her. Was this what Conlon meant about being brave enough to ask about riding the blacksmith's horse? Would this giant take offense and swat her away like a bothersome fly? Trepidation shivered down her spine. She stepped back. Maybe it would be best to slip away before he noticed her.

But the thought came to her too late. The blacksmith turned and thrust the heated metal into a pail of water. Steam hissed and rose in a cloud around him. His inky gaze locked on her, and a slow grin split his face.

"Good evening." His booming voice held her fast. "You must be the captain's daughter."

"I—I am." Glorianna swallowed hard, trying to regain her composure and remember why she was here.

"I'm Josiah Washington." The massive head dipped toward her. "I'm pleased to meet you."

Hot air swirled around Glorianna. She felt light-headed. She gritted her teeth, determined not to faint simply because this man looked like the makings of a nightmare. He sounded friendly enough, and his smile, although crooked, appeared pleasant.

Glorianna forced herself to meet Josiah's jet black gaze. Suddenly, she knew with certainty that this man would never hurt anyone. His eyes were gentle and innocent. She smiled, then relaxed for the first time since approaching the blacksmith's forge.

"I'm sorry to bother you, Mr. Washington. You're right, I'm the captain's daughter, Glorianna. I'd like to ask a favor of you."

"And what might that be?"

"Yesterday, Lieutenant Sullivan took me on a tour of the stables. I happen to love horses. I learned to ride almost before I could walk. When I saw your horse, I wanted to ride him. Lieutenant Sullivan said you wouldn't allow me, but I should ask you myself."

Josiah picked up a rag and swabbed the rivers of sweat off his face. He looked at her, the smile wiped from his face as well. "I don't let anyone ride Sultan, Miss Wilton. I'm sorry to disappoint you, but he's a bit picky about who rides him."

"I'm used to handling difficult horses." Glorianna heard her voice rising, hating the sound of it. "Perhaps, if you give me a chance."

"I would gladly share anything I have with you, Miss Wilton." Josiah held her with his steady gaze. "But the truth is, I know that horse. He isn't just difficult; he can get mean. His former owner didn't treat him so good. I've seen him throw a man and then turn to pound him into the ground. I'd never forgive myself if something like that happened to you."

Glorianna stood silent, watching the gentle giant. Now she understood why no one but Josiah even fed the horse. For some reason, the horse trusted him. He might not feel that way about her or anyone else. Josiah wasn't denying her out of selfishness; he wanted to protect her.

"Thank you, Mr. Washington, I understand."

Before she could turn to go, Josiah spoke again. "There are plenty of good horses in that stable, Miss Wilton. I'm sure the lieutenant will be happy to pick one out for you."

Heavy footsteps thundered across the front room. Glorianna looked up from where she sat cross-legged on her bed writing a letter to Kathleen. A thread of fear wove its way through her. "Who's there?"

"Kitten, it's me." Glorianna cried out at the sound of her father's deep, rumbling voice. Tossing aside her pen and paper, she hopped off the bed and ran to him. Her father wrapped his arms around her, holding her tight.

"I'm so sorry," he murmured. "I had no idea Dirk would try such a thing."

"It's not your fault, Daddy." Glorianna smiled up at him through her tears. "Everything turned out fine, thanks to Lieutenant Sullivan."

"I hear he's been taking good care of you." Her father grinned down at her. "I've heard stories of his fighting snakes of all kinds."

Glorianna could feel the heat of a blush on her cheeks. She pushed back from her father, not wanting to admit how grateful she was for Conlon's protection. "He only did his job." She sounded petty, even to her own ears.

"I'd say he went beyond duty." Her father's reprimand made her feel like a child. His quick smile eased her discomfort. "I do want to say that I've released Dirk. He says it was only the liquor. He won't be around you, though." Her father hugged her again. "Now, enough about that. I've brought a couple of things for you from Tucson. Come with me."

Glorianna followed her father into the kitchen. A young girl turned from the cupboards to face them. Her dark hair and eyes blended with her olive complexion. She looked down and shuffled her bare feet on the floor.

"This is Maria. Maria, this is my daughter, Glorianna." He turned back to Glorianna. "Maria will cook for us and keep the house. If you need anything, just ask. She speaks quite a bit of English."

"Hello, Maria." Glorianna smiled at the pretty Mexican girl. "Thank you for coming to help us out."

Maria nodded quickly and smiled. "Happy to, *Señorita*. Make good food for you."

Slipping her hand onto her father's proffered arm, Glorianna allowed herself to be escorted out of the kitchen. Her father grinned at her. "Now, I have something outside for you."

Glorianna stared in amazement as she stepped into the muted evening sun. Conlon Sullivan stood in the shade of a paloverde tree holding the reins of a beautiful horse. Her sorrel coat and flaxen mane and tail reminded Glorianna of Josiah Washington's Sultan. Four white socks colored her trim legs and a slender white strip ran down her nose. Small ears perked forward as Glorianna and her father approached.

"I know how much you like horses, Kitten. This spunky little mare needed a good home, and I thought of you."

"She's mine?" Glorianna gasped. "Oh, she's so beautiful." She gently stroked the soft neck. She looked across the mare at Conlon and smiled as the horse leaned her head over and rubbed her ear against his arm.

"She seems to like you, Lieutenant." Glorianna turned to her father. "What's her name?" Excitement made her chatter like Alyce.

"She doesn't have one." Her father shook his head. "I guess you'll have to think of a suitable name for her."

"Oh, I don't know." Glorianna paused as she stroked the soft muzzle. "She's such a sweet little girl. Do you have any ideas, Lieutenant?"

"I'd say you just named her." Conlon grinned, his blue eyes sparkling. "Little girl in Spanish is *nina*. That sounds like a good name."

"*Nina*," Glorianna whispered. "I like it. When can I ride her?" She swung around toward her father.

"You may go now if Lieutenant Sullivan will accompany you."

Glorianna turned back to Conlon. She wanted so much to ride Nina, even if it meant going with Conlon Sullivan.

He chuckled in obvious delight with the prospect. "I'm ready to go. Champ is saddled at the stables. I'll get him while you change into your riding habit."

Scampering inside, Glorianna couldn't contain her excitement. *I'll just pretend I'm riding with Kendrick,* she concluded, not at all sure she would manage the pretense.

Chapter 6

Nina's smooth, rocking gait thrilled Glorianna. Her father had given her the perfect gift. She missed the riding she had done in the East. On the days her mother didn't need her so much, she always took the opportunity to go for a refreshing ride. Nothing equaled the feeling of freedom that came from sitting on a spirited horse.

"Where shall we go, Lieutenant?"

Conlon took a long look around them, as if trying to decide the best direction. "It occurred to me that you haven't seen much of our desert. You probably have no idea that we have a river near the camp."

"A river? Here?" Glorianna couldn't mask her astonishment.

"That's right." Conlon laughed aloud. "Would you like to ride down to the Verde with me?"

"I'd love to." Glorianna followed Conlon down a wide trail. Memories assaulted her, the freshest one also the most painful. . . .

§

"Glorianna." Her mother's weak voice barely reached her.

"What is it?" she asked, hurrying to take her mother's thin, dry hand in her own. "What do you need?"

"Please ride to the river. See if you can find some spring flowers and bring me a few." Her mother collapsed back into the pillow, weakened by the speech. "I want to see their beauty one more time." Glorianna leaned close to hear the words.

Glorianna galloped to the river as fast as she dared over the uneven ground. Was her mother dying? Dr. Prince told her only yesterday that it wouldn't be long. She wasn't ready though. She would never be ready. Tears streamed down her face, the whipping wind drying them as they fell.

At the river, Glorianna slipped off her horse near a patch of bluebells, her mother's favorite. As she bent to pick a bouquet of the delicate flowers, a tinkle of laughter caught her attention. Her horse's reins in one hand, flowers in the other, she rounded the bend of the river.

Seated on the riverbank were three girls and a group of five boys. The boys were all friends of Kendrick's. The girls all attended the same church as Glorianna and her mother. Glorianna took another step closer and noticed a couple seated on the ground, partially hidden by a huge oak tree.

Kendrick and Melissa Cornwall—syrupy, beautiful, wealthy Melissa Cornwall—were engaged in intimate conversation. He leaned back against the tree and she rested her hand on his chest, batting her blue eyes at him. Glorianna wanted to scream. How could he look at her like that?

Glorianna backed out of sight and swung back on her horse. On the way home, the tears weren't for her mother; they were for her and her inability to fight for the man she wanted to marry.

At home she put away her horse, wiped her eyes, and headed toward the house. "You won't get away with this, Melissa," she whispered. "Kendrick is mine and I'll not let you have him."

She put the small bouquet of flowers in a vase and took it to her mother's room. Her mother was no longer there. Only her body remained, an empty shell. Her spirit had gone home to be with the Lord.

Within a few days, Glorianna was heading west to be with her father. She had no chance to fight for Kendrick.

She had to get back before it was too late and Melissa won.

🌵

"Miss Wilton?" Conlon called for the third time. He reined Champ closer and touched her hand where it rested on the saddle. She started, and her green eyes focused on him for the first time in several minutes. "Are you okay?"

A slight shudder shook her slender frame, and Glorianna said, "I'm fine, Lieutenant. I apologize for my lack of manners. I was just remembering my last ride before I came west."

"Do you want to talk about it?" Conlon studied her pale face. "You looked so sad."

Glorianna shrugged, a sad, faraway look on her face. "I rode to a river near us to bring some flowers for my mother." She paused, then continued in a near whisper. "She died before I returned."

"I'm sorry," Conlon said, reaching over to squeeze her small hand lightly. She didn't pull back, and he clasped her cool fingers for a moment to warm them.

Glorianna attempted a smile. "I know she's happier with the Lord. It's just that I miss her so."

As if she realized her vulnerability, Glorianna pulled her hand from his. "Maybe this isn't the best time to ride to the river. I'd like to go back home, please."

Conlon nodded and let Champ follow Nina as Glorianna reined her around in the road. *Why does she seem so open, then suddenly close up on me? Just when I think we're starting to become friends, she puts up a wall and shuts me out.* He stroked Champ's sweaty neck and watched Glorianna's fingers whiten on her reins. *Something is bothering her,* he thought. *Lord, help me learn how I can reach her and help her through this difficult time. I know she misses her mother, but it's more than that, I think.*

🌵

"Glorianna! Conlon!" Fayth waved wildly from her seat in the ambulance. The boxlike wagon was often used to transport cavalry wives and children to various destinations. "Come with us," Fayth said as Conlon and Glorianna drew near. "We're going to the Verde River to bathe and cool off." Beyond the wagon a group of cavalrymen sat astride their horses.

Conlon looked at Glorianna and shrugged, giving her the opportunity to answer. "I don't know, Fayth." Glorianna tried to smile. "I don't have any other clothes with me."

"I took care of that." Fayth held up a wrapped bundle. "I was hoping we'd run into you, so I brought some extra things. Come on," she pleaded. "Alyce will love having you along, and it will feel wonderful to be cool for a few minutes." Alyce clapped her hands as if agreeing with her mother.

"All right." Glorianna laughed at the toddler's antics. "I guess we'll just ride behind you."

"If you would like, Miss Wilton, I'll take Nina back to the camp. You can ride in the ambulance with the others."

"Aren't you coming, Conlon?" Fayth frowned at him.

"I want to get some clean clothes. I'll catch up with you," Conlon said. "Don't worry, I won't miss out on a chance to cool off."

Conlon dismounted and helped Glorianna into the wagon. She settled onto the seat next to Fayth. Alyce climbed over to snuggle into her lap, and Glorianna hugged the tiny girl, drawing comfort from her.

The ambulance jolted into motion, nearly unseating several of the women. They laughed and chattered with one another. Glorianna tried to ignore the emptiness gnawing a hole inside her.

"Has anyone told you about the cactus here?" Fayth leaned close to be heard over the other women's chatter.

Glorianna looked at all the strange plants by the side of the road and shook her head. "I don't know much about them. I wouldn't know what to avoid and what's safe."

"Just in case you're ever watching Alyce, let me explain which ones she shouldn't play near." Fayth grinned. "The last thing I want is a daughter that comes in looking like she's been in a fight with a porcupine." They both laughed. For the remainder of the ride to the river, Fayth pointed out various plants and explained their dangers or purposes.

Before long, they arrived at the Verde River. Having caught up with them, Conlon joined the men tromping along the path leading farther down the river. The women slipped and slid down the nearest trail to the cool water.

"Hey, stop that," Glorianna laughed as Alyce splashed water in her face. Alyce chuckled and did it again. "I'll get you wet if you don't stop," Glorianna warned. Alyce squealed and slammed both hands down on the water, shooting a spray into Glorianna's face.

"Alyce, you behave." Fayth's lips pursed as if she held back a smile.

"Don't worry. We're just having a little fun." Glorianna splashed water on Alyce's stomach. They laughed, enjoying the cool river water.

Later, as Fayth, Alyce, and Glorianna relaxed in the shallow water, Fayth asked, "Are you upset about Dirk being released?"

Glorianna shrugged and watched Alyce pick up rocks from the river bottom. "He said he only did it because he was drunk. I'll just stay away from him." She picked up a handful of rocks, then dribbled them back into the river. "I guess I am a little nervous."

Alyce's head nodded forward. Fayth chuckled as she picked her daughter up. "I think you're about to fall asleep in the water." She stood and began to wade toward the bank.

"I'll go up to the wagon and fetch our clothes," Glorianna called. "I'll only be a minute."

Following the faint path up from the river to the road, the sounds of women's laughter faded away. The quiet peacefulness of the desert settled around Glorianna. She hoped none of the men were at the wagon yet. She didn't like the idea of them seeing her in wet clothing, particularly a certain lieutenant who had the bad habit of catching her off guard.

Glorianna peered into the wagon, searching through the bundles of clothing for the one Fayth wrapped up for them. She lifted the bulky garments and turned back to the trail down to the river. Hands grabbed her arms. Before she could react, she was crushed against a wet body.

"Well, well, looky who we have here." Dirk's fetid breath didn't smell of alcohol this time. Glorianna's heart almost stopped, then beat a frantic rhythm as she struggled to free herself from his iron grip.

"Let me go, now," she hissed, "You won't have the excuse of being drunk this time. You know what my father will do."

He laughed. Glorianna turned her head, trying to avoid his foul breath and the unsightly glimpse of rotted teeth. She pushed against his chest, hitting him with her fists.

"That's what I like, sweet thing. A woman with spirit. You and I will get along fine." He laughed and tried to pull her closer. "You just need a little time to get used to the idea of us together."

"Leave me alone." Glorianna's body was taut with fear. "If you don't let go, I'll scream. You know that help isn't far."

A hand clamped over her mouth before she could say more. "Then I guess I'll just have to keep you quiet." His sinister laugh sent a chill coursing down her spine. "No one will hear you now. They're all having too much fun in the river."

Glorianna strained against Dirk as he tried to pull her tighter against him. She wanted to bite his hand and loosen his grip just long enough to get out a scream, but he pushed it painfully tight over her mouth. She relaxed, hoping he would think she was giving in and let down his guard for a minute.

"That's right, sweet thing." Dirk leaned closer to her. "I knew you'd understand. No one will help you this time."

"No one, Dirk? I think you're wrong there." Conlon's voice held a deadly calm. Dirk whirled, releasing Glorianna. She fell to the ground. He crouched low. A knife appeared in his hand as if by magic. Without thinking, Glorianna swept her feet forward, knocking them into Dirk's legs. He lost his balance and stumbled forward.

Like a streak of lightning, Conlon's fist caught Dirk on the jaw, knocking him backward. With his other hand, Conlon grabbed Dirk's arm and banged it against the wagon. The knife clattered to the ground.

Glorianna scooted backward, trying her best to put some distance between herself and the fighters. She winced as Conlon picked Dirk up from the dirt and hit him again. Blood from Dirk's nose streamed down the front of his shirt. Conlon's eyes were dark with anger. He pummeled Dirk, knocking him back against the ambulance.

"I warned you once," Conlon snarled. "I told you to stay away from Glorianna."

Dirk dodged Conlon and wiped his nose with his sleeve. "You just want her for yourself, Lieutenant. You figure you're the Cap'n's pet so you should get her. Well, you aren't the only one in the game."

Conlon let out a low growl and lunged for Dirk. Glorianna screamed. Yells and the pounding of heavy footsteps sounded in the brush. A moment later, Timothy Holwell and several of the other men appeared from the river path. Timothy grabbed Conlon while the other men restrained Dirk.

"Tie him up," Conlon ordered. "We'll take him back to the camp and let the captain handle this."

Timothy loosened his hold, and Conlon walked over to Glorianna. He slipped a hand under her elbow and helped her over to the wagon. "Are you okay?" he asked, concern evident in his voice.

"I'll be fine." Glorianna tried to keep her voice steady. She wanted Conlon to take her in his arms and comfort her, but knew he wouldn't with all the men around. The excited voices of the women were coming closer as they climbed the path from the river. "Thank you for rescuing me again, Lieutenant. You seem to do it very well."

Conlon grinned down at her, his eyes a deep warm blue again. "It's truly my pleasure."

⁂

Conlon lay on his cot watching the panorama of celestial splendor overhead. But a mental image of a beautiful redhead with vivid green eyes overshadowed the stars. She seemed so sad today when they were riding. He longed to hold her and comfort her.

His hands clenched as he remembered finding Glorianna once more in the clutches of Dirk. Never had he felt such rage. The thought of that lowlife touching

Glorianna filled him with fresh anger. At least it wouldn't happen again. The captain had agreed to lock Dirk up until they could ship him to Fort Lowell in Tucson. Conlon wanted to hang him.

God, I'm sorry I'm having such a hard time with forgiveness here. Please help me. Teach me how to reach out to Glorianna without being pushy. I'm so used to getting what I want that I'm having trouble waiting for You, Lord. I want to learn patience. I know I'll need it throughout life, and I may as well start right now.

Conlon drifted off to sleep, a smile relaxing his face. Memories of sweet rose scent and silken fiery red hair filled his thoughts and dreams.

Chapter 7

L ooks like rain might finally be a possibility." Fayth pointed at the sky as she and Glorianna left the mercantile.

Over the desert, billowing clouds played hide and seek with the sun. The wind whipped the women's dresses against their legs. The blowing sand stung as it tried to imbed itself in their tender skin. Fayth handed her package to Glorianna and sheltered Alyce's face against her neck.

"The summer storms are late this year." Fayth led the way across the deserted parade ground. "Usually, we've had some rain by now and the dust isn't so bad as this."

"What exactly are they?" Glorianna squinted against the wind. "Isn't one storm like another?"

Fayth shook her head and leaned farther over Alyce. "These are more than normal storms. They bring lightning, strong winds, and, we hope, rain. The temperature drops drastically. Sometimes, we don't get the rain. Then the lightning starts fires in the dry brush of the desert. The early ones are always a little scary because the desert is so dry. Of course, it's possible these clouds won't amount to anything."

Fayth opened the door to her house. Glorianna stepped in and started to close the door when a shout stopped her. She turned to see Conlon striding toward her; his eyes fastened on her, disregarding the strong breeze. Her heartbeat quickened, and she tried to ignore how much she looked forward to seeing him.

Conlon waved something at her, his mouth moving, but the words were ripped away by the wind. He strode closer, then called again, "I have a letter for you."

Fayth returned to take the packages. Glorianna tried to remain calm as Conlon approached. She didn't know whether her excitement stemmed from seeing him or from getting a letter. Oh, it would be good to hear from home.

"It looks like you heard from someone back east."

Standing in the doorway with Conlon on the steps below her, they were almost the same height. She had no trouble gazing into his sparkling blue eyes. In fact, she had trouble looking away. Mesmerized, she watched the wind play games with his dark hair, flinging it on his forehead, then sweeping it back over his brow.

"Your mail, Miss Wilton."

Glorianna started, then felt the heat of a blush rising. She'd been staring at Conlon like a sentimental schoolgirl. He held out her letter, grinning as if he knew her every thought.

"Thank you, Lieutenant," she stammered. Struggling to regain control, she stared at the envelope, then called to Fayth, "I've gotten a letter from my cousin Kathleen. I'm going to run home and read it." She brushed past Conlon, trying to ignore the feelings he caused, trying to forget the impish grin that set her heart pounding.

Clasping the precious missive to her chest so it wouldn't blow away, Glorianna hurried to get inside. She closed the door and ripped open the envelope.

Glory,

I thought I should tell you about Kendrick. I know you had your heart set on the scoundrel, though I can't understand why. Half the girls around here feel the same way you do. I'm glad he never overwhelmed me.

But, enough with the lecture. I'm sorry to carry on like that. I wanted to write and let you know that Kendrick and Melissa Cornwall have announced their engagement. They are planning a November wedding. I know you can't be here for it and probably wouldn't want to anyway. I'm sorry to be the bearer of bad news. You should get on with your life. I've heard there are plenty of men in the West and not many women. I'm sure you can find a godly husband, once you forget about Kendrick.

Glorianna set the rest of the letter down on the bed. Tears blurred her vision so that she could no longer make out the words. Kendrick couldn't marry Melissa. She wasn't at all right for him. She would surely be whiny and critical like her mother. Poor Kendrick would lose all his sense of adventure in no time.

Without deliberation, Glorianna began to change her clothes. As she struggled to fasten the buttons on her riding habit, confusion reigned. She needed to be alone and focus on this problem. Since she did her best thinking on long horse rides, she would saddle up Nina. She brushed aside Conlon's caution about riding alone. She wouldn't be gone long. What could a short ride hurt?

𝆕

As evening drew on, Glorianna waited until the soldiers turned the other way, then she slipped out of the camp, hoping to be hidden by the brush and growing dusk. Getting this far without being seen hadn't been difficult. Most people were indoors preparing for supper. The wind whipped across the desert in a hot, dry wave.

Nina, normally a sweet-tempered mare, wasn't happy about being out. She had not wanted to leave her sweet hay and the comforts of her stall. She fought the bit, trying to turn toward home each time Glorianna relaxed her grip on the reins. If she hadn't been such an experienced horsewoman, she knew they wouldn't have gotten this far. For safety, she urged Nina to take the road to Yuma. Wider than the trail to the river, this road would lessen her chances of getting lost.

"Nina, I have to figure a way to get back east to Kendrick."

Nina's ears flickered and she snorted.

"Don't you start in on me, too. I'm telling you Kendrick is wonderful. That's why all the girls like him, isn't it?"

Nina pranced on without comment.

Could she be wrong about him? Glorianna relaxed her grip on the reins as she pondered her decision to marry Kendrick. She'd wanted this for so long that she couldn't remember her original reason for deciding to marry him. He was handsome, but so were a lot of men, especially Conlon. She frowned. Where had that thought come from?

Could her father be right? Was Kendrick's penchant for changing jobs due to his shiftlessness? Would he care for a wife and family properly? Should she wait and see what happened or should she do her best to get back home?

The low rumble of thunder startled her. "How did it get so dark, Girl?" She patted the horse's neck. "We'd better get back. That storm looks like it means business."

Glorianna swung the mare around. She had no idea how long she'd been riding, but Camp MacDowell couldn't be too far.

A flash of lightning lit up the black sky. Rain-laden clouds lumbered closer. A crack of thunder shook the ground. Nina jumped, then spooked again as the wind peppered them with debris from the ground. Glorianna worked hard to hold the frightened mare steady. Her nervous prancing took them sideways down the road.

Glorianna squinted against the wind. Hidden in blackness, the road was difficult to see, much less follow, until an occasional flash of lightning illuminated the desert. She searched the countryside for shelter during those brief moments of light. The flat landscape held no hope of refuge. Gnarled mesquite trees and prickly cactus offered no protection from the intensity of the storm. Where had this storm come from so fast?

She longed to urge Nina into a canter, hoping there would be something up ahead, something to block out the wind and the inevitable rain. Nina spooked constantly, afraid of every lightning flash and boom of thunder. Glorianna knew she shouldn't have left the camp when she did. Most of all she regretted going alone.

Had she lost the road? There weren't any high spots near here so that she could get her bearings. What if she found no shelter? Would anyone find her in this desolate place? A growing fear threatened to overtake her.

Unbidden, Conlon's face came to mind. She smiled and relaxed slightly as she remembered the comforting feel of his arms around her. She knew the look in his brilliant blue eyes as he gazed at her. He loved her. She tried to push thoughts of him away for she knew he wasn't God's plan for her, even if Conlon believed he was. But, Glorianna knew with certainty that if she got lost, Conlon would find her. No matter how bad the storm, no matter how far from the road she strayed, he would come for her.

The first of the rain spattered in huge drops against her cheeks. She hunched over the saddle, urging Nina to go faster. They must be getting close to the camp and to shelter. She wasn't prepared for the hard-hitting deluge that dropped from the sky. Lightning seared the clouds, thunder rocked the heavens, and a curtain of rain descended that cut everything else off.

Nina reared and jumped sideways, throwing Glorianna off balance. The rain-soaked desert floor, slippery as ice, gave way beneath the mare's hooves. Nina crashed to the ground. Glorianna flew from the saddle, her head connecting with a rock. Darkness enveloped her.

♯

"Lieutenant Sullivan!" Captain Wilton's roar as he slammed open the door to the officers' quarters made Conlon jump. He winced as the needle he held pierced his finger. He set down the shirt and button he'd been sewing and crossed the room.

"Yes, Sir." He snapped to attention.

Captain Wilton looked as if he had just realized how gruff he sounded. He sighed and ran his hand through his wind-rumpled hair. "I'm sorry, Sullivan. I didn't mean to sound like an angry bear." At Conlon's nod he continued, "Have you seen my daughter?"

Conlon frowned and shook his head. "I haven't seen her since this afternoon when I delivered a letter to her."

"Where was she then?"

"She had just helped Fayth carry home some purchases from the mercantile. She took the letter and went home. Why do you ask?"

An uncharacteristic look of fear clouded the captain's eyes. "She's disappeared. She isn't home or at the Holwells'."

"Did you ask Maria?"

"Yes, she hasn't seen her for a couple of hours. She had to go to the mercantile, and when she returned, Glorianna was gone."

Conlon reached over to the peg by the door where his cap hung. "Let's go see what we can find out."

The wind blew against them and made walking a chore as they crossed the open area to the captain's house. In order to be heard, Conlon shouted at the captain. "Did you check with the other women?"

Captain Wilton nodded. "None of them have seen her this afternoon. The wind and blowing sand kept everyone indoors." He paused and waited until they stepped into the house to continue. "Glorianna knows what time you eat supper. I can't imagine where she is."

"Did you ask Fayth what she thought? She and your daughter have become good friends."

"She said Glorianna helped her some this morning. Fayth says she was fine then."

"What about the letter? Could there have been bad news from back east?"

Captain Wilton frowned. "I don't know. I haven't seen any letter."

Conlon couldn't stand around any longer. An uneasy feeling settled in the pit of his stomach. He had to do something to find Glorianna before it was too late. Too late? He frowned at the thought.

"Why don't you check her room, Sir? See if you can find that letter. I'll talk to Maria again."

The clip of his boot heels echoed down the hall as the captain headed for his daughter's bedroom. Conlon crossed quietly to the kitchen, trying to ignore the growling of his stomach when the rich aromas of simmering vegetables hit.

"Maria?" The petite Mexican girl turned at his call. "We're trying to find Glorianna. Have you noticed anything that might help?"

Maria broke off a piece of dough and began shaping a small tortilla before she answered. "*Sí, Señor,*" she said, hesitantly. "I think something might help." She spoke rapidly in Spanish, then stopped suddenly, looking embarrassed. "Sorry," she said. "Forget speaking English sometimes."

"That's okay." Conlon forced a smile, trying to put the nervous girl at ease. He wanted to pick her up and shake her. "Just tell me anything you can."

"Señorita's riding clothes gone, *Señor.*"

"Her clothes?" Conlon glanced around at the ironing board in the corner of the kitchen.

"I washed yesterday. Today I iron. Her riding clothes were here. Now they gone."

"Thank you, Maria." Conlon turned and headed out of the kitchen toward the bedroom. A sense of impending doom weighed heavily on him.

"Lieutenant, come here." Captain Wilton looked grim as he strode out of Glorianna's room, a piece of paper fluttering in his hand. "Apparently, Sullivan, my daughter did receive bad news. At least, it's bad to her."

"What is it, Sir?" Conlon reached impatiently for the letter, but the captain pulled it away.

"I can't let you read it, Sullivan. The letter is personal. Believe me, though, I know she's upset. The man she wanted to go back and marry is getting married to a girl Glorianna despises. There's no telling where she's gone."

Conlon raced across the parade ground to the stables, ignoring the grit of sand in his eyes. The sweet scent of rain hung heavy in the air. Foreboding built inside him like the massive clouds overhead.

Nina's stall was empty. Conlon stared for a moment as reality sank in. Glorianna had gone riding. She would be caught in this storm.

"What did you find, Sullivan?" Captain Wilton strode toward him down the center aisle of the stables.

"Her horse is gone, Sir." Conlon hated the look of fear in the captain's eyes. He knew his thoughts were on the storm and his daughter braving the elements. "I'll go after her, Captain. I'll bring her back."

Captain Wilton placed his hand on Conlon's shoulder. His voice sounded husky against the rising howl of the wind. "Find her for me, Sullivan. She's all I have. She doesn't understand these desert storms."

Conlon had barely enough time to decipher which road Glorianna had taken before the rain swept out of the skies. Champ pranced momentarily, then calmed down and slogged ahead through the wind, rain, and slippery desert.

She's on the road to Yuma, he thought. *Does she think she can return home and win her boyfriend back? God, I don't understand this. Please, keep her safe. Help me to find her.*

Lightning struck a nearby mesquite tree. The resulting thunderclap vibrated the air around them. Champ reared, startled by the brilliant flash and loud noise. Conlon brought him down easily, then leaned to run his hand down the horse's wet neck. He did his best to soothe the trembling beast.

Hours seemed to pass before the rain eased up to a slow, steady shower, yet Conlon knew it hadn't been that long. He strained to see through the moonless night. Champ lifted his head and nickered softly. Conlon leaned forward trying to see. He wished for one more flash of lightning to illuminate the night.

A movement ahead caught his attention. Out of the darkness, Nina's soft whinny reached them. By the next flash, they saw her. She stood, her reins held fast among some rocks, her left front hoof lifted off the ground. Conlon swung down from Champ and approached the mare, dread making him shake.

"Easy, Girl." He ran his hands over the drenched horse. The mud caked on her knees told of her fall. Her foreleg was tender, but he couldn't feel any sign of lasting damage. He couldn't feel any sticky blood on the saddle, as he ran his hands across it.

"Where's Glorianna, Girl?"

Conlon stepped around the horse. His eyes strained against the inky blackness. *Please, God, help me find her,* he begged again. As if in answer to his prayer, lightning flashed, and the image of her crumpled body was forever burned into his memory.

Chapter 8

*D*ear God, no! Conlon wanted to call out. His throat constricted in fear, and he only mouthed the words that his mind screamed. In two long strides, he reached her side. He knelt by her rain-drenched form.

"Glorianna," his voice cracked. She didn't move. The rain and the fall had loosened her long braid. He swept the sodden curls back from her face. Her pale skin shone in the blackness. She didn't move, didn't appear to breathe.

Oh, God, please, let her be all right. Don't let her die like this. A slight movement caught his eye. He reached down and slipped his fingers around her slender, cold hand. Ever so slowly, her fingers tightened around his. Tears trickled down his cheeks, lost amidst the raindrops. Conlon's head bent forward. *Thank You, Lord. Thank You.*

Conlon hurried back to Champ and retrieved the extra rain slicker and blanket he had thought to bring with him. Placing the blanket over Glorianna's still form, he put the slicker over that. He hoped she would be able to warm up a little. Her fingers and cheeks were like ice. He wondered if it was due to her being soaked and the drop in temperature or from her injuries.

Gently, he checked for broken bones, trying to determine how badly she had been hurt in the fall. As he ran his hand over her head, he felt the lump and the rock she rested against. Now he knew why she lay so still.

She groaned. He leaned closer to her. "Glorianna? Can you hear me?"

Her eyelids fluttered. Her forehead puckered and her eyelids twitched again. They quivered once more, then opened slightly.

"Don't try to talk, Sweetheart. I'm going to take you back to the camp. I'll do my best not to hurt you."

She tried to nod. Her face paled even more at the effort. Then, her eyes drifted shut again. Conlon wanted to lift her into his arms and comfort her. He wanted to take away her pain and make her well, but it wasn't in his power. Instead, he went to bring the horses closer. He tied Nina's reins to Champ's saddle, then returned to Glorianna.

Cradling her head in his arms, Conlon rewrapped the blanket and slicker around her. She weighed almost nothing. He pulled her close. The faint scent of roses wafted around him. He pressed his cheek to hers, willing her to be okay, to be strong for the ride back to camp. The storm had eased. Moonlight pierced through the clouds and chased away the inky darkness.

Champ seemed to understand the need to walk. Nina hobbled beside them.

Glorianna rested against Conlon's chest. Her breathing was even and a faint flush tinted her cheeks. He prayed it wasn't the start of a fever, but her true color coming back.

Swaying in the saddle with the rhythm of Champ's walk, Conlon gazed down at Glorianna. Her long, dark eyelashes rested on creamy white cheeks. Her petite nose turned up slightly. Rosebud lips curled in a secret smile, making him long to brush them with his own.

He had to do something to distract his thoughts, so he began to talk, even though he knew she couldn't hear him. "Glorianna," he whispered. "You are well named. You are a glory to look at." He paused, smiled, then continued. "In fact, I believe from now on I'll call you Glory. Every time I do, you will remind me of the glory of God and how He made you for me. I know you don't believe me about that, but it's true." Conlon reached up and brushed a lock of hair from her face. "For years, I've prayed for you. I asked God to give me a wife like my mother." He laughed softly. "I didn't know you would be as feisty."

He smiled. "You see, my mother is tiny, just like you. She has the same red hair and fiery temper. I learned at a young age not to cross her." He paused a moment, swallowing a lump in his throat. "But the thing I loved most about my mother was her love for my dad. She loved him with everything in her. And she loved God the same way."

He leaned forward and pressed his lips lightly on Glorianna's temple. "I want you to love me like that, Glory. I think you already do, you just haven't realized it yet. Most of all, I want you to follow God's will."

"As for the man back east you think you want," Conlon clenched his teeth, trying to keep the anger from his voice, "remember this, Glory; if he passed you by for that other girl, then he isn't worth the bother. You deserve better."

With a sigh, he pulled her even closer, trying to keep her warm. The wind had died down and the rain had slowed, but she was wet clear through. Champ's pricked ears told him they were nearing Camp MacDowell.

He gazed down at her, his fingers trailing down her cheek. He leaned forward slightly, giving in to temptation and followed the path of his fingers with one of light kisses. He sighed. "I love you so much, Sweetheart. Please don't make me wait forever, although I will, if need be."

Arriving at Camp MacDowell, Conlon roused the guard with a shout. A cavalryman ran to take Nina's reins from him. "Rub her down and tend to her leg," Conlon said. "Send someone for the doctor. I'll take Miss Wilton to her house."

At the sound of hoofbeats, the door to Glorianna's house flung open. Her father, Fayth, and Timothy stood framed in the light. "I have her, Sir."

"Thank God." Captain Wilton rushed from the house. "Is she okay?"

Leaning forward to hand Glorianna to her father, Conlon found himself reluctant to let her go. "Be careful. Her horse fell with her. She hit her head on a rock and hasn't regained consciousness, except for a moment."

Fayth let out a cry, her hand quickly covering her mouth as she looked at Glorianna's still form. "Bring her in. Hurry. We need to get these wet things off her. I'll get Maria to help me. Conlon, did you get the doctor?"

Without waiting for his answer, she rushed into the house ahead of the captain.

⚜

Light pierced her eyes, like a dagger stabbing through to the back of her head. She snapped them shut and held them there tightly. Maybe if she refused to let her eyelids open, this blinding pain would go away. Glorianna tried to breathe in shallow breaths, hoping to settle the churning in her stomach. Her efforts didn't work.

She inched her eyelids apart. The light didn't hurt quite as much, but the ache was still too much to bear. She closed them and relaxed slightly. She now knew she was in her bedroom, lying in bed. How had she gotten here? The last thing she remembered was the lightning and thunder and Nina's rearing in terror.

Booted feet clunked across the floor. Why were they stomping so hard? Couldn't whoever it was walk a little more softly? She would tell them.

"Are you awake?" The note of concern in Conlon's voice almost made her smile. Then, she remembered she needed to tell him to walk quietly before he stomped holes in the floor.

Glorianna opened her eyes and attempted to sit. Conlon knelt by her bed and reached for her hand. Too late she knew she had made a mistake. Before she could turn away, her stomach emptied itself all over her, the bed, and the man who claimed to love her. Horrified, Glorianna dropped back on the bed. As everything faded into darkness once more, she knew she would never be able to face him again.

The next time Glorianna awoke, pale moonlight illuminated the room. She eased her eyes open, hoping her memory of throwing up on Conlon had only been a dream. *A nightmare, actually,* she thought. The pounding in her head had eased, and her stomach felt more settled than it had earlier.

"Kitten?"

She turned her head toward her father. She wondered if the smile she forced looked more like a grimace than a smile. "Hi," she rasped, her voice not cooperating with her. "How long have I been asleep?"

Her father leaned close. "You've slept for two days now. We were pretty worried. The doctor said there was nothing to do but wait."

She tried to nod. A cool night breeze brought the scent of rain to her. "Did it rain again?"

"We got a little monsoon tonight. Not like the other one, though."

She closed her eyes to shut out the pain written in her father's gaze. "I'm sorry. I wanted time to think. I didn't know the storm would come so fast."

"It's okay, Kitten. The weather here takes some getting used to."

She tried to nod and tell him she might have been wrong, but her head began pounding again. She closed her eyes and barely heard the scrape of the chair accompanied by her father's whispered, "Good night," before drifting back to sleep.

"Good morning, Sleepyhead." Fayth's cheerful voice and the tread of her steps in the bedroom made Glorianna wince.

"Good morning." The words rasped in her ears.

"Maria tells me you haven't eaten much of anything." Fayth settled into the chair next to the bed. "I have her fixing some broth. I want you to try your best to eat." She grinned. "I hope to keep you from throwing up on me like you did on Conlon. I don't think he's recovered yet."

"Every time I try to eat, I get sick to my stomach. I don't have any appetite yet."

"It's been four days since Conlon brought you in looking like a drowned rat. We need to get you well." Fayth leaned forward and brushed the hair away from Glorianna's forehead. "Today, we'll try a little harder." She smiled to soften her words. "I think we need to start with some serious prayer about your health and about that gentleman that made you ride off alone."

"Why should we pray about Kendrick?"

Fayth sighed. "I don't know why you're so determined to marry him. Can you tell me?"

"Because it's what God wants."

"How do you know?"

Glorianna stirred restlessly in the bed. For some reason Fayth's question made her uneasy. "I guess, I just feel it. He's so handsome and fun loving. I'm sure he's perfect for me."

"You know, it isn't wise to trust our feelings unless we can back it up with God's Word."

"What do you mean by that?" Glorianna stared at the ceiling, trying to avoid Fayth's knowing gaze.

"Have you checked to see what God thinks about Kendrick's attributes?"

"God loves everyone. I'm sure He loves Kendrick, too."

Fayth frowned. "Of course, God loves us all," Fayth agreed. "However, God hates sin, and He doesn't want us to be unequally yoked with someone who doesn't know Him in the same way we do."

"Kendrick goes to church sometimes." The defense sounded lame.

"But does he put God first in his life? Will he put God first in your marriage?" Fayth lifted Glorianna's hand from the covers and squeezed it lightly. "These are questions you need to pray about. Only you can find the answers."

Glorianna listened in silence as Fayth prayed for God to give her wisdom in the decision she needed to make. A lump settled in her throat and she realized that maybe, just maybe, she wanted to marry Kendrick so desperately that she assumed God wanted it, too. How did Fayth know what God wanted if she didn't go by feelings?

Maria entered the room quietly, carrying a tray. The smell of broth drifted across the room. For the first time, Glorianna felt a faint stirring of hunger. Perhaps good health wasn't so far away after all.

After eating as much as she could hold, Glorianna listened to Fayth talk about Alyce and her latest antics. When she couldn't hold her eyes open any longer, she heard Fayth whisper that she would be back later.

The early morning chill felt refreshing after the scorching desert days. The sky softened slowly from dark gray to deep blue. Conlon breathed in the fresh, crisp air, looking forward to the special time he shared every day with God. Arizona sunrises were God's handiwork at its best.

A family of jackrabbits browsed through the brush looking for the most succulent plants to nibble. Their long ears waved in the breeze. Extra-large hind legs made them look as if they were ready to topple over on their noses. Conlon grinned at the thought. He wasn't sure how a coyote ever caught one of the fleet-footed rabbits.

He turned his face to the sky and noted the clouds building already. It would probably rain again today. He frowned. There were rumors of Apache uprisings. The captain might send a troop to scout around the Superstition Mountains. He hoped he didn't have to go with them, but he felt certain he would.

"God," he whispered, "the truth is I don't want to be away from Glorianna. I don't want to shirk my duty, either, but I feel so protective of her."

Seven days had passed since he brought her home that stormy night. The feeling of holding her in his arms had haunted him ever since. "I love her so much, Lord. What am I supposed to do?"

The sky lightened, and the first faint traces of color began to form among the clouds. "God, I know Josiah says I should be patient. He keeps quoting from Psalm 37, 'Rest in the Lord, and wait patiently for him.' " He sighed, a sound wrenched from deep in his soul. "I don't know how long I can rest, Lord. Help me to be patient with her today. Maybe if I take it one day at a time, it will be easier."

He picked up a rock and flung it in the direction of the grazing rabbits. They bounded away across the desert faster than one might imagine possible.

"I haven't even seen her since the day after I brought her home. She won't allow me in or talk to me at all." He kicked at a rock, sending it skittering away. "I don't know if she's embarrassed or if she won't ever want to see me again. She can't hide forever.

"Should I forget her, Lord? Please don't say I should. I know I couldn't on my own. But if Your will is that I not marry her, then give me the strength to accept it." Conlon hung his head. A feeling of despair threatened to destroy his early morning ritual.

As if God were ready to talk, a brilliant display of colors washed across the eastern sky. Pinks, purples, and gold blended with the blue, painting a dazzling picture. He looked up and smiled through the glittering tears in his eyes. Only God could do this kind of artwork.

"Oh!" The gasp from behind him startled Conlon. Had someone been listening to his private conversation with God? He whirled around, then stared in astonishment.

Chapter 9

"Glorianna!"

As Conlon closed the gap between them in two quick strides, she tore her gaze from the colors rippling across the sky to focus on him. He swept her into his arms, crushing her in a fierce hug. "I'm so glad to see you up and around, Sweetheart."

His blue eyes, darker in the morning light, held her fast. His earthy scent washed over her, and her heart began to pound. He lowered his head, his lips coming closer to hers. For a fleeting breath of time, Glorianna wanted to feel his lips on hers, to be swept away by his kiss. Instead, she turned her head, and his lips brushed her cheek. She struggled against him, but he seemed oblivious. "Lieutenant." She pushed him. "Lieutenant, let me go!"

Glorianna freed one hand. Swinging as hard as she could in such close confines, she slapped his cheek. He stepped back from the embrace, a look of surprise and confusion clouding his eyes.

She stepped back to put some distance between them. Her body, taut with emotion, felt like a leaf in the wind. "Lieutenant, I am not your sweetheart. Neither did I come out here for your pleasure. In fact, I heard you mumbling to yourself and was leaving."

"I was praying."

"I couldn't make out the words. I didn't mean to intrude."

He studied her for a moment. His features relaxed slightly as if he was relieved about something, but she didn't know what. She tried to calm her breathing, hoping her cheeks weren't as red as they felt. "Why did you come out here?"

Her face burned at the thought of his thinking she came looking for him. "I couldn't sleep. I wanted to get some air and think. Now, if you'll excuse me, I'll get back."

She turned before he could say more and walked back toward the camp, forcing herself not to run. Tears crowded together in her eyes and threatened to overflow. Dashing at them angrily with the back of her hand, she headed for the stables. Maybe a talk with Nina would help sort out her confused feelings about Conlon.

The stables were quiet. Most of the horses were resting. Nina's soft nicker comforted her when she leaned over the stall. The mare limped as she moved to the door. Dirty smudges covered the wrap on her leg. Glorianna made a mental note to put on a fresh bandage today.

"Good morning, Girl," she whispered as she stroked the soft, questing nose.

"I didn't bring you a treat, but I'll see that you get one later today. How's your leg?"

"I believe that leg is gonna be fine, Miss Wilton." Josiah Washington's booming voice echoed through the stables, eliciting a startled cry from Glorianna.

"Mr. Washington," she gasped. "I didn't know you were here."

"I like to get an early start on the day." The blacksmith grinned at her. "I came to check out some of the horses, like that pretty little mare of yours. Her leg is mending right nice."

Glorianna relaxed. Nina nudged her, demanding more attention. She wanted to bury her face in the mare's neck and cry. What did the Lord want from her? Why couldn't she have the peace Fayth spoke of having? Inner turmoil had her stomach in knots. She turned her head away and hoped Josiah hadn't seen the tear that trickled down her cheek.

"Are you all right?" Josiah's soft voice reflected his concern.

"I'm fine." She nearly choked on the lie. "I guess I'm just glad Nina wasn't hurt too bad when she fell."

Josiah chuckled, a deep rumbling sound like distant thunder. "I think you should be glad Lieutenant Sullivan found you."

Swiping away the tear, Glorianna looked up at the huge blacksmith. "What do you mean?"

"I mean, it was crazy to be out in that storm. You were off the road in the desert. I believe only a miracle from God made him notice you."

"But, I was careful to stay on the road."

"Maybe you were careful, but it was dark and stormy. I'll bet Nina wasn't calm and sweet like usual, was she?"

"She was a little edgy," Glorianna admitted. "But, then, I'm an experienced rider."

Josiah's grin lit up the stables. "Conlon told me you're a good rider, Ma'am, but I'll tell you something. There isn't another man in this company who would have risked his life riding after you in that storm."

Glorianna wanted to run from the truth he forced her to see. She had put another person's life in danger.

"Conlon loves you, Miss Wilton." Josiah studied her, speaking softly. "I hope you at least thanked him for saving your life. Good day."

Glorianna watched him leave as she reflected on the elements of nature gone crazy during that horrendous storm. Why would anyone want to be out in that unless he had a mission for the person he loved or thought he loved? She had done some deep soul-searching in the past few days and knew she had been wrong about Kendrick. Now she must wait for God to show her His will for her life. Was Conlon the answer?

Lost in thought, she nervously clasped and unclasped her hands as she made her way back outside the camp. Would he still be there? Would he even want to see her? What would she say to him?

She quietly wove through the prickly desert plants. The brilliant colors had faded from the sky, leaving it a pale, washed-out blue. Conlon sat on the rock, his back toward her. His head rested in his hands; a look of utter dejection and defeat surrounded him. Glorianna stopped, overwhelmed by the need to run to him and feel his embrace.

❦

Conlon heard footsteps behind him. *Oh, God, make them go away. I can't face anyone right now. Why did I do that? Why couldn't I see that she doesn't love me? She has no idea how she haunts my every thought. I can't sleep if I don't see her each night. Every day I look forward to being around her. This last week has been awful without her. When I saw her standing there, I couldn't help myself. I just had to hold her. Now she'll hate me. Lord, help me to trust You. Show me what to do.*

"Conlon?"

He froze. Had he heard Glorianna call his name or was he imagining things? She never called him Conlon. Hesitantly, almost afraid of what he would find, Conlon stood up and swung around.

It was Glorianna. She looked like an angel. The pale yellow dress danced lightly in the breeze. Her red hair shone with the sun's highlights. Her pale cheeks accented the brightness of her green eyes and ruby lips.

He tried to speak. His mouth opened, but nothing came out. Why had she come back?

Glorianna licked her lips. Her hands were clasped in front of her. "I want to thank you."

Thank him? She wanted to thank him? He never expected her to say something like that. Why was she thanking him? For mauling her? Because he was such a stupid oaf? He couldn't seem to find his tongue to ask.

She took a step toward him. "I want to thank you for saving my life. I didn't mean to put you in danger when I went riding last week. I didn't know the storm would come so fast." She rambled on as if unable to stem the flow of words now that they were started.

When she paused to catch her breath, he gestured toward the rock. "Would you like to join me? The sunrise colors are gone, but maybe we could just talk until time for breakfast."

She nodded, then went over and eased herself onto the rock. He sat beside her, careful not to come too close, although he longed to wrap his arm around her. Her rose scent beckoned him, but he fought the temptation.

The moments stretched on in silence. There were a hundred things he wanted to ask her, but all of them were wrong. Would she ever be able to love him? Did she still love Kendrick? Could she be happy married to a cavalryman? He couldn't ask any of them. So he kept his peace.

"I hear you love horses." She broke the silence.

He looked at her, nearly losing himself in her liquid green eyes. "Someday

I'd like to raise horses." He smiled as the dream took shape once again in his mind. "Not just any breed, either. They have to be the best."

"And where do you intend to raise these horses of yours?"

"I've been up north in Arizona. There's some of the best pastureland I've ever seen in those mountains. I could raise some fine horses there." The picture of mountain pastures and towering pines was so real, he could almost feel the cool air and see the horses grazing in grass up to their knees.

A light touch on his arm brought him out of his reverie. Glorianna quickly withdrew her hand as he smiled down at her. "It sounds like a beautiful dream." She returned his smile, causing his heart to pound. "I can almost see it from your description."

The clear notes of a bugle brought him back to the present. "I have to get back to camp and so do you. Your father will worry if he can't find you." He stood and offered his hand to help her up. She hesitated, then placed her small fingers into his hand. Once again, he fought a battle to keep from pulling her into his arms.

"I come here every morning. If you find you can't sleep, you're welcome to join me."

"I just might do that." She smiled once again, her countenance rivaling the beauty of the sunrise.

At the Verde River, Glorianna laughed at Alyce as the little girl put her face in the water, then came up chortling while it dripped off her nose and chin. She had never seen a young child enjoy the water as much as Alyce did. They had to guard her constantly because she showed no fear of the river.

Laughing, she reached out to hug Alyce. Fayth hadn't been feeling well. She stayed home, and Glorianna promised to watch Alyce. She really wanted to give Fayth some time to rest without the active toddler to oversee. Alyce made the whole bathing trip more fun, anyway.

Settling the laughing girl in her lap, Glorianna's thoughts drifted as Alyce played. Conlon and the other men were downriver, washing and cooling off. She sighed, thinking of the morning talks she and Conlon had shared in the past few weeks. They had come to enjoy their quiet time watching the sun change the sky from dark to brilliant color.

She remembered what Fayth said about checking for the qualities God would want her to look for in a man. Conlon had those qualities. Every morning he shared something new and exciting he had learned about God. He loved to read the Bible, and his greatest regret came from there being no formal gathering of Christians in the area. He missed his church.

They had begun to share their hopes and dreams with one another. At first, Glorianna was hesitant, thinking Conlon would become impatient and forward. She had been wrong. He modeled gentility. Sometimes she could see the desire to touch her in his eyes, but he always refrained as if waiting for her to signal her readiness.

Every day she liked him more. Liked him? She wasn't sure if that was the right term anymore. Did she love him? She loved his devotion to the Lord. She loved the way his eyes sparkled with humor. She loved his joking. She loved to look at his handsome face when she thought he wouldn't notice. Come to think of it, there was quite a lot she loved about Conlon.

"Go'wy." Alyce tugged on Glorianna's clothes. "Out. Play there." She pointed at the shore.

Glorianna smiled. Alyce had trouble saying her name, but it was so cute. Conlon sometimes mimicked the girl, but most of the time he called her "Glory." Kathleen was the only other one who had ever called her by that nickname.

"Okay, Sweetie, let's go." Glorianna picked Alyce up and headed for the path up to the wagons. They would dry off, then play peekaboo in the brush, Alyce's second favorite thing to do.

"Where are you?" Glorianna called after they had dried off. Alyce giggled loudly, and Glorianna could barely keep from laughing. She could see the girl standing with her face toward a tree. Her hands covered her eyes, and she thought she was invisible. "Where are you?" Glorianna called again, biting her lip to stop the laughter.

"Peekboo." Alyce's deep chuckles were infectious. Glorianna couldn't believe how much the girl had changed in the last few months. Her second birthday was only two months away, and every day she acted more like a little girl than a baby.

Alyce churned her chubby little legs into action as she headed into the brush to hide once more. "Wait, Alyce, don't go far."

Glorianna hurried after her, ducking around a gnarled mesquite tree. Alyce stood with her hands covering her face, waiting for Glorianna to look for her. A low buzzing noise filled the air. A remembered fear stopped Glorianna.

Frozen in place, she looked for the source of the noise. Under the bush beside Alyce, a rattlesnake lay coiled, his spade-shaped head poised to strike. Glorianna didn't know what to do. If she screamed for help, Alyce might get scared and move.

She had no gun to shoot with, but looking at the ground, she noticed a small rock beside her foot. Ever so slowly, she stretched down for the stone. With its weight in her hand, she straightened, trying to pray, remembering that David defeated a giant with one stone and the Lord. *Please, God, help me,* she prayed, hoping He could direct her aim.

As soon as the rock left her hand, Glorianna leapt forward to snatch Alyce away before the snake could strike. Her aim wasn't quite true. The rock missed the snake's head, thudding into its coiled body. The rattler's head darted at Alyce's leg. Glorianna jerked her up and jumped back. The girl's scream told her she hadn't been fast enough.

A gunshot echoed along the riverbank. The snake exploded, and Glorianna whirled away in revulsion. Conlon grabbed her and pulled her out of the brush.

"Did she get bit?" he asked roughly.

Glorianna didn't have to look to know something was wrong. Alyce screamed and twisted in her arms.

"Hold her still while I check her," Conlon ordered.

Trembling, Glorianna tried to obey. Alyce threw herself from side to side, resisting their efforts to help her. Glorianna knew she needed to be calm in order to keep the girl quiet.

"It's okay, Sweetie," she crooned. "It's okay." She smoothed the hair back from Alyce's forehead, praying for the girl.

From the corner of her eye, she watched as Conlon removed Alyce's shoe. Briefly, he worked on the leg, then went to a nearby mud hole. He brought back a handful of mud and slathered it over Alyce's lower leg.

Conlon looked up at her, his face grim. "We have to get her back to camp. I've done what I can, but she'll need to see the doctor."

Glorianna's mouth felt like cotton. She tried to speak, but nothing came out. Tears burned in her eyes. How had this happened? Fayth had trusted her to watch over Alyce and now she might die. Fayth would never forgive her for this.

Chapter 10

Numbness settled over Glorianna as Conlon lifted Alyce from her arms. As though enveloped in a dense fog, she heard the shouts and cries of the men and women who raced up from the river to see what had happened. She still knelt on the ground as confusion reigned.

She tried to listen to Conlon as he spoke with Timothy about his daughter. His deep voice soothed her, but she could only pick up a word here and there. Conversation about the snake, Alyce's shoe, and the doctor drifted past. Some of the women tried to talk to her, but Glorianna couldn't answer. Grief and guilt consumed her.

Loud creaking grated on her nerves. The mules strained to pull the ambulance back to the camp. The thunder of hooves told her someone was hurrying to the camp to alert the doctor and Fayth. Soon it would start. Fayth would hear the news, and they would no longer be friends. Tears began to slide down her cheeks, splatting unheeded on her folded hands.

"Glory?" Conlon squatted on the ground in front of her. "Sweetheart, she's going to be okay."

He reached out and lifted her hands in his, wiping the tears from them. Holding her hands fast in one hand, he touched her wet cheek with the other. His fingers traced the path of her tears. Glorianna closed her eyes and welcomed his soothing touch.

Taking her chin in his hand, Conlon lifted until her eyes met his. His blue eyes were filled with compassion. She wanted so much for him to hold her, but she knew what she had done made her unworthy. She closed her eyes again to shut out the pain.

"Glory, look at me."

She couldn't.

"She's going to be okay, you know."

Glorianna's eyes flew open. "Alyce?" she whispered, as if hearing him for the first time. "How do you know?"

Seated on the ground, Conlon pulled her close, letting her lean on him. "When you hit the snake with the rock, its aim changed. Then you grabbed Alyce. When the snake struck, it hit her shoe."

"Then she didn't really get bit?" Glorianna swung around to face Conlon. She held her breath, hoping it was true.

"Oh, she got bit all right."

Her hopes sank as quickly as they had risen.

"But, it was a grazing bite."

She searched his eyes for a reason to hope. "Will she. . .does that mean. . . ?"

"I'm sure she'll be just fine." Conlon's smile felt like a balm to her wounded soul. "She'll be a little sick and her leg will hurt, but that should be all. Fayth will need your help."

Glorianna stood and turned away, crossing her arms over her stomach. "Fayth won't want to see me ever again."

Conlon stood, put his arms around her, and pulled her against him again. "Now why would you say that? Fayth thinks you're wonderful."

"Don't you see?" She whirled around, anger making her words loud. "She trusted me with her child and I betrayed that trust." Tears of self-directed anger and shame washed down her cheeks.

Conlon grabbed her. His eyes darkened. "Don't you realize you saved her life? If you hadn't thought and acted so quickly, Alyce would be dead. This wasn't your fault."

"Yes, it was." She tried to back away from him. He pulled her against his chest, embracing her. She gripped his shirt in her hands and sobbed. "Every time I'm supposed to take care of someone, she dies. Alyce will die just like my mother did."

"Oh, Sweetheart." Conlon tenderly tightened his hold, his cheek pressed against her head, one hand softly rubbing her back. When her sobs quieted, he spoke. "Your father told me about your mother. It wasn't your fault she died. There was nothing you could have done to prevent it. Your father doesn't blame you. If anything, he's struggled with his own guilt for having left you in charge when he knew she was dying."

He lifted her chin, placing a tender kiss on her forehead. "Come with me now and talk to Fayth. She will understand."

Glorianna nodded, wondering why this man had the ability to comfort her like no other person could. She thought she would be happy to stay forever in his embrace.

❧

Glorianna smoothed her dress with shaky fingers as she approached the Holwell house with Conlon. Conlon had sent one of the men with the ambulance, keeping his horse for her to ride. During the ride back from the river, she hoped fervently Alyce would be okay and that Fayth would find it in her heart to forgive. *Oh, please help her forgive me. I don't think I can bear to lose her as a friend.*

Timothy swung the door open, grinned, and beckoned them in. "Fayth," he called. "They're here."

Before Glorianna had time to be afraid, Timothy engulfed her in a hug. Then Fayth was there, crying, thanking her, and holding her as if she would never let go.

"I don't know how I can thank you enough." Fayth stepped back, her hands still holding Glorianna's. "You saved my little girl, and all I can do is say thank you."

She turned to Conlon and hugged him. "Thank you, too. The doctor said that you helped by having the foresight to put fresh mud on the bite."

Glorianna barely knew when Conlon wrapped his arm around her. Exhaustion made her want to lie down and sleep right then. Elation made her want to sing and dance. She'd been forgiven. She didn't understand why, but she knew Fayth still wanted her as a friend.

"I have to get back to Alyce." Fayth turned back to Glorianna and hugged her again. "You look worn out. Why don't you get some sleep and come by tomorrow. Alyce will want to see you, I'm sure."

Numbly, Glorianna nodded and allowed Conlon to lead her home. Twilight settled over the desert. Crickets sang, and in the distance, coyotes raised their voices in a motley chorus. Peace wrapped around her like a soft blanket as Conlon pulled her once more into his embrace.

"Get some sleep, Glory." His husky whisper sent a tingle through her. "I can't wait to see you in the morning." He kissed her forehead and disappeared in the dusky evening.

The next morning, Glorianna stuck her head through the Holwells' door. "Fayth?" She didn't want to call loudly and risk waking Fayth or Alyce if they were sleeping. She waited a moment, listening. A faint sound of singing drifted through the house. She smiled. Fayth loved to sing to Alyce. She said it helped her sleep.

Glorianna tiptoed across to Alyce's room and peeked through the door. Alyce's eyes were closed, her eyelashes dark against her pale cheeks. Fayth stroked her daughter's head and crooned a song about Jesus being her friend.

Fayth looked up and smiled at Glorianna, beckoning her to enter the room.

"Sit down." Fayth patted the chair beside her. "She's finally asleep. It's been a rough night for her."

Alyce looked frail and vulnerable in the morning light. Fayth, too, seemed drawn and tired.

"Did you get any sleep last night?"

Fayth smiled. "Timothy watched her for awhile so I could rest. You'll find out when you're a mother, though, that it's impossible to sleep when your child is sick or in pain."

Glorianna bit her lip, trying to swallow the lump closing her throat. She didn't want to cry again. "I'm so sorry this happened. I don't know how you could forgive me."

"What?" Fayth's eyes widened. "Why would there be anything to forgive? You saved Alyce's life when you grabbed her away like that."

"But, I'm responsible for her being bitten in the first place." Glorianna wiped angrily at her eyes. "I should have been more careful."

"Glorianna, listen to me." Fayth's smile faded. "You have treated my daughter like she was your own. You did not intend for that snake to bite her. It was an accident. How could you help that?"

"I don't know. I just feel like this is my fault. I was so scared I would lose you as a friend."

Fayth hugged her. "I can't begin to think of not having you for a friend. And I know Alyce would be lost without you to play with her. Besides," she smiled, "you have to help with the baby."

"What baby?" Glorianna frowned.

"Why, the baby I'm expecting." Fayth laughed. "That's why I've been so tired and sick lately."

Glorianna gasped. "A baby! Oh, that's so wonderful. I can't wait." She hugged Fayth with enthusiasm, then pulled back. "Now, I insist you let me sit with Alyce while you get some sleep. Just tell me what to do and I'll be fine."

Fayth nodded and gestured to a bottle and packet on the table. "We've made a poultice of vinegar and gun powder. If she wakes, you can bathe her leg and put more of that on. It helps to draw out the poison."

"Fayth?"

"Yes?" Fayth turned back to look at Glorianna.

"I don't understand how you can still trust God so much in spite of all this."

"Because I know He has a plan for my life, for Timothy's, and even for Alyce's."

"But how do you know His plan is right?"

Fayth smiled and took Glorianna's hand in hers. "I know there have been times when I doubted God and His direction. But I've learned that I can't depend on what I feel. I have to trust what God tells me in the Bible."

"And what does He tell you?" Glorianna whispered.

Tipping her head to one side, Fayth looked at Glorianna a moment. "One of my favorite bits of wisdom from the Bible is Proverbs 3:5 and 6. It says, 'Trust in the Lord with all thine heart; and lean not unto thine own understanding. In all thy ways acknowledge him, and he shall direct thy paths.' You see, all I have to do is trust Him, and God will take care of the rest."

Fayth squeezed her hand. "Does this questioning have to do with a certain handsome cavalry officer?"

Glorianna felt the heat of a blush in her cheeks. "I suppose so. But don't you say anything. Promise?"

At Fayth's nod, she continued. "When I'm with Conlon, it feels so perfect. But sometimes I'm confused about what's right. I can't really explain what I mean."

Fayth stood up, leaned over, and hugged her. "Keep asking God to lead you and He will. You'll know the right way when you have God's peace."

✦

Conlon held Champ's foot aloft as Josiah measured to see if the last shoe fit properly. "Not quite," Josiah announced, heading back to the forge. "I'll just need to bend this side in a little more."

Josiah thrust the horseshoe back into the red embers. Yellow flames licked eagerly at the metal, then died down. "I hear you had some excitement at the river yesterday."

Conlon shook his head. "I'm beginning to think there's something about Glorianna that attracts snakes. There was the one under her cot, the one at the river, and the worst snake of all, Dirk."

Josiah laughed. "At least that's one snake who won't be bothering her again. He's long gone."

"Well, the other two are even farther from reach. They're dead. Sometimes I agree with those who say the only good snake is a dead snake."

Josiah pulled the reddened horseshoe from the coals. Placing it on the anvil, he studied the glowing metal, then began to pound. He plunged the shoe into water before walking back out to Champ with Conlon.

"I agree. I don't know why God allows some snakes to live." Josiah lifted Champ's foot and aligned the shoe. "But, we have to remember that God knows more than we'll ever know. You can trust Him with her. No matter how many critters are out there."

"You're right." Conlon grinned. "Here I am wanting to take over for God again."

Josiah laughed. "We all want to do that on occasion." He pounded the last of the nails into the horseshoe and dropped Champ's foot. "By the way, how's the problem with the future wife? Has she picked out her wedding dress yet?"

"You're asking for trouble." Conlon smiled. "It so happens that she's getting very fond of me. In fact, I think in no time at all I'll be able to ask her to marry me, and she'll jump at the chance."

Putting his tools away, Josiah smirked at Conlon. "You just may be in for a surprise. God has a way of taking us down a notch sometimes. I have a feeling you may be in for a rough time before your little filly agrees to a wedding."

"Exactly what have you heard?"

"Me? I haven't heard a thing. I just know God has a sense of humor. I'll eagerly waiting to hear you say those vows. But I also know nothing has gone smoothly so far for the two of you."

Conlon started to lead Champ back to the stables. "Everything has changed, Josiah. You'll see," he called back.

⚘

That evening, Timothy answered Conlon's knock and pulled him into the house. "Come in. I'm glad you could join us on such short notice."

Conlon smiled at Glorianna, seated across the room beside her father. "What's the occasion?" Conlon asked.

"Oh, good, you're all here." Fayth clapped her hands together and peeked into Alyce's bedroom. "Alyce will be awake soon. Timothy, you tell them why we invited them."

"We thought we would celebrate Alyce's recovery." Timothy crossed the room and put his arm around Fayth. "We're so glad to have friends like you, and this is our way of saying thanks."

"I think Emily has the meal almost ready," Fayth said. "I'll check and be right back."

Conlon pulled a chair alongside Glorianna's and sat down. He wanted to take her hand in his, but refrained. The green dress she wore brought out the green in her eyes and accented the burnished copper of her hair. He longed to touch her again.

"Lieutenant Sullivan?" Captain Wilton pulled his attention from Glorianna. "Do you remember the Dentons?"

Conlon frowned at Timothy, whose face split in a huge grin. "I remember them," he admitted reluctantly. He thought of Major Denton and his overbearing wife, who had been determined that Conlon would marry their only daughter, Chastity. The woman followed him wherever she could, her loathsome daughter trailing behind. He hadn't had a moment's peace while they were at the camp, and he didn't want to repeat the experience. For Captain Wilton's sake, he had been polite, but he didn't know how he had managed.

Captain Wilton interrupted his reverie. "The Dentons are traveling back to Tucson from up north. They will be staying here for a few weeks. I gather Mrs. Denton wants a rest. Also, the major and I need to discuss troop movements and some of the problems with Indians in the area."

"They're staying here?" Conlon glanced at Glorianna. Could Josiah have been right? Was disaster, in the form of Chastity Denton, right around the corner?

Chapter 11

The early morning air caressed her cheek with chilled fingers. Glorianna took a deep breath, savoring the fresh scent of rain-washed earth. The predawn darkness faded, preparing for another gorgeous sunrise.

Glorianna padded out of the fort in eager anticipation of another morning visit with Conlon. Every time they met, she found something else to admire about him. Today she wanted to ask him about his family. He always hedged around that question, but for some reason she couldn't let it drop.

Conlon sat with his back to her, head bowed. She hesitated, wondering if he was praying. Most mornings he spent time with the Lord. Maybe she should leave him alone. She considered this, then with a shake of her head, she wound through the desert plants toward their rock.

As she drew near, Conlon stood and turned to her. "Good morning, Glory." His mischievous smile set her pulse racing. Blue eyes, brighter than daybreak, held her gaze. She longed to reach up and touch his cheek, to run her fingers through his disobedient hair.

"And how do you know this is a good morning?" She smiled, enjoying his teasing.

"Every day the Lord makes is a good one. You should know that by now." The intense look in his eyes took her breath away. "Besides," he continued, softly, "if the morning starts with seeing you, it has to be good."

The heat of a blush stole up her cheeks, and she thought for a moment about returning to the safety of her home. Could she trust herself around this charming man who brought out the best and worst in her?

As if reading her thoughts, Conlon gestured to their rock. "Come on and sit. The show's about to begin."

She relaxed and settled herself on the rock, trying to ignore the tingle that shot through her as his arm brushed against hers. *This should be a bigger rock,* she thought. But there weren't any other rocks big enough to sit on. She leaned away from him, fighting an inner urge to rest her head on his shoulder.

They watched the changing sky in awed silence. Brilliant colors swept across the gray panorama like a wave washing up on the beach, reaching out with all its might, then slowly ebbing back to the ocean.

Conlon took her hand in his. Her small fingers felt at home engulfed by his large ones. The silence wrapped around them like a familiar cloak, comfortable and warm. Oh, how she wanted to know this man better.

"Conlon?" She tried to keep from getting lost in his morning glory gaze. She wanted to remember her objective. "You know so much about me and my family. Why won't you ever tell me about your family and where you come from?"

A look of pain flitted across his face. It happened so fast, she wondered if she had imagined it. He released her hand and bent to scoop up a handful of rocks. He toyed with them as she tried to be patient.

After what seemed an eternity, he looked at her, his expression almost grim. "For years, I never talked about my family and my past. Finally, I did tell Josiah, but only because I had to talk to someone. He's been my friend and encourager in the Lord. He got me through some pretty bad times."

Glorianna swallowed, her mouth suddenly dry as dust. Did she really want to know his past? What if he had done something terrible? Could she forgive him? "If you don't want to tell me, you don't have to." She wanted to grab the words back as soon as they popped out of her mouth. She knew a friend should always be willing to listen.

"No. Josiah tells me it helps to talk about the past, and he's usually right."

He rolled one of the small pebbles between his fingers, then tossed it at a nearby cactus. The plunk of the rock startled a jackrabbit. The rabbit hopped off, his oversized back legs propelling him forward.

"I grew up in a small town near Chicago, I'm the oldest. I had two younger sisters and a younger brother." He paused to throw another rock. "My parents owned a small dairy herd and supplied milk to the town."

He stopped, staring at the gradually lightening sky. Sighing, he looked down at her and smiled sadly. "You'll have to excuse me. I'm not very good at talking about my past. It's hard."

She nodded. "I understand."

"I always helped Dad with the milk route. We worked hard, but that didn't bother me."

Conlon studied his hands as he spoke. "As a teenager, I looked forward to Sundays. We finished our work early, then went to church. But. . . ," he shook his head slowly and sighed, "I loved going to church for all the wrong reasons. I liked seeing my friends and being sought after by the girls. I was always the center of attention. The girls and I flirted constantly. To me that was the sole reason for going to church. I never thought about the Lord back then. I was too full of myself."

Conlon's shoulders sagged, and Glorianna found herself wanting to wrap him in her arms. She wanted to take away the pain of his past and help him heal.

"I've always had a problem with patience or, I should say, a lack of patience. One Sunday, we were running late on our milk run. My dad was sick, and I had to do most of the work. We barely got home, and he collapsed in bed. All I could think about was getting ready for church. Suzanne, one of the cutest girls in town, had promised to sit with me that morning, and I didn't want to miss such an opportunity."

A rock arced out and thudded against another unlucky cactus. "I didn't even help Mom get Dad in bed. All I could think about was me, me, me. Usually, Dad and I got the horse hitched to the wagon so Mom and the girls could ride into town. That morning, my sisters were fighting, so they weren't ready yet. My brother, the youngest of the family, wasn't ready, either. Mom called after me, but I acted like I didn't hear her. I jumped on my horse and left for church, soothing my conscience by saying church was more important than family. Besides, I tried to tell myself that my brother, Andy, could get the horse hitched up just fine."

He tossed the rest of the rocks on the ground and wiped his hands on his pants. "I knew better than to do that. We had a new horse, fresh broke and feisty. Andy didn't have much experience with horses yet. He'd been sickly from the time he was born. Small and frail. He couldn't do the same work I had done at his age. I didn't take that into account. Didn't want to. I only wanted to get to church before someone else claimed my seat beside Suzanne."

He sat in silence for so long, Glorianna didn't think he would finish his story. His shoulders slumped, and the glimpse she had of his blue eyes made her realize they threatened to overflow. Her heart ached for him.

Gently, she placed her hand on his arm. She could feel the muscles knotted beneath his shirt. He looked down at her, and she tried to give him a comforting smile, hoping to relieve his obvious distress.

"We all do things we regret," she spoke up softly. "Especially when we're young and self-centered. Believe me, everyone goes through that at some time." Her words, meant to comfort, had the opposite reaction. His eyes darkened in anger, whether directed at her or himself she didn't know. She fought the urge to back away from him, keeping her hand on his arm.

"You don't understand," he exploded. Closing his eyes, he took a few deep breaths as if trying to calm himself before he continued. "I'm sorry. I didn't mean to get angry." He gave her another sad smile that tore at her heart. "Let me finish, and then maybe you'll see what I mean."

Once more his hand enveloped hers, this time with a feeling of desperation. "We were halfway through the church service when one of our neighbors burst through the door shouting for Doc Riley. I'd been fighting a growing fear and guilt because my family hadn't shown up yet. I knew how much going to church meant to my mother."

He paused and Glorianna spoke up. "Your father was seriously ill, wasn't he?"

"No, it was Andy who needed the doctor." Conlon cleared his throat. "Andy tried to get the new horse hitched to the wagon. The horse must have sensed his fear and inexperience and began to act up. Andy wanted to please Dad and Mom, I'm sure, so he continued trying. Finally, I guess the horse had enough. He reared up, throwing Andy to the ground. When the horse came down, his hoof hit Andy in the head." Conlon choked and couldn't continue. A solitary tear rolled down his cheek.

Glorianna could feel tears flowing down her cheeks, as well. She gripped Conlon's hand tightly, trying to ease his pain from these horrible memories. "Did Andy. . .?" She didn't know how to ask the question.

"He died two days later." Conlon raked his fingers through his hair. "My oldest sister had started out to help him. She saw what happened, but couldn't get there in time. My dad recovered from his illness, but never from his grief. Even Mom, with her strong faith, had a sadness about her that I couldn't take. I blamed it on my selfishness and impatience."

"Is that why you left home?"

He nodded. "I know they didn't really blame me or if they did, they forgave me. Still, I couldn't live with the blame I put on myself. I ran. Like a coward, I ran and haven't been home since."

"You mean you haven't heard from your parents since you left home?" Glorianna couldn't keep the astonishment from her voice.

Conlon looked at her and shook his head. "For years, they had no idea where I was, so they couldn't write to me."

"Have you thought about writing them now?"

He smiled and squeezed her hand. "When I came here I was angry and confused. Josiah stepped in and helped me find my way to the Lord. Now, I don't attend church because there isn't one, but I have a relationship with the Lord that gives me peace about the past. I wrote to my parents. I apologized for everything that happened and told them where I am and what I'm doing. That was several months ago, and I still haven't heard from them."

"Maybe they've moved. Sometimes letters take awhile to reach people."

"Maybe." He sighed. "Then again, they may just want to forget me."

The sound of a trumpet drifted through the morning air. "I guess that's my call to get back inside. Thanks for listening."

Conlon stood, and she let him pull her to her feet. "Thanks for telling me. I know how hard that was for you."

For a long minute, he stood looking down into her eyes. Her heart began to pound, and she wondered if he would kiss her. She wondered if she would let him. Then, he leaned over and kissed her lightly on the forehead before tucking her arm in his and heading to the camp.

⚜

Josiah gave a final blow to the horseshoe on the anvil, then looked at Conlon, his eyes dancing with merriment. "Why the long face this morning, my friend? Are the wedding plans on hold?"

Conlon shrugged. "They're right on target, I think."

Josiah wiped his hands on his blacksmith apron and studied Conlon for a moment. "Something's wrong," he stated. "You haven't looked this bad since before you asked Jesus into your heart. What happened?"

"I don't know how you do it." Conlon grinned, feeling a peace settling over him.

Talking about his past always hurt. He didn't know why being with Josiah helped him so much. "I think God must tell you exactly what I'm thinking and feeling."

Josiah laughed. "Well, someone has to tell me because you sure won't unless I make you."

"I talked to Glorianna this morning." Conlon leaned against the side of the blacksmith shop and watched for Josiah's reaction.

"I thought you talked to her every morning."

"I mean, I talked to her about my family."

Josiah straightened up from throwing wood into the forge. "And?"

"You know, I didn't want to tell her, but now I'm glad I did. She really seemed to understand. She didn't condemn me like I might have done in her place. She's very concerned about my being in touch with my family."

"I knew that girl had something special." Josiah's grin lit up his face. He laughed. "You'd better get her to marry you quick or some other lucky man will get her first."

"Not a chance. I won't let them get close."

"By the way, I heard the captain's looking for you. Maybe he wants to know when you're setting the date." Josiah laughed.

Conlon strode toward the captain's office. With every passing minute, he felt better about having talked to Glorianna. He hadn't wanted to hold anything back from her, and now he knew nothing stood between them. Perhaps Josiah spoke the truth. He should talk to the captain and his daughter about a wedding. He smiled as he thought of finally being able to hold Glory in his arms without letting her go.

He stepped into the captain's office and stood at attention, waiting for him to look up from the papers on his desk. The early morning sounds of the camp blurred into a drone through the thick walls. Finally, Captain Wilton looked up, his face set in a frown. Conlon felt a first prick of uncertainty. What did he want?

"Lieutenant." Captain Wilton's booming voice almost startled him. "I'm afraid we have a little problem. I received word that some Apaches are making trouble over toward Pinal City. They were last reported heading into the Superstition Mountains. I want you to take some men and check it out."

Conlon stood frozen, wanting to protest, knowing it wouldn't be wise. *But I want to stay here with your daughter,* he wanted to say. *I don't want to miss my morning talks with her.* Despite all his protesting thoughts, he replied, "Yes, Sir."

With a heavy heart, he spent the rest of the morning looking over maps and making plans with the captain. He tried hard to forget his red-haired beauty and the Sonoran sunrise they loved to share.

Chapter 12

Conlon leaned back against his saddle, his long frame stretched close to the campfire. Millions of stars paraded across the dark sky like tiny twinkling fireflies. The sounds of the desert descended upon him, the high-pitched yips of a pack of coyotes cut short by the unearthly scream of a cougar. Good thing he had posted guards around the camp.

He rolled to his side and stared at the fire. For two weeks, he and his small troop of men had searched the Superstition Mountains for the band of Apaches reported to be terrorizing the countryside. Each moment of the two weeks had been sheer torture. Every day he thought only of getting back to Glorianna, seeing her bright smile, and talking with her in the mornings. How he longed to run his fingers over her smooth cheeks. He wanted to watch the rose blush travel over her apple blossom complexion like the sunrise traveled across the sky. Glorianna, How he missed her.

He knew the men thought him totally inept. He kept running them in circles, forgetting the direction from which they had come. Thank God, Timothy had been assigned to the group. Without his encouragement, Conlon would have given up days ago. Timothy understood how hard leading could be when you had a woman on your mind.

Another week, he thought. *I'll give this scouting expedition one more week. If we don't see more than some old tracks, we'll head back to Camp MacDowell. There's no need to wear ourselves out when the Indians have already moved on to other parts. They're probably miles from here laughing at how easily they fooled us. We've never even gotten a glimpse of them. Of course, it doesn't help when we don't get word about them until they've had a week's head start.*

He shifted on his bedroll, hoping the hard ground would get softer. *You'd think after two weeks I'd be used to sleeping on the ground. But, then, after two weeks I should be over thinking about Glory all the time, too.* A sudden longing made him grit his teeth in frustration. He could almost feel his arms around her. He could see her rosebud mouth smiling up at him. How would it feel to press his lips to hers? To run his fingers through her silken hair? To hear her say, "I love you"? Smiling, he drifted off to sleep as the coyotes, once again, began their nightly chorus.

Morning dawned, bright and clear. Conlon hurried the men through their breakfast, determined they would find some sign or direction today. As soon as these Indians were controlled, he could return to Camp MacDowell and Glory. The very thought of seeing her made him smile.

73

Four hours later, hot and discouraged, his small troop rested in the shade of a side canyon. They had followed old hoof prints along the side of the canyon, hoping to find a place where the Indians had hidden. It turned out to be a dead end. The only way out was a steep cliff that a horse could never climb.

"Where to, Lieutenant?" Timothy crouched next to Conlon.

"I guess we'll head toward the north end of the mountains. It's closest to Pinal City, and we haven't gone all the way around yet."

Timothy squinted up at the sun. "I wish there weren't so many places to hide in these mountains. You know, they come here because of that. They can disappear without a trace, wait for us to give up, then continue their raids whenever they want."

"I know," Conlon agreed. "I wish I knew a better way. We don't have the knowledge of the land like the Indians do. They can survive on almost nothing and hide behind the smallest bush."

Conlon stood and stared off into the empty desert. "Let's go, men." They mounted and headed back into the open. The intense heat seemed to suck the life out of them one step at a time.

"Lieutenant." Timothy shaded his eyes, staring ahead. "There's a dust cloud ahead. Riders are circling the mountains."

"Fall into formation, men," Conlon directed. "Let's ride."

Even the horses seemed to sense the excitement of the moment. They lifted their heads and rolled into a canter, manes and tails streaming in the wind. Maybe this would end their search. Maybe this was their long-sought quarry.

For long minutes they kept up the pace. Then, the distant dust cloud drifted away. Conlon slowed the column to a trot, wondering if, once again, the Indians had simply disappeared without a trace. Had they imagined the horses ahead? What if the desert heat and the desire to fulfill their mission made the whole company see a mirage? He shook his head. The very idea was ridiculous.

Topping a rise, Conlon raised his hand, calling a halt. Below them a group of horses and riders gathered close. They were so intent on each other, they obviously didn't see the small group of soldiers above them. The riders' saddles creaked. Sunlight glinted off their gun barrels. The yellow stripes on their pant legs caught the eye. These weren't Indians. They were cavalrymen.

Conlon allowed Champ to pick his way down the slope. As small rocks skittered down the hill ahead of them, the men stopped their conference and looked up. Conlon counted a dozen, some in uniform, some in regular clothes. As he and his men approached, the soldiers pulled back, leaving two older men to face them. Clearly, they were in charge.

For a moment, he studied the two men. The one on the right had a commanding air about him. He didn't wear a uniform, but his bearing conveyed the message of his military position. Only an officer of rank could do that with such ease.

The second officer looked vaguely familiar. His grim face sported a huge mustache that covered his mouth and dripped well past his chin. Bushy eyebrows drew together in a frown as he studied Conlon.

"Lieutenant Sullivan, Camp MacDowell, Sir." Conlon held himself erect, watching the reaction of the two men.

"Sullivan?" The heavy mustache opened to release the words. "Are you the Sullivan serving under Captain Wilton?"

That voice tickled a memory somewhere. Conlon nodded. "Yes, Sir."

The mustache split in a grin, a deep chuckle issuing forth to break the man's angry countenance. "I guess you don't remember me, Son."

Son? Who was this man to call him son?

The man continued. "I'm Major Denton."

"Yes, Sir, I remember." *And want to forget,* he thought. "I believe Captain Wilton is expecting your family to visit Camp MacDowell."

"That's right." The big man frowned. "We've had a slight delay, but we plan to get there soon." He gestured to the man on the horse next to him. "You've probably heard of General Crook. General, this young lieutenant took quite a liking to my daughter. He's the reason she's so anxious to return to Camp MacDowell." A hearty laugh followed.

General Crook's gaze hadn't faltered or changed visibly, but Conlon felt the intensity increase just the same. *Took a liking to his daughter?* Conlon wanted to groan in frustration, but kept his expression neutral, pasting a smile on his face.

"Pleasure to meet you, General. I've heard a lot about your campaigns from Arizona Territory to Montana." Conlon had long admired General George Crook and his expertise in tracking and fighting the Indians. He was a legend among the cavalry.

"You know, General," Major Denton said, "Lieutenant Sullivan may be the answer to our problem."

At Crook's nod, Major Denton turned back to Conlon. "We're camped a few miles from here. We were on our way to Camp MacDowell when the general found us. I agreed to help him round up the Apaches who are causing trouble, but we didn't know what to do with my wife and daughter."

Forcing himself to stay calm, Conlon didn't want to hear what the major was thinking. *Please, God, don't let him ask me what I think he wants to ask.*

"Why don't you and your men escort them to Camp MacDowell? Then, we can use all our men and really get after these Indians."

"I'd love to help you out, Sir, but Captain Wilton sent us on a mission to find the marauders. I don't think he would want me to quit before we had tried everything we could to catch them."

"Nonsense." The bushy eyebrows drew together in another frown. "The general and I are superior officers here. If we give you a different set of orders, your captain can't possibly object. Besides, I'll be at the camp as soon as I can and settle the matter."

"We'll send you written orders, Lieutenant," General Crook said. "The ladies need to be someplace other than a rough camp in the desert."

Conlon ordered his men to fall in line for the trip to the major's camp. *God, please give me the patience for this,* he pleaded. *If Mrs. Denton and Chastity are as bad as before, I may be tempted to leave them for coyote bait in the desert.*

Then again, he smiled ruefully, *what do I have against the coyotes?*

❧

"Lieutenant Conlon Sullivan." The high-pitched squeal made Conlon groan all the way down to his toes. Chastity stood before him, batting her blue eyes and fluffing her blond curls, trying her best to look coy. Her attempts failed.

"Hello, Miss Denton."

"Oh, none of this 'Miss Denton' business." She dipped her parasol and smiled impishly. "We know each other too well for such formality. Just call me Chastity." She placed her hand on his arm possessively.

He felt like his face would probably rival the deep pink sky of the sunrise. *God, I can't take Chastity to Camp MacDowell with me. What will Glorianna think? The two of them will be like cats with their tails tied together.* He groaned inwardly, thinking of Josiah's warning of impending doom.

❧

Dearest Kathleen,

I can't thank you enough for writing to me about Kendrick. I don't know why I was so blinded by his charms. I believe he always represented adventure to me. All the other girls were wild about him, and I followed along for some unknown reason. Actually, I guess the reason was pretty obvious. I wanted to fit in.

Because of Mother's illness and our travels as I grew up, I didn't have many friends. You are my only friend there and, believe me, you were enough. I thank you for standing by me even when my thickheaded ways threatened to undo me.

I do have a friend here. I wish you could come out and meet Fayth. She's older than I am and married. She has the sweetest little girl, Alyce. If we didn't live in such a remote area, I would invite you to come out here. Maybe someday I will anyway.

Glorianna stopped and chewed thoughtfully on the end of her pen. Kathleen, sweet and steady, always confided her longing for marriage and a family. Unfortunately, a birthmark splashed across her cheek marred her looks. Despite her deep faith in God and His purpose for her life, Kathleen grieved because none of the eligible young men would notice her. Glorianna frowned; at least they didn't notice her positively. They constantly made hateful remarks and tormented her because of her looks. Not one of the louts took the time to see Kathleen's inner beauty.

As I am writing, I remember Father saying he expects to get a transfer this fall. Maybe we'll go someplace near a city and you could join us. Being in a camp like MacDowell is a little lonely, but I'm told there are some nice cities in Arizona Territory. Maybe we'll even go to Fort Lowell just outside of Tucson. I've heard it's a nice town.

She stopped writing again, thinking how to word the next part of her letter. Laughing blue eyes danced across her vision. How she missed Conlon. For a few mornings, she continued to go to their rock and watch the sunrise. It wasn't the same with Conlon gone. The colors seemed pale without him there to talk to. She couldn't wait for him to get back.

You were right about something else, Kathleen. There are other men. I've finally realized that. In fact, I've met a man I feel is right for me. Fayth recommended the same thing you always did. She said I should look for godly attributes in a man. Conlon Sullivan is just that—a godly man.
We've been meeting in the mornings to watch the sunrise. Conlon always gets up to have a time alone with God. I happened to find out and began to join him. Now, if I don't see him early, my day isn't the same. Right now he's off with some men tracking down renegade Indians. I can't tell you how much I miss his presence. I do wish you could meet him. I know you would love him, too.

She could just picture Conlon and Kathleen together. He wouldn't even notice her birthmark, or if he did, he would only comment on how the star-shaped mark enhanced her beauty. And they wouldn't be empty words, either. Conlon cared about people and saw beauty where others didn't. As she thought, the conviction grew that she needed to bring Kathleen out west to help her heal from life's hurts.

A knock at the door interrupted Glorianna. She carefully put the pen in the inkwell and hurried to answer. Fayth and Alyce beamed at her from the front step.

"Come in. I'm glad you dropped by." She laughed. "I'm so bored, I'm actually writing a letter to my cousin. She'll be shocked to hear from me so soon. I'm terrible with letters."

Fayth's eyes twinkled. "I have some news for you."

"What?" Glorianna held her breath, hoping this was the news she wanted to hear.

"They've been spotted. The men will be here in about half an hour."

Alyce clapped her hands, then held them out to Glorianna. "Daddy, home."

Glorianna swung the girl up in the air. "You're right. Daddy's home, Sweetheart. I'll bet you'll be glad to see him."

"I'll bet you'll be glad to see someone, too." Fayth's knowing gaze sent heat creeping up Glorianna's cheeks.

"I couldn't possibly know what you mean." Glorianna tilted her head and fluffed her hair. Then she dissolved in giggles and kissed Alyce on the cheek. "I can't wait to see him. It seems like forever."

Later, at the mercantile, Glorianna dropped off the letter she'd written to Kathleen, then hurried to follow Fayth across the parade ground. The milling horses and men told them the troop had returned. Her heart raced as she searched the crowd for Conlon's familiar face. She couldn't wait to see him.

"Oh, dear." Fayth's soft whisper barely reached her ears.

She turned to look in the direction Fayth was looking. Conlon stood at the side of a wagon, reaching up to help a young woman down. He swung her easily to the ground. She wrapped her arms around his, leaned on him, and smiled up at him.

Melissa? Glorianna couldn't believe it. How could Melissa Cornwall have come here? The slim form and the blond curls looked just like Melissa's. First Kendrick and now Conlon. Would she never be rid of her rival? Her insides began a slow burn, gradually building in intensity as she watched that brazen female ooze all over Conlon.

Chapter 13

Conlon remembered, years before, falling in the muck of the pigpen after a good rain. The slimy goo stuck to his clothes, his skin, his hair, and everywhere. He thought he would never get it washed off. Chastity Denton reminded him of that slimy goo. She clung to his arm like a leech, a leech he feared he might never dislodge.

Tugging his arm in an attempt to at least loosen her grip, he glanced up to see disaster heading his way. A red-haired, green-eyed ball of fury rolled across the ground on a collision course with him. Desperately, he searched for a way of escape. From the other direction the ultimate catastrophe approached. Like a ship parting the waters of the ocean, Mrs. Denton sailed through the milling soldiers toward them. *God, don't leave me stranded here,* he begged, hating the helplessness of the situation.

"Lieutenant Sullivan." Sounding like a train making an emergency stop, Mrs. Denton had everyone's attention. Conlon winced and tried to turn away, moving his shoulder perilously close to Chastity's head. She took advantage of the situation by leaning against him and rubbing her cheek on his arm. He gritted his teeth and groaned.

"What is going on here?" Glorianna's normally melodic voice could cut through solid rock. Conlon watched helplessly as her green eyes flashed a fire that pierced his heart. He begged her with his eyes, hoping she'd understand his dilemma, but his silent plea didn't seem to help.

Taking a deep breath, Conlon knew he had to do something to redeem the situation. Sending up a silent prayer, he made one more unsuccessful attempt to dislodge Chastity before speaking.

"Excuse me, ladies." For the moment he had their attention. "Glorianna, I'd like you to meet Mrs. Denton and her daughter, Chastity." He tried to move his arm in a gesture, but the leech clung to him. "Mrs. Denton, Chastity, please meet Glorianna Wilton, Captain Wilton's daughter."

The three women eyed each other like vultures prepared to fight over their prey. To his relief, some of the fire faded from Glorianna's eyes as she studied Chastity.

"I'm pleased to meet you ladies." Although softer, her tone still had an edge.

Mrs. Denton sniffed, looked Glorianna up and down, and then nodded in her direction in obvious dismissal. The insult fanned the flames of fury, and the green eyes flashed fire again.

Chastity followed her mother's example. Lifting her nose in the air, she once more began to rub against Conlon's arm like a cat begging for attention.

"Lieutenant Sullivan," Mrs. Denton spoke sharply, "you will show us to our quarters. I believe the captain's quarters will suffice. They were pleasant enough when we were here last."

From the corner of his eye, Conlon watched Glorianna's jaw drop. "I'm sorry, Ma'am." He talked fast, hoping to calm the threatening storm. "The captain and his daughter are there. I'm sure our guest quarters will be fine."

Mrs. Denton, no doubt unaccustomed to having her orders questioned, began to resemble a lobster tossed in a kettle of boiling water. "We will stay in the captain's quarters, Lieutenant." Her tone brooked no discussion. "The captain and his daughter can stay in the guest quarters if they wish."

"What?" Oh, no, Glorianna had finally found her voice.

"Mrs. Denton. Chastity."

Conlon almost cried in relief as Fayth stepped forward, a smile lighting her face. "It's so good to have you visit us again."

Mrs. Denton stared hard at Fayth, whose smile never wavered. "Oh, yes, I remember you. Your husband is one of lower rank." The condescending tone and pointed insult made Conlon wince.

"I'm Fayth Holwell. We heard you were planning to join us. The guest quarters have been freshened and cleaned just for you."

"You forget, Mrs. Holwell, I've seen your guest quarters. We will stay in the captain's house as we did before." Mrs. Denton's features softened as she looked at her daughter. "Besides, Chastity needs a room of her own rather than a front room everyone tramps through."

Glorianna stepped up to Mrs. Denton looking undaunted. The larger woman towered over her. "My father and I are using his quarters, Mrs. Denton." Glorianna's slow, deliberate speech betrayed her anger. "You and your daughter may stay in the guest quarters like any other visitors to Camp MacDowell."

The two combatants faced one another in silence for what seemed an eternity. Mrs. Denton pulled herself up to her full height and turned from Glorianna.

"We'll see about this. Come, Chastity, I'm going to talk to the captain." With that she sailed off through the crowd.

Chastity unwound herself from Conlon and followed her mother with hesitant steps. She turned back for a moment and smiled coyly at Conlon, her ice blue eyes freezing his blood. "I'll be back." Her sultry tones nearly set the ground on fire. "We can take up where we left off then." She turned and sashayed after her mother.

Glorianna swung around and faced him.

God, Conlon prayed, *this would be a good time for an earthquake. Let the ground just open up and swallow me. Or maybe an Indian arrow between the shoulder blades would be nice. Anything but what I'm facing, Lord. I do believe I might be a little cowardly in this instance.*

Glorianna's mouth opened, and he winced, waiting for the diatribe. Her mouth closed again without having issued a sound.

She's speechless! Lord, I didn't know You could do miracles like this. Thank You.

"Glory, I know you're angry, but please let me explain."

Fayth stepped up beside Glorianna, her arms crossed over her chest.

Oh, Lord, not Fayth, too.

"Glory, Chastity and her mother determined the last time they were here that I would make a perfect husband for Chastity." He swallowed hard, trying not to shudder at the memory. "I've never encouraged her. I don't want to marry her. I don't even like her."

Did he detect some softening in both women? Taking a deep breath, he continued, "Please believe me, she means nothing to me."

"Then why was she draped all over you like a winter coat?" Glorianna's voice could still cut iron.

"Because I can't seem to convince her that I'm not good husband material." Desperation began to set in. "I don't know what to do to change her opinion of me. Once Mrs. Denton and Chastity decide something, they never change their minds."

Fayth's sudden smile felt like the sun after a rainy day. "He's right. Mrs. Denton runs her own household like a general and assumes she can run the rest of the world, too." She sighed. "I don't mean to speak ill of the woman, but her last visit was far from pleasant. She had the whole camp in an uproar by the time she left."

Conlon couldn't take his eyes off Glorianna's lips. They were lifting into a smile, a sight he thought he'd never see again. He could only think about how those lips would feel meeting his own. A sudden longing to hold her close almost overwhelmed him.

"I understand a little better." Glorianna smiled. "Just think about the desert heat and remember you don't need a winter coat."

"I'll do that." Relief flooded through him. "Now, if you ladies will excuse me, I need to see to the men." He started to turn away, then wheeled back around to Glorianna. Taking her hand in his, he ran his thumb over the soft skin. "I can't wait to see the sunrise tomorrow."

✤

That afternoon, Glorianna gritted her teeth and stared in stony silence at the desert rolling by the ambulance. They were heading for the Verde River for their evening time to bathe and cool off. She knew she needed more than a river to help her cool off. The heat of anger had been building all day, ever since she first saw Chastity Denton and her mother.

Sighing, she recalled the talk she and Fayth had earlier that afternoon.

"*Glorianna, you have to realize that Conlon is a cavalryman. It's his duty to follow orders and please his superiors. If that means escorting a beautiful girl around, then that's what he has to do. It doesn't mean he likes it.*"

"*But I hate the way she leans on him and smiles up at him. She acts like she owns him.*" Glorianna detested the whine in her voice.

"*You know Conlon is not interested in her. It only takes one look at his face to see he's miserable around her.*"

"*I suppose you're right.*"

"*I am right. Conlon only has eyes for one beautiful girl, and that's you.*"

"*So what should I do?*"

"*Try to remember what a good Christian should do. You love her and treat her like you want to be treated.*" Fayth reached out and gave her a quick hug. "*I know that's far easier to say than to do. With God's help, you can, though.*"

"*I'll try,*" Glorianna promised.

⚜

Of course, that promise was made before she knew the extent of Mrs. Denton's formidable power. She soon learned that even her father quailed before the enemy. She knew he felt he made concessions, but it didn't help her at all. He finally decided that he would sleep in the officers' quarters. Mrs. Denton and the major, when he arrived, would have her father's room. The worst part was that he expected her to share her room with Chastity. That would be like crawling into bed every night with a rattlesnake or, even worse, a viper.

To her credit, Chastity hadn't been happy about the situation, either. She whined and pleaded to no avail. Chastity knew when she pushed as far as she could. Since then, she had done her best to irritate Glorianna at every turn.

The wagon pulled to a stop, and the women began to climb down. The men tied their horses and hurried to help before they continued down the river to their spot. Glorianna watched Chastity, sitting with her parasol twirling over her head, her blue eyes fastened on Conlon.

"Lieutenant." The sultry tone made Glorianna nauseous. "Help me down." Chastity cocked her head to one side and held out her hands, batting her blue eyes. Her ruby lips pursed in a sensual smile.

She could be Melissa's twin, Glorianna thought. *She has the same eyes, the same hair, the same coquettish attitude, and probably the same low standards, judging from the way she plastered herself to him earlier.*

Conlon approached the wagon, his jaw muscles tense, his eyes dark and narrowed. He did not look pleased with Chastity. He reached up, grasped her small waist, and fairly threw her to the ground. She barely caught her balance when he circled away from her to the front of the ambulance where Glorianna sat.

He stopped beside her, and Glorianna could see his struggle to control his anger. "May I help you down, Glory?" he asked softly. His words carried in the silence as the whole group watched the exchange.

"Thank you, Conlon." Glorianna tried to make her smile especially bright for him. The next moment his hands were circling her waist. Wrapping her fingers around his arms, she felt the tensing of his muscles as he lifted her effortlessly over the side of the wagon. He gently deposited her on the ground in front of him, holding her longer than necessary. For a moment she thought he might kiss her. Instead, he ran one finger down her cheek, smiled, winked, and stepped back.

She glanced at Chastity, gratified to see her red face and angry stance. Mrs. Denton stood near her daughter, doing an amazing resemblance of a thundercloud during a summer rainstorm. "Come, Chastity." Mrs. Denton's voice grated in the silence. "Let's not watch such a tawdry display."

Glorianna noticed Fayth and Timothy turning away, trying to hide their smiles. Several of the others chuckled quietly. Activity resumed. The men headed down the path to their part of the river. Glorianna followed Fayth and Alyce down the slope of the riverbank, hoping she could control her dislike of Chastity and her mother.

Awhile later, Alyce laughed with glee as she watched Glorianna spurt water in the air by pushing it up through her hands. Alyce loved water games, splashing her chubby hands and squealing when the water sprayed her face. She made a dive for her mother, going under the water before she reached her. Fayth pulled her up, shaking her head as Alyce sprayed them with water while she spluttered and laughed.

"Alyce, I don't think my heart can stand more of this." Fayth shook her head. "You have no fear of this water. I think it's time to get out."

Glorianna laughed and watched the pair head for the bank. She didn't notice who moved up beside her until Chastity spoke in her ear. The sultry tones had changed, sounding like a lower-pitched version of Mrs. Denton.

"So, you think Lieutenant Sullivan is going to be yours. I just want you to know you're wrong," Chastity said.

Glorianna reluctantly swung around. Ice blue eyes bored into her.

"He's mine," Chastity hissed. "My mother promised me I'd marry him, and she always gets what she wants."

"I believe Lieutenant Sullivan can choose a wife for himself." Glorianna tried hard to push her anger down.

"Oh, but you're wrong there." Chastity's smile could freeze fire. "He's a military man. My father has a lot of rank on him. Lieutenant Sullivan will have to do what he's told."

"Marriage is a little different than following orders on a parade ground."

"My father can make his life miserable. Is that what you want for your precious lieutenant? If you really feel something for him, you'll give up now."

Chastity's smirk proved too much.

"If you excuse me, I believe I'll join Fayth and Alyce at the wagon." Glorianna stood. She started to take a step, then wobbled. Her arms windmilled. In a flash, she fell on top of Chastity, pushing her beneath the rippling water of the Verde River.

Chastity pushed back, and Glorianna leaned harder on her, acting like she couldn't get her balance. The other women began to rush toward her. Just before they reached her, she sat back. Chastity broke the surface, gulping in air, looking like a drowned rat. Her blond curls, now limp, hung in a tangled mass.

"Do forgive me," Glorianna purred. "These rocks can be tricky. I must have slipped on one." With that, she rose and, as gracefully as possible, left the river.

Chapter 14

Glorianna leaned against the house, rubbing her arms against the early morning chill. Stars still twinkled overhead, their light not yet dimmed by the approaching dawn. A dove's haunting cry echoed over the chirp of crickets. In the distance a lone coyote howled a message about the night's hunt.

Her eyes burned. She fought against the tightening in her throat and chest. She hated crying. She wouldn't give in to tears over some flirtatious fool like Chastity Denton. A lone teardrop traced a wet, cool path down her cheek.

"What am I to do?" Glorianna whispered to the night. "I'm going crazy staying in a room with her." For the last three weeks, she had shared her room with Chastity while Mrs. Denton took over the rest of the house, running it like some sort of queen. She told Glorianna what to wear, how to act, and where she could go.

Visiting Fayth hadn't been high on the list of things Mrs. Denton encouraged, either. *After all,* Glorianna could hear her say, *your father is a captain and you have certain standards to which you must measure up. You must watch whom you befriend.*

Well, her mother hadn't felt that way. She loved everyone, welcoming anyone into her house. But her mother also taught her to respect her elders. Glorianna determined not to disappoint her mother or her father.

The hardest part of the last few weeks had to do with Conlon. They hadn't had a minute alone. Mrs. Denton insisted he escort Chastity everywhere. His only break came when he had military duties to perform. Even some of those were given to the other men so he could be at the Dentons' beck and call.

Oh, she knew he didn't enjoy the duty. Having to be attentive to Chastity's every whim was taking its toll. Dark shadows ringed Conlon's eyes. His face seemed drawn and haggard. His blue eyes rarely held their merry twinkle. At least, when she got close enough to him to see his eyes. Chastity made sure he and Glorianna kept their distance.

"Mother, I wish you were here." Glorianna's whispered words echoed the ache in her heart. "Daddy is letting this woman run over the top of him. I know you would have been able to set things right. You were always good at settling disputes among the ladies everywhere we went. Now, I don't know where to turn."

Tears ran down her cheeks. She bit her lip to stifle a sob. She didn't want to wake Mrs. Denton or Chastity. She didn't want them to know she'd slipped out early to be by herself. Today, for the first time since they had arrived, she had managed to get out of the house without Mrs. Denton's waking and demanding to know where she was going before daylight.

Glorianna pushed away from the house. She hoped Conlon would be at their rock today. Maybe, just maybe, they could have a few minutes together. She crossed the parade ground, going first to the stables. Despite the dark, she knew the way well enough. The sound of an occasional stomping foot thudded against the floor. She had to see Nina. Even her horse had been forced to desert her. Chastity demanded the right to ride her and had, of course, gotten her way.

"Hey, Sweetie." Glorianna stroked the satiny muzzle. Nina nickered and blew against her hand. "I'm sorry I don't have a treat for you. It was too risky to go in the kitchen for a sugar lump. I'll try to bring one later."

She wrapped her arms around Nina's neck. "Sometimes I want to get on you and ride away from here." She breathed deeply, drawing comfort from the horse's earthy scent. "I can't do it, though. I've fallen in love with Conlon, and I can't leave him behind." The horse's thick neck muffled her sobs of despair.

❧

Conlon dropped down on the rock. He rubbed his face with his hands, then swept his hair back from his forehead. *God, I'm sorry I've been so lax in my meetings with You lately. Those women are making me crazy. Mrs. Denton is sure I'm the perfect husband for Chastity. She doesn't even care what I think of the idea. All I've done these last few weeks is pamper a spoiled child—for that's exactly what Chastity is.*

The skittering sound of a night animal running for shelter interrupted his thoughts. He watched the sky for a moment, knowing that before long it would begin to lighten in preparation for another day. *Another day wasted,* he thought. His mouth twisted into a grimace of disgust. How could he manage to be polite to Chastity and her mother? How much more could he take before he really exploded?

What he wanted to do was spend the day with Glorianna. How he missed their mornings together. He missed her lilting laugh. He wanted to touch her, talk to her, tell her how much he loved her. A groan escaped as he thought of the sweet scent of roses that belonged to Glory. *God, what am I to do? How long must I wait?*

He hadn't slept well lately. Thoughts of Glory and Chastity fought a war in his head every night. How could he resolve this dilemma? *I guess the truth is, I can't do a thing, Lord. Once more, I have to leave this in Your hands.*

Memories of the previous night drifted before his eyes. Chastity, always too forward, nearly threw herself at him when her mother wasn't looking. Mrs. Denton kept prattling on about his speaking with the major when he arrived tomorrow. She expected him to ask for her daughter's hand in marriage when, in truth, he couldn't stand the thought of even touching Chastity's hand.

Late last night, by the light of a candle, he searched his Bible, looking for some word from God. Psalm 37:7 kept coming to him over and over. "Rest in the Lord, and wait patiently for him. . . ." Conlon shook his head, wondering again how long the Lord expected him to be patient and wait.

Recalling long rides and even longer walks with Chastity made his stomach turn. He couldn't stand the way she flaunted herself. Always one to get her way, she expected him to put her first in everything they did. She never gave a thought to anyone else's feelings.

The scrape of a shoe on the sandy desert startled him. *Oh, God, please don't let Chastity have found me so early.* He groaned. Pushing himself up from the rock, he turned to face the intruder. To his surprise, it wasn't Chastity or her mother coming to begin their daily torments.

"Glory!" He longed to rush to her and scoop her up in his arms. Something held him back. He gestured to the rock. "Come and join me. We have a little time to talk before the sunrise."

"I'd like that." Glorianna's smile warmed him. "We haven't had many chances to see each other these past few weeks."

He waited until she made herself comfortable, then he allowed himself the luxury of sitting next to her. He inhaled, closing his eyes for a moment to enjoy the clean, rose scent that drifted to him. He wanted to pull her close, to bury his face in her soft hair, but he mentally shook himself in order to maintain control.

"I haven't been able to get away from Mrs. Denton long enough to come out and watch the sunrise." She looked so forlorn, it broke his heart. "I miss our morning talks."

He nodded. "I miss them, too. I've had some trouble getting here of a morning myself. I know God understands. I still have a short time with Him at night, but nothing is quite like these early morning meetings."

"You look tired, Conlon. Are you all right?"

"I'm fine." He tried to smile. "I am a little tired of having my schedule directed by someone other than your father."

Glorianna laughed a dry, humorless laugh. "I think the whole camp is tired of being run by Mrs. Denton. I want to blame Daddy, but I know he tries. Despite his best efforts, she has taken over."

He grinned. "I wonder what will happen when the major shows up tomorrow?"

"Does she run him like she does everyone else?"

"She sure does. I remember the last time they were at the camp; she had everything turned upside down. I don't know how one woman can cause so much disorder in so many lives."

"Conlon." Glorianna's voice barely reached his ears. "I don't know how much longer I can take her interference before I explode. I've tried to be nice, but I'd really rather take her out and tie her to a cactus."

"That would be interesting." Conlon chuckled.

"I can't stand spending another night with Chastity. All she talks about is you."

"And what does she tell you about me?"

She shrugged, silent for a moment. "She talks about how much you love her, about how you plan to ask for her hand in marriage when her father gets here, and how wonderful you will be as a husband."

Conlon watched Glorianna as she talked, hope filling his heart. Was she jealous? Just then the sky overhead burst into color. Conlon barely noticed as he stared at Glorianna, drinking in her beauty.

"Glory, I don't plan to be her husband." He tried to speak firmly, to wash away the despair he thought he could see in her eyes.

"But, she says you're in the cavalry and you have to do what her father says. He's a higher rank."

He couldn't help it; the laughter just bubbled up from deep inside. She was jealous. He understood now. The only way she could be this worried about Chastity was if she truly cared about him.

"In a way she's right." Conlon tried to calm the thundering of his heart. "I do have to obey my superior officers. But that only pertains to military matters. My personal life is my own."

"I know Major Denton can't order you to marry his daughter, but she says he'll make your life miserable if you don't marry her."

He watched the colors fade from the sky, trying to think of the best way to answer her. He took her small hand in his, running his thumb over her soft skin. "Glory, look at me." He waited until her tear-filled green eyes looked into his. "There is no way Major Denton could make me more miserable than I would be if I married his daughter. I can't think of anything worse."

Her emerald gaze held his for a long time. Slowly, he became aware of the pressure of her fingers as they gripped his. He smiled and almost laughed with joy as an answering smile lit her face.

"Tell me, Glory." He pulled her close, tucking her arm against his side. "What do you want most?"

For a long time she looked lost in thought, then she turned to him. "I used to think all I wanted was a little cottage. I wanted a white picket fence and a flower garden where my friends could come and visit with me." Her eyes took on a dreamy look. "I pictured sitting there with my children, watching them play and laugh."

A look of sadness washed over her face. He longed to touch her and wipe the look away. "What happened to that dream?" he asked.

She took a deep breath and released it slowly. "I just realized something was missing."

"What's that?"

A faint blush stained her creamy cheeks. "You'll think this is silly, but I always dreamed of friends and children. I never had a husband at my cottage."

"Not even Kendrick?"

"Not even him," she spoke thoughtfully. "I see now it was a shallow wish, only for me."

"So what is your dream now?" He held his breath, not daring to hope.

She pursed her lips and tilted her head to one side, looking up at him. "I don't think the cottage and white picket fence matter anymore. I'm sure I'll have friends wherever I go." She paused, then lowered her eyes before continuing. "I guess what matters most to me now is finding the right husband."

His heart raced. He wanted to grab her up and kiss her. He wanted to waltz her around the cactus. *God, please don't let me be impatient here. Help me to have the right words for Glorianna.*

Conlon opened his mouth to speak, but the words wouldn't come. Glorianna looked up; and for a long minute, he lost himself in her eyes. He reached up and wrapped a strand of her silky hair around his fingers. The burnished red gleamed in the first rays of sunlight.

He tried again. "How will you know when you've found the right husband?" His voice sounded raspy with emotion. He held his breath, waiting for what seemed an eternity for her answer.

Glorianna pulled her hand free from his, leaving his fingers empty. She reached slowly up and softly brushed a stray lock of hair back from his forehead. "I'll know," she whispered. He gasped at the feelings that raced through him. Oh, how he loved this woman.

Releasing her hair, Conlon traced his fingers down her cheek. He remembered doing this once before, but she hadn't been aware of him then. Now, she watched him with wide green eyes. She didn't pull away. In fact, she leaned closer.

Ever so slowly, he lowered his face to hers. His eyes took in the dusting of freckles on her creamy skin. Her scent pulled him closer with rose-perfumed fingers. His lips met hers. He wanted the moment to last forever. He slipped his arm around her slender waist.

"I see you were right, Chastity." The harsh, grating voice interrupted their moment. Glorianna pulled back, her face turning pink. Mrs. Denton, with Chastity peeking from behind her, stood like an avenging judge. Her hands on her hips, she glared at Glorianna.

Chapter 15

I will have a talk with your father, young lady. You are nothing but a seductress trying to take away my daughter's future husband."

Glorianna flushed a deep red and leaped from the rock. Her foot slipped, and Conlon reached out a hand to steady her. He, too, stood and faced their accusers. Keeping a light hold on Glory's arm, he could feel her tremble.

A sudden anger swept through Conlon as the weight of Mrs. Denton's accusation sank in. "You have no right to judge Glorianna's actions." Clenching his jaw to keep from yelling, his words came out soft, spoken with a deadly calm. "She's done nothing wrong."

Mrs. Denton narrowed her piglike eyes even further and leaned forward. "She knows you and Chastity will be getting married. She has no right to be sneaking around, meeting you in the middle of the night like this."

Glorianna tensed. "This is not the middle of the night, and I did not sneak around."

"Did you tell anyone where you were going?" Mrs. Denton folded her arms across her ample bosom.

"I don't have to tell anyone where I'm going." Glorianna spat out the words. "My father trusts me. I don't fawn all over men like a cheap girl would."

Mrs. Denton's mouth fell open. Her face flushed a cherry red.

"I have not asked for Chastity's hand in marriage." Conlon tried to diffuse the situation. "Nor do I intend to, Mrs. Denton."

"Mama." Chastity began to sob.

"Be quiet, Chastity." Mrs. Denton took a few steps toward Conlon and Glorianna. "Lieutenant, the major will be arriving tomorrow. He will talk to you about this matter. Chastity has counted on your asking for her hand since we were here the last time. You will not disappoint my daughter. Not over a woman like that." She gestured toward Glorianna.

"Now, you," Mrs. Denton lashed out at Glorianna, "will return to the house. I'll speak to your father about your behavior."

Before he could stop her, Glorianna jerked her arm free from his grip and closed the distance between herself and the Dentons. "Mrs. Denton, I have done nothing wrong." Glory's tone showed her barely contained fury. "You have no right to speak to my father or to reprimand me."

Mrs. Denton leaned forward until her nose nearly touched Glorianna's. "You were out here in the middle of the night kissing my daughter's future husband.

I realize your mother is dead, so I'm taking on a mother's responsibility by speaking to the captain about this. I want you to return to the house. Now."

Narrow eyes locked onto Conlon. "I will expect you at the house as soon as the drills are finished this morning. Chastity has a full day planned. You will be her escort." Mrs. Denton whirled about before either one could speak and sailed back toward the camp.

Chastity smirked at Glorianna and sidled closer to Conlon. "I'll see you soon. Bring Nina and Champ. We'll start with a long ride by ourselves." At her laugh of triumph, Conlon's hands balled into fists. He gritted his teeth, knowing he couldn't hit her, but picturing it anyway. Chastity sashayed after her mother.

"Glory, I'm sorry." He reached out to embrace her.

She stepped away. "Leave me alone." Tears ran down her cheeks. Her voice cracked. "I hate that woman. I hate Chastity, too. Somehow, I'll get even." She turned and ran away from the camp.

"Glory, wait," Conlon called after her. The sound of the bugle call from the camp told him he had no time to chase after Glorianna. After drills he would find her and settle this matter. Then he sighed, remembering. After drills he had to escort Chastity.

⚜

Blinded by tears, Glorianna stumbled off into the desert. She had to get away. Away from Conlon. Away from the Dentons. Away from all the misery she felt inside. A paloverde tree, its green branches waving in the breeze, gave her a shaded sanctuary. She sank to the ground, burying her face in her hands. Deep, racking sobs shook her body.

What am I to do? What will that woman do next? Can she make Conlon marry Chastity? The memory of the kiss stilled her tears. Her first kiss. Her first wonderful kiss. She hadn't wanted the moment to end. Her heart pounded at the remembrance. She longed to be back with Conlon. She wanted to feel his arms around her again. She needed the comfort of his closeness.

Mother, I wish you were here. You would know how to handle this. Whom can I turn to now? Thoughts of Fayth, her friendship and kindness, made Glorianna sit up and wipe the traces of tears from her face. "Fayth," she spoke aloud. "She'll listen. I know she can help."

A short while later, she slipped quietly through the gates, avoiding the drills being performed on the parade ground. Dust hung heavy in the air from the horses milling around. The dust would help to hide her from the prying eyes of Mrs. Denton and Chastity. She circled around to the houses, hoping no one would notice her. She didn't want anyone to know where she was until she had talked to Fayth.

At the Holwells's, she knocked, then pushed the door open. "Fayth?" she called.

"Glory, is that you?" Fayth stepped from Alyce's room, a welcoming smile lighting her face. "Come on in. What are you doing here? I thought you'd be watching Conlon on the parade ground." Fayth pulled chairs together for them to sit in.

"Why aren't you out watching the drills?" Glorianna avoided Fayth's question with one of her own.

"Alyce isn't feeling well. It's nothing serious. She's asleep now," Fayth hurried to add. She put a hand on her stomach. "Besides, this one is objecting to everything I eat. I wasn't sure I wanted to lose my breakfast in front of the whole camp."

Leaning forward, Fayth took Glorianna's hand in hers. "Is something wrong?" she asked, concern softening her voice.

Despite her resolve to be strong and not cry, Glorianna's throat began to tighten and tears welled in her eyes. She clasped her hands together, digging her nails into her palms, fighting her emotions. Then, Fayth's arms were around her and the dam broke. For long minutes she cried, unable to stop.

"I'm sorry," Glorianna hiccuped, wiping her eyes and nose with a handkerchief Fayth handed her. "I always seem to cry on your shoulder."

"I don't mind," Fayth laughed. "I think that's why God made shoulders. They're a wonderful place to support someone in need of comfort." She reached out to brush back a strand of hair from Glorianna's face. "Do you want to talk about it now?"

Glorianna took a deep breath and began in a shaky voice. She told about the strain of the last three weeks, trying to be nice to a tyrant, sharing a bed with Chastity, listening to Chastity's bragging about Conlon, and finally the heartache of not knowing how Conlon felt.

As she related the morning's events, anger replaced the hesitancy she'd been expressing. She told Fayth about Conlon's kiss, Mrs. Denton's accusations, and Chastity's parting words. "Can she really make him marry her daughter?"

"Glorianna, look at me," Fayth insisted. "Conlon is a strong man. Maybe a weaker man would give in to Mrs. Denton's demands, but he won't. He loves you, and I know his feelings for Chastity don't even begin to resemble love."

An inner rage welled up. Glorianna spat out, "I hate her. I hate them both. Somehow, I'll get revenge on them."

Fayth sat back, a startled look on her face. "I don't think that's the answer. Perhaps we need to pray about this."

Glorianna stood and began to pace the room, fighting the urge to lash out at her friend. "I don't want to pray about it. I'm not sure God even cares about me anymore."

"Oh, but God does care about you." Fayth's eyes filled with tears.

Glorianna sank back into her chair and grasped Fayth's hands. "I didn't mean to hurt you. I'm just confused about God."

"You didn't hurt me." Fayth wrapped her hands around Glorianna's. "It's God you hurt."

"Well, God has hurt me plenty, too." She hated sounding like a petulant child, but she couldn't hold it in anymore. "He took my mother from me. We prayed every day for her to get well, and she died. He wanted me to marry Kendrick, and look what happened. Why should I even try to pray anymore?"

"Glorianna, do you know what the Bible says about heaven? It says there will be no more sickness. God answered your prayer to heal your mother. She's in a place where there is no pain or tears or sickness. Don't you agree?"

At Glorianna's reluctant nod, Fayth continued, "As for Kendrick, you told me you were wrong. Remember, after you were hurt in the storm? You admitted it had been you wanting him, not God wanting him for you."

"But still," Glorianna's voice was almost a whisper. "He brought the Dentons here. I can't take this."

"God always allows trials. They're not a punishment, but meant to strengthen our faith." Fayth squeezed her hand. They sat quietly for a few minutes, and then Fayth spoke again. "I want to ask you something, Glorianna. I don't want to make you angry, but I have to know."

"What is it?"

"This may sound funny, but I feel I need to know if you're a Christian."

Glorianna straightened and tugged at her hands. "Of course, I'm a Christian! I've always been one."

Fayth held her fingers tight. "But how do you know?"

"Well, I was born in a Christian home." Glorianna wanted to feel indignant, but for some reason she knew she needed to hear what Fayth wanted to say. "My parents have always attended church whenever possible. So have I. And I pray and read my Bible. I even help others. You know, doing good deeds."

Fayth shook her head, a look of concern crossing her face. "That isn't what makes a Christian. Who you know or what you do doesn't make you a follower of Jesus. Praying and reading the Bible are good, but that's not where salvation comes from."

"But, the church. . ."

"Church attendance doesn't make you a Christian, either."

Glorianna stared down at her hands clasped with Fayth's. She wanted to be angry, but for some reason she only felt confused. Was there something more to being a Christian that she'd missed all these years? A vague memory of her mother talking about salvation and choices surfaced. Had her mother tried to talk to her like this? Was God trying to get her attention?

"Do you know who General Crook is?" Fayth asked.

Surprised at the change in questions, Glorianna looked up at her friend. "I've heard of him. Conlon talked about meeting him."

"That's right." Fayth smiled. "You know who General Crook is, but do you know him personally?"

"Of course not," Glorianna said. "He's never been here or back east where we were. How could I know him?"

"The point I want to make," Fayth continued, "is that it's one thing to know who someone is and quite another to know him personally. It's the same with Jesus. You may know Who Jesus is, but to be a Christian you need to know Him personally. Do you?"

"I don't know." She took a deep breath. "You mean all these years I thought it was right to do good works and it wasn't?"

"Oh, no, it's always right to do good to others," Fayth assured her. "But if we could get to heaven by our good works, church attendance, or anything that we can do ourselves, then Jesus wouldn't have had to die on the cross for our sins. But Scripture tells us, 'For by grace are ye saved through faith; and that not of yourselves: it is the gift of God: Not of works, lest any man should boast.'"

"So, salvation is a gift?"

"That's right." Fayth smiled. "The Bible says that none of us deserves salvation. But God knew that from the beginning, and He provided a way for us."

"I want to know Him." Glorianna tightened her hold on Fayth's hands. A sudden urgency gripped her. "Tell me how, please."

"It's very simple. Do you believe Jesus died on the cross to take away your sins?"

Glorianna nodded, unable to speak.

"Do you believe God raised Him from the dead?"

"Yes, I believe that." The words barely made their way past the lump in her throat.

"Then all you have to do is ask Jesus into your heart."

As one, the two friends knelt by their chairs. They took turns praying, Glorianna's prayer hesitant yet joyful, Fayth's sure and thankful. Time seemed to stand still. Glorianna felt a healing and peace that she had never before known. Was this what her mother had talked about? This must be the peace that comes from knowing God.

Two hours later, Glorianna walked home. She felt as if her feet never touched the ground. The sky looked bluer and the desert more beautiful than she remembered. She looked forward to seeing how God would work things out. She had an assurance now that He would always care for her.

"Glorianna." Her father's booming voice startled her from her reverie.

"Yes?" She smiled at him, ignoring the frown on his face.

"I've been looking for you. We need to talk. Please come to my office."

As they crossed the parade ground, Glorianna noticed Chastity and Conlon returning from their morning ride. Chastity patted her hair and grinned wickedly at Glorianna. Conlon flashed her a smile that set her heart racing. Suddenly, she couldn't wait to tell him about her new relationship with Jesus. She knew he had the same closeness and would be happy to hear about hers. For once, she wasn't jealous of Chastity for riding Nina or for being with Conlon. God was in charge, and He cared for her.

Mrs. Denton stood on the porch of her father's office. A smug look settled on her face at the sight of Glorianna and her father. She stepped forward to intercept them.

"Captain, would you like me to assist you with your daughter? I understand it's difficult for a father to reprimand his child. I'm more than willing to help."

Glorianna calmly watched her father face Mrs. Denton. She stood nearly as tall as he did, yet he didn't appear overwhelmed by her. "I believe I can handle this, Mrs. Denton. I thank you for your concern."

With that, he crossed over to his office and beckoned Glorianna to come in. For the first time since praying with Fayth, she began to doubt God's ability to work this out. Looking at her father's smoldering eyes, she couldn't help but tremble. *Dear God, please help me remember I'm Your child now. Help me to trust You, no matter what happens,* she prayed as her father shut the door with a resounding thud.

Chapter 16

Glorianna tried to still her trembling. She'd seen her father this angry only once before. She thought of the time a few years earlier, before her mother had gotten too sick to remain out west at the various cavalry posts. Her father had been stationed at Camp Apache, up near where the Black River and the White Mountain River join. The countryside, with its stately pines, canyons, and tall mountains, took her breath away. But the Apaches and wildlife in the area could be dangerous. Going outside the camp was strictly forbidden.

Glorianna, never one to follow the rules, wanted to explore the forest. Innocently enough, she slipped away one afternoon, planning to climb to the top of the closest mountain. Somehow, she managed to get turned around. Night fell, and she had no idea what direction to turn. After hours of searching, the soldiers from the camp found her and carried her home.

Her mother wept while her father paced the floor, ranting about the danger of her thoughtless actions. When he calmed down, she realized his eyes were nearly as red as her mother's. He wasn't so much angry with her as he was scared that something terrible could have happened.

Suddenly, Glorianna understood her father's anger. It wasn't directed at her, but at her situation. She swung around to look at him. Love shone in eyes that only moments before had been smoldering with anger. Could that anger have been directed at Mrs. Denton and not her?

"If not for the grace of God and my respect for the major's leadership abilities, I would lock that woman away," her father growled. He pulled her close in a tight, safe hug. "I'm so sorry she's here, Kitten. I know how hard it is to put up with her and with that spoiled daughter of hers. Please try to persevere."

He pulled back and looked at her. His warm hazel eyes glowed with love. Glorianna reached up and patted his cheek. How she loved her father. He had always been the best he could be, even when it meant he had to be away from his family.

"Daddy, I'm sorry I said things to Mrs. Denton earlier that upset her. I have tried to be respectful." She sighed. "It isn't always easy."

He chuckled. "Yes, I'll certainly agree with that."

"I will apologize to her. I promise."

"You will?"

Her father's surprise reminded Glorianna of how self-serving and demanding

96

she'd always been. "I know I've been difficult. I'm sorry." She took a deep breath and stepped back from her father. Looking him in the eye, she straightened to her full height. "I'm a different person now." She paused, trying to figure how to word what she needed to say. Then, with a short prayer for guidance, the words seemed to flow as she told him about her time with Fayth and the giving of herself to the Lord.

"Oh, Kitten." Her father hugged her again. This time she knew his tears were ones of joy. "I can't tell you how many times your mother and I prayed for this. I know she's in heaven rejoicing with the angels. Thank you for telling me."

He held her away and looked at her for a long time. "Now, what are we going to do about the Denton ladies?"

Glorianna tilted her head to the side and studied her father. "I think we should treat them like we would want to be treated, and let God do the rest. For my part, I'll try not to be jealous of Chastity. I'll be as nice as I can to Mrs. Denton." She paused and tapped a finger on her lip. "And I believe I'll avoid them as much as possible so I can maintain a Christian attitude."

They both laughed, although they tried to keep it quiet so Mrs. Denton wouldn't hear them. She was sure to be standing outside waiting to see how their "talk" had gone.

Leaning close, her father spoke in a low tone. "I think we should sit down and discuss this. After all, she'll think you're getting a long lecture. That should make her happy."

For the next hour, they talked about camp life, the Lord, her mother, and myriad other things they never made the time to talk about. Glorianna warmed to her father's good advice and wonderful sense of humor, although they had to remember to laugh quietly.

"Try to look contrite," her father whispered as he prepared to open the door.

Glorianna forced her eyes to open wide, attempting a surprised look. "Me, look contrite?"

He grinned. "You were always a good actress. I'm sure you can do it."

She wrinkled her nose and crossed her eyes, watching him struggle to maintain his composure. He opened the door. Mrs. Denton shot up from the chair near the door. A frown drew her features into a hound dog expression. Glorianna wondered for a moment if she would begin to bark, then banished the thought before it became her undoing.

"I do hope the matter of Glorianna's improper behavior is settled, Captain." Mrs. Denton lifted her chin, speaking in an imperious tone.

Glorianna stepped forward, halting before the tyrannical woman. "I do want to apologize for any problems I've caused, Mrs. Denton. I appreciate your concern for me. I. . ." She felt a nudge from her father as she started to continue. He wouldn't want her to overdo it.

"Well, I do hope we won't have any more incidents like this morning. If you need an example to follow, you can watch my Chastity. She's a wonderful daughter." Mrs. Denton's face twisted into what she must have thought was a smile. "I know your mother was sick and probably unable to teach you as she should. That accounts for your lack of manners. I'll be happy to fill in."

Anger at the mention of her mother's lacking anything swelled up inside. Her father, as if seeing the danger, spoke up. "I'm sure Glorianna will be fine now, Mrs. Denton. I promise to keep a closer eye on her. You seem to have your hands full watching your own daughter. I've noticed her forward behavior."

Mrs. Denton narrowed her eyes, staring at Captain Wilton. "Thank you for your concern, Captain," she said before she turned and stalked away.

That afternoon, Glorianna curled up with her mother's Bible. Her mother used to spend hours reading and making notes. Now those observances spoke to her about her mother's desire to live her life in a way that pleased God. After rereading Ephesians 2:8 and 9, she had to stop reading and talk with God.

God, thank You for my salvation. I feel like I ought to do something to pay for this, but You say in the Bible it's a gift from You. Please be patient with me as I learn. I want to trust You with my life.

Your Word says here in verse 10 that You have good works for me to do. God, I want to do that, but You need to show me what those works are. Fayth says I need to start by seeing people the way You see them. If that's right, Lord, then it won't be easy. How can I possibly care for Chastity and her mother? Especially Chastity. She's trying her best to steal Conlon away from me. I love him, Lord. Please help me to see a good part or maybe some reason why I should love Chastity.

Tears ran down her cheeks. She tried to think of a redeeming quality for Chastity, but nothing came to mind. As she continued to read and pray, she marveled at the way the Bible made sense to her now, when it used to be so confusing. She felt like she'd never read these words before.

Late that afternoon, Glorianna hurried to Fayth's house to help get Alyce ready to go to the river. She'd lost track of time and knew the other ladies were already waiting by the stables.

"Fayth, are you ready?" she called through the open door.

A wailing cry was her only answer. She stepped in, calling again, heading to Alyce's room. Inside, Fayth, her hair in disarray, her face worn and tired, rocked her flushed child.

"Fayth, is she all right?"

A tired smile lit Fayth's face. "Her fever is higher now. I won't be going with you today."

"I'll stay and help you." Glorianna felt bad for not checking back in after this morning.

"No, you go," Fayth insisted. "I don't think Alyce will agree to let you hold her right now. Besides, Timothy will be here soon. He'll help out."

Panic stricken, Glorianna said, "But I can't go to the river without you. What will I do about Chastity? I need you there."

"Glory, you don't need me. You have Jesus. Just listen to Him."

Glorianna prayed all the way to the ambulance, trying to find a reason to stay behind. *God, I know You want me to trust You, and so I will. Please help me.* She looked up to see Chastity sitting astride Nina, so close to Champ that her knee occasionally brushed against Conlon's. The look of defiance on her face grated on Glorianna.

She swallowed her pride, forcing a smile. "I'm glad you like Nina, Chastity. It's nice you're willing to give her some exercise." A look of astonishment crossed Chastity's face. Glorianna climbed into the wagon with the other women.

The trip to the Verde River was miserable. Glorianna spent her time trying to ignore Mrs. Denton's loud lecturing to the wagon's occupants and her daughter's obvious flirting. At least she could tell Conlon would rather be just about anywhere than riding with Chastity.

At the river, she moved away from the others, needing to be alone. The refreshing water not only cooled her physically, but soothed her ragged emotions as well. She dipped her head beneath the surface, rubbing her fingers through her tangled hair, washing the dirt free.

"I suppose you're trying to figure how you can get more time alone with Conlon." Chastity's snotty voice greeted her as she lifted her head out of the water. "My mother will be watching for you to sneak off and meet him in the mornings. That ploy won't work anymore."

"I didn't sneak off this morning." Glorianna tried to keep her tone even. "I simply went for a walk and met him."

"Are you saying you weren't in the habit of meeting him?"

"We enjoy watching the sunrise together. There's nothing wrong with that."

"I think there's something wrong with a young lady's spending so much time with a man when they aren't chaperoned."

"We weren't exactly alone." Glorianna struggled to control her temper. "After all, the night guards were watching. Besides, what about your rides together? You don't have a chaperone."

"Well. . .we. . .we aren't sitting together on a rock. Or kissing. . . ," Chastity sputtered.

Glorianna scooped some of the water in her hands and rubbed her face. Maybe the water would cool her anger. *God, I still can't find anything to love about her. Please, help me.*

Remember your childhood, came to her as clearly as if a voice had spoken out loud. She ducked under the water again to get a moment to think. What about her childhood? Then, understanding came in a rush. The years of constant moving, going to different forts and camps where there were only adults and few, if any, children. The terrible loneliness and longing for a friend. She remembered how glad she was to finally be back east where she and Kathleen could be friends.

She burst up from the water, catching Chastity unaware. The forlorn look on the girl's face confirmed her suspicions. *Thank You, God, for showing me the answer.*

"Tell me, Chastity," she said, watching the girl's expression closely. "Have you and your mother always followed your father wherever he was stationed?"

"Of course. What's wrong with that. Didn't you?"

"When I was young we did." Glorianna tried to pick her words with care. "Then, when my mother got sick, we had to go back east. We were there two years before she died."

"So?"

Glorianna took a deep breath. "The one thing I missed the most out here, the thing my father couldn't provide, was another girl my age. I didn't have a close friend until I took care of my mother. Then, my cousin Kathleen and I became best friends." She noted the look of longing that flitted across Chastity's face. "Have you ever had someone like that, Chastity?"

"My mother is my friend." Chastity looked over toward her mother and the other women.

"My mother was my friend, too," Glorianna said. "But didn't you ever want to be close to a girl your age? Someone to share a joke with or someone to stay up all night talking to?"

Chastity remained silent for a long time, still staring at the other women. Finally, she scooped water from the river, running her hands over her face. When she turned back to Glorianna, her shiny eyes spoke of tears unshed. "I don't need a friend." Her voice was a hoarse whisper.

She began to edge away. The other women were moving to leave the river, and Chastity started to follow them.

Before she could get too far, Glorianna called softly, "If you want a friend, I'm willing to be one."

Chastity stopped and turned toward her. "Why?" she asked bluntly.

"Why what?"

"Why would you want to be my friend?"

Glorianna tried to think from Chastity's point of view. Since arriving at Camp MacDowell, she had done nothing but torment Glorianna. She'd gone out of her way to steal Conlon, tried to alienate her father, and, in general, done her best to give Glorianna a bad name around the camp. She knew Chastity couldn't understand an offer of friendship under those circumstances.

Her heart pounding in nervous fear, Glorianna said, "I know I haven't been friendly to you before. This morning, my life changed. I gave my life to Jesus, and now I want to try to be like Him. I know I always needed a friend, and I'm sure Jesus wants me to be that to you."

Chastity whirled away and waded from the river. Glorianna followed, wondering if there was some other way that she could have answered the question better. At the top of the bank, Chastity waited for her. The others were already near the ambulance, laughing and chattering.

Speaking in a low tone, Chastity hissed, "I don't need your friendship. I don't want to hear about your religion, either. I have Conlon. He'll marry me soon, and I won't need anyone else."

She stormed away toward the wagon. Glorianna didn't think she could hurt anymore if she'd been slapped across the face. *God, what did I do wrong? I tried to follow what You told me. It didn't work. How will I manage? I don't think I can stand to live if she marries Conlon.*

Trust Me, spoke a still, small voice.

Chapter 17

The rhythmic creak of the rocking chair sounded loud in the room's stillness. Glorianna laid her cheek against Alyce's hot forehead to see if her temperature had gone down. For the first time since she'd come by this evening, Alyce had ceased crying and fallen asleep. Although her face still bore the flush of fever, she felt a little cooler.

Removing the warm rag from Alyce's forehead, she dipped it in the basin of cool water on the stand beside her chair. She swirled the piece of toweling in the water before squeezing it out and placing it over Alyce's brow. The child barely moved. Only a slight puckering of her mouth showed she felt anything.

"Oh, Alyce," Glorianna whispered, "I hope love isn't so difficult for you." She couldn't quit thinking about Conlon. When they returned from the river, Chastity insisted that he come for her after supper so they could go for a walk. She knew he must have begged Timothy to go with them. Fayth wouldn't agree until Glorianna said she would stay with Alyce. After all, she'd pointed out, Fayth needed a break. A walk in the cool evening air would be refreshing.

The ache in her heart beat in a dull rhythm. She knew Conlon loved her, but would his love be strong enough to overcome Major and Mrs. Denton? Would they allow Chastity's wishes to dictate their lives and Conlon's? She wished her father could help, but his hands were tied when it came to superior officers. He could only make suggestions, and the Dentons didn't take kindly to suggestions about raising their daughter.

The sound of a door opening and muted voices drifted through the house. Fayth and Timothy stepped quietly into Alyce's room. Fayth looked much better than she had earlier. Her cheeks, hollow and drawn from her inability to keep her food down, now had a bit of color.

"Is she sleeping?" Fayth's whisper barely reached across the room.

"She fell asleep about half an hour ago. I think her fever has gone down a little."

Fayth quietly crossed the room as Timothy slipped back into the front room. Glorianna could hear voices and wondered if Conlon had come back home with them.

"Let's put her in bed." Fayth pulled back the covers and centered the pillow. "It will probably be better if I don't take her. Do you think you can put her down?"

"I'll try." Glorianna stood, gritting her teeth against the ache in her arms.

How did Fayth manage to hold this child for hours? She crossed to the bed, leaned over, and gently slipped Alyce into the bed. Alyce sighed and rolled to the side. The rag from her forehead dropped on the sheets. Fayth retrieved it and put it back in the bowl of water.

Touching Alyce's forehead, Fayth nodded. "I think you're right. She does feel cooler."

"You look much better, too. I think the walk was a good idea."

A high cackling laugh drifted through from the front room. Fayth's eyes met Glorianna's.

"We invited Conlon and Chastity to come in for awhile." Fayth glanced at the door and lowered her voice. "I think Timothy did it out of sympathy for Conlon. That girl needs some lessons in propriety."

"I don't think I can go out there." Glorianna sank down in the rocker. "I told you what happened at the river. How am I supposed to be civil to someone who only wants to make me look like a fool?"

Fayth pulled a chair over by Glorianna's. "Remember that while we were completely unlovable, God loved us. You have to follow His example. Jesus loved those who cursed Him, spit on Him, and beat Him."

"You're right." Glorianna sighed. "If He can do that, surely I can love a lonely girl."

"I know you can." Fayth hugged Glorianna, then checked Alyce one more time. "Come on, Alyce is fine for now. Let's go visit."

Conlon and Timothy stood as they entered the room. Chastity edged her chair slightly closer to Conlon's. A smug smile twisted her features when she noticed Glorianna watching her. She settled back in the chair, her gaze never leaving Glorianna's. When Conlon sat down, he would be within easy touching distance for Chastity.

"I see we need another chair." Conlon glanced around. "Here, Glory, why don't you take mine and I'll get another one. No, it's all right." He motioned Timothy to sit down. "I can get the chair."

Normally, Glorianna wouldn't have wanted to come so close to Chastity, but this time she knew it would keep Conlon from being next to the little vixen. Attempting her sweetest smile, she ignored the daggers flying from Chastity's eyes. "Why, thank you, Conlon." She crossed the room. Lowering herself to the chair, her elbow poked into Chastity's arm.

"Oh, excuse me." She lifted up and moved her chair. "I didn't realize your chair was so close."

"You did that on purpose," Chastity hissed.

Glorianna widened her eyes. "Did what?"

The anger faded from Chastity's face, replaced by a sugary smile that coated her features as Conlon walked toward them carrying a chair.

"You can sit next to me, Conlon." Chastity made it sound like an order.

"I think there's more room over here," Conlon replied, placing his chair on the other side of Glorianna. He settled into the chair, so close his sleeve brushed against her arm. She wanted to reach out and touch him, but knew it would only cause trouble between him and the Dentons.

Timothy asked about Alyce and a buzz of conversation drifted around Glorianna. She couldn't seem to concentrate on what they were saying. Her thoughts, instead, centered on the nearness of Conlon and her desire to tell him about her salvation. She forced herself not to fidget, picturing his excitement when she finally told him.

She didn't know how long her mind drifted, but a sudden uncomfortable silence in the room brought her back to the present. Sometime in the last few minutes, while her mind toyed with other thoughts, her fingers had become entangled with Conlon's. It felt so right that she hadn't even noticed and wasn't entirely sure he had, either. From the tension in the room and the look on her face, she knew Chastity was aware that they were holding hands.

Glorianna loosened her grip, thinking Conlon would allow her hand to drop. Instead he tightened his. Was he determined to make Chastity mad? Didn't he realize she had to sleep in the same room, the same bed, with the girl?

Chastity stood, red-faced, her eyes sparking with anger. "I believe I'll go on home. The hour is getting late." She stopped and looked back at Glorianna. "Come on, Mother will expect you home at the same time." Her eyes didn't leave their locked fingers.

"She's right." Glorianna stood. "I know Fayth is tired. Alyce may have another restless night, and they all need their rest."

"I'll walk the two of you home." Conlon, who stood when Chastity did, lifted his hand, pulling Glorianna a step closer. He didn't let her hand leave his. She wondered at his defiance of Chastity. *Oh, Lord, don't let him make trouble because of me,* she prayed.

The cool evening air wrapped around them as Conlon and Glorianna strolled the short distance to Glorianna's house. A pack of coyotes yipped and howled their nightly chorus, sounding as if they were next door rather than out in the desert. Chastity marched ahead of them, her back straight, head held high. She looked like a soldier on a mission.

Chastity stomped up to the door, flung it open, then turned to glare back at them. Without a word, she stepped inside, closing the door with a resounding thud. Conlon chuckled with what sounded like relief.

Glorianna squeezed his fingers. "You'd better be nice. Don't make me start laughing. If you do, I'll lie in bed giggling, and she'll know it's because of her."

"I'm not sure how you manage, Glory." Conlon's face was so close his breath tickled her ear. "Personally, I'm wishing I was anywhere but near Chastity Denton."

Glorianna turned to him, trying to ignore how close they were. "I have something to say." Now that the time had come, she felt shy and nervous.

"I wanted to tell you what happened to me."

"I heard." His chuckle returned, louder this time.

"Did Fayth tell you?" Glorianna tried to hide her hurt.

Conlon looked puzzled. "Fayth didn't tell me. Timothy and some of the others told me yesterday. That was all the ladies could talk about—your dunking Chastity while pretending to fall. I forgot to mention it this morning."

She gasped. "You mean, they knew I did it on purpose?"

"Of course, they did. The men all got a good laugh. Too bad you didn't fall on Mrs. Denton, too."

"Conlon, stop." She glanced toward the house. "They'll hear you." She bit her lip, trying not to succumb to laughter. "Besides, that's not what I have to tell you."

He took a deep breath as if trying to get himself under control. "I'm sorry. The picture of your holding Chastity under the water nearly did me in. What did you want to tell me?"

Suddenly, she couldn't put it into words. What would Conlon think? Would he think her foolish for thinking she was a Christian all these years only to find out she wasn't? Did it matter so much if she told him? *Confess with your mouth,* she could hear Fayth say.

"I prayed with Fayth today," she blurted out.

He tilted his head to one side, the shadows hiding his eyes from her. "Did you pray for Alyce?"

"No. . . I. . . Yes." She stopped, knowing she wasn't making any sense. She stepped back from him, pulling her hand free, hoping the distance would help to calm her thoughts.

"Fayth pointed out to me that, although I've always gone to church, I've never had a personal relationship with Jesus. We prayed about that." Twisting her fingers together, she waited for his laughter.

Strong arms engulfed her. Conlon crushed her against him in a fierce hug. "Oh, Glory, this is an answer to prayer. Thank you for telling me."

His genuine feelings touched her. Tears welled up in her eyes. "I thought maybe you would laugh."

He held her away. The rising moon glinted off the tears on his cheeks. "I can't tell you how happy I am about this. I can't tell you, but I can show you."

He dropped to one knee. Grasping her hands in his, he kissed her fingertips. "Glorianna, will you marry me? I'll talk to your father tomorrow morning. Tonight, I want to make sure you will have me."

She could barely talk. "Yes. Yes, I'll marry you, Conlon Sullivan."

He stood and pulled her into his arms. His kiss was sweet. She felt so safe and content held in his embrace.

"Glorianna Wilton, you get in here right now." Mrs. Denton's voice grated in the night.

"Why does she always interrupt?" Conlon squeezed her hand, then traced a finger down her cheek. "I'll see you in the morning. I'll talk to your father as soon as I can."

"Good night." Glorianna wanted to say more, but didn't dare with Mrs. Denton standing guard. Already she felt empty at his leaving. Dreamily, she brushed by Mrs. Denton and floated to her room. *Mrs. Conlon Sullivan, Glorianna Sullivan,* she thought. *It sounds perfect. Thank You, God.*

"It's about time you came inside." Chastity's petulant whine brought reality crashing in. "What were you doing out there for so long? Kissing again?"

Glorianna felt like the smile she couldn't wipe from her face must certainly give her away. There was nothing Chastity could say that would take away this happiness. Conlon wanted to marry her.

"I suppose you think he's going to marry you." Chastity's words made Glorianna wonder if she'd read her mind. "Well, I'll tell you this, my father arrived early. He's here right now. By morning he'll have told Lieutenant Sullivan exactly what his orders are. Those orders don't include you."

For the first time since coming inside, Glorianna really looked at Chastity. Her eyes flashed anger and possibly hatred. Her blond hair straggled around her face, which was covered with red blotches. Her lips were pinched into thin lines. She felt sorry for this girl, who had missed out on so much by focusing on herself.

Lord, help me talk to her. I don't know what to say. She doesn't want me for a friend, and I can't force my friendship on her. Help me to be like You, no matter what she says or does to me.

"I'm glad your father finally got here, Chastity. I know you wanted to see him. Maybe in the morning we can get some of this straightened out."

"There's nothing to straighten out," Chastity sputtered. "You think you have the right to waltz in here and claim the man who's going to be my husband. Well, you don't. The last time we were at Camp MacDowell, it was decided that Conlon and I would marry."

"Did he propose to you?"

"No, he didn't propose. We had an understanding, though." Chastity glared at Glorianna. "He would have asked me to marry him by now, if you hadn't interfered."

"I don't know how I've done that." Glorianna turned away to pull on a night-dress, hoping to keep her anger down. *Lord, help me keep my tongue under control.*

"You don't consider meeting my intended in the middle of the night, holding hands with him, and kissing him as interfering?"

Glorianna blew out the lamp and climbed into bed beside Chastity. She bit her lip, determined to hold her angry thoughts and words at bay.

"You'll see," Chastity hissed in the silence. "Tomorrow my father will tell him what's what."

"Your father hasn't any authority over Conlon's personal life. Conlon is free to make his own decisions. That includes choosing for himself the woman he wants to marry."

"I suppose you think that will be you."

Glorianna ground her teeth together, fighting a losing battle for control. "I know it will be me." She couldn't keep the words inside. "He's never had feelings for you." As the words left her mouth, she longed to pull them back, but it was too late.

A sniffle sounded in the silence. Then Chastity spoke in a tear-filled voice. "Just wait until tomorrow. You'll see."

"Chastity, I'm sorry. I. . ."

"Leave me alone, Glorianna. I don't want to talk anymore."

Glorianna could feel the bed move as Chastity turned over. *Oh, Lord, I want to be like You, but I can't. I let my mouth get the best of me. Please, forgive me. Now I'll never be able to get Chastity to open up to me. I'm so sorry, and I'm so scared that she's right. Can her father really make Conlon marry her? Please, don't let that happen. Please.*

Sleep took a long time coming.

Chapter 18

Whistling slightly off key, Conlon strode toward the captain's office. He couldn't help whistling. Even though Glorianna hadn't gotten away to meet him this morning, he felt as if he were walking on air. She loved him. She wanted to marry him. Now the captain had summoned him to the office. This would be the perfect time to ask for his daughter's hand in marriage. Of course, he didn't doubt the captain's answer. After all, he had readily agreed to let him court her.

Leaping up the steps, he paused, amazed at the difference in the world around him. The sky stretched overhead like a taut blue canvas, blank, waiting for God to paint His signature for the day. Birds trilled, men shouted, horses called for their breakfast, all with a clarity of sound that hadn't been there before. The whole world gleamed with the knowledge of his and Glory's love for one another.

Nodding to the private who worked for the captain, Conlon knocked on the office door.

"Come in."

He pushed open the door and confronted the first bit of concern since rising this morning. Captain Wilton wasn't alone. Major Denton filled the office with his commanding presence. When had he arrived? Suddenly, Conlon felt a pinprick of dread worm its way inside his heart. Why had the captain summoned him?

"Good morning, Lieutenant. I'm sure you remember Major Denton."

Standing stiff, Conlon nodded at the major. "Yes, Sir. Good morning, Major. I'm glad to see you've arrived. I trust you and General Crook were able to round up the renegades?"

"General Crook is a remarkable man." Major Denton's voice rattled the walls. "We made short work of rounding up the Apaches and getting them back where they belonged."

"Lieutenant, please have a seat. There's a matter we need to discuss." Captain Wilton's voice sounded lackluster.

Conlon studied the captain as he lowered himself into the chair. Something was wrong. He could feel it. The captain's eyes were dull, his face drawn, and sadness hung over him like a pall. Conlon decided to sit quietly, waiting for the captain to tell him the bad news.

Major Denton's thunderous voice startled him. "I believe I've upset your captain this morning, Lieutenant. I've brought some news he hadn't expected. He doesn't seem to agree with me, but sometimes that's the way it is with the military."

Conlon swung around to face the major. The feeling of dread spread through his body like a disease, consuming him. He felt weighed down, as if his whole body were covered with lead.

"Those papers on the captain's desk are your transfer orders."

Once, in a fight at school, a boy had punched Conlon in the stomach, knocking the breath out of him. He had fallen to the ground, unable to breathe or respond at all. That same helpless, wheezing feeling overtook him now. The major's words dimmed, and for a moment he feared he would not get hold of himself.

"Excuse me, Major." Conlon didn't care if he was interrupting. "What did you say?"

Major Denton laughed, tilting his head back and allowing a full throaty chuckle to issue forth. "I told you he'd be glad to get away from this post, Captain. This is the most forsaken country I've ever seen. Any soldier would be grateful to get a reprieve."

Conlon glanced at Captain Wilton. "Did I hear him right? Am I getting a transfer?" At the captain's nod, Conlon asked, "When? Where?"

"Your orders state immediately." The captain's voice echoed in the silence.

"Yes, Sir, Lieutenant." Major Denton slapped him on the back. "You'll enjoy Fort Lowell outside of Tucson. It's a great place. Most of all, you'll enjoy being where my daughter is."

"Your daughter isn't there, Sir, she's here."

Major Denton laughed again. "Only for a short time. Right now, she and my wife are packing. They are leaving with us just as soon as we all get ready to head out."

Confusion and anger fought a battle inside him. Conlon stared at the major. "You mean I have to go now?"

"That's right. Your orders are immediate. I brought them in myself last night. Sorry there isn't more notice, but in the cavalry you have to be ready."

"But, I don't want to go to Fort Lowell," Conlon blurted, feeling stupid for coming up with such a weak statement. "I mean, I needed to talk to the captain about something personal this morning. I have some private matters to settle before I can leave here." He forced himself to stop babbling, fighting down the panic welling up inside.

"Son, I understand your private matters have to do with my daughter. We can discuss them on the way to Fort Lowell. We'll have plenty of time."

"Sir, the private matters have to do with the captain's daughter."

Major Denton chuckled. "I've heard she'll be mighty disappointed to see you and Chastity together, but she'll have to get used to the idea."

"But, Sir. . ." Conlon's objections died as the major dismissed him with a wave of his hand.

"Not now, Soldier. We need to talk about your plans for leaving here."

Conlon bit his lip to keep from snapping at the major. Couldn't this oaf see that he wasn't interested in marrying his whiny daughter? He wanted to grab him by the shirtfront and set him straight. He looked at the captain, hoping he would intercede, yet he knew Captain Wilton could do nothing to countermand an order by a superior officer.

"But don't we need to wait for a replacement for me?" Conlon asked, grasping for any excuse.

"No need for that," Major Denton said. "I brought a young lieutenant with me last night. He'll mature nicely under Captain Wilton's command."

"May I have a moment to speak privately with Lieutenant Sullivan, Major?"

"Certainly." Major Denton rose. "Don't take too long, though. My wife is anxious to leave. I'm sure they'll be ready within the hour, and the lieutenant still has to get his things packed."

Silence stretched tautly when the major closed the door behind him. Conlon forced himself to look up and meet the captain's sad eyes. How differently this moment was turning out compared to what he dreamed about last night.

"You wanted to talk to me?"

Conlon leaned forward in his chair, his elbows on his knees. "Last night I asked Glorianna to marry me. I told her I would speak to you this morning. I'd like your permission, Sir."

"You realize the Dentons expect you to marry Chastity."

"Yes, Sir." Conlon sat up straight, anger making him determined. "I've never once given Chastity or her parents any reason to suspect I would marry her. I've only done my duty by following orders and escorting her around. They have assumed things. I love your daughter. I want to marry her."

"How does Glorianna feel about this?"

"She loves me, too, Sir. Last night she agreed to become my wife. I can't leave now." Conlon noticed his fingers twisting his cap as if they had a mind of their own. He forced himself to stop. "Couldn't you at least get a delay in my orders, Sir?"

Captain Wilton sighed. "I don't know what I can do. I'll pray about it. Right now, you need to go pack. Let me see if there's any other way. You realize the Dentons are used to getting their way, don't you?"

Conlon stood, pulling his cap back on his head. "Yes, Sir, but there's also God's way. I believe He has a way to make this right. We'll both pray about it."

"Conlon?"

He stopped with his hand poised over the doorknob. The captain had never called him by his first name before. "Yes, Sir?"

"You have my blessing. I would be happy to have you for a son-in-law."

"Thank you, Sir."

In a daze, Conlon left the captain's office and crossed to his quarters. The sky had lost its brilliance, the birds' songs grated on his nerves, and he wanted to yell at God for not watching over him like He promised in Scripture. He'd waited all this time. He'd been patient, yet look what happened. For all the faithfulness he'd shown to God, God was turning His back. *Why,* he cried silently, *why did You let this happen? Just when Glorianna is willing to marry me, I'm jerked away like some puppet. How can any good come out of this?*

"Conlon?" Josiah's deep voice cut through his thoughts.

"Come in," Conlon called, not sure whether to be resentful of the intrusion or glad to have a friend when he felt so low.

"I heard." Josiah, always blunt, sank down on the cot.

Conlon continued to gather his things in silence, not knowing what to say. The hurt ate at him, stealing his reason, stealing his voice.

"You know God has a plan here." Josiah's statement hit a nerve.

"I know that's what the Bible says." Conlon couldn't hold back his anger. "I also know He told me to wait patiently. I did. Now look what I've got to show for it."

"And what would have happened if you'd not been so patient with Glorianna?" At Conlon's silence, Josiah continued. "You know very well you would have lost her. If it's meant to be, God will see things through. Trust Him and be patient, just like He asks."

"But, last night Glorianna said she would marry me. This morning I felt like God was in charge of everything. Then I got my orders and all that changed."

"So, what's different?" Josiah asked quietly.

Conlon knelt on the floor in front of his bedroll. He covered his face with his hands. Josiah didn't interrupt his thoughts.

"You're right, Josiah," he sighed. "It isn't God Who changed. It's my outlook." He bowed his head and whispered, "Oh, God, I'm sorry I didn't trust You totally. Please see me through this. Help me to wait on You."

When he finished the prayer, he felt Josiah's arm around his shoulders. His friend knelt with him on the hard floor, praying for the guidance only God can give.

"Thank you," Conlon said gruffly. "I don't know what I'll do without you, either."

Josiah grinned. "You won't have to be without me for long. My hitch is up in a couple of months. I'm planning to get out."

"You didn't tell me." Conlon couldn't suppress the surprise. "When did you decide this?"

"I've been praying about it for awhile," Josiah said. "I feel the Lord directing me to set up my own blacksmith shop in Tucson. I'll look you up when I get there."

"I'll look forward to it," Conlon spoke sincerely. "I just hope you'll be able to look up Glorianna and me."

"We'll keep praying about it. God brought you this far. Be patient and let Him do the rest."

With tears in her eyes and a pain in her heart so severe she thought she might die, Glorianna watched the ambulance being packed. This morning, as soon as she got out of bed, Chastity blurted out the news that they were leaving and Conlon had orders to go with them. The triumph in her eyes made Glorianna want to scratch the orbs from her face. Chastity told her that she and Conlon would be married before Thanksgiving for sure. After all, there wasn't a parson anywhere around here, but in Tucson it wouldn't be hard to find one. Glorianna's stomach had been tied in knots ever since.

God, how could You allow this? I know Fayth says You allow trials, but haven't we gone through enough? I don't know how I can live life knowing Conlon is married to Chastity and not me. Please, God, I have the feeling if he leaves with them, I'll never see him again. Help me. Help us.

She clutched the handle of her parasol, not caring that it wasn't even tilted right to keep the sun off her face. What were a few freckles compared to life without Conlon? She wanted to rush to his quarters and beg him to stay. But that was foolish. He couldn't disobey orders. The matter was out of his hands. Even her father couldn't change things. She knew he had tried. She'd overheard him talking to the major.

Trust. The voice wove a soft pattern across her heart. *Lean not on thine own understanding.*

Lord, I know in my head I can trust You. But my heart won't listen. I feel like everything is falling apart. I feel like You're not in control.

Glorianna thought about Fayth and the Scriptures they'd discussed since she arrived at Camp MacDowell. Over and over, Fayth reminded her that you can't trust in your feelings, but you can trust in God's Word.

Okay, God, even though it seems hopeless, I want to trust You. Help me just to look at You and not at the circumstances around me.

"Well, I hear you won't be lonely." Chastity sauntered over from the wagon. "My father says he brought a new lieutenant with him. Maybe you can get him to marry you."

Glorianna wanted to wipe the smirk off Chastity's face. She closed her eyes and said a quick prayer. Peace flooded over her, filling every part of her with a sense of well-being, of knowing God could and would take care of everything.

"Chastity, I know you're lonely and need a friend," she said softly. "But I want you to stop and think about what you're doing. Forcing a man to marry you when he doesn't want to isn't the answer. Soon he'll turn bitter, and your life will be miserable."

Chastity's eyes narrowed, and Glorianna hurried on before she interrupted. "I know somewhere the right man is waiting. Conlon isn't that man. Please don't make him do something that both of you will regret."

"You just want him for yourself," Chastity snapped. "I know he'll be happy once we're away from you. Mother and I plan to have the wedding as soon as we get to Tucson."

Chastity whirled and stalked back to the ambulance, where her mother directed the two soldiers loading their trunks. *God, I don't see how You can work this out,* Glorianna prayed, watching the duo prepare to leave. *I'm trying not to listen to my understanding, but to trust You.* She turned and trudged toward the stables, hoping to find Conlon before he left.

"Conlon?" He had his back to her, saddling Champ. She ached to touch him, to tell him it would be all right. She knew by the sag in his shoulders how discouraged he was.

"Glorianna." He swung around, not losing his grip on the cinch he was tightening.

"I heard you're leaving." She tried to say more, but the lump growing in her throat held back the words.

He nodded. "I tried to get out of it, but I can't." He dropped the cinch strap and reached for her. His arms wrapped tightly around her, pulling her close. "I'll miss you so much, my morning Glory. Somehow, this will work out."

She gazed into his deep blue eyes that overflowed with love. "I love you," she whispered, then stepped back, hearing the major call for him. Watching him ride down the stable aisle, she felt like she were being torn in two. Was he right? Would this work out, or was this the last time she would see him?

Chapter 19

The outline of the business district at Florence barely broke the skyline when Major Denton called a halt. Conlon watched the weary soldiers swing down from their equally tired mounts. They should have arrived at Florence yesterday, for the major and the ladies to take the stage to Tucson, leaving the cavalrymen to follow with their belongings at a more leisurely pace. None of them counted on the various mishaps that had beset them on the way.

On the morning of the second day, one of the wagon wheels dropped into a rut, splintering several spokes. It took hours to fix the wheel, and they traveled late to make up lost time. Then, this morning, they rose before dawn to resume the trip. In the predawn darkness, one of the horses pulling the ambulance stepped in a hole, breaking its leg. They lost even more time disposing of the horse and bringing in a replacement. What should have been a two-day trip had taken them three long days.

"Lieutenant."

Mrs. Denton's voice twisted the knot in his stomach. She had done nothing but complain over the delays. Between her bossiness and Chastity's whining about being uncomfortable, he wanted to throttle them both. How did the major stand it? Perhaps this explained why he spent so much time in the field.

"Yes, Ma'am?" Conlon tried to keep his voice polite as he kneed Champ closer to the wagon.

"Why are we stopping?" Mrs. Denton demanded. "We need to get on to Florence so Chastity and I can rest."

"I would assume we stopped to let the horses get their wind," Conlon tried to explain, knowing Mrs. Denton wouldn't be listening anyway. "We've been traveling hard, and the strain is telling on the horses. We'll be in Florence in time for you to catch the evening stage."

"Conlon, I need to get out and walk," Chastity whined. "I want someone to escort me." She tilted her head to one side, as if trying to look coy.

Reining Champ away from the wagon, Conlon called back, "I'll send someone to walk with you. Now, if you'll excuse me, I need to see the major." He quickly urged Champ to a faster pace, hoping they wouldn't call him back. Gritting his teeth, Conlon determined he wouldn't spend any more time with Chastity Denton than absolutely necessary. Nor would he cater to her whims. He didn't have to, now that his actions weren't hurting the captain.

"Lieutenant." Major Denton beckoned to him. "I've just heard that there's a detachment of soldiers from Fort Lowell in Florence. I want to ride ahead and see why they're there. Will you accompany me? I believe the ambulance will be well escorted without us."

Falling in beside the major, Conlon tried to remember what he had planned to say. All the arguments that came so easily last night disappeared now. *God, I need You to give me the words,* he prayed. *Please, don't let me offend this man. Prepare his heart to really hear what I have to say and to accept it. Thank You, Father.*

"You know, Sullivan, my wife and daughter seem determined to have a wedding the minute we arrive in Tucson." Major Denton glanced over at Conlon.

Conlon nodded, waiting to see what the major was leading up to. Had God already worked in this man's heart, or was he going to help plan the wedding?

"When I mentioned your marrying my daughter, I thought I detected some reluctance on your part. Is that correct?"

Taking a deep breath, Conlon prayed again for the appropriate words. "Yes, Sir, you're right."

"I'm thinking you might have some feelings for the captain's daughter."

Conlon nodded again, not sure where this was leading.

"Why didn't you just say so? Why did you continue to escort my daughter?"

"Well, Sir, to be honest, I was concerned about the captain." At Major Denton's questioning look, Conlon continued. "The last time you were at Camp MacDowell, I tried to discourage Chastity. If you remember, Sir, Captain Wilton came under fire for my behavior."

"I do recall some of that," Major Denton admitted. "My apologies. I realize my wife and daughter can be rather determined once they set their minds to something. However, I've been doing a lot of thinking in the past few days." He paused, his dark eyes watching Conlon. "I don't want my daughter marrying a man who doesn't want her. That would make for a disastrous marriage. Don't you agree?"

"Yes, Sir."

"I've decided to intervene. I know my wife. She won't like it, and Chastity will cry for awhile, but I think it's best if you don't marry her."

"Thank you, Sir." *Thank You, God,* Conlon added silently. "I'm sure your daughter will find the right man someday, but I'm not him. I can't marry her when my heart belongs to another. I hope you can see that, Sir."

Major Denton pulled his horse to a halt. He stretched out his hand, and Conlon grasped it in a firm handshake. "I understand completely, Lieutenant."

"Thank you," Conlon repeated. "I am afraid, Sir, that it won't be easy to convince Mrs. Denton and Chastity to call off the wedding."

"You let me handle that." Major Denton chuckled. "I'll break the news and then ride out for a week or two with some soldiers. I've found it's the best way to handle those two."

At the outskirts of Florence, Major Denton gestured to a group of cavalrymen gathered by their horses. Conlon followed him as he urged his horse to a canter, changing direction to intercept the troops. They looked as if they were preparing to mount up and ride out until Conlon and the major came riding over.

A young lieutenant handed over the reins of his horse to another cavalryman and walked over to meet them. He saluted as the major dismounted.

"Lieutenant Rourke, Sir."

"Lieutenant." Major Denton returned his salute and finished the introductions. "What are you men doing so far from Fort Lowell? Is there trouble?"

"We were tracking a soldier, Sir. We had one who'd gone bad. He was coming up for trial and he broke out. He killed the soldier guarding him and escaped."

"Did you catch him?" Major Denton asked.

"No, Sir, we tracked him all the way to the Superstition Mountains. We lost him in the canyons there."

"That's a miserable place to try to find someone," Major Denton said.

"True," said Lieutenant Rourke. "We finally gave up after we lost one of our men."

"How's that? It wasn't Indians, was it?" Major Denton looked tense.

"No, Sir." Lieutenant Rourke paled slightly, as if the memory of what happened still plagued him. "One of the men left camp by himself. A cougar got him." The lieutenant rubbed a hand over his face. "We'd heard the cat scream the night before, but didn't think about it being out in the daylight. We couldn't understand why it was taking O'Reilly so long to get back. When we found him, it was too late."

"We were tracking some Indians in the Superstitions a few weeks back and heard a cougar." Conlon shuddered at the thought of losing one of his men that way.

Lieutenant Rourke choked for a moment before he could continue. "O'Reilly was a good man. One of the best. Judging by the tracks, the cat was a big one. We decided to leave Smith to the cougar. I didn't want to risk any more men."

"Who?" Conlon tried to calm his sense of panic. "Who were you chasing?"

Major Denton and the lieutenant were both staring at him. "The man's name is Smith, Dirk Smith. I believe he used to be at Camp MacDowell, so maybe you know him."

Conlon felt the world shift beneath his feet. Dirk! He was back in the area, and Glorianna didn't know. What if he tried to get to her? He turned to the major, urgency taking the place of everything else.

"Major Denton, I have to go back to Camp MacDowell. We originally sent Dirk Smith to Fort Lowell because he attacked the captain's daughter twice. The first time he was drunk, but the second time he fully intended to take advantage of her. He may try again."

Major Denton studied him for a long minute. "Go on back, Sullivan. I'll take care of your orders. I'll have them delayed for a few weeks. We'll send you notice."

"Be careful of him, Lieutenant," Rourke warned. "He's a dangerous man. He's killed once and probably won't hesitate to do it again."

Running to mount Champ, Conlon prayed, *Please, God, protect Glorianna. Don't let that madman get his hands on her.* Anger began to build as he thought of Dirk's touching Glorianna. He had to get back in time.

※

"Glorianna?" Fayth called through the open door. "May we come in?"

"Go'wy." Alyce's high voice mimicked her mother.

Glorianna smiled as she crossed the front room to the door. "Of course, you may come in." It felt good to smile. She hadn't done much of that since Conlon rode off with the Dentons, taking her heart with him. Life now consisted of a constant ache within as she longed for his return.

"How are you doing?" Fayth's steady gaze seemed to look right through her façade and uncover the misery beneath.

"I miss him so much." Glorianna fought back the tears. "I'm so glad I have God now. Despite all the hurt, deep down I have a peace I can't explain. I know things will work out. I just don't know if they will work out the way I want them to."

"At least you know things will work out God's way. Right?" Fayth asked softly.

"Yes," Glorianna said. "But, of course, I do wish I had one more chance to dunk Chastity in the river. Maybe I wouldn't let her up so soon," she teased.

Fayth laughed. "Sometimes I think I'd like to help you with that. Oh, by the way, I came to bring you a letter. Timothy brought it by a little while ago."

Glorianna held the cream-colored envelope in her hand for a moment, savoring its heaviness. "It's from Kathleen. I miss her so much. She was my only friend until you." She tore open the letter before her eyes got too watery. She had been crying entirely too much lately.

"If you want, we'll leave so you can have time with your letter."

"No, please stay," Glorianna urged Fayth. She pulled Alyce up on her lap. "Besides, I won't let Alyce go, so you have to stay. Let me tell you what Kathleen has to say."

She opened the letter and read for a minute. A blush heated her cheeks. "Oh, my." She slapped a hand over her mouth. "It seems that Kendrick and Melissa are married now."

"So soon?" Fayth asked. "I thought they weren't getting married for a couple of months."

"That's what everyone else thought, too. But it seems Melissa's father visited Kendrick with a shotgun, and the two of them were married very quickly."

Fayth gasped and covered her mouth with her hand. "I hate to say this, but I'm glad you didn't marry him if he's that kind of man."

Glorianna hugged Alyce against her. "I thought I'd be upset when they got married, but I find I don't care at all. I believe that if I had gotten to know Kendrick, I may not have liked him so much. I realize now I only liked him because all the other girls did. That's a poor reason to marry someone."

"Unfortunately, when we're young, we can be easily influenced that way. I wonder if God brought you out here to get you away from that situation."

"I know now that God has my best interests at heart. I only want to trust Him, even though it's hard for me not to tell Him what I think those best interests are."

Fayth grinned. "I think we all have that problem."

Slipping the unfinished letter in her pocket, Glorianna tickled Alyce, making her giggle. Alyce's deep chuckle was contagious, and they all laughed.

"I've been moping around here long enough," Glorianna declared. "Why don't we go for a ride? I haven't ridden Nina since Chastity took her over. Would you go with me?"

After leaving Alyce with Mrs. Peterson, Fayth and Glorianna hurried to the stable for their horses. They planned a late evening meal, which would give them a couple of hours to ride.

"Are you sure you'll be able to ride?" Glorianna asked again. "I don't want you to do this if it will hurt the baby."

"Don't worry about this baby. He's too feisty to be hurt by anything as simple as a horseback ride. I think getting away for awhile will be the best thing for me."

Glorianna settled into Nina's easy walk, relaxing completely for the first time in days. She hadn't been this direction before. This road led to Pinal City and the Florence turnoff. Conlon had ridden this road only four days ago. Was he in Tucson by now? Had Chastity made him marry her? She pushed the thoughts from her head before worry set in once more. Trust. That's what God wanted her to do.

"This is a beautiful time of day." Glorianna savored the peacefulness of the desert. "I love to watch the rabbits and coyotes. I don't even mind a snake if it keeps its distance."

"Oh, look." Fayth pointed ahead and to the left. A herd of antelope raced over a slight rise. They bounded effortlessly across the desert, leaping over bushes and weaving around the cactus. Pulling the horses to a halt, they watched the graceful animals until they were out of sight.

"I wonder what startled them." Fayth frowned. "Maybe we should head back to the camp."

"But we still have at least an hour to ride." Glorianna didn't want to give up this time. "Why do you want to go back? Are you feeling ill?"

"No." Fayth glanced over her shoulder. "I just feel uneasy for some reason." She shrugged. "I'm being silly, I guess."

They rode down the side of the hill where the antelope had run. At the bottom stood a clump of trees. As they approached the trees, Nina pricked her ears forward. She nickered softly.

"What is it, Girl?" Glorianna patted Nina's neck. "What's out there that interests you?"

"It might be me." Dirk stepped from behind a tree, grabbing Nina's bridle so swiftly Glorianna couldn't react.

Chapter 20

Heart pounding, Glorianna jerked futilely on the reins. Her worst nightmare stood before her. A gash, crusted over with dirt and dried blood, covered part of one unshaven cheek. Judging from the redness surrounding the wound, infection had set in. Brown patches of what might be dried blood spotted his clothing. She shuddered, not wanting to know if it was Dirk's or someone else's. Bile rose in her throat, and she covered her nose to ward off the stench of his unwashed body. His dark-circled, haunted eyes glared at her. Her stomach churned. Where had he come from?

"Let go of my horse." Glorianna hoped to keep her voice steady. Then, before he could say anything, she called, "Go, Fayth, get help."

Dirk's hand snaked out even as she uttered the words. He grabbed Fayth's horse before she could turn him. "Not so fast," he warned. "You're both coming with me." Blackened teeth showed through his grin.

"My husband and the others from the camp expect us back soon, Mr. Smith." Fayth's words steadied Glorianna. "You won't get away with this."

A mirthless laugh filled the air around them. "I heard the little lady say you still had an hour before you had to be back. That will give us plenty of time to put some distance between us and the camp."

Dirk jerked the reins away from them and led the horses into the trees. A horse, tethered to a tree, waited for him. Dirk mounted, never letting go of their reins. He turned his horse east, riding parallel to the road, but off of it.

"Where are you taking us?" Glorianna bit her lip, knowing he heard the fear in her voice.

Dirk grinned back at her. "I have a little place all picked out for you and me. We'll be together from now on, so you'd best get used to the idea."

"But what about Fayth? You don't need to drag her along."

He chuckled malevolently. "Oh, I'll let her go soon enough. Then, it'll just be the two of us. I didn't know you were so eager."

Glorianna shuddered. She looked at Fayth, hoping desperately for a way out of this. Fayth's closed eyes and moving lips reminded her that she had other help with her at all times. How could she have forgotten?

God, help us, her prayer screamed out inside her head. *You can't let this happen.* Taking a calming breath, she tried to gather her thoughts.

Jesus, I know You are my Protector, my Shield, and my Help in time of trouble. You asked me to trust You and lean not on my own understanding. But where are You? How can You allow something like this? What about Fayth and the baby?

Glorianna bit her lip. She knew she was repeating herself. She closed her eyes, and reassurance gradually eased her fear. She knew Fayth would be praying, too. *Oh, Lord, if only Conlon were here. Why did he have to leave? But, there I go, questioning You again. Please forgive all my doubts.* A gentle peace crept over her. She sighed, feeling as if someone was there with her, holding her close. *Thank You,* she said silently.

"Are you all right?" Glorianna asked Fayth.

"Shut up," Dirk barked. "If you talk, I'll have to gag you."

Glorianna bit her lip, wondering if she had turned pale. The thought of being gagged with some of Dirk's clothing almost made her retch.

When he turned back around, Fayth reached over and quickly squeezed her hand. "I'm fine." She mouthed the words silently. Her smile helped Glorianna relax. *God is in charge,* she told herself. *Remember that.*

Dirk set a fast pace, heading toward the Superstition Mountains. The road to Florence was a ribbon of brown in the distance. They could only see pieces of it when they topped a rise in the desert. Each time, Glorianna looked at the road with longing. A quiet despair began to settle over her as she wondered if anyone would ever find them. She remembered Conlon's saying how hard it was to find Indians once they made it to the Superstitions. There were myriad places to hide there.

Two hours later, the sun dipping low in the west, Glorianna knew she had to speak up. Fayth could barely stay upright in the saddle. Pain etched pale lines in her face. "Mr. Smith, we have to stop. Fayth can't go on like this."

Reining in his horse, Dirk turned to look at them, his eyes filled with anger. "We have to get to the mountains. We aren't stopping just because one of you can't keep up." He swiveled back around and jerked the horses' reins to start again.

Fayth's eyes filled with tears. Her whitened fingers gripped the saddle as if trying to ease the jolting gait. Each time her horse stumbled on the uneven ground, Fayth would bite her lip to keep quiet.

Desperate to do something to help Fayth, Glorianna began to form a plan. Seeing a clear space ahead, she slipped her feet from the stirrup. Glancing at Fayth, hoping she would be quiet, she lifted her leg over the saddle. Saying a quick prayer, she jumped from Nina's back. Her feet hitting the hard sand sent a jolt through her body. She swung her arms, fighting a losing battle for balance. Falling to the side, she rolled away from Nina and lay still for a moment to catch her breath.

Dirk whirled around, pulling the horses to a halt. "What are you doing?" he yelled.

She sat up as he jumped from his horse and rushed over to her. He grabbed her arm, jerking her to her feet. The smell of his filthy body revolted her. She clenched her teeth, knowing she had to be strong for Fayth and the baby.

Glaring at him, she snapped, "We have to stop. Fayth is tired and it's almost dark. We can't keep riding in the desert after dark." She straightened up, attempting to tug her arm free from his grasp.

He grimaced and tightened his hold on her. "You'll do what I say. I've seen for some time you need to be told a thing or two. Your father is too lax with you." Leaning closer, his soft-spoken words sent a chill down her spine. "Now you'll be my woman, and you'll do what I tell you. I've trained many a stubborn mule. I guess I can teach you something."

Dear God, help me think of something. Fayth can't even sit straight in the saddle. If we continue, she could lose the baby. Please help us.

Taking a deep breath, Glorianna tried to calm her thoughts. "If we ride in the dark, the horses could walk into a cactus. We can reach the mountains more easily in the morning. We're almost there. Why can't we just spend the night here?"

She forced herself to meet Dirk's gaze as he studied her. Finally, he gave a short nod.

"Get your friend down. We don't have any bedrolls, so you'll have to use the saddle blankets." He released her arm and ran a gritty finger down the side of her cheek. She flinched away, and he grinned. "Then again," he said with deadly calm, "maybe Fayth can have the blankets, and I'll keep you warm."

Glorianna gasped and stepped away. *God protect me,* she whispered in her soul. *Trust Me,* came the answer written across her heart.

Hurrying to help Fayth, Glorianna shuddered at the thought of Dirk's suggestion. Fayth slipped from the horse and hugged Glorianna. Peering over the horse's back, Fayth turned back to her.

"God can handle this," she whispered. "I know Timothy and the others are following us by now."

"But how will they know where we are? We didn't stay on the road. They won't think to look in the desert for us."

"God knows where we are. He will show them the way," Fayth assured her.

"What are you doing?" Dirk growled. He pulled the horses away and glared at them. When they didn't answer, he spat on the ground. "There won't be any way to cook food. I don't have much anyway. Do I have to tie you or will you stay?"

"Mr. Smith, it's too far to walk. I'm not sure we would find our way from here anyway," Fayth assured him.

He studied her, then led the horses to a tree and tied them securely. Removing the saddles, he carried their blankets back to them. Glorianna spread them out to dry before the night chill set in. A sweaty blanket wouldn't be much of a comfort.

Sinking down by Fayth, Glorianna watched Dirk. In the gathering darkness, she could see him studying her. Fear twisted a knot in her stomach. Would he follow through with his threat to keep her warm? What if no one found them? What if Dirk forced her to do something she didn't want? What could she do to stop him? Where was Conlon? She needed him.

She closed her eyes, squeezing tears away. A picture of Conlon swam before her. She could see his black hair, the wayward lock falling across his forehead.

She could picture his blue eyes, brightly reflecting his love for her. If there was any way, he would come for her. In her heart she knew how much he loved her. Somehow, he would find a way to get away from Chastity. He had to.

Nearing exhaustion, Conlon pulled Champ to a halt. They were less than an hour's ride from Camp MacDowell. In the growing twilight, he watched the cloud of dust approaching. The thunder of hoofbeats filled the air. A sense of dread wrapped around him like a mantle.

A few minutes later, his uneasiness grew stronger as he watched the grim faces of the cavalrymen surrounding him. Timothy pushed his horse close to Conlon's. "What are you doing here? Have you seen Fayth and Glorianna?"

Conlon shifted in the saddle. "What do you mean, have I seen them?" He wanted to shout his impatience. He needed to know what was happening.

"They went for a ride this afternoon and haven't returned," Timothy said. "The guard saw them head this direction, but we haven't found them yet."

Forcing his fear away, Conlon replied, "I just rode here from Florence. I haven't seen any sign of them. You're sure they came this way?"

Timothy and several of the others nodded. "We saw fresh tracks on the road. There's no question." Timothy looked torn between fear and anger. "I can't imagine why they would get off the road."

Conlon knew he had to tell him, although he dreaded the reaction. "I might know the reason," he admitted reluctantly. "I'm here because we met a patrol in Florence. They had just come from tracking a criminal to the Superstitions." He paused, looking at the men. "They were tracking Dirk Smith. He killed a man before he escaped and headed this direction. I think he might be after Glorianna."

Timothy paled. "You mean that crazy fool might have Fayth and Glorianna?"

Conlon couldn't speak for a moment, caught in the panic he knew his friend felt. "I hope I'm wrong," he spoke hoarsely. "But I'm guessing he has them."

"What do we do? They could be anywhere." Fear echoed in Timothy's voice.

"I think he'll try to head for the Superstitions. It's the closest place to hide." Conlon turned to look at the forbidding mountains in the distance. "I'll head over there and try to find their tracks."

"I'll go with you," Timothy said. He turned to the others. "The rest of you go back and tell the captain what's happened. He'll probably want to send some of you to help."

"You'll most likely have to wait until morning," Conlon added. "We'll try to leave some sign so you can find us."

When they were alone, Timothy faced Conlon. "Do you think he'll kill them?"

"He won't kill Glory." Conlon hated to think about the women being at Dirk's mercy.

"What about Fayth?"

"I don't know," Conlon answered honestly. "I hope we catch him before he has to make a choice." Deciding to keep silent his fears of what Dirk would do with Fayth when he wanted to be alone with Glorianna, Conlon instead turned Champ toward the mountain range. "Let's ride while there's still daylight. The closer we get, the better our chances of catching them before they disappear in the Superstitions."

They rode until the night drew too close around them, then halted. *Lord, please watch over Fayth and Glory. Be their protection.* The spine-chilling scream of a cougar interrupted his silent plea.

Chapter 21

Glorianna took a sip of water from her canteen. Her stomach ached from hunger and fear. They had ridden most of the morning to reach the edge of the mountains. Dirk looked even worse this morning than he had last night. He hadn't slept, probably because he was afraid they would take the horses and run. He had been right. She slept lightly, waking several times during the night, hoping he would be asleep and they could escape. Every time, his eyes were on her, the wicked gleam in them making her uncomfortable.

Dirk turned his horse back to theirs. "You." He gestured at Fayth. Handing her the reins to her horse, he said, "You can go back now. Tell them not to follow us. I've got what I want." He grinned lecherously at Glorianna. "I know she puts on a good show, but she's really glad to go with me. You can tell the captain and Lieutenant Sullivan that."

"I won't leave Glorianna." Fayth nudged her horse closer to Nina.

"Then you'll die," Dirk snarled. He whipped his knife up, lunging at her throat.

Fayth jerked back. Glorianna screamed.

"Now get out of here." At Dirk's command, Glorianna gave Fayth a pleading look. Fayth turned her horse and rode away, glancing back at Glorianna only once.

Dirk nudged his horse next to Nina. "Now it's just the two of us." His rancid breath made her cough. "Let's get lost in these mountains."

He tugged on the reins, and Nina followed. Tears filled Glorianna's eyes as she watched Fayth disappear. She felt all her hopes vanish as well. *Trust Me. Lean not on thine own understanding,* a voice whispered.

Minutes later, Dirk jerked the horses to a stop. He stared back into the desert and cursed. Glancing behind them, Glorianna could see a rider racing toward them. Her heart beat wildly as she thought she recognized the lean form. It couldn't be, could it?

She nearly fell when Dirk forced the horses to plunge ahead. He turned up a steep slope. Evidently, he thought the rocks would offer shelter. Glorianna loosened her feet in the stirrups. Perhaps she could jump off again. That would give the rider a chance to catch them. One look at the sharp incline they were traveling up convinced her it wouldn't be a good idea. She clung desperately to Nina's saddle, hoping to think of something.

"Get down." Dirk's raspy voice echoed in the stillness.

He dragged her to the rocks, making her climb in front of him. When they were hemmed in on all sides by the huge boulders, he pulled her down.

"Smith, you may as well give up. I know you're up there."

Glorianna gasped and tried to rise up. It was Conlon. He had come for her.

"She's mine, Sullivan. She's always been mine."

"If you think she wants you, then why don't you let her decide?" They could hear Conlon working his way up the slope as he talked.

Dirk stood, pulling Glorianna up in front of him. "Stop right there," he ordered. His knife blade flashed in the sunlight. He stuck it under Glorianna's chin, making her tip her head back to avoid the blade. She didn't dare breathe. "If you come any closer, I'll cut her. Then neither one of us will have her." His maniacal laughter filled the air.

From the corner of her eye, Glorianna could see Conlon pause. He held his rifle loosely in his hand. She'd seen him on the drills and knew the speed with which he could swing the gun into firing position.

"Let her go, Dirk. She doesn't want you." Glorianna wondered if he felt as relaxed as he sounded. "By now the troops are on their way. You can see their dust from up there. You won't get away with this."

"I don't know how you found us, but I'm not letting her go. You may as well go and tell the captain. Now get out of here before I hurt her."

While he was talking, Dirk's knife eased away from Glorianna's throat. She lowered her head slightly, getting a better view of Conlon. She watched him open his mouth to reply, then pause, his gaze going to the rocks above them.

"Smith." Conlon's voice lowered. "There's a cougar on the rocks above you."

"Don't try to bluff me." Dirk's knife swept up under Glorianna's chin, forcing her to lift her head again. "Now head on back to your horse and ride out of here."

In the silence that followed, Glorianna strained to look at the rocks above them. The knife blade kept her from turning her head, but she could hear the rattle of tiny rocks sliding down from above. She began to tremble.

"Please, he isn't bluffing."

A low growl above them confirmed her fears. Dirk whirled. His grip loosened. Glorianna dropped to the ground. She could see Conlon swing his rifle up in one smooth motion. Fire and smoke belched from the end of it.

The rifle cracked. The cougar roared. Dirk's frantic scream washed over her. A heavy weight landed on her back, knocking the air from her. In one continuous motion, the body rolled over the top of her and off the rocks. She thought of the long drop to the hillside below and shuddered.

"No!" Glorianna screamed as hands wrapped around her arms, lifting her. She lashed out, struggling to get free.

"Glory, Sweetheart, it's all right." Conlon's soothing voice finally broke through her fear.

Sobbing, she collapsed in his arms. He held her tight, running his hand over her hair. "It's over, my love," he whispered.

"What happened?" Glorianna tried to turn and look over the side of the rocks.

"Don't look," Conlon commanded, pulling her back around. "I shot the cougar, but in its fall, it knocked Dirk off the rocks. He's dead, Sweetheart. He won't bother you again."

Glorianna pushed away slightly, tilting her head to look into Conlon's brilliant blue eyes. They were even more wonderful than she remembered. She reached up to brush the lock of hair from his forehead, savoring the touch.

"What happened to Chastity? How did you get here?" She covered her mouth with her hand. "Fayth, she's out in the desert. We have to find her."

He grinned, running a finger down her cheek, tracing the outline of her lips before he answered. "Timothy and I met Fayth. He's taking her back to the camp. She told me where to find you. As for Chastity, the major decided I wasn't the right son-in-law for him. He sent me back to Camp MacDowell for a time."

"For how long?" she asked, fearing losing him again.

"Long enough to get married," he whispered. "That is, if you'll still have me."

"Yes. Oh yes," she breathed as his lips settled over hers in a kiss that made her knees weak.

Epilogue

L oud pounding on the door startled Conlon as he scraped the razor across his face. "Ouch!" He winced as a tiny line of red welled up on his jaw.

"Hey, Conlon, you too high and mighty to talk to a friend?" Josiah stuck his head through the door and grinned. "Here you are in the guest house like you're some high-falutin' fancy pants."

"Can't you knock a little softer? You almost made me cut my throat." Conlon tilted his head and pointed to the blood.

Josiah's laughter rumbled through the room. "If you had your head out of the clouds, you would have heard me knock the first two times."

Leaning over the basin to rinse his face, Conlon hoped to hide his embarrassment. Josiah was right. Today was his wedding day, and for the last week or so, he couldn't seem to do anything right. Even Champ had been giving him funny looks.

He knew the disorientation had to do with finally getting to be with Glory again. For the past two months, he'd been stationed at Fort Lowell in Tucson. Major Denton, true to his promise, had sent Mrs. Denton and Chastity back east for a visit after breaking the news to them that Conlon wouldn't be marrying Chastity.

The major had insisted that Conlon come to Fort Lowell. He wanted him to work as a cavalry liaison officer, acquiring new horses for the troops and making sure they were properly broken. Only the separation from Glorianna marred his happiness. This job was the beginning of his dream. He now had the opportunity to learn where the best horses could be found when he was ready to start his ranch. Glorianna had been very understanding about the separation. She encouraged him in what she called "their dream," the hope that someday they would have a ranch where they could raise quality horses.

Conlon patted his face dry, taking care not to make the cut bleed again. Did all bridegrooms nick themselves on their wedding day? He grinned at the thought and turned to Josiah. "You're just jealous because I've been writing Glory all those letters instead of sending them to you."

A crooked grin split Josiah's ebony face. "You've got that right. Did you know the mail carrier's horse's legs are two inches shorter than they used to be? Poor thing's been running back and forth between here and Fort Lowell so much, he's worn to a frazzle." He slapped Conlon on the back, then sank into a chair. "Speaking of letters, I hear you had an important one waiting for you when you arrived."

Conlon reached into his pocket and pulled out an envelope. For a moment he couldn't speak as emotion made a tight knot in his throat. He ran his fingers over the fine print on the crinkled paper. Even after all these years, he'd recognized his mother's handwriting.

"My mother wrote." He looked up and saw the compassion in Josiah's eyes. "My father died last month. The doctor said his heart gave out."

He pulled out the pages of paper he'd already memorized and opened them up. "Mom says my letter reached them not long before Dad got real sick. She said the news of my becoming a Christian helped them all. Dad's only regret was not getting to see me again before he died. He wanted to tell me how much he loved me and that he forgave me years ago for what happened to my brother."

Conlon leaned forward and rested his elbows on his knees. "You know, I miss Dad, but I've been thinking all night long that now I'll be able to be with him in heaven someday. A few years ago, I wouldn't have had that comfort."

Josiah reached over and engulfed Conlon's hands in his callused hands. "I'm glad you wrote them. This will really start the healing. Knowing you're forgiven will help you to forgive yourself." Josiah stood and stretched. "Now, we'd better get going, or you won't be at the ceremony in time. I can't wait until you see your bride in that pretty dress."

"Dress?" Conlon grimaced. "I wanted to bring a special one for Glory. I knew she wouldn't be able to get the right material here, but I couldn't find the time to shop in Tucson. Where did she get a dress?"

"She didn't tell you last night?"

"I got in so late, we didn't have much time to talk."

"I'll bet there was time for a kiss or two." Josiah chuckled.

Conlon laughed, feeling his face warm. "That's possible. Now, tell me about the dress."

"Her cousin Kathleen, from back east, sent Glorianna's mother's wedding dress. It came in on a shipment last week. On the same train that brought your letter." Josiah clapped Conlon on the shoulder and steered him toward the door. "Anyway, your bride has been crying ever since. Seems she had given up the idea of having a decent dress to wear for her wedding day."

Thank You, Lord. What a gift for Glory and me. Conlon felt light as air as he followed Josiah outside. He couldn't wait to see Glorianna. When Captain Wilton first insisted he stay in the guest house, he'd objected. Now he was thankful for the privacy he would have with his bride.

※

"Oh, Fayth, I wish my mother could be here today." Glorianna smoothed her hand over the pure white of her wedding dress. Her mother's dress. The skirt fell in soft folds to her feet. Lace trimmed the long sleeves, the neck, and the hem. The simplicity of the pattern made the dress beautiful.

"Your mother would be so happy for you." Fayth finished the last of the tiny buttons, then came around and gave Glorianna a hug. "I know she'd love

Conlon." She took a moment to adjust the lace collar. "Kathleen must be such a blessing to you. I can't believe she even sent these ribbons to weave in your hair. She must have known we would have no flowers around here."

Glorianna brushed her fingers over her hair. "She is wonderful." She closed her eyes and bit her lip. "Fayth, I'm so nervous, my stomach is jittery. I don't think I can do this."

Fayth laughed and hugged her again. "I know just how you feel. I felt the same way right before my wedding. You'll be fine. Ready to go?" She walked around Glorianna one more time as if looking for anything out of place, then gestured to the door.

⚘

Conlon held himself stiff, hoping he didn't show any nervousness. Most of the camp had gathered in the dining hall for the wedding. The pastor from Florence had ridden in with him, and he waited now with Conlon, watching the door for Glorianna to enter.

The last rays of the sun streamed in as Glorianna stepped through the doorway. In that moment, the golden glow seemed to surround her in a haze. Conlon's chest tightened, and he fought for a breath. *Oh, God, she's so beautiful. Thank You for this gift. Please help me to be worthy of her love.*

She glided down the aisle between the rows of people. Her gaze never faltered from his. As she drew closer, he could see the silent promise she offered, the promise of her love and commitment for a lifetime.

He stepped forward and joined his hand with hers. With a smile, he returned her promise with one of his own—to love and cherish her forever, just the way God intended.

Sonoran Star

To Marie and Ellen,
sisters extraordinaire.

Chapter 1

Quinn Kirby finished digging the splinter from his thumb, wiped the blade on his pants, snapped the pocketknife shut, and pushed it into his pocket. The thrum of horses' hooves, accompanied by the rattle of the stage, echoed down the quiet street. He turned to the right and leaned his shoulder against the rough-hewn boards of the mercantile. Glancing down to make sure his deputy badge still shone from last night's polishing, he continued his patient wait for the stage.

Every day was the same. The afternoon stage would arrive, and Quinn would be waiting—waiting for her, so he could arrest her. He knew one day the thief, known as the Veiled Widow, would show up here in Tucson. When she did, he'd be ready. Quinn wasn't afraid of arresting a woman. From the reports coming in over the wires, the Widow was getting bolder all the time.

Her modus operandi—he rolled the fancy police term around in his mind, fighting the faint smile that touched his lips—involved showing up in a town and acting helpless. She targeted older, well-to-do gentlemen. She stayed long enough to get the gentleman to cough up a tidy sum, then she disappeared. No one would hear about her for weeks until she came out of hiding to strike again. Her appetite for wealth seemed to be growing. In the last few months, she'd struck with alarming frequency.

The stage rattled to a stop in a cloud of dust that settled to the ground in a slow waltz. White lather flecked the horses' harness straps. Quinn straightened. Eight weeks ago the Widow had robbed and wounded a man in Texas. She seemed to be working her way west. To Quinn's way of thinking, that made Tucson a likely destination. He was here to make sure she didn't carry out her manipulations on any of the fine citizens of the town he'd sworn to protect.

The driver climbed down from the top of the stagecoach. His bones creaked as loud as the stage. He opened the door, stepped to the side, and held out his hand. Quinn brushed the handle of his pistol. The driver wouldn't be helping a man from the coach.

The sight of a small foot encased in a black shoe made Quinn's heart accelerate. Muscles tense, he flexed his fingers, and he held his breath. The woman climbed out, one hand holding her dark green skirt up so she wouldn't trip. A dainty matching hat trimmed with a pheasant feather and no veil perched atop her gray-streaked hair. Mrs. Baker. She and her husband must be getting home from their trip to Albuquerque to visit their daughter. Lena Baker smiled at the driver. Richard Baker climbed from the coach and took his wife's arm to help her to the side of the street. A young man, thin and gawky, clambered from the stage, grabbing the door just in time to keep from falling in the dust.

Quinn watched as the young man righted himself and turned to help catch the luggage being lowered to the ground. Some of the tension drained away. He'd had such hopes that she would be on the stage today. In fact, he woke this morning with the feeling that he would arrest her today. He could almost picture the black veil covering her face, her trim figure decked in a black traveling dress, slender long-fingered hands holding the skirt up in a delicate manner as she stepped down. Quinn jumped. He wasn't just thinking this; he was seeing her. The lanky youth finished helping the woman, came close to falling again as he offered her his arm, then reddened as she turned and walked away from the stagecoach straight toward the elderly Mr. Ash, one of the richest men in town.

After pushing off from the dry adobe wall, Quinn began the stalk. His left hand brushed against his deputy badge, his right shifted his Colt pistol, making sure the gun was loose in the holster. A breeze crept across the street, ruffling the woman's veil. Quinn itched to rip the cloth away. Back stiff, the woman lifted her skirts again to step over a pile of manure. Before her foot touched ground, Quinn had her by the elbow. His grip wasn't gentle. No way would he lose the Veiled Widow.

She gasped. Her arm jerked.

He tightened his hold.

"Ouch. Let me go." She tugged hard, stumbling to the side.

"I don't believe I will, Ma'am. You're coming with me."

She turned her head toward him. "I will not. I don't even know you. Now, if you'll let me go, I'm expecting someone."

Quinn shook his head. "You are despicable. You haven't even been in town two minutes, and you already have your victim picked out." He wrapped his hand tightly around her slender arm.

"If you don't release me right now, I'll have the authorities called."

Lifting his hat with his free hand, Quinn smiled. "I am the authority, Ma'am. Deputy Quinn Kirby at your service."

"What?" She stopped struggling. The stage passengers stared as they waited in the shade of the building.

"Let's go, Widow. I have some mighty fine accommodations for you."

"Widow? Accommodations? I don't know what you're talking about. Did my cousin send you?"

Fine dust curled up around their legs as Quinn marched her down the street. He had to admit she was good. From her tone, he could almost believe she had no idea why he was arresting her. No wonder so many lawmen and businessmen had succumbed to her charms. "I don't know your cousin. I'm here to arrest you for robbery."

"What?" Despite his grip, she stopped in the middle of the street. Wrenching her arm to the side and getting loose, she staggered back.

Quinn lunged at her before she could get her footing. This woman was one slippery character. He misjudged the distance and smacked into her. They both tumbled onto the roadway. Quinn twisted in midfall so he wouldn't drop on top of her. His shoulder landed with a splat in a fresh pile of manure.

The Widow fell hard beside him. Her hair tumbled loose. The hat with the veil attached dropped to one side. Quinn found himself gazing into the most incredible hazel eyes he'd ever seen—green, dotted with flecks of yellow, bordered by a ring of darker green. He forgot the horse manure. He couldn't remember why he wanted to arrest her. All he could think of was how much he wanted to stay here and look into those amazing eyes.

She blinked. Her lips twitched. A picture flashed through Quinn's mind of him lying in the street with horse manure dripping from his cheek. No wonder she wanted to laugh. Before he found himself chuckling with a known criminal, Quinn leapt to his feet. He offered her a hand up. She accepted and turned her face to the left as she rose. All humor faded from her beautiful eyes.

"My hat." She started to bend over and pick it up.

Quinn jerked her to his side. "Oh, no, you don't. I'm not giving you a second chance to escape."

"Please, I'm not trying to escape. I need my veil." She continued to tilt her head to the side. Her peaches-and-cream complexion had a light sprinkle of pale freckles. Long, dark eyelashes brushed against her cheek as she blinked. Mahogany hair shone in the afternoon light despite a light coating of Arizona dust.

"Why do you want a veil? What are you trying to hide?" Quinn wondered, then realized he'd spoken the words aloud. He caught her other arm and pulled her around. His eyes widened in surprise. On her left cheek, marring the perfection, was a star-shaped birthmark. The reddish-brown blemish covered a large portion of her cheek.

⚜

Kathleen O'Connor felt heat flush her face. Deputy Kirby stood gawking at her like the school kids had when she was a girl. That's why her parents had taken her out of school. The familiar taunts came flooding back. *"Hey, devil girl." "She's Satan's spawn."* The whisperings, the mothers who forced their children to the other side of the street when she passed by. The years of horror washed over her.

She flinched. Trying to free her hand, she longed to cover her cheek. The deputy held her tight. Dipping her face to the left, Kathleen did her best to hide her birthmark-stained cheek with her shoulder. *God, please, help me.*

Deputy Kirby released her left arm. She pivoted away from him. He bent down, picked up her hat and veil from the dirt, and knocked them against his leg. Then he handed them to her. She wanted to cry. She didn't know why it mattered that this handsome man with his riveting blue-gray eyes wanted her face covered. She knew she wasn't fit for anyone to look at. Hadn't she been told that most of her life? Now she felt more shame than she'd known in years.

"Thank you." She nearly choked on the words.

Using her free hand to try to put the hat in place, Kathleen glanced at the deputy. His eyes glittered. He turned away and pulled her down the street. *Were those tears in his eyes? Does he feel sorry for me?*

"I don't need your pity."

"What?" He looked at her, his mouth set in a grim line.

"I said I don't need your pity. Just because I have a birthmark doesn't mean I'm evil."

They reached a small adobe building. The deputy opened a door that creaked in protest and pulled her inside. Kathleen blinked, trying to adjust to the dimness.

Kicking the door closed, the deputy motioned to the desk in one corner. "Leave your bag on the desk." He gave her a long look. "I don't pity you for the mark on your cheek. I pity you for the way of life you've chosen."

"My way of life?" Kathleen gaped. "Exactly what do you know about me?"

He snorted. "I've been following your career for months. I knew you'd turn up in Tucson eventually. Criminal sorts tend to find their way here. You think you can hide out here or that we'll be easy marks. Well, it didn't work this time. I was ready for you."

He dragged her across the small room to a cell. The deputy pulled the door open, ushered her to the cell, and slammed the door shut behind her.

"What are you doing?" Kathleen had never felt such outrage. "Why am I being locked in a jail cell? I demand you let me out of here. And I don't know why you called me a widow. I am not a widow."

"Then why are you wearing black?"

"My mother gave me her old mourning dress. She said it's sensible for travel."

The deputy stepped away and hung the ring of keys on a nail near the cluttered desk. He hooked his thumbs in his belt loops, turned to face her, and relaxed his slim frame against the wall. "Don't think you can fool me. I know your type. You think you can shed a few tears and a man will do exactly what you want. Well, this man won't. You can cry all you want, and it won't do you any good."

Kathleen's mouth dropped open. "I've never in my life done that. I have no idea what you're talking about. I'm not a widow. I'm not a thief. I came to Tucson to visit my cousin. You have no right to put me in this cell." Anger welled up inside. Who did he think he was, dragging her off to jail and accusing her of such ridiculous things? She glared at Quinn, using the practiced glare that always made her siblings cringe and do exactly what she'd asked of them.

Quinn appeared unaffected. Walking around the desk into the shadows beyond, he began to unbutton his shirt with a studied nonchalance. Kathleen turned her back, unwilling to watch. The rear door banged. She could hear water splashing as he cleaned the manure from his face and shoulder. She'd nearly laughed at the deputy when she'd first seen the manure splashed across his ear. Then, as now, the seriousness of her situation sobered her.

A feeling of helplessness wrapped around her. *God, what is going on here? Why am I in jail? I've never done anything against the law.*

The rough boards of the floor echoed like a hollow drum as the deputy clumped to the desk and pulled a different shirt from a peg on the wall. Kathleen tried not to watch. He had to be the handsomest man she'd ever laid eyes on. A slightly hooked nose added strength to his face. With his hat off, she could see the dark blond waves in his hair. She wondered if they gleamed even more in the sunlight than they did in the shadow. If looks were all a woman needed in a man, this one would make a fine husband.

What am I thinking? This man threw me in jail for no good reason, and all I can do is admire him. Kathleen wanted to kick herself. . .or maybe someone else.

After crossing to the front of the small cell, Kathleen wrapped her gloved fingers around the metal bars. She wondered how many truly desperate characters had gripped the bars this way before her. "I'd like to know how long you plan to keep me in here. My cousin's husband should be here any time to pick me up. What about my trunks? If someone takes them, you'll answer for it."

Deputy Kirby pulled out the chair, settled into the seat, and lifted his booted feet onto the scarred desk. "I'll send someone to fetch your trunks. We can store them for a time. Where you're going, you won't be needing them."

Waves of red-hot anger blurred Kathleen's vision. "Exactly where do you think I'll be going, besides my cousin's house?"

The deputy reached up and ran a hand through his unruly waves of hair, leaving them in even more disorder "Why, Ma'am, I reckon you'll either be going to prison for a good, long time or swinging from a gallows when I'm done with you."

Chapter 2

Kathleen could feel the blood draining from her face. Her grip tightened on the bars as her knees began to shake. She refused to show weakness before this lout who was bent on intimidating her. There must be some way to get him to see reason. Her cousin, Glorianna Sullivan, would be expecting her today. She'd sent a telegram at the last major town to let Glory know exactly what day she would arrive. *Lord, let someone tell Glory or her husband where I am. Please, help me.*

"I can't imagine the good townspeople in Tucson would allow you to hang an innocent woman." Kathleen fought a wave of dizziness at the thought of a hanging. "Our justice system is better than that."

"It is—if you're innocent." The deputy pulled a knife from his pocket and began to clean his fingernails as if he hadn't a care in the world. "Of course that fella in '73 claimed to be innocent too. Didn't do him any good." He paused, his light eyes gazing at her with the intensity of a hunter watching his prey. "The townsfolk hung him anyway, along with those three Mexican fellas who murdered Vicente Hernandez and his wife. Mrs. Hernandez was expecting their child. Folks were riled up real good. When folks out West get riled up about something, they're hard to reason with."

"Didn't anyone try to stop them? Didn't they get a fair trial?"

"Naw." Deputy Kirby's chair legs thumped on the floor as he sat up. He shoved the knife into his pocket and pulled out his pistol. "Old Milton Duffield tried to convince the boys to stop. He got a lump on the head for his troubles and slept through the whole lynching."

Nausea swept through Kathleen. Her legs felt as if they would give out. She leaned into the bars. "And where were you, Deputy? Didn't you try to stop them, or were you at the head of the mob?"

His eyes narrowed. "I'm here to uphold justice, not to take it in my own hands. If I'd been in town, I would have tried to stop them. So happens, I was out of town on business."

Pulling out a rag, he began to polish his pistol. "I reckon you'll come up before Doc Meyer in a couple of days."

"A doctor? I don't need a doctor. I need to get out of this jail."

He grinned, and his handsome face took on a boyish quality. "Oh, Doc Meyer isn't really a sawbones. He runs the drugstore. He's also our justice of the peace. He hears all the cases like yours, then decides what we should do."

Slipping his pistol into the holster, he strode across to her cell. "Ma'am, if you hold any tighter to those bars, you might leave marks on them. Why don't you have a seat on that bunk in there, and I'll run out and fetch you something to eat. There's one thing I know about riding the stage—you can build up a mighty thirst and hunger."

"I'm not hungry." Kathleen knew her dry throat could use something. "I would appreciate a drink, though, if you're sure it won't be wasted on someone who's to die so soon. I'd also like to speak to the sheriff."

"You'll have to talk mighty loud then. The sheriff is off with a couple of U.S. marshals on a manhunt up north." His eyes twinkled, and she found she couldn't turn away. "Now, Ma'am, I wouldn't have it said we mistreat our prisoners here in Tucson. I'll be back with your food in two twitches of a burro's ear."

She couldn't resist a parting shot. "I suppose lynching isn't considered mistreatment?"

He laughed. "No, Ma'am. Not when the criminal is as guilty as you."

The door creaked shut behind him. Kathleen could hear the scratch of the key turning in the lock. Tears burned in her eyes. What was going on here? She'd just come to Tucson to visit Glory and help her with the new baby. Everything seemed to be going wrong. The trip out here was miserable. The stage broke down twice, and the driver's stories of Apache attacks nearly scared her to death. Now, here she was so close to her destination but locked in a stinking jail on false charges, threatened with being hung. What next?

She released the bars. On legs that promised collapse at any moment, she made her way to the cot. She sank onto the dingy mattress, closing her eyes in relief at being able to sit. The next moment, the smell of stale sweat and unidentified odors assaulted her. How could these people claim to be civilized when their jail was little better than a pigsty?

Slipping her gloved hands beneath her veil, Kathleen covered her face. Even through the gloves, she could feel the raised mark on her cheek, the mark that set her apart from others. She didn't understand why God had allowed her to be like this, but she tried not to question, only trust. Today, trust seemed too far from her grasp. She felt ugly, unwanted, and abandoned. All the feelings of hatred and fear directed at her from childhood seemed to crash over her now. She wept, silent tears dampening her travel-stained gloves.

❦

"Thank you, Señora Arvizu." Quinn smiled at the widow as she placed the plate of food in front of him. He inhaled the spicy scent of chilies. "I'll need another plate to take to the jail with me in a few minutes." The señora nodded, then squeezed her way past him to set a plate in front of Edward Fish, owner of Tucson's first steam-powered flour mill.

"Have you heard the good news?" Ed moved close to Quinn.

Scooping beans onto his fork with his folded tortilla, Quinn gave Ed a questioning look. "What news would that be?"

"The new schoolteachers have been hired and will arrive in a few weeks."

"Schoolteachers? They need two teachers to replace one?" Quinn shook his head, puzzled at the expense the town was taking on.

"Two female teachers." Edward's lips twitched with a rare smile. "Unattached teachers." He straightened and forked a bite into his mouth.

Quinn stared as he chewed. In this town, unattached white females would be a novelty. "This is the stupidest thing I've ever heard of. Don't they realize this is a waste of money, hiring women for the job? Unless they're the worst women in the world, they'll be married off within six months, and then the town will have to look for another teacher."

"That's true, but think of the advantage we single men have. Since I lost my wife, I've wanted to remarry. Maybe one of these young ladies will be just right for me. You can bet I'm willing to give them a chance."

"I still think the board should have given John Spring the raise he asked for or the assistant he needed."

"Well, if one of these ladies proves to be good marriage material, I'll be grateful to Spring for the uproar he caused. The school board was right. They can easily afford two female teachers for the one hundred twenty-five dollars a month they were paying him. His demand for an assistant or a raise of twenty-five dollars a month so he could hire his own assistant was ludicrous."

Quinn shoveled the last mouthful of beans into his mouth, swallowing before he continued. "I don't know. I think bringing women out here is a mistake. Not too long ago, we were having Apache attacks. This is man's territory and should remain that way until it's safe for women." He stood. "Besides, before I'd consider getting married, I'd have to meet a woman who's got plenty of spunk and courage." A vision of hazel eyes and a star-marked cheek floated through his mind. He pushed the thought away. He refused to be attracted to a criminal.

"Nice talking with you. I'd better get back to the jail and feed my charge." Before Ed could ask more, Quinn pushed his way through the crowded tables and collected a plate of food to take with him.

The outside air had cooled as the sun dropped low in the sky. Quinn drew in a deep breath, then wrinkled his nose. Despite washing, the scent of manure still clung to him. Then again, it could be the smell of the Tucson streets, known for piles of dung. With all the freight traffic through town, no one seemed to be able to find a solution for the mess the horses and mules left behind.

Few of the town's inhabitants wandered the streets at this hour. Most were at home for their evening meal or somewhere like Señora Arvizu's eatery. Quinn grimaced at the thought of spending the night at the jail. He couldn't leave a female occupant by herself all night even with the door locked. He'd have to set up a cot. Sleeping on an uncomfortable bed made the thrill of catching the Widow fade a little. Pushing away the thought, he resumed the walk toward the jail, thinking instead of the stir of excitement that would sweep the territories when he sent a telegram tomorrow announcing the capture of the Veiled Widow.

The jail door complained loudly as Quinn pushed it open a few minutes later. The Widow was rubbing at her cheeks when he glanced her way. Had she been crying? In the dim light, it was hard to tell. Quinn snorted softly as he set the plate of food down and went out to fetch a cup of cold water. Just like a woman to resort to tears to get someone to feel sorry for her. Well, he wasn't letting down his guard around this woman. If he did, who knew how many more people would end up robbed or killed before her criminal activities ceased?

"I brought you some supper." Quinn slipped the plate and cup through the appropriate slots in the bars. The woman eased off the bunk and took the meal from his hands.

"Thank you." She balanced the plate on the cot, lifted her veil a bit, and drained the contents of the cup.

Guilt washed over Quinn. He should have given her some water before he went to find supper. He would have treated his horse better than he treated this woman. Just because she was a criminal didn't make her any less human. He could almost hear the lecture his pa would give him about treating others fairly despite their outward appearance.

"I'll get you more water." He put his hand through the bars. She gave him the cup, then sank onto the cot and picked up the plate as he left. A minute later, he carried the full mug back to find her staring at the plate balanced on her knees. "Is something wrong?"

"I. . .um. No, nothing." She picked up the tortilla, unfolded it, and turned it over as if examining it for some reason. Cocking her head to one side, she turned her face to him. "I don't mean to be rude, but can you tell me what kind of food this is?"

Quinn chuckled. "I hadn't thought this might be your first time eating Mexican food. That circle of dough in your hand is a tortilla. The Mexicans use it like bread. They scoop up their food into the tortilla or use it to get food on the fork. The other food is beans with chilies and some meat with peppers and vegetables mixed together. The taste is good, but you might find the food a little spicier than what you're used to."

She nodded and took a tentative bite, lifting the veil with the back of her hand. Quinn caught a glimpse of her perfectly formed chin before she dropped the veil and began to chew.

"You might have an easier time eating if you were to take off that veil. Seems to me the thing must get in the way a lot."

"I'm fine." She must have decided she liked the food. Other than taking the time to retrieve the cup of water he held, she continued to eat with dainty bites. Quinn walked back to his desk and sat down, trying to ignore her. He didn't want to think about how vulnerable she looked as she bent over her plate, her delicate hands trembling just enough to notice. How could this woman appear so miserable when she was covered from head to toe in black? Instead of giving the image of an austere matron, she portrayed that of a vulnerable, needy lady in distress. No wonder so many men had fallen under her spell.

The Widow stood and crossed to the cell door. "I've finished. Thank you for the food and water."

Quinn retrieved the utensils, placing the cup on his desk. Snagging his hat from the rack by the door, he hesitated before walking out. "I need to return these to the eatery. Then I'll be making my rounds. The door will be locked so no one will bother you."

Jamming the hat on his head, Quinn slammed the door behind him. Why had he said that? Since when did he need to explain himself and his actions to some common criminal? He stalked down the street, stopping at Señora Arvizu's to drop off the plate and fork. His foul mood stayed with him as he went throughout the town, checking doors of businesses already closed and greeting those still on the streets. Quinn hurried to get to the jail before full dark set in, since he'd left without his lantern. What had this woman done to him? He'd never gone off with his thoughts so mixed up before.

"Deputy Kirby. Quinn." A man's voice called out to him. Quinn turned. A man in a cavalry uniform moved slowly down the street, a woman heavy with child on his arm.

"Conlon." Quinn felt himself relax somewhat at the sight of his good friends. "What are you and Glorianna doing out so late? Taking a walk?"

Even in the dimness of the evening, Glorianna Sullivan's eyes flashed fire. "Quinn Kirby, did you or did you not arrest my cousin?"

"Now why would I arrest your cousin? I don't even know who your cousin is."

Glorianna Sullivan could be a formidable force to reckon with when she was angry. Right now she appeared to be furious.

Conlon gave Glorianna a grin, pulled her closer to his side, and patted the hand she'd wrapped around his arm. "Glory's cousin, Kathleen, was supposed to arrive on the stage. I got home from the new fort site a little late. By the time we got there, the stage had gone. Kathleen's trunk was waiting by the side of the street, but she wasn't there. We heard you arrested a woman who got off the stage, so we've been looking for you."

A feeling of impending doom settled heavy on Quinn's chest. "I arrested a known criminal who came in on the stage. I didn't ask her name."

"What did she look like?" Sparks flew from Glorianna's green eyes.

From the storm building in Glorianna, Quinn knew his description fit that of her cousin. He felt like squirming, wishing the dark would close in and he could hide. That forlorn woman sitting in the dingy jail cell was Kathleen O'Connor, not the Veiled Widow. How would he ever explain this?

Chapter 3

Long hours in a swaying stagecoach, uncertain about her safety, had taken a toll on Kathleen. Though normally very optimistic, right now she was so weary, she couldn't think straight. Every muscle in her body cried out in agony from the constant shifting on the long ride to Tucson. Road dust covered every inch of her body. She felt as if she hadn't had a bath in weeks rather than days. In fact, she smelled almost as bad as the filthy mattress underneath her. Despair became her companion in this cell. The dirt walls, probably made of the adobe bricks Glorianna had written to her about, started to close in around her.

Kathleen pulled the small but stylish hat from her head, sticking the hatpin through the side to keep it safe. She felt naked without the veil, yet she didn't care anymore. What did it matter if people saw her face? Her mother's gasp of shock at the thought filled her mind. Mother had always been embarrassed at having a marked daughter. Although treated well enough at home, Kathleen had to hide behind the veil when she went out in public. Even then, her mother never stood close to her or sat with her at church as if, by distancing herself, she could avoid the taunting and ridicule Kathleen received.

Curling in a ball, Kathleen sank onto her side on the cot. Her tired brain barely registered the scratches dug into the adobe bricks. Prisoners before her had carved their initials or little notches, perhaps to count the days spent in this dismal place. Her eyes drifted shut. She knew she should pray for strength, for comfort, for the will to live—but she couldn't.

※

"Now, Glorianna, please calm down. If this is your cousin, I've taken good care of her. She even had supper from Señora Arvizu's." Quinn bit his tongue to keep the stupid thing from flapping anymore. He'd rather be caught between a mother grizzly and her squalling cubs than to face an angry Glorianna.

The trio continued down the darkening street. Lamplight shone through windows. They kept to the edge of the walkway to avoid any refuse that might have been thrown out. Quinn knew the cities back East had a system for getting rid of sewage that kept their streets from smelling and looking so awful, but Tucson still hadn't advanced that far. Only in the past year had the Apache uprisings been brought under control, paving the way for more people to immigrate to the Southwest.

Deep shadows covered the door of the jail. Metal clanked against metal as Quinn inserted the key into the lock. Beside him, Glorianna tapped her foot.

Conlon's low chuckle made the heat rush to his face. The cavalry lieutenant must know his spunky wife was making Quinn nervous. A grating sound accompanied the turning of the key. The door swung open.

"If you'll wait here, I'll light the lamp so you don't trip in the dark." Quinn stepped through the door. Silence greeted him.

"Do you mean you left Kathleen in the dark?" Outrage echoed in Glorianna's voice.

"Now you don't know if this is your cousin for sure." Quinn tried to defend himself. "Just wait until you get a look at her. I'm telling you, she fits the description I got of the Veiled Widow."

Flame flared, causing Quinn to squint as he lit the lamp. He lowered the wick, then turned to beckon Glorianna and Conlon inside. Glancing at the cell, he thought at first his prisoner had escaped. Lifting the lantern high, he was at the door in two strides. The black lump on the bed proved to be the woman, curled in a tight ball, her face resting on one palm. If not for the soft cadence of her breathing, he wouldn't have known she was alive.

"Kathleen!" Glorianna grasped the bars with her hands, trying to tug them open. "Quinn, you open this cell right now. That's my cousin, Kathleen. She is not the criminal you're looking for."

Quinn hesitated. "Are you sure? I don't want to let you in there if you're not positive she's your cousin. I can roust her so you can be sure."

Glorianna swiveled around to face him. Her fisted hands dug into her hips. Quinn fought a smile at her feistiness.

"I'd suggest you let my wife in the cell." Humor crackled in Conlon's tone. "I don't know of a criminal anywhere who could stand up to her. Do you?"

Quinn couldn't help the chuckle as he reached over to shove a key into the lock. "I see your point, Conlon. Maybe I should caution Glorianna not to harm my prisoner."

The door creaked as it swung open, but the woman on the cot didn't stir. With her knees drawn up near her chin, she reminded Quinn of a little child. A powerful longing swept over him to sit down, pull her into his lap, and let her know everything would be all right. He mentally shook himself as he stepped aside for Glorianna. He couldn't afford to become soft, or every lawbreaker this side of the Mississippi would be heading this way for the easy pickings.

"Kathleen?" Glorianna started to kneel by the cot, then leaned over, instead. Quinn figured her condition hindered her movement. She brushed a hand across the woman's creamy cheek, getting no response. "What have you done to her? Did you knock her out so she wouldn't try to escape while you strolled around town at your leisure?"

"Now, Glory, you know Quinn wouldn't do such a thing."

She sighed and sank down on the edge of the bed. "I know. I'm sorry, Quinn. You're only doing your job. I've been as cantankerous as a grizzly bear lately."

Conlon chuckled, then sobered as she glared at him. "I imagine Kathleen is exhausted from the trip across the country. That's enough to wear anyone out."

Glorianna nodded as she continued to stroke Kathleen's forehead. "What should we do? We can't leave her here all night. We don't have the wagon for her to ride home in, either. When we found her bags, Pedro took them on home. I suggested to Conlon that we could walk to Señora Arvizu's to see if Kathleen was waiting there."

"Tell you what." Quinn hoped to get in Glorianna's good graces with his suggestion. "I noticed Doc Meyer's buggy tied up in front of the drugstore. Why don't I run down there and see if I can borrow it to take you home?"

A frown creased Glorianna's forehead. "Don't you let Doc Meyer drive us, though. That man goes faster than a hawk can dive. He's a danger to this town."

Conlon laughed. "He's never run over anyone. Besides, maybe he's trying to create a little business for himself."

By the time Quinn returned with the buggy, Glorianna informed him they'd decided to not wake her cousin since she appeared to be so exhausted. As Conlon helped his wife outside, Quinn picked up Kathleen. Amazement streaked through him at how light she was. How could he have made such a mistake? He gave a silent groan as he considered that he hadn't even asked her name or the identity of the person she planned to meet. What kind of lawman was he?

Turning sideways to ease past the bars, Quinn noticed the black hat and veil still resting on the cot. He paused, gazing down at the birthmark on her cheek. Some people would say it marred her beauty, but he knew differently. This was one special woman. The star-shaped mark proved that. He would leave the hat and veil here. Tomorrow, when she'd had a chance to recover some, he would show up at the Sullivans' home to apologize and return her belongings. Then he would have one more chance to see those gorgeous hazel eyes.

※

The aroma of bacon frying tried to draw Kathleen out of her sleep. She fought waking, burying her face in the soft pillow, breathing in the freshness of newly washed laundry. Her eyes snapped open. A pillow? Clean, sweet-smelling sheets? Last night she'd fallen asleep in a grimy jail cell. Where was she?

She lay on a mattress on the floor of someone's parlor. A tall writing desk stood in one corner, the top open, with pen and paper ready for use. A small bookshelf stood nearby, holding several volumes. An oval braided rug covered most of the floor, the mix of colors testifying to someone using scraps of material from her sewing.

Kathleen sat up. A momentary wave of dizziness washed over her. She couldn't remember when she'd been so worn out. It was hard to even think. How had she come to be in this house? Surely that deputy wouldn't have allowed her to leave. . .and if he did, how did she get here when she didn't recall a thing?

A table near the doorway held a large pitcher and basin. A cloth for washing and a towel lay beside them. Kathleen stood on protesting legs and made her way over. Right now, washing up sounded like the biggest treat she could have. The cool water refreshed her, giving her a renewed desire to find out where she was. She turned to the bed, pulled the covers down, and searched for her veil. Her headgear was nowhere to be found. How could she go anywhere without it?

Soft footfalls sounded in the hallway outside the room. Panic shot through Kathleen. She gave the room a frantic glance, wondering where she could hide even when she knew hiding was futile. Whoever brought her to this place knew she was still here.

"You're awake." Glorianna's familiar voice brought Kathleen around. Tears of relief burned in Kathleen's eyes.

"Oh, Glory, it's so good to see you." Kathleen rushed into her cousin's embrace. She had no idea how she'd gotten to Glorianna's, but her heart sang a song of thanks to God. Had the jail and her arrest been only a bad dream? Somehow in the light of day, with her cousin's arms around her, it seemed that way.

"I thought you were going to sleep until Christmas." Glorianna's green eyes sparkled.

"What time is it?"

"Almost time to start some lunch for us. You'd better take time to eat a little breakfast first." Glorianna began to tug on her arm to pull her down the hall. "We can talk while you eat, then I'll see to getting you some bath water. I remember traveling out here and how much I wanted a bath."

"That sounds like heaven." Kathleen could feel the heaviness of yesterday fading. The smell of food made her mouth water and stomach growl. She waited to speak until she was seated at the table with Glorianna, a plate of food in front of her.

"I feel so disoriented. I remember falling asleep last night in a jail cell. Was that a bad dream? How did I ever get here without remembering anything?"

As Kathleen ate, Glorianna filled her in on the previous night's events and how their friend, Deputy Quinn Kirby, had mistaken her for a desperado. In the bright light of day, with a stomach full of food and the promise of a bath, Kathleen could finally see humor in the mistake.

"Tell me about the baby, Glory." Kathleen reached over to give a soft pat to Glorianna's rounded stomach. "When do you think the little one will arrive?"

"Not soon enough." Glorianna groaned and relaxed in the chair. "This one has to be a boy with six legs and eight arms. He kicks and pushes on me all the time. I had no idea babies could be so active before they were born. Who knows how I'll be able to keep up with him once he's here."

Kathleen laughed. "Sounds to me like you might be having a girl like you. I remember your mother making a few complaints about the trouble she had with you."

"Me?" Glorianna batted her eyes, then laughed. "I'd say that I hope the baby would be more like Conlon than me, but I've heard from his mother, and he wasn't an angel, either. I think we're doomed no matter what. This one will be the terror of Tucson."

"Speaking of Conlon, when will I get to meet this mysterious husband of yours?"

"He'll be home this evening. Every day he rides out to oversee the building of the new Fort Lowell. It's about six or seven miles from town. The first buildings are almost done."

"I thought you were living at the fort." Kathleen took a long drink of water to finish washing down her breakfast.

"We were." Glorianna sighed and shook her head. "Conlon decided I needed to be somewhere else. Because of the old fort's location, there's too much sickness. That's why the cavalry is building the new one outside of town." She leaned forward and rubbed her back. "It should have been done ages ago, but they have had so many delays for money, goods, and all. I can't wait to move there. Maybe in a few days Conlon can drive us to see what they have done."

Kathleen frowned. "If the drive is that long, maybe we should wait until the baby comes."

Glorianna stood. "I don't know. Maybe the rough wagon trip will convince the baby to get here faster. Come on, I'll show you to your bath. I had Pedro draw the water for you."

A sigh of contentment escaped as Kathleen sank into the warm water. The tub was smaller than the one she used in her parents' home, but this one felt better. Her aching muscles protested every movement, and she hoped the warmth would loosen them. Glorianna left her with a bar of lavender-scented soap and instructions to be sure to take her time. She was to rest up for a few days anyway. Kathleen didn't argue. She had to smile at the changes she'd seen in Glorianna— the calmness and peace she didn't used to have. There was still the same bossy girl underneath, however, this time tempered with God's love.

After washing the grit from her hair, Kathleen frowned at the dingy water left in the tub. Who would have thought a person could get so dirty just from traveling? This water looked as if a bunch of hooligans had trekked through mud, then bathed.

Donning a fresh gown retrieved from her trunk before bathing, Kathleen felt almost presentable. She combed her long hair, twisting it up on her head in the latest fashion. The only things missing were her hat and veil. She didn't mind leaving her face uncovered around Glorianna, but she couldn't go out of the house without being concealed. Maybe Glorianna knew where it was. She'd have to ask.

Her shoes clacked noisily on the floor as she headed for the kitchen. Glorianna said she would probably be there working on lunch. At the time, Kathleen couldn't imagine eating anything else, but already her stomach seemed to have ideas of its own. She'd never had an appetite like this.

"Glory, have you seen my hat and veil? I can't find where I placed them last night." Seeing her cousin at work near the stove, Kathleen stepped through the kitchen door.

Glorianna turned, a smile lighting her face. "I believe you'll find them on the table."

Puzzled, Kathleen turned, wondering why she hadn't noticed they were there when she ate breakfast earlier. Deputy Quinn Kirby sat at the table, a grin on his face, her hat and veil dangling from his fingers. Kathleen slapped a hand to her cheek and wished the floor would open up and swallow her.

Chapter 4

Turning her face to the side so her birthmark was away from the deputy, Kathleen held out her hand for her headgear. She couldn't imagine why Glorianna allowed this man in here. Then she remembered all the times Glorianna lectured her on not hiding her beauty behind that veil. Glorianna always thought Kathleen's mother had done her a disservice by convincing her she should conceal her shame.

From the corner of her eye, Kathleen could see the deputy grinning at her. Was he making fun? Did he think he could waltz in here after the fiasco yesterday and laugh at her? Anger swelled through her in a mighty wave.

"I believe you have something that belongs to me." She reached out to grab the items from him. "And I see no reason to laugh at someone for a deformity."

The infuriating man swept her hat and veil to the side, out of her reach. His grin faded to be replaced by a look of astonishment. A faint red flush colored his cheeks.

"I am not laughing at you, Miss O'Connor." He stumbled to his feet as if he'd just recalled his manners. "I had no intention of coming here to gloat at your expense." He moved closer. "Besides, I smiled in an effort to ease the way to an apology since I mistook you for a criminal yesterday. It was an honest mistake, but one I'm heartily sorry for."

Kathleen considered stepping away as he approached. After what he'd done to her yesterday, she had every reason to dislike him. Instead, she found herself drawn to him. *Most likely as a moth is drawn to a flame,* she chided silently.

He reached out and grabbed her hand, sending a shock through her. "Here are your belongings. They were left at the jail." He still held her. She wanted to pull free, but couldn't seem to move.

"Furthermore, I can't stop you from hiding behind that silly thing, but I will say this: I think it's a fool thing to do. You have beautiful eyes and a beautiful face." He tugged her an inch closer, his eyes gray with emotion. "I don't know why you're ashamed of yourself, but I think it's too bad."

"I beg your pardon." Kathleen found the strength to try to free herself from his grasp. He held tight. "I am not ashamed of myself, and if I were, it would be none of your business."

"If you're not, then why do you hide behind that veil? You sure acted embarrassed yesterday when you lost it."

Kathleen tried to think of something to say. Was he right? Had her mother's shame become her own? For so long, she'd convinced herself she wore a covering to protect others. That had to be the reason.

"I know how people are horrified to see something like the mark I have. I'm simply saving them from embarrassment."

An emotion she couldn't identify swept across his face. Was it sympathy? Understanding? His expression softened, and a small smile lifted the corners of his mouth.

"I do understand. Perhaps more than you know." His grip loosened, and she pulled free, clasping her hands together to keep from shaking. He glanced down, then up into her eyes. "If I've offended you, I apologize. I still think you're hiding a lot of beauty. I'd appreciate your not wearing that contraption around me."

He slapped his hat onto his head and stepped toward the door. Nodding to Glorianna, who for once had been silent during the whole interchange, he opened the door. He looked at Kathleen and tipped his hat. "Remember what I said. I'd hate to mistake you for some criminal and have to arrest you again."

The door had barely closed behind him when Glorianna burst into peals of laughter. She clutched her sides, gasping for air. Kathleen didn't know whether to join her cousin laughing or to stomp her foot in anger. She looked at the pathetic scrap of netting in her hand and decided merriment was much better than anger.

"I declare, Kathleen." Glorianna's face nearly matched her red hair. "I believe you two are meant for each other."

The laughter died in Kathleen's throat. "I can't believe you said that." Horrified, she stared at her cousin. "You know I can't be serious about any man— especially not one like that."

"I only know I haven't seen sparks fly like that since Conlon and I met." Glorianna grinned. "Besides, I know nothing of the sort about you not being able to get married. That was your mother's notion and a wrong one at that. My mother always encouraged you to consider marriage." Setting the pot on the stove to simmer, Glorianna crossed to the table, where a pile of sewing waited.

Sinking into a chair across from her cousin, Kathleen watched Glory's needle dip in and out of the white material. What looked to be a baby's nightgown rapidly took shape beneath her nimble fingers. Glancing at the pile of diapers waiting to be hemmed, Kathleen took up a needle, thread, and a diaper and joined Glorianna in her work. She needed time to think.

There had been a mistake here. She felt no attraction to the deputy. *The very handsome deputy with the compelling eyes*, she found herself thinking. The needle poked into her finger. She wiped the blood on a scrap of cloth before continuing.

How many times had her mother cautioned her to stay away from men? "You'll end up with a child just like you." Her mother would stand there lecturing, her hands on her hips, brow furrowed in a frown. "Imagine putting a child through the agony you've gone through. I don't see how you could ever want to do that."

Kathleen never summoned the courage to tell her mother that her life would have been bearable if she'd had some support at home. Instead, all she faced were more shame and ridicule. The only satisfaction she got was being in charge of her younger siblings. They loved her for who she was, not for how she looked.

Her aunt and Glorianna, on the other hand, always loved her and accepted her as a special child of God. The memory of the day the three of them sat sewing while Mother was out came flooding back. She could clearly recall her aunt's gentle voice. "Kathleen, someday you will make some young man a wonderful wife. Don't deprive yourself of one of God's greatest gifts. Consider yourself as worthy as any other girl to marry and have children. God loves you so much. He wants the best for you."

Did God truly want her to marry? She understood God loved her as she was, but could someone else love her the same way? How could any man get past her outer ugliness?

⚘

Flipping the reins over his horse's neck, Quinn swung into the saddle. He needed some time alone, and he'd promised Conlon he'd come out to the new Fort Lowell to see how the building was progressing. Ever since the contract came through for Lord and Williams to supply the adobe bricks for the buildings, Conlon had been hard pressed to have any free time. Quinn knew he chafed at leaving Glorianna for so long each day, especially with the fort so far from town. Having Kathleen here would be a relief for him.

Quinn tipped his hat to the mayor, John Allen, as he urged his horse to a faster pace near the edge of town. Being a deputy certainly had good points and bad ones. Keeping the peace and making sure people were safe gave him great satisfaction. Dealing with the officials could sometimes give him a headache, even if they were good men.

The sun shone bright, warming the crisp, clear day. Quinn's thoughts began to drift to the subject he wanted to avoid thinking about—his visit with a certain young lady this morning. A groan escaped as he thought of the stupid way he'd acted in front of Glorianna and Kathleen. When Kathleen entered the kitchen, he'd been so enamored, he'd forgotten his manners, sitting there with a coyote-that-caught-the-chicken grin on his face. His horse slowed to a walk, something the beast did whenever Quinn wasn't paying close attention. Quinn eased in the saddle and let him walk as he envisioned Kathleen bright-eyed and without her veil.

Her hair, still damp from washing, shone in the morning light. She wore it wrapped up in a very becoming fashion, but he wondered what she would look like with it hanging loose about her shoulders. He could still recall yesterday when she fell in the street and her hair loosened, allowing more than a few tendrils to come down. Even that wasn't like seeing it all flowing freely around her.

Quinn frowned. The only problem with the woman was her idea that people would dislike her because of the birthmark on her left cheek. His finger itched to trace the line of her intriguing star. He couldn't imagine how she'd gotten the idea that the birthmark detracted from her looks. She was a beauty who had been hidden for too long. He'd have to see what he could do about that.

The ride to the fort passed by too quickly. Quinn would have liked a little more time to get his thoughts in order before facing Conlon. He knew his friend wouldn't resist ribbing him for arresting Glorianna's cousin. Conlon didn't know, and Quinn hoped he wouldn't guess, that Quinn was the one most relieved that Kathleen wasn't a criminal. He'd hate to think he could have such an immediate attraction to someone who lived her life outside of the law. The most important measure in determining a person's worth should be their ability to live within the law.

"Hey, Quinn! Over here." Conlon waved from across the parade ground. Quinn waved, swung down, and watered his horse before tying him in the shade. The buzz of conversations from men at work droned in the air. Glancing around, he could see a lot of progress since his last visit to the site. The men had been working hard.

" 'Morning." He greeted Conlon with a slap on the back. "You sure accomplished a lot."

Conlon grinned. "I figure we need to work fast before the government decides on better ways to spend the money and takes the rest. Follow me, and I'll show you where everything will be. By the time Glory and I move out here, we'll have our own doctor and hospital in case anything should happen. That's one of the worries Glory always had about being so far from town."

Quinn followed Conlon about the fort, admiring the buildings and the setup. "Has Glorianna been out here lately?"

A frown creased Conlon's brow. "She wants to come awful bad. I want her to wait until the baby arrives. She's getting so big, I figure the baby could come any time. I refuse to be between here and Tucson and have to deliver a baby."

Quinn laughed and clapped him on the shoulder. "I imagine you've delivered a colt or two. You should be able to handle one little baby."

Conlon chuckled. "The only way I know to deliver a baby is to rub the mother with straw to wipe the sweat off and rub her nose whispering things like, 'Good girl, you're doing fine.' Somehow, I don't think Glory would appreciate that."

They both laughed as they walked toward the parade ground. "I went by your house this morning to deliver some things Glorianna's cousin left at the jail. Your wife seemed pleased to have her cousin visiting."

"And how was Kathleen this morning? Since she was sleeping when I left, I still haven't met her." Conlon's intense blue eyes studied Quinn, making him want to squirm. Why had he mentioned Glorianna and Kathleen?

"She looked refreshed from the trip. I do believe she liked her accommodations at your house better than the ones at the jail. She didn't seem particularly happy to see me."

"She doesn't know you." Conlon strode across to the stable area. "Why don't you come to supper tonight? I'm sure Glory won't mind. She loves company. That way you can get to know Kathleen in a more relaxed atmosphere than the jail."

"Naw, you need the time to get to know her without me intruding."

"You aren't intruding. I invited you." Conlon slung a saddle on his horse and began to adjust the cinch. "If I didn't know better, I'd think you might be a little sweet on Miss O'Connor, Deputy."

"I only met her yesterday—and then I thought she was a criminal. How could I be sweet on a woman that fast?"

Conlon swung up on his horse. "Well, I knew the minute I met Glory that she was the one for me. I'd been praying for a wife, and when I saw her, I knew God brought her all this way just for me. Now, how about we head for town? I need to get Josiah Washington to do some shoeing for the cavalry."

Quinn tugged his horse's reins free and mounted. "Well, I haven't been praying for a wife. If and when I decide to get married, I don't need any help from anyone, God included."

Conlon's shoulders stiffened, and Quinn knew he'd hurt his friend again. He hadn't meant to. Conlon and Glorianna couldn't seem to understand why he didn't mind them believing in God and praying. If that worked for them, fine. They could worship however they wanted. Quinn's parents were Christians, but he knew he didn't need anyone bossing over him. He could manage his own life quite nicely. If he decided to pursue Kathleen, then that would be his choice—not something brought about by a God who lived in some far-off place watching over everyone. He had parents as a boy. Now, as a man, he answered to no one.

Nudging his horse, Quinn caught up with Conlon. "I didn't mean to offend. I'm glad your God brought you a wonderful wife, if that's what you believe. All I'm saying is, I'd like to pick out my own wife when the time comes."

"I understand, Quinn." The smile had faded from Conlon's face. "I used to feel the same way you do. I'll pray you turn your heart to God before it's too late."

The thunder of hooves interrupted them. A horse raced around a bend toward them. They rode ahead to meet the rider. Tugging the reins, the young boy almost lost his seating as the horse slid to a stop. Conlon reached out to grab the horse's bridle.

"Paulo, what's wrong?"

Quinn recognized the son of Pedro and Alicia Rodriquez, the couple who worked for Conlon and Glorianna. Paulo looked pale and ready to fall from the horse.

"The señora. She is having baby." Paulo looked frightened. "Doctor say to get you home."

Panic crossed Conlon's face. "Something must be wrong. Why else would they send for me?"

Chapter 5

Swallowing a grin, Quinn urged his horse to catch up to Conlon's. He couldn't understand what possessed a normally rational, in-charge man like Conlon to fall apart at the mention of a woman having a baby. Glorianna was healthy and fit. Didn't women have babies all the time? Most of the families he knew had several children, and the wife was just fine. This wasn't the Dark Ages. Between the doctor and women with midwife experience helping Glorianna, this baby's birth should be easy.

The doctor shouldn't send for the father until the baby arrived. That would save hours of floor-walking distress for the husband. After all, what could he do at the house? Husbands weren't allowed to help with the delivery, although Quinn couldn't imagine why a husband would want to. The father always seemed to be in the way as the doctor's helpers hurried from one task to another. A father-to-be should be left at work, content in his ignorance, until the baby made an appearance.

The day had turned warm, and Quinn could see the sweat starting to lather up on Conlon's horse. Ridden like this, the animal would be overheated by the time they arrived in town.

"Conlon, slow down." Quinn urged his gelding to a faster pace and drew up alongside his friend. "Running your mount into the ground won't help Glorianna or the baby."

Blue eyes, glazed with worry, glanced his way. As if he suddenly realized what he was doing, Conlon pulled on the reins. Both horses slowed, their breaths huffing out in sharp pants. Patting his mount's neck, Conlon grimaced.

"Sorry. All I could think of was getting home to Glory. I hate being so far from her when she needs me." Panic swept across his face again.

"She's got the doc looking after her. Don't worry." Quinn spoke in the soothing voice he used when calming a skittish mount or an angry drunk. "Besides, you know Alicia is there. She's had six kids of her own and probably delivered who knows how many others."

A shuddering sigh rippled through Conlon, making his shoulders quake. "I know you're right. I'm fine now." He rubbed a hand over his face. "I don't know why I can't trust God with everything the first time, but even now I run off trying to take care of everything myself." He grinned. "When will I learn? All I have to do is pray, and God will handle everything else."

Quinn groaned. Not another religion lesson. Conlon must have read his look, because he tipped his head back and laughed. How could the man be in a panic one minute and completely at peace the next? An uncomfortable reminder pricked Quinn's conscience. This was the same kind of peace his parents demonstrated when they went through difficulties. They would go off together, pray, then not be bothered by anything.

The steady thump of the horses' hooves in the dry dirt had a calming effect. Small waves of dust blew into the brush at the side of the road, coating the deep green leaves of the mesquite trees and creosote bushes with a layer of tan. Conlon appeared to be deep in thought, probably about his wife and child. Quinn began to relax.

Almost a mile passed with Conlon urging the horses on at a trot, fast enough to speed the trip home, slow enough to keep their mounts from overheating.

Conlon glanced over, his forehead furrowed. "Do you mind if I ask you a personal question, Quinn? One friend to another."

Quinn studied Conlon for a long moment, trepidation making him hesitate. "I guess I don't mind. That doesn't mean I'll answer." He cracked a grin. "If you're asking me what to name the baby, I'll have to tell you the only names I've ever given were to dogs and horses. How would Glorianna like a daughter named Brownie or a son named Buster?"

Conlon chuckled. "I'm glad I wasn't asking for help with names. I think Glory and I can manage that quite nicely." His grin faded. "I wanted to ask something about your growing up."

Quinn's horse snorted and pranced to the side as Quinn's legs tensed.

"You told me once before that your parents are as bad as me and Glory when it comes to talking about the Bible and the Lord. I don't want to be nosy, but I'm curious as to why you're so against anything Christian when your parents are firm believers."

The reins dug painful grooves into Quinn's palms. He and Conlon had grown pretty close in the last few months since the Sullivans moved to Tucson from Camp MacDowell. Their respective jobs brought them in close contact, and the friendship had developed from there. Conlon was easy to talk to. He often listened when others jumped to conclusions without considering the surrounding circumstances. Maybe if Conlon understood his reasons for turning away from God, he would leave him alone. After all, if Christians could go around explaining their faith to everyone, why couldn't he explain his beliefs, especially since Conlon asked?

"I used to think like you do." Quinn forced his hands to relax on the reins, and his horse settled into a steady walk. "I went to church every Sunday with my family. I joined them in prayer at mealtimes and even listened at night when my dad read to us from the Bible. I agreed with most everything they said until about a year before I left home."

The silence stretched as long-forgotten images flashed through Quinn's mind. He could see his sister, Elizabeth, seated on the floor, a book in her lap.

His mother would be in the rocking chair working on the never-ending pile of mending, while his dad's deep voice filled the house, sometimes sounding like what Quinn thought of as the voice of God Himself.

"What happened to change you?" Conlon appeared genuinely interested.

"A new family moved to town." Buried anger burned in Quinn's gut. "They had a boy a little older than me. Rupert Magee was the biggest bully I've ever met. He and his dad were large men, and both thought they should rule over everyone. Rupert took a dislike to my family for reasons I won't go into. He hated my sister, Elizabeth. At first he only yelled taunts at her in front of her friends. That hurt, but she and my folks prayed about it and said it would be all right. I wanted to pound Rupert into the ground."

Quinn's horse began to prance sideways down the road. "My dad tried talking to Rupert's dad, but Mr. Magee always defended his son. He said Elizabeth deserved what she got. Since they never did more than talk, there was nothing the law could do."

"I remember my mama saying words only hurt you if you let them." Conlon reined his horse around a gopher mound. "I think it's impossible for kids to ignore something said in cruelty. That kind of hurt is hard to heal. Did he ever do more than taunt her?"

Quinn's jaw tightened. "Not openly. Rupert took to following Elizabeth, but she didn't say anything for fear that I would get riled. Two days before I left, he followed her home from town and pelted her with rocks. We found out he'd done it before, but he'd never hit her. This time she came home with a knot on her head, the cut beside it bleeding all over. She also had a bruise on her back from a rock.

"I wanted to fight Rupert so bad, I could feel my fists hitting him. My pa stopped me, saying we needed to do this legally. We went to the sheriff. He was afraid of Rupert and his daddy. He wouldn't do a thing. Pa said that was God's answer."

"That would be enough to rile any boy," Conlon said.

"You're right. I was angry at my dad, angry at Rupert, and most of all, angry at God. All this time I believed God would protect His own, but now I knew different. I knew I couldn't stay around and believe in a God who made promises He didn't keep."

The clop of the horses' hooves and the jangle of their bits grated in the quiet. "Did you leave then?"

"I gave God one more night to do something. I thought maybe He was busy or Elizabeth wasn't important enough to take care of right away. Nothing happened, and I realized I had to handle things myself. When I had the chance, I packed a bedroll and loaded my horse. I didn't tell my folks I was leaving. I was so angry with them, I didn't think they deserved to know.

"That night I waited for Rupert at a spot I knew he'd pass by on the way home from a friend's house. I beat him almost senseless. After I had my revenge, I told him he'd better never even look at my sister again, or I'd hear about it and come looking for him. Then I climbed on my horse and haven't been home since."

Conlon's brows drew together. "So how do you know he listened to you?"

"Because he's a coward. Bullies are always that way when someone stands up to them. Besides, I did write to my folks. After I cooled down, I wrote and asked them about Rupert. They said he left town shortly after I did. He and his dad moved, and no one knew where they went."

The first houses on the outskirts of Tucson came into sight around a curve in the road. Quinn's horse settled to a quiet walk. "I suppose you'll say what I did was wrong, but I don't agree with you. I took care of my sister that night, and I've been taking care of myself ever since. I don't need a God like yours to interfere with my life."

Conlon flashed a cocky grin. "I know how patient God is. When you're tired of doing everything yourself, He'll be waiting." He urged his horse to a trot. "Now, let's go see if I'm a father."

Quinn noted the relief he felt at finally sharing his story. Conlon hadn't rejected him for what he'd said. In fact, he didn't appear surprised at all. As they tramped from the stable to the house, Quinn clapped his hand on Conlon's shoulder.

"Thank you for listening and not lecturing me."

Blue eyes twinkled as Conlon glanced at him. "Who am I to chide you on your attitude toward God? Lecturing won't help. Only prayer will work, and you can bet I'm doing plenty of that."

The door snapped shut behind them. Alicia stood over the stove, dipping water out of a pot, sweat beaded on her round face. She gave Conlon a tired smile as she turned to leave the room.

"Wait, Alicia. How's Glorianna?" The calm appeared to have left Conlon. Before he could ask more, Alicia disappeared through the doorway. Conlon pulled off his hat and glanced at Quinn. "I don't know if that's good or bad."

Biting back a laugh at the lost little boy look on Conlon's face, Quinn took his elbow and ushered him over to the table. "Why don't you sit down while I rustle up some coffee? I'm sure everything is just fine. Alicia was just a bit rushed."

Continuing his one-sided conversation, Quinn lifted the coffeepot from the stove. The weight told him there was enough of the brew for both of them. After finding the cups, he poured coffee that must have sat on the hot stove all day. It looked strong enough to eat the cups, but that might be just what Conlon needed.

"Here, drink this." He placed the brew on the table in front of the dazed father-to-be and sank into a chair across from him.

Conlon's fingers wrapped around the mug. He took a drink, choked, grimaced, and took another swig. A high, thin wail caused Conlon to jerk, sloshing coffee on the table. His eyes widened. He relaxed, then grinned.

Standing, he looked at Quinn as if wondering how he'd gotten there. "I think that might be my baby."

Setting his cup on the table, Quinn swallowed a mouthful of coffee. "That's either your baby or a cat that got its tail stepped on."

Conlon gave a nervous chuckle at Quinn's attempted humor. "Should I go see if Doc will let me in?"

"I think you'd better wait." Quinn heard the tap of light footsteps. Kathleen hurried into the kitchen, her dark hair in disarray, her dress rumpled and damp. The ever-present veil hung askew, though it still covered her face. Even so, Quinn had never seen a more charming sight. She grabbed a pile of snowy towels and started to rush out of the kitchen, acting as if she hadn't seen the men frozen in place, watching her.

"Kathleen," Quinn said.

She stopped, her back stiffening. Quinn realized then that she'd been so focused on her errand, she hadn't seen them. "Kathleen, I think Conlon would like to know how Glorianna and the baby are doing."

Without turning, Kathleen replied. "The doctor will be out soon to talk to you. Glory's doing great." Then she disappeared as fast as she'd come.

Time stood still as Quinn tried to imagine the agony his friend felt. Had something gone wrong with the birthing? The baby wasn't crying. He knew a thousand problems were racing through Conlon's mind right now, and he didn't know how to help him. There wasn't a thing he could do.

Conlon sank into the chair, curled his fingers around the coffee cup, and bowed his head. Quinn knew he must be praying. He'd seen his parents this way many times. The tension in Conlon's shoulders slowly relaxed. His grip loosened. An air of peace seemed to wrap around him.

A baby's cry once again echoed through the house. Conlon's head snapped up. Tears sparkled in his eyes.

A few minutes later, the tap of footsteps, moving at a slower pace, sounded in the hallway. Kathleen, her veil straightened and hair fixed, came into the kitchen. She carried a bundle of blankets in each arm. Halting just inside the doorway, she turned to face Conlon. He rose from the table and stepped toward her.

Lifting the two small bundles, she spoke in an awed voice. "Conlon, this is your son." Her head dipped as if she were looking from one blanket to the other. "And this is your daughter." A note of delight crept into her voice. "You have twins."

Chapter 6

Kathleen hummed a soft melody as she rocked Angelina, Glorianna and Conlon's baby girl. Andrew lay fast asleep in the cradle, his shock of black hair sticking out from beneath the blanket covering him. She brushed her fingers through Angelina's deep red curls. They were downy soft and wrapped tightly around Kathleen's fingers.

Blinking away tears, Kathleen lifted the baby and kissed her soft cheek, breathing in the soapy smell of the infant. She hadn't realized how much her heart ached to have a child of her own. Knowing that could never be made this a bittersweet experience. These babies were so precious.

Thinking of the day three weeks ago when the twins were born, Kathleen chuckled aloud. She would never forget the look on Conlon's face when she introduced him to his new son and daughter. Sheets had more color than his face did at that moment. She'd been afraid he would pass out from the shock.

She couldn't help feeling a flutter of anticipation when she remembered the surprised look on Quinn's face. He had stopped by every day the last three weeks on one pretext or another. He always waited to see her if she was busy elsewhere. Glorianna did her best to leave the two of them alone despite Kathleen telling her not to. Glory said Quinn was sweet on her, but that didn't matter. She could never marry and preferred not to be tempted.

Tipping her head back against the rocker, Kathleen closed her eyes. Immediately, the image of blue-gray eyes, twinkling with humor, flashed across her vision. She had to do something to get Quinn interested in someone else. If he kept coming by, she wouldn't be able to deny the attraction between them.

The soft whisper of footsteps alerted her that company had entered the room. She opened her eyes to find Glory bending over the cradle. She sat up, and Glory straightened.

"Who is the one needing the nap? You told me you were taking the babies to put them down, and here I find you taking a siesta." Glorianna grinned and reached for Angelina.

"I wasn't sleeping, just resting my eyes and thinking." Kathleen tried to sound miffed, then giggled.

"I think we're all a little tired. Who would believe something so small could make enough noise that would wake the entire household?" Glorianna settled her daughter into the cradle beside her brother, rocking the tiny bed to ease their restlessness. "Conlon's men have been teasing him about the circles under his eyes, and he isn't even the one getting up in the night. I'm so glad you're here to help."

"I've been meaning to talk to you about that." Kathleen followed Glorianna to the kitchen, where they poured coffee and sat at the table. "You have such a small house. I thought maybe I should plan to leave so you could have the place to yourselves." At Glorianna's panicked look, she continued. "I won't do it right away. In a couple of weeks you'll have your routine down."

Glorianna's fingertips whitened on her coffee cup. "I'm so sorry you have to stay in the parlor. I know it isn't very private or comfortable. Our quarters at the new fort will be much better, but I don't know how soon we'll be able to move in." Her eyes glittered with tears. "Oh, Kathleen, I've enjoyed having you here. I can't bear the thought of you leaving. The trip east is so long. I thought you would stay through the winter."

"Glory, I didn't mean to leave the city. I want to stay. I love it here." Kathleen reached across the table and twined her fingers with her cousin's.

"I've heard that Mrs. Monroy, down the street, is letting rooms to young ladies. I thought I would talk to her about one. Her house is so close, I could walk over every day to visit and help out with the babies."

"But how will you afford to stay there?" Glorianna's shoulders relaxed as she took a sip of her coffee.

Excitement made it hard for Kathleen to sit still. "I've been thinking about that. The wives here aren't able to keep up with the eastern fashions. I've just come from there, and I'm an excellent seamstress. I thought I could offer my services to sew the latest in clothing for the ladies and men in Tucson. I brought the latest E. Butterick and Company's catalog with me. As the fashions change, I can have Mama send me the new catalogs showing the various styles. I can order material through the mercantile."

Kathleen forced herself to sit still and wait for Glory's opinion. Now that she was out from under her mother's oppressive guardianship, she wanted to stay here. The freedom she'd always longed for seemed attainable. Only one question remained unanswered. Could people accept her despite her birthmark? Would they consider her an equal or someone cursed, as her classmates once taunted?

"Would Mrs. Monroy let you run a business like this from her house?"

"I don't know. I need to ask. It would mean entertaining ladies in the parlor and in my room." Kathleen tried to control her eagerness, but knew she wasn't doing a good job. "Once I get started, I could look for a small building to let and have a little shop."

Glorianna frowned. A lump formed in Kathleen's throat. Did her cousin disapprove of her idea? Would she have the courage to continue with her venture if Glory didn't agree?

A smile lit Glorianna's face. "I think this is a wonderful idea. You'll have to adjust some of the patterns for the Southwest. The heat in the summer makes the tight dresses unbearable. You'll have to learn about using lighter fabrics too."

"That won't be hard at all. I know a lot about different materials already. You can help me, and I'm sure the other ladies here will help out as well. Do you think. . . ?" Kathleen stopped, afraid to voice the question that scared her the most.

"Do I think what?" Glorianna's smile vanished.

Kathleen's hands twisted in her lap. She couldn't look at her cousin. The question burned inside, yet she feared to say anything.

"Kathleen, what is it?" Glorianna retrieved the coffeepot and filled their cups, giving Kathleen a few moments to compose her question.

Waiting for Glory to sit down again, Kathleen took a quick sip, scalding her tongue. She drew in a deep breath and faced her impatient cousin. Glorianna's foot tapped a rapid rhythm on the floor.

"I wondered if you thought people would be able to accept me."

"Accept you? What do you mean?" Glorianna leaned forward, eyes narrowed, looking as if sparks would soon fly. "Are you referring to the way you were treated in school?"

Kathleen nodded.

"I can't believe you even considered people out here might reject you because of a little birthmark. I don't know why you insist on wearing that ugly veil. The only reason I can think of is your mother's negative influence."

Glorianna moved to a chair beside Kathleen. She pulled Kathleen's hands into her lap and held them. "Listen to me. You are a beautiful person. You are not cursed. You know God loves you." Her grip tightened, becoming almost painful. "Trust me in this. No one will reject you because of your birthmark. God made you special. Don't be ashamed."

Kathleen glanced up, blinking rapidly. Glorianna caught Kathleen's gaze. She grinned. "Besides, you know you have one admirer in town, and he's seen you at least twice without your veil. You haven't scared him off yet."

A sharp knock rattled the kitchen door. Kathleen tugged at her hands, but Glorianna wouldn't let go.

"Come on in, Quinn." Hidden laughter gave Glorianna's voice a musical lilt. The door opened. Kathleen heard the deputy sheriff's heavy footsteps. She tried to focus on her coffee cup on the table, but the pull of his gaze drew her eyes upward. When their eyes met, the connection was instant and powerful. Kathleen could feel the flush staining her cheeks.

"Good morning, Kathleen." Quinn smiled, twisting his hat in his hands. For some reason, she knew he wasn't at all uncomfortable seeing her without her veil. Even so, she would have covered her cheek with a hand if Glorianna hadn't held them both tight.

"Good morning, Deputy. Could I get you a cup of coffee?" Kathleen knew if he said yes, Glorianna would have to let her go. She could pour a quick cup, then dash to the parlor and retrieve her veil.

Still holding Kathleen's hands, Glorianna stood and offered her chair. "Here, Quinn, have a seat. I'll pour your coffee, then check the babies."

Kathleen gritted her teeth in anger. Glory knew exactly what she'd planned and had managed to keep her from escaping. Quinn settled in next to her.

"Did you know Kathleen is thinking of leaving us?" The sweetness in Glorianna's tone let Kathleen know her cousin was up to something. Quinn's eyes widened as he looked from Glorianna to Kathleen.

"Are you going back East so soon? Traveling so far in the winter months can be hazardous." A note of panic matched the look on his face.

"Oh, she's not leaving Tucson; she's only leaving our house." Glorianna handed Quinn his coffee. "She wants to rent a room from Mrs. Monroy and open a dress-making shop. If you're not too busy, maybe you could escort her to see about it."

Taking a long swig of coffee, Quinn studied her. Kathleen wanted to squirm.

"I have nothing pressing to do right now. If you're ready, I'll walk down the street with you. I'm sure the ladies in town would welcome a seamstress who is familiar with eastern fashions." He downed the rest of his coffee. "Shall we go?"

Standing, Quinn slapped his hat on his head and offered Kathleen his hand. She felt trapped. Part of her wanted to place her hand in his and walk out the door without a care; the other part feared the reaction of others on the street and wanted to hide.

"I have to get my hat and veil before I can go."

"The hat, I can understand. Ladies always want to wear a hat when they go out." Quinn frowned. "The veil you don't need." He started to touch her cheek, and she jerked away. "You have nothing to hide." His eyes were warm and compassionate.

"I'll get your hat." Glorianna hummed a light melody as she swept from the kitchen, returning momentarily with Kathleen's hat minus the veil. "Here you are. You tell Mrs. Monroy hello for me."

Before she knew what happened, the kitchen door banged shut behind them, and Kathleen was standing barefaced beside Quinn in the bright fall sunlight. She stepped away, ready to turn and rush into the house. As if he sensed her fear, Quinn placed her trembling hand on his arm and smiled at her as if he hadn't a care in the world.

"I can't do this." Kathleen backed against the door. "I'm sorry. It has nothing to do with you. I'm just not ready yet." With a sad smile, Quinn opened the door and waited while she retrieved her veil.

On the short walk down the street, Quinn waved to the occasional rider or wagon passing by on the road. He kept her close to his side as if trying to reassure her that she would be fine. Kathleen began to relax.

"I'm guessing the kids you grew up around used to tease you about your birthmark."

Kathleen jerked at Quinn's blunt statement. No one had ever dared speak so openly to her.

"I used to know someone with a mark similar to yours. She got called names, accused of being cursed or of the devil. She was the sweetest girl. None of those accusations were true for her, and they aren't true for you." His serious gaze held hers.

"Maybe the person you knew didn't deserve the accusations, but I'm not that person. Please don't judge me by the same standard." Kathleen pulled her hand free. "Here is Mrs. Monroy's house. I believe you have other duties, Deputy Kirby. I can see myself home." She turned up the walkway to the large adobe house, hoping he couldn't see the regret eating a hole in her heart. No matter how painful she found it, she had to discourage him. This couldn't continue. She'd heard Conlon talking to Glorianna about Quinn's lack of faith. Even if she were free to marry, she could never wed someone who didn't share her love of the Father.

"You won't get rid of me that easily, Miss O'Connor."

She held her stance rigid as she knocked on the door, waiting for Mrs. Monroy to let her in. She refused to give Quinn the satisfaction of knowing how much she wanted to see if he was still there.

Lydia Monroy, a large woman with plump cheeks and kind eyes, exuded a warmth Kathleen found comforting. Chattering away, Lydia told of being a widow for three months and how she decided to take in boarders because her large home was lonely. She and her husband had never had children. All her family lived in the East. She wanted company to talk to during the long evenings.

"Breakfast and supper will be provided. When you move in, I'll let you know the schedule. We'll all sit down and eat at the same time." Lydia smoothed her hair and frowned. "I have two boarders arriving next week. Both new school-teachers will be staying here. With three unattached young ladies in the house, I'll have to make rules about gentlemen callers. I'll expect you to abide by them."

"That won't be a problem. I don't expect to have any callers." Kathleen looked around the airy room they'd entered.

"These will be your sleeping quarters." Lydia gestured around. "Now, you mentioned being a seamstress." She stepped to a door and opened it. "This room hasn't been used for years. If you're willing to help clean it up, you can use it for a shop. There is an outside door, so patrons can come and go without disturbing the rest of the house."

Kathleen peered into the dusty room. Cobwebs and layers of dust covered various items piled in the room. This would be perfect. She clasped her hands together to still the shaking.

"I'm sure we'll be able to come to terms." Lydia smiled at her. "I can't wait to be your first customer."

Kathleen was almost singing as she said good-bye to Lydia Monroy. They agreed she would come by every day to work on the room and could move in at the end of two weeks. She wanted to wait at least that long to continue helping Glorianna.

"You're looking pretty cheerful."

Kathleen clapped a hand to her mouth to stifle a shriek. Quinn lounged against a tree at the edge of the road.

"What are you doing here?"

"I told you, I'm not easy to get rid of." His lazy smile warmed her in a way she'd never felt before. He took hold of her hand and wrapped it around his arm, starting down the street toward Glorianna's house. "I'm afraid you may as well plan on seeing me around a lot. I've decided someone needs to introduce you to everyone in town so you can get used to us all. As a deputy, I know just about everyone." He grinned, and she couldn't remember why she hadn't wanted to be with him.

Chapter 7

Waiting for the stage's arrival, Quinn couldn't seem to keep his mind on his duty and off of Kathleen. Yesterday, she had moved into her new quarters at Mrs. Monroy's boardinghouse. For the past two weeks, she had been hard at work helping Glorianna with the babies. Then, when they were napping, she would slip away and go to work on the room that would become her seamstress shop. He couldn't believe how she'd taken a dingy, cobweb-infested place and made it into an airy, inviting room. Yellow curtains draped across clean windows. Sunlight-brightened walls held swatches of colorful materials.

Although Kathleen continued to discourage his visits, Quinn couldn't make himself stay away. He'd never wanted to be tied down with a wife and kids, but for some reason, since he'd met Kathleen, that didn't matter so much. She still didn't feel comfortable going into town without her hat and veil firmly in place. He accused her of hiding her beauty from the world when, in reality, he only wanted to be able to see her himself. He didn't care if any of the other men in town could see her. There were so few single women here that those who came were pursued by so many men, they often had trouble choosing one to marry. He didn't want that to happen with Kathleen. She should be for him alone.

A cloud of dust roiling in the air heralded the arrival of the stage. Quinn checked his pistol, lifting it, then dropping the gun into the holster. His badge shone. Although he didn't move other than to check his gun, his whole body tensed with readiness. Maybe today the Widow would be arriving on the stage. He still waited for her every day, hoping to catch her before she had the chance to harm one of the citizens under his protection.

The driver eased down off the coach, nodding at Quinn. After placing the small step stool on the ground, he opened the door and reached up to help someone down. Quinn tensed. His hand flexed above the handle of his pistol. A foot encased in a brown boot reached for the step. A woman in a gray dress, her hair upswept and topped with a matching gray hat, stepped down from the stage. She gave the driver a tired smile and moved away before turning around, as if waiting for someone else.

Some of the tension eased out of Quinn. He wondered who the new arrival was and if her husband accompanied her. Once more the driver reached up to help someone from the stage. This time a slender foot extended encased in black. Excitement coursed through Quinn. He gripped the butt of his gun. The woman who stepped down was garbed in black with a hat, but no veil. Dark hair, grayed by the road dust, was drawn up into a high, loose bun. Even from here, he could see a set of lively dark eyes taking in the town. She nodded to the driver and moved to stand beside the first woman. The two waited for bags from the top of the stage.

Neither of these two women was the Widow. Quinn sighed and dug his toe into the dry road. Why didn't she just show up? He was ready and waiting. The Veiled Widow wouldn't get past him. He'd been taking care of himself for years and had been a lawman in various cities for the past six years. His hunches always seemed to pay off. . .and right now, those hunches told him she would show up here in Tucson. When she did, he would be ready.

The huffing of a person in a hurry sounded from behind him. Quinn glanced around to find John Allen approaching at a faster pace than the man generally moved. His partially balding pate glistened with sweat as he removed his hat. He wiped his head with a handkerchief and slapped the hat back on.

"Afternoon, Mayor."

"Afternoon, Deputy. Sure is a warm one for November."

"Might be best to slow down." Quinn grinned. He rarely saw the mayor in such a hurry. "You act like you're heading for a fire."

Mayor Allen wiped a drip of sweat that ran down his nose. "I almost missed the stage. Have they arrived?"

"Who?" Quinn followed the mayor's gaze to the two women now standing next to a pile of trunks and bags at the side of the street. "Are those ladies relatives of yours?"

"What? Who?" Mayor Allen scrubbed at his mouth, looking flustered. "No, they're not. I'm here to meet them in an official capacity. These are the new schoolteachers the town hired. I sent for a boy to bring round a wagon to take them to their rooms. They'll be staying at Mrs. Monroy's boardinghouse."

Mayor Allen tore his gaze away from the two young women and glanced up at Quinn. A bright flush crept up his cheeks. "I can see we'll have a number of men interested in meeting these ladies."

Quinn chuckled and straightened from the wall. "Don't count me among them. I'd better be off on my rounds. Good day."

Striding down the street in the opposite direction of the jail, Quinn couldn't help wondering how Kathleen would take to the new arrivals. Would she hide her face from them, too? A couple of times, he'd caught her working on the room without the veil, but she still wore the contraption around the house. Quinn gritted his teeth as a wave of anger swept through him. What he wouldn't give to have the chance to trounce the kids who'd taunted Kathleen when she was young. Whoever did this to her had done a thorough job. Parting her from her veil would be a major undertaking—one he considered a challenge.

A half-hour later, the low rumble of his stomach alerted Quinn that evening had crept up on him. Turning in the direction of Señora Arvizu's eatery, he quickened his pace. When he arrived, several tables were already taken. The buzz of conversation carried a hint of excitement.

"Quinn, join us." Ed Fish waved an arm in the air. Quinn threaded his way through the crowd to the table occupied by Ed and John Wasson, owner of the *Citizen* newspaper.

"Evening." Quinn sank into a chair next to Ed and signaled to Señora Arvizu. She would bring his usual. "What's all the excitement?" Ed and John looked at him as if he'd grown an extra head.

"Haven't you heard?" Astonishment crossed Ed's face. "The new schoolteachers are here. We've seen them. I went with John to ask about interviewing them for the *Citizen*."

Quinn's lips twitched. "I didn't know you did articles for the paper, Ed."

Ed flushed. "I don't. John asked me to go along and meet the teachers. As a business owner, I wanted to make them feel welcome."

"It didn't hurt to see that they were pretty, either." John chuckled at his friend's obvious discomfort. "We didn't actually get the interview today. They were just moving in, but we did set up an appointment to talk with them tomorrow."

"I can't wait to read the article." Quinn picked up a fork as the señora placed a plate loaded with steaming food in front of him. "Did you happen to meet Glorianna Sullivan's cousin while you were there?" He tried to sound casual, hoping his friends wouldn't suspect where his interests lie.

Ed pushed his empty plate away. "Is she the one who always wears the veil?" At Quinn's nod, his brow furrowed. "I can't figure out why she does that. Any ideas?"

Shoveling a forkful of beans into his mouth, Quinn hoped to avoid the question. He'd brought this on himself by inquiring, but now he didn't want to answer. He shrugged.

"I haven't seen her," John said. "I've heard talk, though. Most people think she's a little standoffish. Maybe she's so ugly, she doesn't want anyone to see what she looks like."

Quinn choked. Ed pounded him on the back. Quinn took a deep breath, then a long swig of coffee.

"Have to be careful with that hot chili." Ed spoke with the conviction of one who knew. "I breathed in one of those chilies last week and thought I was gonna die." John nodded his agreement.

Pushing his plate to one side, Quinn stood. "I better be off again. 'Bout time to start my evening rounds."

"Hey, you goin' to the fandango next week?" John asked.

Quinn shrugged again.

"I'm going." Ed grinned. "I imagine every bachelor around will be there. Those new schoolteachers will have their feet worn off by the end of the night. I plan to try to get in my share of dances."

John rubbed his chin. "You know, Ed, I imagine those ladies will step around the floor more with the men they already know. What do you say to wandering over to the boardinghouse and getting better acquainted?"

Ed stood so fast he knocked over the bench he and Quinn had been seated on. His face reddened, and with Quinn's help, he straightened the bench. The three walked out into the fading light together.

"Why don't you come along with us, Quinn? Maybe one of these ladies will take a shine to you." Ed clapped him on the shoulder.

"Nope, I've got work to do. You boys go on ahead. Besides, if I were to show up, you two wouldn't have a chance with the ladies." They all laughed as they headed off in opposite directions.

The urge for Quinn to go by and see Kathleen was tempered by the knowledge that Ed and John would be there visiting the new schoolteachers. Quinn didn't want them to realize his interest lie in the mystery woman, not in the two unattached teachers who had just come to town. Tomorrow morning, he would go by and see how her shop opening had gone. He'd check to see if she'd gotten any sewing assignments, and if not, he would try to spread the word. Then again, Mrs. Monroy would be her best customer for awhile, and she knew everyone in town. News would get around.

❦

Kathleen's muscles ached from sitting so rigidly. For the last hour, she'd been trapped in the parlor. She'd been visiting with Mrs. Monroy and the two new schoolteachers, Maria Wakefield and Harriet Bolton, when the callers began to arrive. First, two of the town's prominent men came: John, the owner of the paper, and Ed, who owned the flour mill. She couldn't remember their last names.

A knock rattled the front door. Mrs. Monroy left the room.

Ed stood, his hat in his hands. "It's sure been a pleasure meeting you ladies. We'd best be on our way."

John jumped up. He followed Ed in lifting Maria's hand to his lips for a quick kiss. He turned to Harriet, lingering a little over her fingers. Kathleen nearly groaned aloud at his obvious infatuation with a woman he'd only known for an hour. Maria and Harriet stood to walk their admirers to the door, chatting easily. Kathleen relaxed her tense muscles and prepared to escape to her room. Confusion reigned in the hallway, keeping her inside the parlor until it was too late.

"Here you go, gentlemen." Mrs. Monroy gestured to the two chairs recently vacated by Ed and John. Maria and Harriet slipped into the room and resumed their seats.

"Kathleen, these are Thomas McKaye and Robert Beldon. They've come by to meet the new ladies in town." Mrs. Monroy beamed as if having all these men stop by had been her idea.

Thomas, a tall, lanky man with a droopy mustache, nodded his greeting. Robert, as short and rotund as Thomas was tall, gave a grin that showed all eight of his teeth. They seemed to be waiting for Kathleen to say something. She opened her mouth, but nothing came out. Just as with Ed and John, she could think of nothing to say. She'd never had experience with small talk like this. Her mind went blank.

"Are you ladies planning to go to the fandango?" Robert gave another grin.

Maria smiled. "The last two gentlemen mentioned a fandango, but I'm afraid we easterners have no idea what you're talking about."

Thomas tapped the toe of his boot on the floor. He twisted his long mustache with a finger and thumb, giving himself a lopsided look. "Why, a fandango is just a dance. The Mexicans here are fond of having them. All the soldiers like to attend, and we want as many of the single gals as we can get. There's usually quite a crowd."

"If you ladies would like, we could escort you to the dance." Robert looked hopeful as he stared at Maria and Harriet and pointedly ignored Kathleen.

Maria and Harriet exchanged glances. "I believe we'll be attending with Mrs. Monroy. Perhaps we'll see you gentlemen there," Harriet said.

The conversation continued as Kathleen sat still as a stone. She hoped no one would remember her presence if she didn't move or speak. Sitting in a parlor with men was a nightmare. She could only imagine how much worse attending a dance would be. *Please, help me find a way to stay home from this, Lord. You know how Glorianna likes to socialize. She'll expect me to go with her. I simply can't do that.*

She closed her eyes and pictured the horror of trying to learn dance steps that everyone else was good at, when she'd never done such a thing in her life. Other people didn't realize how hard a simple thing like walking was when you were wearing a veil. Of course, Glory's answer would be to leave the veil at home. How could she? Didn't Glorianna know how everyone stared at her with the veil? How much worse would it be when they could see the ugly mark disfiguring her cheek?

Before the next round of visitors could intrude, Kathleen escaped to her room. She stood in the dark, relief making her tired. A soft, rattling sound came from the room next door. Her heart began to pound. Someone was coming into her dress shop. Picking up a candlestick in one hand and a lamp in the other, she crept toward the door separating her room from her shop.

The figure of a man stood outlined against the window. As she moved the lamp to shine through the door, the gleam of a badge caught her eye.

"What are you doing here?" She hissed the words at Quinn, hoping everyone in the parlor wouldn't hear.

"I'm supposed to check on businesses and see that they're locked up for the night. I'm just doing my job." Quinn didn't look as certain as he sounded.

"You could get me kicked out if Mrs. Monroy caught you sneaking in here."

"I'm not sneaking; I'm checking."

"Well, everything's fine, so leave before you get caught."

Quinn's thumb rubbed across his badge, and he grinned. "I'll leave just as soon as you promise to go to the fandango with me. It's next week."

"I know when it is." Kathleen's voice began to rise above a whisper, and she glanced over her shoulder. "I can't go to a dance. I've never done such a thing, and I don't intend to start now."

"Have you ever heard me sing?" Quinn's question caught her off guard. He opened his mouth.

"Don't you dare. My reputation will be ruined. Now, leave quietly."

He grinned. "Just give me your word." She remained silent. "Okay, here's my favorite cowpoke song. I learned it not long after I left home." He opened his mouth again.

"No." Kathleen's teeth clicked together over the word. "All right, I'll go. But this is blackmail, and I believe it's illegal, Mr. Deputy Sheriff."

He chuckled and tipped his hat as he backed out the door. "I guess you'll have to tell the sheriff the whole story or arrest me yourself."

Chapter 8

G lory, I can't do this." Kathleen tugged at her skirt, straightening it again. The green taffeta dress was the latest fashion. Beside her on the writing desk lay a matching green hat complete with a dark green veil.

Glorianna picked it up, stretched, and pinned the stylish hat in place. "You will be just fine, Kathleen. You've never seen anything like this fandango. The music is different. The dancing is fast and fun. Relax and enjoy the evening."

"But I told you what Quinn did. He blackmailed me into going. I can't go with him."

Glorianna placed her hands on her hips. "Why can't you go with him? The man is crazy about you. He asks Conlon questions every day."

"He doesn't believe in Jesus Christ, Glory. You know what the Bible says about being yoked to unbelievers. We're not to do that. Besides, someone like me can't marry."

"Aha." Glorianna crossed her arms and tapped her foot on the floor. "Now the truth is coming out. Are you still listening to what your mother told you about never having children?"

Kathleen could feel the heat in her cheeks. She bit her lip, trying to think of a quick answer that would satisfy her cousin and still not be a lie.

"I thought so." Glorianna took a step closer. "Now you listen to me. I know you remember my mother talking to you about your cheek. There is no reason for you to be ashamed."

Her tone softened, and Glory placed her fingertips over Kathleen's mark. "My mother told you this is as if God took a star from heaven and touched it to your cheek before you were born. I always loved that thought. In fact, for a long time, I was jealous that God never did anything so special for me."

Tears glistened in her cousin's eyes, and Kathleen swallowed hard around the lump in her throat. She could still remember the day her aunt made that comment. She'd treasured the thought for years, even though she knew the rest of the world didn't view her deformity the same way.

"Kathleen, you were denied the fun most young women experience. You've let your mother's fears become your own. Give the people here a chance to know you. They aren't the children you grew up with."

"But I can't go with Quinn." Kathleen's voice sounded gritty from emotion.

"He's not asking you to marry him. You need to get out and meet the townspeople. Quinn knows everyone. He'll make sure you're introduced around."

Glory smiled and stepped away. She tapped a finger on her lower lip. Kathleen wanted to cringe under the scrutiny of a cousin who knew her too well.

"Are you afraid of your feelings for him?"

Cold fingers of dread wormed their way through Kathleen. Did she have feelings for Quinn? She knew without thinking that her answer had to be yes. Over the last few weeks, she'd come to look forward to having him around. He had seen what she looked like and never made fun or acted as if she was different from any other woman on the street. When he stopped in at the boardinghouse, he was polite to Maria and Harriet but paid special attention to her. For the first time in her life, Kathleen was being courted by a man—one she found thoroughly attractive, no less. Somehow she had to deny these feelings before they carried too far. There were too many reasons she couldn't have a relationship with the handsome deputy.

A faint knock sounded from the front door. They heard the thump of booted feet as Conlon strode down the hallway to answer. Kathleen had told Quinn she would be at Glorianna's getting ready. Conlon and Glorianna were going to the fandango, too. Glory insisted the babies would be fine. Usually, the older women loved to care for the babies while their mothers danced. This would be the first time they'd get to watch Glory's twins, and Kathleen had heard there were several ladies vying to be the first to hold them.

"Kathleen, Quinn's here." Conlon stuck his head in the room, his black hair in total disarray, his clothes unchanged. He grinned at Glory's look of dismay. "I'm a fast dresser. I'll be ready before Angelina cries." They heard him rush down the hall to the bedroom.

"When he grins at me that way, I wonder how his mother could ever punish him." Glorianna sighed. "I can almost see the cute little boy he was. I'm hoping Andrew doesn't ever grin at me like that, or he'll get away with anything."

Tamping down her nervousness, Kathleen gave a strangled sound she hoped passed for a laugh. "You always were one to let the boys' smiles get to you." She glanced at the door. Her fingers twined together, squeezing until she wondered if the bones would crack. *Jesus, help me. I have to find a way to discourage Quinn. . . . And he's the most persistent man I've ever known.*

A faint wail sounded from Glorianna's bedroom. "That sounds like Angelina. I guess that means Conlon is ready to go." Glorianna chuckled and swept from the room to retrieve her unhappy child.

Kathleen watched her cousin leave. Quinn was waiting in the sitting room. She should be happy to be going to the fandango with such a handsome man. Why, all the girls there would probably want to dance with him. Kathleen gasped. That was the answer to her problem. Relief swept through her. Her fingers unclenched, and she touched her hat to make sure it was firmly pinned in place. Straightening her shoulders, she marched out the door and down the hallway to meet Quinn.

Quinn stared out into the darkness, the lamp behind him giving an eerie reflection in the glass. A leather vest stretched taut across his chest, his only concession to the cool November evening. Cold rarely bothered him. Here in Tucson the weather didn't get chilly enough to worry about. When he'd worked up in the northern territories, the cold had been fierce enough to make a man want to hibernate right along with the bears.

A gleam caught his eye. He'd wondered about leaving his badge and gun at home but thought better of it. He never knew when conflict could break out at one of these dances. Usually, it wasn't anything too big. Some fella would get jealous of another, probably because of a pretty señorita they both wanted to dance with. Quinn grinned to himself and rocked back on his heels. He had the advantage over all the other men in town. He knew where the prettiest girl lived, and they had no idea. Maybe tonight Kathleen would leave her veil at home. Being seen at the fandango with her on his arm would give Quinn no end of pleasure. All the unmarried men in town would burn with jealousy.

More and more, he heard speculation about why Kathleen wore a veil all of the time. Although he hadn't said anything, Quinn had been chuckling to himself, wondering what these men would say if they knew the truth. Meanwhile, every day he made some excuse to visit her. A few times lately, she had even allowed him to come into her shop and talk when she had removed her veil to do some of her work. She admitted that sewing was impossible to do with heavy gauze blocking the view. Even taking measurements and writing were probably a challenge. Several times, he'd seen her copying Scriptures on a paper, and she never wore her veil for that, either.

The firm click of shoes on the hard floor alerted him to her approach. Quinn turned as Kathleen walked into the room. Disappointment flashed through him. Heavy green netting covered her face and part of her slender neck. An urge to rip the fragile material away made him clench his fists, lest he follow through with the desire. The beauty of her green dress stole his breath. The finely ruffled blouse over a straight skirt with ruffles at the hem and an overskirt of intricate ruffles and bows displayed her feminine charms. He could only imagine how the green of her dress would bring out the color in her eyes. What he wouldn't give to see them.

Kathleen paused. "Is there something wrong, Deputy?"

Quinn realized he still had a frown on his face from seeing her with her veil in place. He relaxed and smiled. "I had hoped you would accompany me without the veil. I can't imagine how hard it must be to have everything around you muted by the covering over your face. Can I convince you to leave it behind tonight?"

She stiffened. "I can see just fine. If my veil embarrasses you, we can cancel our plans for the evening."

"Oh, I'm not embarrassed. In fact, I was just considering my advantage over the other men in town."

"Your advantage?"

He reached to pluck his hat from the hat rack. His grin widened. "Of course. I'm the only single man in town who knows just how beautiful you are. The others don't have any idea how lucky I am."

"And just why are you so lucky, Deputy Kirby?" Her frosty tone almost made him glance up to see if snow was in the air.

"Why, because I'll be the gentleman at the fandango with the most beautiful woman on my arm. I know we got off to a rough start, but I think you have to admit to enjoying my visits."

Her slender hands clamped onto green-clad hips with enough force to make Quinn wince. Pulling herself up to her full height, which meant the top of her head might reach his chest, Kathleen looked like she was prepared to wage a war.

"Oh, good. You two are ready to go." Glorianna swept into the room, a well-bundled baby in her arms. Conlon strode in behind her with the other twin snuggled on his shoulder.

"Good evening, Quinn." Glory stretched up and kissed his cheek. "Whoever would think I'd be so excited about a silly dance?" She sighed. "I've been cooped up here for weeks; and before that, I couldn't dance because I was so big, my husband couldn't get his arms around me."

"I believe you must be talking about someone else, my dear." Conlon gazed fondly at his wife. "I seem to remember my arms being around you a number of times."

Glorianna blushed. "If you two will help us with our cloaks, we'll be ready."

Quinn accepted the dark gray cloak Glorianna handed him and stepped toward Kathleen. She had relaxed her stance somewhat but still acted a bit miffed. He couldn't resist letting his hands linger a minute on her shoulders as he settled the cloak there. Giving her a little squeeze, he released Kathleen and stepped to her side.

"Shall we go?" Quinn offered his arm. Her head inclined to the right, and he thought he could see the faint shadow of a smile through the veil. Her slender fingers rested on his sleeve, their slight pressure making him long to see her expression clearly.

"Would you like me to carry that for you?" Quinn gestured at the satchel containing the babies' belongings. Conlon still hadn't figured out how to carry a baby, a satchel, and offer his arm to his wife. Quinn wondered how he would manage if he were in his friend's shoes. Before meeting Kathleen, he would have scoffed at taking the thought seriously. Now, the idea didn't scare him. Maybe being a husband and father could be right for him.

Although the fandango wasn't far, Conlon had arranged for a buggy to transport them. He told Quinn he wasn't sure Glorianna was up to walking so much yet. Besides, he wanted to have plenty of dances with his wife without her being worn out.

Strains of guitar and violin music drifted to them on the evening breeze long before they arrived. Cowhands and cavalrymen milled around the door, laughing and sharing stories as they watched the pretty girls inside. The men would be picking the one they wanted to dance with, then building courage before entering the hall.

Reaching up, Quinn put his hands on Kathleen's waist to swing her down. She must be made of air, because she sure didn't weigh anything. Once again, he chafed at the veil keeping him from seeing her expression. He thought maybe she enjoyed his company and his touch and longed to see for himself what her eyes would tell.

Kathleen hesitated as they faced the crowd of men around the door. She seemed to draw nearer to him. Quinn tightened his arm, pulling her close, wanting to comfort her.

"These men are noisy and a little rough sometimes, but they're harmless." Quinn leaned close, his cheek brushing her veil. He thought he could feel a slight tremor pass through her. "Shall we go on in?"

Conlon and Glorianna were disappearing through the group. Many of the cavalrymen called greetings to them. Kathleen stiffened her shoulders and nodded. Quinn led her in, not wanting to give her time to be afraid. She'd admitted to him a few days ago that being in public had been a rare occurrence in her life. He wondered if she was afraid of saying or doing something wrong. Perhaps she feared the careless remarks said by people who didn't stop to think before they spoke.

"Evenin', Deputy."

Quinn nodded at several of the young men crowding the door and returned a few greetings. Curiosity filled more than one gaze as the men parted to let them pass. Stifling a grin, Quinn again thought how lucky he was to have Kathleen at his side. He could feel the shaking of her hand on his arm and knew she would stick close simply because he was someone she knew and felt partially comfortable with.

Chattering women and uncomfortable-looking men crowded the inside of the hall. Most husbands would rather stay at home, relaxing for the evening. The women seemed to blossom in the charged social atmosphere.

At one end of the hall, several musicians seated on a raised platform tried out their various instruments. Even though they hadn't begun a formal song, the partial tunes they played made the people tap their toes, anxious for the dancing to begin.

A tug on his arm reminded Quinn that Kathleen stood beside him. He glanced down to find her gazing across the large room at a group of young women. Harriet and Maria, the new schoolteachers, stood with several other girls. Pulling his arm, Kathleen began to work her way through the crowd to reach her friends from the boardinghouse. Quinn hoped she didn't intend to stay with them all night.

By the time they reached the girls, the first strains of the opening song called the dancers to gather on the floor. Kathleen plucked the forgotten satchel with the babies' things from Quinn. Taking her hand from his arm, Kathleen pulled Maria forward.

"Maria, Quinn is dying to get started dancing. Would you mind joining him while I deliver these things to Glorianna?" With that she swept off, leaving a stunned deputy in her wake. Maria gave a shy smile, her brown eyes not meeting his as she stretched out her hand. As if in a dream, Quinn led her to the dance floor, his heart following the veiled beauty as she left him behind.

Chapter 9

H ere's the bag with the babies' necessities, Glory." Kathleen stepped into a small anteroom. Chairs were grouped in a corner, and several baby beds stood to one side of the floor. A few older ladies bent over some of the beds. Others sat with infants on their laps. At Kathleen's entrance, they looked up and seemed to realize for the first time that Glory and her twins were there. They rushed in an excited ensemble to surround the new mother and her sleeping newborns.

Glorianna handed Angelina to a stout, black-clad woman, then retrieved Andrew from Conlon, who made a hasty retreat. Handing Andrew, then the bag Kathleen carried, to the women, Glorianna drew her cousin to a corner of the room.

"What are you doing in here?" Glorianna looked suspicious. "Why aren't you with Quinn?"

"I had to bring you the babies' things." Kathleen breathed a quiet sigh of relief that Glory couldn't see her face. Even without the visual, Glory would probably know she was omitting something. Kathleen knew she couldn't hide what she'd done forever.

"Conlon is waiting for you out there. You'd better get a start on the dancing." Kathleen pushed Glory toward the door. Conlon turned, peering into the room. He pulled his wife onto the dance floor, where they began a lively step Kathleen had never seen.

After Glorianna disappeared from sight, Kathleen slipped into the nursery. She would do her best to hide here. Holding babies was much more to her liking than attempting to dance when she had no idea how to do such a thing. Her mother never allowed her to attend a function like this. There was always too much chance that her mark would be seen and shame the family. Kathleen still felt uncomfortable appearing in public even with her face covered.

Growing up, she met a few friends at church. Those friends kept her up on the latest happenings and romances in the community. They described picnics at the park, box socials, and dances in great detail, but Kathleen never experienced them in person. As a teenager, she'd longed for a normal life, but now she was comfortable with the way things turned out. She didn't need love and marriage and family. She could be content with where God had her. Maybe the mark on her face was special to God.

"Look at this, Kathleen." Mrs. Monroy settled onto a chair beside her. Her plump cheeks creased as she smiled at Andrew nestled in her arms. "Have you ever seen such a sweet thing?"

"Not since looking at his sister." Kathleen grinned at the matron's startled expression.

Mrs. Monroy chuckled, her plump body shaking like jelly. "I reckon that's true. This has to be the prettiest pair of babies I've seen in years. Of course, with the parents they have, how could they be anything but beautiful? Glorianna and Conlon make a fine-looking couple."

Andrew scrunched his face in a scowl. Mrs. Monroy patted him until he burped and settled quietly to sleep. She snuggled the baby close and glanced over at Kathleen. "Of course, I'm wondering if there isn't another couple who look pretty good together."

"Is it someone I know?" Kathleen shot a glance at the door leading to the dance floor. Laughter and music drifted in, and she tamped down the longing to see the festivities.

"You're half of the couple, so I guess you know them." Mrs. Monroy smirked. Kathleen tried to keep her surprise from showing. "The other half is that handsome deputy sheriff who keeps showing up at my house. Funny thing is, I don't ever remember Quinn Kirby dropping by my place until you moved in. Now he's there every day."

A plump hand patted Kathleen's knee. "I don't know why you always wear that veil, Kathleen, but there are other ways of being beautiful than through one's looks. You have a caring, godly demeanor. Once these ladies get to know you, they can see for themselves what a beauty you are."

Once again someone was after her to rid herself of the veil. She knew Mrs. Monroy wasn't being bossy or nosy; she only intended to encourage and help. Kathleen wondered at the number of times she'd recently been asked to remove her veil. Always before, she spent most of her time around her family. She hadn't been alone with anyone long enough for them to care to look at her.

"I can't possibly take off my veil. People would stare and talk." Kathleen blurted out the truth before she could stop herself.

Mrs. Monroy's eyebrows shot skyward. "Take a look around you, Honey." She gestured to the women on the far side of the room. As soon as Kathleen looked their way, they acted as if they weren't watching her.

"You see, these women aren't used to seeing someone covered by a veil. They're all wondering what you have to hide. Believe me, the things they're imagining are probably much worse than the reality."

Kathleen's eyes burned. What were these people thinking of her? She hoped coming out West would be a new start for her, away from the gossip and memories of childhood. Maybe she couldn't escape the horror after all. Perhaps she should just return home and spend the rest of her life secreted in her mother's house. The thought of that miserable existence terrified her.

Mrs. Monroy eased up from the chair and stepped toward the baby beds with the sleeping Andrew, then returned. "Whatever you're hiding, I know there will be some who might make crude remarks. You can't ever escape that, Honey, but the ones who count will accept you just the way the good Lord made you." Her hand cupped Kathleen's chin through the veil. "Give them a chance."

Watching Mrs. Monroy cross the room and join the other women seated in a group, Kathleen felt so alone. Her foot tapped out the beat of the music being played in the other room. Everyone but she seemed to have a place. All her life, she'd been an embarrassment to her family. Now she had no idea how to fit in with others. Glorianna interacted with the townspeople so naturally. Kathleen didn't think she could ever do that. She would always be aware of the mark on her cheek that set her apart from others. She would never be one with these people. Even now, she could still see the women casting glances in her direction and imagined the questions they were asking Mrs. Monroy.

"There you are, Kathleen. Why are you still in here?" Glorianna sank onto a chair beside her and wiped the perspiration from her brow. "Whew, the music is so fast here. I feel like I've run a few miles, and we've only done a few dances. I don't know how I'll make it through the evening." She grinned. "Of course, I'll figure out some way."

Reaching over, Glory grabbed Kathleen's hand and tugged. "Come on. I saw Quinn with one of the new schoolteachers, looking as uncomfortable as a man can. You have to come out there and rescue him."

"He's still with her?" Kathleen sat forward. A stab of jealousy cut through her. This was ridiculous. Her plan was working, and she didn't want it to. She forced her feelings to recede and tried to look on the positive side. "I think I'll stay here a little longer. I'm sure Quinn won't mind."

"Wait a minute. What's going on here?"

"Nothing. I was in here, talking to Mrs. Monroy." Attempting to look nonchalant, Kathleen relaxed in the chair. "Besides, next to you, I'm the woman who knows the twins best. My being in here assures you a much-needed evening with your husband. Now get out there before he comes looking for you."

Before Kathleen could react, Glorianna lifted the veil, pushing it up over her hat. "You are up to something, Kathleen, and I intend to find out what. You're not going to hide from me." Glory's eyes flashed as she stared into Kathleen's eyes. "Now you tell me why Quinn would bring you to this fandango, then spend the night dancing with other women."

Glancing across the room, Kathleen could see the ladies staring in their direction. She turned her head so they wouldn't be able to see her cheek and reached to lower the veil. Glory caught her hand.

"I told you, I can't allow Quinn to be interested in me. He's not a Christian. Letting him court me is just too dangerous." Kathleen twisted her skirt in her hand. "I decided to get him interested in some of the other available young women. Then he won't want to see me."

"Kathleen, Conlon and Quinn have done quite a bit of talking lately. Did you know Quinn was raised by Christian parents? The more I hear his story, the more I believe he's a lot like me. As a child, he thought he would get to heaven because of his family connections. Then, when things got tough, he didn't have the faith he needed to stand, so he turned away from God. I agree that you can't marry a nonbeliever, but I also believe God is working in Quinn's life."

"Don't you see? I can't take the chance of being around him." Kathleen choked and couldn't continue.

Tears glistened in Glory's eyes. "Because you already care too much for him. Am I right?"

She couldn't deny the truth any longer. Kathleen nodded. "You see, even if I were free to wed, I couldn't marry someone like him, an unbeliever."

Glorianna pulled her close and gave her a hug. "I understand. Conlon and I are praying for his salvation. God can do mighty works when you trust in Him. Look what He did for me."

The line of dancers stretched before Quinn. They seemed to go on forever. Maria clung to his arm once again, smiling up at him whenever he looked her way. She was pretty, with dark hair piled high on her head and eyes that sparkled with merriment. He had seen the way some of the fellows from town watched her. Ed Fish, who rarely attended a social event, was here tonight. He hadn't taken his eyes off the schoolteacher but appeared too bashful to ask her to dance. Quinn groaned. Except for one time with Harriet, to the obvious jealousy of John Wasson, he'd spent the whole evening with Maria. He hadn't even had a glimpse of Kathleen since they'd arrived and she disappeared in the vicinity of the nursery.

He couldn't understand why Kathleen had paired him off with Maria. Although she was nice, he couldn't get her to say two words. She had to be intelligent, or she wouldn't be qualified to teach school, but so far he hadn't even learned where she hailed from. Dancing together, smiling at one another, and blushing occasionally weren't his ideas of an entertaining evening.

The music ended. In the moment of quiet, he heard a soft voice. "I believe I'd like a cup of punch."

Quinn stared at the woman standing next to him. She'd spoken a whole sentence. He smiled. "Why don't you wait with your friends, and I'll see that you get some."

He escorted her across the floor to the gaggle of giggling young ladies, then departed. Working his way through the crowd, Quinn craned his neck, looking for the person he sought. Ed stood against the wall with John, talking and watching the proceedings. Weaving around some couples, Quinn approached them.

"Ed, I need a favor." The thin man didn't look happy to see him. He must think Quinn was trying to steal the girl he liked. "I need to find Kathleen. Would you take a cup of punch to Miss Wakefield and keep her company for awhile?"

Ed pushed off from the wall, his gaze straying to the group of girls across the room. "I reckon I can do that."

Quinn turned to leave, then halted. "John, I would imagine Miss Bolton might enjoy some, also. She seems to be a little tired."

The two friends strode off in the direction of the refreshment table. Quinn grimaced. Now he had to find the girl he came with and discover why she'd disappeared. Throughout the dancing, he hadn't seen her in the hall one time. She must still be in the nursery with the babies. Usually only the older women stayed there. Why would Kathleen hide there this long? Was she that uncomfortable with people?

As he moved around the edge of the floor to avoid the dancers, Quinn returned greetings from many of the townspeople. Pondering the question of Kathleen's reason for hiding from him, he stopped at the door of the nursery room. Several women gathered across the room, their heads close together as they visited and laughed. He could hear someone speaking behind the open door and started to enter until he heard his name. Glorianna and Kathleen were talking about him. He recognized their voices. Quinn stilled, unsure whether he should leave or step into the room. He knew better than to eavesdrop, especially when he was the topic of conversation.

Before he could make a decision, he heard Kathleen's reason she was avoiding him. His lack of Christianity stood between them. Teeth clenched, he listened a moment longer. Quinn stalked to a side door and stepped outside. What difference did his beliefs make? He wouldn't keep Kathleen from believing the way she wanted. This was what he hated about Christians. If you weren't one of them, you weren't good enough. Well, he'd done just fine taking care of himself. Other than a few rough times, life treated him fine. Everyone had a few difficulties. It was to be expected.

When he realized he was pacing, Quinn forced himself to stop. The Christians he knew would use any form of trickery to get someone to accept their religion. Well, two could play at that game. What if he convinced Kathleen he believed the same as she did? He would have to be careful, but he could do it. Having been raised in a Christian household, he knew all of the lingo. He could pray with the best of them, spouting meaningless words that sounded spiritual.

Quinn moved into the open and stared up at the sky. He didn't know about God being real. God was for those who were weak and needed a crutch. He didn't need that, but he would convince Kathleen that he did. Turning to go into the hall, he ignored the prick of his conscience reminding him that men like Conlon weren't weak. Conlon recently told him he believed in Jesus because of the sin he committed—not because of a weakness. Sin could be a weakness of character, he argued silently. He didn't have that fault.

In a matter of minutes, Quinn stood in front of Kathleen. "I believe we have a dance to share." He held out his hand. She looked nervous, but accepted. To do otherwise would be rude. Leading her to the dance floor, he squeezed her hand. "I promise I'll go slow and teach you the steps. You'll be fine."

The music began, a slow melody designed to give the perspiring dancers a rest. Quinn drew her into his arms. "I know you miss having a church to attend." He ignored her start of surprise. "I heard from the wires today that a traveling evangelist is going to be here for a few weeks. I thought you'd like to go to the meetings with me."

Her sharp gasp and speechless silence were all the answer he needed. His plan was going to work.

Chapter 10

The feel of Quinn's hand on her back did disturbing things to Kathleen's equilibrium. She'd never been this close to a man other than the members of her family. The scent of soap and leather mingled together. A powerful longing to rest her head on his shoulder and surrender to the unnamed feelings sprang up inside her.

When he'd invited her to attend the evangelist meetings with him, she hadn't known what to say. Had she heard right? This independent, self-reliant man wanted to hear the Word of God? He would willingly accompany her? Somehow, his invitation didn't ring true; but she would go with him, if only to get him there. Glorianna mentioned she and Conlon had been praying for Quinn. That meant at least three people consistently prayed for his salvation. Maybe the preacher could bring the message that would touch Quinn's heart. The thought thrilled her.

"Are you always this quiet when you go out?" Quinn's low drawl close to her ear sent a shiver down her spine.

"I don't go out."

He drew away, staring at her veil as if he could see her face through the gauzy material. "What do you mean, you don't go out? Don't tell me you've never gone to a dance or at least a social of some sort."

She shook her head. "I didn't go many places when I lived at home. I went to church on Sunday morning and that was about all."

His eyes widened in amazement. "Why?"

Turning her head, Kathleen tried to think of a way to hide the truth but couldn't. Quinn had seen what she looked like. Surely he would understand her mother's position and reasoning. "You should be able to guess, Deputy. I didn't want to disgrace my family."

His mouth dropped open, and he gaped for a few minutes before he spoke. "First off, I wish you would stop calling me Deputy. My name is Quinn, and you're welcome to use it."

His eyes snapped with anger. "Second, why would you disgrace your family? You're a kind, God-fearing person. The only thing you do that's shameful is wearing this veil to cover one of the prettiest faces I've ever seen."

This time her mouth fell open. "How can you say that? You've seen my face."

"If I remember right, there's nothing wrong with how you look. Your eyes could make a man lose his sense of direction." His face reddened and he grinned.

"You've managed to make me lose my savvy. I don't know when I've paid a woman a compliment like this."

"Mr. Kirby." Kathleen paused when she saw the anger darken his eyes again. "Quinn. My parents had good standing in our community. Having a daughter with a mark on her face could have hurt their reputation. People are often unkind in what they say. My mother taught me early to cover my deformity so the family wouldn't be ostracized."

Quinn's arms tightened around her. She hadn't noticed how he was moving closer to the outer door each time they came around the floor until he swept her outside. As the last notes of the song faded, he released his tight hold but kept a firm grip on her hand.

"Let's walk for a minute. We need to talk." He growled out the words, a scowl wrinkling his forehead.

The cool night air felt good after the warmth inside. With all the dancers and crowds of people, the building had become stuffy. Kathleen took a deep breath of fresh air, trying to calm her jangling nerves. How could she explain her mother's actions to Quinn? Even Glorianna didn't understand.

"Are you telling me you've never attended a church social or been courted by a young man because your family might be embarrassed?" The muscles of Quinn's jaw clenched and loosened as he talked.

"Mr. K—Quinn, you mustn't think this was a terrible hardship. I'm glad to sacrifice for my family. I remember quite clearly the early years before Mother had the idea for me to be veiled. The children were horrible with their taunts. Sometimes they even resorted to violence against me."

The quiet stretched between them. Her fingers were becoming numb from Quinn's grip. She wasn't sure he even realized he held her hand.

"Didn't your father talk to the parents of the children who did this?"

Kathleen sighed. "That wouldn't have helped. You have to understand that the community we lived in was superstitious. Many times, people of all ages would cross to the other side of the street when they saw me coming. They kept their distance, as if the mark on me would rub off on them." She tried to keep the bitterness out of her voice.

"But the people of your church should have treated you right."

"Religious people tend to be easily swayed. They can be so eager to watch for Satan's traps that they see him everywhere rather than looking for God." Quinn nodded, and she continued. "Many of the taunts and remarks made about me originated from the people in our church. Some of them believed I was marked by the devil. 'Satan's spawn' was a common jeer the boys yelled at me."

Quinn halted and pulled her around to face him. His eyes narrowed as he studied her. "I'd like to say I'm angry with your parents for not standing up for you, but I've experienced something similar. My sister too was the brunt of jokes and pranks. My father refused to do more than pray with her and teach her Scripture that said God loved her no matter what." He looked off down the street, his thoughts seeming to be far away. "I could never understand why God would allow someone like my sister to suffer so much."

Shaking his head, Quinn said, "I believe it's high time you experienced some of the things you missed as a girl. Tomorrow I'll come by for you. I want you to be dressed for a picnic. I know a beautiful spot down near the Santa Cruz River."

Kathleen couldn't think of an argument. A picnic. She'd always wanted to go on one. Excitement made her tremble. Maybe just this once she could agree to go with Quinn and fulfill her longtime dream. As a young girl, she used to picture going on an outing with a handsome man who made her laugh and feel beautiful.

The dance was winding down. People gathered their things, preparing to go home. Kathleen hurried inside to help Glorianna with the babies. She did her best to ignore the townspeople who stared at her as she worked her way through the crowd. No matter how many years she lived, she would never get used to everyone gawking as she passed by. If she removed her veil, would they stop ogling her as Mrs. Monroy suggested, or would they then begin to sling ugly comments along with the stares?

✤

"Ouch!" Kathleen pricked herself for the tenth time this morning. Picking up a rag, she quickly dabbed at the drop of blood. The tip of her finger had never been so sore. At this rate, she wouldn't have Mrs. Monroy's new dress done for another week.

What had possessed her last night to agree to go with Quinn? The romantic evening, dancing in his arms, and his sweet compliments all caused her to lose her common sense and agree to something dangerous. Even if Quinn were to become a solid Christian sharing a like faith with her, she couldn't marry him. She could never allow that. She shuddered to think of bringing a child into the world to suffer as much as she had.

All morning she'd prayed and tried to think of a way to get excused from this afternoon's outing. Yes, she would enjoy the picnic and seeing the river, but not with someone as attractive as Quinn. He made her lose her common sense. A sudden idea made her sit up straight in the chair. She folded the unfinished dress and placed it on the table beside her. This plan just might work.

✤

Quinn stretched the wanted poster out and tacked it to the wall behind his desk. The bounty on the Veiled Widow just went up. She'd made her way to California, leaving two men dead and several more a lot poorer. The woman had to be stopped. What was the matter with the lawmen in the cities where she struck? Weren't they watching for her? Did she come to town without her disguise? If so, why couldn't anybody identify her? The only picture on the poster was that of a slender woman dressed in black, her face covered by a veil like the ones Kathleen often wore. This could be any woman.

He retrieved his hat from the rack and stepped outside. Señora Arvizu had prepared a basket lunch for him, and he'd made arrangements to rent a buggy from the stables. Whistling, he left to gather what he needed. He and Kathleen could have a picnic, and he would still be back in time to meet the evening stage. No one in Tucson could say Quinn Kirby wasn't doing his job. Protecting the citizens of this town was his first priority. A grin stretched across his face. Courting a certain hazel-eyed beauty was his second priority. He chuckled. Maybe even his third, fourth, and fifth priorities.

The smell of fried chicken wafted out of the basket next to Quinn's feet as he drove the buggy to Mrs. Monroy's boardinghouse and pulled to a stop. He jumped over the side, tied the horse, and strode up the sidewalk. He rapped on the front door, then fiddled with his hat as he waited for someone to answer. By the third knock, he realized no one was home or they were in a part of the house where they couldn't hear. Where was Kathleen? She'd said she would go with him. She'd even acted excited about the idea.

Quinn strode around the side of the house to Kathleen's shop. A bell trilled as he pushed the door open.

"I'll be with you in a minute." Kathleen's voice came from the adjoining room. She sounded a little winded. Quinn smiled. She was probably excited about the outing.

A few minutes passed before Kathleen entered the room accompanied by another younger woman, Luisa Espinosa. Quinn had seen her around town and knew her father but had never met Luisa. She appeared nervous, her hands fiddling with her skirt. Her long, dark hair was smoothed back and fastened with a bow. Long ringlets draped over her shoulders. Dark eyes peered from beneath long lashes, sought his, then glanced away. A deep gray dress hugged her slender figure, making him wonder about her age. She looked to be still in school, yet she seemed ready for a gentleman caller, so perfect were her dress and demeanor.

Kathleen, on the other hand, looked like she'd run out to the new fort and then home. Her hair straggled down in strands from the hat perched at an unnatural angle on her head. Wrinkles and a few stains marked her dress.

"Quinn, have you met Luisa?" Kathleen tried to straighten her hat and sweep up the falling tendrils of hair as she spoke. Her ministrations didn't meet with success. The instant she released her hold on the hat, it tilted sideways once more. Quinn longed to rip it off so he could see her with the shining locks falling around her face. He could imagine how charming she would look. For a moment his fingers ached to reach up and tug her hair free, allowing the heavy dark mass to float down around her shoulders. Would it fall to her waist?

"Quinn?"

He jumped. His face flamed. He'd forgotten her question.

"Quinn, are you all right?" At his nod, she asked again, "Have you met Luisa Espinosa?"

"I know her father. I've seen Luisa around town, but I don't believe we've been introduced before." He nodded at the young girl. "Pleased to meet you, Miss Espinosa."

"Luisa is here for a fitting. I'm making a dress for her and one for her mother. They want them done by next week. I also have to finish Mrs. Monroy's dress. She's talking about ordering another."

"Sounds like you're getting busy."

Kathleen's sewing business was taking off. He knew she would feel better about herself if she were able to make her own way in the world.

"The ladies here are very excited about getting the newest styles. Mrs. Monroy says they sometimes don't see the catalogs for two years after they've come out. I brought some with me, so several of the women in town have taken to dropping by and looking at the patterns."

Quinn mumbled something he hoped was appropriate. He couldn't understand women's fascination with fashion. Who cared whether you had the latest design or not? As long as the clothes fit and wore for a good length of time, what more did a person need?

"I'm told there are a couple of freighters in town who might be able to get me materials if I order by the bolt. Do you know them?"

"Of course." Quinn frowned, trying to decide who would be more likely to fill Kathleen's order. "Pinkney Tully and Estevan Ochoa would be the ones to talk to. Charles Lord and Wheeler Williams do freighting, but theirs is mostly government contracts. They haul in a lot of the lumber and outfitting for the new fort."

"Then I'll seek out Mr. Tully and Mr. Ochoa tomorrow morning." Kathleen folded her hands in front of her.

"Are you ready for our outing?" Quinn didn't want to be rude, but he could picture some dog wandering down the street and smelling that basket full of chicken. There would go the lunch his stomach was calling for.

"Oh, the picnic." Kathleen's hands crossed over her breast. "I'm not at all ready to go. In fact, with all the work I've just been given, I don't know how I can get away right now." She pursed her lips as if she were thinking. Her hands clapped. "I know. You can take Luisa with you. That food shouldn't be wasted. Luisa, are you free to go?"

At the Mexican girl's bright smile and nod, Quinn knew he'd been set up again.

Chapter 11

The last leg of chicken sat like a rock in the pit of Quinn's stomach. He glanced at the sweets Luisa popped into her mouth with great abandon and almost groaned. With maturity, Luisa would make some man a wonderful wife. Right now, she couldn't seem to think beyond the next meal to fix or the next dress to purchase.

"I just adore pink. Don't you, Deputy Kirby?" Luisa batted her impossible eyelashes and gave him a coquettish smile. "I believe I'll have Kathleen make me a gown of bright pink for next summer. With winter approaching, I prefer darker colors. Perhaps a red or even a burgundy. One with plenty of those fashionable satin ruffles. What do you think, Deputy?"

"I'm sure the young men will enjoy them. You'll be the belle at the next fandango for sure."

Luisa moved closer, careful not to leave the shade of the huge mesquite tree they rested under. "But what about you, Deputy? Will *you* enjoy seeing me in those dresses?"

Quinn tugged on the collar of his shirt. Glancing at the sun, he saw they hadn't been here nearly as long as it felt like. "I'm sure you'll be beautiful in any color, Miss Espinosa." He began to gather the food. "I hate to end the fun we're having, but I need to meet the evening stage."

Luisa laughed, a high-pitched giggle that grated like Patty McGregor's nails on the blackboard. "We have plenty of time, Quinn. You don't mind if I call you by your given name, do you?" He stared, speechless, and she continued. "The stage won't be in town for another two hours. That gives us the chance for a little stroll along the river." She simpered, "We have to do something after that delicious meal, don't we?"

Quinn rose and gave Luisa a helping hand up, trying to keep his disgust from showing. Kathleen would hear about this. He thought his plan to pretend to be a Christian was foolproof and she would fall for him in a minute. There must be some other obstacle to deal with before she would succumb. Gritting his teeth as Luisa sidled close and clung to his arm, he determined to discover the problem between him and Kathleen. He would let her know in no uncertain terms he wasn't looking for anyone else.

For another thirty minutes, he endured Luisa's chatter about clothing, styles, and colors. She talked about the fandango, how many boys she'd danced with, and how she would rather dance with him than any of them. Once she even knocked his hat into the river with her parasol. He had to clamber down the bank, soaking his best pair of boots in the process. All in all, his mood was foul and getting worse by the minute.

A steady drum of hoofbeats thundered on the road. Quinn peered toward town and saw a rider racing for them. Ed Fish pulled his big roan to a stop, scattering sand over Quinn's damp boots.

"Quinn, you got to hurry." The tall man was breathless with excitement.

Grabbing the reins of the prancing horse, dread raced through Quinn. He was Tucson's protector. What happened while he was out here wasting time?

"What is it, Ed?"

"One of Lord and Williams's wagons just pulled into town. They got attacked by Apaches and lost most of the men and all of the rigs but this one. Lord and Williams are in a bind. Those wagons carried all the supplies for the officers' housing in the new fort. The cavalry is being notified. They want to get a detachment ready to see what they can salvage."

Ed's horse pranced sideways, as if it sensed the excitement of the news. "The townspeople are riled up. They're talking about a posse. William Oury's trying to stir up trouble again."

"Ed, will you escort Miss Espinosa home for me? I'll take your horse." Quinn gestured downriver. "Our things and the buggy are in that stand of trees just down a ways. Luisa can show you."

Swinging down, Ed nodded to Luisa and offered her his arm. Quinn made his apologies and swung up onto the tall roan. As he raced away, guilt began to eat at him. He shouldn't feel so relieved when a tragedy was the reason he'd escaped such an uncomfortable situation. Never again would he escort Luisa Espinosa anywhere.

⚜

A crowd of angry men surrounded the remaining Lord and Williams freight wagon as it stood in the street outside Doc Meyer's drugstore. The team of horses was being unhitched. Their heads hung low. Looking at them, Quinn wondered if they'd even make it to the livery where Lord and Williams kept their stock.

Without dismounting, Quinn faced the angry townsmen. "Boys, I want you to go home. I'll look into this matter, as will Lieutenant Sullivan from Fort Lowell. We'll get this resolved. If we need to deputize some of you to help out, we'll be letting you know."

"What about the woman?" one of the men shouted.

Quinn glanced around. "What woman?"

"The one who was injured." Manuel spoke up from the front of the crowd. "Doc Meyer has her inside, trying to fix her up."

"I didn't know a passenger was with the freight wagons." Quinn was puzzled. How had a lady come to be with the Lord and Williams party? "I still want you gentlemen to return to your work or homes. I'll check in with Doc Meyer. We'll make an announcement about what happened as soon as we know. You might watch for the article in the *Citizen*. I'm sure John will be reporting on this."

Grumbling and talking among themselves, the crowd broke into small groups and headed in different directions. A sigh of relief escaped Quinn. He could see William Oury glaring at him as the big man stalked off, surrounded by a few of his cronies. Quinn didn't want trouble. This would be a matter for the cavalry, and Conlon would be the one to get things going.

The door of the drugstore creaked as he stepped inside. He blinked, giving his eyes a moment to adjust to the dim interior before he moved toward the rooms where Doc Meyer saw patients. Usually, Charles Lord took care of the serious injuries, having been a physician in the Civil War; but he'd traveled east to make arrangements for more government contracts. When Dr. Lord wasn't in town, everyone's welfare fell to Charles Meyer.

Low voices spoke in hushed tones as Quinn entered the room. Conlon stood on one side of an examining table and Doc Meyer on the other side. A young woman lay between them, her face waxy, her appearance disheveled. She seemed to be unconscious. Blood soaked the right side of her dress from the shoulder to the waist. Doc Meyer was in the process of cutting away the sleeve and shoulder of her dress.

"Afternoon, Conlon, Doc. Who's this?"

Conlon's smile looked more like a grimace of pain as he glanced up at Quinn. Doc Meyer kept working.

"We're not sure who she is." Conlon's words were so soft, Quinn had to step closer to hear. "The driver said she talked to the head man about riding along with the train for safety purposes. He said she kept to herself, and he hadn't even heard where she was headed for sure. She had a traveling companion—a younger woman who appeared to be a servant. The servant died in the attack. The men working with the train were told to stay away from her and her companion."

The three men studied the silent form as Doc exposed the wounded shoulder. He eased her up, exposing the exit hole for the bullet. Doc grunted. "At least I don't have to dig out a bullet. I'll get the wound cleaned and dressed. She should be fine in a few days. She'll be a little sore."

The woman groaned as Doc eased her down on the table. Sweat beaded on her forehead, but she didn't open her eyes. Her lips moved, but even when he put his ear close, Quinn couldn't make out what she tried to say. He figured she wasn't really aware of what was happening, but she wasn't all the way under, either. When Doc started working, she would probably lose consciousness completely.

Light brown waves of hair had once been pulled into a bun. Sometime during the attack or the flight afterwards, her hair had come loose. It now flowed down off the table. Lines creased the corners of her eyes. An old, jagged scar streaked across her right cheek, adding a mystique to her beauty. Her maroon traveling dress was ruined even before Doc cut the shoulder away. A maroon hat with a veil lay on the floor beside her. He assumed it had fallen there. Who was she? Why had she been traveling with freighters in dangerous territory? Where had the Lord and Williams train encountered her? Questions raced through Quinn's head at a dizzying pace with no answers forthcoming. He would have to wait to ask her until at least tomorrow. He knew Conlon had some inquiries of his own. The cavalry would need to know where the attack occurred and as much information as this woman and the driver could provide. Then they would be looking for this renegade band of Apaches.

Chewing didn't help. The bite in Kathleen's mouth refused to be swallowed. A lump in her throat blocked the way. She couldn't understand how Quinn and Conlon could eat so calmly, as if nothing unusual had happened. . .as if several men and at least one woman hadn't died a violent death out in the desert. Another woman lay in the last room at Mrs. Monroy's, severely injured. If infection set in, she could die too.

The bite seemed to grow larger. Kathleen thought she would be sick if she didn't get it out of her mouth soon. Glorianna sat across from her, pale and silent, stirring her food on her plate. She, too, had been affected by the sad story of the attack. At least the twins slept. Babies and men. Maybe the two had something in common—the ability to shrug off catastrophic events. Then again, perhaps Conlon and Quinn had had more time to adjust to the horror. She knew they felt badly for the woman who lay wounded and unconscious. Comparing them to infants who had no knowledge of right or wrong hadn't been fair.

With a force of will, Kathleen swallowed. She could feel the slow path the bite took down her throat. Closing her eyes, she hoped it wouldn't want to come right back up. Pushing away her plate of food, she took a small sip of water.

"Did the woman have any belongings with her?" Glorianna's soft question came at a lull in the men's conversation.

"The driver said they didn't have time to gather anything. He said he whipped the horses to leave, and the woman jumped to grab the wagon. She was almost up when the bullet hit her shoulder. If he hadn't grabbed and pulled her aboard, the Indians would have killed her too. I don't think she even has a valise of her personal things." Conlon frowned. "Maybe when the men and I ride out there in the morning, we can recover some of her belongings."

"It would be nice to have her regain consciousness so we can find out some more about her and her companion. I'm sure there will be others to notify. Do you think she could have been traveling here to meet someone she knew or some family?" Quinn asked.

Conlon shrugged. "Hard to say. I haven't heard anything, but then I don't have the contact with townspeople the way you do."

"Well, I don't remember anyone saying anything about expecting relatives or company." Quinn drained his coffee. "I'd better get on patrol. I want to keep an eye on some of the men. There are those who would stir up trouble just for the sake of hunting down Indians, whether they've done anything or not."

Quinn's blue-gray gaze caught Kathleen, sending a jolt of awareness through her. He studied her, then looked at Glorianna. "I apologize, ladies." Conlon seemed to follow his lead in noticing Kathleen and her cousin. His forehead furrowed.

"We've been talking about matters that are upsetting to you without thinking." Conlon reached across the table and cupped Glorianna's pale cheek. "I should have known when you were so quiet." He smiled, trying to lighten the mood. "We should have saved this discussion for later, when Quinn and I could be alone. You all right?"

A strand of Glorianna's hair tumbled down as she nodded. "I wish we could do something. Do you think Kathleen and I should take turns sitting with the woman? I'm sure Mrs. Monroy can't be there all the time."

"That's a fine idea, Sweetheart, but I think you've got plenty of your own to do. Andrew and Angelina might have something to say about you running off and leaving them—no matter how good the cause is."

"Let me get these dishes done, then I'll go right over and offer to sit with her." Kathleen rose and began to gather the plates. She hadn't meant to stay for supper, but she'd been helping Glorianna when Quinn and Conlon showed up with the news. Somehow they all ended up sitting down together, although only the men ate.

"You'll do no such thing." A bit of the old fire tinged Glorianna's tone. "The least I can do is wash up a few dishes. You go right on over and see how that woman is doing. When she wakes up, she'll need someone to be there to care for her."

"I'll walk you home." Quinn stood and reached for his hat. "I'd like to see if she's regained consciousness. Maybe she'll feel like talking a bit."

"Quinn Kirby, don't you dare tire that woman. She's been through enough."

Eyes widened, Quinn gave Glorianna an innocent look. "If she's too tired, I promise to hold off asking questions until tomorrow." He plunked his hat on his head and held out his arm to Kathleen. "Besides, Kathleen will be right there, watching to see that I behave myself."

"That's right." Kathleen bent over and kissed Glory's cheek. "Don't you worry about her. Just pray." She reached for her hat and veil, which she hadn't been wearing during the meal—proof that she was beginning to feel very comfortable with Quinn and Conlon.

A cool evening breeze made Kathleen draw her shawl closer. She hadn't expected to be out this late.

Quinn held her hand on his arm and tugged her close. Lifting her veil, he smoothed the gauzy covering over her hat. He moved around until he was gazing into her eyes. "There isn't anyone around, and I want to see your face. I believe you and I have some talking to do. I don't appreciate you sending me off with other women. I want to spend time with you, and I think we need to clear this up."

Kathleen felt a chill race through her that had nothing to do with the weather.

Chapter 12

Through the cool night air, Quinn could feel Kathleen's hesitance. He knew she didn't want to talk about her deception. She was putting up a barrier between them, and he intended to bring it down before the wall grew too high to breach. This woman was special. She cared so much for other people. He could picture her being the kind of daughter-in-law his mother would love. She had spunk, but she also had compassion and a strong faith. Even though he didn't need the faith she believed in, he had no reservations about her clinging to her beliefs.

Moonlight peeked through the trees, bathing the ground with a golden glow. The night brought quiet to this part of Tucson that was rarely disturbed. Most of the action was closer to the downtown area where the businesses were. Quinn knew he couldn't stay here long. He needed to check on the men and make sure they weren't getting stirred up unnecessarily. Walking slowly, he tried to sort his thoughts before he began.

He cleared his throat, the sound loud and coarse in the darkness. Kathleen started. He patted her hand. "I want to know why you agree to do something with me, then back out. At the fandango, you ran off and left me dancing with Maria. Today, you promised to attend a picnic with me, something you've never done with anyone before. When I came to pick you up, you had Luisa ready to go."

He could almost see Kathleen cringing at his words, but he refused to stop. "When I ask you to go somewhere with me, it's you I want to spend time with—not anyone else, I believe you've enjoyed my company. Perhaps I'm wrong, though. Are you trying to say you don't have feelings for me?"

Her head bowed as if she were mulling over her answer. Silence stretched between them as they strolled closer to the boardinghouse.

"I do enjoy your company." Kathleen tugged on her hand, which he held fast. "No matter what I feel for you, this relationship can't go anywhere other than with us as friends." Quinn thought he caught a glimmer of tears in her eyes as she met his gaze for a moment.

"Why do you say that?"

"Because we have different convictions. I follow what the Bible teaches. God says I shouldn't be yoked with an unbeliever."

"So you're saying I'm an unbeliever and not worthy of you? Isn't that a harsh judgment on your part?"

Kathleen drew back as if she'd been struck. Her eyes widened. "I'm not the

193

one passing judgment. I'm only repeating what you've said yourself."

Knowing he had to step carefully to convince Kathleen of his sincerity, Quinn thought a long moment before he spoke. "I was raised to go to church. I've read the Bible and know who God is and what He expects of His children. I do believe in God, but I also believe in the goodness of His creation, mankind. I believe God put us here on earth, and what we do with our lives is up to us. We can live right, which I think I'm doing a good job of; or we can live wrong, like a lot of folks do. I don't see that I'm any different from you."

He hadn't meant to talk so long. Convincing Kathleen they were compatible in religious matters might be more difficult than he expected, considering the hesitant look on her face. Going to hear the evangelist should show her he was right with God. After all, how did God have time or energy to direct the lives of everyone on earth? Did He really care enough to do that?

"There's another reason we can't be more than friends." Kathleen halted at the porch of Mrs. Monroy's house. She touched the mark on her cheek. "I can never marry and have children. Passing on something like this to a child would be cruel beyond measure. I can't do that."

Sadness made Quinn's heart break. "I have no idea who taught you such nonsense, Kathleen." His fingers skimmed across the chocolate mark on her cheek. "There is nothing wrong with you. Besides, there is no guarantee you would pass this on. Do either of your parents have one? Do any of your sisters or brothers?" She shook her head, her eyes lowered.

"I didn't think so. You may have a passel of children and not one of them would share that mark with you. Or, you may have one or more that do. It wouldn't matter to me. I would love them even more if they carried that part of you."

She stopped cold. "How can you say that? You have no idea what life is like when you're different. People are cruel, especially children. As long as I have a choice, I will never subject a child to the kind of life I've lived. Never."

Swiveling around, Kathleen jerked her hand from his arm. She pulled the veil over her face and ran to the door before he could stop her. Quinn didn't know whether to follow her or let her think for awhile and talk to her in the morning. A rapid succession of gunshots made the decision for him. Things were heating up downtown. He'd better make an appearance and try to cool some tempers before someone got hurt.

❦

The front door pressed against Kathleen's back as she waited to see what Quinn would do. An overpowering longing to have him come after her, declare he could make everything right, and tell her how much he loved her weakened her knees until she thought she might collapse. *Lord, why am I so attracted to this man? I tell him how I don't ever want children and why, but that's more to convince myself than him. I do want children, Lord. I love to hold Andrew and Angelina. You know how sometimes I pretend they're my own. I'm so confused. I don't know what You want me to do.*

194

Tears dripped onto her dress, leaving dark spots in the fabric. Exhaustion claimed her. Kathleen started to push away from the door when a volley of gunshots echoed from far away. Fear stilled her. Quinn. The commotion would draw him to his job. A sudden image of Quinn facing a mob of angry, armed men made her gasp. What if he were hurt? Or worse, what if he were killed?

Whirling around, she struggled to pull open the door. Her fingers, still wet from wiping away tears, slipped on the knob. With a cry of exasperation, Kathleen wrenched the door open. She rushed onto the porch, her eyes straining to adjust to the darkness. She could hear the pounding of footsteps moving fast, far down the street toward the center of town. She knew Quinn raced headlong into danger, heedless of what might happen. He believed keeping peace in this community to be his utmost responsibility, and nothing would keep him from his job. Wrapping her arms around her waist, she prayed for his safety, but mostly for his salvation. From their troubling discussion tonight, she knew he didn't fully comprehend God's plan of salvation. She hadn't felt the timing was right to share Bible teachings with him since he was so adamant about his beliefs. Now, she prayed for a softening of his heart so he would be willing to listen when God's Spirit spoke.

The night's soft breeze dried the wetness from her cheeks. She began to shiver and knew she needed to get out of the cool air. The low babble of voices in the parlor greeted her as she shut the door. Maria peered into the hall.

"There you are, Kathleen. We heard the door a few minutes ago and thought you were here, but you didn't come in. Then we heard the latch click and were just wondering if there were haunts at work." Maria's smile warmed Kathleen.

"I did come in, but then I heard some gunshots and stepped outside to see if Quinn was still here." Kathleen tried to keep the shaking from her voice. "He'd already gone."

Harriet stepped up beside Maria. "I imagine he has to stop some revelry that's gotten out of hand." She shivered and crossed her arms over her bosom. "I'll pray the Lord keeps him safe."

"Thank you." Warmth surrounded Kathleen, making the chill of the day's events ease. "How is the woman Quinn and Conlon brought here? Has she regained consciousness?"

Sadness filled Maria's eyes. "She's still not awake. Mrs. Monroy has been sitting with her most of the evening. We were going over our lesson plans for tomorrow, then hoped to take a turn with her."

"Don't worry." Kathleen held up her hand, palm outward. "I can gather some of my sewing and do my work right in her room. You get your school lessons planned." She smiled. "Besides, you two need your rest. It's hard to imagine being in charge of all those children when you're refreshed, let alone when you're tired."

After she'd grabbed a basket from her sewing room, Kathleen filled it with the dress she was working on and all the thread and necessities. Much of the evening had passed, but she knew she couldn't sleep now anyway. After hearing of the day's events and thinking about the crisis Quinn faced, she might be awake for hours.

Mrs. Monroy sat in a rocking chair next to the bed, her knitting needles held motionless in her lap. Her ample chin tilted down. Soft snores vibrated in the air. The woman on the bed lay still and pale as death. Brown, wavy hair fanned out on the white pillow beneath her head. Kathleen stared for a long moment, frozen in the doorway, until she saw the slight movement of the sheet covering the woman's chest. She still lived.

Giving herself a mental shake, Kathleen moved into the room to waken Mrs. Monroy. Quinn had told her and Glorianna that Doc Meyer had confidence the woman would be fine, but a gunshot and bleeding could never be scoffed at. This woman hadn't received immediate attention because of the harrowing ride to town on the racing wagon. Even though the ride saved her life, the jolting must have cost blood she couldn't spare.

"Mrs. Monroy." Kathleen gave the woman's shoulder a gentle shake. "Mrs. Monroy."

The older woman snorted awake, her fingers taking up the knitting needles as if she'd never stopped working. Sleep-laden eyes gave Kathleen an uncomprehending look.

"Mrs. Monroy, I've come to sit for awhile. Why don't you go on to bed?" Kathleen lifted the basket. "I'm wide awake and have some sewing to work on."

Heaving up from the rocker, Mrs. Monroy groaned as her joints popped. "Thank you, Kathleen. I haven't heard a peep from the lady. She seems to be resting fine. I couldn't find any evidence of a fever." The older woman walked with mincing steps to the door, leaned against it, and looked back at Kathleen. "If she needs something, don't hesitate to wake me. I'll be right down the hall. I have some broth in the warmer of the stove if she needs something to eat. Doc says not to give her regular food right away."

"Don't you worry. We'll be fine." As Mrs. Monroy shut the door behind her, Kathleen set the basket of sewing beside the rocker and crossed to the bed. She gave the woman's forehead a light touch but found no fever. Her steady breathing sounded clear.

A jagged scar stood out in bright relief on her pale cheek. Kathleen touched the old wound with her fingertip. What had happened to make such a scar? Had she been young then or was this a more recent mishap? Her features were pretty, but Kathleen noticed the hat and veil on the dresser. Had she too hidden her shame behind a veil?

Kathleen settled into a rocker and pulled the dress onto her lap as she listened to the woman's soft, steady breathing. The lamp on the table next to the chair gave plenty of light to see for stitching seams. The finer work would have to wait until daylight. Time sped by as she went from thinking of her growing feelings for Quinn and the dangers involved with loving him to wondering how her family fared and if they missed her. She missed her younger siblings, but being out from under her mother's negative influence had only been a relief. Guilt consumed her when she acknowledged those feelings.

Silence settled over the house as Maria and Harriet checked on Kathleen, then headed off to bed. A brisk wind rattled the windowpanes on occasion. Kathleen found herself straining to hear more gunshots as her thoughts continually strayed to Quinn. Every unusual noise set her nerves on edge.

When she pricked her finger for the fourth time because she kept drifting to sleep, Kathleen folded the dress and placed it back in the basket. She glanced a final time at the still figure on the bed, lowered the lamp wick, and rested against the rocker. Her heavy eyelids refused to stay open any longer. Peace stole over her as she drifted off to sleep.

"Water."

The hoarse whisper startled Kathleen awake. She glanced around the darkened room, wondering where she was.

"Water." The woman on the bed stirred and moaned as if the movement caused her great pain.

Raising the wick on the lamp, Kathleen crossed to the bed. Mrs. Monroy had set a pitcher of water and a cup on a night table. Kathleen lifted the woman's head, helping her to get some of the precious liquid into her dry mouth. After a few sips, the woman nodded that she'd had enough. A sigh, probably of relief, escaped as Kathleen lowered her onto the bed.

"Thank you." She sounded stronger and gave a wan smile.

"I'm sorry if I hurt you." Kathleen straightened the covers. Taking a damp cloth, she wiped the woman's brow and checked her for fever even though her clear eyes denied any weakness.

"What happened?" The woman grimaced as she tried to move.

"Stay still." Kathleen rested her hand lightly on the woman's uninjured shoulder. "Your party was attacked by Indians. You were shot. The doctor already cleaned your wound and says you'll be as good as new in a few days. Do you remember any of what happened? Can you tell me your name?"

Pale blue eyes gazed at Kathleen. Panic made her eyes brighten. She started to rise up off the bed, and her face paled with the effort. She fell back with a moan. "Cassie. What happened to Cassie? Where is she?"

Sorrow closed Kathleen's throat, making speech difficult. She swallowed. "Is Cassie the girl traveling with you?" The woman nodded. Kathleen wished anyone else were here to relay the sad news. "The man who brought you in said the other woman died. You and the driver were the only ones who survived the attack."

"No." The cry echoed through the small room. Turning her head away, the woman wept. Silent tears streamed down her cheeks.

Chapter 13

A light knock preceded Quinn poking his head around the door of Kathleen's shop the next morning. Eyes gritty from lack of sleep, Kathleen gave him what she knew had to be a tired smile. She couldn't even muster up a giddy feeling of relief to see him alive after the uncertainty of last night. Before dawn this morning, the woman, who finally identified herself as Edith Barstow, had fallen into a fitful sleep. She'd insisted on Kathleen repeating everything she knew of the attack and of the cavalry's plans to recover the bodies and belongings this morning. After Edith had fallen asleep, Kathleen barely managed to drag herself to her own room. She'd dropped onto her bed fully clothed and fallen asleep before she could pull up the covers.

"Morning. You look a little tired."

"I've had nights with more sleep." Kathleen rotated her shoulders, trying to ease the stiffness. "In fact, most nights have included more rest." She gestured at a chair. "Come on in."

Settling into the chair beside hers, Quinn reached out and took her hand. "Thank you." His blue-gray gaze held hers.

"For what?" She couldn't imagine what she'd done that made him want to thank her.

"For this." He reached out and traced her bare cheek, sending a tingle through her.

"I. . .I guess I'm so tired, I forgot." Kathleen glanced at the veil on the table with her sewing.

"Maybe you're getting used to me and don't think you need to hide anymore." Quinn smiled. Kathleen couldn't breathe. She couldn't think of a reply. For a moment she couldn't even recall why she wore a veil.

Quinn blinked. The air seemed to lighten. Kathleen felt her face flush and wished she had her veil on to hide the redness. Did he know how much his presence affected her?

"I heard the gunshots last night." Kathleen picked up her sewing from her lap, concentrating on the stitches. "Is everyone all right?"

"There was a little trouble down at the saloon. Some of the boys got to arguing about who should do what to the renegades, and shots were exchanged. No one got hurt. I guess it was their way of letting off steam." He crossed his legs at the ankles. From the corner of her eye, Kathleen could see him watching her with a smug sort of smile on his face.

"Were you worried?"

She pricked her finger. Yanking the injured digit away from the needle, she stalled for time. "I thought maybe the men would try to take vengeance themselves. Remember, you once told me about the lynchings that happened a year ago or so? I didn't know how they would take to the news of what happened yesterday." She found herself reluctant to say anything about the actual attacks. The horror, relived with Edith last night, lay fresh on her mind.

"William Oury is the main one I'm worried about." Quinn's eyes turned hard. "That man is good at organizing and getting people to do what they wouldn't normally do."

"I don't believe I've met him."

"He was at the dance the other night." Quinn seemed almost angry at the thought. "He's a big man, with a long, dour face. William always looks like he's just sucked on an early lemon."

"I take it this William is not one of your favorite people."

Quinn sighed. "I know my parents used to preach forgive and forget, but sometimes the wrongs people do shouldn't be forgotten. If you forget the evil, then you may not be ready to stop them from doing the same again."

Surprise made Kathleen pause in her work. She'd never seen Quinn so angry. Although he still looked relaxed, he was actually as tense as a cat ready to pounce. What had Oury done to warrant this kind of dislike? She wasn't sure she wanted to know.

"Back in '70 and '71, the Apaches were causing a lot of trouble." Although Quinn spoke, his eyes had such a faraway look, Kathleen didn't think he was in the room with her. She stitched while he continued. "There were a lot of raids. Ranchers and farmers outside of Tucson were hit the hardest. The townsfolk didn't get attacked because of the number of people here.

"William Oury led a party to Florence to see General Stoneman about getting help. The general said there weren't enough people in the Santa Cruz valley to warrant a cavalry troop coming down here."

Kathleen gasped. "You mean he didn't even try to help out?"

"Nope." Quinn frowned. "The raids continued. People died. Oury and some of his friends were angry. I can't fault them for that." He stopped and met her eyes. "I don't agree that the Indians were right to do the raiding and killing, but what Oury did was worse than that."

"What could be worse than killing innocent people?"

"In the spring of '71, Oury led a party of men, mostly Papagos, up to Aravaipa Canyon near Camp Grant. A group of Apaches had come to the camp, seeking refuge. The camp commander vouched for them and said they weren't responsible for the trouble."

"Mr. Oury wouldn't believe the commander?"

"I don't know why, but he decided these were the Indians responsible for all the troubles of the people in this valley. He led almost one hundred and fifty men on a dawn raid of the village."

"Didn't the cavalry troops at Camp Grant try to stop them?"

Quinn shook his head. His eyes sparked with anger. "The Apaches set up camp several miles up the creek from Camp Grant. The commander had no idea of the raid until it was over." He rubbed his eyes. Kathleen clutched the material, her sewing all but forgotten.

"All the young men were gone on a hunting expedition. Oury and his men waged war on women, children, and a few old men."

"Surely they stopped when they realized the men they thought responsible weren't there." Ice raced up Kathleen's arms. She shivered and wished for something to take the chill away.

"I told you what they did was worse than anything the Indians did. Oury and his men killed and mutilated most of the tribe. What they did to the women isn't something I can tell." He stopped, a pained expression making him look sick. "The children who weren't killed were taken captive so the Papagos could sell them as slaves."

"No." Kathleen's hand flew to her throat. "We fought a war against slavery. How could that happen?"

"That war was in the States. Arizona is a territory, and slavery among captives has been a part of Indian life for generations. Before anyone knew what happened, those twenty-eight children were already sold and taken to other places."

"Were Mr. Oury and his men punished?"

Quinn gave a harsh laugh. "Oh, they went on trial all right. The raid happened in the spring of '71, and they went on trial in December. It took the jury a whole nineteen minutes to decide they were innocent of all charges. The whole trial was a travesty of justice."

Kathleen blinked. Her eyes burned as she thought of the horrible deaths suffered because of this man and his perverted sense of justice. Quinn's hand closed over hers. She hadn't even heard him move. He raised her hand to his lips and kissed her fingers.

"I'm sorry. I shouldn't have told you that story. After yesterday's attack, I worry about what Oury will do. Conlon believes the man will let the cavalry handle the matter. I hope he's right."

A shudder raced through Kathleen. Quinn tightened his grip, his thumb tracing a path across her knuckles. She fought to keep from leaning toward him. Never had she wanted to be held as much as she did now. The desire to feel Quinn's arms around her, comforting her, strengthening her, almost overwhelmed her good sense.

⚜

Guilt filled Quinn. Why did he tell Kathleen that story? What was there about her that made him want to bare his soul? He knew the answer to that one. She not only listened; she cared. He couldn't remember meeting anyone except his mother who had such compassion. Kathleen saw what others needed or wanted, and she reached out to them. Even with a birthmark she considered a handicap, she still thought of everyone else before she thought of herself. His father had talked to him many times about that trait as being one Jesus demonstrated. Compassion for certain people came easily for Quinn. Men like Oury didn't deserve forgiveness or caring.

Kathleen's hands still trembled in his. They felt like ice, as if she were frozen from the inside out. He knew rubbing his thumbs over her knuckles wasn't enough to warm her. She needed a distraction.

"I almost forgot the main reason I came by this morning." He smiled, hoping to ease her discomfort.

"What's that?"

"I wanted to see if the woman we brought over yesterday had regained consciousness."

Nodding, Kathleen drew her hands from his. "She woke in the middle of the night. Her name is Edith Barstow. She's very bewildered. I had to tell her what happened."

"She didn't remember the attack?"

"She remembered parts of it. Her shoulder was causing her so much pain. Doc Meyer had given her something that might have left her confused too. Anyway, after I mentioned the attack, she began asking for the girl traveling with her, Cassie."

"Cassie who?"

"She didn't give a last name. For hours she cried and moaned. I thought she might be getting a fever, but she didn't feel hot. Finally, just before dawn, she dropped off to sleep."

"I'll need to talk to her as soon as I can."

"Why don't you wait here? I'll see if she's awake." Kathleen put on her hat and adjusted her veil before slipping from the room. In a few minutes she returned and beckoned to Quinn. "Mrs. Monroy gave her permission for you to go to Edith's room, although men are not usually allowed beyond the sitting room. This is a special circumstance since Edith is still too weak to get up."

The door to the woman's bedroom flew open as they approached. Mrs. Monroy came out, carrying a tray with dishes stacked on it. She leveled a stare at Quinn. "Deputy, Edith has been through a lot. I don't want you tiring her. Understand?"

Feeling like a schoolboy called up in front of the class, Quinn nodded. "I'll do my best, Mrs. Monroy. Kathleen will be there to make sure I don't ask too many questions."

Edith Barstow looked thinner than he remembered from yesterday. A strong breeze could blow her away. Although she had a trace of pink in her cheeks, her color almost matched that of the sheets. Her nightdress showed dark traces of bloodstains. The wound had bled through the bandage at some time during the night. The white line around her mouth told of her pain.

"Miss Barstow, this is Deputy Quinn Kirby. He'd like to ask you a few questions." Kathleen smoothed the hair from Edith's brow. Edith's pale eyes turned to him.

"Good morning, Miss Barstow. I'm sorry to bother you, but I need to find out what happened as soon as possible. I'm working with the cavalry, and we'd like to catch the party responsible."

A tear traced a path down her pale cheek, following the jagged line of the scar. "You're too late, Deputy. Cassie's dead. There's nothing you can do to help that."

"Can you tell me who Cassie was?"

"She was my sister." Quinn bent down to hear the whispered reply. "We'd just gotten together and were traveling to Tucson to begin a new life. Now she's gone. I tried so hard." She choked and turned her head away. An involuntary cry of pain escaped as she moved the injured shoulder.

Kneeling by the bed, Kathleen clasped Edith's hand in hers. "Can you tell Deputy Kirby about the attack, Edith? Any details you can remember will help."

Edith's chest jerked as a sob wrenched from her. "I'll try. There were so many of them. They were everywhere at once. We had just finished taking a break so the horses could have some water and a rest. That was to be the final stop before we reached Tucson. We were so close." She covered her mouth with her hand, as if to hold back the horror.

"That's fine, Miss Barstow." Quinn squeezed the rim of his hat. "Why don't you relax, and I'll talk to you later. I'll be riding out to the site of the attack with Lieutenant Sullivan and a troop of cavalrymen."

She brought her head around to stare at him with tear-drenched eyes. "Cassie. . . Will you see to her? I can't bear the thought of her lying there like that." Another sob shook her, making her face lose the bit of color she had.

"We'll see that she gets a proper burial, Miss Barstow. Don't you worry about that." Quinn slipped his hat on and caught Kathleen's attention. He motioned toward the door and she nodded.

"I'll walk Deputy Kirby out, then come back to sit with you, Edith. Is there anything you need?" Edith shook her head, and Kathleen rose to precede Quinn from the room.

In her shop, Kathleen brushed the gauze from her face and began to gather some of her sewing together, placing what she needed in a basket. Quinn could see the dark circles of fatigue around her eyes.

"Don't you think you should get some sleep before you sit with her again? I'm sure Mrs. Monroy would be happy to do that while you nap."

Kathleen gave him a tired smile and shook her head. "After all that woman has been through, the least I can do is lose a little sleep." She paused, toying with a thimble. "I felt so badly for her last night. She kept repeating how she and Cassie had gotten together and were starting a new life. I didn't know they were sisters."

"I wonder what she meant by that?"

"I don't know. She just kept saying, 'I worked so hard to get her free, and now it was all for nothing.'" Kathleen looked at him, a frown wrinkling her forehead. "I kept wondering why Cassie wasn't free before."

Quinn shrugged and reached for the door. He had to leave before he couldn't resist the urge to pull Kathleen into his arms and try to erase the tired look from her eyes. "That sounds like quite a mystery." He gave her a saucy wink that he hoped set her heart pounding and stepped out into the sunshine.

Chapter 14

Quinn sat at his desk, his head resting in his hands, staring blankly at a wrinkled wanted poster. He'd failed. His job in this town was to protect the citizens. From the talk in town and the nervous way the townspeople acted, he knew they were all upset about the raid on the freight wagons. There hadn't been an Indian attack for over a year now, but this one shook everyone. Deep down, he knew preventing Indian uprisings wasn't his responsibility, but he still felt guilty.

This also shook the foundation of his beliefs. He'd already berated himself for holding the conviction that he could take care of most anything. Lately, he hadn't been able to prevent a lot from happening. As he thought about his trust in the goodness of mankind, now he wondered how he could have allowed such a delusion. The actions of men like William Oury, who butchered innocent people and justified—even bragged—about what they had done, shook his faith. Even the Indian attacks showed the worst in man, didn't they? After they'd lived peacefully for so long, why did the Indians take innocent lives? Where was the goodness in that?

Quinn scrubbed his hands over his face. Stubbornness rose up inside him. His beliefs were right. Time had proved that mankind was basically good. Look at Kathleen, Glorianna, and Mrs. Monroy. They were charitable people. What about Conlon? Quinn couldn't ask for a better friend. He pushed away from his desk and stood. Just because a few people had no redeeming qualities in them or had moments of weakness didn't mean everyone was evil. He had to cling to that. After all, for the last eight years of his life, that idea had carried him through most anything. He refused to let himself be deluded.

He plucked the poster from his desk and turned to tack the picture next to the poster of the Veiled Widow on the wall. The woman seemed to stare out at him, the mocking smirk on her face hidden by the dark covering. Still, he knew the taunt was there. She thought no one would find her, but she was wrong. Someday she would make the mistake of coming to this town, and he would be waiting. He could feel her evil in his bones. She was close, and he had to be ready.

The door swept open. Early morning chill rushed in as Conlon stepped through. "The men are waiting for us. You about ready to go?" Conlon's serious expression told of the grimness of the expedition. They were riding out this morning to bury the bodies of those killed in the attack and recover any belongings they could.

Quinn couldn't help the heaviness weighing him down as he followed his friend out the door. Riding out of town, the cavalry troop stayed silent as if they were already displaying a respect for the dead. Even the clink of bridles and the creak of leather sounded loud in the early quiet. At the end of the column, a wagon loaded with shovels and picks lumbered after them.

Vultures wheeling in lazy circles marked the site of the attack. The men could see their destination long before the grisly scene came into view. Most of them covered their mouths and noses with their neck scarves. Despite the relatively weak winter sun, the smell wasn't pleasant.

Conlon split up the men, directing some to begin digging graves while others would help gather any salvageable belongings. They would trade off jobs to relieve those using shovels in the difficult desert soil.

Quinn followed Conlon past the bodies of teamsters, some with arrows still protruding from them, most dead from gunshot wounds. Quinn knew that, like him, Conlon searched for Edith's sister. What if the woman hadn't been killed during the attack? What if the Indians had taken her captive? Would they be able to rescue her? A shiver ran down his spine as he recalled the stories of the Oatman family who was attacked by Mohave Indians in 1851. The two girls survived the attack and were taken captive. Years later, their brother rescued Olive from the Indians. Her sister died in captivity. Olive's beauty was ruined by the facial tatoos the Indians forced on her. He could only imagine the horror she had lived through. He didn't want Miss Barstow's sister to have to suffer in a similar way.

"Here, Quinn." Conlon stopped on the other side of a group of rocks. His face paled under his tan.

The sour taste of bile filled Quinn's mouth. He'd seen death plenty of times, but the young girl sprawled on the ground beside the rocks was the worst. She couldn't have been much older than his sister. Even in death, her face bore a look of innocence. The gunshot through her chest must have caused an instant death. Quinn breathed a sigh of thanks for that.

"Look at this." Conlon motioned to her arm and her neck where the dress had torn. Greenish-yellow bruises marred her skin. Conlon frowned. "Someone hasn't treated this girl right."

Quinn shuddered. "Who would do such a thing? She looks as if she's been choked and beaten sometime in the last few weeks." A shawl lay on the ground near the girl. Quinn picked it up and covered her exposed limbs the best he could.

"We'd best have some of the men move her down to the burial site. Then we can start looking for any belongings the Indians left behind. I'm hoping to find the bags these two women were carrying."

"I've thought of that, too." Quinn nodded in agreement. "Miss Barstow will feel a little better if we can find something of her sister's for her to hang on to."

For the next hour, Quinn and Conlon searched through the goods strewn across the landscape. Most of the foodstuffs had disappeared, and the other things were badly damaged or destroyed. Some of the wagon pieces had been piled together and set afire. A pall of smoke still hung heavy in the air, making Quinn's throat ache long before they finished their search.

"Here, Sir." One of Conlon's men gestured from across the battle scene. They hurried over, slipping on the rocky ground.

"Would these be the ladies' bags, Sir?" The soldier gestured to two valises, their sides scraped and covered with dirt. "I found them under the pieces of this dresser. This must have fallen off a wagon and covered the bags. No one saw them."

Conlon knelt down and opened the closest satchel. A pile of feminine clothing, scented with a faint lavender, showed these indeed belonged to Miss Barstow or her sister. Conlon straightened.

"Thank you, Kent." He nodded to the young soldier. "Why don't you load these on the wagon, and we'll see that they get to Miss Barstow when we return to town."

Kent carried the two satchels down the hillside. Conlon and Quinn gazed at the wreckage around them. Many of the articles had been furniture items for the new fort. This would set them back as they waited for more to be shipped.

Conlon gathered what little sign of the Indians he could find. He and Quinn discovered where the raiding party had approached the unsuspecting wagon train and where they rode off after the raid, their horses heavier for all the extra food they carried. All the teams were missing too—probably taken by the Indians.

"Ready to go?" Conlon looked as gritty as Quinn felt. They watched the column of smoke from the burning goods ascend. "I could use a bath and some cool water." A sad smile creased Conlon's face. "I could also use some time with my family. Somehow, after seeing something so horrible, I always want to hold Glory and now the babies too." He acted embarrassed at having said something so personal. "I suppose that sounds funny to you."

"Not at all." Quinn swung up into the saddle. "The only thing that's kept me going this last hour is the thought that I'll get to see Kathleen this evening." He could feel his face flush and wondered at his temerity in letting Conlon know of his interest in Glorianna's cousin.

"You two getting pretty close?" Conlon signaled for the men to fall in behind them as they moved out into the road.

Heat ran down into Quinn's collar. "I just admire her spunk. She's been through a lot and is the most caring person I've ever met. In her shoes, I think I might have ended up bitter and angry at the world."

"That's true." Conlon frowned. "From what Glory's told me, Kathleen went through a lot with the people in their neighborhood, but the worst came from her mother."

"Her mother?"

"Yep." Conlon shook his head. "It's pretty sad, but her mother was so

206

ashamed of Kathleen, that she kept her hidden away from the world. Kathleen wasn't allowed to go to school with the other kids or do anything they did. Church was the only function she could attend outside the house, and then she had to wear a veil. It's no wonder she's afraid to let people see her face."

"I don't understand a mother who would do that to her own child." Anger coursed through Quinn. His horse danced sideways.

"Glory says in some perverted way, Kathleen's mother thought she was protecting her from further harm." He shrugged. "That's in the past. I'd like to see Kathleen become comfortable with her looks. It will take time and patience."

"I intend to have plenty of those." Quinn grinned and urged his horse to a faster walk. All this talk about Kathleen made him long to see her. He had to continue convincing her that his beliefs wouldn't stand in the way of their relationship. Tomorrow would be the first service with the evangelist who'd arrived two days ago. Quinn planned to check with Kathleen tonight, letting her know he would pick her up in plenty of time to make the meeting.

⚑

Kathleen hummed a soft melody as her needle flew through the shiny material of the dress she was making for Mrs. Monroy. She should have this finished in time for her landlady to wear it to the evangelist's meeting tomorrow. The steady pace of her needle matched Edith's soft breathing. A couple of hours ago, Doc Meyer had come by to check her wound. The pain from changing the dressing had been enough to make Edith faint. An angry red was beginning to surround the wound, and Doc Meyer left a powder to make a poultice twice a day for her shoulder. He also gave her laudanum to help her sleep.

"Rest will be the best healing agent." His gravelly voice made him sound gruff, but Kathleen could see the caring underneath the stern exterior. "Don't let her move any more than she has to. We don't want to aggravate the wound."

At a light knock on the door, Kathleen set aside her sewing, lowered her veil, and opened up to see who had come. Quinn stood in the hall, freshly scrubbed and shaved. He looked so handsome, her breath caught in her throat and she couldn't speak. She brushed the gauze out of the way. Quinn held her gaze for what seemed an eternity before gesturing to the floor beside him.

"I brought some things I believe might belong to Miss Barstow. We found these two bags of ladies' clothing. I thought she would want them right away."

"Come on in, Dep. . .Quinn. Does Mrs. Monroy know you're here?" Kathleen glanced down the hallway toward the sitting room.

"Yep, she's the one who let me in. She said Miss Barstow is sleeping." He picked up the bags and stepped inside the room.

"Yes, Doc Meyer gave her something to help her rest. I don't know when she'll wake up." Kathleen could see the disappointment on Quinn's face. "Did you have something you wanted to talk with her about?"

"Nothing particular. Just a few more questions. I figure I can't ask too much at one time, so I'll come by every day to interview her a little. How's the wound healing?"

"Doc's worried about infection setting in. He showed me how to treat the wound." Kathleen tried to hide her uncertainty. "I've never done anything like this. I worry about hurting her instead of helping."

Quinn placed the bags at the foot of the bed. Following behind him, Kathleen wasn't prepared for him to turn around so fast. They were only inches apart. She couldn't breathe. She could see that he wanted to hold her in his arms as much as she wanted to be held. Silence stretched as taut as a rope. The only sound in the room was Edith's steady breathing.

His hand, warm against her cheek, startled, then thrilled Kathleen. She hadn't noticed him reaching up to touch her. Never had she felt like this about anyone. *Why now, Lord? Why Quinn?* Kathleen closed her eyes and stepped away. She couldn't let this happen. Somehow, she had to discourage him. Guilt ripped through her as she watched pain flash across his face. She didn't want to hurt him.

His hand dropped to his side. "I'm sorry. I didn't mean to offend you. For the last few hours, all I've thought about is looking at you and touching you. You are so beautiful, Kathleen, so alive."

Understanding jolted her. He'd spent the day out at the site of the attack. After viewing all that death, he needed comfort. How could she deny him that? Would it be so wrong in this instance? Kathleen ignored the check in her spirit and stepped closer to Quinn.

"I'm sorry, too. I misjudged your intentions. After what you've been through today, I can see why you need a person's touch." She reached up and traced her thumb along his strong jaw. His eyelids lowered. His hands caught hold of her upper arms, drawing her to him. Like a moth drawn to a flame, Kathleen couldn't seem to stop him as he lowered his head to hers. She closed her eyes. In the back of her mind, she wondered what her first kiss would be like. Never before had she allowed herself to even dream of such a thing happening.

Quinn's lips settled over hers in a warm caress. He slid his hand around her, drawing her even closer. Time stopped. A wonderful feeling of contentment settled over Kathleen. She didn't ever want this to stop.

"Kathleen, is that deputy still in there?"

At the sound of Mrs. Monroy's voice, Kathleen jerked away as if she'd been burned. Her cheeks felt on fire. Quinn gave her a lazy smile that made her heart sing.

Chapter 15

Tugging his string tie to tighten it, Quinn gazed at his image in the mirror. Clean shaven, his hair a little damp from the bath, he looked ready to pick up Kathleen for the church meeting. He didn't feel ready. What he was about to do would break his parents' hearts. They'd always taught him deception was the same as lying. A sin. He hadn't thought of that word in years.

I'm not deceiving anyone. Quinn wasn't sure who he tried to convince. *Religion is important to Kathleen. She is important to me. Because of that, I can go with her to church and make this sacrifice. After all, I do believe in God. Someone had to make this world. All I'm doing by going to this church meeting is supporting the woman I care about.* Quinn stared at his reflection. He could read the guilt still present in his eyes. He turned away, grabbed his hat, and dusted off the brim. Settling it on his head, he stalked out of the room. He wouldn't allow these feelings to interfere with what he planned to do. He wasn't doing anything wrong. Wincing at the prick in his conscience, Quinn shoved the feeling deep inside, where he hoped it wouldn't surface again today.

The packed meeting hall showed how much the townspeople missed regular church services. For the last three days, the evangelist had been scouring the town, encouraging everyone to come to his meetings and hear the Word of God. A buzz of excitement filled the room as men and women settled onto hard benches.

Quinn steadied Maria's elbow as they inched through the crowd to find a seat. Harriet and Kathleen followed behind. Once again, Kathleen had managed to pair him up with a girl he didn't want. Maria was nice enough. So was Harriet, but neither one could hold a candle to Kathleen. At least, that was his opinion. Ed Fish and John Wasson seemed to have other ideas. The two glowered at Quinn from across the room. They must think he had orchestrated this himself, leaving them out when he knew they were interested in the new schoolteachers. They couldn't be more wrong.

Part of an empty bench showed up on the left. Quinn directed Maria down the aisle. There should be enough room for the four of them if they sat close together. He fought a smile at the thought of sitting close to Kathleen. Quinn began to urge Harriet in beside Maria. She stopped, waiting for him, a smile on her face. Kathleen was nowhere in sight.

With a groan, Quinn stepped in next to Maria and waited for Harriet to take her place on the other side of him. Ed and John would believe for sure that he had designs on their girls, even though they hadn't declared their intentions.

"Where did Kathleen go?" Quinn tried to keep his distance when he asked the question.

Harriet didn't have the same reservations. She almost rested against his arm, holding her fan in front of her face as if to hide something. "She went to help Glorianna with the babies. Conlon got stopped by some of the men outside, and Glorianna couldn't handle them alone."

How had this woman known so much, when he hadn't even realized Kathleen left them? Quinn sighed and glanced across the crowded room. He caught sight of Conlon moving down the outside aisle, then saw Glorianna seated beside Kathleen, each of them snuggling one of the twins. As Conlon reached his wife, Quinn prepared to stand and beckon to Kathleen so she would know where they were sitting. Kathleen seemed to refuse Conlon's offer to take the baby. She looked across the room at Quinn and waved. She had made her choice of with whom to sit. Because of the veil covering her face, Quinn couldn't even see if she was disappointed or happy that they were apart.

For a moment, Quinn considered getting up and leaving before the meeting started. After all, he'd come here to prove to Kathleen that they were compatible despite their different beliefs. "Well, getting up and leaving won't prove a thing to her." He mumbled the words to himself.

"Did you say something?" Harriet's shoulder touched his as she spoke. Quinn could almost feel John's gaze burning into his back. How would he ever get out of this one?

"Nothing." Quinn shook his head at her.

The hum of conversation died as the evangelist stepped up on the platform. A slight breeze from Harriet's fan slid across Quinn's face. The moving air felt good. There were too many people crowded into this closed building. Already, the warmth made Quinn want to loosen his collar. By the end of the service, this many bodies would smell worse than a pack of javelinas.

The preacher greeted the crowd, introducing himself in case some of the people hadn't met him yet. He began to speak, and Quinn shut him out, choosing to let his mind wander to other things. As a boy, he'd heard enough sermons to last him a lifetime. Of course, in those days, he hadn't listened much, either. He spent most of the time ogling the girls or daydreaming about the plans he had to leave home and become a lawman. Those plans had been fulfilled.

The crowd laughed, and Quinn glanced in Kathleen's direction. Despite her veil, he knew she watched his reaction to the message. He'd better at least try to look interested and react the same way the crowd reacted. That shouldn't be too hard. He smiled, and she faced forward once again.

"I want to spend my time talking to you folks about whom you trust." The preacher pulled out a rag and wiped it across his beaked nose. "I've found something disturbing as I've traveled across the West." He glared out at the congregation as if accusing them of a terrible crime. "People out here trust in a lot of things, but they don't trust in the Lord."

One elbow on the pulpit, the preacher pointed in Quinn's direction. "Over here I see your fine deputy. I haven't met him yet, but I've heard about how he cares for this community. After talking with folks about him, I'm sure the deputy feels responsible for your welfare. He takes that charge seriously."

Sweat dribbled down Quinn's spine. People turned to stare at him as he sat between the two schoolteachers. Why was this man singling him out?

"I'm sure you folks think you can trust this deputy to provide protection for you and your families, and you can. . .to an extent."

Jaw muscles tense, Quinn fought the anger burning inside him. Had this preacher just sullied his name and reputation?

"Then, there's this fine lieutenant over here."

All heads turned in Conlon's direction.

"The other day, he and his men performed a horrible duty. I'm sure you all know about the attack, so I won't go into that. Your community is blessed to have the cavalry here to help watch out for you. I'm sure they do their best to avoid incidents like the one that happened this past week. You can trust in them. . .to an extent."

A murmur passed over the crowd. Heads moved close together as everyone seemed to wonder at the unusual way this man made his points. Quinn glanced over at Conlon, expecting to see anger. Instead, Conlon and Glorianna both had smiles on their faces. Didn't they realize what this man had said? He might be causing the whole town to doubt their ability to protect and defend. Quinn clenched his fists, longing to leave this place before he enacted violence on the preacher.

"I'd like to look at a problem the Israelites had with their protection." The evangelist peered over the pulpit, rubbed his nose, and smiled at the crowd. "You see this problem has been around since God first revealed Himself. The Israelites, during the days of Joseph, went to live in Egypt. I'm sure you remember that story. Well, there came a time when God wanted His people to leave Egypt and trust in Him. That introduced a load of suffering." He chuckled and stepped around the pulpit. Absolute silence filled the hall.

"The Israelites liked putting their trust in the Egyptians. Those Egyptians had fancy chariots and plenty of them. They had horses that were trained for war. And their horsemen had such strength everyone marveled at them."

A baby wailed. Quinn glanced at Kathleen and saw her jiggling the infant she held, probably Andrew. He could tell from the blanket. The crying ceased.

The preacher stepped behind the pulpit again. He looked down at the Bible he'd placed there. "I'd like to read a verse from the book of Isaiah the prophet in the thirty-first chapter. 'Woe to them that go down to Egypt for help; and stay on horses, and trust in chariots, because they are many; and in horsemen, because they are very strong; but they look not unto the Holy One of Israel, neither seek the Lord!' "

Looking up, the preacher gave a moment for the words to sink in. "Isaiah says later in the chapter that the Egyptians are not gods. Their men and horses are only flesh and blood. The Israelites weren't wrong to trust in the Egyptians and their tools partially, but God says don't forget to seek Him. You folks can trust in your cavalry and your deputy. That's a good idea, because these fine people will do their best to protect you from harm.

"But they are only flesh and blood. Put your trust in the Lord, Jesus Christ, who is able to always take care of you. I tell you today, He is not flesh and blood; He is God, and He is worthy of your trust."

The rest of the evangelist's words buzzed past Quinn without him hearing them. This teaching was wrong. He knew for a fact that God did not always protect His people. He didn't always have their best interests at heart. How could this man stand up there and say these things? Gripping the side of the bench, Quinn held on to keep from jumping to his feet and shouting out the hypocrisy of the message spoken here.

At the end of the service, Quinn excused himself from Maria and Harriet. Pushing through the crowd, he approached Ed and John. The two gave him looks that would make him cringe at another time. He ignored the animosity.

"Ed, John, would you two mind escorting Miss Bolton and Miss Wakefield home?"

Surprise gave the pair a startled look. They nodded, and Quinn once again pushed off through the crowd. People were milling around, chatting about the message and how wonderful this speaker was. Quinn couldn't believe how gullible they were. No wonder the Bible called these people sheep. They couldn't even see the truth for themselves.

Several men clapped Quinn on the back in greeting. He nodded and pushed past them, working his way toward Conlon. As he arrived, Glorianna and Kathleen stepped into the aisle.

"Conlon, could you give Kathleen a ride home?" Quinn almost winced at his harsh tone.

"Why, sure." Conlon shot a surprised glance at his wife.

Quinn didn't wait to see Glorianna's or Kathleen's reactions. Once more, he set off through the gaggle of people. He wanted to mow them down to get outside and away from here. Getting free couldn't happen fast enough. Shutting out all sound and focusing on the door, Quinn plowed through the mass of townsmen, heedless of the startled glances he received. Let them wonder what his hurry was. He didn't care.

The nip of winter in the air outside chilled the sweat on Quinn's face. He searched the yard for the horse and buggy he'd brought the women in. He should have offered Ed and John the use of the buggy in case they had walked or come on horses. For a moment, he pondered going inside to see if they needed the conveyance. One glance at the crush behind him and he banished the idea.

"Deputy Kirby." Mayor Allen grabbed his hand and stopped him. Quinn cast a longing glance at the buggy waiting for him. The mayor pumped his hand like he wanted to get well water to flow. "Good to see you here, Deputy. Mighty fine sermon today."

"Yes, Sir." Quinn tried to extract his hand. People were beginning to pour out of the building. He had to get away from here. The sense of urgency was overpowering.

"I heard about that woman you rescued from the wagon train attack. Fine piece of work. That's why we hired you."

Confused, Quinn stopped and gazed at the mayor. "But, Sir, I didn't rescue her. One of the drivers brought her to town."

"That's not the story I heard." Mayor Allen beamed. People were stopping to listen, and he continued. "I heard you carried her into Mrs. Monroy's house, and you've been there several times to check on her welfare. I'm proud to have a deputy who does his job so well."

An embarrassed flush burned Quinn's cheeks. Had the whole town been talking like this? They didn't know the real reason he went to Mrs. Monroy's so often was to see Kathleen. Yes, he wanted to hear Miss Barstow's story, but her account wasn't that important. He'd already heard the driver's story. Miss Barstow couldn't have much to add other than the reason she'd been traveling with her sister.

People crushed up against him, shoving him close to the mayor. "Sir, I'll stop by and discuss this with you tomorrow." Sunlight glinted off the shine on the top of Mayor Allen's head. Quinn pulled his hand free. He started to step away.

"You do that, young man." Mayor Allen beamed in his direction. "I'll be looking forward to a full report from you. I want to hear how you single-handedly ran off those Indians and rescued that young woman."

Quinn stopped. His mouth fell open. A murmur ran through the people standing outside. What would they think? What stories would be passed around the town now? Gritting his teeth, Quinn strode across the yard and yanked the reins free. The horse jerked its head away from him, startled at his quick movement.

"Easy, Girl." Quinn calmed the horse, then stepped around to the side of the buggy.

Quinn felt someone touch his arm. He almost groaned aloud. Not another person thinking he was some kind of hero. Looking down, he stared in shock at Kathleen standing beside him. Through the gauze of her veil, he could make out a shadowy smile.

"Conlon and Glorianna are taking you home." He gestured at the hall. "I'm sorry; I have to leave."

"Do you have an emergency?" Her soft voice touched a chord in his heart.

"No, I just need to go."

"Then I'm going with you." Kathleen stepped around him and lifted her skirts to step into the buggy. "I came to the meeting with you, and I'll return with you."

He stared up at her as she folded her hands in her lap. Blocking her face with her hand, she lifted her veil a bit and smiled at him. "Are you coming?"

Chapter 16

Gripping the seat between them, Kathleen did her best to maintain her balance as the buggy raced down the street. The muscles in Quinn's jaw stood out in tense relief, a testimony to the anger he must be trying to hide. What had upset him so? She could still recall the urgent feeling that raced through her when he asked Conlon to take her home. God had spoken to her heart as if in audible words, letting her know she had to go with him. She didn't know what she was to say to Quinn, but the Lord wanted her here for a reason.

The buggy careened around a corner and raced out of town. Kathleen wasn't sure where they were going, but this wasn't the way to Mrs. Monroy's boarding-house. Relieved that Maria and Harriet weren't with them, she clung to the rocking conveyance, praying they would stop soon and that they would be safe.

As the bank of the Santa Cruz River approached, Quinn pulled on the reins, slowing the horse. He turned off the road and guided them into a small stand of trees. Sweat coated the horse's hide. The bay tossed her head, jangling the bridle and sending a long string of saliva into the air. Kathleen thought the poor horse wasn't used to being treated this way. Quinn swung down and tied the mare where she could reach some grass.

"I still can't get used to such mild weather this late in the year." Kathleen noted the way Quinn jumped at the sound of her voice as if he'd forgotten he'd brought her. "Back home we'd have ice on the ponds—even snow—and each person would be wearing enough clothes to cover two families." She almost hated resorting to such inane conversation, but she had to break the silence between them.

The anger in Quinn's eyes eased somewhat. His forehead smoothed. Kathleen breathed a little easier. Whatever had upset him must have happened during the service. Had the preacher said something? She couldn't think what. The message had been one of the best she'd heard in a long time.

Quinn crossed to her side of the buggy and reached up to help her down. Her feet settled on the ground, but Quinn kept his hold on her longer than necessary. His eyes, more gray than blue today, gazed at her. She could almost see the pain inside and wondered anew at the cause.

Kathleen unpinned her hat and placed the veiled head covering on the buggy seat. Once more, she looked up at Quinn, wishing he'd know he could talk to her. She didn't want to appear to be hiding.

"Quinn, what's wrong?" She thought to reach up and touch his cheek as she had the night before, but the memory of the kiss they shared still startled her. If she did that again, she would seem forward, and that would be the wrong impression to give.

His eyes darkened. Quinn turned toward the meandering river, his jaw tense once again. Kathleen grasped his arm, hoping he wouldn't storm off, leaving her here.

"Did the preacher say something that bothered you?"

Quinn's body jerked. She could feel his muscles tighten. His fists clenched.

"He said a lot that bothered me. In fact, he didn't say much of anything I liked. I have no idea how people could sit and listen as he insulted everyone there."

"I didn't hear him insult anyone." Kathleen tried to remember the preacher's exact words to see if there was something she'd missed. Her hand slipped from Quinn's arm as he strode over to the riverbank. Lifting her skirts to clear the brush, she followed at a slower pace.

Whirling around, Quinn faced her. Deep lines dug into his forehead. His eyes flashed. "Didn't you hear what he said about Conlon and me? We do our best to protect the people in this town, and this man comes along and kicks us in the teeth. On top of that, the people applaud him for it. I felt as if no one cared whether I do my job or not."

Shock raced through Kathleen, robbing her of speech. Quinn felt his credibility had been attacked. Being a lawman was his life, and he took his duties seriously. Now, the work he'd devoted his life to had been questioned. Even if no one else in the service this morning viewed the pastor's words that way, Quinn did. His anger covered a multitude of hurts.

"Another thing." The muscles in Quinn's jaw jumped as he spoke. "That man didn't know what he was talking about."

"Why is that?" Kathleen kept her tone soft, hoping to ease Quinn's distress.

"He said that God would protect us when we needed protecting." Quinn started to rake a hand through his hair and knocked his hat to the ground. He picked the hat up and banged it against his leg. "That was a lie. I know for a fact God doesn't protect those who love Him. He allows all sorts of bad things to happen to them, and no one ever knows the reason. It's as if He can do whatever He wants and we, insignificant as we are, aren't to question Him."

Oh, Lord, how do I answer all these years of hurt and anger that he's allowed to build up? I feel You are speaking to Quinn's spirit. Otherwise, he wouldn't be so angry over this message. Please, give me the words to answer him. Help me to reach out in the right way. Kathleen waited for God to give her the wisdom to speak, but nothing came. She could only watch as Quinn turned away and stared across the river to the fields beyond.

Stepping up beside him, Kathleen took Quinn's hand in hers. This might be a bold move, but she knew he needed someone right now. If he wanted to talk, she would listen. If he wanted to stand quiet and be angry, she would stand with him and pray. Until God gave her the words, she would be silent and wait.

Long moments passed in silence. When Kathleen was almost ready to concede nothing would happen, Quinn began to speak. She held still in order to catch his quiet words. He told her the story of his sister, how she'd been different, but everyone learned to accept her as she was. Then, the new family moved in. The torment began. Bitterness made Quinn's voice harsh as he told her the story of Rupert Magee and his own part in saving Elizabeth from the bully.

"So you see, my sister loved God. My parents loved God. At that time I thought I loved God." His mouth twisted in a grimace. "All that love didn't help her at all. God refused to protect her."

"Did the boy hurt her permanently?"

"No, the bruises and cuts would heal. She could even get over the cruel taunts." Quinn's hand gripped hers so hard her fingers were going numb. He looked down at her and cupped her chin with his other hand. He stared with an intensity that was hard to face. "Don't you see? A God who protects His people should always be there for them. How would I look if I allowed bad things to happen one time and not the other? I wouldn't be a very good deputy, and I would lose my job." He shook his head. "Well, that's what happened to God. As far as I'm concerned, He lost His job."

Tears burned in Kathleen's eyes. She lowered her lids to try to hide them. How she wanted Quinn to believe in Jesus. He needed the comfort of a Savior now more than ever. A wave of compassion washed over her. All these years, Quinn hid his love for God behind indifference and anger. His hurt now was because he truly wanted to trust God, but felt he couldn't.

"Quinn, maybe you should talk to the preacher. Tell him why you disagree with him." Kathleen refused to release his arm as he tried to turn away. "Quinn, if you were doing your job and someone disagreed with what you'd done, would you want them to be angry at you or come to you for an explanation of why you acted in the manner you did?" Afraid to even breathe, Kathleen waited to see if Quinn would understand the analogy.

Emotions played across his face like clouds across a sky on a windy day. When his eyes met hers again, she could see understanding and a sort of peace. He ran his thumb across the reddish-brown star. Her heart began to pound. She thought he might try to kiss her again. She didn't know whether to lean toward him or back away.

"Thank you." He smiled and the air warmed between them.

Her heart pounded. "What are you thanking me for?"

"For this." He stroked her bare cheek again with his thumb. "For caring enough to come with me when I was so angry. For reminding me of the right thing to do." He pulled her close and rested his cheek on the top of her head. "I'll go talk to the preacher. I don't expect anything to come of it, but I'll give him a chance to explain."

Kathleen drew away. "I'd better get home. I need to check on Edith. We all left her alone while we went to church. She'll need someone there soon to tend her needs."

"Do you think she's strong enough for me to talk with her?" The serious expression of a lawman changed Quinn's demeanor. "I'd still like to ask her some questions about her sister and herself. Maybe I can find out if she wants me to notify anyone of her sister's death."

Sadness tugged at Kathleen. "She's taking the news hard. I think even though she knew her sister probably died in the attack, she still held out a hope you would bring her back alive when you and Conlon rode out to the site. She says she has a black dress for mourning in her things, and I promised to help her change this afternoon."

Quinn slipped a hand under her elbow to steady her on the uneven path. The horse lifted its head and nickered at their approach. "I think she wants to get to the stable for her oats." Quinn helped Kathleen climb into the buggy. "I'm afraid she'll be disappointed to find out she isn't going straight home."

On the ride to town, Kathleen didn't have to hang on tight. The slower pace and the closeness to Quinn made a heady combination. She didn't want the ride to end even though she knew they had no chance together. That small, rebellious part inside her longed for a relationship with Quinn, marriage, and a family of her own. No matter how hard she tried to rid herself of those desires, they were buried deep and would come to the surface at all of the wrong times.

Now was one of those times. She could picture Quinn with a son or a daughter. Pride would shine from him. He would make a good father. Even now, he took the time to talk to them and play with Andrew and Angelina. Unlike many unmarried men, he wasn't afraid of holding the small babies. Kathleen sighed at the picture her thoughts made and pushed the impossible dreams away.

The boardinghouse echoed when they walked inside. As they drove into town, they'd seen Maria and Harriet walking down the street with Ed and John. They were going to Señora Arvizu's for supper. The foursome looked like they belonged together. Quinn had shot Kathleen a warning look as if to let her know she couldn't set him up with either of them again.

Mrs. Monroy had informed all the girls before church that she would be going to a friend's house after the service. She wouldn't be home until after the evening meal, so they would have to find something to eat themselves.

Opening the door to Miss Barstow's room, Kathleen stuck her head in, hoping she wouldn't be waking her. Doc Meyer insisted Edith needed a lot of rest from all her blood loss. When Kathleen peered around, Edith rolled over to look at her. Her swollen, red eyes told of the crying she'd been doing.

"Edith?" Kathleen slipped into the room, blocking the door so Quinn would have to wait until she had permission to let him in. "The deputy is here to talk to you. Do you think you can manage?"

"Could I wash a little first?" Edith wiped at her eyes with a hanky.

Kathleen relayed the message to Quinn, then slipped in to help Edith. By the time Quinn entered the room, Edith had pillows behind her to help her sit up a little, her face was washed, and her hair combed. She hadn't tried to cover the scar on her cheek, although she did turn her head to the side, as if to hide the blemish from them.

Amazed, Kathleen listened as Quinn questioned Edith in such a gentle manner that she didn't get very upset. He answered her questions, her main concern being that her sister hadn't been tortured or suffered, but had died quickly.

"Do you mind telling me why you and your sister were traveling to Tucson with a bunch of freight wagons rather than waiting for the stage?" The chair Quinn sat in creaked as he moved.

Picking at the blankets covering her, Edith avoided his gaze. Her face paled even further, causing the scar to stand out like a jagged bolt of lightning on a dark night.

"Is there someone you'd like me to notify? Your parents?" At Quinn's gentle question, Edith's eyes widened in horror.

"No." She tried to sit up, cried out in pain, and dropped onto the pillow. "No. He'll kill me if he finds out. Don't tell anyone."

Chapter 17

Clicking open Edith's valise, Kathleen glanced at the woman asleep on the bed. Edith started to move, moaned, and lay still again. She'd been so distraught after Quinn's question about notifying the family, Kathleen feared she would tear open her wound. After doing her best to calm the woman, she finally gave her some of Doc Meyer's medication to help her sleep. Then she shooed Quinn out of the house and sat by Edith's bed, assuring her everything would be fine, praying she told the truth.

Once again questions raced through her mind. Who was the man who would be angry enough to kill Edith if he found out what happened? Had her sister been a favorite and their father would be so grief stricken, he would resort to violence even though the girl's death hadn't been Edith's fault? What comfort could she offer Edith? Prayer came to mind, so she petitioned God while Edith sank into a fitful sleep.

Earlier in the day, Kathleen had talked to Edith about unpacking her bag. After all, Edith would be staying here until she gained enough strength to look for another place. She might even want to rent a room at Mrs. Monroy's. A young woman living alone could cause talk, and Kathleen knew Edith would do best to avoid that. Already rumors were flying about town since the Barstow sisters were traveling with a group of teamsters.

Kathleen laid the things from the valise on the dresser top, deciding which items to put where. Miss Barstow certainly had been traveling light. When asked where their trunks of clothes were, she'd said they had none. All they carried were the two satchels and the dresses they wore. Kathleen wondered if perhaps other belongings would be sent as soon as Edith notified someone where to ship them.

In the bottom of the bag a black dress lay folded with a black veil beside the dress. Pulling them out, Kathleen noted the dress seemed a little more worn than the other things in the valise. Had Edith experienced another death in the family recently? Was that why she seemed unusually distraught right now? She shook her head and sighed. If one of her sisters died in such a horrible manner, she would be just as upset as Edith—maybe more so.

With the clothes put away, Kathleen took the empty valise and set it on the floor to push under the bed. Letting go too soon, she noticed a thump as the bag landed. She frowned. If the bag were empty, where did the noise come from? After picking up the valise, she snapped the catch open and peered inside, wondering if she'd missed a shoe or something. Empty space greeted her.

Reaching in, she ran her hand along the bottom to see if she could feel anything. Her fingers ran across the hidden catch twice before she realized what the lump was. Starting to ease the catch open, Kathleen halted. Edith had agreed for her to unpack the bag, but would she agree to this? *Maybe there's something in here that can help me understand why Edith is so afraid.* Kathleen ignored the twinge of guilt that said she was only being nosy, not helpful.

Easing open the false bottom, Kathleen could see a rather large beaded bag and a pistol nestled together. She lifted the expensive-looking bag from the valise. The black beads shone in the lamplight. For some reason Kathleen shivered as she gazed at them. Her fingers closed over the object in the purse. She frowned. Why would Edith have this in her bag?

Edith stirred and moaned. Kathleen jumped. Heart pounding, she watched as Edith plucked at the covers, then lay still again. Her breathing evened out once more. A sigh of relief escaped Kathleen. She shoved the beaded bag into the valise and shut the hidden compartment. Determined not to snoop anymore, she pushed the bag under the bed. With quiet steps, she moved to the chair by the lamp where her sewing waited and sat down. Picking up the dress and her needle, she couldn't keep her thoughts from the object in the beaded bag.

Ψ

The door to the telegraph office slammed shut after Quinn. He paid little attention as he thought of the message he'd sent across the wires. Something about Edith struck him wrong. Why would she get so upset about her family being notified of her sister's death? So far, she hadn't even told anyone much of anything about her sister. Yes, she'd cried knowing Cassie died in the attack, but she also seemed to be hiding something or from someone. The lawman in him couldn't let that go. He had to make some inquiries about Edith and see if he could figure out who she was.

Striding down the street, Quinn found himself thinking as he had all day about the message he'd heard at the church yesterday. For the hundredth time, he chastised himself for reacting the way he had. Here he'd planned to show Kathleen how compatible they were, and the first chance he got, he'd blown up over a sermon that shouldn't have mattered. He didn't care about that stuff anymore. He didn't believe it, either.

This morning, when he'd stopped by to see how Miss Barstow was doing, Kathleen assured him she was resting peacefully. Before he left, she pressed a bundle of folded papers into his hand.

"I copied these Scriptures, Quinn. They've helped me in tough times. Please take the time to read them and think about them. I know you're angry with God, but I'd still like you to talk to the preacher."

"I'm planning to see him today sometime." Quinn backed toward the door. "I have a lot to do, but if I can find him, I'll ask him some questions."

He'd run like a scared rabbit, folding the thick sheaf of papers and shoving them in his vest pocket. Later, he'd take the time to read what she'd written.

Touching his pocket, Quinn felt the bulge where the papers rested. He still hadn't looked at them. Even though Kathleen had given them to him, he still didn't want to be pushed. From the look of the writing on the paper, he guessed she'd copied whole passages from the Bible. His father used to carry Scripture with him, memorizing and quoting what God said, but that hadn't helped his sister, either.

Making his way down the street to the jail, Quinn ignored the activity around him. Why did everyone think they had the right to tell him how and what to believe? Every time he and Conlon were together, the man had to get in some remark about God and how Quinn should believe in Him. Kathleen didn't preach at him, but he knew she held back because of his lack of faith. She said she would never marry because of her birthmark, but he could see the longing in her eyes when she held one of the twins. If any woman deserved a husband and a family, Kathleen did. Quinn determined that somehow he would find a way to overcome their differences and become her husband.

Shaking the ring of keys, he located the one to unlock the door of the jail when he stopped. This wasn't right. His stomach couldn't take any more of this indecision. He had to prove to Kathleen that he was right when he said God would not protect His people. She wouldn't believe him, but if he could convince the preacher to talk to her, then she would have to concede the point. Most of the time, God just left His people at the mercy of whatever happenstance came along. He didn't really care, and Quinn knew it.

Shoving the keys into his pocket, he headed down the street to the home where the evangelist stayed. Several of the families in the area had offered to put him up during the weeks he would be in Tucson. Quinn couldn't imagine wanting to have someone in your house who might start preaching at any moment.

Mrs. Dooley smiled a welcome as she opened the front door. A toddler clung to her skirts, eyes peeping out at Quinn as if he might be some monster from the dark.

"Hello, Deputy Kirby. What can I do fer you today?" Mrs. Dooley's smile displayed a tooth chipped off at an angle, the rest yellowed and stained.

"Mrs. Dooley, did I hear that the evangelist is staying with you this week?"

She beamed as if this fact made her the most important person in town. "Why, yes, he is."

"Do you think I could speak with him?" Quinn wanted to turn and run. "If he's too busy, I'll talk to him later."

"He's out back. That man sure is a worker. He's repaired my porch and fixed the fence around my chicken pen. We won't have any coyotes stealing chickens for awhile." She shuffled aside, gesturing for Quinn to come inside.

"That's okay, Mrs. Dooley. It sounds like he's a busy man. I'll come by another time."

"Oh, no, you don't. That man needs a break. I just made him sit down for a drink. You join him, and he'll rest a little longer. He don't have enough meat on his bones to be working so hard." The toddler peeked out again with his finger in his nose.

Taking his hat off, Quinn stepped in the house. Mrs. Dooley swept the child up into her arms, pulling his finger out of his nose. Quinn followed her to the door leading outside. There in the shade sat the preacher, his thin frame resting against the wall of the house, his eyes closed as if he were asleep.

Before Quinn could stop her, Mrs. Dooley called out, "Reverend, you've got company."

The man smiled and quirked open one eye. His eyebrow rose as if asking who would be visiting him in a town where he knew almost no one. With one fluid motion, he rose from the chair belying the ungainliness his tall, lanky body displayed.

He held out his hand to Quinn. "Name's Reilly, Son, Matthew Reilly."

Quinn took hold of his hand, surprised at the strength. "Deputy Quinn Kirby, Sir. I, uh, just stopped by to welcome you to town. I haven't had the chance to do that yet. I didn't mean to disturb your rest."

Matthew Reilly laughed as if he'd never heard anything so funny. "My rest will be when I get to heaven and live with my Lord, Son. Right now, I take a moment to sit down and pray once in awhile. Otherwise, work is the best medicine. Idle hands are a tool of the devil, you know."

Quinn nodded as if he knew exactly what the man meant. He sidled toward the corner of the house. Coming here had been a mistake. He had to leave before the conversation went further.

"Here you go, Deputy." Mrs. Dooley came out with a cup of coffee and a pot to refill the preacher's cup. "Now, you two just sit and visit awhile. I've got to run out and do some errands."

"Thank you, Ma'am." Preacher Reilly flashed her a wide smile. As the door closed behind her, he motioned to a chair beside the one he'd been resting in and sat down. Not seeing any way out, Quinn perched on the edge of the chair, his coffee warming his hands.

"I believe you were at the meeting last Sunday. Am I right?" Reilly had dark green eyes that seemed to see right into Quinn's soul.

"Yes, Sir, I was there." Quinn took a long swig of coffee and grimaced as he burnt his tongue.

"You weren't real happy with what I said."

Trying to hide his surprise, Quinn searched for the words to say. "I, uh, it's been a long time since I've been in church."

Reilly nodded. "I've had a lot of experience watching the faces of people I preach to. Some people don't listen; some thrive on the words I speak, and others get angry like you did. I admire a man who's not afraid to face what makes him mad. Now, if you don't mind, I'd like to hear what I said that you objected to."

His mind scrabbling, Quinn tried to think of a way to get out of this. Why had he come here? Who was he to try to tell this man he was wrong? Then he remembered his sister, what she'd gone through, and he could feel the anger rising up all over again. The anger and bitterness of years of hating God for what happened to his innocent sister poured out. Matthew Reilly sat silent as Quinn told the whole story, including his accusations that God didn't care what happened to the people who loved Him.

The shadows were growing long when Quinn finished talking. He couldn't look at the preacher. His eyes would be full of condemnation at Quinn's charges against God. Even knowing this, Quinn couldn't bring himself to rise and slink away like the whipped dog he felt he resembled.

"Tell me, Son, how would your sister have felt if your father refused to let her go anywhere because something bad might happen to her? In fact, what if your father made you stay at home and never let you decide anything you wanted to do whether right or wrong?"

"My father wouldn't have done that." Quinn looked at Reilly in surprise. "He loved us too much to treat us in that manner."

A faint smile lit the preacher's eyes. "That's a good father, then, wouldn't you say?"

Quinn nodded. "He was always a good father. He guided us, but he also let us make some mistakes."

Reilly's dark green eyes gazed at the sky as a few clouds scudded past. "You see, Son, that's sort of the way God did things too."

Quinn blinked in surprise.

"When God made the garden for Adam and Eve, He made it a perfect place. Every day He came down and talked with Adam and Eve. He wanted them to do right always, but He wanted the choice to be theirs. You know what happened?"

A lump filled Quinn's throat. He nodded.

"They committed the first sin." Reilly rubbed his chin. "Seems to me we've been doing that ever since. You see, God didn't want us to be like the animals. The Bible says He wants us to fellowship with Him. Do you know why He allows us to make our mistakes?"

Tightness wrapped around Quinn. He felt like he couldn't get a breath.

"Because He loves us so much." Reilly's eyes were serious. "Just like your daddy let you and your sister make choices that weren't always right, God lets each one of us make our own decisions. You see, some people make pretty poor choices and everyone suffers for that."

"But why didn't God step in and protect my sister?" The tightness almost made speaking impossible for Quinn.

"How do you know He didn't?"

"She got hit with a rock and hurt pretty bad."

"Maybe that rock should have hit her hard enough to kill her." The preacher sat forward and clasped his hands over his knees as if in prayer. "You see, we can't know the mind of God. Who's to say how much He protected Elizabeth?"

Stumbling up from his chair, Quinn mumbled something. He set his coffee cup on the porch railing, then almost ran around the house to leave. He couldn't stay longer. This couldn't be right. Had he been wrong all these years? Had he misunderstood what God had done? Half running down the street, all he could think of was his need to escape the thoughts careening through his head.

Chapter 18

Andrew gurgled and stretched a tiny hand up to Kathleen's face. He grabbed her lip and tugged.

"Ouch." Kathleen loosened his fingers one by one as Andrew gave her a toothless smile. "You are so proud of yourself." She tried to act angry at the fat baby. "I'll have to get you now." She lifted him and nibbled his neck, causing him to give off infectious chuckles that soon had them both laughing.

"Are you spoiling that boy again?"

Kathleen jumped. Andrew started, his face puckering as if he were about to cry. "Oh, don't you cry, Sweetie. Your mommy just scared me, that's all." She frowned at Glorianna. "Next time don't sneak up on us. I could have dropped him."

Putting Angelina on the rug in the middle of the room, Glorianna grinned. "A team of horses in a full gallop could have sneaked up on you two, you were laughing so loud." She reached for Andrew, gave him a kiss on the cheek, and put him down with his sister. Glorianna sank onto the settee beside Kathleen and collapsed with a sigh. "I was prepared for one baby to make me tired, but two are double the work. Some days, I don't know what I'd do without you and Alicia helping out."

Watching the two infants, Kathleen couldn't help but smile as Andrew began to look around at the various objects within his sight. Angelina did her best to follow the voices talking. "You are a very good mother, Glory. These babies are such blessings."

"You need some of your own." Glorianna put a hand on Kathleen's arm. Her eyes filled with compassion.

Hurt and anger swept through Kathleen. She stiffened at her cousin's touch. "I can't marry, Glorianna, and you know that."

"Can't or won't?" Fire sparked in Glory's eyes.

"Can't." Kathleen tried to hold onto her resolve in the face of Glory's determination. She'd never been able to win an argument with Glory.

"I am getting tired of listening to you feel sorry for yourself because of a little mark on your cheek." Angelina and Andrew both looked their direction as their mother's tone became firm. "You always lectured me about not being afraid to step out and be what God wants me to be. If that's true, then why are you still hiding behind that veil? Why can't you believe God made you as you are, and to Him and to those who know you, you're beautiful?"

Angelina whined, a sure sign she was getting ready to cry. Glorianna ignored her and took Kathleen's hands. "You're going to ruin God's plans for you by not allowing Him to work." Glory's eyes filled with tears. "Take off that mask, Kathleen. Quit shutting yourself away from everyone. Allow people the chance to love you as much as I do. Let God know you trust Him to protect you, no matter what."

The words felt like physical blows that battered Kathleen from one side, then the other. She tried to fight down a surge of anger. "You have no idea what my life has been like. How can you expect me to live like that?"

"Do you think you're the only one ever to be made fun of? Imagine how I felt, moving around so much with Daddy in the cavalry. I was always the new girl." Glory's eyes narrowed for a moment. "I can't tell you how many people have asked about you since you arrived. They care, Kathleen. They aren't children. Why can't you give them a chance?" Glory's fingers dug into Kathleen's arm.

Jumping to her feet and rushing for the door, Kathleen almost fell over Angelina. The baby began to wail. Glorianna reached for her daughter as Kathleen backed away, groping for her hat and veil.

"I have to go." Kathleen choked out the words as she turned toward the door.

"Wait." Glory's voice halted her in midstep. "Kathleen, you were so brave to come all the way out here like you did. All your life, your mother kept you shut away from the world. Your only real memories are those of cruel taunts you suffered as a child. Trust God. He's done a good work in you, and He's longing to do more."

After stumbling off the porch, Kathleen made her way down the path to the street. Tears blinded her even worse than the blackness of the veil over her eyes. What would happen if she were to rip this gauze off? She shuddered. Horror crept up her spine, sending chills racing down her arms. Glory didn't understand. She'd never been made fun of to the extent Kathleen had. No one could understand that unless they'd been through the same.

A picture of the Bible description of Jesus at the mercy of the soldiers who arrested Him flashed through her mind. She gasped. Last night she'd read that very story in her Bible time. Jesus had done nothing wrong. He was perfect, yet they spit on Him, mocked Him, and called Him names. What they did to Jesus was far worse than anything anyone had ever done to her. What had He done to them? He'd asked forgiveness for the very ones who abused Him.

Going around to the back of Mrs. Monroy's house, Kathleen took out the key to her sewing room. Her hand shaking, she missed the lock twice before the key slipped home and turned. The door swung open. Kathleen fell through, her hand covering her mouth to hold in the sobs. *Oh, God, have I been disobedient? Have I been hiding and not trusting You to protect me? Lord, I know how You suffered, but I feel so alone and unable to face something like that. Help me.*

Kathleen ran to her room, fell to her knees, and rested her forehead against the bed. For a long time she stayed there, resting in the touch of her Savior's hand as He comforted her. When she stood, she removed the veil from her hat. Walking to where she kept her scraps of cloth, she threw the bit of fabric into the discard pile.

"Jesus, thank You for helping me to forgive. Now, help me to have the courage to walk out of here like this." Kathleen closed her eyes. "This is the way You made me, Lord. Help me to rejoice and be glad." Lightness filled her. She felt as if she could float on the clouds. Laughter bubbled up, escaping into the room. She hadn't realized how heavy her burden had been until she gave her fears to the Lord. Tears of joy streamed down her cheeks.

"Kathleen, are you in there?" A knock sounded from her bedroom door. Mrs. Monroy called out to her. Wiping the wetness from her cheeks, Kathleen hurried to open the door. Mrs. Monroy started to speak, then stopped with her mouth open. She stared at Kathleen.

"Why, young lady, you are a beauty. Why have you been hiding under that veil?" She took hold of Kathleen's chin and turned her face. As the birthmark came into view, her expression softened. "Look at that." Her hand covered the star on Kathleen's cheek. "When I was a girl, our neighbor had something like this. My mother used to call it an angel's kiss. That's no reason to hide, Honey. I hope you know that."

Her throat ached. Kathleen managed to nod. "I understand now."

Mrs. Monroy straightened. "I want you to speak with Miss Barstow. Something is wrong with that woman."

"What's happened?" Kathleen started to reach for her hat and veil before she remembered. She took Mrs. Monroy's arm and led her out the door.

"She's become like a different person. I came to her room after lunch to find her up and getting dressed. She says she's got work to do. I ask you, what kind of work can a woman do when she has a gunshot wound in her shoulder? When I told her to get back in bed, she gave me such a cold look I near froze to death."

"That doesn't sound like Edith." Puzzled, Kathleen hurried to the injured woman's room, Mrs. Monroy huffing along behind her. Giving a light knock, she opened the door and peeked in. "Edith, may I come in?"

"I can't stop you." The cold voice sounded so different from the near invalid Kathleen had stayed with for days. Then she'd been quiet, acquiescent, so withdrawn Kathleen had wondered if she would ever recover. Now, she sounded almost brassy, defiant—a different person than the one who'd been in this room previously.

Miss Barstow stood before a small mirror, trying to pin up her hair with one hand. The lush, brown waves were not cooperating. Several pieces of hair straggled down around her face. As if exasperated, Edith started to lift her injured arm to do the job two-handed. A grimace of pain crossed her face. She dropped the brush, which fell to the floor with a sharp crack.

"I'll leave you to see what you can do," Mrs. Monroy whispered behind

Kathleen. Her heavy tread receded down the hall.

"Let me help you with your hair." Kathleen stepped in and shut the door. "I don't know how I could do mine with one hand."

Edith yanked out the pins she'd already used, sending her hair cascading to her waist. Glancing around, she caught sight of Kathleen and turned, her eyes wide. Kathleen's hand itched to cover her cheek. She smiled at Edith.

"I hope your brush isn't hurt."

"I'm sure it's fine." Edith continued to stare. Kathleen picked up the brush and, as she stood, Edith stretched out her hand to touch Kathleen's face. "Is this why you always wore the veil?"

Kathleen nodded.

Placing a hand over her jagged scar, Edith seemed to lose her anger. "I'm sorry I spoke harshly with you. You've been so kind to me. Thank you."

"Where are you going?" Kathleen glanced around the room. "I see you have your bags packed."

Edith turned. Her brown hair looked pale over the black of her dress. "I need to get something from town, then I'll be leaving."

"I thought you planned to live here."

"That's before my sister died." Edith's shoulders sagged as if a great weight sat on them. "I want to return home. There's some unfinished business I have to attend to."

"Can I help you with anything?" Kathleen longed to put her arms around Edith. She seemed so alone in the world.

"If you'd help me with my hair, I would appreciate it." Edith sat in a chair so Kathleen could do the chore. Tension seemed to radiate from her as Kathleen brushed her hair, then pinned it up. The waves were so becoming. Edith turned and smiled her thanks. Picking up her hat and veil, she paused at the door. Her light eyes hardened, all compassion gone.

"I know you care for that deputy. You might want to go visit him and keep him company."

Before Kathleen could respond, Edith pinned the hat in place and disappeared out the door. What had she meant about Quinn? Had he been here today looking for her? The thought of seeing him set her blood racing, but having the courage to walk down the streets in the open proved daunting. Instead, she returned to her rooms and organized her sewing, rearranging items that didn't need it.

Sinking onto a chair, she buried her head in her hands. "I'm so sorry, Lord. Just this afternoon I promised to have courage and trust in Your protection. Mrs. Monroy and Edith were both so kind. There's nothing for me to be afraid of, but I'm scared. Will You take my hand and walk with me to see Quinn?"

Taking a deep breath, Kathleen stood, walked out the door, and locked it behind her. For some reason, Edith's comment about Quinn bothered her, but she couldn't decide why. Her steps quickened, an urgency building inside. Beside her, she felt a comforting presence as if the Lord walked there, lending her His courage.

✤

Rubbing a hand over his unshaven jaw, Quinn winced at the raspy sound. His vest hung open, his shirt wrinkled. Even his badge appeared tarnished and off center. He felt as if he were falling apart and didn't know which way to turn. All night long, he'd wrestled with the questions raised by the preacher, but the answer he sought seemed as distant as ever. Walking the streets last evening to keep tabs on the action in town, he'd been surly to at least a dozen people. He would have to look them up and apologize, but right now the retraction would be worse than the offense.

Touching the side of his vest, Quinn thought of the Scriptures Kathleen had given him. She said they were verses she'd memorized and that they'd helped her. Some of the papers were worn; others looked as if they'd only been copied in recent days. Off and on during the night, he'd read from the verses, thought on the preacher's conversation and sermon, and argued aloud that this wasn't true. God didn't care about anyone. Somehow, he'd been unable to convince himself. If what he believed was true, then why were so many of the people he admired adamant about their belief in God's protection?

Pounding hooves raced down the street outside the office. Quinn grabbed his hat and surged to his feet. Whoever was on that horse was traveling too fast. He tugged at his vest, too much in a hurry to straighten his clothes anymore. Before he could reach for the handle, the door burst open. Paulo Rodriquez fell to the floor, springing up again with the agility of youth.

"*Señor, andele, por favor.*" He turned to rush out the door. Quinn caught hold of the boy's shirt and hauled him back.

"Whoa, Paulo, speak slow and in English." Paulo panted, his open mouth dragging in great gulps of air. His black eyes were wide with fear. "Sorry, Señor. You must hurry, please."

"What's the problem?"

Paulo danced from foot to foot. "She's here. Come on." He took Quinn's hand and tugged so hard Quinn almost lost his balance.

"Who's here, Paulo?" Last night's lack of sleep made Quinn want to grab the boy and shake him until his teeth rattled. Taking a deep breath, he stooped and looked Paulo in the eye, trying to help the boy calm down.

"The lady, Señor deputy. She's here, and she has a gun. You have to come."

Quinn frowned. A lady with a gun? Most women didn't carry guns.

"What lady and what is she doing with the gun?"

Paulo's eyes filled with tears. "The lady in black. She has her face covered. She wants much money."

The lady in black? Face covered? A veil! Quinn snapped up, his brain struggling to register the information. He'd been so distraught over talking with the preacher, he hadn't met the stage yesterday evening. Had the Veiled Widow come to town on the stage the one day he missed being there? That couldn't be. Grabbing Paulo's shoulders, Quinn tried to get control of himself. He could see the fear in the boy's eyes and knew he was the cause now.

Easing his grip, he tried speak calmly. "Paulo, tell me where the woman is. Who is she pointing the gun at?"

"At the offices of Lord and Williams, Señor. She says they owe her, and she wants money and two horses. I was there with my papa. He helped me sneak out the door so I could come and get you. Please, Señor, hurry."

"Paulo, I want you to go home. I'll take your horse, but I don't want you to follow me. Understand?"

Paulo nodded, and Quinn headed for the door. As he raced for the horse, he checked the pistol strapped to his side. He had to stop this woman before she killed someone.

Chapter 19

A small body hurtled into Kathleen's as she rounded the corner of the street leading to the jail. Her breath whooshed out. She grabbed the person, trying to keep both of them from falling.

"Paulo, what are you doing?" Kathleen gasped. Her stomach ached from the hit.

Big, black eyes gazed at her with terror. He didn't recognize her without her veil. She'd seen him a few times with his mother at Glory's house, but she'd always been careful to keep the covering in place when they were around.

"Paulo, it's okay. I'm Kathleen, Glorianna's cousin. I usually have a veil on. Remember?"

He nodded, his brow furrowed as if he recognized the voice, but not the face. His small chest heaved, out of breath from his headlong dash. His eyes still held a look of fear, but she didn't believe she was the cause anymore.

"He said I have to go right home." Paulo hopped to one side. She kept her hold on his arms.

"Your father sent you home?"

"No, the deputy. He said I shouldn't follow him, but I should go home." Paulo glanced behind him as if Quinn would be watching and know he wasn't hurrying home.

"Have you been bothering Deputy Kirby?" Kathleen couldn't figure out why Quinn had been so harsh with the boy. Paulo loved to talk with Quinn, and Quinn enjoyed the boy too.

Paulo whispered, as if imparting a confidence. "He's going to shoot her, and he doesn't want me to see."

Kathleen could feel the color drain from her face. "Who's he going to shoot?" Paulo's brow knit as her grip tightened on his arms. She forced herself to relax.

"The lady in black." Paulo glanced behind him once more. "She is going to shoot someone at the office of Lord and Williams. I told Deputy Kirby, and he will shoot her and save my papa."

The woman in black. Kathleen recalled all the times Quinn referred to this criminal and how he arrested her, thinking she was the Veiled Widow. Fear wrapped around her as she thought of Quinn facing this danger.

"Paulo, I want you to go on home." She released the boy. He hesitated.

"Don't go where the black lady is. She scares me. She talks like a *bruja*, a witch." His black eyes widened. He looked terrified.

"Don't worry about me, Paulo. You go on home to your mama."

The boy raced past her. She knew she should watch to make sure he continued home, but the urgency to get to Quinn made her gather her skirts and race off in the opposite direction. Heart-pounding scenarios began racing through her mind as she hurried down the empty roadway. Pictures of Quinn lying still and pale with blood on his shirt made her pray harder than she ever had before.

The buildings she sought came into view. The street was deserted except for a few horses tied at hitching posts. An ominous quiet huddled over the town. Kathleen slowed her headlong pace, trying to catch her breath. Heedless of the danger, she pushed through the doors into the offices of the Lord and Williams building.

A slender woman in black faced Quinn. His back was to the door, but Kathleen could read the tension in the set of his shoulders as he trained his pistol on the woman. As Kathleen rushed in, the woman glanced at the door. She took a step closer to the rear door. Quinn didn't move, his gaze never wavering from the woman, his gun not faltering.

Time seemed to slow. Kathleen noted several things at once. A black beaded bag dangled from the woman's wrist; she held a pistol pointed at Quinn; several men cowered in one corner of the office, and a lock of wavy, light brown hair hung loose on the woman's shoulder. Kathleen gasped.

"I'm telling you for the last time, Widow, put the pistol down."

The woman's head turned from side to side as if she were looking between Quinn and Kathleen. The barrel of the pistol wavered, then lowered. The thump of the pistol hitting the floor echoed in the silent office. The woman's shoulders sagged. She took another step.

"Quinn." Kathleen had to tell him.

His head whipped around for an instant. "Kathleen, get out of here."

The woman moved again as Quinn's attention left her. Kathleen could feel the stares of the men in the room. Her hand brushed her cheek as she remembered she wasn't wearing her veil. *Lord, help me.* A surge of peace settled over her.

"Stop." Quinn's command halted everyone. The veiled woman froze in midstep. "You aren't sneaking out of here. I've waited and watched for you. . .and now you're coming to jail with me."

Somehow, the woman had slipped her hand in the bag dangling from her wrist. Panic began to overwhelm Kathleen. She had to stop this.

"Quinn, you've got to listen."

"Kathleen, get out of here now." Anger infused Quinn's voice.

The woman took another step as if she thought Quinn too distracted to notice. Any minute, she would be close enough to dash through the door and attempt an escape. The shot from Quinn's gun startled Kathleen. The Veiled Widow jumped, then raised her beaded bag.

"No, Edith." Kathleen tried to rush forward. The sound of a second shot broke the tension. Quinn stumbled. His gun bucked, and the woman cried out. Quinn clutched his chest and folded over on himself, collapsing to the floor. The woman fell straight back, her small body making little noise as she hit the floor.

Quinn heard the door crash open behind him. He saw the Widow start and glance in that direction. He didn't move. She had never been known to work with anyone or have an accomplice of any kind. This was probably Paulo disobeying his directive. The boy would be in trouble when this was over. Right now, Quinn refused to be distracted.

He gave the order for her to drop her gun. Shocked, he watched her obey. Events began to unfold fast. Kathleen was here. He didn't want her here. The woman he loved shouldn't be in danger. Loved? Warmth rushed through him at the thought. Would she ever be able to love him? He pulled his thoughts away from such dangerous territory and forced them to return to the matters at hand. He saw the Widow trying to make a break for the door. His finger closed over the trigger, and he shot into the floor next to her, wanting to frighten her into complying with him. He couldn't lose her after waiting so long.

She raised her hands as if she were surrendering. The black, beaded bag dangled from her left wrist. Her right hand was inside the bag. Kathleen shouted Edith's name for some reason. A blow slammed into his chest. His hand jerked up. His finger tightened on the trigger. The gun fired, then fell from his hand. He couldn't breathe. As he crumpled forward, the light in the room faded away.

Voices called his name from a distance. He heard Kathleen. Opening his mouth, Quinn tried to speak to her, but the sound wouldn't come. In the dimness he felt a presence. Peace stole over him. Was he dying? If so, he didn't seem to care. Somehow, he knew everything would be all right.

A wave of pain washed over him. His left side ached as if he'd been kicked by a mule. Booted feet clumped on the floor near his head. Hands touched him. Voices spoke, hazy, but getting clearer. The room began to come into focus.

"I think he's coming to." A man's voice spoke.

Kathleen knelt beside him. Her veil had fallen off. He'd never seen a more beautiful sight than the star-shaped mark on her cheek.

"Quinn, can you hear me?" Her beautiful lips formed the words. Fascinated with the way she spoke, he wished to stay still and watch her. She didn't seem to have the same desire. Her hand cupped his cheek. "Quinn, you were shot, but you're okay. She had a derringer in her bag. Because of the papers, the bullet only penetrated the skin. Doc Meyer already popped the lead out."

Memories of what happened flooded over him. He tried to get up. What happened to the Veiled Widow? Was she getting away?

Kathleen pushed down on him. "Quinn, stop." The sharpness of her voice halted him. "Don't worry. You shot her. She's alive, and the doc is looking at her."

"Am I hit bad?" Quinn knew with certainty he didn't want to die. He wanted a long life. A life filled with days spent with Kathleen and a family.

She smiled. "I've never seen a better example of God's protection than this." She held up a thick sheaf of folded papers. They were the Scriptures she'd copied. He'd read them, folded them tightly, and put them in his inside vest pocket. He remembered thinking they were so thick folded up that they made the vest bulge out. The center of the papers held a bullet hole. The Word of God had slowed the bullet. Once more, the preacher's message came rushing back to him.

Gritting his teeth, Quinn eased up to his feet. A trickle of blood stained his shirt. He refused to consider what would have happened if her gun had been a bigger caliber or if he'd been standing closer. By tomorrow, he'd be sporting a whopper of a bruise. He could see Doc Meyer working on the woman. He took a step in that direction when Kathleen halted him.

"Quinn." She waited for him to look at her. "It's Edith—Miss Barstow."

He glanced over at Doc, then at Kathleen. Had he heard right?

"Edith is the criminal you've been looking for. I didn't figure it all out until I saw her here. Then I knew. When I put her things away, I found the guns in her valise. That's how I knew she had the little, hidden derringer. I tried to warn you."

"I don't understand. Why was she traveling with her sister?"

"No one knows." Kathleen's eyes reflected such sadness, he couldn't resist taking her hand. "If she doesn't live, we may never know."

"Your veil." Quinn brushed a finger across Kathleen's velvety cheek. "Where is it?" She smiled, and he couldn't breathe.

"Glory gave me a tongue lashing that I sorely needed. I realized I needed to trust God to protect me from mean comments. I had to quit hiding. It's been hard, but these people are wonderful." She gestured to several of the men talking in small groups at the rear of the office.

Jerking his hand away, Quinn limped across to where Doc worked on Edith. Doc gave him a grim prognosis, and Quinn stalked from the room, ignoring the hurt look on Kathleen's face. He couldn't stay longer. Every time something happened lately, he had to hear about God's protection. *God, won't You leave me alone? My life was fine, but now I don't even know which way to turn.*

❦

A chill wind blew down the street, making Quinn wish he'd put on his jacket. Standing outside the meeting hall, he could hear the people singing. He didn't want to go inside. This was the last service before the preacher moved on. An invisible force seemed to drag him here. For several nights, he hadn't slept well. He felt like he was in the middle of a battle, and he didn't know which side would win.

Ever since Edith Barstow had died from the gunshot wound he'd accidentally inflicted on her, he'd avoided all the people he cared about. The desire to see Kathleen had become a physical ache over the days. A sense of justice kept him from seeking her out. He didn't think he could keep from asking her to marry him;

yet he knew because of his lack of faith, she would say no. He couldn't bear that.

The music ended. Quiet settled over the hall. He could almost see the lanky preacher walking to the pulpit and opening his Bible. The wind gathered behind him, pushing with enough force to make him take a step. He tried to fight. His feet seemed to have a will of their own, dragging him through the door to an empty seat in the back.

"I'd like to read a Scripture from the book of Jeremiah the prophet, chapter seventeen." Matthew Reilly looked over the crowd, his eyes meeting Quinn's. " 'Thus saith the Lord; Cursed be the man that trusteth in man, and maketh flesh his arm, and whose heart departeth from the Lord. For he shall be like the heath in the desert, and shall not see when good cometh; but shall inhabit the parched places in the wilderness, in a salt land and not inhabited.' "

I'm cursed, Lord. All this time I thought I was so smart trusting in man's goodness. It wasn't true. God forgive me. Quinn fought tears that threatened to overflow. He wanted to run out of the building, but he couldn't seem to move.

"Now I want to read you the next part of that passage." The preacher's voice cut in on Quinn's thoughts. " 'Blessed is the man that trusteth in the Lord, and whose hope the Lord is. For he shall be as a tree planted by the waters, and that spreadeth out her roots by the river, and shall not see when heat cometh, but her leaf shall be green; and shall not be careful in the year of drought, neither shall cease from yielding fruit.' "

Hope burned like a flame in Quinn's heart. *Lord, I want to trust in You, not in myself, not in man. I want to believe in Your protection. Help me, Lord. Forgive me for all these years of doubting You.*

The service ended. Quinn heard nothing more than the passages of Scripture and the preacher asking for those to come forward who needed prayer or salvation. As if in a dream, Quinn made his way down the aisle.

⚘

Kathleen snuggled Angelina against her breast. She brushed her cheek against the sleeping infant. The touch of soft skin against hers never failed to amaze her. Glorianna gasped beside her. Kathleen glanced at her cousin. Glory had tears in her eyes. Conlon, too, had shiny eyes. Kathleen turned her gaze to the front, where the preacher knelt praying with a man. Quinn? Was that Quinn, the man she loved, kneeling at the altar? Tears ran down her cheeks as she gave her thanks to God for another miracle.

People began milling around, some making their way out. Kathleen watched as Quinn stood, spoke to the evangelist for a few minutes, then began to search the crowd. Her heart did a little dance in anticipation. Quinn's eyes met hers. He smiled, and she knew. She knew without a doubt that he loved her as much as she loved him. She handed Angelina to Glory. As the crowd thinned and they could see one another better, Kathleen watched Quinn mouth the words that made her heart sing. "I love you."

Epilogue

Gripping the side of the buggy with one hand, Kathleen stared out at the velvety, green grass and trees lining the road. Her other hand rested on the small mound of her stomach. She smiled at Quinn, reveling in the love that shone in his eyes. They'd been married six months, and she'd finally agreed to go with him to visit his family.

"Are you. . ."

"Kathleen, for the thousandth time, I'm sure my family will love you just as you are and just as much as I do." Putting his hat on the seat, he pulled the buggy to a stop and kissed her. "I think you keep asking me that just so I'll stop and kiss you." His eyes twinkled.

She could feel her face flame. "I do not." She wrinkled her nose at him. "Well, you don't seem to be complaining."

He kissed her again. "You're right; I don't." He rattled the reins, urging the horses to go. "We'll be there in about half an hour."

The sun shone with a golden warmth that felt good. Kathleen knew she would get too hot later in the day, but right now she needed to be warm. Since the day she'd stopped hiding behind her veil, she'd become so free. The people in Tucson proved wonderful. No one ever made her feel unwelcome. Glorianna said if Kathleen thanked her one more time for confronting her on that issue, she would give her the twins for a whole week. Kathleen smiled. Those twins were a handful.

Her only worry was that Quinn's family would find her lacking. He'd assured her many times they wouldn't, but she'd lived with years of doubt. Quinn even said that after they visited his folks, they would travel on to see her family. She couldn't repress a shudder. Her mother would be horrified to see her face uncovered. Quinn insisted he would set the matter straight, and somehow Kathleen knew he would.

Since the day Quinn became a Christian, he'd changed so much. Even though he hadn't admitted it to anyone, he blamed himself for Edith's death. As a lawman, he felt so responsible for everyone, even the criminals. Before she died, Edith had awakened enough to talk to Kathleen. She told her the whole story of how her father, in a drunken bout of gambling, sold her sister to a horrible man. This man forced her to do unspeakable things, often beating her for the sheer pleasure the violence brought him. Edith's father didn't care about anything other than where his next drink was coming from. Edith's mother was dead, so Edith knew that she was the only one who could rescue Cassie.

Edith had no money, and her ploy of getting cash or gold from men had begun innocently. She'd always been beautiful. The scar she'd received as a young girl seemed to add to her mystique. She preyed on the men only to get the means to help her and her sister make a new start somewhere they would never be found. Before she died, she told Kathleen where to find the remainder of the money so at least some of it could be returned. Quinn and Kathleen talked for hours about how Edith's need to protect her sister rather than turning to God for protection had brought only heartache and grief.

"Are you still with me?" Quinn's arm slipped around her shoulder.

"I'm sorry. I was thinking about Edith."

Sadness stole over Quinn's face. He pulled Kathleen close. "At least she has a chance for true happiness. After you talked to her, I believe she understood her need for Jesus. That's the best gift you could show her."

Resting her head against his shoulder, Kathleen sighed. She'd never thought she could be so content.

The buggy rounded a corner. Quinn guided the horse around a turn onto a narrow lane. Before them, a house and outbuildings sprawled against the landscape. Several horses in a corral raised their heads and whinnied. The door to the house opened, and a man stepped out. Even from this distance, Kathleen could see the resemblance to Quinn. The way he stood, then his stride as he came toward them made her wonder if she would mistake him for his son in the dark. Coming closer, she could see the strong jaw and thick blond waves of hair like Quinn's. Even his eyes seemed to be the same color of blue-gray.

Quinn pulled the buggy to a stop and hopped down. His father halted a few feet away, and the two faced each other for the first time in years. Kathleen held her breath, waiting to see what would happen.

Mr. Kirby took a long stride forward and embraced Quinn. "Welcome home, Son. It's been too long."

Tears burned in Kathleen's eyes as she watched the reunion.

"Quinn." A woman raced out the door and across the yard. Her face shone with excitement as she almost threw herself at Quinn.

"Mom." Quinn sounded choked as he hugged the small woman. Her head only reached his chest, and she looked as if a strong wind would blow her away.

"Who's this?" Quinn's father was standing by the buggy studying Kathleen.

Releasing his mother, Quinn turned to help Kathleen down. Her legs felt unsteady. Grateful for Quinn's arm around her, she leaned against him for support.

"This is my wife, Kathleen. Kathleen, my parents, James and Mary Kirby."

With a cry of joy, her mother-in-law embraced Kathleen. Quinn's father shook his hand, then kissed Kathleen on the cheek—right on top of her star-shaped birthmark. "Welcome to the family, Kathleen."

Mary shot Quinn an accusing look. "You could have sent a letter telling us. That telegram only mentioned you coming for a visit." She grabbed Kathleen by the arm. "Let's go into the house. It sounds like we have a lot of catching up to do."

Kathleen followed her mother-in-law into the frame house. Bright rag rugs decorated polished wooden floors. A few wooden toys lay scattered in one corner of the room. Quinn and his father followed them in after watering the horse and turning the tired animal loose in the corral.

"I just finished baking a dried apple pie." Mary brought out some plates and lifted the cooling pie from the counter. "Elizabeth and her family will be here for supper. She'll be so excited to meet you, Kathleen. I can see you two have something special in common."

Quinn sat beside Kathleen and wrapped her hand in his as if he understood her discomfort. His smile and eyes spoke of his love without a word. Warmth and peace flowed through her.

"I didn't know Elizabeth married." Quinn gave his mom a puzzled look. "Why didn't you write and tell me?"

Mary gave James a glance Kathleen couldn't interpret. She seemed hesitant to answer Quinn's question.

"I don't believe you've written in awhile." James accepted his piece of pie, giving his wife a smile. "You sent the telegram saying you were coming, but that was the first we knew you were in Tucson. Your mother wrote to you at the last address we had in Colorado, but the letter came back to us with a note that they didn't know where you were."

Quinn's face reddened. He gave his parents a sheepish look. "I guess I haven't been too good about writing." He cut a bite of pie. "So, tell me about Elizabeth and her family. Who'd she marry?"

Another uneasy glance passed between his parents, but Kathleen didn't think Quinn noticed. She wondered what was wrong.

Mary began to talk in a tone that sounded contrived and unnaturally cheerful. "Elizabeth's been married over two years. She has a boy, Seth, and a new baby girl, Emily Anne. She's the sweetest little thing."

Swallowing a bite of pie, Quinn seemed to catch on to the tension in the room. "Who'd she marry?" He asked the question in a soft voice, placing his fork on the plate beside his uneaten portion of pie.

James pushed away from the table and stood. "Son, why don't you and I go outside? I'll show you some of the changes we've made to the place."

The muscles in Quinn's jaw bunched. Kathleen rested her hand on his arm and could feel the tightness there.

"Dad, you're avoiding the question. What happened to Elizabeth, and who'd she marry?"

Sinking into his chair, James rubbed his hands over his face and reached over to take Mary's hand. Her brow knit as if she were worried.

"Elizabeth is now Elizabeth Magee. She married Rupert."

"What?" Quinn surged to his feet. Kathleen caught his hand and began to pray. She hadn't seen him this distraught since before he'd become a Christian.

"How could you let her do that? Did he threaten you? Or her?" Quinn's free hand bunched into a fist. "I should have stayed to make sure she'd be safe."

James rose to his feet. Anger shone in his eyes. "Sit down." At his command, Quinn sat down, and his dad followed suit. "I want you to listen to this story before you go jumping to conclusions."

"You told me the Magees left town."

"They did. The day after you left, they packed up and moved. There was a lot of speculation about what happened. No one around here regretted their leaving." Mary took hold of her husband's hand, and Kathleen appreciated the love between the two of them.

"Three years ago, Rupert returned by himself. His father died the previous spring." James seemed uncomfortable about going on. "I don't know how you feel about the Lord these days, Quinn. When you left home, you were dead set against believing."

Bowing his head, Kathleen thought Quinn must be remembering with regret the words spoken in haste before he left and the years following. "I turned my back on Jesus. I was hurt and angry and thought I could do everything on my own without God. Last fall, I found out different. I gave my life to Jesus—partly because of Kathleen's prayers and witness."

Mary gave a cry of joy. Tears sparkled in her eyes. She came around the table and gave Quinn a long hug. "I'm so happy, Quinn. We've prayed every single day for you."

He nodded and cleared his throat. "Thank you for that. But, I'd like to know what this has to do with Magee."

"Well, you see, Rupert returned for one reason. He came to apologize to Elizabeth for the way he treated her when he lived here. Through a series of events, he too became a Christian." James paused to study his son. "I have a feeling you've changed a lot in the last few months. Am I right?"

Quinn nodded. Kathleen couldn't help smiling as she thought of the considerate, caring man he'd become.

"Well, Rupert is the same way. He's no longer brash and obnoxious, demanding his way. You couldn't ask for a better husband for your sister. He treats her like a princess, and he loves those kids in a way most fathers never do."

Kathleen could almost see the thoughts turning in Quinn's head. Since he'd left home, he had hated Rupert Magee for what he'd done. They talked about his need to forgive and prayed about God helping him find forgiveness. All those feelings of animosity must be coming back. Once more, Quinn would have to find it in his heart to forgive with a completeness that would heal the relationship.

When Quinn found out that Rupert and Elizabeth owned the farm next to his parents, he insisted on going over by himself. "I have to settle this thing with Rupert." He pulled Kathleen into his arms in the privacy of the bedroom they'd been given. "I trust my parents' and Elizabeth's judgment, but I have to make amends with Rupert myself."

"I understand." Kathleen breathed in Quinn's familiar scent, contentment wrapping around her. Exhaustion made her weak.

"I want you to rest while I'm gone." Quinn put his hand over her rounded belly. "Carrying this little one is tiring without all the traveling we've done. I'll tell Mom you're napping, and I'll wake you up when I get back." He put her in bed and kissed her before leaving. Kathleen drifted off, praying everything would be settled in a peaceful manner.

✤

Lord, You have to help me here. I'm so new at this forgiveness. I've harbored ill feelings toward Rupert for so long, I'm not sure I know how to truly forgive. Help me do that, Jesus, and show me right from the start that he's truly changed. Quinn nudged his horse to a faster walk as he finished praying. Peace settled over him as the buildings of Elizabeth and Rupert's place came in sight. The hollow knock of an axe chopping wood reverberated in the air.

Pulling his horse to a stop, Quinn sat at the edge of the yard taking in the neat, welcoming appearance of the property. This didn't resemble the Magee's disorderly home at all. He could see Elizabeth's happiness in the bright flowers along the house. He could also see a caring man's touch in the well-mended fences and tall woodpile ready for winter.

Swinging down from the horse, Quinn stepped up on the porch. The door flew open, and his sister flung herself into his arms. "Quinn, I can't believe you're here. I've missed you so much."

He held her away and looked at her. Cupping her cheek, he fought the emotion clogging his throat. "It's been a long time, Sis."

The door creaked open once more. Quinn's hold on his sister tightened for a moment, then relaxed. He looked up and met Rupert's hesitant gaze. This wasn't the braggart he'd fought so long ago. Quinn could see this was a man at peace with himself and God. Rupert Magee, one-time bully and braggart, exuded compassion.

"Afternoon, Rupert." Quinn held out his hand.

"Quinn." Rupert's large hand engulfed Quinn's. There wasn't a contest of wills, as Quinn would have once had. Instead, a feeling of utter peace seemed to flow between them. Elizabeth took her husband's hand, concern furrowing her brow.

"I hear we're brothers in more ways than one." Quinn grinned as Rupert raised his eyebrow. "Last fall I became a Christian. That makes us brothers through marriage and through the Lord. Welcome to the family."

Rupert's eyes glittered with moisture. Tears ran down Elizabeth's cheeks. Quinn stepped forward, and the two men enfolded Elizabeth in a long-awaited hug.

✤

Voices and the delicious smell of roasted meat woke Kathleen. She could tell from the shadows that evening approached. The bedroom door swung open, and Quinn peeked in.

"Awake at last?" He crossed to the bed and kissed her. "My sister is here. You have to meet her."

Kathleen stretched and swung her legs off the bed. "How's Rupert?" She tried to keep the question light.

"He's great with my sister." A rueful smile quirked Quinn's lips. "Once more, I see where God's hand was at work when I couldn't understand. He used Elizabeth's godly response to Rupert's meanness to eat at him until he yielded his life. They make a wonderful couple and are even talking about taking a trip to Tucson to visit us in a year or two."

Fixing her hair, Kathleen couldn't help putting her hand over the birthmark on her cheek. Quinn's parents hadn't said a word, but she knew they noticed. How could anyone not see the mark?

Quinn's hands settled on her shoulders. He brushed a kiss on her neck, sending a tingle down her spine. "You are so beautiful, my love. Come meet my sister, and you'll understand a lot."

Hand in hand, they walked into the kitchen, where Mary and Elizabeth were visiting. A tiny baby slept in a cradle in the corner.

"Here she is." Mary beamed at Kathleen. "Your new sister."

A young woman as tiny as Mary with wheat-colored hair turned to greet Kathleen. Her eyes were a darker blue than Quinn's. Her smile radiated joy. Kathleen's throat became tight. Her eyes burned. She could feel Quinn's arms tighten around her as she gazed at his sister, a beautiful girl with a dark brown birthmark staining her left cheek.

"Kathleen, I'm so happy to meet you." Elizabeth came forward and opened her arms. Kathleen stepped into her embrace. No wonder Quinn hadn't looked at her star as a deformity. He'd grown up with a sister with a mark like hers. Now she understood all his comments about Elizabeth being tormented and teased. That's why he'd been so drawn to her and so protective of her.

"Is this my new sister-in-law?" The deep voice boomed across the kitchen. Elizabeth released Kathleen and turned to the huge man standing beside her father. He came over and wrapped an arm around Elizabeth, love and gentleness radiating from him. "I hear you're visiting from the great Sonoran Desert."

"That's right." Quinn slipped his arms around her. "Rupert, I'd like you to meet Kathleen, my Sonoran Star." He leaned around and kissed her on the cheek.

Joy such as she'd never thought possible filled Kathleen.

Sonoran
Sweetheart

Chapter 1

The ring of the blacksmith's hammer striking against hot metal reverberated through the air, making Lavette Johnson's heart pound in time to the beat. Like primitive, rhythmic music, the sound drew her, intoxicating and unavoidable. She moved to the doorway of the shop, past horses waiting at the hitching post, neat piles of tools, and various utensils waiting for repair. Extra aprons for protection against heat and sparks hung on hooks by the door. A workbench with a variety of hammers and tools laid in orderly rows stood along one side of the three-sided room.

Stepping out of the bright sunlight, Lavette squinted against the dimness of the forge. She blinked, then stared at the giant of a man who swung the huge hammer as if it were a child's toy. His shirt, the sleeves torn and frayed at the shoulders, clung like a second skin to his bulging muscles. The blacksmith switched the hammer into his other hand and didn't lose a beat. His ebony skin glistened, the glow of the fire in the forge making tiny light particles dance across his arms.

Lavette sucked in a breath, pulling hard to get more air. Black dots danced across her vision. In a recess of her mind, she wondered if this was the way Miss Susannah felt before she swooned in order to get some handsome boy's attention. Lavette shoved the thought away. She didn't like to remember the years she'd spent as a slave to Miss Susannah's family before her people were liberated at the end of the war. Free! She scoffed at the word. She would never be free. She wasn't then, and she wasn't now. Lavette refused to listen to people talk about emancipation. She'd resigned herself to a life of servitude in one form or another. She didn't understand why she had to be in bondage, but she knew her place.

She also knew she had no room in her life for a husband or children. She'd seen what happened to her papa and mama when their older sons and daughters were sold off one by one, many of them leaving while they were still too young to be separated from their parents.

"We need to do this while they're young enough to train right," Miss Susannah's papa said. Lavette didn't believe a word of it. He was cruel and greedy, only looking at the money he would make from the sale. He always seemed to delight in the weeping and moaning of the parting relatives.

Unable to take her eyes off the man working at the forge, Lavette knew she had to leave. This blacksmith had been recommended as the best, but Lavette knew better now. He was a dangerous man. Oh, he probably was the best in Tucson, but her heart could tell he was a threat to her. The sight of him heightened her senses. She used to dream about the kind of man she would marry. Of course, that was before she knew she would never be a wife. This man with his great height, treelike arms, and good reputation fulfilled all her girlish dreams. She always imagined a big, strong husband who could shelter her from all the pain of life. Part of her longed to race forward in excited anticipation, the other part desired to race away in absolute terror.

Terror won. Lavette stepped back to make an exit. Her movement must have caught the blacksmith's eye, for he looked up. Like a rabbit caught in a snare, she froze. Intelligence shone from his black eyes along with something else she couldn't quite name. He stared, his hammer poised for a blow that never fell. Now that he faced her, she could see he was as handsome as she'd dreamed he would be, with rounded cheeks and a slightly flattened nose. His face split in a wide grin. Lavette couldn't breathe. Oh, she was right. This was a dangerous man.

Josiah Washington usually lost himself in the rhythm of his work. Once, he'd loved the solitude and the pounding beat of the hammer falling on the metal. During these times he felt closest to Jesus. Lately, he'd needed that closeness. Although he had friends in Tucson, an ache of loneliness had begun to needle at him. He watched his friends Lieutenant Conlon Sullivan and his wife Glorianna, and now Deputy Quinn Kirby had married Kathleen O'Connor. They were so happy. They shared something special between them. Every time he saw them together, Josiah couldn't stop the heart-wrenching anguish that filled him.

Shame filled him. He should be thankful to God for the friends he had. Before he'd led Conlon to the Lord, he'd had no friends as such. Since then, he'd become close with the Sullivans, the Kirbys, and friendly with the other Christians who worshipped with them. These believers agreed with 1 Samuel 16:7. Instead of looking at his skin color, they looked at his heart. He should be content with that.

Jesus, I don't mean to complain, but I'm tired of being alone. If this is Your will that I remain single all my life, then please remove the desire I have for a wife. But, Lord, if You have someone in mind, let me know clearly when I see her. Thank You, Jesus.

With a lithe movement, Josiah slipped the hammer from his right hand to his left. He hated the thought of ending up with one arm bigger than the other like some blacksmiths did. When his father taught him to shoe horses, he also showed him the trick of working the metal with either hand. Josiah made sure to keep in constant practice.

Something moved at the front of the shop. Josiah looked up, expecting to see one of his regular customers bringing him a new job. He'd never lacked for work since leaving the cavalry and coming to Tucson. Some of the other blacksmiths complained because their steady customers preferred Josiah's work to theirs. He didn't intend to take away their clients, but he wouldn't compromise his work ethics, either.

The heat from the hot metal he was working rose in undulating waves in front of him. A mirage. That's what he was seeing. She certainly wasn't one of his regulars. Delicate bone structure gave her heart-shaped face an ethereal look. Her flawless complexion, dark coffee with a touch of milk, made his fingers twitch with a longing to touch. Josiah's chest began to ache. He realized he'd been holding his breath. He exhaled and drew in a deep, ragged breath. This was the woman of his dreams, the woman God made to be a helpmeet for him. Oh, that she could be real and not a vision.

She moved. Josiah caught his breath. She took another small step backwards. Suddenly he knew she wasn't a mirage, vision, or dream. She was real—a living, breathing person. *God, is this Your answer? Is she the one?*

Josiah's hammer clattered to the floor. They both jumped. He hadn't even realized he was losing his grip on the heavy tool. He glanced down at the iron scraps the hammer had fallen on, feeling stupid as he tried to pull his thoughts together. When he looked back at the door, she had stepped close enough to it to be framed by the bright sun. Wisps of curly black frizzed out from the rest of her hair, which was pulled back into a neat bun at the base of her neck. A look of uncertainty or fear widened her already large eyes. A burst of compassion such as Josiah had never known raced through him. He wanted nothing more than to care for this woman and to protect her from whatever she feared.

She turned to leave.

"Wait." Josiah stretched out his hand, wishing he could reach across and stop her. Panic rose up at the thought that she might go, and he would never have the chance to find out her name.

She hesitated, her face still turned away.

Stepping around the bench, Josiah closed the distance between them in two quick strides. In slow motion, she twisted back around to face him. The scents of cinnamon, fresh bread, and wood smoke wafted up from her.

"Cinnamon."

"What?" The vision's melodic voice matched the rest of her.

Horrified, Josiah realized he'd spoken his thoughts aloud. "I, uh." He glanced around, hoping to come up with something that would sound plausible. He didn't. Josiah shrugged. The truth was always best anyway. "You smell like cinnamon."

She looked down, her impossibly long eyelashes brushing like delicate butterflies against her cheeks. Josiah was in the act of lifting his hand to touch her face when he caught himself. What was he doing? He didn't even know her name. For some reason, he couldn't think clearly. Frantic that she would disappear, he struggled to think of something to say. Why was she here?

"Oh." Josiah's gasp of the word caused the angel to look up. "Is there something I could help you with, Miss?"

"Johnson." A small smile flitted across her lips.

Josiah stared at her. He couldn't figure out what she was saying. He couldn't remember what he'd asked.

"Lavette Johnson. My name is Lavette Johnson." She tilted her head back and managed to look at him. Even her eyes reminded him of spices. The rich brown depths glowed with intelligence and humor.

"Josiah. Washington." Josiah knew she must think him a complete dolt. He couldn't drag his gaze from the multitude of wiry strands of hair framing her face like a troop of fairies dancing in pure joy at her beauty. He could feel from the stretching of his cheeks that he must be grinning at her, but he couldn't seem to quit.

Lavette took a step away, then held out her hand. "It's a pleasure to meet ya, Mr. Washington."

For the first time, he noticed her pronounced Southern accent. He thought he could listen to her talk all day, even if she never said anything even halfway important.

"We don't stand on much formality out here." Josiah did his best to scale down the overpowering grin to a smile. "You can call me Josiah."

Once more, her eyelashes rested on the gentle slope of her cheek. "I don't believe I know you well enough for that, Mr. Washington. Perhaps if we become friends, I will consider using your given name."

Friends? Had she said they might become friends? Josiah wanted to do cartwheels like that young fellow who worked at that sideshow had done.

"Hey, Smithy."

Josiah tensed. Even the smile left his face. He straightened and turned toward the opening of his shop. Bertrand Mead. He'd know that voice anywhere. One of the drawbacks of being in business was the necessity of serving the public, no matter how difficult they were. Bertrand Mead was worse than difficult. Mead owned a hostelry and saloon. To all intents and purposes, he gave the appearance of being a well-to-do businessman. Josiah knew differently. He knew about the secret houses Mead was suspected of running. There was even talk about him bringing in young girls from back East to work there—girls too young to work anywhere except doing chores for their mama or papa. The thought of such an immoral action made Josiah's blood boil.

Stepping around Miss Johnson, Josiah nodded at the fancy-dressed man seated in a small buggy. "What can I do for you, Mr. Mead?" Josiah's voice must have held a warning, for Lavette moved a step closer, like she was trying to hide behind him.

"I want you to take a look at my team." Mead gestured at the matched bays hitched to his buggy. "They haven't been shod in awhile. I think the mare is getting ready to throw a shoe."

Standing several feet away from the horses, Josiah could still hear the faint click of a loose shoe as the mare fidgeted. "Would you like me to stop by and get the horses, or do you want to leave them now? I can take care of them as soon as I finish the job I'm working on, if you like." Although he didn't care about pleasing this customer, Josiah did his best to keep contact with Mead to a minimum. The faster he finished the man's horses, the sooner he could be out of his oily presence.

"I have a little business down the street, so I'll leave them now." Mead stepped down, landing gingerly in the dust, careful of his polished shoes. He brushed imaginary dirt from his pant leg, then tossed the lead rope toward Josiah. The mare jerked her head away, white showing around her eyes. In one swift move, Josiah swept up the rope. He stepped closer and began to soothe the startled horse, wondering if Mead abused the animal to have her react like that.

"Well, well, what have we here?"

Josiah whirled around at Mead's question. He'd forgotten that stepping toward the mare would expose Miss Johnson. When he moved, she was no longer concealed from Mead's sight.

Lavette stared at the ground in front of her. Her hands clenched the folds of her skirt. Small white teeth caught at her bottom lip to keep it from quivering. She looked terrified. Josiah understood. The Southern accent. The hesitance at meeting his eyes. She'd once been a slave. She knew the power a white man had over a black girl. No wonder she was so scared.

Wrapping the lead rein around the hitching post, Josiah let his long stride carry him between Mead and Miss Johnson. "I'll have those horses ready for you in an hour, Mr. Mead. You can go ahead and take care of your business."

Mead moved to the side of Josiah. His shifty gaze traveled over Miss Johnson in a way that made Josiah want to wipe Mead's face in the dirt. *Vengeance is mine, saith the Lord.* Josiah wanted to groan as the verse popped into his head. Most of the time he found it easy to allow the Lord to work. Right now, he wanted to take over and do things his way rather than wait for God to handle matters.

"I don't believe I've met this young lady." Bertrand looked at Josiah. His ice blue eyes glinted with an evil look. "Perhaps you could introduce us."

Clenching his teeth, Josiah stepped to Lavette's side. "Miss Johnson, this is Bertrand Mead. Mead, Miss Johnson."

Mead bowed low, sweeping the hat from his head. "This is truly a pleasure, Miss Johnson. I'm sure I can't wait to get to know you better." He lifted her hand to his lips.

With a small cry, Lavette yanked her hand back. Lifting her skirts, she raced away down the street.

Chapter 2

Closing the kitchen door behind her, Lavette leaned back against the wood, her legs trembling so hard, she wondered how she managed to make her way home. She'd gone from total elation to complete terror so fast, her mind was still catching up to her body. When Bertrand Mead had touched her, all she could feel were the times Miss Susannah's father would catch her alone and put his slimy hands on her. She shuddered. Bile rose in her throat. What was she to do? Would Mr. Mead find out where she lived?

Her breathing slowed, and Lavette made her way to the bucket of water by the stove. Wetting her face, she thought how nice it would be to wash away her troubles as well. She hadn't been around Master Brennan, Susannah's father, in nine years, yet she could still see and feel him as if he were here in this room. Growing up, she'd lived in terror of the man. Even when she was a young girl, Mr. Brennan would look at her in a way that made her uncomfortable. As she grew older, she learned to never be near him without Miss Susannah close by.

"Lavette? Are you here?" A thin, quavery voice came through the doorway, followed by deep, hacking coughs. A bell tinkled.

Lavette dried her face and hurried to the front bedroom where Mrs. Sawyer rested. The elderly woman lay on her side, her translucent skin taking on a slightly bluish cast. She held a handkerchief to her mouth as the coughs racked her frail body. Her gray-white hair, flattened on one side, curled around her face.

Moving to the basin of water on the night table, Lavette wet a clean rag to wipe the perspiration from Mrs. Sawyer's brow. The features on the left side of Mrs. Sawyer's face still sagged a little, refusing to work properly just as her left arm and leg gave her problems. Eight months ago Lavette had come home from shopping to find Mrs. Sawyer lying on the floor, pale as death. The doctor diagnosed the problem as apoplexy. He assured Lavette that her mistress might improve, but the improvements would be slow and would take a lot of work. Then he showed Lavette how to help Mrs. Sawyer exercise her limbs and suggested she encourage her to talk, even though the sounds were garbled.

For the first few weeks, Lavette felt nothing but despair as she tried to help the kind lady. The muscles refused to respond. Mrs. Sawyer couldn't seem to say the simplest words that once flowed with ease. As the day wore on and she tired, the responses were smaller. By evening, Mrs. Sawyer would be in tears, and Lavette often felt like joining her.

Lavette refused to give up on the exercises and made Mrs. Sawyer repeat certain words every day. Bit by bit, she began to improve. Now, after eight long months, her speech faltered only a little, and she walked a short distance with Lavette's assistance. Her movements were still very slow, but even the doctor praised them both for the progress they'd made. It hadn't been easy coming out here. They'd taken the trip in short distances, and each day had taken its toll. Still, they'd made it. Now, although she had a nasty cold, Mrs. Sawyer seemed to be gaining strength.

"Is Gretta coming by today?" Mrs. Sawyer's gaze sought Lavette's.

"She'll be here in time for the evening meal." Lavette forced a smile and a light tone, not wanting Mrs. Sawyer to know the horror she'd faced this morning. After all, this woman wouldn't understand the terror and the power white men had over her.

"I need to get up and dressed." Mrs. Sawyer's voice was hoarse from all the coughing. Sweat popped out on her brow as she tried to sit up unassisted.

"Not yet." Lavette put her arm behind Mrs. Sawyer for support as she plumped the pillows and piled them behind her. Then she eased the older lady back until she rested against the cushioning. "Dinner is a long way off. You need to rest so you'll be ready for those rambunctious grandsons of yours."

Mrs. Sawyer's pale blue eyes lit with some of their old sparkle. "They are quite a rowdy trio. I wish I felt good enough to get up and run with them. Why are they coming so late?"

"Your son-in-law will be able to join you for tonight's meal. Your daughter will be here in the afternoon with the children, then he will join you at dinnertime."

Mrs. Sawyer gave Lavette a smile that shone with sincerity. "He's such a wonderful young man and so good to Gretta and the children."

"I'm sure he's as wonderful as you say." Lavette finished straightening the covers.

"I'll bring you some breakfast, then you can rest for awhile." Lavette hurried to the kitchen, having noted the tired circles beneath her mistress's eyes. She wouldn't be awake for long and needed some nourishing food to continue gaining strength.

The familiarity of the routine gave Lavette time to think as she worked. Her thoughts strayed back to this morning, to the time before that repulsive Mead had accosted her. Instead, she could clearly recall the blacksmith's warm smile and dark eyes. Had his eyes shone with interest in her? Her pulse quickened, and for a moment, she allowed the childhood dream of husband and family to wash over her. She imagined the patter of bare feet racing across the floor and the eager smiles on the small faces. Those smiles all resembled the friendly grin of a certain blacksmith.

With a final tap, Josiah finished the last shoe on Bertrand Mead's mare. He patted her, rubbing down her neck and scratching her ears. She sure was a sweet horse. If he ever found out Mead was mistreating her, he'd take her away from the man. No one should be allowed to own animals if he abused them.

"Have you finished?"

Josiah turned around at the sound of Bertrand Mead's voice. The bay pressed close against Josiah's side.

"Yes, Sir." Josiah patted the mare's neck, hoping to reassure her. She tried to dance away as Mead stepped closer.

Mead raised the short buggy whip, his eyes flashing with anger. "Stupid horse. I should sell her and get a decent one."

"Would you like me to hitch her to the buggy?" Josiah stepped in front of the mare, hoping to keep Mead from hitting her.

"Fine. See to it." Mead crossed to stand in the shade near his buggy, the whip flicking against his leg in a steady rhythm.

Doing his best to soothe the skittish mare, Josiah urged her back into the traces next to the other bay. Her eyes rolled as she tilted her head to keep an eye on her owner. Nostrils wide, she snorted and stamped, the opposite of the sweet, contented horse he'd finished shoeing.

"There you go, Sir." Josiah strode to her head to give her a final pat as Mead climbed into the buggy. "She's a fine animal. They make a smart-looking team."

"Of course they do." Mead's icy gaze chilled Josiah. "I wouldn't have anything less." He leaned forward, his gaze riveting. "Speaking of smart looking, who was the young lady with you earlier?"

"I introduced you to her." Josiah wanted to walk away and ignore the question. He could picture slime dripping from this man.

"Yes, I remember her name." Mead slapped the whip against the side of the conveyance, causing both horses to jump. Mead jerked the reins. "I want to know who she is, where she lives."

Josiah breathed a silent sigh of relief. At least he could answer honestly. "I only met her this morning. I don't know where she stays."

Mead's pale eyes fastened on Josiah's with a gaze that would have intimidated many men. A slow, feral smile tilted his lips but didn't reach his eyes. "I have plans for that girl. You don't often find beauty like hers." His eyes took on a thoughtful gaze. "I wonder if she can sing as pretty as she looks. Imagine what she would do for my business. Of course, there are other ways a beautiful girl can be useful."

Anger swept through Josiah. He clenched his fists tightly against his legs. Every part of him wanted to drag this man from the buggy and wipe that insolent look from his face. *Vengeance is mine.* The voice of the Holy Spirit seemed to whisper in his mind. The anger drained away, and Josiah stepped back to watch Mead drive off, whipping his horses to a quick trot.

Stalking back into the shop, Josiah stoked the fire, then picked up his hammer. The heavy instrument felt good as his fist tightened around the handle. He couldn't wait for the ore to get pliable in the heat. Was this why the Lord made him a blacksmith—so he could take out his anger and frustrations on metal instead of pounding men like Mead?

Stirring the coals, Josiah shoved a piece of iron in to heat up. Impatience tore at him, making him want to pull the rod from the fire long before it would be ready. At last, he plucked the bar out, shaking the remnants of red-hot coals from the shaft. After swinging over to the anvil, Josiah hefted the hammer in his hand and began to pound with a vengeance that sent sparks flying.

Jesus, help me. You know I want to think about this being Mead instead of a piece of iron. Help me to forgive, to find something about the man that is lovable in Your eyes. I surely can't see anything from my point of view.

The redness faded as the bar cooled, and Josiah turned to thrust it back into the coals for a second heating. He did feel better. Praying and working always helped. Blacksmithing was a noisy occupation and gave him plenty of time for prayer and thinking.

When he finished talking with God, his mind strayed from Bertrand Mead to Lavette Johnson. Never had he seen such a beautiful woman. He could picture Adam's reaction to Eve in the garden when Adam said, "This is now bone of my bones, flesh of my flesh." Adam must have been as bowled over by Eve as Josiah was with Lavette. She had to be the one for him. He could still remember the prayer, then looking up and seeing her.

"I don't think I've ever seen anyone so excited over his work before. Have you, Quinn?" Conlon Sullivan stood in the door of the shop next to Deputy Quinn Kirby. Both of them had thoughtful expressions on their faces.

"Nope. I don't believe I have." Quinn frowned and shook his head. "I love my job, and I know you love yours, but we don't go around wearing a grin that stretches our cheeks out of shape while we're doing our work."

Heat other than from the forge warmed Josiah's face. He put the metal bar back by the coals, trying to give himself some time to get over the embarrassment of being caught thinking of Lavette. At least with his dark skin, his cheeks wouldn't show red like Quinn's usually did. He wiped his hands on a rag.

"Afternoon, Conlon, Quinn. What brings you over this way? Got time to sit a spell?" Gesturing at a bench outside in the shade, Josiah waited for the pair to lead the way, then followed.

Conlon slumped down and tilted his hat forward to lessen the sun's brightness. "We may not have come for anything in particular. That bright light drew us."

"That's right." Quinn pretended to rub his eyes. "The glow from your smithy made the sun look dim for awhile. We didn't realize you could make a place shine like that."

"If Glorianna and I ever run out of lamp oil, we'll have you come over and light up the house."

"All right." Josiah thought about tipping the bench over and sending his joking friends into the dust. "If you don't want me to dunk you in the horse trough, lay off."

"Did you hear that, Deputy? I believe this man is threatening us."

Quinn frowned. "I may have to consult the judge on this one. I'm not sure of the penalty here."

Josiah laughed. He couldn't help it. These two were his friends, and they wouldn't quit until they wormed every bit of information from him they could. "Aw, what do you guys really want? A tool repaired? Horses shod?"

Blue eyes twinkled as Conlon chuckled. "I did have some business, but now we want to know the reason for that idiotic grin. A smile that dazzling doesn't come along every day."

With a groan, Josiah shook his head. Conlon wouldn't give up until he told him. They'd been friends for too long. He couldn't hide anything anymore.

"A girl came by the shop this morning." Warmth flowed through Josiah at the thought of Lavette.

"A girl?" Conlon raised an eyebrow. "Just any girl? Is this someone we know?"

"Naw. She's new in town. I don't even know where I can find her. She ran off before I could find out where she's living."

"If she's that afraid of you, maybe you should give up before you start." Conlon's remark started Quinn chuckling.

"She wasn't afraid of me. Bertrand Mead showed up."

Quinn and Conlon sobered. Quinn frowned. "He's enough to make anyone run away. I wish I could find something to pin on him, but that fella is slipperier than a wet snake."

Clapping Josiah on the back, Conlon nodded. "So tell us what you know about this girl."

"Her name is Lavette Johnson. She's the most beautiful woman God ever made." Josiah gave a sheepish grin. "I'm not saying Glorianna and Kathleen aren't beautiful, but Lavette is special. From her Southern accent and the way she acted around Mead, I'd say she grew up on a plantation as a slave."

"Did Mead do something wrong?" Quinn asked.

"Everything Mead does is wrong." Josiah groaned. "Sorry. I have a hard time finding something likable about that fella. Anyway, he was cocky and tried to touch her. She ran away."

"Did he go after her?" Quinn had a mean look in his eye.

"No, he let her go, but he knows her name, and he wants to find her. Who knows what he'll do if he does?"

"Well, I guess you'll have to find Miss Johnson before Mead does." Conlon stood and stretched. "If I wasn't needing to get business over with, I'd take the time to tell you all about the man in my regiment whose mother-in-law came to town with a servant who used to be a slave."

Chapter 3

S urging to his feet, Josiah didn't know whether to grab Conlon and hug him or shake him. "You know where she lives?"

"How many head of horses did you need shod, Conlon?" Quinn pulled out his knife and began to clean his fingernails.

"That's right." Conlon snapped his fingers. "Josiah, I wanted to see how soon you can come to Fort Lowell and check the horses. Several of them need new shoes before we go out on maneuvers again." Conlon studied the cloudless blue sky.

Josiah knew they were funning with him, so he bit back a groan. "I have to know where she lives. Tell me the man's name." Josiah wanted to get down on his knees and beg Conlon at the same time his stomach clenched in anticipation.

"Now, Josiah, you know I'm not a gossiping man. I'll have to go back and check with the gentleman involved and see if I can give out that information."

"Conlon, I will never shoe your horse again if you don't stop this."

"Josiah's a mite touchy, wouldn't you say, Quinn?"

"I will tell Glorianna, and you won't have a hot meal or a moment of peace for weeks." Josiah leaned forward, his fists on his hips.

Conlon winced. "Aw, you're getting downright mean." He sighed. "All right. I wouldn't want you bothering Glory about this, and I can see you're determined. Paul Ashton's mother-in law arrived two weeks ago. She's had an attack of apoplexy, and his wife wanted her to come here to visit since they couldn't go back East. I think she's hoping her mother will decide to stay."

"So where are they living?" Josiah once again resisted the urge to shake the information out of Conlon.

"I don't know that." Conlon lifted his hat, ran his hand through his thick black hair, and settled his cap back on his head.

"What do you mean, you don't know?"

"Paul told us about them coming, but they aren't staying at the same house because Paul has three very rambunctious boys. They thought his mother-in-law would be able to rest easier in a separate house."

Josiah groaned. "Where can I find this Paul Ashton so I can ask where they're living?"

"He'll be out at the fort all day. Then I believe he said something about coming to town for supper tonight." Conlon grinned and clapped Josiah on the back. "I'll ask him tomorrow, so when you come to shoe the horses, I can tell you where to find your lady."

"That might be too late." Josiah rubbed a drip of sweat from his temple.

"Why are you so certain you need to find her right away?" Quinn snapped his knife shut and slipped it back into his pocket.

"You didn't see the way Mead looked at her or hear the comments he made about her. That man has something in mind, and I don't think it's anything good."

Sauntering after Conlon, Quinn swung up onto his horse. He grinned at Conlon and gave him a wink. "You know that little adobe house about a block from Mrs. Monroy's boardinghouse?" Josiah felt a surge of hope as Quinn continued. "It's the house that sits back a ways from the road and has been deserted for several months."

Frowning, Conlon gave a quick nod. "Yeah, I remember the place."

"I heard the other day that someone moved in there. Some lady from back East who's convalescing. I believe she has someone there helping her out."

Josiah let out a whoop. "I could drag you off that horse and hug you, Quinn Kirby. Of course, that's right after I yell at the two of you for tormenting me like this."

"I think that means we should leave." Quinn laughed and urged his horse after Conlon's.

"I'll be out to the fort on Thursday, Conlon," Josiah called after the two riders, the grin once more splitting his face. This afternoon, when he'd finished his work, he'd clean up, mosey over to that house, and welcome those newcomers. He'd show them the people of Tucson were mighty hospitable. He chuckled to himself. At least he wanted to show one of them how friendly he could be.

※

Straightening from putting away the last of the dishes, Lavette put her hands on her hips and rotated her shoulders to ease the ache. Moving Mrs. Sawyer around in the bed got harder every day. The older woman was gaining strength and weight. At times like tonight when Lavette's back felt like she'd been kicked by a whole herd of mules, she had to wonder if Mrs. Sawyer's continued recovery wasn't a mixed blessing. Shaking her head, she sighed as she wiped a few errant crumbs from the table. She'd come to care for Amelia Sawyer too much to want her to stay sickly. For years, she'd wanted to hate the woman but couldn't because Mrs. Sawyer had to be one of the most caring people she'd ever been around. Once Mrs. Sawyer believed a person worthwhile, she was very loyal to them.

Glancing out the window, Lavette could see the sun sinking lower in the sky, but still giving plenty of light. What would have been fall days back home proved to still carry summer warmth here in Tucson. A gentle breeze blew outside, and she relished the idea of sitting on the porch with the mending she intended to do this evening. That breeze would feel good, and she knew the house sat far enough from the street that most people wouldn't notice her. She had no desire to have anyone stop by for a conversation with her. She preferred the peace and quiet of her own thoughts after a day such as this one. Fixing supper and helping with

Gretta's children while the adults ate always wore her out. Those boys were terrors, although adorable ones.

Settling into the chair at the end of the porch nearest the parlor, Lavette tipped her head back, allowing the soothing wind to cool her face. From here, she could hear her employer if she needed anything; yet with the trellis and vines coming down over the porch, she wouldn't be easily visible to those passing by. This position was almost as good as the weeping willow she used to sit under as a child, trying to hide from the ugliness of slavery.

Her thoughts turned to her family so far away. She hadn't seen them in years. By now her brother Toby would be eighteen. Was he married? Did he still work with her father, or had he moved out on his own? Lila and Nellie, her sisters, would be fourteen and eleven now. Lila would be starting to attract the attention of some of the young men in the area. Before long, they would be all grown up, and Lavette would have missed watching it happen. She blinked back tears, knowing they did no good and hating the weakness of them.

Placing her mending in her lap, Lavette watched the street. This small cottage sat back from the road, the view partially blocked by the large house in front of and to the side of this one. Although only a small portion of the roadway was visible, Lavette could see a few people strolling past. Evenings here seemed to be a time of getting out and visiting with neighbors. She was thankful her distance from the street gave her privacy.

A low moan came from inside the house. Lavette jumped up and set the skirt she was working on in the vacated chair. Walking quietly, she moved into the house and peeked into Mrs. Sawyer's room. The elderly woman had thrown off her covers, drawing her knees up to fight a chill. After tucking the blankets back around the woman, Lavette smoothed Mrs. Sawyer's hair and waited until her breathing evened. She tiptoed from the room. Quite often since they'd traveled west, Mrs. Sawyer woke from dreams that made her restless. Lavette hoped this wouldn't be one of those nights, or she wouldn't get much sleep, either.

The shadows were growing when Lavette stepped back out onto the porch. Her slippers whispered soft against the boards as she headed for her chair. When she bent to pick up her sewing, a shadow at the edge of the porch moved. Lavette clapped her hand across her mouth to avoid a shriek that would surely wake Mrs. Sawyer. Her heart pounded.

"Sorry to startle you, Miss Johnson. I saw you go inside. You left your mending on the chair, so I figured you'd be back out. I hope you don't mind that I waited." The huge blacksmith's grin banished the shadows.

Forcing herself to take a few deep breaths, Lavette waited a moment for her heart rate to slow. "You scared the insides out of me."

He twisted the hat in his hands until she wondered if the thing would survive the torture. "You rushed off so fast this morning, I didn't find out what you needed." Josiah looked chagrined, as if he knew the story sounded contrived.

"Is there something I can do for you?"

Clasping her hands together, Lavette hoped Josiah wouldn't notice her trembling. For some strange reason, she couldn't control her emotions around this man. She couldn't even seem to concentrate on what he asked.

"Excuse me?" She felt stupid, staring at his wonderful smile and missing what he'd said.

"I wondered if there were some business I could help you with."

"I—uh, no I don't believe so."

He frowned, the fading of his smile allowing the shadows to close in. He arched one eyebrow. "Are you sure? You must have come by my shop for some reason. Do you have a horse that needs to be shod?"

A horse? His shop? Her brain tried to grasp his question. Remembrance flooded over her. "Oh, this morning." Heat suffused her cheeks. "I wanted to ask about a few things. They weren't important."

"Please sit down." He gestured at her still-vacant chair. Picking up her mending, she slid into the chair. His smile returned. Her heart sped up.

"If those things you wanted to ask about were important this morning, then they're still important now. Why don't you tell me what you need, and I'll see if I can help?"

"I—we arrived in Tucson a couple of weeks ago. Mrs. Sawyer plans to stay another six weeks. I wanted to inquire about getting a knife repaired and possibly getting another one to use while we're here. I thought perhaps you made tools as well as shoeing horses." She twisted the torn skirt in her hands until the prick of the needle stuck in the cloth startled her.

"I have several knives and other utensils at my shop. I'll see that you get what you need." Josiah settled his large frame back against the rail, which creaked under the pressure.

"We'll only be here a short time before heading back East." Lavette couldn't meet his eyes. Maybe his interest would be discouraged if he thought she would be leaving soon.

"There's no reason your stay can't be as comfortable as possible." Josiah's voice was a deep rumble that calmed her. No wonder the man was so good with horses. She thought she could sit and listen to him talk all night. He spoke in such a slow, easy manner.

"I've heard you're here to visit Paul Ashton and his family. Where do you come from?" Josiah's eyes gleamed like obsidian in the shadows.

"We came here from Virginia." Lavette lowered her gaze from his, unable to meet his intense study for long.

"Have you always lived there?" Josiah crossed his arms over his massive chest. He acted like he planned to stay for a long time. Lavette couldn't think of a way to get rid of him fast without being offensive, and she didn't want to insult this gentle giant.

"I lived in Alabama before moving north with Mrs. Sawyer because of her health." Smoothing the skirt she was mending, Lavette couldn't seem to quit talking so he would leave. "Mrs. Sawyer had to leave the South because of the damp in the air. The doctor said the moist night air was bad for her lungs, and the only hope for her to improve was to get her up north in the cooler, dryer climates. He wanted her to go to New York, but she insisted she didn't know anyone there. Her brother lived in Virginia, so we moved in with him."

"So when Mrs. Sawyer leaves, she'll return to her brother's house?"

Lavette's gaze jerked up to meet those twinkling eyes and that wide grin that affected her. She looked back down at her sewing. Had he meant to suggest she might not be returning with Mrs. Sawyer? If so, he didn't understand her position here. She had no choice about what she would do.

"Mrs. Sawyer's brother passed on last year. He never married. His solicitor has instructions to see that she is well cared for as long as she chooses to reside there. We'll be going back to Virginia as soon as this visit is over." Lavette wanted to ask Josiah to tell her about his background, if for no other reason than to hear his voice, but she didn't want him to think her interested. She wanted to discourage him, not encourage him.

"Tucson is a lot different than the cities in Virginia." Josiah shifted, uncrossing his arms and resting more on the porch rail. "Do you prefer the busier lifestyle back there?"

"Oh, no." Lavette found herself meeting his gaze before she thought. She looked away quickly. "I like the quiet here. It's so peaceful. Nobody rushes anywhere."

Josiah chuckled. "That's true. Around here, the summer heat teaches everyone to move slower to survive. Do you miss the green?"

Frowning, Lavette considered the difference from their lush surroundings in Virginia and the sparse growth of the desert. "This is different and takes some adjusting." She looked off at the mountains rising starkly against the sky. "There's a beauty here that can't be compared to my home. Everything seems bigger and wider, maybe grander." She stopped, embarrassed to have said so much.

"Sounds to me like you would enjoy living here. Why don't you plan to stay when Mrs. Sawyer goes back East? She can find someone else to work for her. I'm sure there are a lot of young women who would gladly accept a position."

"I can't do that." Lavette jumped up from her chair, her mending falling to the porch floor. Scrabbling to gather everything up, she wondered how this conversation had gotten so personal.

Josiah's shoulder brushed against hers. Lavette froze. He took her hand, turned it over, and placed her needle and thread in her palm, then closed her fingers over the implements. "I don't know why you can't do that, but I intend to find out."

Lavette fled into the house, letting the door slam shut behind her. She leaned back against the closed door, her whole body shaking. Why? Why did she have to meet this man now? Her life was set out before her, and she knew her place. She'd been comfortable with that until Mr. Washington entered the picture.

The sound of his heavy tread echoed on the boards of the porch. She held her breath, waiting for him to leave. As she began to relax, thinking he'd gone, the wooden entryway she rested against began to vibrate as he knocked.

Chapter 4

Amazement swept through Josiah as he watched the door slam shut behind Lavette. He still knelt on the rough boards of the porch, his hand tingling from the contact with hers. The warmth of her fingers lingered as if he still held them. Why had she rushed off like that? Had he said something he shouldn't have? Had he been too forward, inviting her to stay in Tucson when they'd only met today? He hadn't meant the invitation to sound so personal.

A deep sigh escaped him. She was as beautiful this evening as she'd been in the early morning light—maybe even more lovely, now that he'd had the chance to watch her. Although he enjoyed the glimpses of her cinnamon eyes, he loved watching those long eyelashes curl against her cheek. Since they'd begun to talk, he'd hardly been able to take his eyes from her long, slender fingers. Helping her pick up her sewing supplies had been a gift from God because he'd wanted so much to touch her, to hold her hand.

Lord, You need to guide me. I don't know why she wants to run back east when she seems to like it here in Tucson. Help me to not be too pushy. I know she must be the one for me. Otherwise, You wouldn't have brought her by the shop right when I asked You about a wife. Now, please help me convince her that she's the one.

Standing up, Josiah noticed a basket of other mending pushed behind her chair. He grinned. All he had to do was ask and God answered. This was the opportunity he needed to see her again so soon. Maybe he could even understand why she'd run off like a scared rabbit. That frightened look in her eyes reminded him of an animal cornered by a hunter. No way did he want her to be afraid of him.

After picking up the basket, he strode across the porch. No sound came from inside the house. He wondered where she had gone, what she was doing and thinking. Taking a deep breath, he rapped his knuckles on the door, careful not to shake the old wood too much.

He waited. No tap of footsteps sounded. Where had she disappeared to so fast? Out the back door? Was she helping Mrs. Sawyer and didn't hear his knock? The door flung open, and he stepped back in startled surprise. Lavette faced him, still clutching the needle and thread with the skirt draped over her arm. Several more tight curls had pulled free from her bun and wound around her neck like a fine, wiry chain.

"Yes?" She sounded breathless, like she'd run a long distance. There hadn't been any footsteps, though. Realization made his grin widen. She'd been waiting on the other side of the door. Had she wanted to see him again?

"You left the basket on the porch." He held out the mending. She stared at it, seeming unsure whether she should reach out or not.

"Thank you, Mr. Washington." She grabbed the basket and stepped back into the house. "I have to go. I should check on Mrs. Sawyer."

As the door closed with a soft click, Josiah turned and sauntered off the porch. He pursed his lips and began to whistle the tune to the words running through his head.

> There is a fountain filled with blood,
> Drawn from Immanuel's veins
> And sinners, plunged beneath that flood,
> Lose all their guilty stains.

Ever since the night he'd heard that song at a revival meeting and later accepted Jesus, he'd felt the fountain hymn was his. Music often swirled through his head as he worked at the forge, the pounding of his hammer beating a rhythm while he whistled or sang a tune.

Taking in a deep draught of air, Josiah tried to sort out his tangled emotions. Lavette had to be the one the Lord sent for him. Hadn't she appeared right after his prayer this morning? Didn't she admit to liking Tucson and the slower paced lifestyle here? She wasn't someone enamored with big city life and the luxuries to be had back East.

So why did she insist she had to go back when Mrs. Sawyer left? Why did she run away when he mentioned her staying here? He could see from her reaction to his touch that she must feel something for him. "Why is she so afraid of me?"

"Probably because you're so mean looking."

Josiah jerked to a stop. He hadn't realized he'd spoken the words aloud. Quinn Kirby leaned against a building, his face red, trying his best not to laugh. Josiah drew his eyebrows together, attempting to look angry. "I don't recall asking your opinion."

"Then who were you asking?" Quinn let loose a long laugh and grasped his sides.

"Maybe the Lord and I were having a private discussion." Josiah bit back a grin.

Quinn clapped him on the shoulder. "Come on. I'm heading your direction. You can tell me all about why you think she's afraid of you. I'll be happy to give you any advice you need."

Josiah snorted. "As if you know it all." Shaking his head, he fell in beside Quinn, matching his longer stride to Quinn's shorter one.

"I'm gathering you went to see Miss Johnson, right?" The deputy gave Josiah an inquisitive glance.

"Yeah." Josiah waved his hand back toward the house where Lavette and Mrs. Sawyer were staying. An easy silence rested between the two men. In the past year, since Quinn had become a Christian, he often sought out Josiah to talk about a Scripture or a problem he needed advice on. Because of Conlon, Quinn often came to Josiah for scriptural advice. Sometimes the two commented on how he should have been a preacher with his understanding of the Bible and his love for Jesus. Because of his and Quinn's deepening friendship and the serious discussions they'd shared in the past, Josiah didn't hesitate to open up to him.

"You know this morning when I first met Miss Johnson?" At Quinn's affirmative, Josiah continued to relate the story of how God seemed to answer his prayer by sending Lavette at the precise moment Josiah asked for a wife.

Stopping beside the walkway to his house, Quinn turned to Josiah. "If you haven't eaten, why don't you join Kathleen and me for supper? She always fixes plenty of food, especially now that she isn't sick with the baby anymore."

Josiah chuckled. "I remember my mama being that way. She would be so sick for awhile, I thought sure she would die. The sickness used to scare me until my pa told me most women were that way when new babies were coming. After she got over the sickness though, she ate everything in sight."

"Lately all Kathleen does is eat and sleep." Quinn grinned. "I'll bet she thinks she does a lot more than that. In fact, I always have a tidy house, clean clothes, and a hot meal. She makes it look so easy, I think she's doing nothing."

The pair turned up the walkway. Many an evening, Quinn had invited Josiah to eat with him and Kathleen. Often Conlon and Glorianna Sullivan joined them. As much as Josiah loved his friends, he sometimes felt like he didn't belong. Tonight, however, he would enjoy talking with Kathleen and Quinn. Maybe they could help him make sense of these roiling feelings.

Leading the way around to the kitchen door, Quinn hesitated. Josiah took a deep breath. The air smelled of something burning. As Quinn reached to open the door, the portal flung open, and a billow of smoke engulfed them. Josiah coughed and blinked his stinging eyes.

"Kathleen?" Panic rang in Quinn's voice.

The smoke danced away on the breeze, and there stood Kathleen, tears streaming down her face, a smoking pot clutched in her cloth-covered hands. Quinn grabbed the cloths and the pan. Moving around Josiah, he set the smoking kettle on the ground. Standing next to Quinn, Josiah held his breath and peered down at what once might have been a piece of meat. The charred remains didn't look at all appetizing.

A long shuddering sob sounded behind them. Quinn and Josiah turned back to see Kathleen wiping her face with a handkerchief.

"Oh, Quinn, I'm so sorry." She covered her face with the hanky and turned her back on them.

"What happened?" Quinn moved up the steps and put his arm around his wife's shaking shoulders.

"I fell asleep again." The words came out in a wail. "I was so tired and thought if I could rest a few minutes, I'd be fine. I didn't even lay down in the bed, but sat in the chair in the living room. The next thing I knew, I was choking on smoke."

Quinn pulled her around into his embrace. "You know, this looks like a beautiful evening. Why don't we open the windows? Then we can stroll down to the Widow Arvizu's eatery with Josiah and have some supper." He brushed a strand of hair behind her ear. Watching Quinn wipe a tear from Kathleen's cheek, the tenderness of the moment gave Josiah an ache that settled in his heart. He longed so much for a woman to look at in the same way.

"You help Kathleen get ready, and I'll open the windows." Josiah clumped up the steps and past the couple before he succumbed to the emotion of the moment. He choked as the strong smell of burning meat and smoke hit him. He didn't want to think how close Kathleen had come to catching the house on fire. Although the walls were made of adobe and wouldn't burn readily, the contents would have caught fire.

By the time Kathleen washed and fixed her hair, fresh air had blown most of the heavy smoke from the house. Eyes puffy, Kathleen gave Josiah a watery smile. "I'm sorry about this, Josiah. I had a feeling you might be here for supper and planned to make plenty."

"I'll be proud to sit beside you at Arvizu's." Josiah knew Señora Arvizu's was the only place he was welcome to eat in the same room with the whites in town. "I'll even split the cost with Quinn. Of course, then I'll charge him extra on his next horseshoeing." He chuckled and Kathleen laughed.

Stepping through the door, Quinn held it open. Kathleen took his arm, and they all set off down the street. Stars twinkled overhead in a sky that seemed to go on forever. Josiah took a few deep breaths, careful not to let Kathleen notice. The smell of smoke lingered in his nostrils. His throat ached, and he wondered how Kathleen's felt.

"Did you know Josiah has a sweetheart?" Quinn's question jolted Josiah from his reverie.

"What?" Kathleen turned to look at Josiah. Her eyes sparkled in the light of the rising moon. "When did this happen?"

"He only met her today. She walked into his smithy, and he was smitten."

"Truly, Josiah? Tell me all about her."

Josiah groaned. His face warmed. "I'd rather talk about the fine weather we're having."

Kathleen sighed. "Now, Josiah, Quinn's the deputy. If you won't talk, I'll have him lock you up. Then you won't be able to escape my questions."

Quinn's laugh startled a dog at the side of the road. "You may as well give up. She'll keep after you until she knows every detail."

Shaking his head, Josiah heaved an exaggerated sigh. For the rest of the short walk to Arvizu's, he related once more the events of the day and his experience with Lavette. He could see Kathleen's excitement. He tried to keep the discouragement from his voice when he told her about Lavette leaving to go home soon.

"How much longer did she say she would be here?"

"I don't recall if she said an exact time. I think she mentioned a few weeks." Josiah could see the light spilling out of the Arvizu eatery. His stomach protested the lack of food today. "I can't force her to stay. Maybe she has some reason to return to Virginia."

"Does she have a beau? She may be promised to someone already."

Reaching to open the door, Josiah shook his head. "How am I supposed to ask something like that?"

Kathleen swept through the door. She acted as if her burned dinner had been completely forgotten in the quest to solve his problems. Crossing the room to an empty table took a long time. Between Quinn and Kathleen, they knew everyone and stopped to chat several times. Josiah thought he might faint from hunger before they reached their destination. Waiting for Kathleen to be seated, he paid no attention to those around them or the few stares he received. He knew there were some who didn't accept his presence here. Only through the grace of God did others welcome him.

After Señora Arvizu explained all her problems, health and businesswise, to Kathleen and took their order. Kathleen turned to Josiah with a sweet smile on her face. "I know what you need, Josiah. You need someone to help you out with your cause. I'll get Glory, and we'll go to visit Mrs. Sawyer and Lavette."

"No." Talking ceased. People stared. Josiah shrank back onto the bench. He hadn't meant to be so loud. She'd surprised him. "I'll find a way to ask her."

"Nonsense." Kathleen patted his hand and winked at Quinn. "We'd heard there was someone new in that house. I've been meaning to wander over there for several days. Glory is always looking for a way to get out with the twins. She'll enjoy the walk."

Josiah knew he must have the look of doom on his face. Kathleen laughed.

"Don't you worry, Josiah. Glory could get a cactus to tell its life history. When she bats those lashes of hers, people fall all over themselves to tell her anything she wants. We'll find out all you need to know to court Lavette in a way she won't be able to resist."

Señora Arvizu placed steaming plates of food in front of them. The spicy scent made Josiah's stomach twist in anticipation. He bowed his head for a short prayer, then lifted his fork. How could he stop Kathleen and Glorianna? What if they said the wrong thing to Lavette and ruined his chances altogether?

"You may as well give up, Josiah." Quinn lifted a bite of beans to his mouth.

"What's that?" Josiah frowned, trying to decide what Quinn meant.

"Once Kathleen and Glorianna get something in their heads, stopping them is like standing in front of a locomotive with your hand out to halt the machine."

Kathleen smoothed a napkin in her lap. "I promise we'll be as discreet as possible. Before she knows what's happening, that girl will be dreaming of you all day long."

Quinn chuckled. "Maybe when we leave here, we can go to the telegraph office and send off for a preacher. We could even go to the mercantile and order the wedding gown."

Josiah hunched his shoulders, wishing he could disappear. Why had he ever talked about Lavette in the first place?

"I'd say you shouldn't consider your suit a sure thing."

The nasal voice behind him struck a chill down Josiah's back. He could see the stillness in Quinn's face and the dislike Kathleen tried to hide. Placing his fork on his plate, he turned to face Bertrand Mead.

"I don't know what you have to say about anything." Quinn spoke before Josiah had a chance.

The false smile on Mead's face turned Josiah's stomach. Pale, narrow eyes, filled with arrogance, looked down at him. "The girl will be mine. I happened to hear her singing this afternoon. She's incredible. When I've had the chance to talk to her, I'm sure she'll be willing to come and work for me. With a good voice and her looks, she won't want for opportunity." He gave a mirthless laugh. "I'm sure the men of this town will enjoy her immensely."

Chapter 5

Bile wormed its way up Josiah's throat, although he barely noticed the burning. His hands clenched into fists. Pushing against the table, he started to rise. Quinn clamped his hand over Josiah's. Their eyes met, and Josiah could read Quinn's message. Even though he wanted to ignore his friend, Mead wasn't worth a night or more in jail. This wasn't the South, but even so, blacks didn't have the freedom others did. For him to strike a white man would bring certain disaster upon himself and would affect those who stood by him.

Easing back onto the bench, Josiah forced his hands to relax. He pulled in a deep breath, praying as he did so.

"Mr. Mead, perhaps Miss Johnson will prefer to sing for our evangelist meetings when we have a preacher in town." Kathleen's voice carried a little too much sugar.

Josiah knew she was trying to help him.

Mead stepped to the side. Josiah could see him from the corner of his eye. The man settled his hat on his head as if making a fashion statement. Putting his walking stick under his arm, Mead nodded in Kathleen's direction. "Perhaps that's true, Mrs. Kirby. I'll go by tomorrow and discuss this with the lady in question." He straightened his coat. "However, it's been my experience that a lucrative offer such as I plan to give Miss Johnson will usually be too tempting to refuse."

Anger burned through Josiah as he watched the dandy stride from the restaurant. He felt so helpless to stop him. What Mead planned for Miss Johnson shouldn't be done to any woman. Taking advantage because she was a servant was despicable.

"Josiah, ease up." Quinn spoke low, but with a firmness that caught Josiah's attention. "If Miss Johnson is a respectable person, she'll turn him down no matter how lucrative his offer is. If she's the woman God has for you, then she's a decent person."

The swell of noise from the chattering diners wrapped around Josiah once more. He didn't know if they'd all quit talking or if he'd been so focused on Mead that he'd shut out everything else. For a moment, he wondered how so many people could be going about their business like nothing had happened when he'd been so shaken.

A soft touch on his hand startled Josiah. He looked down to see Kathleen's small hand covering his larger one. Lifting his gaze to meet hers, he knew she hurt with him.

"Josiah, if this were Quinn or Conlon, what would you tell them to do?" Kathleen's soft words were almost lost in the cacophony around them.

Letting out the deep breath he hadn't realized he held, Josiah gave a tired smile. "I'd tell them to pray."

Kathleen smiled and patted his hand. "And I'll bet your mama would have said to finish your supper. Then you can go home and spend time in prayer. God knew this would happen, and you'll have to trust His plan even when you can't see it." She picked up a forkful of beans. "Tomorrow I'll get Glory, and we'll go by to visit Miss Johnson. You come for supper tomorrow night, and I'll tell you what we find out. This young lady won't be able to resist your charms with all of us praying for her and praising you."

Quinn shook his head. "I don't know who to feel sorrier for, Josiah or Miss Johnson."

Smiling, Josiah picked up his fork. *Thank You, Lord, for friends like these. Please protect Lavette from Mead. You know he's up to no good.* The rest of the meal flew by. Between Quinn's stories of his day's adventures and Kathleen's tales of the Sullivan twins' escapades, Josiah didn't realize he'd finished his food until he looked down to find his plate clean. Standing, he thanked his friends and excused himself. He wanted to get home, spend some time with Jesus, and maybe even dream a little about expressive cinnamon eyes and wiry curls around a heart-shaped face.

❦

"My Father, how long, my Father, how long, my Father, how long, poor sinner suffer here?" Lavette's heart ached as she sang. When she closed her eyes, she could still see the line of slaves marching to the fields, shoulders stooped from years of bending over plants, their voices lifting up this sad song. So many times, she'd felt guilty that her physical burden was lighter than theirs. She didn't have to suffer the hard labor they did. As she grew older and garnered the attention of Miss Susannah's father, Lavette often wished for the chance to be a slave in the fields, rather than one in the house.

Sprinkling the bread dough with a little more flour, Lavette folded and pushed the mass as if this were someone she had a grudge against. She tried to recall her mother's face or voice, but only a vague idea came to mind. She couldn't clearly see her family's faces anymore. Once in awhile, she could hear her mother's voice, but those times were getting fewer as the days went by. Oh, how she missed them all.

A light knock rattled the kitchen door. Shaking the excess flour from her hands, Lavette wiped the rest on her apron. Wishing she could check her hair, but having no time, she crossed to open the door. Two young women stood on the porch. One of them had red hair, the other had a star-shaped birthmark on her cheek. Each held a young child on her hip.

"May I help you?" Lavette smoothed her floury apron.

"Hello." The dark-haired woman held out a luscious-looking cake. "I'm Kathleen Kirby, and this is my cousin, Glorianna Sullivan. We heard someone had moved into this house and thought we'd drop by to say hello."

"Thank you. My mistress is sleeping right now. I don't know when she'll be ready to receive callers. She hasn't been feeling well for some time." Lavette stared at the ground. One glance told her she didn't deserve to look at these women. They might be like Miss Susannah.

"Maybe we could come in and visit with you for awhile. Then, if your mistress is still asleep, we'll come by another time."

Not knowing what else to do, Lavette opened the door. As Glorianna stepped past Lavette, the little boy in her arms leaned back until his face was under Lavette's. He chortled, reaching his pudgy hands toward her. Bright blue eyes, full of mischief, stared at her.

"Andrew, come back here."

The boy disappeared from sight as the woman pulled him upright. Lavette chanced a glance at the other baby. The little girl had a thumb in her mouth, her wide green eyes taking in everything in the house. Red hair, a shade lighter than the other woman's, surrounded her head in a halo of curls.

"Oh, you have fixed this little place up so nice." Kathleen turned so Lavette could no longer see the baby, only the woman's back. "Are you making some bread?"

"Yes, Ma'am." Lavette followed the two women into the kitchen where her unfinished bread dough waited for more kneading. If she didn't get back to it soon, the whole batch would be ruined.

"You go right ahead and finish." Kathleen seemed to read Lavette's mind. "We don't want you to have to start over with this."

"Do you mind if we put the twins down?" Glorianna's question caught Lavette off guard.

"No, Ma'am. They won't hurt anything." Lavette watched as the twins were put on the floor. Andrew began to take hesitant steps across the room, stopping to give his mother a toothy grin. The little girl plopped down on her padded bottom, one hand twined in Kathleen's skirt as she examined the room from there. Lavette began to knead the bread, feeling a little uncomfortable. Should she go in and wake Mrs. Sawyer to let her know the ladies were here? Mrs. Sawyer was gaining strength, but Lavette didn't want to tire her.

"Mrs. Sawyer needs a lot of rest. She takes several naps during the day. Would you like me to wake her?" Lavette squeezed the bread, hoping to keep her hands from shaking. She never felt right around white folks she didn't know, and she hated the way she couldn't seem to stop from chattering. "Would you like to wait in the parlor where the chairs are nicer? We're only here for a short time, so the house isn't very fancy."

"We heard about you visiting Gretta and Paul. My husband is the lieutenant over Paul at Fort Lowell." Glorianna had a smile in her voice. "We do want to visit with your mistress, but we also wanted to call on you."

Lavette's hand stilled. Her gaze flitted up, catching both women looking at her. She dropped her gaze and continued to work the dough. "I'm not sure why you want to see me. I didn't do nothing wrong."

"Miss Johnson, we heard about you from a friend. He told us so much about you, we had to come and meet you for ourselves."

Lavette paused, trying to think who would be talking about her. "I don't know anyone here."

"You met Josiah Washington at the blacksmith shop yesterday. He speaks very highly of you."

Andrew toddled over to Lavette and wrapped his arms around her leg. Her skirt bunched up as he leaned against her, giving her the same charming grin he'd given Glorianna. She smiled and winked at him. He rested his head on her leg and stuck a finger in his mouth.

"I met Mr. Washington." Lavette didn't know what to say. She didn't want to admit that she'd been thinking of the man all day. Last night she'd had trouble falling asleep remembering the warm smile he'd given her as he left the house. She'd never heard of a black man being friends with whites. How could this be?

"Josiah is a wonderful man, don't you think?" Glorianna seemed to be the one doing all the talking. "He sure is taken with you."

Glorianna's comment sent a rush of pleasure spiraling through Lavette. Did Josiah think about her as much as she thought about him? He must be considering her some, to have told his friends about her.

"He seems like a very nice man, but I won't be here long enough to get to know him well. My time is taken with caring for Mrs. Sawyer."

"Josiah said you like the desert." Kathleen spoke up, and Lavette wondered at the change in subject.

"Oh, I do." She couldn't keep the enthusiasm from her voice. "I've heard the weather is very hot in the summer, but I'd rather face the heat than the ice and snow of the East. I grew up in the South and have never adjusted to the colder climate."

"So why don't you stay here when Mrs. Sawyer returns home?" Glorianna sounded pleased about the chance to ask the same question Josiah had asked. "Do you have someone special waiting for you?"

Anger swept through Lavette. How could these women understand her reasons? Had they ever belonged to anyone as a slave? Well, she had, and so had her family. In fact, she still belonged to someone. Freedom was something she would never experience, no matter how many wars were fought.

Smoothing the dough, Lavette covered the mass with a towel to let it rise. Stepping to one side, she waited for Andrew to let go of her skirt so she could move to the wash basin. She washed her hands, drying them on her apron. "I'll go see if Mrs. Sawyer is awake yet. If you ladies will follow me, I'll show you into the parlor where you can wait for her." Lavette knew her tone held a chill that would leave Glorianna and Kathleen wondering what had upset her, but she couldn't talk to them. They wouldn't understand.

No white person would.

Wriggling her shoulders, Lavette arched her back to ease the ache as she settled into the porch chair, her basket of mending beside her. She'd finished giving Mrs. Sawyer a bath and getting her to bed. The work today had exhausted her. All the lifting was taking a toll on her strength. Not only that, but the tension of the last two days and the lack of sleep last night added to her distress.

Pulling a nightgown from the pile of clothing that needed to be repaired, Lavette broke off a length of thread. Soon she would have to go to the mercantile to get more sewing supplies. The constant lifting and moving of her mistress proved to be hard on the clothes, both hers and Mrs. Sawyer's. Her needle wove in and out, repairing the tear as her thoughts strayed to last night on this same porch.

She could almost feel Josiah standing by the railing near her chair. He had such magnetism, it seemed to linger long after he left. The thought of his wide grin and deep voice set her heart fluttering. She stopped sewing a moment to fan her face. Never had a man affected her like this. Perhaps she should encourage Mrs. Sawyer to return east early so she could get away from Josiah's influence before she lost her heart to him. Surely that hadn't happened yet. How could she have fallen for him in such a short time? Inside, a small voice let her know that even if she left the man now, he'd already changed her life. She would never forget him.

"Evenin', Miss Johnson."

Lavette jumped. The needle slid smoothly into her thumb. "Ouch." She jerked her thumb away, nursing the small wound. The man she'd run from at Josiah's blacksmith shop yesterday stood in front of her, his hat tilted at a rakish angle. A black stick cane with a carved silver head stuck out from under his arm. Lifting his hat, he nodded at her.

She clutched the sewing to her breast, wanting to run. Since he stood between her and the door, there was no escape this time. The feral gleam in his eyes reminded her of Miss Susannah's father. That's why she'd fled yesterday, and that's why fear paralyzed her today.

"I thought we could talk for a few minutes." He leaned closer. She could smell the cloying scent of some lotion.

"I got to get back inside."

"But you just came out here." His lips tilted in a lascivious smile. "Why don't you relax? I won't hurt you."

"What do you want?" Nausea burned Lavette's throat.

"Why, I only want to make you an offer, Miss Johnson. Nothing more." He took a step closer. She backed farther into the chair.

"I'm not interested." She grabbed up her basket of sewing without taking her eyes from Mead.

"But you haven't heard my offer." He chuckled, a menacing sound that reminded her of the way a snake petrified its victims to catch them. "I heard you yesterday. I'd like for you to come and sing in my establishments. You will earn a good wage and have people wait on you for a change. That's not a bad offer, is it?"

She stood so fast, the chair tipped back with a crash. "I can't do that." She eased past him to the door. "Leave me alone. I can't work for you."

"Oh, but I think you can, Miss Johnson." His hand closed on her arm, and a foreboding chill raced through her. "You see, I've found out things about you already. I know the reason you're here with your mistress, and I know how to make you mine." Releasing her arm, he swiveled around and stepped off the porch. Whistling a jaunty tune, he ambled down the path to the street, leaving Lavette shaking with terror that he would be able to carry through on his threat.

Chapter 6

Two days had passed since Josiah had visited Lavette. He hadn't been able to stay away any longer. The excitement of seeing her again made him feel like a little boy with a secret so big, he couldn't stay still with wanting to tell someone. He wanted to run and shout with the sensation. The grin on his face must be showing everyone he passed exactly what he was thinking and feeling.

The bag dangling from his hand rattled with his movement. He glanced down, hoping this offering would make Lavette more receptive to him. Maybe she wouldn't run away this time. Perhaps they could sit down together, and he would find out why she feared getting to know him. He knew this was too soon to consider touching those slender hands of hers, but the thought made his heart race anyway.

Last night Josiah ate supper with the Kirbys and the Sullivans. The resulting conversation proved very enlightening. Glorianna and Kathleen told him all about their conversation with Lavette, but the best part came from Conlon and the talk he had with Paul Ashton about his mother-in-law and her servant. Paul said Lavette had no beau waiting that he knew about.

Whistling his favorite hymn, Josiah turned up the path that led to the Sawyer house. He wiped his damp palms on his pants, glad he'd taken the time to bathe and change before coming over here. Working a forge wasn't the cleanest job, but it was honest labor. Josiah could remember all the times he worked alongside his father, learning about horses and shoeing. He'd never regretted learning the blacksmith trade.

Tapping softly on the door, Josiah waited. He didn't want to wake Mrs. Sawyer if she was resting. No one answered, and he couldn't hear any movement from inside. He knocked a little louder, then tilted his head to one side listening. From somewhere he could hear the sound of an angel singing. The music drifted in and out on the breeze, tantalizing the senses and leaving him wanting to hear more.

Stepping off the porch, Josiah walked around the corner of the house. The singing got louder, although it still seemed faint. The angel must not want anyone to hear. At the back of the house he halted, amazed at the vision that greeted him.

Lavette stood with her back to him, pulling laundry from a clothesline. As she folded a heavy sheet, a soft melody issued from her—a slow, sad tune about suffering. The song made him want to weep and beg for more at the same time. Her voice brought to mind butterflies in the summer sun or birds soaring in the heavens. Never in his life had he heard anything more beautiful.

The tune and the words were simple enough. Josiah didn't know how long he stood there before he found himself humming along. As Lavette started on another verse, he caught the idea and joined his bass to her lovely voice. He couldn't have stopped himself if he tried. The music seemed to be drawn out on its own free will without asking his permission. For a moment, their voices blended in a beautiful harmony as if God created them for this express purpose. Lavette stopped mid-note. She whirled around. The nightgown in her hand almost dropped to the dirt.

A silly grin stretched Josiah's cheeks. He could stand here all day watching her. Lavette was taller than most women, although she was still several inches shorter than he. Lithe and willowy, she moved with the grace of one of those ballerinas he'd seen when he lived back East as a boy. Of course, he'd never seen them dance, but he remembered the time he and his father were driving Mr. Bellingham somewhere. Those dancers seemed to flow.

"Whatever are yah doin' heah?" Lavette's Southern accent seemed more pronounced now, when she was upset.

"I didn't mean to scare you." A clink from the bag at his side reminded Josiah of his excuse. He lifted the bag in the air. "I brought you some things I thought might be useful."

She stared at him, suspicion appearing to make her cautious. After folding the nightgown, she placed it in the basket at her feet. "I don't recall us needing anything."

"The other night you mentioned wanting another knife. You didn't give me the one you wanted repaired, so I brought a couple of new ones for you. Cooking can be a mite difficult when you only have one." He reached into the bag and pulled out a poker. "I also brought some utensils and tools I thought you might use. Since you're only here for a short time, I thought maybe you wouldn't have all you needed. You can return them before you go home." His heart clenched as he added the last.

Brushing a mass of curls from her forehead, Lavette reached for the last piece of clothing on the line. The wayward curls landed back on her brow before she had time to lift her hand away. They gave her a sweet look that somehow reminded him of his own mother when she worked with her hair frizzing in mad disarray.

Slinging the bag of utensils over his shoulder, Josiah hurried after Lavette as she carried the full basket to the house. He stretched out a hand to open the door for her. Lavette turned to him, her mouth open like she planned to invite him in. Her fingers closed around the latch, and his covered hers before he could stop. Lavette's eyes widened. Josiah couldn't breathe. Time seemed to stand still as they stood transfixed, gazing into one another's eyes.

Lavette moaned and tugged her hand from under his. Josiah pulled the latch and opened the door.

"Can I get the basket for you?"

She darted through the open door, her gaze downcast. "No, thank you. I'll put the clothes in the other room and be right back. Please have a seat." Her skirt swished as she crossed the room.

Stepping inside, Josiah closed the door behind him. His hand still tingled from the contact with her. His arms ached with the desire to hold her close. Shaking his head, he put the bag of utensils on the table and began to examine the room. How could he feel this way about a woman so fast? Until a few days ago, he hadn't recognized the longing inside as loneliness and a suppressed desire for a wife. Was he reacting to Lavette simply because he'd finally admitted the truth to himself?

"May I offer y'all a drink?" Even her speaking voice carried a trace of the melodic singing he'd heard outside. "We have some cake from last night's supper too."

He grinned. "I believe you said the right words. I'm never one to pass on a piece of something sweet and a cup of water or coffee. Will you join me?" He waited while Lavette dished up two pieces of cake, a tiny one for herself and a huge one for him. His mouth watered, and his stomach growled.

The corner of her mouth turned up at the sound. "Sounds like you must be starving. Did you miss your lunch today?"

He chuckled. "If I haven't eaten in the last hour, my stomach thinks I'm dying of starvation."

"We can't have that, then." Lavette carried the plates to the table. Turning to the stove, she lifted the coffeepot, then brought two cups. "Do you want a little milk or sweetening in your coffee?"

"No, thank you, but you can leave the pot here. I'll probably need a refill." Josiah held the chair for Lavette, then sat across from her. He wasn't sure if he could take his eyes off of her long enough to eat, she was so beautiful.

"Mmm. This is delicious. Kathleen Kirby makes a cake exactly like this."

Lavette's mouth twitched. She began to giggle. Even her giggle didn't sound girlish, but musical. Josiah wanted to shake himself. He must have it bad, whatever this was.

"You seem to find that funny. Did you get the recipe from Kathleen? She told me she visited you yesterday." He stared as Lavette broke into peals of laughter. Tears streamed down her face. She pulled a handkerchief from her pocket and wiped her cheeks.

"I'm sorry." She gasped for a breath. "Mrs. Kirby brought the cake over yesterday when she and Mrs. Sullivan came to visit. I didn't mean to make you think I baked this. I'm not sure why I'm laughing."

Josiah began to chuckle. "I'm not either, but I'd rather see you laughing than throwing something at me."

"Like the cake?" She laughed harder.

"Like the cake." He grinned as he watched her struggle to control her mirth. This woman was as changeable as a cat he used to have. One day the beast would be friendly, the next, a tigress ready to attack. He'd loved the cat, though, because she was never boring. He thought life with Lavette would never be dull, either.

⚘

Giddiness welled up inside Lavette. She couldn't seem to stop laughing. *What is the matter with me?* Since the moment Josiah's fingers closed over hers on the door latch, she hadn't been able to think straight. *No, that's not true.* A small voice whispered the words in her mind. Since the moment she'd heard his deep bass blending with her voice, she'd lost the ability to think rationally. Something had snapped, and she thought it must be the protective covering she'd put over her heart long ago.

When his hand touched hers, she was transfixed. The look in his eyes mesmerized her. She found she wanted to have him hold her, to feel those strong arms around her lending strength and comfort. The sudden desire to belong to the man of her dreams had been almost more than she could bear.

Now, he was sitting here, trying to eat cake, and all she could do was cackle like some lovesick hen. That thought made her start laughing all over again. She could see Josiah strutting around like a rooster. No, he wasn't like that at all. He wouldn't think the world of himself, but he would think the world of his wife. If he strutted around, it would mean he was proud of her.

"You have the most beautiful soprano I ever heard." Josiah's words were like cold water and sobered her in an instant.

"Thank you." She ducked her head and began to cut a bite from her cake.

"I remember Mrs. Thompson back home. She had a fine voice. We would hear her every Sunday when she stood up and sang at church." Josiah's bright gaze caught hers when she looked up. "But Mrs. Thompson couldn't sing at all compared to you. You make me think the angels are listening so they can take lessons."

Fire burned in her cheeks. Miss Susannah's papa talked about how pretty her voice was, too. He even took her with him to a house where he wanted her to sing for the folks. She hated the memory. The women there hadn't been dressed right. The men were smoking and drinking. The talk made her ears burn, and she was sure God would never forgive her. Maybe He hadn't; look what all had happened to her. Miss Susannah's papa insisted that when Lavette grew up, that was all she'd be good for—to entertain and work in one of those places. For so long after the war, she'd been terrified to sing.

"Do you enjoy the music in church at your home?" Josiah must not be able to see the turmoil going on inside her. She thought it would be obvious for anyone to notice. "We don't have a regular church here." Josiah continued without noticing her distress. "Sometimes we get a pastor passing through, and he stays for a few weeks to preach to us, but mostly we get together with friends and share Scripture."

Lavette pushed away from the table and picked up her plate with the uneaten cake. Before walking to the washing tub, she scraped the cake into the scrap bucket. She knew what would happen when she told Josiah about her beliefs. He'd be gone so fast, she wouldn't hear him leave. She could tell from looking at him, he was a decent man. He wouldn't want to be seen with the likes of her.

"Maybe this Sunday you could join me when I meet with the Sullivans, the Kirbys, and some others."

She gripped the edge of the washtub, willing her hands not to pick up the plate and throw it at him. Didn't he understand? Not only was she not worthy of him, she wasn't free to love him, either. She would never be free. Anger at that thought bubbled up like acid, eating through her.

"I don't go to church." She spat out the words.

"This isn't like church exactly." He stood and brought his empty plate and cup over to her. "We're friends, taking time to share some Bible and to pray. Afterwards, we eat the noon meal together. They're good people, and I'm sure you'll love them as much as I do."

Taking his dishes, she plunked them into the basin. Whirling around, she was startled to see he still stood there, a solid mountain of a man. She tilted her head back to look in his face. The anger drained away. How could this man affect her so? Every fiber in her being was aware of him. He was like a magnet, drawing her to him, and she was helpless to resist.

"I have to take care of Mrs. Sawyer."

"I heard her daughter and son-in-law are taking her to their house for the day. That means you'll be here all by yourself, unless you have other friends in town that I don't know about." His grin softened, and he leaned closer.

Lavette wanted to move back, but the wash basin wouldn't allow that. "I don't go to church."

"You said that before, but this isn't going to church. This is friends getting together." His grin widened. "The only one of us that bites is little Andrew, and then only when he's getting another tooth."

She couldn't help herself. She chuckled. "I've met Andrew. He's adorable, and I don't think you're very nice to say mean things about him."

He pretended to be stricken. "Oh, I'm not being mean. I'm telling the honest truth. The last time he cut a tooth, I carried the evidence on my thumb for a week." He touched her arm, sending her emotions awry. "Will you come, please?"

"I don't even have a Bible." What a feeble excuse. *Maybe I should tell him I'll be sick by Sunday. After all, thinking of spending the day with all of them talking about God could make me ill.*

His huge hand touched her cheek. The warmth in his gaze stole her breath. When he spoke, his voice was husky with emotion. "That's no problem. I'll share mine."

Chapter 7

The door of the mercantile squeaked as Lavette pushed it open. A mixture of smells rushed out to greet her. The earthy scent of burlap, spices, leather, and an undefined musty odor all combined in an aroma that made identifying the more subtle fragrances difficult. High walls lined with shelves were packed full of assorted necessities. Her hand tightened on the short list she'd brought.

A group of men in the back of the store glanced up. Their stares made her want to fidget as the door creaked shut behind her. The brightness of the sun and the dim interior made distinguishing the men impossible, but she knew they'd stopped talking and watched her. Fear clutched at her with icy fingers. She wanted to fling the door open and run home as fast as she could.

Blinking, Lavette forced her feet to carry her to the counter, where a middle-aged man waited. His large mustache wiggled as he smiled at her. "May I help you?"

"I need some things." She tried to keep her voice from quaking but knew she hadn't succeeded. Holding out her trembling hand, she placed the crumpled list on the counter.

"Let's see." He frowned and put on a pair of spectacles. Squinting at the writing, he glanced up at her. "Thread, a pound of sugar, beans." He continued reading the list silently. "I'll have these things ready in a few minutes, if you'd like to look around."

She shook her head. "Thank you. I'll wait here." She kept her gaze lowered, trying to keep from seeing what the men in the back of the room were doing. One of them let out a loud guffaw, followed by laughter from the rest. She glanced around for the clerk. He wasn't in sight.

Murmuring and snickering alternated from the group in the back. Lavette could feel a trickle of sweat inching down her back. Her muscles ached from staying still so long. Where was the man who took her order? Could she leave the cash on the counter and come back to pick up the goods later? She knew that wouldn't work. What if someone came along and took the coins before the man returned? Then, she would be in trouble with him and with Mrs. Sawyer for wasting money.

The ribaldry grew louder, along with a few comments that made her ears burn. Reaching into her bag, she fished around for the change Mrs. Sawyer had given her. She could hardly hear the jangling over the racket from the back of the store. Why hadn't she waited until tomorrow, when Mr. Ashton would be able to go to the mercantile for them?

From the corner of her eye, she saw one of the men sauntering in her direction. She froze, her fingers clenched so hard around the coins that they cut into her palm.

"Well, hello there, Miss Johnson. What a pleasure meeting you here." Bertrand Mead's nasal whine sent a chill racing down her spine. She shivered.

"I've been telling some of the boys here about you and how well you can sing. They were wondering if you would give us a little preview." Mead stopped next to her. She gagged on the nauseating scent of him. "I told them you would be entertaining in one of my establishments soon, and they are very excited. How about a song?"

"No." Her lips trembled. "Leave me alone."

Mead turned toward the men. "She's a little shy. Perhaps if you were to make it worth her while, she would give us a tune." His voice lowered. "She might even remember you favorably when you come to my place."

A chorus of hoots and laughter jolted Lavette. She jumped and began to sidle closer to the door. She didn't care about the items she came to buy. All she wanted was to get away from these men. Oh, why was the door so far away from her?

"Now, don't think you can run off, Miss Johnson." Mead took hold of her arm and began to drag her back to the table where the other men sat. Lavette couldn't look up. She didn't want to see the stares. Memories from her childhood haunted her, wrapping her in a cloak of terror.

"My, my, these gentlemen really do want to hear you, Miss Johnson." Mead pulled her to a stop beside the table. She could see a pile of coins thrown in the center. Mead's fingers held her in a painful grip. "Let's hear you do something for the men." His grip tightened, and she feared he might break her arm.

"Well, if you won't sing for us, let's at least let them get a look at your pretty face. I'm sure these men will want to look you up when you belong to me." Mead clasped her jaw and forced her head up. She closed her eyes, wishing the ground would open and swallow her.

"Here you are, Miss." The clerk swept through a curtained-off area at the back of the store. "I'm sorry I took so long. We were out of the thread you needed, and I had to find the new shipment in the back. Will this be all?"

Mead released her as the clerk swept past them, his arms full of packages. Lavette ran after him in her haste to get away from Mead and his cronies. Her heart pounded. Her hands shook so badly, she dropped the money she pulled from her reticule. Scrambling on the floor, she did her best to retrieve it all. Laughter rang from the table at the back of the mercantile.

"Thank you." Lavette managed to get the words out as the clerk finished wrapping her purchases together in a paper and tying them with a string. She could feel Mead's gaze on her. What if he followed her? What could she do?

Stepping outside, Lavette reveled in the warmth of the sun. Her body felt chilled, as if she'd been exposed to the worst winter storm imaginable. Starting off down the street, she wanted to run but knew that was foolish. Mead was probably laughing about her with his friends. She'd been someone they made fun of, not someone he was truly serious about.

A door creaked behind her. Her heart pounded. Stomach churning, she glanced over her shoulder. Bertrand Mead stood outside the mercantile, watching her. With a deliberate smile, he began to stalk after her. Feeling like a rabbit running from a fox, Lavette quickened her pace.

She could not get to the house before he caught up with her. Mead's legs were longer. Even if she could run that far, he could easily outdistance her. She had no defense against him.

Hurrying around the corner, Lavette began to trot. Her skirts caught at her legs, slowing her down, threatening to trip her. Heavy footsteps sounded from behind. A cruel snigger let her know what Mead thought of her efforts to elude him. A sob tore through her chest. *Help me.* She wanted to scream the words aloud, but couldn't get them out.

Please, someone help me. No one paid attention to her. Some even pointedly ignored what was happening.

The footsteps were closer. Mead would have her in a moment. She picked up her skirts and raced full tilt around a corner. The wall she ran into wasn't brick. For a moment she didn't realize she'd run into a person. Only when arms came around her, did she understand. One of Mead's men must have gone out a back way to catch her. How stupid she'd been to fall into such a trap.

Lavette twisted and fought to no avail. The package of goods she'd bought fell to the ground. The arms holding her felt like iron. He spoke, but she refused to listen. This man might be stronger than she, but she would at least put up a fight before they dragged her away.

"She doesn't seem to want you, Blacksmith." Mead's whine cut through her fear. Lavette stilled.

"I'm taking her home, Mead. She doesn't want to go with you." Josiah's deep voice rumbled in his chest. Lavette's ear pressed tight against him.

Josiah. He would protect her. She quit struggling and rested against him, so exhausted, she knew if he let go she would fall. He smelled of horses, smoke, and sweat, reminding her of her father and comfort. She wanted to stay there forever, to hide from the evil of the world.

"You all right?" Josiah's question spoken close to her ear sent a shiver down her spine, a very different kind of shiver from the one she got when Mead spoke to her.

She nodded. He seemed to understand, for his arms tightened a moment, then eased their hold.

"Let go of the girl." Anger gave Mead's voice a shrill sound. "I'll take her home. I need to talk to her owner, anyway."

Josiah stiffened. "No one is her owner. She's employed by Mrs. Sawyer. We aren't slaves anymore, Mead, no matter how much you want us to be."

Lavette tensed. Not slaves anymore? Was he blind? Didn't he understand they would always be in bondage? She started to push away, but Josiah's arms tightened, holding her close.

"Oh, I know they fought a war for emancipation, but this girl still belongs to the lady. She'll be for sale, and I'm going to buy her. If you don't believe me, ask her. For now, you can have her, but she'll be mine soon enough, and you won't get near her."

Lavette could hear Mead's heavy steps fading as he returned the way he had come. Fear tore through her. What if Mrs. Sawyer agreed to let Mead have her? Money could buy most anything. Hadn't she seen that, growing up on Wild Oak plantation?

"I have to get home. Thank you." Lavette pushed back, and this time Josiah let go of her. She stepped away, unable to look at him. Her foot bumped against the package from the mercantile. Picking it up, she hugged the goods to her, wishing she were back in Josiah's arms.

"What did he mean? Why does he think you're still a slave?" Josiah stood like a mountain in front of her.

"Mrs. Sawyer will be expecting me. I need to get back to her." Lavette eased to one side.

"Wait." Josiah's command halted her. His huge fingers cupped her face, lifting until she looked at him. "We have to talk. Maybe now isn't the time. I'll come by this evening after you put your mistress to bed. We can discuss this on the porch."

She could see the compassion in his eyes. His touch warmed her, banishing thoughts of Mead and his associates. Tears clogged her throat. She blinked and nodded. Telling her story was too painful, but for some reason, she felt confiding in Josiah would help. Maybe he would understand why they had no future. Before she came to care for him more than she already did, she should tell him the truth. Then he would leave and never see her again.

✦

Josiah stopped in the shadow of a paloverde tree as he turned onto the path leading up to Lavette's house. He could see her seated on the porch, her head bent over her mending. Clenching his fists, he recalled the fright in her eyes when she barreled into him while being chased by Bertrand Mead. At the time, he hadn't known what he wanted more—to beat Mead to pulp or to hold and protect Lavette. In the end, common sense won. Although she fought like a tiger at first, his arms well remembered the feel of her trembling against him once she'd realized who held her.

After Mead left and she'd calmed down, he'd walked her home. Lavette insisted he didn't have to do that, but he wouldn't have trusted Mead not to sneak around and meet up with her. Of course, he hadn't suggested that to Lavette. He wouldn't want to scare the poor girl more than she already was.

He admired her spirit. As he'd pointed out to his friends, she'd been born a slave, and that's all she'd known until the war ended. Having been raised in the North by parents who'd been set free, Josiah had never been a slave, but he'd heard plenty of stories. Even as a child, a beautiful girl like Lavette would have caught the attention of the male owners of the plantation. He gritted his teeth. What had she endured that made her so afraid?

All afternoon, as he worked, Josiah hadn't been able to banish the thoughts of Mead and his words about Lavette belonging to Mrs. Sawyer. How could that be? He'd tried to think of every way he could imagine, but nothing made sense. There were no more slaves in the States, and that's where Mrs. Sawyer and Lavette came from.

Lavette glanced up from her sewing and started when she noticed him. Josiah strode forward, not wanting her to think him someone else in the fading light. If all she saw was the outlined figure of a man, she could easily mistake him for someone who would frighten her. That would never do.

"Good evening, Miss Johnson." The boards of the porch creaked under his weight.

"Evenin'." Lavette seemed to huddle deeper into the chair, her hands clutching the mending against her breast. She appeared to want to run rather than talk to him.

Walking quietly to avoid bothering Mrs. Sawyer, Josiah was surprised to see a second chair waiting beside the vine-covered trellis on the other side of Lavette. She must have brought the chair out after he'd walked her home today. Josiah couldn't hide the grin of satisfaction in knowing she might have looked forward to seeing him at least a little. He sank into the chair and faced her, drinking in her beauty before the light faded. He knew he would never tire of watching Lavette Johnson.

"Did you have a lot of work today?" Her soft, Southern accent thrilled him. She picked at the loose thread on the garment in her lap.

"This afternoon I went out to the fort again to do some more horses for Conlon. I fixed a buggy wheel for Doc Meyer and did a few other odd jobs." Josiah eased to one side of the chair to avoid a knot in the wood that poked his back. He didn't want to make small talk. He wanted answers to his questions, but now that he was here, he hesitated to force Lavette to talk. She seemed so frightened, and he didn't know why.

"Have you eaten? I could fix you something, or we have some dried apple pie if you'd like a piece."

"I already ate, but I never turn down apple pie." Josiah's mouth began to water at the thought.

Lavette jumped up. The thread clattered to the porch floor and rolled to a stop by Josiah's boot. They both reached for the spool at the same time. Lavette's slender fingers closed over Josiah's. She glanced up, her eyes wide. Jerking away, she straightened. Josiah picked up the thread and handed it to her.

Holding tight to the spool, Josiah caught Lavette's hand as she reached out. "I'd love a piece of your pie, but this won't keep me from asking what I want to know. Why does Mead think he can own you? The war ended nine years ago. Slaves were set free. I want to know why you're so afraid he'll get control over you."

Lavette tugged her hand free. "I don't care if the war is over. I'll never be liberated. I'm still in bondage and always will be." She turned and rushed into the house, letting the door slam behind her.

Chapter 8

Lavette's hands shook as she lifted the generous slice of pie from the tin. How could she have acted that way toward Josiah? He only wanted to help her. He cared, while most people in her life didn't. She blinked back tears as she poured a cup of coffee. This was the reason she hadn't wanted to get to know Josiah. She didn't want to lose her heart to a man she couldn't marry. She picked up the pie and coffee, trying to keep from sloshing the liquid. Was she too late? Had she already lost her heart to this gentle giant?

The evening breeze carried a welcome hint of cool, wiping the traces of tears from Lavette's eyes as she stepped through the door. Josiah still sat in the chair, bent forward, his arms resting on his knees. Head bowed, he looked as though he were praying, although not a sound issued from him. Lavette recalled the times her papa and mama prayed together. They hadn't been quiet.

The porch creaked. Josiah raised his head. The anguish in his eyes tore at her heart. She longed to tell him everything would work out fine. She'd been in servitude most of her life and adjusted to the idea. Most of the time, belonging to someone else didn't bother her. The only time she'd lived differently had been a miserable period in her life. Remaining enslaved had been her choice, a decision she rarely regretted as she recalled the good her sacrifice had done for her mother.

"Here's your pie, and I brought you a cup of coffee." His fingers brushed against hers as he accepted the plate and cup. Lavette couldn't help the tremor of delight that raced up her arm.

"Thank you." Josiah set the mug on the porch beside his chair. He leaned back and placed the pie on his massive leg as if the appendage were a table. He left the sweet untouched as he crossed his arms over his chest.

"I'd like to hear why you think you're still a slave. I can understand it would be hard to discuss, but we need to talk."

"Why?"

"Because I care what happens to you. I don't want you to be afraid every time you walk down the street, thinking you might end up belonging to someone like Mead."

Lavette shuddered. She rubbed her arms. She couldn't look at Josiah, but stared at the black gleam of his coffee. "I can't tell you without relating how this happened. It'll take too long."

"I've got time." Josiah rested his ankle on top of his knee, leaning back farther into the chair. He picked up the pie and cut a bite, chewing like he had forever to sit on this porch. "Why don't you start by telling me about your family."

"My mama and papa were slaves on the Wild Oak plantation in Alabama. I was born about the same time as Miss Susannah, the owner's daughter. Since we were the same age, I became her playmate. She had four older brothers, but no sisters." Lavette twisted her fingers together in her lap.

"Some people thought I had it easy because I didn't have to work in the fields." Terror rose up like bile in her throat. "I can't tell you how many times I wanted to be in the fields and away from the horrors of the house."

She glanced up to see Josiah holding the still-unfinished pie. His look held compassion and knowing. He'd probably heard the tales of what happened to girl slaves when they were at the mercy of their masters' whims. She rubbed her arms again, hoping he would think the evening air caused the chill.

"Did you get to stay with your folks? I know a lot of children were separated from their families."

"I think I was kept at the plantation because of being Miss Susannah's playmate. My two older brothers and one older sister were sold off before they were half-grown. That like to broke my mama's heart."

"Did you find them after the war?" She could hear the anguish Josiah was trying to hold back.

"My papa tried to find them, but he couldn't. I have a younger brother and two younger sisters. Papa didn't have much time to go off looking for the lost ones when he also had to feed all of us."

"Where are your parents now?"

Feeling cool air on her cheeks, Lavette reached up to wipe away the tears with the back of her hand. "Alabama. Papa's job at Wild Oak was in the stables. He has a knack for working with horses." She drew a shaky breath.

"At the end of the war, Papa worked hard to provide for us. Mama grew a garden, and Papa found what jobs he could. Out in the country, there weren't many. Most of the plantation owners were ruined. No one could afford to hire Papa or Toby, my brother, to work for them very often. Papa finally found a job on a big farm. It wasn't much different than being a slave. The landowner didn't pay enough, but he allowed us to get what we needed from his store on credit. Papa tried hard to keep from doing that. He didn't want to be indebted to anyone. We were barely gettin' by when Mama had the accident."

Lavette stared down at the mending in her lap. Josiah's hands engulfed hers, warming them, offering her comfort. She had no idea when he'd moved closer.

"What happened?"

"We were in town getting a few things. I had to watch Lila and little Nellie while Mama crossed the street to get to the tanner's. Mama stepped into the street to come back over just as a man in a buggy whipped around the corner." Lavette's throat closed. The memory filled her with horror all over again.

"Did she get trampled?"

Lavette shook her head. "No, the buggy tilted, catching my mama and throwing her to one side like a rag doll." Her voice dropped to a whisper. "I can still see the look of horror on her face. I can hear the driver yell as he jumped away, hitting his head against a watering trough. The horses' ears were laid back, its eyes wild. My mama didn't have a chance."

Pulling a hand free, Lavette covered her mouth. "We heard later the driver died. The doctor said Mama was lucky to have been hit by the wagon instead of being run over. She had a broken arm, some broken ribs, and bruises, but she was unconscious for days. We didn't think she would ever wake up. When she did, she couldn't recall what happened. Sometimes I didn't think she really remembered us.

"For a long time, Papa couldn't work enough to feed us. I tried to find food in the woods. A few others tried to help us, but most people we knew were as bad off as we were. There were many nights when the baby, Nellie, would cry herself to sleep because she was so hungry. I thought we would all starve. Papa couldn't let that go on, so he began to borrow from the store. We got deeper and deeper in debt."

Josiah's callused hands rubbed hers with a gentle, soothing motion. His quiet strength seemed to give her enough courage to continue.

"One day, Michael Sawyer came to see us. We'd almost given up hope. Food was so scarce, I didn't know what we would eat the next day." Lavette drew in a shaky breath. "It turned out that Mr. Sawyer's son-in-law was responsible for the accident. When he heard what happened, Mr. Sawyer felt beholden to find us and try to make things right. The problem was, he didn't have much after the war, either. While he was talking to Papa, I came home from foraging in the woods. He said he had an idea and told Papa he would return the next day."

For several minutes, Lavette sat in silence, unable to continue. Josiah's thumb rubbed the palm of her hand. "What did he do?"

"He said his mother needed someone to work for her. His mother, Mrs. Sawyer, had some health problems. The doctors thought she would improve if she moved north to get away from the damp air. Her brother up North would help her, but she needed someone to go along to care for her."

"Lavette, being a servant isn't at all like being a slave. You're free to quit and find work somewhere else."

"That's what her son feared. To keep me from quitting and leaving her alone, he offered me a contract similar to an indentured servant's. He would give my father enough money to pay off his debt. Papa would be able to move to the city, where he could find better work. In fact, Mr. Sawyer had a friend in the city looking for a good man to take charge of his livery. He promised medical help for Mama, too." She drew in a shaky breath. "He also said I would earn a small monthly wage."

"What did your father do?"

"He turned him down. He said he'd watched three of his children be sold off, and he wouldn't sell his own daughter, not for any amount of money. Mr.

Sawyer said he would give us some time to think about it and would return in a couple of days."

Josiah's knees brushed hers. He leaned forward, his body and his face betraying his tension.

"Mama still wasn't strong. The girls were old enough to start helping out, though. I couldn't let Papa turn down such a generous offer. I waited until everyone except the two of us was sleeping. Then I told him that I chose to become Mrs. Sawyer's servant. That way, he wouldn't be selling me off. I would be offering my services. I begged him to let me do this for him and Mama. They could go to the city and get a better job. Maybe Mama could even get some help for the headaches she continued to have."

"But you couldn't have been very old." Josiah cleared his throat and blinked.

"I wasn't too old, only seventeen. Living as a slave, a person grows up fast. Some girls were married by that age. I'd been caring for my brother and sisters for a long time. Since Mama had been sick, I'd pretty much run the house." She didn't object when Josiah rested his forehead against their joined hands.

"When Mr. Sawyer came back, I told him I'd take care of his mama, but I couldn't do it until my family had paid their debts and moved to the city. He gave Papa the money right away and gave us the address of a man he knew who wanted to hire Papa. It didn't take long to pack up the meager belongings we had. Within a few days, I was a slave once more." She shrugged and gave a small smile. "Oh, I know this is a little different. I had a choice, but still I'm not free to decide what I want to do."

"How much longer is left on your contract?"

"I signed the contract for ten years. I have two years left. There's no way of knowing where I'll be then. Mrs. Sawyer only made plans to stay here for six to eight weeks. She wants to return back East. If she does that, I'll have to accompany her."

Night had fallen. Lavette grimaced, knowing she'd done most of the talking. This was the first time she'd told anyone the whole story. For the last eight years, she hadn't had a friend to confide in. She didn't want to think why she felt so comfortable with Josiah when she'd only known him such a short time. In her heart, she felt she'd known him forever. After all, he was the image of the handsome stranger who swept her off her feet in her childhood dreams.

A pack of coyotes began to sing their nightly chorus. The unearthly yips escalated, the voices of the younger coyotes making a sharp contrast with the more mature adults. Lavette knew many people hated the sound, but she found the cries a sign of freedom. Even the wild animals had more independence than she did. They could lift their muzzles and howl as much as they wanted, and no one could do a thing.

Josiah sighed. "I thought being an indentured servant wasn't done anymore—hadn't been done since the last century. I can't believe this."

Pulling her hand free, Lavette touched his cheek, making him look at her.

His dark eyes swam with unshed tears.

"I felt a little bitter at first." She knew she had to make him understand. "Then I would remember that I helped my family by doing this. Who knows what would have happened to us if we had to continue on where we were? The last time I saw them, my mama was back to running the house. Papa loves working with horses again." She smiled. "I think you and Papa would get along well. You both have that interest in common."

He leaned his cheek against her hand, but she pulled back. "My only regret is that I can't have a relationship with anyone. I can be your friend for a short time, but that's all." Her heart begged him to understand what she was saying.

"But your family." Josiah's brow creased in a frown. "Don't you miss them?"

"Of course. Don't you miss your family?"

He nodded. "I guess I see your point. That isn't a good argument. I find that I want to get angry and say this isn't right."

"There's no need to fret." Lavette stood and stretched, arching her back to ease the ache. "I've come to terms with freedom, or the lack of it. Even when my time with this contract is up, I have the feeling I still won't be delivered. Something will happen. I don't know what, but I can feel it."

She picked up Josiah's discarded plate and cup. "We all have burdens to bear, and mine is being a bondwoman to some master or mistress. I can live with that. I have to."

Backing toward the door, she hoped he would leave. Her stomach ached from holding back her emotions. She wanted to lie on her bed in the dark where no one could hear her and cry. Talking to Josiah brought up the resentment she'd buried. She hadn't told him the truth. She would never get over the idea of being a slave and the indignation accompanying that. Inside, she would always long for freedom—even if she never found it.

"Wait, Lavette." Josiah reached her in two quick steps. "Let me pray with you about this. God didn't bring you all the way out here for no reason. He has a purpose, and I believe His purpose involves the two of us."

Anger bubbled up, making Lavette's words come out in a bitter torrent. "I don't ask God about anything. He quit caring about me and my family a long time ago. For years my mama said Jesus would set us free and things would be better. Well, look what happened. My mama got sick, and I ended up in bondage again."

Pushing the door open, she flung her parting words in a hushed voice. "I can't stop you from praying, but don't ever ask me to pray with you." Stepping inside, only the thought of Mrs. Sawyer sleeping kept Lavette from slamming the door in his face.

Chapter 9

Josiah slipped the rod into the hot coals, twisting it with the tongs until the metal lay settled among the glowing embers. Next to the bar, he placed a crucible with iron to melt. His left hand automatically found the cord to the bellows. He pulled, sending a steady stream of air to intensify the heat. The coals glowed from reddish-orange to white hot. Tiny flames, lissome dancers, rose up and swayed across the embers in a graceful, ethereal rhythm. Mesmerized, Josiah heard nothing around him.

As he waited for the ore to heat so he could begin work on the nails and the new axe head one of his customers had ordered, Josiah tried to ignore the inner heaviness that weighed on him this morning. Lavette's parting words yesterday evening had kept him awake most of the night. He knew he could never marry someone who didn't share his love for and belief in Jesus Christ. All this time, he'd taken Lavette's faith for granted. He'd assumed she loved Jesus as much as he did. He should have known better. The voice of his mother reminding him that a young lady's spiritual beauty would always be more important than her physical charm rang through his mind.

When Lavette appeared at his smithy that first morning, he'd known she was a gift from God. He hadn't questioned, only accepted. Now he knew that he should have discussed her faith at the first opportunity rather than have his heart broken when he discovered her disbelief. How could he have been so blind? What should he do now?

Lifting the crucible from the fire, Josiah checked to see if the iron was ready, then placed the partially molten ore back in the heat. Using the tongs, he turned the iron bar. He couldn't seem to focus today. Of course, he hadn't been thinking right since Lavette walked into his life. She'd managed, in a very short time, to turn his reasoning upside down.

After running his hand over the smooth face of his anvil, Josiah went on to check over his tools. He knew the importance of caring for the implements of his trade. He'd made most of them himself, although a few were ones his father had given him when he left home. With these tools and the knowledge he carried, he would always be able to make his way. His father had seen to that.

The long tongs fastened onto the glowing shaft. Josiah lifted the hot iron from the embers, careful to keep away from the sparks. The small scars dotting his bare arms bore testimony to the dangers of the flying ash and coal.

"That's what I like to see—a man hard at work."

Josiah swung around to grin at Conlon. "Have you ever thought of trying it for yourself, or do you spend so much time watching those soldiers of yours, you don't have time to do any physical labor?"

"A cruel blow." Conlon tried to act affronted, but the sparkle in his eyes told the truth. "You have no idea the mental anguish I suffer from forcing all those cavalrymen to do their jobs every day."

Josiah shook his head. Sometimes Conlon didn't have a serious bone in his body. That's one of the reasons they were able to stay so close. They seemed to both have the ability to laugh and forgive. Then too being brothers in faith helped build a strong bond between them. God had worked a miracle by giving him such wonderful friends.

"So, how many horses do I need to shoe for you today?" Josiah gave a light tug on the bellows rope, then moved away from the heat.

A wounded look crossed Conlon's face. "I didn't bring you work. It so happens I need a valuable opinion, and you were the first one I thought to ask."

"What have you done now? Is Glorianna making you sleep in the barn with the horse?"

Conlon chuckled. "With those twins walking and getting into everything, that might not be so bad." He pursed his mouth in a thoughtful expression. "Come to think of it, the horse doesn't pull my hair, climb all over me, or scream in my ear, and I never need to change his diapers."

"Your horse wears diapers?" Josiah raised his eyebrows, feigning surprise. "That must be an interesting sight."

Conlon's grin turned to a chuckle, then a roar of laughter. His eyes crinkled, tears of mirth winking in the light of the fire. Gasping, Conlon wiped his eyes with the back of his hand. "I have to admit that would be a funny sight." He continued to chuckle. "No, my horse doesn't wear diapers. If he did, I would probably take him inside at night. I think he would be great at helping corral those kids of mine."

Glancing at the forge, Josiah could see he needed to check the heating metal. Tongs in hand, he picked up the bar and moved it to the edge of the fire. After placing the crucible next to the iron, he turned back to his friend.

"So, what kind of advice can I give you?"

"I'm interested in purchasing some new horses for the cavalry. I went to look at some yesterday, and I wanted to see if you know of them. Eduardo Villegas has them for sale. I know he's honest, because he's been selling cattle to the cavalry for a number of years. Now, he's raising horses too. Have you seen them?"

Josiah nodded. "I know Villegas. He has some fine stock. He's been working to build a herd for awhile now. I'd think he would be a good one to buy from. He treats his animals right. Do you want me to go with you to look them over?"

"I think I already had my mind made up, but if you get the chance to look at them, you might give me your opinion." Conlon rubbed the back of his neck. "His horses are a mite more money than some others, but they seem sound. I wanted to see what you thought before I spent the extra for them."

"He's been after me to do some work for him. When I'm there, I'll look over his stock."

Conlon gave Josiah a devilish grin. "Now that we have business out of the way, how's the sweetheart? Shall I have Glory and Kathleen start working on a wedding dress?"

Josiah resisted the urge to make a face. Instead, he turned to check the forge. With the tongs, he carefully plucked the crucible from the midst of the burning embers. After setting the fiery hot container on the bench, he lifted the lid and put it to one side. Heat waves undulated up from the molten mass. In a ritual he'd practiced since he was a boy, Josiah lifted the pot and poured the melted iron into the molds he had ready. Conlon stood silent, watching the whole process, a serious expression replacing the levity of moments before.

Placing the empty jar in its proper place, Josiah turned to inspect his work. He didn't want to ignore his friend, but right now, he wasn't sure he could talk about his relationship with Lavette. After last night there couldn't be any relationship, and that thought was eating a hole in his heart.

"Okay, Josiah." Conlon's hand on Josiah's arm halted him in midstep. "I think we need to sit down and talk. Have any coffee around here?" Conlon glanced to the corner of the smithy where Josiah usually had hot brew ready to share with a customer.

"I'll get you some." Josiah pulled free with little effort and filled two cups. This was the problem with having a good friend. Conlon could read him like a book. In a way, he wanted to confide in Conlon, knowing he would get godly advice. At least Conlon would care enough to listen; however, what he felt for Lavette seemed so precious, Josiah didn't know if he could bare his heart even to his best friend.

Conlon took a long sip of coffee and made a face. "When did you make this stuff—last week?"

Leaning back against the side of the shop, Josiah shrugged. "I can't afford to make fresh coffee every five minutes in case you show up and want some." He took a sip. "You could be right. This tastes like it's left over from a month ago." He chuckled, a hollow sound that echoed in his broken heart.

"So, care to talk?" Conlon blew the steam across the top of his cup, then slurped noisily. He grinned and winked at Josiah. "I can't do that at home. Glory would look daggers at me. Now, what happened between you and Miss Johnson? The last I heard, she was the best thing since store-bought boots. Isn't she as sweet as you first thought?"

Josiah couldn't help the smile that creased his cheeks. "Oh, she's sweet all right. I've never met a more delightful gal."

"Then what's the problem? She doesn't go for a big oaf like you?" Conlon grinned.

"I'd say she's a mite taken with me." Josiah rested his elbows on his knees, the steam from his coffee wafting past his eyes. "The problem is, last night when we were talking, I found out she and I don't share a faith in Jesus. In fact, she's carrying a mighty big grudge against God."

For several minutes, Conlon sat silent, sipping and listening as Josiah related the events of the previous evening. "She was so angry when I mentioned praying that she almost slammed the door in my face. I'll still pray for her, but I can't consider pursuing anything serious. Even if, as a child, she did believe in Jesus, right now she's full of resentment and anger toward Him."

"So, you're going to give up on her?" Conlon set his empty mug on the bench.

"I'm not giving up. I've been begging Jesus to help her all night and all day." Josiah tried not to be angry at his friend. "I don't know what more I can do."

"I apologize." Conlon gripped Josiah's shoulder. "I seem to remember a friend of mine telling me to be patient and let God have a chance to work. Why don't we agree to pray together for Miss Johnson? You know the power of that. I'll even get Glory and the Kirbys to join with us."

"I'd appreciate that." Josiah stood and stretched. He had to get back to work. "I don't know that there's any chance she's the right woman for me, but that doesn't matter as much as her getting over her anger at God."

Conlon stood and handed Josiah his cup. "You know, Glory and Kathleen have already visited her once. Maybe they could stop by again and invite her to our Sunday morning meeting. If the invitation comes from them, maybe she won't find it as easy to say no."

The heaviness in Josiah's heart eased. "I'll pray specifically that she'll agree to come." He nodded at Conlon. "Thanks. Tell Glory hello for me." Josiah turned and walked back into the smithy with a lighter step than he'd had since last evening.

Lavette folded the bread dough over and pushed, sending a whoosh of yeasty smell into the air. She folded and pushed again, kneading the pockets of air out of the dough, making it smooth. Patting the mound into a ball shape, she placed it on a bed of flour and covered the mass with a soft cloth to keep the flies away while the leavening worked.

On the counter near the stove, a batch of cinnamon rolls was rising, nearly ready to pop into the oven. Two pies cooled on the open windowsill. Ever since last night when she'd exploded at Josiah, Lavette couldn't seem to stay still. She'd gotten up early from a restless night and begun baking. The familiarity of the routine helped to calm her ragged nerves.

Guilt ate at her. She could recall her mother and father talking in hushed whispers about the Lord Jesus and how He would come to take them to gloryland one day. Her mother taught her songs about climbing a ladder into heaven and other spirituals. Their master didn't allow the slaves to have formal services, but even he couldn't stop the secret meetings that occurred after dark when they were supposed to be too tired to talk. Lavette could still remember curling up in a corner of the room, wide-eyed, as her parents and other couples would share bits of Scripture they'd learned. Early on she caught the excitement of a Savior who would one day deliver them. For years, along with many of her relatives and friends, she'd clung to that hope. Had she been wrong to turn her back on God when He let her down? Where were all those promises? Why had God said one thing, then done another? If she couldn't trust God to keep His word, then how could she trust Him with her life?

By the end of the War Between the States, she'd been sure Jesus was setting His people free. Then she would have all the privileges of independence like Miss Susannah. That hadn't happened. Instead, she and her family suffered even more, and within a short time she was once again a slave. Oh, they didn't call her that, but she was one all the same.

Anger churned in her stomach. She pushed away the bitterness and tried to recall her mother's face and the reason she'd given up so much for her family. They were worth the cost, weren't they? If she had the chance to choose again, she would do the same thing. Only this time she wouldn't go into servanthood with any misconception that Jesus would come along and rescue her. Reality had long ago overturned that delusion.

The tinkle of a bell chimed from the other room. Mrs. Sawyer must be finished with her lunch. Lavette took the cloth off the cinnamon buns and slid the pan into the oven. She wiped her hands on her apron and hurried down the hall.

"Thank you, Dear." Mrs. Sawyer gave a smile. "I can't tell you how wonderful I feel today. It must be this warm, dry air. I'd like to sit in the parlor for awhile and look out the window. Would you mind helping me?"

Lavette returned her mistress's smile. In the past days Mrs. Sawyer had made a vast improvement. A pink flush tinted her cheeks, and her eyes sparkled with life. Her cough had disappeared. Lavette couldn't remember the last time Mrs. Sawyer was this well.

"I think you've been enjoying your daughter and those sweet grandchildren." Lavette steadied Mrs. Sawyer with one arm holding her around the waist and the other on her closest shoulder. "This visit has done you a lot of good."

"I believe you're right." Mrs. Sawyer took several steps and stopped to rest, leaning against Lavette for support. "I think I shall get up every day and try walking a little farther. Maybe if I start sitting up more, I'll gain some strength."

"As long as you don't tire yourself too much." Lavette helped her through the door to the parlor and into the chair by the window. "Would you like me to bring a blanket for your lap? I don't want you chilling."

"That would be very nice." The light appeared to shine through Mrs. Sawyer's paper thin, blue-veined hands as she held them in the sunlight that streamed inside. Plucking a lap quilt from the back of a chair, Lavette spread the comforter over Mrs. Sawyer's legs, tucking the edge under to hold in the warmth.

An odd rapping issued from the front door. Mrs. Sawyer's countenance brightened. "Oh, I do hope that's Gretta come to visit. Did she plan to come today?"

"I don't believe she did." Lavette frowned. "I'll see who it is and be right back."

At the front door she stopped, her hand trembling on the latch. What if Josiah had come back? The thought made her heart leap even though she'd done her best to scare him away for good. The rapping began again. Lavette took a deep breath and pulled the door open. Her hand tightened on the wood. She couldn't speak. She began to quake—not from anticipation, but from fear.

Chapter 10

G ood day, Miss Johnson." Bertrand Mead's smooth tone sent dread racing through Lavette. He still held his silver-headed cane aloft, ready to rap on the door once more, should it close on him. "I came to speak with your mistress, if you'll let her know I'm here. She is available for company, isn't she?" His small eyes narrowed. "I've heard she's getting stronger and is able to receive callers."

Lavette opened her mouth, but nothing came out. The door latch cut into her palm, the pain easing some of the fear. She wanted to slam the door shut and pile every stick of furniture in the house against it to keep this man away. The devil himself couldn't have been much scarier.

"Well, may I come in?" He bent toward her, and she could smell again the cloying aroma of whatever he used after he washed. Her stomach roiled like she was rocking on a storm-tossed ship.

"Lavette, Dear, who's here?" At the sound of Mrs. Sawyer's quavery voice, Mead raised one eyebrow, the corner of his mouth lifting in a contemptuous smile.

"I'll go announce you." Lavette took a quick step back and started to shut the door. Mead inserted his cane, striking the door with an audible thump.

"I'll step inside while you notify Mrs. Sawyer of my presence." His shoes clicked smartly as he moved past her and slid the door closed behind him.

Lavette backed away, doing her best to repress a shudder as his slimy gaze flicked over her. Rounding the door to the parlor, she breathed a sigh of relief. Her whole body shook.

"Why, whatever is the matter, Girl? You look a little peaked." Mrs. Sawyer bent forward, peering intently at Lavette.

"I believe I've startled your servant without intending to, Ma'am."

Lavette whirled to find Mead standing in the doorway behind her. "Mrs. Sawyer, Mr. Bertrand Mead is here to see you." Her voice sounded hollow and shaky.

"What a pleasure. I don't get much company. Come in and sit down, young man."

Lavette moved to the side, hoping Mead wouldn't touch her as he walked past. He crossed the room and bent over Mrs. Sawyer, lifting her hand for a gentleman's kiss.

"Good afternoon. I'm acquainted with your son-in-law, Paul Ashton. He talks so much about you, I decided to come by and see for myself if you are as wonderful as he says."

Mrs. Sawyer giggled. Lavette's stomach clenched, the contents threatening to come up.

"I'll have none of that flattery, Mr. Mead. Sit down here beside me. Lavette, why don't you bring us something? I'm sure Mr. Mead would enjoy some refreshments."

"Why, yes, I would." Mead's eyes bored into Lavette, reminding her he intended to own her. "If I'm not mistaken, I smell something delicious baking. Paul's commented on your servant's excellent cooking skills. I'm sure they're only the beginning of her talents."

Lavette's hands shook so much, she almost dropped the pan of rolls as she pulled them from the oven. The sweet cinnamon scent that she loved nauseated her this time. What was Mead doing here? What did he really want? The possible answers frightened her so much, she wanted to run.

She took her time putting the cups, coffee, and buns on a tray. The thought of facing Mead again was more than she could bear. Perhaps she could accidentally spill coffee on him and he would have to leave. Lavette shook her head and sighed. The way her hands were shaking, the spilling wouldn't be hard to imagine.

Picking up the tray, she steeled herself for the ordeal of seeing Mead again. The question of his real reason for calling on Mrs. Sawyer nagged at her as she carried the refreshments into the parlor.

"Ah, here's Lavette with some of her famous cinnamon buns. This girl is a wonder." Mrs. Sawyer gave her a lopsided smile, but Lavette could see the tired lines beginning to show around her mouth and eyes. As soon as the pair finished eating, she would suggest that her mistress needed to rest and get Mead out of the house.

Mrs. Sawyer waved away the roll and coffee Lavette offered to serve her. She knew the lady had trouble eating when she began to tire. Although she grew stronger every day, Mrs. Sawyer still didn't have the stamina for long visits. Lavette forced her face to be void of expression as Mead deliberately caressed her hand as he took the plate from her. She straightened and moved toward the door.

"I'll be back in a few minutes." Lavette faced her mistress. "You'll need to rest soon."

"Let me visit a little longer." Mrs. Sawyer seemed to wilt more each moment. "This gentleman is telling me about his business prospects. We can talk a few more minutes, then perhaps you can return another day, Mr. Mead."

Bertrand Mead caught Lavette's gaze. She hurried from the room. Resting her forehead against the painted wall of the hallway, Lavette let out a slow breath. She hadn't feared a man this much since she'd gotten away from the plantation. Mead reminded her of Miss Susannah's father—the way he used to watch her and try to catch her alone. His touch had been as repulsive as Mead's.

She tried to ignore the low rumble of voices as she fought to get her emotions under control. Whatever Mead had to say about himself, she didn't want to listen to his lies. Lavette knew he continued to flatter her employer from the number of girlish giggles issuing from a woman who should be old enough to see Mead's compliments for what they were—lies.

"I really must be on my way." Mead's words cut through Lavette's thoughts. "Before I go, I would like to speak with you about your young servant, Miss Johnson. I had the pleasure of hearing her sing. She has the voice of an angel."

Lavette wanted to run. She knew she shouldn't be listening, but her feet seemed rooted to the spot.

"Because my other business ventures are doing so well, I thought I should try to bring some of the sophistication of the eastern cities to our little town."

"What are you thinking of doing?"

"I would like to start a theater of sorts to present the arts to the citizens of Tucson. I thought perhaps Miss Johnson could sing for us as a regular part of the entertainment."

Lavette could hear the frown in Mrs. Sawyer's voice. "I'm not sure I approve of that, but there won't be a chance, anyway. We leave to return home in a few weeks. Lavette won't be here to perform."

"Paul did mention that you would be returning to your home. At first, I thought to offer Miss Johnson the opportunity to remain here when you leave, but Paul says she has a contract to fulfill. I came today to ask you to consider allowing me to purchase her agreement before you leave."

"Why, I don't know that I can do that." Mrs. Sawyer sounded shocked.

"I'm not asking you to give me an answer today, dear lady. I'm only requesting that you consider my offer. You might speak with your daughter and son-in-law too. Now, you look tired. I'll see myself out, and you get some rest. I'll be back to visit soon."

Before Lavette could move, Mead rounded the corner into the hall. His narrow gaze fastened on her. The sneer lifting the corner of his mouth gave him a triumphant appearance. She flattened against the wall as he started past. He stopped. She stared in silent terror as he roughly stroked his thumb over her cheek. "You'll be mine." He mouthed the words, gave her a feral smile, stalked to the door, and disappeared.

An hour later, Lavette eased the back door closed behind her. She still couldn't believe the control she'd shown as she prepared Mrs. Sawyer for her nap and finished putting the bread in the pans to rise. Any thoughts of Mead and his threats and conversation with her mistress were blocked for the moment. She'd floated through the hour in an air of unreality, feeling like she watched herself at work, rather than doing the chores in person. Now, the truth began to seep inside. Her stomach knotted, fear replacing the calm.

She wondered if she could run away. Maybe the little bit of money she'd saved over the years would be enough to purchase a ticket for the stage. Hope sank as she realized her funds weren't enough to get home to her family, and anywhere else she went would leave her vulnerable to other types like Mead. Who would hire an unknown girl with no visible means and no references?

Hurrying across the backyard, Lavette began to wander the quiet side streets. Walking always helped her think, and right now she had to come up with a plan to escape before Mead figured a way to make her his. Despair clutched at her with painful fingers. *Oh, Papa, I need you. I don't know what to do. You wouldn't let him hurt me. Was I wrong to become a bondservant when you didn't want me to? Is this the cost of disobedience?*

Tears blinded her. She hurried on, her head lowered, not watching where she was going. Dashing a hand across her watering eyes, Lavette did her best to stop the panic welling up inside.

"Well, well, what have we here?" Mead's question stopped her cold. He stood beside a tree, his hands resting on top of his cane. His eyes raked over her in a way that made her want to hide. She felt like a rabbit caught in a snare, with no strength to run.

In two strides, Mead stood beside her, close enough that she could smell alcohol on his breath. She tried to turn away to avoid the unpleasant smell. Mead's well-manicured fingers grasped her arm, forcing her to face him. Her heart pounded.

"Looking for me, were you?" He chuckled, a predatory rumble that held no mirth. "You must be eager to begin working for me. I know your singing will please the crowds, but I'll train you in other areas too."

Lavette gasped. Jerking back, she tried to break free. His hold didn't loosen. Why did this street have to be so deserted right now? Why hadn't she gone where there would be other people? Did it matter? They would probably refuse to help her anyway.

"Oh, no, my sweet. I'm thinking I should give you an early trial. Why don't you accompany me? My Jackrabbit Saloon isn't too far. You can give the boys a song or two." He slipped his cane under his arm and began to run his fingers down her forearm to her wrist. "Maybe you can even give me a little private entertainment." He began to pull her close.

Pure panic swept over her. Lavette jerked back. She kicked, and her foot met his shin. Mead grimaced. His grip tightened. She bent forward, trying to ease the ache in her arm.

"Let me go." She couldn't look at him. She already knew what she would see in his eyes. "I need to get back before Mrs. Sawyer wakes up. She'll expect me to be there."

"Oh, we won't keep you all that long, my dear. I simply want to give the men who visit my establishment a taste of what's to come." He took a firm hold of her upper arm, propelling her down the street. "This way when I convince your mistress to sell me your contract, the men will be waiting and eager. Word will spread about your wonderful voice and beauty."

She wanted to shout at him. She wanted to yell, *I can't sing for you. I won't.* Years of slavery and beatings when she refused to follow her master's orders left her unable to find the courage to say the words. Instead, the clench of foreboding made her too afraid to keep pace. Despite his tight hold on her arm, her steps flagged enough that he too began to slow. A few men passed by, but rather than help her, they averted their faces.

"If you think going at the pace of an ant will give you time, you're wrong." Alcohol fumes made her wrinkle her nose as he tugged her close. "I'm going to get hold of you and never let you go."

Lavette stumbled as Mead released her. His arm swept around her back, yanking her against him again. Like an iron band, he held her tight. She couldn't breathe. He began to lower his mouth. Lavette tried to kick and squirm to no avail. She turned her head. His lips brushed her cheek. Mead cursed.

"Let her go, Mead."

At the soft-spoken command, Mead looked up. His grip eased, but Lavette still couldn't get away.

"Why, Deputy, we're only having a little discussion. There's no need to interrupt."

"Let the lady go."

Mead's eyes flashed. His lips thinned. Lavette felt his hold loosen a bit more, and she began to push away. Mead released her. She stumbled back and would have fallen if not for the hands that caught her. She could see the star pinned to the man's chest.

"Now get on back to the hole you crawled out of, Mead." Anger gave the deputy's voice a menacing quality. "One of these days, you'll make a mistake, and I'll be waiting. I want you to leave this young lady alone. Understand?"

"Why, I had no intention of hurting Miss Johnson." Mead smirked. "I was acting the gentleman and showing her around. Good day." He tipped his hat and strolled away, the silver of his walking cane sparkling in the sunlight.

"Miss Johnson, is it?"

Lavette nodded. The deputy had a kind voice when he wasn't talking to Mead. She still didn't dare look up.

"I believe my wife met you the other day. I'm Deputy Quinn Kirby. My wife is Kathleen. She said she and Glorianna Sullivan dropped by to see you."

"Yes, Suh, they did."

"Are you all right? Mead didn't hurt you, did he?"

Rubbing her arm, Lavette knew she would have bruises. Those would heal. The hurt Mead intended to inflict wouldn't mend easily.

"I'm fine." That wasn't true, but Lavette didn't want to say more to the deputy. The realization that she was safe sank in. Her knees began to quake. She wasn't sure she could even walk. A lump lodged in her throat. Tears burned in her eyes. She knew she had to get out of here before she began to cry. The strain from the afternoon's events proved too much. A lone tear trickled down her cheek and dripped onto her dress. She turned her head away, hoping the deputy hadn't noticed.

Deputy Kirby picked up her hand and tucked it into the crook of his arm. "Why don't you come with me?" He acted as if he didn't know she was crying, yet he must have noticed. "I left home a few minutes ago. Kathleen and Glorianna were having a visit. If I'm not mistaken, you could use a lady to talk to about now."

She'd gone off without her hanky. Lavette sniffed, wishing the tears would stop. They came harder. She bit her lip. Deputy Kirby opened a door and ushered her into a kitchen that smelled of fresh-baked bread and roasting meat. She wanted to turn and run the other way.

"Why, look who's come for a visit, Kathleen."

From the corner of her eye, Lavette could see Glorianna's red hair as the small woman swept toward her.

"Welcome to my house, Lavette. I'm glad you could come over." Kathleen stopped by Lavette, stretched up, and kissed her husband on the cheek. Lavette heard the door close behind her. A dam broke. Sobs began to wrack her body. She barely felt the arms that hugged her close, giving her the comfort she desperately needed.

Chapter 11

Lavette, what's wrong?" Kathleen's voice was soothing. Her hand rubbed circles on Lavette's back, seeming to understand the ache she had there. "Come on in and sit down."

Sobs still shook her body as the two women led the way to the kitchen table. Lavette could see that Kathleen had been the one holding onto her. Glorianna thrust a hanky into Lavette's curled fist. Mopping the tears and wiping her dripping nose, Lavette wished she could crawl under the table. She didn't even know these women well. How could she have behaved this way? Her mother would never understand.

"Would you like a glass of water or a cup of coffee?" Kathleen sat close, her hand still stroking Lavette's shoulder.

Cool water sounded so good, Lavette almost groaned at the thought. How could she ask this woman to wait on her, though? She was the servant. A white woman didn't bring something to a black person. She shook her head, then held her breath, trying to stop the hiccups that always seemed to follow crying. If she could only get hold of her emotions, she would be able to thank Kathleen and Glorianna and leave.

"Did we mention the other day that we're friends of Josiah's?" Glorianna pulled a chair close on the other side of Lavette. "He told us you haven't seen your family in a number of years. I would imagine that's pretty hard, not being able to talk with any family. Then you come out here to Tucson, where you don't know a soul."

"Lavette, we'd like to be your friends." Kathleen's voice had a soothing quality that reminded Lavette of her mother. "I don't know what happened, but something upset you a lot. Is Mrs. Sawyer all right?"

Lavette nodded.

"Are you having trouble working for her?"

Lavette shook her head. The hiccups and sobs stopped, but she still trembled, remembering the way Mead had looked at her and touched her.

Glorianna brushed a lock of Lavette's hair back from her face. "Did you fall or do something to hurt yourself?"

Once more, Lavette shook her head. These women seemed so kind, but she couldn't bring herself to talk to them. She hadn't wanted her mama this badly since she was a young child, and she wasn't sure her mother would know what to do about Mead.

Kathleen patted her shoulder once more and rose. "I'd like a cup of coffee,

Would you like one, Glory?"

Still smoothing Lavette's hair in a gesture so calming, Lavette thought she might start purring if she were a cat, Glorianna said, "That sounds good. I might like a little water too."

Dishes clinked as Kathleen busied herself near the stove and the water bucket. Before long, she set two cups of water on the table in front of Lavette and Glorianna, returning moments later with coffee for each of them. From the aroma, Lavette knew the coffee must be freshly brewed. Kathleen made one more trip, bringing back the same drinks for herself. Lavette knew they were doing this to make her feel comfortable. She marveled that they would consider waiting on her like this.

"Thank you." The whispered words came from her. She picked up the water and took a long sip. The cool liquid soothed the ache in her throat. She swallowed some more before placing the glass back on the table.

"Lavette, can you look at me?" Kathleen took Lavette's hand in hers as she spoke. Lavette glanced up. The gold and green of Kathleen's eyes mesmerized her. She'd never seen anyone with that color of eyes before. Of course, she rarely looked at a white person. She knew better.

"My husband told me when Josiah first met you, Bertrand Mead happened by." Kathleen's hands squeezed as a chill raced through Lavette. "Has he been bothering you again?" Kathleen's soft question pricked Lavette. Could these women understand?

"I need to get back home before Mrs. Sawyer wakes up from her nap. She'll be expecting me." Lavette began to quake at the thought of walking home alone. Even though it wasn't far, Mead could be anywhere. She forced herself to stand. "Thank you so much." Her voice shook.

Glorianna stood and stretched. "I hate to say this, Kathleen, but I'd best get home too. The twins are probably awake, and Alicia will need help with them." She touched Lavette on the arm. "My house isn't far from yours. Shall we walk together?"

Gratitude made Lavette's knees weak. "That'd be fine." She couldn't keep the relief out of her tone.

As they made their way down the dusty streets, Glorianna kept up a light chatter. She talked about her husband and the new fort. They would be moving there soon. He'd wanted to live there already, but Glorianna had begged him to wait until after Kathleen had her baby. They were cousins, and Glorianna wanted to stay close for now.

She talked about her twins, Andrew and Angelina, and the trials and blessings of having babies. Lavette learned more about Glorianna and Conlon than she would have thought possible in such a short time. Although she hadn't said a word, Lavette felt warmed by Glorianna's offer of friendship. This wasn't the type of companion Miss Susannah wanted. Glorianna seemed to care about knowing

Lavette, something Lavette had never had from a white woman.

They reached the door of Mrs. Sawyer's house. Without looking at Glorianna, Lavette spoke. "Thank you. I baked some pies and rolls today. Would you like some to take home to your family? We have more than we can eat with just the two of us."

"Why, I do believe I'd love that. I doubt if Alicia's gotten much done today in the way of baking. She's had her hands full while I was at Kathleen's."

Not wanting to disturb Mrs. Sawyer if she still slept, Glorianna insisted on staying outside. Lavette brought out a pie and rolls wrapped in a cloth to keep the flies and dust from getting on them. "Thank you for walking me home."

Balancing the sweets on one hand, Glorianna gave Lavette's fingers a gentle squeeze. "We'll talk again soon. Before I go, I do want to invite you over to my house this Sunday morning."

"Me?"

"Yes, you. We don't have a church here in Tucson that we can attend. Some of us get together on Sunday. We sing, share Bible verses, and pray. Then we all eat together." Lavette could hear the smile in Glorianna's voice.

"I don't usually attend church."

"Well, this is more like friends getting together. Please come."

Lavette nodded. "I'll try, but only if Mrs. Sawyer's daughter will be coming to take her to her house."

"I hope you'll be there." Glorianna gave Lavette's fingers another squeeze, then walked off down the path. Lavette watched her go, Glorianna's red-gold hair shimmering in the light. Could she trust this woman to be her friend? Her heart wanted to say yes, but her experience said no. The hope that started to blossom faded at that thought. She had no friend, no one to confide in, and right now, she needed someone.

✢

Josiah whistled as he strode down the street toward Conlon's house. Sunday, his day of rest, always made him want to make music. Then too Josiah knew he needed the day off.

This had been a rough week. As much as he liked Lavette, he hadn't been by to see her after their talk about praying. He'd struggled with that decision, especially after his conversation with Conlon. Still, he felt God wouldn't want him becoming attached to a woman who was too angry at God to pray.

Quinn had stopped by on Thursday to tell him about rescuing Lavette from Mead. Josiah had to stop work and spend time alone in prayer to keep from looking Mead up and confronting him. Mead would never listen to him. He might end up doing more harm than good.

For the first time since becoming a Christian, Josiah felt as if he were walking alone. Always before, God seemed so close. In prayer time, he could feel the presence of the Holy Spirit. When he went through a trial, Jesus was right there, lighting the way and giving him comfort to carry on. This time, Josiah couldn't sense God anywhere. Maybe this morning's meeting with the other Christians would help.

Striding up the path, Josiah glanced up at the Sullivans' porch. A slight figure stood at the door, her hand raised to knock. She lowered her fist, raised it, then lowered it again. She turned and began to leave.

"Lavette?" Josiah couldn't believe what he was seeing. She started and nearly dropped the dish she held.

"Oh, you scared me." She looked embarrassed as she shuffled to one side, allowing him to go past her.

"Isn't anybody home?" Josiah frowned. "We were supposed to have our meeting here."

"I think they're home." Lavette stared at the ground, her fingers kneading the cloth covering what smelled like fried chicken. Josiah's mind crept back to the times when he stood by his mother as the pieces of chicken popped and spattered in a pan full of grease. The memory brought a strong ache for home and family that he hadn't experienced in years.

Shaking off the reverie, Josiah recalled Conlon saying Glorianna intended to invite Lavette to the service. "Are you here for the Sunday get-together?" He smiled and guided her to the door, his hand on her back. "Come on. I'll help you in and introduce you around."

Lavette glanced up, her eyes wide and fearful. "I don't know."

"Come on." Josiah chuckled. "Remember, the only ones who bite here are Andrew and Angelina. Since they're babies, you can't blame them." He guided her up the steps. "Take warning, though. Don't stick your finger in the mouth of a child that young."

She giggled, a wonderful sound. "I don't recall my brother so much when he was a baby, but those girls were terrible. They chewed everything. My papa said they were worse than a whole litter of puppies."

He laughed. He hadn't been this lighthearted since the last time he'd seen her. How he wanted this to mean she was changing toward God! Maybe she would hear something this morning that would help her get rid of her anger and bitterness—something that would help her make peace with Him.

The Sullivans' parlor couldn't hold many more people. A pleasant buzz of conversation wound through the air. A mixture of smells emanated from the kitchen area: meats, spices, and sweets. The aroma of cinnamon reminded Josiah of the first day he met Lavette. He took his hand from her back to keep from turning the touch into a caress.

"Lavette, I'm so glad you could come." Glorianna threaded her way through the gathering to greet them. She took Lavette's free hand and patted it.

"Does this mean you aren't glad to see me?" Josiah tried to look offended.

"Oh, Josiah, don't get your feathers ruffled." Glorianna wrinkled her nose. "We see you all of the time, and you know how special you are." She smiled at Lavette. "If I'm not mistaken, you've brought fried chicken to share. That smells delicious."

"Yes, Ma'am." Lavette's response could barely be heard over the noise of the crowd. "Where would you like me to put the dish?"

"I'll take it for you." Glorianna reached out.

Lavette glanced up, her eyes wide, the whites giving her a look of absolute terror. "Oh, no, Ma'am. I—you have—" Her gaze skimmed the room before settling on Josiah's face. The pleading look in her eyes begged him to intervene.

"I'll show her where to put the chicken." Josiah hoped Glorianna would understand Lavette's fear of having someone else waiting on her. He grinned to lighten the moment. "I might even have to sample a piece. Maybe two."

Hands on hips, Glorianna glared at him. "Don't you dare, Josiah Washington. If I know you, once you start, you won't stop until everything in there has been tasted." She gave Lavette a look of mock exasperation, although Josiah wasn't sure Lavette noticed since her gaze was once again directed toward the floor. "I'll let him show you, Lavette, but you keep a close eye on him. Don't let him eat all our lunch before we even have the services."

The kitchen table and every other available space was piled with cloth-covered dishes and baskets of food. Josiah couldn't stop his stomach from protesting the fact that he could only look and smell, but not eat. With only coffee for breakfast, he knew he might be embarrassed during the quiet moments of the meeting. Perhaps he could slip just one piece of chicken. He peeked in Lavette's direction and saw that she watched him, a knowing smile lifting the corners of her mouth.

"You wouldn't really tell on me, would you?" He started to lift the corner of the cloth over the chicken.

"Oh, no, you don't." She swatted his hand. "I remember my papa trying the very same thing. Mama always laughed and slapped his hand."

"What did your papa do?"

She grinned and tugged his arm away from the dish. "Well, he didn't starve to death."

Josiah gave an exaggerated sigh. "Come on. We'd best get back before they start, or Glorianna will be thinking I am sampling all the goodies." He gestured at the door, but Lavette hesitated. She glanced at him, then at the floor. "Hey, what's wrong?"

"I don't feel like I belong here. Are you sure my coming is all right?"

He put a finger under her chin, tipping her head back until her gaze met his. "Lavette, we're all glad you're here. Believe me, Glorianna wouldn't have invited you if she didn't want you to come." He began to escort her out, then stopped.

"One more thing." He waited until she looked at him. "You don't have to always examine the floor." He smiled to take the sting from the words. "You can look at these people and not be afraid. Maybe if you see their expressions, you'll be more comfortable speaking with them. God has blessed these Christians with a love for all people." He could feel her withdraw at the thought and waited to give her time to adjust to the new idea.

"I don't think I can." Lavette peered at him, her cinnamon eyes bright. "I'm so afraid sometimes."

Josiah's heart ached as he pulled Lavette close. He didn't want to think about what she'd gone through to make her so fearful of others. Leaning his cheek against her head, he whispered, "Stay close to me. Everything will be fine."

Chapter 12

Squeezed in beside Josiah in one corner of the room, Lavette tried to make herself even smaller, hoping no one would notice her. What had possessed her this morning? Yes, she'd made a promise of sorts to Glorianna. When Mrs. Sawyer announced that she planned to spend the day at her daughter's house, Lavette felt obligated to attend the service here. She even got permission to fix food to bring. Now, she wished she'd stayed home alone. Josiah was the only one here whom she knew very well, and he'd seemed to be avoiding her lately.

Peeking at the faces of the people clustered in the room, Lavette couldn't help wondering about those gathered here, as each seemed to have a look of excited expectation. Then again, why shouldn't they? Other than Josiah, none of the people in this room would have ever suffered the indignity of being bound. To her, God appeared to be the deity for this kind of people. They had every convenience and comfort. He provided well for them while her people suffered all sorts of trials.

Josiah leaned forward and clasped his hands together. Lavette moved to the side, allowing his broad back to hide her further. She twisted her hanky with her fingers to keep from touching him. The thought of resting her cheek against his back, the comfort that would bring, seemed so real she could almost feel the rough cotton of his shirt against her face.

Conlon stood. The conversation died away. An expectant hush settled over the room broken only by the whine of a baby unsure at the sudden change. "Glory and I want to welcome you all to our house. I've asked Josiah to lead the singing this week because we all know he's the only one who can carry a tune." Conlon grinned and everyone chuckled. Gesturing at Josiah, Conlon sat back down.

"Before we begin, I'd like to introduce you to someone new. In case you haven't met her, this is Lavette Johnson." Josiah reached back and plucked Lavette from her hiding place, pulling her forward so everyone in the room could stare at her. She wanted to die, yet at the same time she was filled with wonder that these people were willing to let Josiah speak up like that.

"Miss Johnson is here for a few weeks, and we hope she will join us often."

A spattering of applause met his statement. Lavette tried to look at the people. She'd been introduced to a few of them before being seated, but she knew she would never be able to put names with faces since she hadn't looked up at them. No matter what Josiah said, she couldn't do that. Even after they'd been given freedom at the end of the war, her family always had to show reverence for white folks by lowering their gaze when in the presence of a person of authority. Relief raced through Lavette when Josiah took his hand from her arm, allowing her to sink back behind him once more. From this vantage point, she could peek out at the men and women nestled together like birds in a nest. One of the men across the room seated next to a woman who looked like she'd eaten a green crabapple, stared back at Lavette, a strange expression on his puff-cheeked face. Lavette ducked back behind Josiah, wondering if she'd seen the man before.

Josiah began to lead the singing. Most of the songs weren't familiar to Lavette, so she sat silently, listening to Josiah's strong bass. He had a wonderful voice. She began to relax, lulled by the sound of music. Her father used to say that the only way to quiet her when she was an infant was to sing. For as long as she could recall, music brought out her heart and soul. She could hear a song in everyday noises that most people ignored.

The hymns ended and Conlon stood. "Glory and I have been studying the story of Joseph in the book of Genesis. I know most of you are familiar with the tale of how Joseph was a favorite of his father, Jacob. His brothers were so jealous, they sold him into slavery and told Jacob that Joseph died."

Conlon glanced down at Glorianna. She smiled and nodded. Lavette thought he must not be used to standing up and speaking before others like this. Longing stabbed through Lavette as she watched Glorianna's obvious devotion to her husband. As Conlon spoke, Glorianna's eyes shone with love. *Some day I want to feel that way about a man.* Brushing the thought away, Lavette turned her attention back to Conlon's dissertation.

"As a young boy, Joseph had several dreams about his brothers and father bowing down to him. Knowing those dreams came from God, I wondered if he got discouraged during his years in bondage. He even spent time in prison for something he didn't do."

Watching Josiah, with his open Bible on his lap, nodding at Conlon's account of Scripture, Lavette could see he wasn't upset or angry at all. Why did she feel such anger toward God? Hadn't Joseph suffered in slavery? She could picture Joseph being enraged at his brothers and at the unjust sentence he received. If those dreams truly came from God, then Joseph deserved to be mad. She had chosen to remain in servitude for a good reason, but Joseph had no choice. Lavette couldn't recall the story in detail, but she knew if she were Joseph, she would never forgive her brothers.

"I know a lot of people who have been betrayed by relatives or friends. They usually struggle with resentment, hatred, and anger. Joseph didn't have those feelings, and I intend to show you how I know that." Conlon ran a hand through his hair, leaving some of it to stick up in spikes. Glorianna started to rise, as if she would smooth his hair down. Kathleen, seated next to Glorianna, put a hand on her arm. Glorianna settled back in her chair, an amused twinkle in her eye.

"God began to bless Joseph. I think He did that because Joseph, rather than think of himself and allow those negative feelings toward those who betrayed him, tried to trust God with his life. After years in prison, Joseph became a very powerful man in Egypt because of God's plan.

"Finally, Joseph was able to confront his brothers. He had power over them. In fact, his dream came true: His brothers had to bow down to him." Conlon rubbed the back of his neck, staring at the page open in his Bible. "You know, I've thought and thought about this story. I can't imagine being as godly as Joseph. Is everyone familiar with what Joseph said to his brothers after their father's death?" Conlon paused. A few heads nodded, indicating they knew the verse he referred to. "I'd like to read this part to you."

As Conlon ran his finger down the page to find the verse, Lavette shifted forward on the seat. She couldn't wait to hear what Joseph had to say. He'd been a slave and unfairly imprisoned. They shared something in common. Surely, what he said would reflect her feelings, too.

Conlon cleared his throat. " 'And Joseph said unto them, Fear not: for am I in the place of God? But as for you, ye thought evil against me; but God meant it unto good, to bring to pass, as it is this day, to save much people alive. Now therefore fear ye not: I will nourish you, and your little ones. And he comforted them, and spake kindly unto them.' "

Stunned, Lavette ignored the murmured comments of the others in the room. Joseph let them off without any blame? Had she heard right? Did Joseph say it was all right for him to be made a slave and thrown into prison because God planned it that way? *If that's true, then what about me and my family, God? Did You intend our slavery to be for our good? I can't believe that.* Lavette fought the familiar anger coursing through her. For so long, she'd blamed God for all the terrible things that happened to her. Now she had a Scripture to show He was responsible. Even so, she couldn't understand why, and she couldn't seem to keep her anger. Instead, a hollow ache filled her.

Conlon raised a hand, and the whispered conversations faded away. "I've had to think this week about all the times I've blamed others for my circumstances, when all along maybe God had a bigger plan. I have the feeling if I'd stayed at home as a young man, I would never have met Jesus in a personal way. Even though I had a lot of rough years, I'm grateful for what I went through simply because God taught me so much. Glory feels the same way. I'd like to open a discussion this morning, where we can share how God used the trials in our lives to help bring us closer to Him."

Finished speaking, Conlon sat down. Glorianna gave him a loving touch on the shoulder, and he winked at her. She slipped her small hand into his, and Lavette could imagine how wonderful that would feel. Glimpsing at Josiah's work-roughened hands, she thought of the way her father's callused palms felt on her as a child. What she wouldn't give to feel a comforting touch right now. She was so confused.

Kathleen began to share her story, telling how her mother was ashamed to have a daughter born with a birthmark. She told of the years of hiding, too embarrassed to let people see her face, and how God taught her compassion for others because of what she endured.

Deputy Kirby told of the anger and hatred he carried with him and how God showed him the need to forgive others. Unbeknownst to him, the man Quinn despised married his sister. If he hadn't met Jesus before he went back home and discovered that truth, he might have been responsible for misery in his sister's life. He smiled and picked up his wife's hand, saying he was grateful to God for using the trials to bring him and Kathleen together.

Several others shared a testimony of God leading them through difficult times and the resulting good that came from it. Lavette wanted to scoff because none of the ones who were talking had ever been a slave, yet after the story of Joseph, she couldn't say anything. He had been a slave and not only forgave, but when his brothers felt guilty over what they'd done, Joseph comforted them and took care of them and their families.

The sound of Josiah's stomach rumbling brought Lavette out of her reverie. He grinned at her. She bit her lip to keep from laughing, wondering if anyone else heard.

"I think we should end the meeting with a song, then eat before Josiah starves." A spattering of chuckles followed Conlon's announcement.

"Josiah, why don't we try that song you taught us this week?" Glorianna and Kathleen spoke at the same time. They grinned at each other and Glorianna continued. "We can do all the verses if you have the strength."

"I can probably manage." Josiah rubbed his stomach. "I'll do much better if you promise I can be first in line for lunch."

"Oh, no, you don't." Quinn glowered at Josiah in mock anger. "We want some food left for us."

Josiah held up a hand in surrender. "I promise to save you a little. After all, I wouldn't want to be arrested for stealing all the grub." They all laughed.

"Like I told the Sullivans and the Kirbys, I hadn't heard this song for years. In fact, I forgot I even knew it until I heard Lavette singing one day. Hearing the words brought back memories from when my mama and her friends used to sing this." Josiah flashed Lavette a wide smile. His dark gaze warmed her.

"My Father, how long, my Father, how long, my Father, how long, poor sinner suffer here?"

The people began to join in with Josiah. Lavette listened a moment to the familiar song she'd learned as a young child. Closing her eyes, she could see her mother sitting in the rocking chair with a baby in her lap, singing "My Father" in a soft voice. Letting the melody take over her soul, Lavette joined her high, clear soprano to Josiah's bass.

"We'll soon be free, we'll soon be free, we'll soon be free, de Lord will call us home."

The second verse ended. Lavette drew a breath to begin the chorus when she realized she and Josiah were the only ones singing. Every eye in the room was trained on the two of them. Kathleen, Glorianna, and their husbands were staring openmouthed. Chagrined, Lavette stopped and sank back to hide once more.

"Lavette." Glorianna came and knelt on the floor by Lavette's feet, waiting until Lavette looked up. "You have the most beautiful voice I've ever heard. You and Josiah are wonderful together. Please sing some more." Her green gaze held Lavette's.

"I'm not used to having everybody looking at me." Lavette's throat scratched with dryness.

"Well, you'd better get used to it." A chill filled the warm room as the tight-lipped woman across the room spoke up.

"Whatever do you mean by that, Mrs. Laughlin?" Glorianna looked over her shoulder at the older woman.

"I've heard where she's planning to sing." The woman's mouth looked even more pinched. Beside her, the man with the heavy jowls leered at Lavette, then, when the woman glanced at him, changed to an expression of indignation.

Mortified, Lavette couldn't imagine what the woman was talking about. Peering at the woman and the man next to her, Lavette thought again that she'd seen him somewhere before. Her mind flashed back to the day in the mercantile when Bertrand Mead confronted her. He'd dragged her back to where there were several men, telling them she would be performing for him. This man had been there—in the mercantile.

A cacophony of confusion reigned in the room as men and women began to question one another. The discussion grew in volume until Quinn stood. Although he wasn't a huge man, his presence commanded their attention. Quiet settled over the gathering.

"Mrs. Laughlin, Miss Johnson is a friend and guest. We'd like to know what you're implying with your comments."

The thin woman sat erect, her black clothes and thin face giving her the look of a bird of prey about to dive on some unsuspecting creature. "My Lyle came home the other day and told me what happened at the mercantile. This woman came in, supposedly to buy some things for her employer. She was really there to meet with Bertrand Mead, the owner of those heathen establishments." Her glare bored into Lavette like red-hot bullets. "Mead even introduced her to the men in the store. He bragged about how her sweet singing would bring him all sorts of money. I think it's a shame she had the gall to come to our meeting today."

Dead silence followed the woman's accusations. Lavette could feel the chair pressing into her back as she tried to sink from sight. These were all lies, yet no one in this room knew her well. Who would they be willing to believe—someone they'd only met recently or a long-time friend? She knew the answer to that question before she even asked.

Chapter 13

Josiah surged to his feet. Conlon shot him a warning glance. Glorianna appeared ready to spit fire at the Laughlins. Coming up out of his chair with an air of grace, Conlon moved to stand beside Quinn, effectively making a block between Mrs. Laughlin and Lavette. Josiah understood now. Conlon and Quinn would handle the affront; he should be there for Lavette. She would need someone to lean on right now.

He sank into his seat and half-turned so he could keep one eye on the proceedings, yet still see Lavette. She huddled against the chair back, her eyes downcast. Her lower lip trembled, her tiny white teeth making a sharp contrast as they bit into the lip in an obvious attempt to control her emotions.

Placing one of his hands over her clenched ones, Josiah could feel her tension. She must be on the verge of breaking down. Over the last several months, their group had tolerated the Laughlins' sporadic visits, hoping to reach them. Now, Josiah wished they'd been less congenial. As she'd done with others before, Mrs. Laughlin deliberately attacked Lavette with what he knew to be lies.

Josiah noted most of the room's occupants were involved in the discussion going on between Conlon, Quinn, and the Laughlins. He brought his head close to Lavette's, hoping she would realize their conversation would be private even in such a crowded place.

"You okay?" He could feel her trembling and wanted to wrap her in his arms. "This is not the first time Mrs. Laughlin has attacked someone. No one will listen to her."

"They're lies." A tear rolled down Lavette's cheek. Josiah wiped the drop with his thumb.

"I know she's lying. So do several of the others here. Gossip travels fast in this town. We've heard two stories: the one Mead told and the truth. The Christians will listen to the truth."

"They'll never believe my story against that of a white woman." Lavette's hurt made him ache.

His thumb caressed her cheek as he lifted her chin until he could see her eyes. They glittered with unshed tears and pain. He sympathized with her. "Everything will work out fine, Lavette. Trust me." He smiled, hoping she would relax a little. She turned her face away, trying to hide her feelings.

"Excuse me, Josiah." Glorianna stood next to him, Kathleen beside her. "Conlon asked that the women leave while the men take care of this situation.

We'd like for Lavette to come with us."

Josiah glanced around the room, noting that Glorianna, Kathleen, and Lavette were the only women left in the room besides Mrs. Laughlin, who sat stiff-backed in the chair opposite him. The only men left were Mr. Laughlin and the ones well grounded in Scripture, who could be trusted to look at a situation through God's eyes. He looked back at Glorianna. He didn't want to let Lavette go.

"We'll take good care of her, I promise." Glorianna smiled and stretched out a hand. Josiah nodded and turned back to Lavette.

"You need to leave. Glorianna and Kathleen will be with you until we're done here. I want you to stay with them. Will you?" He waited until Lavette nodded, then gave her a hand up. It took all his willpower not to follow the women from the room so he could accompany Lavette. She looked so vulnerable and alone.

Twenty minutes later, Josiah took a deep breath as he stepped into the kitchen behind the other men. Discipline was never pleasant, but he couldn't fault the way Conlon handled the chore. He'd admonished the Laughlins not only for this occurrence, but for other times they hadn't displayed Christian charity to people who chose to worship with the group. Conlon then reminded them the meetings weren't for perfect people, but for those who wished to worship together because all are sinners. Mrs. Laughlin had turned beet red and exploded. She had the tongue of a shrew and wasn't afraid to use it. She and Lyle had left in a huff, even though they'd been invited to stay for the meal. Josiah had to admit he wasn't sorry to see them leave.

The women were chattering and laughing as they set out the various dishes of food. Josiah's stomach rumbled again, but the general hubbub covered the growl. Lavette sat in a corner of the room with one of the twins on her lap. The other, Andrew, stood beside her, his thumb in his mouth, his gaze fastened on her face. She smiled down at him, looking to Josiah like an angel. Angelina caught one of the loose wisps of Lavette's hair and tugged, pulling the tendril toward her mouth. As Lavette pried open the baby's fist to release her hair, she saw Josiah across the room. The smile she gave him made him wish they were alone. All this time he'd been afraid she would feel abandoned, and here she appeared nearly as comfortable as the other women. What had Glorianna and Kathleen done?

Within a few minutes, the blessing had been said, and people were starting to fill their plates. Josiah wanted to shove everyone aside to get to Lavette. He longed to be with her. He needed to talk to her about what had happened today and why she seemed so at peace when such hurtful things had been said.

He watched as Glorianna took the twins, their faces greasy from the chicken legs clasped in tiny fists. Lavette stood and helped her clean them up. Then Glorianna disappeared with the pair, probably to take them to their room for a nap. Lavette saw him watching her, looked away, then returned his gaze. She smiled again, and Josiah began to work his way through the crowd to her. He couldn't wait any longer.

Standing in front of her at last, he couldn't think of a thing to say. Her cinnamon eyes were wide, the long lashes grazing her cheeks when she blinked. He couldn't stop staring and knew he was making a perfect fool of himself. None of the people in this room would doubt how he felt about Lavette after this. Even he couldn't deny his feelings. He only hoped she had changed her attitude toward God this morning. If she hadn't, it would break his heart to turn away from her.

"You have the most beautiful voice I've ever heard." Josiah could have kicked himself. Why had he opened his mouth and brought up the most painful subject possible? Of course, she wouldn't want to be reminded of that incident so soon after it happened. He wouldn't blame her if she walked away and never spoke to him again.

"Thank you." She gave a shy smile. "I love to sing, and that was my favorite spiritual. I didn't know the other hymns you did earlier, but I'd like to learn."

Josiah tried to make his mouth shut. He knew his jaw had almost hit the floor. She didn't sound upset or angry at all. What had Glorianna done?

"I think I'd like something to eat." Lavette peeked around him. Most of the others had taken their food outside to where a temporary table was set up. Josiah's stomach gave a low growl. "I guess you'd like some, too." She giggled.

"I've been hungry since I smelled that chicken of yours. I sure hope there's some left. No one knows how to make fried chicken like someone who's raised in the South. My mama grew up there and made the best in the world." He stopped. "At least, she's made the best I tasted so far."

She giggled again. "That's fine. I wouldn't want to make a man doubt his mama's chicken. I believe there's plenty left. Glorianna put the plates over there." She pointed to a spot on the table where two plates waited for them.

Outside, there were two places at the table. Lavette seemed much more comfortable with the others. She even glanced up at the women sometimes when they talked to her. Josiah wanted to ask what had been said before he got to the kitchen, but he didn't quite know how to put it.

The meal wore on, people returning to the kitchen, the men for a second plate of food, then everyone for a piece of pie or cake for dessert. Josiah couldn't keep up with the conversation. He heard bits and pieces about Fort Lowell, the school, the changes needed to the less savory parts of town, and the need for a church with a pastor in residence. Most of the time he simply enjoyed being next to Lavette, watching as she listened to everyone else.

"May I walk you home?" Josiah could smell the hint of cinnamon that seemed to cling to Lavette as if she just stepped out of the kitchen. "That is, if you're ready to leave."

She gazed up at him, her light brown eyes probing. "I should get home. Mrs. Sawyer may be coming back from her daughter's any time, and I'll need to be there. She gets so tired on these long days, but she loves seeing her grandchildren."

He followed her to the kitchen, where she gathered her empty dish and said her good-byes to the women there. On the way from the house, Josiah nodded to Conlon, Quinn, and some of the other men to let them know he was leaving. Taking the cloth-covered bowl from Lavette, Josiah ushered her out into the late afternoon sunshine. A cloudless blue sky stretched overhead. The sun blazed down, not overly hot, but enough to make them willing to stroll rather than rush down the street.

A hummingbird darted past Josiah's ear, pausing to hover beside a flower long enough to extract a bit of sweetness, then flitting away. The iridescent green of the tiny bird's body gleamed in the sunlight.

"That thing can't be bigger than my hand." Lavette's dulcet tone held a hint of awe.

"They may be small, but I always want to duck when they fly past. The way their wings go so fast makes them sound like a swarm of bees on the attack." Josiah grinned. Lavette's hand tucked in the crook of his arm felt comfortable.

"I'm sorry if I'm nosy, but I have to ask you something."

Lavette studied him, her eyes wide and questioning. "What?"

"When you left the parlor with Glorianna and Kathleen, you looked like the world was coming to an end. Then, when I came in the kitchen, you were smiling and playing with the babies. What happened?" Lavette frowned, and Josiah wondered if he'd overstepped his bounds. "If you don't want to tell, that's fine. I'm curious; that's all."

"I don't mind talking about it. I don't know if I can explain what happened." Lavette slowed, and Josiah matched her pace, waiting for her to continue.

"Glorianna and Kathleen didn't take me to the kitchen where the other women were. Instead, we went to Glorianna's bedroom. We all sat on the bed. I thought they were going to tell me they didn't want me coming around their house anymore."

"They wouldn't do that."

Lavette flashed a smile. "I know that now, but I didn't then."

"So what did they talk about?"

"Well, that's the funny part." Lavette worried her lower lip for a moment. "They didn't talk to me at all. Kathleen started praying, and Glorianna took up when she stopped. I've never heard anyone talk to God like He was standing right next to them. I think Mama may have prayed like that, but only in private."

Josiah bounced on the balls of his feet, trying to be patient. "Did you join in?"

"Not out loud." She shook her head. "No, I don't think I did, but something happened. Between what Conlon said about Joseph forgiving his brothers and these women praying as if they truly cared about me—" She gave Josiah a bewildered look. "I can't explain what happened. One minute, I was afraid and angry, and the next minute this wonderful sense of peace filled me. I don't think I'm mad at God anymore, but I can't tell you why. I'll have to consider this."

They walked in silence. Josiah couldn't believe what she'd said. God was at work in her heart. She might not understand it, but he did. He knew God would work everything out for him and for Lavette. He couldn't recall the last time he'd been so happy.

"Would you like to learn some of the songs we sang this morning?"

She glanced up, her eyes sparkling. "Oh, yes. I liked the one about the fountain. Could you sing it, and I'll try to follow along?"

"That happens to be my favorite hymn." Josiah squeezed his arm closer to his body, pulling Lavette to him. "There is a fountain filled with blood—" By the time he reached the chorus, she'd added her lovely soprano. Her words were hesitant, but Josiah was amazed at how much she'd caught from the singing earlier that morning.

"What beautiful words." Lavette sighed. "I've always loved to sing, but sometimes I'm afraid to."

"Why is that?"

She looked to the side, something in her posture telling him she wasn't comfortable talking about her reason. They turned on the path leading up to Mrs. Sawyer's house. Lavette halted, turning to face Josiah. Her mouth opened, then snapped shut. She stared at the front of his shirt, not looking up at him. Josiah waited, even though he wanted to grab her and make her tell him.

The smell of roasting peppers floated on the breeze. Josiah's stomach rumbled.

Lavette chuckled, a strained sound. She glanced up. "How can you possibly be hungry after all you ate today?"

"Would you believe I'm a growing boy?" Josiah widened his eyes and tried to look forlorn. Lavette laughed.

"No, but I would believe you need a lot of food. I wish I had some more chicken to offer, but I'm afraid it's all gone." She met his gaze. Josiah realized his free hand rested on her shoulder. With only a slight pull, she would be close enough for him to hold her and kiss her. The urge nearly overwhelmed his senses.

A door banged somewhere close. Josiah stepped back. Lavette reached for her dish. Josiah took her elbow in his hand. He turned her toward the house. He'd better get her inside and leave before his emotions took over.

"May I come by in the evenings? I could teach you some more of the songs before next Sunday."

"I haven't sung with anyone in a long time." She looked out at the street, a faraway look in her eyes. "I think I need to, though." She smiled. "I'd be happy to have you come by tomorrow. Do you think we can do the fountain song one more time before you go?"

Josiah followed her example and closed his eyes. He let the words and music wash over him. Their voices seemed to blend in a way few did. He could imagine God in heaven enjoying the words and the sound. Silence hung heavy as the last notes floated away. Clapping startled him. Josiah's eyes flew open. Lavette backed against him. Bertrand Mead stood a few paces away on the path.

"I'm so glad to hear you practicing, my dear. I spoke with Mrs. Sawyer again. I believe she'll be ready to sell me your contract very soon. Then you can perform for me and my patrons."

Chapter 14

The heat from Josiah should have chased away the chill that shook Lavette. Instead, she trembled like a leaf as she huddled next to him. She wondered if the heat came from the force of his anger. He put his arm around her shoulders to protect her from Mead. She could feel the tension in his taut muscles. His fingers dug into her shoulder, yet she drew comfort from the touch.

"You have no hold over Lavette, Mead. Leave her alone."

"Or what?" Mead's lip lifted in an expression of contempt. "You gonna call on your deputy friend to cover for you? There are some things he can't do. When I own Miss Johnson, everything will be legal."

"Mrs. Sawyer won't do that." Lavette's voice shook. "I've been with her for eight years. She can't sell me off like a piece of furniture, especially to someone like you."

"Oh, but that's where you're wrong, my dear. Your employer is considering staying with her daughter, Gretta, rather than returning home. If she does that, she'll need to get rid of you. Gretta already has help, and with the size of the house, they'll have no room for you."

She would never let someone like you have me. Lavette wanted to scream the words at him, but terror kept her silent. She knew Mead could read the fear in her.

"In case you're wondering, Mrs. Sawyer's son-in-law, Paul, believes me to be a fine, upstanding citizen. You see, he put in a good word with her today. I believe we'll have everything worked out within the next few weeks." He chuckled, and the sound sent a shiver of dread through Lavette. "Keep practicing that singing, my beauty. Soon you'll have an audience who will appreciate your talents."

Mead lifted his hand to touch Lavette's cheek. Josiah caught him by the wrist. His grip must have been tight because a flicker of pain crossed Mead's face. His eyes narrowed.

"Let me go, Boy. This is not your business."

"I believe it is." Josiah moved more in front of Lavette without releasing her or Mead. Mead's expression tensed as if Josiah were adding more pressure to his arm.

"You don't have any say over what I do here. I'll see to it you regret interfering. Let me go." Mead's voice sounded tight with anger.

With a slight shove, Josiah released the man. Mead stumbled back, then caught himself. He rubbed his wrist, anger giving his face a ruddy tint. "You'll pay for this." He snarled the words, gave Lavette a look that made her skin crawl, and strode past them down the path.

Lavette's heart pounded so hard, she wondered if Josiah could feel the beat. What was happening? Would Mrs. Sawyer sell her contract to Bertrand Mead? Did she intend to live with her daughter instead of returning home?

"You okay?" Josiah's low voice in her ear startled, and comforted, Lavette. This man felt like a solid wall of strength. Somehow, being near him made her feel protected from all the wickedness that could erupt around her.

"I'm fine, just a little shook up." She pushed away from Josiah's warmth. "I need to get inside and see to Mrs. Sawyer."

Josiah guided her to the door, his hand a comforting touch on the small of her back. "I want to know what your employer has to say about this. I don't understand why Mead thinks he can buy your contract." He studied her, his eyes full of concern. "Right now, I think you're too tired to explain. If you have the time tomorrow, you're welcome to stop by my shop in the afternoon. Usually, business is a little slower then."

She nodded, her throat aching from the tension. "I'll see if I can get there." She slipped through the door and listened to his footsteps clump across the porch and recede down the path. *Lord, I don't know what's going on in my life. Something changed in me today. Help me to understand what.* Maybe tomorrow she could bring herself to talk to Josiah about her confusion. Perhaps he could help her understand.

"Lavette, is that you?" Mrs. Sawyer's voice trembled as it did when she was very tired. She'd been gone since early morning. Even if Gretta tried to get her to take a nap, her grandsons were too noisy for her to rest much. Lavette couldn't help wondering how they would manage if Mrs. Sawyer chose to stay here with Paul and Gretta.

"I'm right here. Have you been home long?" Lavette tried to make her voice light so her employer wouldn't guess the turmoil brewing inside. Judging from the lines of exhaustion on Mrs. Sawyer's face, her efforts weren't needed. She appeared to be beyond caring about anything but rest.

The next two hours felt like weeks to Lavette. She hadn't been able to get any information from Mrs. Sawyer before the older woman fell asleep. Lavette worked around the house, catching up on some of the little chores. She wanted to sit and pray or read, but uncertainty kept her from relaxing enough to do that. Where had all the peace gone that she'd felt this morning? Memories of the horror from her childhood rose up to haunt her. Could she share all of her past with Josiah? He was a godly man. Would he turn his back on her when he found out what Miss Susannah's father had done? *Maybe I'm a fool,* she thought, *but I can't see Josiah doing something like that. Lord, help me to trust Josiah with the truth, if that's the right thing to do.*

The tinkling of a bell roused her from her reverie. Mrs. Sawyer was awake. *Oh, please let her tell me what she said to Mr. Mead.* Lavette hurried in to find Mrs. Sawyer struggling to sit up in bed.

"Here, let me help you." She slipped her arm around the woman's shoulders.

"Thank you, Dear. I get so impatient these days. I want to be able to do everything on my own." Mrs. Sawyer sighed and let Lavette help her dress. "Old age isn't much fun at times, but I wouldn't miss being here and seeing those babies of Gretta's."

"Did you have fun with them today?"

"Oh, my goodness, yes. The boys put on a wild animal show for me." She chuckled. "They read somewhere about a man putting his head in a lion's mouth. Imagine that."

Lavette gasped. "That can't be true. Why would anyone do something so dangerous?"

"Oh, you know these men. Always trying to find something to do that no one else has ever done." Mrs. Sawyer stayed quiet for the walk to the parlor. Lavette put her in the chair by the window and opened the latch to let fresh air inside.

"Marcus was the animal tamer, and Winston and Harold were the beasts." Her eyes crinkled with humor. "Winston growled and acted so fierce. He even tried to bite Marcus a couple of times. I'm afraid Marcus will have to get a friendlier animal to tame."

Lavette couldn't help giggling at the picture of the boys and their show. "I've heard the men who work with wild animals in shows use big whips to control them. I hope Marcus didn't have one of those."

"Oh, no. He wanted to, especially when the tiger tried to bite, but his papa said no. Paul gave the boy a feather and said tickling would be a better torture for his beast. The next thing we knew, all three boys were rolling on the floor, cackling like a bunch of chickens." Her eyes twinkled. "Now, don't you tell those fierce beasts I compared them to something so tame."

"Never." Lavette adjusted a shawl around Mrs. Sawyer's shoulders in case the evening air was too fresh. She tried to keep the strain out of her touch and voice. "You're going to miss that family when we leave."

Mrs. Sawyer tensed. She gestured to a stool on the floor near her. "Sit down, Child." She stayed silent until Lavette was seated. "I'm not sure I'll be going back to Virginia like we planned. Gretta and Paul want me to stay here. Paul seems to think he wouldn't have much trouble making me a small private room at the back of the house."

"But the children. Would you be able to rest enough with them there?" Lavette didn't want to discourage Mrs. Sawyer from staying with her daughter, but the thought of being sold off terrified her.

"As long as I have a room of my own where I can retreat when the melee gets too intense, I'll be fine." Mrs. Sawyer paused, studying Lavette. "The main problem with my staying here is what to do with you. Gretta has two girls who work for her already, and she doesn't have the room for another. I can't send you back home by yourself."

"Maybe I could share a room with the girls who work for her."

"I'm afraid that would never work. Their room is very small. I've talked to Mr. Mead. Paul knows him. He's a fine, upstanding businessman here in Tucson. He's willing to buy the last two years of your contract. You would work for him for that length of time, then be free to do as you choose."

Bitterness rose like bile in Lavette's throat. She stared at the floor, afraid to look up lest Mrs. Sawyer see the emotion in her eyes. "You can't sell me off." The words came out as a hoarse whisper.

"This man, Mr. Mead, will take good care of you. He's quite a gentleman."

"He's not what you think." Lavette couldn't look up. It took all her willpower to get the words out.

"Are you suggesting Paul doesn't know what he's talking about? He said some good things about Mr. Mead. You would be a great asset to him in his business." Mrs. Sawyer's tone held a note of dismissal. Lavette stood.

"I'll fix you something to eat before you retire." She managed to hold back the tears until she got to the kitchen. There she grabbed a towel, held it over her face, and sobbed. What would become of her? She knew what Mead wanted to happen. Two years with him would be like a lifetime. "What am I to do?" She whispered the question to no one in particular. Josiah's face flashed before her. She could almost hear his low voice and feel the touch of his hand. Tomorrow afternoon while Mrs. Sawyer napped, she would talk with Josiah. Maybe he would understand and have an idea how to help her.

※

Cottonball clouds dotted a brilliant azure sky as Lavette made her way downtown the next afternoon. Her eyes burned, and her head felt fuzzy from lack of sleep. Every time she'd fallen asleep, she'd dreamed of Mead dragging her off to a noisy saloon where she was forced to sing in front of drunken men who shouted lurid taunts. She would wake covered with sweat, the blanket tangled around her like a shroud, only to fall asleep to a variation of the same dream. Lavette shuddered despite the warmth of the day. Had her dream been a portent of her life to come?

An Indian woman trudged down the street, a *giho* on her back, carrying baskets for sale. A strap running around the woman's forehead held the *giho* in place so the large carrier wouldn't tip as it hung down her back. Lavette had heard about the woven goods the Tohono O'odham Indians sold in Tucson. Their baskets, mats, and sandals were made from desert plants. Gretta had given Lavette one to hold her mending and a larger one for the laundry. Lavette watched as the barefoot woman plodded down the street, her burden swaying with her steps.

The few minutes watching the basket seller helped Lavette forget her destination. Mrs. Sawyer once again sent her to purchase items they needed from the mercantile. Dread tugged at Lavette's feet, moving her slower as she neared the store. What if Mead were there again? What about that awful man from yesterday's meeting? She wiped her clammy hands on her skirts. The mercantile stood across the street, its tall facade staring at her with glass eyes.

She pictured Josiah's big frame and wondered if she could ask him to accompany her on her errands. *No, I can do this. I can't depend on someone else to protect me.* The last time was an accident. Like Mrs. Sawyer said, Mr. Mead is a businessman. He'll be working this afternoon, not engaging in idle conversation here. Lavette squared her shoulders and crossed the street.

The murmuring of men's voices ceased as Lavette stepped inside. After the brightness of the sun, the tomblike darkness blinded her. Her heart thudded. She clutched her bag with the money and the list in fingers that trembled. Hushed whispers began before her vision cleared enough for her to locate the counter. The curtain to the back room fluttered as the man who helped her before strode to the front.

"May I help you?" He smiled and nodded. Lavette forced her feet to carry her forward. She didn't look away from the scarred countertop as she fished the list from her bag.

"We need to have these things, please, Suh." She put the scrap of paper down and watched the man's stained fingers as he picked it up.

"This will only take a minute." The owner must have noticed Lavette's nervous glance at the back of the room. "I won't be leaving the front for this order. You'll be fine. I'll see to it."

Lavette tried to smile. The man's voice sounded vaguely familiar. Her brow tightened as she tried to recall where she'd heard it before. A sudden recollection of the testimonies at the meeting yesterday eased her trepidation. This man had been one of the ones to speak. She hadn't recognized him since he'd been all fixed up then, and here he wore work clothing. She wondered if he was the one who told the truth of what happened between her and Mead here at the mercantile.

Chairs scraped against the floor. Lavette gripped the counter with shaking hands. *Hurry, please hurry.* She could hear footsteps coming her way. She squeezed her eyes shut. *Oh, please don't let Mead be here.*

"Here we go." The owner plunked the items she'd ordered down with a thud that made her jump. "Let me get these wrapped up, and you'll be all ready."

Her fingers shook as she fished some coins out of her reticule. One dropped to the floor and rolled a few feet, coming to rest beside a booted foot. Lavette thought about ignoring the money, but it wasn't hers to waste. She glanced up to see the owner of the boots. Bertrand Mead, a superior smile creasing his face, watched her. Keeping his gaze locked on her, he stooped and picked up the coin. In two steps he stood close enough for her to catch the residue of pipe tobacco clinging to him.

"I believe you dropped something, Miss Johnson." He held out the money. She couldn't move, but only stared at his hand.

The man behind the counter cleared his throat, and Mead tossed the coin down. Within a minute, the owner handed her the change and the package. Lavette moved back toward the door, the parcel clutched tightly to her chest. All noise seemed to be suspended as she fumbled for the latch. A well-manicured hand closed over hers.

"Let me help you with that. I want to speak with Mrs. Sawyer again, so I'll walk you home." Something sinister oozed out in Mead's voice. "We wouldn't want anything to happen to you, would we?"

Chapter 15

Heart pounding, Lavette jerked her fingers from beneath Mead's. The door swung open. She darted out. Behind her she heard the shopkeeper shout something, but she didn't stop. Her slippers made little sound as she hurried away, her ears straining for the sound of footsteps following her.

At the corner, Lavette glanced behind to see Mead standing outside the mercantile watching her. His stance suggested cockiness, making him appear so sure of his hold over her that he didn't need to push. She groaned. A tremor raced through her. Moving out of Mead's sight, Lavette sagged against the wall of a building. The shaded adobe bricks were cool on her back. Sweat-drenched, she welcomed the chill.

A horse whinnied. A freight wagon rumbled past. The vibration in the ground ran up her legs, echoing the quivering in her knees. Her breathing slowed. The moisture on her forehead dried. Relief that she hadn't been followed made Lavette weak. Pushing away from the wall, she glanced back before heading for Josiah's smithy.

A brace of mules dozed in the shade outside Josiah's place. Their tails twitched. Long ears jerked back and forth. Their expressions of utter boredom made them appear to be half-asleep. Flies swooped through the air, buzzing from one beast to the other with an annoying drone.

Josiah stood near the forge, outlined by the glow of the fire. In one hand, he held a pair of tongs, which he used to move an iron bar heating in the coals. Lavette stepped out of the sun into the dimness of the shop. She knew Josiah didn't hear her. Peace seemed to settle over her. Merely being in the presence of this man filled her with a calm she'd never felt before. Her heart ached to be close to him. *Why can't I be free? When so many are able to have freedom, why am I still a slave?* Sorrow welled up inside her. Maybe yesterday slavery hadn't seemed so real, but today she knew she would always live in chains. No matter how she craved what others had, she must learn to live with her lot in life, and Josiah would never be a part of that.

He lifted the iron bar from the coals. The end glowed white hot. As he swung around, he glanced up and saw her. His face split in a wide grin. She could see the joy sparkling in his eyes. He beckoned her to come inside.

"Afternoon." Josiah's voice rumbled over the whoosh of the bellows as he pulled the cord. "I was beginning to think you might not come."

"I had to wait until Mrs. Sawyer went down for a nap. Then I had some errands to run."

He frowned. "Did you go to the mercantile?" She nodded, and his brow creased further. "Mead is always there this time of day. Did he bother you?"

She looked down, digging her toe into the dirt floor of the smithy. She shrugged. "He didn't follow me today."

"Did he bother you?" Josiah's stern tone made her glance up.

"Not really." She shrugged, unable to meet his gaze. "I think the mercantile owner said something."

Josiah wiped his hands on a rag lying on the bench beside his anvil. In one step, he stood beside her. She could feel the warmth he exuded and the comfort. She wanted to lean toward him, but made her body stay upright and still. Josiah wrapped one of her wiry curls around his finger.

"If you have to go there again, why don't you come here first? I don't mind walking over with you. Mead won't try anything with me around." His dark eyes glittered in the light from the forge. His bulging muscles flexed. Lavette drew in a deep breath, forcing her thoughts away from how wonderful it would feel to have Josiah wrap her in his arms and hold her tight. To her, he represented safety—a safety she would never be able to have.

"What are you making?" She gestured to the hot metal, hoping to distract him from thinking about Mead and her situation. Josiah couldn't do anything about her predicament. No one would be able to help her. Lavette knew she should leave now and not risk losing her heart further to this giant of a man, but like a moth drawn to a flame, she couldn't go.

"I'm working on some shoes for those mules. One of them has a peculiar hoof and needs a special fit. He went lame when he was shod poorly. I've been trying to adjust the shoes, and he's doing better."

The mules being talked about still stood in sleepy ignorance outside the smithy, the twitching of their long ears the only indication they were awake.

"I remember Papa talking about one of the blacksmiths at Wild Oaks who didn't do his work right. I never quite understood what Papa meant, but he said the wrong fit could ruin a horse."

"That's right." Josiah pulled a stool close enough to the bench so they could talk and she could see, but far enough to be away from the danger of flying sparks. "Here, sit down. I need to work on this shoe so I can finish by the time Mr. Hernandez returns." Josiah picked up the iron bar with a shorter pair of tongs, frowned at the red-orange glow of the heated portion, and thrust it back into the coals.

"I'm sorry to interrupt your work. Did that cool off too much?"

"Yep. In order to work it the way I need to, the metal has to be white hot. Otherwise it won't bend or flatten properly." Josiah strode across the shop and picked up a packing crate with one meaty hand. Placing the wooden box beside Lavette's stool, he sat down, the lower crate putting him eye to eye with her.

"While we're waiting for that bar to reheat, I want to hear about your talk with Mrs. Sawyer." His gaze bored into her, making her want to squirm. She felt like she'd been hiding something from him. "I want to know why Mead thinks he has a hold over you. What did he mean about owning you?"

Lavette fidgeted with the string around the package from the mercantile, which she held in her lap. Josiah extracted the parcel and set it up on a bench lined with rows of tools. He took her hands in his, bringing warmth to her cool fingers.

"Lavette, I don't know how you feel, but I care for you a lot. I've never felt this way about anyone before. If there's any way possible, I want to help you."

Her breath caught as she saw the look in his eyes. He cared for her as much as she cared for him. Was this love? She hesitated to give the emotion a name, not wanting to admit the depth of her feelings.

"I told you about the contract Mrs. Sawyer has on me." She paused as Josiah nodded. "Well, she's considering staying in Tucson with her daughter and son-in-law. They have no room for me, so she's thinking of selling the remainder of my contract. Paul is the one who recommended Mr. Mead." Lavette's throat ached with the need to cry. "After talking with Mrs. Sawyer, I can't see any way you can help me. Soon I'll belong to Mr. Mead, and he can do with me as he pleases."

"What about us?" Josiah's hands tightened on hers.

"There is no us. There never can be." Bitterness made her spit out the words.

"Do you care for me?"

"What does it matter?" She couldn't meet Josiah's gaze.

"It matters to me. Do you care for me?" The heat of his gaze drilled into her. She wanted to deny her feelings for him. All she had to do was to say she felt nothing, then he would leave her alone and be safe. If she admitted her feelings, Josiah might do something foolish that would only end up hurting him. She would never be free, and he had to understand that.

"You are special to me. A friend." *Coward!* She berated herself. "Josiah, don't worry about me. You know what it's like to be a slave. We have no choice in this."

※

Holding Lavette's small hands in his, Josiah stared at the contrast between his dark coffee skin and her lighter, milkier tones. Her fine bones gave her a delicate appearance, while his large frame sometimes made him feel like a lumbering bear. Right now, he felt as stupid as an animal. He didn't know what to say to her. Lavette seemed to be shutting him out when she needed him most. He knew she cared for him. When she looked at him wide-eyed, the longing and love shone like a lantern on a dark night. Being a friend wasn't what he wanted anymore, and he was sure friendship wasn't what God wanted for them.

"Don't you remember the story of Joseph? Conlon talked about it yesterday— how Joseph's brother sold him into slavery and all the bad things that happened, but God was there watching over him. God made good things happen."

Lavette sat back, tugging at her hands. "God doesn't care whether I'm a bondwoman or free. I can't count on Him for anything."

"But, yesterday—" Josiah was stunned.

"Yesterday I felt a measure of peace, that's true. I've thought about it, though. What I felt was because I was with a bunch of folks who've never been enslaved. They don't understand the horror like you and I do."

He knew he had to set her straight, yet he hesitated. Would she equate him with all the others who'd been at the meeting? "Lavette, I've never been a slave."

"What?" She drew back again, her eyes going wide. "But you're black, and the war only ended nine years ago. How could you not have been a slave?"

"My father and mother were slaves. Right after they were married, their master's son, Edward, decided to move north. He didn't like slavery, didn't agree that it was right. His father let him choose two slaves to take with him to care for his needs. He chose my parents. After they were settled in New York, he gave my parents their freedom. I was born six months later to emancipated parents and have always been free." He smiled. "At least in that sense. I wanted to talk to you about the other kind of slavery, spiritual bondage."

"I don't want to hear any more." Lavette jerked her hands free. "No wonder you don't understand what I'm going through. You've never been there. You're no better than one of them." She jumped to her feet.

"Lavette, no." Josiah reached for her. Tears filled her eyes. She turned away, rushing for the door. "Wait."

Feeling helpless, Josiah watched as the girl of his dreams raced away from him. What now? How could he make her trust him again? *Oh, Lord, what have I done?* Head bowed and shoulders slumped, Josiah tried to think of a way to explain things to Lavette. His gaze fell on the parcel from the mercantile that she'd left lying on his tool bench. He touched the wrap with a finger, feeling the paper crinkle in the indention.

A bray from outside startled him. He'd forgotten the mules. Mr. Hernandez would be here shortly and expect his animals to be ready. Glancing at the forge, Josiah could see the iron bar glowing white in the coals. He picked up the tongs and drew the rod out. He would finish the shoes, then take the package to Lavette. By that time, maybe she would have calmed down and they could talk. She had to understand. Perhaps if he admitted his love to her, she would accept his help. There had to be a way to keep her away from Mead.

An hour later, Josiah strode down the street. Mr. Hernandez had taken longer than he thought to return for the mules. Waiting had proved impossible. All Josiah wanted to do was see Lavette again. At least no one else had shown up with more work. One good thing came of the waiting. He had a plan he thought might work. He only hoped Lavette agreed with it.

The sun was dipping toward the western mountains as Josiah hurried up the path leading to Mrs. Sawyer's house. The porch boards creaked under his weight. He sniffed, wondering at the lack of supper smells in the air. Usually, he could at least enjoy the scent of Lavette's cooking. His mouth watered at the thought.

Knocking on the door, Josiah began to shift from one foot to another as he waited. Where was she? The faint ding of a bell came from inside. He frowned. Hadn't Lavette once mentioned Mrs. Sawyer calling to her by ringing a bell? Quiet enveloped him. He couldn't hear talking or footsteps.

Josiah stepped off the porch and started around the house to see if Lavette was in the backyard. Perhaps she was taking down some laundry and hadn't heard anything.

"Help me."

The words drifted out of one of the side windows where Josiah assumed the bedrooms were. He turned and ran back to the front door and lifted the latch. Pushing the portal open he called, "Hello, anybody home?"

"Help." Once more the shaky voice cried out. Josiah rushed in, following the sound. Mrs. Sawyer lay beside her bed, the covers tangled around her legs, a small bell clutched in one hand. Josiah eased her up enough to loosen the blankets, then lifted her gently into the bed.

"What happened? Where's Lavette?"

Mrs. Sawyer closed her eyes, tears tracing a track down her wrinkled cheeks. "I sent her to town for some things while I napped. When I woke, she wasn't here. I've called and called." A hiccuping sob shook her. "I tried to get up myself and fell."

"You mean Lavette hasn't come home yet? She left my place over an hour ago and was headed here." Josiah paused. He'd assumed Lavette was going straight home. Where else would she go?

"When I first awakened, that nice Mr. Mead stopped by. I hadn't fallen then. He promised to find Lavette and see that she came home."

A chill raced through Josiah. Mead was looking for Lavette? He didn't want to think of what could have happened.

"I'll go fetch someone to help you, Ma'am." Josiah crossed the room before stopping to look back. "As soon as I do, I'll go find Lavette. I'll see to it that she's safe."

The front door slammed hard enough to rattle the whole house as Josiah rushed out. He ran all the way to the Sullivans' and banged on the door. Concern wiped away Glorianna's smile as she looked at him.

"Josiah, what's happened?"

"Lavette is missing. Mrs. Sawyer needs help. Can you go or send someone to help her while I look for Lavette?"

Glorianna barely had time to nod her head before he raced away. Where should he start looking? As he neared town, he could hear the faint sounds of revelry. The saloon. If Mead found her, he would take her there. As his footsteps turned toward the seedy establishment, Josiah didn't want to think what Mead would do once he had Lavette in his grasp.

Chapter 16

Raucous laughter and the tinny plink of piano keys jarred Lavette's already-frayed nerves. Cigarette and cigar smoke hung like a pall in the air. Two women, their lips and cheeks brightened unnaturally, sauntered about the room, hips swaying in a saucy rhythm. Lavette cringed, trying to draw away from the nauseating scene.

"I knew you would warm to me." Mead's breath brushed the hair by her ear. Lavette tried to pull away. His grip tightened. "What's the matter? Think you're too good for a place like this?"

"Please, I need to get home." Lavette could imagine the malevolence in Mead's eyes. The man had no heart or conscience. "My mistress will be expecting me."

"Oh, that is true." He seemed to be mocking her. "I visited with dear Mrs. Sawyer, Amelia, a short time ago. I promised I would find you and get you home." He gave a wicked chuckle. "Of course, I didn't say how soon I would return you."

"But, she'll need help getting up from bed." Panic rushed through Lavette at the thought of the partially invalid woman trying to do things on her own and getting hurt. She jerked again, and Mead switched his hold, hitting a nerve that sent a painful tingle down her arm, numbing her fingers.

"The old biddy will have to manage. I brought you here so you could see where you'll be working." He gestured across the room with his free hand at the small platform with curtains around the back. "There's where you'll be performing for the crowds."

Fear caught in her throat. The sharp scent of beer, along with the variety of noises and sounds, brought back too many memories. She could almost feel Miss Susannah's father standing behind her. She tried to glance around, but Mead's gaze caught hers. He pulled her closer. The cacophony in the background faded as terror gripped her.

"Of course, I'll be expecting a private performance." His beady eyes were filled with knowledge and lasciviousness. Turning her head, Lavette tried to remind herself that she was a slave and nothing could be done about that. Josiah's face swam before her. *No, I can't think of you, Josiah, or I'll never be able to live my life in peace. I've got to give you up.* Agony tore through her at the thought.

"Come along, my dear. You'll be the hit of the show, so to speak." Mead began to drag her across the floor. Conversation halted. Men turned to stare. Muttered conversation fluttered about the room as she and Mead passed.

"You see, my sweet, they're all amazed by your beauty, and they haven't even heard your voice. I, at least, already knew of your dulcet tones before I found you here."

Lavette stopped. She couldn't breathe as she took in the implications of what he'd said.

Lifting her arm, Mead forced her to go up the steps to the stage. She felt the patrons' eyes were boring holes in her back. Her stomach burned. She took shallow breaths to fight the nausea threatening her.

"You're surprised that I knew of you." Mead pressed her against his side, his mouth next to her ear. "You see, I was there when you sang as a young girl."

Lavette's heart pounded. Blackness seeped across her vision. He couldn't have been there. He couldn't know her shame.

"I visited a neighboring plantation, a distant relative. This gentleman took me to hear the girl with the marvelous voice." Mead's breath smelled of beer and cigarettes, but Lavette couldn't turn away. "I loved your voice, my sweet, but I wasn't blind. Even though you were so young, I could see the potential beauty you would become. Imagine my delight when I heard you singing in the backyard of Mrs. Sawyer's house. I knew at that moment you would be mine."

"Please don't make me do this."

"Oh, but the men want to hear you. I've told them all about how you sing. They've been clamoring for you. See how quiet they are?"

She didn't think her legs would hold her up any longer. They shook worse than a leaf in the fall wind. Lavette gripped the sides of her skirt, clenching the material tight, trying to draw strength from the fabric.

"You may think you can beat me, my sweet." Mead's thumb rubbed the outside of her arm in a way that sent a wash of revulsion through Lavette. "If you can't bring yourself to sing today, then perhaps we can go straight to the private performance for me. I'll be happy to show you to my room."

"No." Lavette gasped. The subdued noise in the room bothered her more than the din when they first entered. She felt every man in the saloon watching and listening to what Mead was saying to her.

"Ready?" She could hear the triumph in his voice and looked up. He smirked at her. He knew she wouldn't be able to do anything other than what he asked.

"I can't think of anything to sing."

"I'm sure you remember some of the music you learned as a child."

Her face warmed. She'd all but forgotten those horrible ditties she'd been forced to sing. At that age, she hadn't understood the bawdiness of the lyrics. Even now, she didn't fully understand, nor did she want to.

"That was so long ago." She hoped he'd think she didn't recall them.

"I could join you. The men would love that—unless you can think of something else to perform."

She nodded. Mead released her arm, turned her to face the crowd, and stepped to one side. Lavette opened her mouth. Nothing came out. She'd never been this frightened. *Oh, God, did Joseph have to do things like this when he was a slave?*

"Sing now, or you'll regret your silence." Mead's low-voiced threat startled her, and a song popped into her mind.

The saloon doors swung open, but she didn't look up. Lavette closed her eyes and began to sing. Utter quiet enveloped the crowd. As she moved into the refrain, she could feel Mead near her, his anger a palpable thing. At the end of the chorus, she stopped. She only knew the one verse and wasn't sure what to do now. Applause and cheers broke out from the patrons. Mead's fingers clenched on her arm, then eased.

"Only that voice saved you. If they had booed instead of cheering—"

"I believe we'll show the lady out now, Mr. Mead."

Lavette almost collapsed at the sound of Josiah's voice. He stood at the edge of the platform, his face a study in conflicting emotions. When he looked at Mead, she saw the anger held on a tight rein. When he looked at her, she could see concern and love. Behind Josiah stood Quinn, his hand resting on the butt of his pistol.

Mead's fingers dug deep into the flesh of her arm. Lavette gasped.

"The young lady was entertaining the boys. I'm sure she didn't mind." Mead gave them a contemptuous smile.

"Now that she's done, why don't you let Josiah walk her home?" Quinn took a step closer.

Mead released her arm. Lavette started to move to the steps, but Josiah reached up, grasped her waist, and swung her down beside him. Although his huge hands were gentle, she couldn't help wincing when he bumped the arm Mead had abused. Josiah seemed to notice and took care to stay away from that side. He slipped an arm around her shoulders, pulling her close to him as he led her out of the saloon.

She didn't know which helped the most, the warmth of the day or the warmth coming from Josiah, but the chill began to fade as they walked away from the downtown area. Quinn strode beside them, his hand still hovering near his gun. Lavette understood Josiah's wisdom in bringing the lawman to the saloon with him. On his own, Josiah wouldn't have had the power to get her out of there without a fight.

"I must say I've never heard that song sung better or in a place that needed it more." Quinn began to chuckle. "Did you see the look on Mead's face, Josiah?"

A low rumble began in Josiah's chest. He still had his arm around her, and Lavette could feel the vibrations. "As my mama would say, 'You could have knocked him over with a feather.' I think I should teach Lavette the other stanzas, and she can sing for them on a regular basis." Josiah and Quinn both laughed, although the sound still held a note of tension. "What made you sing that anyway?" Josiah gave her shoulder a light squeeze.

"I couldn't think of any songs. He threatened me with—with— Anyway, I asked God if Joseph ever had to face anything like this, and then that hymn popped into my head."

"I'm heading back to the office before I have to get home." Quinn waved at them and turned down the next street.

"Mrs. Sawyer." Now that the ordeal was over, exhaustion made Lavette feel weak. She wasn't sure she could walk home, let alone do all her chores when she arrived.

"Don't worry about her." Josiah took his arm from around her. His large fingers wrapped around hers, and he slowed his stride so she didn't have to walk so fast. "Glorianna was going to go over or send her helper, Alicia, to see to Mrs. Sawyer. The lady will be well taken care of.

"You see how amazing God is?" Josiah's eyes twinkled in the waning light. "You didn't ask Him for help, but He gave you the right song to sing. I'll bet most of those men have never heard that one before."

"The fountain hymn was all that came to mind." Lavette agreed with Josiah on the wonder of it. "You'll have to teach me the other verses sometime." He began to sing and she joined him.

"There is a fountain filled with blood—"

🌵

Lavette hummed softly as she sorted beans. Last night she thought she would never be rested again. After her ordeal at the saloon, she'd come home to find Glorianna and the twins entertaining Mrs. Sawyer. Josiah told her about her employer's fall from bed. He also said he would get Conlon to speak with Paul Ashton about Mead. Josiah suggested maybe something else could be worked out, but he wouldn't say what. Lavette had gone to bed early and awakened with the dawn, surprised she hadn't been plagued by nightmares.

A gentle knock rattled the kitchen door. Lavette hurried to open it. Glorianna stood there, a book in one hand. She smiled.

"Come in." Lavette held the door open. "What have you done with Angelina and Andrew?"

"Shame on me, I left them home taking a nap." Glorianna grinned. "They wouldn't like it if they knew where I was. Those two adore you."

"They are sweet." Lavette smiled as Glorianna snorted. "They remind me of my youngest sister when she was a baby. She was as ornery as the day is long, but she was so cute, you couldn't stay mad at her. When she looked at me with those wide brown eyes and that puppy dog expression, I'd melt inside. I'm afraid we spoiled her."

Glorianna chuckled. "I can understand that. Among Conlon and me, Quinn and Kathleen, and everyone else we know, the twins don't stand a chance." She handed the book to Lavette. "I brought you this Bible." She looked down, seeming uncertain. "When I started out, I thought this was a grand idea.

Then I realized that most of the people who were slaves couldn't read. I don't mean to insult you."

"A Bible." Lavette ran her hand over the cover. She hesitated. Somehow, she knew she could trust Glorianna with the truth. "I do know how to read. I grew up as the playmate to the master's daughter. I had to be with her all day and sometimes at night. Her father had a tutor for her even though Miss Susannah hated learning. I soaked up all her lessons like a sponge. Miss Susannah had to repeat everything so many times, I couldn't help but learn."

Glorianna laughed. "I'm glad to hear that. Did you learn sums, too?"

"Yes. I'm one of the few blacks who are educated. I did teach my family a little. On the nights when I was allowed to go home, they had me spend hours showing them figures or teaching them the letters. We had to be careful not to let anyone know, though."

"That's wonderful." Glorianna tapped the Bible. "I thought you might like to read the story of Joseph for yourself. Have you ever read the Bible?"

"No, Ma'am. I've never even held one before."

"The story of Joseph is found in the very first book of the Bible, Genesis." Glorianna took the book and riffled through the pages. "Here you go. This is the part about Joseph, although you might want to start at the beginning and read what happened before then."

Lavette accepted the Bible and hugged it. "I can't wait." She bit her lip, wondering if she could ask Glorianna what was on her heart. This had been bothering her most of the day, and she needed to talk to someone.

"What is it?"

Lavette jumped. Had Glorianna known her thoughts?

"You look like you wanted to ask me something." Glorianna chuckled. "Don't look so guilty."

Looking down, Lavette sighed and hoped this would be the right thing to do. "I do have a question."

"Yes?"

"I've been angry and bitter at God for a long time. Then last Sunday at your house I felt such a peace after you and Kathleen prayed. I thought all those old feelings would be gone." Lavette stopped, unsure how to continue.

"Then the old bitterness popped up again, and you're wondering if you really felt God's peace or not, right?"

Lavette's mouth fell open. "How did you know?"

Glorianna patted Lavette's arm. "We all have doubts about our walk with God. That's one of the reasons we need to meet together. As Christians, we can encourage one another. When we are alone too long, then it's easy to doubt ourselves or God."

"But what do I do about these feelings?"

"Pray." Glorianna smiled. "It's so simple, yet we often forget. Prayer is the best remedy for fears, uncertainty, or a lack of faith." She pursed her lips in thought. "Did you ever pull a weed, only to have the root break off, and before you knew it, another weed sprang up?"

Lavette nodded.

"Bitterness can be like that weed. We may get the main part of the plant pulled up the first time, but there are still all the little roots that can send up shoots at unexpected times. When they do, don't panic. Pray."

A few minutes later, Glorianna left. Lavette turned to the story of Joseph, wondering what else this man faced while a slave. Had God helped him through the hard times?

Chapter 17

Josiah turned from the anvil to the bench with his tools lined in neat rows. He frowned. "What is wrong with me lately?"

"I don't think I have time to list everything that's wrong with you."

Startled, Josiah tried to act indifferent. He hadn't seen Conlon enter the smithy. Focused on the job at hand and the problems with Lavette and Mead, he hadn't heard a thing. He flashed a grin at his friend. "You'd better not start, or I might be tempted to put your horse's shoes on upside down the next time."

"Threats. I never thought you'd stoop so low, Josiah." Conlon shook his head and sighed. "It's amazing what love will do to a man." He chuckled. "Now, tell me what's wrong."

Josiah gestured at the tool-laden table. "I can't seem to find the piece I need. I always put things in the same spot, but now I need my creaser for this shoe, and it's not there."

"Hmm." Conlon rubbed his chin and peered at the variety of blacksmith implements. His eyes sparkled. "I don't suppose what you're looking for could be in your hand, could it?"

Heat warmed his face as Josiah stared at the creaser in his hand. Conlon gave a guffaw that the whole neighborhood could have heard. Shaking his head, Josiah sighed and gave a sheepish grin. "I don't suppose you'd believe I was trying to see if you knew what a creaser was?"

"Nope. I remember acting like a fool when I met Glory. I'm kind of enjoying seeing you do the same." Conlon smirked. "As I recall, you weren't too sympathetic with me then."

"Hey, what happened to helping a brother?"

"I helped you. I told you exactly where to find what you'd lost."

Josiah groaned. "I give up. Have some coffee while I finish this job. Then we can talk."

Picking up a hammer, Josiah set the creaser along the side of the hot horseshoe. With a few strokes, he made the creases the nails would fit in. Taking up the punch, he made the holes he needed inside the crease, careful to not damage the surface of his anvil. When he finished the last nail hole, he placed the finished shoe to one side to cool while he put his tools away.

"Did you get them all in the right place?" Conlon pretended to examine the tool bench. "I wouldn't want to have to come by every day to show you where everything is."

Josiah slapped his friend on the shoulder, slopping Conlon's coffee over the rim of the mug. Conlon moved the cup to the side to keep the liquid from spilling on his uniform.

"I think you're having trouble taking a joke right now." Conlon wiped the drips from the bottom of the cup and shook his finger. "Glory said you came by to see me this morning. I thought I'd see what you wanted. Maybe I should have stayed away."

Josiah filled his mug with coffee that looked more like sludge than drinkable brew. He tried to look serious. "I guess you're right. I'm as touchy as a bear right out of hibernation."

"Is this a roundabout way of asking for food? That's what those bears always want."

Josiah groaned and shook his head. Conlon gave him a wicked grin. Taking a sip of the scalding coffee, Josiah grimaced. "I don't know why I keep drinking this stuff. I think this could eat the nail holes through those horseshoes."

"I have to agree. Is this the same pot we shared two weeks ago, or have you considered making some fresh?"

"I usually make it fresh every morning, although the way my mind is working lately, this could be from two weeks ago." Josiah took another slug. "I wanted to talk to you about one of your men."

Conlon straightened. His expression changed from joking to serious. "Is something wrong?"

"No, not wrong, so to speak." Josiah rubbed the back of his neck. "It's Paul Ashton. Do you know him well?"

"We aren't close, but he's one of my men." Conlon's brows drew together even farther. "He's the son-in-law of the woman Lavette works for."

Putting his cup down, Josiah rubbed his palms on the legs of his pants. "I don't know if you're aware of what Mrs. Sawyer, Lavette's employer, is planning to do." When Conlon shook his head, Josiah continued. "She plans to stay in Tucson with the Ashtons rather than returning home."

"That's good news, isn't it?" Conlon looked puzzled.

"In a way, yes. The problem is she can't keep Lavette. Paul recommended she sell the remainder of Lavette's contract to Bertrand Mead. He says Mead is a fine, upstanding citizen, and Mrs. Sawyer believes him."

"Has she met Mead?"

"Yep. He's put on such an act that she talks like he's a saint or something."

"So what can I do?" Conlon rested against the side of the tool bench, placing his empty cup beside him.

"I thought maybe you could talk to Ashton. Does he know Mead well? If not, maybe he would see him in a different light."

Conlon lifted off his cap and ran a hand through his hair. "Unfortunately, Paul may not be swayed. For some reason, he spends a lot of his time off in the saloon. I think he knows exactly what kind of person Mead is. In fact, my guess would be that he's doing this at Mead's bidding."

Josiah felt as if someone had knocked the air out of him. He'd counted on Paul Ashton's help. Now what would he do?

"I'll try to talk to him anyway, but don't count on it doing much good. Has Lavette spoken with Mrs. Sawyer about Mead?"

"She tried, but Mead can put on a good act. Mrs. Sawyer won't believe anything bad about him because she hasn't seen that side of him."

"Well, I've got to get back out to the fort." Conlon straightened and slapped his cap on his head. "I'll try talking to Paul." Josiah followed Conlon outside. Conlon swung up on the horse, then paused. "You know, I wish Glory and I had the money. We would go buy Lavette's contract and release her." He shook his head and reined his horse around.

Stunned, Josiah stood where he was watching the dust billow up around Conlon's horse's legs as they trotted off. Why hadn't he thought of that? *Lord, am I stupid? This is the answer, and I didn't see it.* Josiah rushed around the side of the smithy to the rooms at the back where he lived. Dropping onto his knees, he felt for the loose board beside his bed. With a protesting creak, the board lifted, revealing a box in the crevice below.

His fingers trembled as Josiah shook out the coins he'd saved. They fell with a musical clink on his blanket. His heart sank. This was a paltry amount. He had no idea how much Mead was willing to pay or how much Mrs. Sawyer wanted for Lavette's contract, but he knew his savings weren't enough. Scraping the coins back into the bag, he hid them once more. Excitement made his movements jerky. He had a plan now, and this afternoon he would begin to put it into action.

⚜

The comforting melody of Josiah's song floated around her as Lavette took the dry clothes from the line and folded them in the basket. She'd come to think of the fountain hymn as Josiah's song because he taught it to her and loved the words so much. All day she couldn't seem to get the tune out of her head. After last night, she thought she would never sing again, let alone this song. For some reason, though, her heart wasn't weighed down with fear and trepidation over what the future held. Something in her was changing.

This morning she'd tried once again to talk to Mrs. Sawyer about Bertrand Mead. Lavette wanted to tell her mistress what happened yesterday at the saloon, but Mrs. Sawyer refused to hear any of it, saying she wouldn't have such a fine gentleman's character maligned. Lavette knew it wasn't her place to push the point. She'd learned long ago, the hard way, that people weren't interested in her thoughts on anything. Speaking up only brought pain.

Instead of arguing, she'd gone to her room for a few minutes to read more of Joseph's story. She took comfort in the fact that Joseph, despite being chosen by God, had to suffer the same as she and her people had to suffer. Joseph didn't seem to have any resentment to deal with like she did. Perhaps she hadn't given God the chance to work in her life. Lavette frowned, and the melody faltered. Her opinion of God was faltering right now. She didn't know what way to turn sometimes.

"I was getting ready to join you. Don't stop."

Lavette screeched and clutched the sheet she was folding. Whirling around, she faced Josiah. How he'd managed to get so close without her hearing him, she didn't know.

"I didn't mean to scare you."

She folded the cloth, put it on the full basket, and glared at him. "I'm not sure I believe that. My brother used to sneak up on me. He had that same grin on his face when I screamed."

Josiah stepped closer. His gaze held hers. She wanted to grab another sheet off the line and hide behind it. This man set her heart pounding so loud, she couldn't think. He lifted a lock of her hair that had escaped the bun at the nape of her neck, and the strand curled around his finger like it belonged there. He tugged. She took a step closer, tilting her head back to still meet his gaze. His huge hand covered her cheek. She closed her eyes and leaned into the touch. A sigh of contentment escaped to dance on the breeze.

The warm touch of his lips on hers surprised her, then stole her breath away. She'd never been kissed like this before. The only kisses she'd known were the ones forced on her when she'd been a slave at Wild Oaks. Those had been hard, mean, and hurtful—nothing at all like Josiah's kiss. This one could go on forever, and she wouldn't mind.

He encircled her with his massive arms, his touch so gentle. Releasing her mouth, Josiah held her close, his breath warm on her forehead. She rested her cheek against his chest. He smelled of soap, smoke, and the faint scent of sweat.

"That's what I wanted to know." The rumble of his voice wrapped around her.

"What's that?"

"I needed to know how you felt about me." His answer surprised her. She arched back to look at him. He smiled. "I know how I feel about you, Lavette. I love you. Before I put my plan into action, I had to know if you felt something for me too."

She pushed away from him. Love? This gentle giant of a man loved her? Panic grabbed her. She couldn't let this happen. She had to keep him at a distance. Inside she knew it was too late. He'd stolen her heart long ago.

"I can't love you." She ached as she spoke. "This will never work. You have to leave and forget me."

He reached out, and she moved farther away. "Do you love me, Lavette?"

"I can't. You don't know what I've done."

"Then tell me. I can't imagine you doing anything wrong."

Panic and horror closed around her. "I had no choice. When I was at Wild

Oaks—in the early years of the war—"

Josiah lifted her hand and kissed her fingers. "You didn't have a choice when you were there. You had to do what your owner told you to do."

"He used to touch me." Her voice broke.

"Oh, Sweetheart." Josiah pulled her into his arms again. "I know the horrible things women had to do. My mother was forced to do them. That's one of the reasons Mr. Bellingham chose my father and mother to take with him when he went north. He wanted to get my mother away from his brothers." He stroked a hand over her hair. "That's over. All I care about now is if you love me."

"Oh, Josiah."

"Do you?"

She glanced around the yard, feeling an urgency to escape. She couldn't lie to him. Looking up, she saw the anguish in his eyes. "Yes." The word tore from her. Tears filled her eyes. "I love you so much, but I can't let this happen. I'm not free to care that much for anyone."

Josiah glowed. Before she could react, he grabbed her and hugged her to him once more. This time his kiss wasn't as gentle. This kiss claimed her as his. She didn't fight him. She wanted to be his. He set her back on her feet. A silly grin creased his cheeks. She laughed, unable to remember when she'd felt so giddy.

"I need to talk to Mrs. Sawyer. Is she awake?"

Lavette shook her head, uncertain whether she could speak yet.

"When will she be ready for company?"

"I—uh." Lavette stiffened as Josiah grinned wider. His smug look said he knew exactly why she couldn't put a thought together. She smiled and shook her head at him. He was right. His kisses had chased away all her sensibility.

"Let me gather this laundry and we'll go in. If you'd like, I have some pie and coffee. Mrs. Sawyer should be awake soon."

"Let me carry this." Josiah picked up the heavy basket as if it weighed nothing. Leading the way across the yard, Lavette remembered her morning's discovery. At the time, she'd wanted to share the news with Josiah. Now, she wasn't certain of his reaction. She whirled around, almost knocking the laundry from his arms.

"I about forgot to tell you, I think I know what to do about Mr. Mead." Josiah's eyebrows lifted, and she hurried on. "Glorianna brought me a Bible. I was reading about Joseph. Anyway, I read what happened with Potiphar's wife. She tried to do to Joseph what Mr. Mead wants to do to me."

Josiah nodded. "And?"

"Don't you see? Joseph ran away. I can run away from here. Maybe I can hide somewhere, and you can come later." Her voice died away. This had sounded so good when she'd thought of it, but as she put the plan into words, she could see the difficulties involved. How would she escape when she had so little money? Where would she go?

"Lavette, Joseph ran away from the sinful act. He didn't try to escape from his responsibilities. Running away never works. Joseph stayed and faced his troubles. Yes, he spent time in prison, but he trusted God to work everything out, and He did."

"But I don't know if I have that kind of faith. I have doubts that God can work this out. I'm scared." Her voice fell to a whisper.

Josiah set the basket on the ground and pulled her into his embrace once more. Her tears wet his shirt, but he didn't seem to mind. She felt the gentle touch of his lips on her forehead. Peace stole over her. Josiah had such a strong faith. Could she trust Jesus as all her new friends suggested? She wiped her eyes and stepped back.

"I'm sorry. Sometimes I don't think things through."

"We're all that way." Josiah picked up the laundry. His stomach growled. "I believe I heard something about pie?"

She sniffed and gave a light laugh. "I hope I have enough. From the sound of things, you could eat the whole thing. By the way, why did you want to see Mrs. Sawyer?"

Josiah gave her a wide grin. "Because I have a plan to rescue a damsel in distress."

"What? You didn't tell me." Lavette hopped up the steps to open the door. "What is it?"

Josiah stopped to give her a peck on the cheek. "It's a surprise. You'll find out after Mrs. Sawyer agrees with me."

Chapter 18

Lavette danced on pins and needles, waiting for the ding of Mrs. Sawyer's bell. Josiah refused to say more. He ate two pieces of pie and drank his coffee, acting like he didn't have a care in the world. If he wasn't so big, she would pick him up and shake him. He kept saying to be patient, but the anticipation wouldn't let her.

She stirred the coals to life in the stove. The door screeched like a cat with its tail stepped on. Josiah's chuckle brought her around.

"What are you laughing about now?"

"You."

"Me?" She placed her hands on her hips in exasperation. "Why?"

"Because you've been waiting for something, and now you've missed it."

She wanted to stuff her apron in his mouth. At the same time, his lightness of attitude made her long to join him. A bell dinged. She gaped.

"Is that what you're meaning? Did she already ring the bell once?"

He nodded. Lavette gave him a withering glare before starting to stalk out of the room. Josiah grabbed her hand and pulled her onto his lap. His huge hand cupped her cheek, turning her to look at him.

"You aren't really mad, are you?"

"Of course I am." She crossed her arms and huffed. Her mouth twitched, and he grinned. He gave her a quick kiss and lifted her back onto her feet.

"I'll wait until you have her up and ready for company."

Lavette sped down the hall. She had to be careful, or she would be in such a hurry, she would jerk Mrs. Sawyer out of bed, throw her clothes on her, and rush her into the parlor to hear what Josiah had to say.

"Good afternoon, Ma'am. Did you have a good nap?"

"Yes, I did." Mrs. Sawyer's brow wrinkled. "I thought I heard voices. Is someone here?"

"Yes, Ma'am." Lavette lifted her mistress into a sitting position and began to help her dress. "My friend, Josiah, is here. He'd like to speak with you when you're ready."

"Why certainly, although I was hoping Mr. Mead had stopped by. He's such a charming sort." She chuckled. "If I were years younger, I believe I might be taken with the man."

Lavette bit back a groan. She picked up the brush and began to straighten Mrs. Sawyer's hair. How could this woman be so deceived? The man must have missed his calling as an actor in one of those fancy theaters back East. He certainly could cover up his true self.

"There we go." Lavette placed the brush back on the shelf, hoping Mrs. Sawyer didn't notice her impatience. "Are you ready to go out to the parlor? The weather outside is beautiful. I already have the window open, and you can hear the birds singing."

"That sounds wonderful." Mrs. Sawyer eased up with Lavette's help and began to shuffle down the hallway. "I think I'm still a little tired from my visit to Gretta. I don't believe I'll move in with them until Paul has my room done. Those grandchildren are fun, but they wear a person down."

Lavette eased the woman into her favorite chair and arranged a blanket on her lap. "Can I get you anything?"

"I would take a glass of water." Mrs. Sawyer smiled, the left side of her mouth sagging a little more than usual. "I seem to be parched after my nap." Lavette turned to leave when her mistress spoke again. "Oh, and you may show your young man in to see me."

"Yes, Ma'am."

Lavette almost tripped from excitement as she led Josiah into the parlor. "Mrs. Sawyer, this is Josiah Washington. He has a blacksmith shop here in town."

Josiah nodded in greeting, his hat lost in his hands. Mrs. Sawyer indicated the chair next to her, and he sat down. Lavette didn't know whether to leave or stay.

"If you don't mind, Ma'am, I'd like for Lavette to stay. What I have to say concerns her too."

Mrs. Sawyer glanced at Lavette, then back at Josiah. "That's fine with me. How can I help you? I believe you're the young man who rescued me yesterday. I thank you."

Josiah twisted his hat, his fingers kneading the material until Lavette thought it might rip into shreds. "I'm not sure if Lavette has mentioned me, Ma'am, but I've taken quite a liking to her." He hesitated and glanced at Lavette. "In fact, I love her very much."

Lavette put her hands to her warm cheeks and couldn't look at her mistress. She'd had no idea Josiah would say something like this.

"I believe Lavette loves me, too, and I would like to speak with you about purchasing the remainder of her contract. I want her to be my wife, but I know Mr. Mead wouldn't allow that to happen."

"I don't know how you could know Mr. Mead's thoughts if you haven't spoken to him." Mrs. Sawyer's lips drew into a thin line, a sign that she wasn't happy. "The fact is, Mr. Mead has already proposed to buy her contract, should I choose to sell it."

"You mean you haven't actually agreed to let him?" Josiah looked hopeful. "If not, could you give me some time to raise what we need? I have some savings, and I'll work hard for the rest."

"Mr. Mead has agreed to pay me fifty dollars for Lavette's contract. Do you have that kind of money?" Mrs. Sawyer's imperious tone made Lavette clench her fists. How could she talk to Josiah like that?

"No, Ma'am, I don't have that much. Not even close." The sparkle in Josiah's eyes dimmed. He lowered his gaze. Bringing his head up, he smiled once more. "Could I give you what I have and make payments on the rest? I have friends who will vouch for me. I'm honest and I work hard. We could even postpone getting married until Lavette is free."

"That will never work. My son-in-law is using the money Mr. Mead is paying to build a room on his house for me. He needs that paid all at once so he will have the funds for the project."

Josiah nodded. Lavette wanted to cry. He'd tried his best, but it wasn't good enough.

"How do you even know Lavette wants to marry you? Have you asked her?" Mrs. Sawyer leaned forward in her chair.

"No, Ma'am, I haven't asked her yet, but I do know she loves me." He glanced over at Lavette. His eyes pleaded with her to return his love. She moved away from the door where she'd been standing and crossed the room. She knelt down at his feet, took one of his hands in hers, and squeezed. His love was almost visible in the air. She could feel it surrounding her.

"Ma'am, I'd be honored to be Josiah's wife. He's everything I've ever dreamed of." Lavette tore her gaze from Josiah's and looked at her mistress. Mrs. Sawyer frowned at them.

"I'll give you two weeks to earn the money. If you haven't saved enough by then, I'll allow Mr. Mead to have her contract." She nodded, dismissing the two of them.

Tugging on Josiah's hand, Lavette urged him out of the room. This would never work. Fifty dollars was an unheard of amount for people like them. She would have to convince him to give up the idea of the two of them being together.

In the kitchen, she turned to him. He put his arms around her and hugged her to him. "Somehow, I'll get enough." His whispered promise only brought her pain.

"No." She too kept her voice low. "There's no way for you to do that. You have to give up the idea, Josiah. It won't work."

He stroked her hair, smoothing back the loosened tendrils. "You're a gift to me from God. I won't give up." He gave her a light kiss. "There's a man outside of Tucson who wants me to come out and do some work for him. I'll ride out there tomorrow. If he has some big jobs that pay well, I'll stay and do them."

"I wish I could help, but I have only a few dollars saved from my wages." Lavette rested her forehead on Josiah's broad chest. She longed to cling to him forever.

"I have an idea there, too."

"What?" Hope began to push away the doubts.

"Quinn mentioned the other day that Kathleen has more work than she can keep up with in her seamstress shop. With her time so close for the baby, she doesn't have the stamina she used to."

"Josiah Washington, you make her sound like a horse." Lavette giggled. "I can sew. I'll stop by tomorrow and see if she would like some help. I'm sure the pay won't be much, but I do want to help."

"I'd be happy to walk you over there tonight after Mrs. Sawyer goes to bed."

Lavette nodded, her heart full of love and hope for the first time she could remember.

⁂

Josiah couldn't help whistling as he turned up the path to Lavette's house. He could see her waiting in the shadows of the porch. Since Mrs. Sawyer always retired early, they had plenty of time to walk to Quinn and Kathleen's house. The thought of going anywhere with Lavette set his heart singing.

"There is a fountain filled with blood, drawn from Immanuel's veins." Lavette's voice rang out softly. He matched her volume since he didn't want to disturb Mrs. Sawyer.

He jumped onto the porch, ignoring the steps. He felt like he could leap to the moon and back tonight. "Good evenin', Beautiful." Lavette stopped singing. Her head dipped as if she were embarrassed. He wanted to grab her and kiss her again, but kept his hands at his sides.

"Evenin'."

"Ready to go?" Josiah stretched out a hand for hers. "I saw Quinn this afternoon and mentioned we might stop by."

She slipped her small hand into his. He sighed with pleasure at the touch. "I've decided that I need to teach you another verse of my fountain song on the way."

"I like the first two well enough. I'm ready for the third." Her eyes were dark in the twilight. "How many verses are there?"

"I know five. At church we don't always do all of them. Some of the folks have trouble remembering so many."

"Okay, I'm ready."

"Dear dying Lamb, Thy precious blood shall never lose its power, till all the ransomed Church of God, be saved, to sin no more: Be saved, to sin no more, be saved, to sin no more; till all the ransomed Church of God be saved to sin no more." Josiah cleared his throat. Lavette walked in silence beside him.

"Okay, you've heard the words. Now join with me." He opened his mouth to sing, but something wasn't right. Lavette ignored him. A lone tear glistened on her cheek.

"Hey, what's wrong? Was I that bad?" He pulled her around, put a finger under her chin, and lifted.

Her mouth quivered. She tried to smile but failed. He put his arms around her, hugging her close. He couldn't think of anything he'd said or done to upset her, so he waited for her to gather her composure. When she was ready, she would tell him.

"I'm so sorry." Her arms slipped around his waist, and she leaned her cheek against him. "Those words showed me something I think Jesus has been trying to tell me."

"Well, I'm glad I didn't do anything wrong." Josiah gave her a light squeeze.

"No." She drew in a ragged breath. "You know I've been reading about Joseph. I've been angry with God so many years for allowing me to be a slave, that I didn't stop to think there are other forms of bondage than being in chains on a plantation. You tried to tell me that, too, didn't you?"

"Mm-hmm." Josiah leaned his cheek against the top of her head.

"Glorianna shared a verse with me the other day about being free in Jesus. That's what true freedom is, isn't it? Just like I can't pay the debt I owe Mrs. Sawyer, I can't pay the debt for my sins to God, either. Only Jesus could do that." She sniffed. He could feel her tears wetting his shirt.

"When I asked Jesus into my heart years ago, I was as free as I ever would be."

"There are many kinds of enslavement, and the worst is the bondage of sin." Josiah rubbed her back as he spoke. "I've never been a slave in the sense that you were, but for years I was bound in sin. I couldn't liberate myself. I had to have Jesus' help. He's the One who delivered me. I don't care if I'm put in chains for the rest of my life, I'll always be free because of Jesus paying the price for me."

"We're all ransomed like the words in that song say. By Jesus' blood we're set free." She wiped at her cheek. "I've wasted so many years being bitter and angry when all along what I wanted was already mine."

Cocking her head to the side, she frowned. "Another thing—I've always thought Jesus came for the white people. Now, I see He died for us all, didn't He?"

"That's right. He doesn't see any distinction in color or race. He loved us all enough to die for us."

She pushed back, and Josiah let his arms fall to his side. How he loved this woman. He planned to spend as many years as God gave him loving her and getting to know her better.

"We'd better get going, or the Kirbys may think we aren't coming." She held out a hand to him. "Let's do that verse again." She glanced up, and he could see the sheen of tears still in her eyes. "I may not be able to sing it aloud with you right now, but I'll be joining you inside."

Josiah set a leisurely pace as he began to sing once more. They repeated the hymn all the way to Quinn's house.

The rest of the evening sped past. Kathleen was grateful to Lavette for the offer of assistance. She wouldn't be able to pay much, but every penny would be put aside to add to what Josiah saved.

As they strolled home, Josiah couldn't help the melancholy that came over him.

Tomorrow he would ride out to see Eduardo Villegas about the work he needed done. From what Eduardo told him, there was plenty to do. He probably wouldn't be back in town for at least a week. Not seeing Lavette for that long made him want to slow this evening down.

Back on the porch at Mrs. Sawyer's house, Josiah took Lavette in his arms one more time. He marveled at how tiny she felt. She was so perfect.

"I'll be leaving early in the morning."

"You've said that at least six times now." Her light tone told him she wasn't chiding him. "I know because every time you say that, I can't wait for you to return."

"You'll miss me then?" He brushed his lips over her forehead.

"Of course. Who else can teach me the words to the fountain hymn?" They both chuckled.

"I'll miss you more than I can say. As soon as I can, I'll get back to town. I'm hoping I'll have the money we need." He kissed her pert nose. "You start thinking about a wedding. Plan exactly what you want. I'm sure Glorianna and Kathleen will be glad to help."

"I don't care about a big wedding. I just want you." Lavette reached up and gave him a light kiss. "Hurry back. I'll be waiting."

As the door closed behind her, Josiah bounded off the porch. Eager to get going so he could return faster, he ran most of the way home.

Chapter 19

Heavy gray clouds hung low in the sky as Josiah rode into town twelve days later. Huge raindrops spattered against him, the warmth of the air making them feel like ice water. He ducked his head and pulled his hat down tight. Nothing could dampen his excitement at being back in Tucson with enough money to pay off Lavette's contract. By tomorrow morning, she would be free to be his wife. Working for Eduardo had taken more time than he figured, but the reward was earning enough for Lavette.

By the time he stabled his horse, darkness had fallen. The rain increased to a steady downpour unusual in this area, but welcomed to settle the dust. Josiah drew in a deep breath of the moisture-laden air. He'd never been fond of the downpours they had where he grew up, but now that he lived in the desert, he relished the infrequent showers.

Listening to the patter of drops outside, Josiah debated going to see Lavette tonight. He shook his head and sighed. It was late, and he needed some sleep. For close to two weeks, he'd worked long, hard hours. Eduardo had a nice forge already set up on his place. He'd said his father built it and knew how to do blacksmith work, but Eduardo never learned. With a sigh, Josiah blew out the lamp and climbed into bed, longing to see the woman he loved. He groaned. Every muscle in his body ached, but knowing Lavette would soon be his made all the discomfort worthwhile.

Clouds still draped across the sky in the morning. A light breeze gave a chill to the air, although the rain had ceased for the moment. Josiah loved the fresh-washed scent and breathed deeply. His heart raced faster than his feet as he headed to Lavette's. Safe at home, under the floor, was the money he'd earned. He wanted to speak with Mrs. Sawyer first and see when she wanted him to pay her. They would need to have some sort of paperwork done up to show that Lavette was free from her obligation to the elderly lady.

Josiah jumped onto the porch and rapped on the door. Before he could lower his hand, the door swung open. Lavette stood there, her eyes shining and wide, her whole countenance glowing. He swept her up and gave her a resounding kiss. Her arms tightened around his neck as she kissed him back.

"I thought you might not be coming back." She sounded breathless as he set her back on her feet.

"Eduardo had more work for me than I thought. I hurried as fast as I could." He cupped her soft cheek in his hand, unable to resist the contact. His eyes drank in her beauty. "I've missed you so much."

She caught his hand in hers and kissed his fingers. "I've missed you too. Come on in. I've got some fresh cinnamon buns."

Stepping inside, Josiah could smell the heavenly aroma of the sweets. "Mmm." His stomach growled, and he gave Lavette a sheepish grin. "I didn't eat breakfast this morning. I wanted to get over here and see you first."

She laughed and pulled him toward the kitchen. "Come on. I'll make you something to eat." She held a finger to her lips. "We'll have to be quiet. Mrs. Sawyer is still sleeping."

He sat at the table and watched her break eggs into a skillet. The chunk of bacon she'd thrown in sizzled. Contentment washed over him. He could imagine how wonderful life would be when he and Lavette were married. Every morning he would wake up to her beautiful face, and every night he would go to sleep with her beside him.

Lavette set a plate of food in front of him and dropped into the chair on the other side of the table. "I can't wait any longer. Tell me about your work for this Eduardo."

Josiah's mouth dropped open. Shame washed over him. "I'm sorry. How could I have been so thoughtless?" He reached over and took her hands in his. "I have the money."

Her face lit up with a mixture of surprise and joy.

"Here? Did you bring it today?"

"No, I have it safe at my place. I wasn't sure how Mrs. Sawyer wanted to do this. I need to talk to her."

Tears rolled down Lavette's cheeks. She pulled her hands free and wiped the drops away with the edge of her apron. "This is so silly of me." She sniffed. "I didn't want to believe you could earn enough. I only managed to get three dollars from the work I did for Kathleen. How did you get so much?"

Standing, Josiah pulled Lavette up into his embrace. He stroked her slender back, trying to comfort her. "I had some put by already. Eduardo has a lot of horses, but shoeing doesn't pay much. I rebuilt a couple of old wagons for him. That's what paid off." He tipped Lavette's head back and gazed into her bright eyes. "You save what you earned and buy something for yourself. Maybe you could use it for material to make a new dress for our wedding."

"I can't recall ever having a new dress of my own." Lavette gave him a fierce hug. A bell tinkled. She jumped. "Mrs. Sawyer is awake." She pushed Josiah toward the chair. "You sit down and eat that breakfast. The cinnamon buns are on the stove. Help yourself. I'll let you know when we're ready for you."

Josiah watched her rush from the room. He'd never seen Lavette so flustered. She reminded him of a bird trapped in a building, fluttering to and fro, trying to find a way out. He shoveled a bite of eggs and bacon into his mouth. Life with Lavette would be pure joy.

Lavette took most of an hour getting Mrs. Sawyer ready for company. Josiah ate more sweet rolls than he should have while waiting. He was used to working, not sitting patiently. He needed to be doing something.

When Lavette finally escorted him into the parlor, Mrs. Sawyer was sitting in the chair by the window. Her erect posture and stern demeanor told him she wasn't happy to see him.

"Good morning, Ma'am." Josiah gave her a polite nod.

She inclined her head but didn't ask him to sit down. "Lavette said you wish to speak with me again. What is it this time?"

Surprised, Josiah stayed silent for a moment. "I've earned the money needed to purchase Lavette's contract. I came to see how you would like to do this."

"Isn't the time I extended to you already up?" Her cold gaze sent a chill through him.

"I believe you gave me two weeks, Ma'am. Tomorrow would be the last day." Josiah forced himself to stand quietly. He refused to let this woman know how she rattled him with her obvious wish to sell Lavette to Mead.

She nodded. "Mr. Mead and I both believed you would not be able to come up with the money. He plans to be here today with the papers for me to look over. Then, tomorrow the transaction will be final."

"But you gave your word." Lavette's voice shook as she spoke. Josiah could hear the hopelessness in her undertone.

Mrs. Sawyer gave Lavette a hard look. "I'm doing this for your good, Lavette. I have come to care for you over the years."

"If you care for me at all, you'll let Josiah, not Mr. Mead, have me." Lavette twisted her fingers together. Josiah longed to comfort her.

"I'm not at all sure that would be to your benefit. I have heard some rather disparaging things about Mr. Washington's character and background. Until I'm positive he will care for you properly, I can't let you go with him."

"What things have you heard?" Lavette and Josiah spoke at the same time. Josiah glanced at her and could see the disbelief and anger that matched his own.

Mrs. Sawyer studied them both for several minutes. "I have heard that Mr. Washington left the East to join the cavalry because of some trouble he got into. Trouble with the law, I might add."

"That can't be true." Lavette's eyes were wide as she stared at him. Josiah was too stunned to speak.

"Do you have anything to say for yourself, young man?"

"Ma'am, the closest thing I've ever done to a crime was when I was five. I stole a pie my mother had cooling on the windowsill. I ate the whole thing and got sick. My mama said the sickness was a punishment for stealing. I never did that again."

"And how am I supposed to believe that?" Mrs. Sawyer's tone could freeze the sun in the sky.

"I don't know how I can prove myself, Ma'am. All I can say is that I'm a Christian, and I try to live a godly life according to the Bible. I don't know where you heard these stories, but they aren't true."

"Are you saying my very reliable sources are lying?"

"No, Ma'am, I'm saying they are mistaken. They must have gotten the wrong information or the wrong person."

"Mrs. Sawyer, I've never met such a kind, caring man as Josiah. I know he couldn't have done those things." Lavette stepped closer and put her hand on Josiah's arm, as if to add her word to his.

"Can you bring me someone who can vouch for you—someone upstanding in the community?" From her tone, Josiah knew Mrs. Sawyer doubted he could do that.

"Yes, Ma'am, I have a lot of friends here."

"Then you may return tomorrow with your money and your friend." She paused and Josiah turned to leave. "Oh, and Mr. Washington."

He turned back. "Yes, Ma'am."

"Your friend should be someone I'll have no doubts about."

His boots clumped out a rhythm of doom as Josiah crossed to the door. Where had Mrs. Sawyer heard those rumors? His lips thinned to an angry line. Mead. Who else would bother to tarnish his reputation? Lavette trudged behind him in forlorn silence. She held the door as he stepped out. When she looked at him, he could see the despair in her eyes that matched the feelings in him. He held her close and kissed her forehead, wondering if this were one of the last times he would be allowed such a privilege.

"Remember Joseph, Josiah? God always saw him through the times when there didn't seem to be any hope."

"I know, Honey. I'll see you tomorrow." He gave her a quick kiss and stalked down the path. He had some errands to run, then he would work. When he was angry, only talking to God and hard work seemed to bring release.

✤

Lavette knelt beside her bed, her Bible on her lap, open to the book of Genesis. The lamp on the floor beside her cast a circle of light around her. She rested her forehead against the blanket.

"Lord Jesus, help me. I feel like Joseph in the pit, waiting for his brothers to sell him into slavery. You know what will happen if Mr. Mead gets my contract. You know the things I'll be required to do—things that don't honor You. Jesus, I want to run away, but I'm trusting You to work everything out instead. I know Josiah is a good man. He loves You. He loves me too. Please help us. Make Mrs. Sawyer see the truth tomorrow."

She clutched the Bible to her breast, thinking how far she'd come. The thought of slavery didn't scare her so much anymore. She knew Jesus wanted the best for her, and anything that happened would be to His glory. The long talks she'd had with Kathleen over the last two weeks had helped her understand so much about the Bible and the way Christians were to believe. As long as she had Jesus in her heart, she would have the freedom she desired, and the Bible said no one could take Him away from her.

A light tapping at the front door snapped her head up. Josiah? Would he come by this late to see her? Jumping up, she reached for her wrapper. Her bare feet made little noise on the hallway floor. She lifted the latch, her heart thundering in anticipation of seeing the very man she'd been thinking about.

"Good evening, my sweet." Bertrand Mead sagged against the doorjamb, his breath laden with alcohol. Lavette swung the door to slam it shut, but he put his foot in the way.

"Now is that any way to treat your prospective owner?" He grabbed her, his fingers digging into her shoulder. "In the good days before the war, when a man bought slaves, he got to examine them thoroughly. I think I should get the same privilege, don't you?"

"Let me go. You're drunk." Lavette jerked back, but she couldn't break his hold.

"Now, now, my sweet, don't fight me." Mead tugged at the sash on her wrapper.

"Stop that, or I'll scream."

"And who would care about a slave girl screaming?" He chuckled, a malevolent sound that sent chills racing down Lavette's spine.

"I am not a slave. Let me go."

"I'm buying you, aren't I? When I pay my money tomorrow, you'll be mine."

"You won't get to do that." She spat the words at him. "Josiah earned enough. He'll be here in the morning to purchase my contract. You don't have a chance."

His lip lifted in a sneer. He yanked her tight against him. "Your Josiah doesn't stand a chance. A man of his ilk wouldn't be good for a girl like you. You need a man of sterling character like me." He lowered his mouth. Lavette turned her head, and he gave her a slobbery kiss on the cheek. She stomped on his boot, but her bare foot made no impression. He chuckled.

A sob welled up inside her. *Jesus, help me.* She pushed again. Mead stumbled back. He let go. His arms flailed as he teetered on the edge of the porch. Lavette darted into the house, shut the door, and slid the bolt home. Her whole body trembled as she strained to hear if he was gone. What if he tried to force the door or get in a window? Her heart thundered.

Uneven steps clumped to the door. Mead's voice came clearly through the cracks. "I know you're in there, my sweet. The wait will make our time tomorrow night more delightful. Think about that."

She listened to his uneven tread. Silence hung heavy like a shroud. She covered her mouth to hold back the sobs. What would tomorrow bring? Could she trust Jesus with this? *Lord, help me.* She cried the words from the depth of her soul.

A comforting warmth settled about her. She basked in the feeling of contentment. This must be the peace Kathleen told her about, the peace that passed all understanding. She moved down the hall with lighter steps. With Jesus watching over her, she would sleep well tonight.

Chapter 20

Cavelike darkness surrounded Josiah as he stepped from his smithy. Glancing back, he could see the faint glow from the banked coals. Although he'd spent hours working, he still didn't have the tranquillity he longed for. He was in turmoil over what would happen with Lavette. His body couldn't continue. Exhausted after this day and the long days he'd put in for nearly two weeks, he shuffled around the side of the building.

Heavy clouds blocked the moon and stars, so nothing lit the night. He hadn't bothered with a lantern. The path to his door was as familiar as the back of his hand. The dark didn't trouble him. He fumbled in the pitch black for the latch to his door.

Josiah paused. The door wasn't latched. With a slight creak, it swung open. He couldn't hear anything. Had he left the door open by accident? When he'd returned from speaking with Mrs. Sawyer, he'd been so distraught, he might have done anything. He stepped inside.

Pain exploded in his head. Josiah fell back against the wall. Something whooshed past him and thudded on the side of the door close to his ear. He pushed against the wood. The world was spinning. Bile rose in his throat. He fell. Something hard struck him in the back of the head. He pitched forward. Darkness closed around him. All sound faded.

The soft coo of a mourning dove awakened Josiah. The sound echoed in his head like a gunshot. He tried to open his eyes. The gray light of dawn pierced like a needle. He groaned. As he pushed up from the floor, the world began to tilt. His stomach roiled. Blackness surrounded him, and he sank into oblivion.

"Josiah." Someone's hand lifted his shoulder, rattling his brains. "Josiah, can you hear me?"

He groaned. Bright light sent a pain to the base of his skull. He closed his eyes.

"Josiah, I'm going for help. You stay still." The voice that sounded like Conlon quieted, and Josiah drifted off once more.

He awoke again to someone prodding the sore spot on his temple. He squinted and could see Doc Meyer, Conlon, and Quinn hovering over him.

"Good thing he has a hard head." Doc grunted. "I don't feel anything cracked. He'll need a little rest, then he'll be fine." Pulling out some cloth, he began to bandage Josiah's wounds. He stood, dusted off his pants, and picked up his bag from the floor next to Josiah.

"Thanks, Doc." Josiah barely got the words out. He licked his dry lips with a tongue that felt like a rolled-up sock.

"Let me get you some water." Conlon patted Josiah's leg. Josiah did his best to stifle a groan.

"What happened?" He spoke to Quinn, who still knelt beside him.

"I think you were robbed. I'm guessing you came home and surprised the thief. He hit you with this." Quinn held up a poker.

"I always did say you were thick headed for a reason." Conlon knelt beside him and gave him a sip of cool water. Josiah took a second drink and eased up to a sitting position. The room swam in sickening circles. He closed his eyes until the dizziness passed, then opened them slowly.

"My money." He tried to stand, but Quinn pushed him back.

"Oh, no, you don't. You sit right there until you get your bearings." Quinn glanced at Conlon, then met Josiah's gaze. "Did you keep the money you earned in a box under a floorboard?" Josiah nodded and winced. Quinn frowned. "The board's been pulled up, and the hole is empty. Did you get a look at who hit you?"

"No." Josiah's fingers probed the knot on the back of his skull. "It was pitch black last night. I didn't have a lantern. He was in the house when I came in. I didn't even see him coming."

Quinn blew out a breath. "I think we all know who's responsible, but proving that will be difficult." Josiah saw Conlon nod.

"You need to rest, Josiah. We'll help you into bed, then Quinn and I will ask around town to see what we can find out. We'll come by right after lunch and go with you to Mrs. Sawyer's, like we planned."

Josiah had talked to Quinn and Conlon yesterday about being his character witnesses before Mrs. Sawyer. They both agreed and made arrangements to meet at her house this afternoon. Now, he wondered if they should bother.

"I can't go there. If I haven't got any money to buy the contract, how will I face Lavette?"

"She deserves to know what happened." Conlon squeezed Josiah's shoulder. "She's quite a girl. Give her a chance."

After Conlon and Quinn left, Josiah couldn't stop the tears that seeped from his eyes. "Jesus, I've made a mess of things. All along, I assumed my being with Lavette was Your will. I didn't stop to ask what You wanted me to do. I barged ahead on my own. Please, Lord, don't let Lavette suffer for my willfulness. Work this out according to Your plan and Your will. Thank You, Jesus." Josiah drifted into a restful sleep, marveling at the peace he felt inside, when all around him things were in turmoil.

❧

Lavette swung the door open before Josiah finished knocking. She'd heard a wagon draw up outside. Looking out the window, she'd seen a strange sight. Conlon was helping Josiah down as Quinn tied the horses. Why had they come in a wagon? What was wrong with Josiah? Her heart pounded as she raced to greet them.

"Josiah, what's wrong?" She gripped the door, fear clutching at her as she took in the sight of the white bandage on Josiah's temple. He didn't give her his usual smile.

"Someone robbed me last night." He touched the bandage. "They tried to dent my skull but failed." His lips trembled as he tried to smile. "I need to talk with Mrs. Sawyer. I don't have the money we need."

"Oh, Josiah, it doesn't matter." Lavette traced the side of his cheek with her fingers. "I'm so glad you're all right. I know everything else will work out fine."

Josiah nodded. Lavette stepped back for them to enter, embarrassed at her temerity in front of Josiah's friends. They didn't seem to mind. In fact, the two men seemed pleased as they followed Josiah inside. Lavette led the way to the front room. Mrs. Sawyer was already up from her nap and seated by the open window.

"Good afternoon, gentlemen." Mrs. Sawyer looked surprised to see the deputy sheriff and a cavalry lieutenant accompanying Josiah. She gestured to the other chairs in the room, and the men seated themselves.

"Mrs. Sawyer, I brought two of my friends to vouch for my character." Josiah's voice was full of anguish. Lavette stood behind him and placed her hands on his shoulders. He reached up and squeezed her fingers.

"You look as though you've been in a fight. I thought perhaps you were under arrest."

Quinn chuckled and Conlon grinned.

"No, Ma'am." Quinn spoke up. "Josiah is one of the finest men you'll ever meet. I can't imagine him being arrested for anything."

"That's right." Conlon winked at Josiah. "I've known him for several years now. We met when he was still in the cavalry. He's a godly man and one you can trust completely."

Mrs. Sawyer sat quiet, studying the two men. She looked at Josiah. "I guess I can have no further objections to you then. I have the papers in my room. Have you brought the money?"

Lavette felt Josiah's shoulders sag. "No, Ma'am. I don't have it."

"Then you lied to me yesterday? You said you'd earned enough and would bring it today."

"I intended to, but last night I was robbed."

Mrs. Sawyer frowned and started to reply. Before she could say anything, footsteps echoed on the porch, followed by knocking. Lavette slipped from the parlor. She opened the door to find Mead waiting, a twisted grin on his face. Understanding dawned. She knew this man was responsible for what had happened to Josiah. She stepped out and shut the door. She moved down the porch closer to the open window.

❦

Josiah's heart ached as Lavette left the room. That must be Mead. In a few minutes, Lavette would belong to that scoundrel. Josiah couldn't do anything to rescue her now.

Mrs. Sawyer opened her mouth to say something, then stopped. She cocked her head to one side. Josiah could see Conlon and Quinn frowning in concentration. He began to listen.

From the open window, he heard Bertrand Mead speaking. "I'm glad you're so eager to see me this morning. After my reception last night, I thought you might give me trouble today."

"Josiah is here. What makes you think I'll be yours? He earned the money to buy my contract."

"So you said last night, my sweet. I thank you for that helpful bit of information." Mead's words made Josiah clench his fists. "I know he won't be able to come up with the funds he needs."

"And how would you know that?"

"Oh, I have my ways, sweet thing." The boards outside the window creaked. "Why don't you and I go inside and get this business taken care of? Then you can come with me and begin learning how to entertain."

"You said you wanted me to sing. I already know how to do that." Lavette's voice held steady.

"Oh, I intend for you to sing, but I also have other plans for you, my sweet. With your beauty, men will pay a lot. I'm going to make a fortune off of you." Mead chuckled.

Mrs. Sawyer gave a slight gasp.

"You're too late. Josiah is talking with Mrs. Sawyer right now."

"Oh, but he won't have the money he needs." Mead chuckled.

"How do you know that?"

"Because I went to his place and made sure of it last night." The threat in Mead's tone made Josiah tremble with the desire to protect Lavette. "In fact, if it hadn't been so dark, he wouldn't be here at all."

"You would have killed him?" Lavette's gasp drowned out Mrs. Sawyer's.

"Yes," Mead hissed.

Quinn stood and lifted his revolver from the holster. He gave Mrs. Sawyer a long look and stepped from the room. Josiah could hear the front door opening and the creak of the boards as the deputy strode to where Mead and Lavette stood outside the window.

"I believe I owe you an apology, Mr. Washington." Mrs. Sawyer sounded tired. She rubbed her forehead. "When you get the money back from Mr. Mead, come by to see me."

Josiah nodded and followed Conlon from the room.

"Are you ready?" Josiah spoke close to Lavette's ear, sending a shiver of delight through her.

"Josiah, this is silly. Take this blindfold off." Lavette blinked in the bright light as Josiah whisked the cloth away from her eyes. She gasped in delight. There in front of her was a new cottage. She could smell the cut wood on the porch. The rest of the house was made from adobe bricks.

"Come on." Josiah dragged her up the stairs and opened the door.

She stepped inside and marveled at the newness of everything. The kitchen had a stove, newly blacked, shelves with dishes, and pans hanging on the walls. A small table stood at one side. Josiah led her through the rest of the house, grinning at her delight.

"This is our room." He opened the door to the bedroom, and she walked in. White curtains fluttered at the window. A colorful rag rug covered the floor by the bed. What caught her eye, though, was the yellow dress hanging on the wall.

"Oh, Josiah, it's beautiful."

"The dress is a gift from Kathleen. She and Glorianna thought you would look pretty in yellow." He wrapped his arms around her and whispered in her ear. "I think you're beautiful in any color."

"How did you manage this?" Lavette turned in Josiah's arms to face him.

"You can thank Mrs. Sawyer." He grinned. "When I went to pay her the money for your contract, she refused to take any. She asked me where we would live, and when I told her about the room by the smithy, she insisted I use the contract money to build you a house. She said you deserved the best for all you'd given up." He planted a kiss on her nose. "She's right, you know. She also said your freedom would be our wedding gift from her. Paul didn't need the money anymore since she decided to return to Virginia."

"This is like a dream come true."

"I was worried I wouldn't get done before our wedding tomorrow, but other than a few finishing touches, the house is ready to move into."

"You are amazing, Josiah Washington. You're the handsome prince I always dreamed about."

"And you're the sweetheart I never thought I'd get. I love you more than I can say, Lavette. I look forward to spending a lifetime with you."

As Josiah's lips met hers, Lavette couldn't stop the prayer of thankfulness for all the Lord had given her. She'd wanted freedom, and He'd given so much more.

Sonoran
Secret

To Cindy, Janet, and Rella.
Thank you always for being such supportive prayer partners.
You are a blessing to me.

Chapter 1

Arizona Territory, 1870s

E duardo Villegas twisted the tip of his mustache, then smoothed it back into place. In the distance, a cloud of dust heralded the arrival of his bride-to-be. Soon his lonely evenings would end.

"You look a little nervous, my friend. Are you sure you want to go through with this?"

Eduardo glanced over at his friend and pastor, Matthew Reilly. He shrugged, then continued to stare down the road. "I gave my word, Pastor. Besides, the Lord clearly showed me this is the right thing to do."

Deputy Quinn Kirby, another friend of Eduardo's, chuckled. "I know you can trust God. Trusting Diego Garcia is the problem."

"What's to trust? He promised to give me his daughter, Teresa, in marriage. After the wedding, I'll forgive the debt he owes me. It's as simple as that."

"With Diego, nothing is ever easy. That's why I'm here." Quinn brushed his fingers across his holstered pistol. "I wasn't sure Diego would even show up."

Eduardo frowned as the buckboard lurched into view. Quinn knew Diego too well. Diego would do anything to cheat on a bargain. Eduardo didn't know how else to settle the debt between them, short of bringing in the law. When Diego approached him with the idea of marriage to one of his five daughters as a way to pay what he owed, Eduardo prayed about it, then agreed to the arrangement.

Now, Matthew was right. He felt like turning around and running as fast and far as he could. What had he gotten himself into? Did he really hear God saying he should marry Teresa Garcia? He didn't even know the girl. *Lord, I'm a little nervous about this. Please let me know if this is part of Your plan for my life.*

As the wagon clattered to a stop in the grove of trees that straddled the Villegas and Garcia property, a calm descended over Eduardo. He nodded in satisfaction, knowing God answered his prayer with His peace.

Diego Garcia stepped down from the wagon, then turned to take the hand of the young woman clad all in white. The long dress rustled in the quiet as she eased over the side of the wagon. Eduardo couldn't be certain from this distance, but he thought his bride might be missing her shoes.

"Thank God, it's a cool day," Matthew whispered to Eduardo. "Otherwise your wife-to-be would melt in all of those clothes."

Eduardo bit back a smile, knowing the truth of Matthew's words. In the

Arizona Territory, the sun could be merciless. Long-sleeved dresses and gloves in the summer would bring heatstroke in a short time. The heavy veil that covered Teresa's head and blocked out fresh air must be suffocating, despite the cool day.

Diego leaned close to his daughter, speaking words too quiet for the others to hear. She stiffened and took his proffered arm. They moved toward Eduardo. He wondered if he detected reluctance in Teresa's steps. *Brides are always nervous and unsure,* he admonished himself. After all, he'd only spoken to the girl once over a year ago. He remembered her as being a little saucy. She wasn't beautiful, but pretty enough. There were worse things than having a wife who wasn't a beauty. Eduardo recalled her being sturdy. She would be able to work hard and have his children.

Lord, Eduardo lowered his eyes, hoping his friends weren't watching, *I'm trying to have faith in You. I know in my head that Your plans for me are right, but I don't want a wife who's only good for working and bearing children. I want someone who loves You, a wife who will be a friend.*

"Well, here is my future son-in-law." Diego's low, gravelly voice grated on Eduardo's taut nerves.

Looking up, Eduardo stared at the woman encased in white. The long, thick veil, concealing any evidence of her features, draped to cover nearly to her elbows. White, beaded gloves, tucked into the long sleeves of her gown, hid even her small hands from his sight. Eduardo took a deep breath. Part of him was relieved, but part of him wanted to rip the veil away and see how Teresa felt about this marriage. Would she be able to love him? Could he learn to love her? He could clearly recall the way his mother and father looked at one another, their eyes glowing with unspoken feelings. Anger knotted his stomach at the thought of his parents' needless deaths. As if sensing his mood, Quinn nudged him. Eduardo tamped down the rage, refusing to allow it to boil over right then.

Matthew cleared his throat. "Diego, I'm surprised your wife and other daughters didn't wish to attend the wedding. Are they coming later?"

Diego grinned and shook his head. His greasy mustache trembled with the movement. "My wife wasn't feeling well this morning. She needed the other girls to stay home and help her." He pulled his daughter forward a few steps. "Shall we get this over? Eduardo, I'm keeping my end of the bargain. Do you have the papers releasing me from my debt?"

Lifting the envelope in his pocket, Eduardo nodded. "They're right here. I'll hand them over as soon as the ceremony is done." He could almost feel Quinn's approval at his caution.

Diego's beady eyes fastened on the envelope. He licked his lips. "You know, you are getting quite a wife here. Perhaps we should add a little something to even things out on my end of the bargain."

Quinn shifted forward. Eduardo lifted his hand to stop his friend.

"Diego, my father was very generous in his help to you and your family. Your debt to my father, and now to me, is worth more than everything you own. Over the years, you have paid nothing against this debt. I am trying to be just as charitable by agreeing to forgive what you owe me. I believe that is enough of a bride price for your daughter."

Quinn stepped forward, his hand resting on the grip of his pistol. "If you don't think Señor Villegas is right, then he and Pastor Reilly can return your daughter home, and I'll escort you into Tucson. I've got a cozy little cell for you. In fact, I would prefer to have you behind bars."

Sweat beaded on Diego's brow. He held up his hand. "No, Señor Villegas is being very generous. My daughter is pleased to marry him." He pushed her white-gloved hand toward Eduardo. "Please, let's begin the ceremony."

Matthew opened his Bible and cleared his throat. "Would you like me to use your full name, Señorita Garcia?" Her head shook from side to side. The veil fluttered.

"My lovely girl is very nervous. Without her mama and sisters, she gets shy. Just Señorita Garcia will be fine."

Matthew frowned and glanced at Eduardo.

Eduardo gave a brief nod, stepped over beside Teresa, and took her hand in his. She seemed shorter than he remembered. Her fine-boned hand didn't feel as sturdy as he thought it should. A vague sense of unease swept through him, then was gone as quickly as it had come. Eduardo tensed, trying to pin down the strange sensation before giving up, convincing himself that he, too, had a case of nerves. He straightened, took his hat off, and handed it to Quinn.

Matthew flipped through the Bible until he reached the book of Ephesians. His strong voice rang out with the words written to husbands and wives in the fifth chapter. " 'Wives, submit yourselves unto your own husbands, as unto the Lord. . . . Husbands, love your wives, even as Christ also loved the church, and gave himself for it.' " Eduardo wondered if he would be able to love his wife as Christ loved the church. That kind of love would take work and commitment. All his life, his parents had talked to him about the importance of marriage. He was prepared to do his best to love and cherish Teresa.

When Matthew asked Teresa to repeat the vows, she remained silent. Shifting to the side, she turned her head toward her father. The veil rustled.

"I'm afraid my daughter is unable to speak. If you will say the words, she will nod her acceptance."

"Why can't she say the vows?" Quinn's question carried a tinge of distrust.

"Ahh! You know these women. Flighty creatures, they are at times." Diego's strained smile didn't set Eduardo at ease. "My daughter, when she gets nervous, she has trouble talking."

"With some women that would be a blessing."

Teresa stiffened at Quinn's mumbled words.

"It's okay." Eduardo wanted to get this over. "Just get on with this, Matthew."

He wanted to add that, the sooner the marriage ceremony was finished, the faster Diego Garcia would be off his land.

Matthew proceeded to recite Teresa's vows. She nodded her assent. Eduardo said the vows and slipped his mother's wedding ring over his bride's gloved finger. Her hand quivered like a leaf in the breeze. The ring stopped partway up. He knew she could put it on right later. He gave her hand a light squeeze, trying to reassure her.

"I now pronounce you man and wife."

Diego slapped Eduardo on the back. "Well, son-in-law, I reckon it's time to get those papers out and hand them over."

"What happened to kissing the bride?" Quinn leaned forward, his gaze focused on Diego.

A nervous laugh bubbled out of Diego. "I need to get back to my wife. She's sick, you know." He held out his hand to Eduardo. "If you give me the papers, my daughter can change, and I'll be getting home."

"What do you mean, your daughter can change?" Eduardo couldn't keep his apprehension in check any longer.

Waving a hand in the air, Diego forced a laugh. "Oh, you see, this is her mother's wedding dress. This gown must be kept for her sisters."

"Then we'll return the dress later."

"No, I think my wife would be too upset if I returned without her gown. She considers it very precious."

Eduardo fought the urge to roll his eyes. He pointed to the thick stand of trees behind him. "She can go over there and change while we sign the papers."

Diego rushed to the wagon and came back with a bundle of clothes tied with string. Teresa moved off to more privacy. Quinn pushed forward as Eduardo pulled the debt release papers from his pocket.

"Diego, I don't like the sound of this. Something isn't right. If you've tricked Eduardo in any way, I'll make sure you regret it."

"Please, Señor Kirby. I have brought my daughter to Señor Villegas as I promised. You have been here for the whole ceremony. What have I done wrong?"

Quinn growled and stepped back. Eduardo opened the papers, scratched his signature in the appropriate place, and handed them to Diego. After a quick glance, Diego shoved them down in his shirt and headed for his wagon.

"What about Teresa's clothes?" Eduardo gestured toward his own wagon, brought for the purpose of transporting whatever she'd brought with her.

"Thank you for reminding me." Diego whirled around and stalked off into the trees after Teresa.

"Do you want us to stick around?" Quinn's narrowed gaze followed Diego's retreating back.

"I'll be fine." Eduardo tried to sound sure of himself. "I know Kathleen is expecting you home before dark. It's a long ride back. Thanks for coming out."

Eduardo clapped Quinn on the back as he walked with him toward his horse. After all the trouble Diego Garcia caused in town, Eduardo knew Quinn had plenty of reasons to be suspicious.

"Fealdad, where are you?" Diego's words hissed through the air.

Fealdad Garcia shivered. Fear clenched at her heart. She smoothed her skirt and shook her ratted hair so the tangles would conceal most of her face. Fealdad—*ugliness*. That's what her name meant, and that's how she had to appear so her father wouldn't take out his ever-present wrath on her again. As far back as she could remember, she'd been treated differently than her sisters. While they were coddled, she did chores. When excuses were made for their mistakes, she was beaten.

She thought of the man who was now her husband. She'd only seen him from a distance once, when he visited their house to talk to her father about some business. Until today, she hadn't known how handsome he was. He had the thickest, blackest hair she'd ever seen—the kind that made her want to touch it. A long, straight nose and square jaw gave him a rugged, strong appearance. His deep brown eyes drew her in. He'd looked at her with such kindness. Oh, she hoped he would be kind to her.

"Girl, I'd better find you soon, or you'll regret hiding from me." Papa's voice sounded like the warning of a venomous snake.

The sinister threat made her fingers fumble. She slipped her shawl over her head, picked up the neat pile of wedding clothes, and stepped through the thick brush into his path.

"About time." He growled out the words as he jerked the white garments from her. One of the beaded gloves dropped. Fealdad snatched it before the garment reached the dirt. She slipped the glove on top of the pile of clothes, wishing her father would go. His black eyes took on a feral gleam as he looked at her. Fealdad stood her ground, refusing to let him see the terror she felt. He loved to hit her. He always had.

"Diego, I need to get back. I have chores to do." From the sound of his voice, Eduardo was growing impatient.

Diego stared a moment longer. His lip curled into a snarl. "We're glad to be rid of you, Girl. You've never been any good for anyone. You don't do anything right. Ugly and stupid, that's what you are. Villegas thinks he's gotten one over on me, but I'm the one who wins." He pivoted and strode away through the trees. Coming to a halt, he turned and came back. He grabbed her wrist tight enough to make her gasp.

"Your husband is waiting for you." He gave a leering grin. "I'm sure he can't wait to see his lovely bride."

Fealdad tugged at her wrist. Dread clutched her heart. How could she face Eduardo? What man, no matter how kind he was, would want an ugly, worthless person like her? Would he beat her like Papa had? Would she be the cause of him turning to drink as she had with her father? Her insides turned liquid. Her legs felt limp. Stumbling behind her father, she didn't look up until he came to a halt. The polished boots in front of her didn't move. The pull of Eduardo's gaze was like a physical force, moving her chin upward. She lifted her head, hoping this time might be different, hoping she might see some sort of love and acceptance from a man instead of resentment.

Eduardo looked confused. He glanced at her father, then back at her. What might have been surprise or disgust flashed across his face. His eyes narrowed. Anger darkened his gaze. She closed her eyes. Eduardo wouldn't be any different from her father. Had she gone from one horror to another?

"What kind of trick are you trying now, Diego? This isn't Teresa. Where is my wife?"

Chapter 2

This is your wife." Diego thrust her forward. "You married my daughter, Fealdad—Señorita Garcia."

Eduardo's hand flashed across Fealdad's vision. She ducked. Eduardo grabbed Diego's shirt in his fist and dragged him forward. "What are you trying to pull here? You know we agreed that I would marry Teresa. You never mentioned any of your other daughters."

Her father tugged at his shirt with one hand, trying to free himself. Eduardo twisted his fist, knotting the material tighter against Papa's throat.

"Señor Villegas." Papa's face began to darken; his voice sounded raspy and strained. "I never promised you Teresa, only one of my daughters. I have kept my word on this."

Eduardo glanced over his shoulder as if wishing his friends were still there. The muscles in his jaw bunched. Fealdad could almost see his teeth grinding, chewing on the rage over this deception. He pulled her father closer, until they stood nose to nose.

"You will get off my land. Don't you ever come here again. Is that clear?"

Papa nodded, gasping for air. The wedding dress dropped in the dirt. His fingers began to claw at Eduardo's hand. Eduardo released him with a shove, sending him sprawling onto the ground beside the garments. Her father scrabbled to get away, his chest heaving.

"Diego."

Fealdad watched as her father froze. She'd never seen him afraid of anyone before.

"Si, Señor Villegas?"

"Don't forget these." Eduardo nudged the now-filthy gown with the toe of his boot. "I don't want any reminders of you left on my land."

Her father scrambled to gather the clothes. Finished, his gaze flicked to Fealdad.

"She stays." Eduardo's growl sent a shiver of fear through Fealdad. "Before you go, I want to know what kind of name Fealdad is. Why would you call your daughter *ugliness?*"

Standing, Papa backed away toward his wagon. "Look at her. We only named her for what we saw. She will work hard for you, though, Señor." He hesitated. "At least you will have peace and quiet with her. Fealdad can't talk, or at least, she hasn't spoken since she was very young."

With that announcement, her father whirled and raced the short distance to the wagon. After flinging the precious wedding clothes in the bed, he climbed up to the seat. Fealdad didn't know what to do. If she ran after him, would her father take her back home? Would that be better than staying with a husband who had been cuckolded into marriage with a girl he didn't want? How could she stay with Eduardo when he expected someone pretty and talkative like Teresa?

"Come along." Eduardo gripped her elbow none too gently, steering her toward the buggy waiting in the shade. "We may as well get on home."

Straightening her shoulders, Fealdad went with her new husband, hoping he couldn't see how terrified she was. Anger still raged in his eyes. At this point, only her compliance would keep her from a beating. She knew that from years of experience.

"Why didn't you bring any clothes?" Eduardo's hold eased as he stopped by the buggy. She stared at the ground, knowing he waited for an answer, yet unsure how to communicate with him. She shrugged, then cringed inwardly, waiting for the slap that would follow.

"Is Diego right?" He lifted her chin until her tangled hair fell back, and their gazes met. "Can you talk?"

She shook her head. Fear clenched at her heart.

"Are we supposed to go get your things?"

She shook her head again.

His eyes narrowed. "You mean you have nothing to bring? No clothes except what you're wearing?" He raised a hand.

Her eyes widened. Panic swept through her. Although she tried not to, she flinched away from him. His grasp on her arm tightened.

"Get in." He released her long enough to grab her waist and lift her onto the seat.

Before she could react, he untied the horse and sat down beside her. She edged as far away from him as she could, hoping he wouldn't notice. His fingers were white on the reins. Did he want to throttle her or her father? A chill rippled down her spine. She couldn't help feeling sorry for Eduardo. He'd married her in good faith, thinking he was getting Teresa. Now, here he was stuck with an ugly bride who had no clothes and couldn't even talk. He must hate her. She closed her eyes. This wasn't how she pictured beginning a marriage.

The ride to Eduardo's house seemed long. The sprawling adobe house nestled among some large mesquite and cottonwood trees. Off to one side stood a barn, complete with a blacksmith forge at one end. Some corrals and a fenced pasture surrounded the buildings. A smaller house and a long, narrow building—possibly a bunkhouse—were farther away.

Eduardo pulled back on the reins, stopping the horse. He turned to Fealdad. "I can't call you Fealdad. I don't care what your parents named you. I can't do it. Do you have another name?"

All her life she'd only been Fealdad. She shook her head.

"Then I'll call you Chiquita, for now. As tiny as you are, that will be fitting." He climbed down and reached up for her. She tensed. Some of the anger seemed to have gone from him, but she knew how fast a man could be filled with rage.

"Go on in the house. I'll put the horse away. I've got business with my foreman." Eduardo started to turn away, then halted. He looked at her. She could see the tightness in his jaw again. "I'll not hold this against you. I knew how Diego was before I agreed to this marriage." His clipped words buffeted her and felt as painful as a physical blow. He swatted the horse on the rump. The animal snorted.

Fealdad watched him swing into the buggy and drive toward the barn. *Chiquita.* She rolled the name around in her head. All her life, she'd been called ugly and stupid. Eduardo called her tiny. He was right. He wasn't tall, but she only reached his shoulder. A seed of hope sprouted as she questioned if maybe she had misjudged him. Maybe he wouldn't be an angry drunk like her father. Maybe he wouldn't hate her.

⚜

The sorrel mare tried to dance away from Eduardo as he undid the harness. He knew she could sense his distress. He wanted to throw something or hit someone. He hadn't been this angry in a long time. How had he let Diego dupe him like this? Sure, he hadn't known Teresa well, but the day he met her, she had been laughing, talking, and staring at him with her big, dark eyes. That look reminded him of the flirtatious way his mother used to glance at his father. That was the main reason he'd agreed to the marriage and released Diego from his debt. He wanted to have what his parents had had.

Tying the horse to a ring in the wall of the barn, Eduardo began to brush her down. The familiar motion soothed the mare and, after awhile, him. He put his face against the reddish-brown neck and breathed deeply. The familiar animal scent calmed him further. Pushing away, he sighed, finished the brushing, and put the mare out in the pasture. She cantered away, nickering at the other horses standing in the shade of some mesquite trees.

He strode back into the barn and put the tack away. Sudden weariness washed over him, dulling the anger. This was his wedding day. He'd waited a long time for this day, and now it seemed like everything had gone wrong.

A low whicker of greeting came from a stall at the far end of the barn. *El Rey.* His new stallion, named King because he would be the start of a new line. He heralded the beginning of a longtime dream of Eduardo's.

"Hey, Boy." Eduardo rested one hand atop El Rey's withers as he stroked the baby-soft nose. El Rey sniffed his hand and whooshed a warm breath as if disappointed. Eduardo chuckled. "Spoiled, aren't you? I don't have a treat this time."

El Rey didn't seem to mind as Eduardo began to rub his ears. The horse leaned into Eduardo. Since the death of his father, Eduardo had only the animals to talk to. He'd never had other family. Although his foreman, Rico Gonzalez, had been around since Eduardo's father started the ranch, Eduardo hadn't been close to Rico. They could talk about business matters, but that was the extent of their relationship.

"I got married today, El Rey." Eduardo knew the quiet drone of his voice wouldn't be heard from any distance. "I now have a wife I didn't ask for, and I don't know what to do. She can't talk to me. I don't know how we'll ever communicate, but I gave my word. I can't go back on that." He ran his fingers through the horse's walnut-colored mane, working out a tangle.

"I'm not even sure what she looks like. She's so ragged, like one of your mares who's been run through the brush for days." Guilt stabbed him. Here he was comparing his bride to an animal, talking to a horse as if he expected advice on marriage from the beast.

The picture of Feal. . .Chiquita in her clean, but very worn, clothes rose in front of him like a specter. The dress hung on her thin frame. Her hair, washed but uncombed, fell across her face in matted tangles as if she were trying to hide. *Fealdad. That's what her family had always called her. Is she so ugly?* He didn't really know. When he'd lifted her chin to make her look at him, all he'd really seen were her golden-brown eyes, rich and sweet, the color of late summer honey. The thought warmed him. For a moment, he wanted to stalk back to the house and demand one more look.

Most of the time, she'd kept her scarf over her head. She was small. The top of her head barely came to his shoulders. Her hands, although work roughened, were fine boned and slender, with fingernails short and free of dirt. If she kept herself so clean, then why did she dress so ratty?

The sudden image of her ducking when he reached to grab Diego came to him. When Diego started to touch her, she flinched from him, too. Eduardo had been around enough mistreated animals to know what caused a person to do that. Someone had hit Chiquita often enough to make her wary. Was it Diego? His wife? Anger coursed through Eduardo at the thought of a child being treated that way. Did they punish her for not talking? The cause didn't matter. There were other ways of discipline than beating.

El Rey nudged his hand, and Eduardo patted the horse's neck. He had to admire Chiquita, though. If she had been beaten and was afraid, she still had a lot of spunk. Although she flinched and had ducked from him once, most of the time, she held herself straight, with an air of determination that impressed him. She wasn't one to run just because she was afraid. She had strength of character. He could see that in her reaction to Diego and her refusal to back down from him.

"Eduardo?" Rico's voice called from outside the barn.

"In here."

The foreman came into the barn carrying a cloth-covered platter. Eduardo gave El Rey a final pat and headed down the aisle to meet Rico.

"Pilar sent you some food." Rico held out the dish. "She says your bride won't have time to fix something, and she's cooking, anyway."

"Tell her thanks." Eduardo took the warm plate from Rico. Pilar, Rico's wife, did most of the cooking for the vaqueros who worked for Eduardo. Until now, Eduardo usually ate the evening meal with them. He found it hard to work all day and still have time to cook. Pilar never seemed to mind his joining them.

"I guess I'd better take this inside." Once again, guilt stabbed at Eduardo. He'd meant to clean the house before bringing his wife home. Instead she'd been welcomed by a mess. He'd only fired the stove enough to boil some coffee this morning. He'd been too nervous to eat. Even the dishes from yesterday's breakfast still waited. Last night, he'd been so tired, he hadn't found the strength to do much of anything.

"Have you heard from Lucio and Tomas?" The two ranch hands were out checking on some of the cows that were calving. Although most of his cattle were range-bred, Eduardo still liked to keep an eye on them. Between Apaches stealing them and wild animals preying on them, they bore close watching, especially during calving season.

Rico shook his head. "They should be back today. If not, I'll send Jorge to check on them."

The two parted. Eduardo turned toward the house. A tendril of smoke rose from the chimney. Chiquita must have started a fire. He quickened his pace, wanting to get to the house before she began to cook, since they already had a meal prepared. The smell of beef and chilies seeping through the cloth made his stomach rumble. The late spring sun warmed his back.

Opening the door, Eduardo maneuvered into the house with the awkward platter of food. Pilar must have sent enough for them and everyone on the ranch. He almost smiled. Did she think he married a giant of a woman who could eat like a horse? She would be in for a surprise. He doubted if someone the size of Chiquita could eat much. She probably ate more like one of the chickens than the larger animals.

Chiquita's back was to him when he entered the kitchen. She was studying something held in her hands and didn't act like she'd heard him. He eased the plate of food onto the table, noting with surprise the amount of work she'd done in the short time she'd been there. The floor was swept clean, water was warming for washing the dishes that were stacked by the washtub, and in passing through the main room, he could see that she'd straightened his mess there.

"You've been hard at work."

Chiquita gasped and whirled around. The object in her hands crashed to the floor, splintering into pieces. Her hands flew to cover her mouth. She started to step back, then her back stiffened. She stood her ground, staring at him through a fall of matted hair.

"No." A wave of anger swept over Eduardo. She'd broken his grandmother's statue of the Madonna and Child. His mother prized that over anything else in the house. As a boy, he was never allowed to touch the precious figure.

"Do you have any idea what you've done?" He could see her slight cringing as he shouted the words. Even knowing she expected him to hit her didn't dim his anger. He had very little of his family left, and she'd just ruined a part of that.

Chiquita knelt and began to gather the larger pieces with trembling fingers. Eduardo strode over and pulled her to her feet. "I'll clean this up." He snarled the words. Deep inside, he hated what he was doing to her, but he couldn't seem to stop. He could feel a shudder go through her. He loosened his grip on her arm. She stepped back. He bent down and picked up the largest piece of the sculpture, the child's face. Rage coursed through him. He flung the piece against the wall. The tiny features exploded.

Chiquita flinched. Her slender fingers clutched her skirt. She squared her shoulders again, as if knowing what would be coming next.

Chapter 3

E duardo." The kitchen door began to vibrate as someone pounded an urgent rhythm. "Eduardo, hurry. Come quick."

Dragging his gaze from the fear and resignation he could sense in his wife's stance, Eduardo rose and jerked open the door. Anger raced like lightning through his veins. "What?"

Rico bent over, gasping for breath. He pointed toward the bunkhouse on the other side of the barn. "It's Tomas. You have to hurry. There's been an accident. One of the cows gored Lucio. Tomas came to get the wagon to bring him home. Hurry." Rico didn't wait, but turned and sprinted back the way he'd come.

Stepping outside, Eduardo hesitated, his hand on the latch. He glanced back at Chiquita. He could barely make out the gleam of her tawny eyes through the hanks of hair over her face. Her fingers still clenched her skirt, but her shoulders were squared and her head held high. Remorse fought a battle with rage. Eduardo shook his head.

"I don't know when I'll be back. If you need anything, go to Pilar. You'll find her down at the cabin by the bunkhouse." Slamming the door, Eduardo raced after Rico. By the time he reached the barn, Jorge and Tomas had the wagon hitched and the horses saddled, including a fresh mount for Tomas. There would be no time to waste if they were to save Lucio.

"Where'd you leave him?" Eduardo shot the question at Tomas as they mounted.

"Up there, near the base of the mountains." Tomas pointed to the east.

"Tomas and I will ride ahead. Rico, bring the wagon. Jorge, stay here and keep an eye on the ranch."

"Wait." Pilar trotted from the house, a bulky package in her hands. She lifted the cloth-bound parcel up to Eduardo. "Bandages, medicine, some food. You may need them."

Eduardo secured the bundle behind him on the saddle and nodded his thanks to Pilar. Motioning with his head, he kneed his gelding and raced from the yard, Tomas at his side.

The horses were breathing heavily by the time Eduardo pulled them down to a walk. As much as he wanted to get to Lucio, he knew they couldn't risk over-tiring their mounts. Tomas pulled up beside Eduardo.

"What happened?"

"You know the narrow gorge—the one that's impossible to get to the bottom because it's so steep?" Tomas waited until Eduardo nodded. "One of the cows had her calf on the edge of the gorge. The minute the little one would roll over, down he would go. Lucio had me distract the mama while he went to pull the calf to a safer place."

Tomas wiped the sweat from his face with his bandana. "That cow was a mean one with horns a mile wide. She ran at me like one of the bulls in a bull-fight." He frowned. "The look in her eye should have killed me."

Eduardo gripped the reins until they dug into his hands. He wanted to shout at Tomas to get on with the story, yet he knew the importance of letting the events unfold in the young man's mind. Tomas pushed his sombrero back a little. His eyes mirrored the horror of the story he was telling.

"Lucio raced in and jumped from his horse. He grabbed the calf to pick it up. The edge of the gorge gave away. His foot dropped down. He almost went over the side with the baby. I could see him scrabbling to get up. I tried to keep the mama's attention, but the minute she heard her little one cry, she forgot about me. I've never seen a cow move so fast. Lucio didn't have a chance."

A look of panic crossed Tomas's face. Eduardo reached over and squeezed his shoulder. Tomas tried to smile, but only grimaced. "That cow, she hit him hard. I think the only thing that saved him was that she knocked him clear across the gorge so she wouldn't follow."

Eduardo nodded, seeing in his mind the steep gorge, only two feet wide, but about thirty feet deep.

"I jumped my horse across and got to him right away. That mama kept bellowing, running back and forth along the edge on the other side."

"Where did she get him?"

"Her horn caught him below the shoulder on the right side. If she'd caught him low or on the left, he would probably be dead right away."

A twinge of pain lanced through Eduardo's chest, as if he could feel Lucio's suffering. "Did you get the bleeding to stop?"

"No, Señor." Tomas shook his head, his face pale. "I took off my shirt and tore it to make a tight bandage. I don't know if Lucio was able to stay conscious. He was losing a lot of blood. We have to hurry." Tomas urged his horse to a faster pace.

The rest of the trip, they rode in silence. Despite his concern for Lucio, Eduardo couldn't help thinking about what had happened at home. Once more, his anger had gotten the best of him. He'd just made the determination to change because of Chiquita, then he'd gone in and thrown a fit over a piece of pottery that didn't really matter. Yes, his mother had prized the object, but he hadn't—at least, not until Chiquita had broken it.

He knew he'd scared her, yet she was willing to stand her ground. Admiration welled up once again. When this emergency was taken care of, he would have to sit down and talk with her. He frowned. How was he to do that? She couldn't talk. Could she read and write? He knew better than that. Very few ranch people were educated. His parents insisted he go to school in Tucson, making him one of the few learned people around here.

He would see. Maybe Chiquita would want to learn. In the evenings, he could teach her the letters. When she knew enough, they could communicate through writing, even though she couldn't verbalize anything. Surely she would want to do that.

"We're almost there." Tomas pointed ahead.

Glancing over his shoulder, Eduardo could see Rico on the wagon, far below and behind them. He must be pushing the team to even be in sight. Rico would come up a longer route to be on the same side of the gorge as they were. The trip home could be a little slower, but getting to Lucio fast could be the difference between life and death.

The cow lowed, a threatening sound, as she stood over her calf. Lowering her head, she shook her sharp horns at them, as if warning that they would get the same as Lucio if they dared to come close. Urging his horse to a canter, Eduardo jumped the narrow cleft, Tomas just behind him. Lucio lay on the ground, still and limp.

Swinging from the saddle, Eduardo ignored the angry sounds coming from the heifer across the gorge. He knelt beside his ranch hand. The ground around Lucio still looked damp and stained from his blood.

Eduardo's breath froze. He placed a hand over Lucio's heart, then bent over to place his ear on the man's chest. A slow, faint rhythm made him sigh in relief. Lucio still lived. Eduardo strode to his horse and retrieved the bundle Pilar sent with him. Untying the corners, he pulled out what he needed.

"Bring me a canteen."

Tomas, who had knelt beside him, jumped to obey. Eduardo ripped Lucio's shirt, exposing the wound so he could get a better look. The hole appeared enormous. The edges were ugly and torn. Lifting Lucio, Eduardo could see the place in the back where the cow hit him with such force that the horn went completely through. He'd lost a lot of blood, and it still seeped from the wound. Pulling the shirt away caused the flow to increase a little.

By the time Rico arrived with the wagon, Eduardo had done as much as he knew how to help Lucio. He was still unconscious, pale, and sweating. He'd moaned a few times as Eduardo worked, but he hadn't wakened. The bleeding had stopped and hopefully wouldn't start again on the trip home. Rico would drive as carefully as he could over the rough terrain.

Time would tell if the man would live. They needed to get him back to the ranch as quickly as possible, where Pilar could take over. She had considerable skill patching up wounded ranch hands. She even helped care for the injured animals. If Lucio lived through the journey home, he would stand a good chance of surviving.

"Should we chance the trip home or wait until morning?" Rico glanced at the late afternoon sun. They wouldn't be able to make it back before dark.

"I threw in some bedrolls. We could make Lucio comfortable. Maybe by morning, he'll be able to travel better."

Eduardo frowned. "By morning, fever could set in. If we get him back tonight, Pilar can start treating him for infection. I put on the leaves she sent to draw out the dirt, but that may not be enough."

Rico nodded. "You're right. If that wound gets infected, he'll never make it. Let's go."

By the time the lights of the ranch came into view, Eduardo's anger had long faded. Exhaustion and guilt weighed heavily on him. Hunger, too, gnawed at him. He hadn't eaten the food Pilar sent them earlier, although he hoped Chiquita had taken the time to eat. He wasn't sure how he could tell her he regretted his earlier actions, but he had to try. As soon as Lucio was settled, he would go home and face his bride.

⚜

When the door slammed shut, Fealdad felt the concussion throughout her body. She began to shake. Would Eduardo get over his anger, or would he beat her when he came home? Sometimes Papa told her he would beat her, then waited, as if the anticipation added to his satisfaction. He seemed to delight in making her agonize before he began to pummel her. Was Eduardo the same way? His anger had been strong enough.

She watched from the window as the horses and wagon disappeared from the ranch. The woman—Pilar, Eduardo called her—glanced at the house. Fealdad stepped to the side so Pilar wouldn't be able to see her. Right now, she didn't want to have this woman coming to the house. She felt as ugly and stupid as her name. *Chiquita*. Eduardo might call her that, but she didn't feel any different.

The smell of food tickled her nose. She walked to the table and lifted the cloth from the tray there. Her mouth watered as the appetizing smells wafted up. Reaching out, she brushed her fingertips against a warm tortilla. How she longed to eat just a little, but she couldn't. Eduardo would be even angrier to know that she was eating his food when she hadn't done her work. Brushing the cloth back into place, she turned to see if the water was hot enough to begin washing.

Hours flew by as she did the dishes, cleaned the floor, and gathered clothes to begin washing them the next day. Eduardo's house was much bigger than her parents' with its tiny area that barely held the family. Here, the rooms were spacious and plentiful. Besides the kitchen, main area, and bedroom, there were two other rooms with beds—evidently for company. She wondered if Eduardo had a lot of people who came to visit. Did he have family near here? She didn't know anything about her husband.

Much of the house was in a state of disorder, like it hadn't been given a good cleaning in a long time. Dust, thick enough to draw pictures in, covered most of the furniture. The unused bedrooms were the worst, but Fealdad knew she couldn't clean everything in one day. The rugs felt gritty as she walked across them.

Tomorrow, she would have to take them outside and beat them, along with doing the laundry.

In the bedroom that must be Eduardo's, Fealdad found a treasure: books. A shelf along the wall held more books than she thought were in the world. Glancing around to make sure she was alone, she crossed the room to stand before them. Reaching up to touch one, her fingers trembled. She stopped short of making contact. *Does Eduardo know how to read?*

For as long as she could remember, she'd wanted to learn to read. Her mother could read a little and had taught the other girls what she could. Fealdad never had time for the lessons, although her mother constantly scolded her for missing them. Once in awhile, she would hear the girls recite some of their letters and she would try them out, silently rolling the sounds across her tongue.

Heart pounding, Fealdad rested her hand on the shelf next to the books. How many were there? She gazed up and down the long row. More than she could count from the few numbers she'd picked up here and there. It would take her a week just to look through all of them.

A bold idea tempted her. Her heart began to pound. She brushed her hair back from her eyes. Glancing at the door, she made a decision. Trotting back to the kitchen, she peered out the window. There was no sign of wagons or horses returning in the gathering dusk. If the hurt man was far away, Eduardo could be gone all night. Even if they came back soon, surely she would hear the noise of their arrival.

Creeping back to the bedroom, she took a deep breath and tugged one of the precious tomes free. Opening the pages, she lifted it to her nose. The smell of paper and dust made her sneeze. A smile lifted the corners of her mouth for a brief moment. The letters were grouped together in tight rows, marching in two columns down each page. How did anyone decipher which letter was which? How could she ever sort them into words? Running her fingers over the print, she couldn't help wondering what message the writer wanted to convey.

Putting up the first book, she eagerly drew a second from its perch. This time, she gasped as the pages opened. Pictures greeted her. Drawings of animals, mostly birds and wildlife, captured her. She sank to the floor, held spellbound as she turned one leaf after another. The drawings looked as if they could walk out of the book at any moment, they were so lifelike.

Dark settled in. She went to find a lamp so she could continue with her discovery. Eduardo and his men hadn't returned. She assumed they'd traveled too far and wouldn't be back tonight. She knew she should decide where to sleep, but the magic pictures wouldn't let her go. Time flew past, and she ignored the sounds in the background because she was so caught up with the book on her lap.

A loud thump vibrated the floor. She jumped. Her heart began to hammer loud enough to drown out any other noise. She clutched the book to her chest. The bedroom door swung open. Eduardo stood there, his face haggard and grim.

"What are you doing?"

She knew he would swagger across the room in a moment and begin to strike her. She had to protect the book. She stood and backed away, fumbling for a place to put the volume of drawings. Eduardo began to stride toward her. For a moment, she felt a whimper of fear, then she straightened, waiting for the inevitable.

Chapter 4

Tiny flames of fury sped through Eduardo's veins as he approached Chiquita. If Diego were standing before him, he would wring the man's neck. How could anyone treat a child so poorly that she lived in fear of his every action? This had to stop now. He'd seen her flinch as he started across the room. She was waiting for him to begin hitting her.

Lord, help me say this the right way. I don't want to instill more terror. Eduardo took the book from Chiquita and set it on the edge of the bookshelf. Taking her hands in his, he could feel the trembling she couldn't control. He wanted to draw her into his arms, to let her know he wouldn't hurt her. She'd been wounded so many times—most likely by Diego—that Eduardo knew she wouldn't trust him.

With one hand, he swept back her tangled locks and lifted her chin. Her eyes were closed, her lips compressed so tight, they were nearly colorless. He could tell her teeth were clenched tight, as if she was ready for him to do his worst. Closing his eyes for a moment, he tried to calm his wrath at Diego, lest she think his anger was directed at her.

Letting out a deep breath, he traced the curve of her jaw with his thumb. A single tear welled up at the corner of her eye. Had Diego done this, too, just to torment her before the violence began?

"My father bought a horse once."

Her eyes snapped open, studying him, full of fear. Her breath came fast and ragged.

"He didn't need the mare, but he saw the owner mistreating her. The man would get her on a lead and beat her for no reason. Dad said he heard from others how the man would take out his frustration on the poor beast." Eduardo continued the soft caress along Chiquita's jaw.

"You would think that horse would be grateful to be away from such a terrible master." He frowned at the memory. "Instead, she would bare her teeth when we came near. Whenever we groomed her, she had to be well tied because she would always try to bite or kick. That mare was ruined because some man thought he could treat her as mean as he wanted. I worked with her for a long time before I could get her to trust me a little. She never could relax around anyone else."

A tear trickled down Chiquita's cheek. Eduardo caught it with his thumb, brushing the moisture away. She didn't seem to notice.

"A horse is an animal. You can't explain to an animal that you're different. We kept her for the rest of her life, treating her the best we could.

"I've seen the signs, Chiquita. Someone hasn't treated you right, but I want you to know that you're safe here. Maybe you can't talk, but I know you can hear." He sighed. "I know I have a temper, but I promise you I'll never hit you. My parents raised me to respect others, especially women."

Lowering her gaze, Chiquita turned her face from him, trying to hide. She looked like she wanted to be anywhere but here, with him.

Eduardo released her hand and stepped back. He knew she was still scared. He wanted to give her some room. *How can I make her understand? She's terrified, Lord. Help me make her see that I'm different from Diego.*

"I see you like books. Do you know how to read?" He motioned at the bookshelf.

Chiquita glanced at the volume he'd taken from her. Her fingers curled in her skirt, clutching the worn material. She gave her head a quick shake.

"Would you like to learn?"

Her eyes widened. Her gaze sought his for a moment, the golden depths glinting in the lamplight, before she looked away again. Eduardo wanted to grin in satisfaction. For that moment, he'd seen such a longing that he knew this was something she wanted without her telling him so.

"Maybe tomorrow evening, we'll try learning some of the letters. I'll see if I can rustle up a slate to use. For now, I'd like to get something to eat. It's been a long day."

The haunted look returned to Chiquita's eyes as she edged around him to the door. Once past, her steps continued, quick and determined. Eduardo followed her to the kitchen more slowly, wondering how he could make her understand she was safe here.

A crash reverberated through the air, followed by a small sob. Stepping into the kitchen, Eduardo noticed the slump of Chiquita's shoulders. The door of the stove hung askew. He groaned. He meant to fix that before getting married, but he hadn't had the time.

"Here, let me help."

Chiquita jumped. She whirled around, backing away from him. The embers from the fire in the stove flickered to life, flaring as Chiquita moved.

"Stop!" Eduardo leapt forward. He grabbed her up. She weighed almost nothing. He whirled her around. Greedy flames attached themselves to her skirt. The crackle and pop from the stove echoed like shots in the panicked stillness surrounding them. He beat the flames with his hand, hoping he wouldn't burn Chiquita. The heat stung, but he paid no attention.

Rolling the folds of the skirt over on the fire, Eduardo squeezed, smothering them out. Chiquita had stiffened like a board. Tremors ran through her body. Eduardo almost pulled her close, then realized she must be afraid.

"I'm not mad. Your clothes caught on fire. I was only putting them out before you got burned. Are you all right?" He frowned at the ragged skirt with the blackened hole down the length of it. Chiquita clutched the edges together.

"I'm not sure those clothes shouldn't be burned anyway. Let's eat. Afterwards, I'll see what I can find for you to wear, since you didn't bring other clothes." Turning back to the stove, Eduardo stirred the fire, then maneuvered the door closed. "This thing has been giving me fits. I'll try to fix it in the morning before I leave so you won't have to worry about the door falling off."

He glanced over his shoulder. Chiquita seemed frozen in place—a waif so thin and frail, he wondered how she could stand. She must have thought he was angry about the stove and was trying to beat her. All he wanted to do was save her from the fire.

"Did you have some of the food Pilar sent over earlier? I left the platter on the table."

She shook her head, her hair once again covering her face. Smelling the spicy scent of chilies, Eduardo opened the door of the warming oven to find the mounded plate of food. Grabbing a towel, he pulled out the dish.

"The plates are in that cupboard." He indicated the shelves nearest the sink. "I'll bring in some fresh water from the well while you get the table ready." Striding from the house with the bucket swinging from his hand, Eduardo could feel his frustration mounting. *Lord, how am I going to do this? I'm carrying on a one-sided conversation. She's terrified of me. I'm gonna be walking on eggshells to keep from startling her. I don't think I can do it.*

When he carried the sloshing bucket back into the house, Chiquita waited at the side of the table nearest the head chair. The table had one plate, fork, and cup resting where he usually sat.

"Where's your plate?"

Chiquita kept her gaze lowered. She shook her head.

"Did you eat earlier?"

She hesitated, then shook her head again.

The bucket clanked as he set it down and dropped the handle. Chiquita winced. Eduardo crossed to the cupboard and brought out another plate. In silence he readied a place for Chiquita so she would be seated close enough that he could fill her plate. The girl had to get some meat on her bones. Filling two glasses with the cool water, he plunked them down on the table.

"Sit down." He hadn't meant to growl, but he was getting fed up. *Wasn't she used to eating with the family? Did she have to eat scraps like a dog?*

Chiquita slid into the chair he held for her, careful to keep her scorched dress from gaping. She still trembled from the scare. Placing his hands on her shoulders, Eduardo ignored the way she flinched.

"Chiquita, you need food. I don't know why you didn't want to eat with me, but my parents always ate together. They enjoyed one another's company. I hope someday we can be the same way."

Seating himself, Eduardo bowed his head to pray. Chiquita already had her head bowed, but then she'd been that way most of the time he was around.

"Do you pray at mealtimes?"

She flicked a glance at him. She seemed puzzled, almost as if she didn't know what he meant.

Eduardo couldn't help sighing. "That's all right. I'll say the prayer, and you can listen."

A few minutes later, he lifted the covering from the fragrant meal. Although dried a little from the long wait to be served, everything looked delicious. He served Chiquita first, careful not to give her too much. He didn't think she would eat, but with a quick glance in his direction, she picked up her fork and began.

After their silent meal ended, Eduardo left Chiquita to clean up while he lit a lantern and went into one of the back rooms. Putting the light next to an old trunk, he ran his hand over the scarred surface before lifting the lid. A *whoosh* of musty lavender air greeted him, the scent reminding him so much of his mother, he almost looked around for her. Kneeling down, he began to remove the various items packed there. The things he wanted, he put in one pile; the rest, he packed back into the trunk. His mother wouldn't mind giving some of her things to her daughter-in-law. In fact, being able to do so would delight her.

Gathering the items he'd chosen, Eduardo picked up the lantern and headed back to the kitchen. Looking through his mother's things had stirred memories, reminding him of the loneliness that had become his constant companion since his parents' deaths. His heart ached. He wasn't sure marrying Chiquita would ease the ache at all.

❦

Chiquita dipped warm water from the reservoir at the side of the stove. The sight of scorched clothing made her wrinkle her nose. She could still feel the sting of the burns on her leg. She hadn't wanted Eduardo to know about them. The memory of him hitting her, trying to put out the flames, jarred her. At first, she'd thought he had finally behaved like her father. She'd done something so wrong, he couldn't help but beat her.

That hadn't been true. Instead, he'd put out the fire before she was hurt badly, then apologized as if the whole thing were his fault. He didn't blame her at all. He hadn't been mad about her looking at the books, either. A spark of excitement flared in her heart. Would he follow through with his suggestion? Would he teach her to read? Hope, even in the face of a lifetime of disappointments, wouldn't die.

Supper had been so hard. She'd never been allowed to eat with the family. Only after they were finished and gone from the room could she sit down and eat of the few leftovers. Sometimes her father would deny her that, saying she had too much work to do to waste time on eating. She didn't want to displease Eduardo, but the idea of eating at the same time he did was daunting.

He'd remained so silent. She'd wanted him to tell her if the *vaquero* who'd been hurt was all right. She wanted to know all about Eduardo and his family. Who was Pilar? What was she like? How Chiquita longed for her tongue to be loosened, but she knew that wouldn't happen. She didn't think she'd ever really talked.

Finished with the dishes and cleanup, Chiquita listened to the quiet of the house. Where had Eduardo gone? Moving close to the flickering light of the lantern, she pulled apart the scorched place in her skirt. Small blisters dotted the red area on her thigh. She shuddered. A few times over the years, Papa threatened to burn her. The thought always brought terror. If not for Eduardo's quick reaction, she might have been burnt badly enough to die. How could she ever thank him? Did this mean she could trust him?

She thought back to the early afternoon, right before Eduardo had to leave. When he threw the piece of pottery against the wall, she'd been sure he was just like her father. The rage in his eyes looked the same. Looking back, she couldn't help but think he might have resorted to violence if his foreman hadn't come to fetch him.

Then, when he'd come home, he'd acted like a different person. He'd been kind, seeming to know what she'd suffered with her father. She was confused. What was Eduardo— tender and compassionate or violent and hate-filled?

"Chiquita?" Eduardo called from the other room. She quickly pulled the material of her dress over the burns on her leg.

Hurrying to the main room, Chiquita stumbled to a halt. Eduardo stood by the desk in one corner of the room. Beside him lay a pile of clothing. He smiled and pointed to the clothes.

"These were my mother's. I know she would want you to have them." He lifted one of the dresses from the pile, letting the pale yellow material unfold. Chiquita gasped at the simple beauty. She'd never seen anything so pretty before. How could Eduardo expect her to wear something this nice when she worked all day?

"This one can be for the times when you go visiting or when we go to town." He shrugged. "That won't be often, but I remember my mother saying that every woman needed something beautiful, even if she didn't get to wear it much." He folded the dress and placed it on the desk.

"The darker ones will do for everyday work." Plucking up a light gray gown, he held it up for her to see. "My mother was about the same height as you, but she wasn't as slight. You'll probably need to alter them some." He hesitated. "Do you know how to do that?"

Chiquita nodded, amazed at his generosity. She'd never had more than one gown at a time, and Eduardo was offering at least five dresses at once. Her family would be amazed. Of course, her sisters and mother had more than she did, but none of them owned this many clothes.

Moving the pile of dresses, Eduardo stopped and looked uncomfortable. He cleared his throat. "I. . .um, got some of my mother's underthings for you." He gestured at the remainder of the stack. Under the tan, his face took on a ruddy tint.

"There are a couple of nightdresses, too."

Clearing his throat again, he straightened and faced her. "In the morning, I'll bring in enough water for you to take a bath while I'm gone." He looked stern, but not angry. "I've explained to you that I'm different from Diego. I want you to stop hiding." He strode across the room toward her holding something in his hand.

Chiquita's insides quivered. She wanted to flee. She stiffened and waited.

Eduardo stopped in front of her. "Look at me, Chiquita." He waited until she met his gaze. "This is for you to use tomorrow. I'm glad you've kept yourself clean, but I'll expect you to have your hair brushed when I get home tomorrow afternoon."

Chiquita glanced down at his hands. He held out a brush and mirror such as she'd never dreamed existed. Silver, inlaid with turquoise, gleamed in the light. Spots of tarnish stained the handle in places. Eduardo must have kept the set put away after his mother's death. She couldn't possibly use something so fine. What if she dropped the mirror and broke it? Would Eduardo be upset then? Would that be the time he would hit her? He'd been so angry this morning when she broke a simple figurine. What would he do over something this valuable?

She backed away, shaking her head, holding her hands palm outward to him. He understood. She could see the hurt in his eyes for a moment before anger took over. His jaw clenched. He spun around, took the set to the desk, and set them down with a clack that made her heart leap.

"I'm going to bed. You can stay in the bedroom down the hall. You don't have to stay with me until we get to know each other better." He stalked off to his room and slammed the door. She froze, wondering if the anger would grow until he sought her out to ease his rage.

Chapter 5

The sun shining in her eyes woke Chiquita the next morning. She stretched, enjoying the luxurious feeling of sleeping on a mattress covered with sheets and enough blankets to keep her warm. At home, she always slept on a thin pallet on the floor of the room she shared with her sisters.

She jerked upright. The sun was shining. She was late. Eduardo would be expecting her to fix coffee and his breakfast. After throwing back the covers, Chiquita stumbled from the bed and searched for her clothes. She'd carried Eduardo's mother's things into the room and had worn the simplest nightdress. Picking up her own scorched clothing, she wrinkled her nose. The burn spot in the skirt gaped open. She couldn't wear this again. She glanced at the pile of beautiful gowns. How could she ever wear one of those?

Discarding her dress, she ran her hand over the colorful pile of garments. Treating them with care, she chose the plainest brown one and put it on. The length would have been right, but the rest of the dress sagged. She could easily end up tripping over the hem if she wasn't careful. No help for it; she would have to wear this for now. Later in the day, she could take the time to make the fit better.

Chiquita rushed to the kitchen, holding up the skirt to keep from falling. A pot of coffee stood on the back of the stove. A skillet and dirty dishes showed that Eduardo had already eaten and gone. She couldn't feel his presence in the house. She closed her eyes and moaned. He would be furious by the time he came home tonight. How could she have slept late? She needed to make a good start of this marriage, or she would be doomed to a life of pain from him being angry with her.

Stretching up, she peered out the window at the barn and other outbuildings. They appeared deserted. He'd mentioned yesterday having to go take care of some business. He had planned to leave early, so she was too late to try to make up for oversleeping. She sighed and turned to the work at hand, ignoring the twinge of hunger in her stomach. There was too much to do to take time for eating. Perhaps if she spent the day working as hard as she could, he wouldn't be so enraged with her tonight.

A plan began to develop in her mind. She would work hard all day, then fix a supper that would wait for Eduardo's return. Then she would bathe, comb her hair, and don the yellow dress that belonged to his mother. Husbands must be different from fathers. Maybe if she made herself neat as well as clean, he wouldn't be so repulsed like Papa and would be merciful. She would never be beautiful, but perhaps she could be pleasing.

"Eduardo, my friend, come inside where we can talk out of the sun." Antonio Soza strode from his hacienda to greet Eduardo. They were neighbors, although their ranches were several miles apart. Eduardo often consulted with Antonio on matters of business.

"Pepito, take Señor Eduardo's horse for some water." Antonio dispatched the young boy with a wave of his hand. "Come, my friend. Maria will bring us something refreshing."

The dim interior of the adobe house felt cool after the warmth of the day. Eduardo removed his hat and wiped the beads of sweat from his forehead. A cool drink would be welcome.

"So, I'm surprised to see you." Antonio tugged at his full beard as he led Eduardo into his living room. He motioned to a chair. Eduardo sat down, placing his hat beside him. Antonio grinned. "When I sent the message for you to come over today, I didn't realize you were getting married yesterday. Congratulations, my friend. When am I to meet the lucky bride?"

They were interrupted by Maria, one of Antonio's helpers in the house. She brought them glasses of lemonade. Eduardo took a long drink of the tangy liquid before he spoke. "I married one of Diego Garcia's daughters."

Antonio's heavy eyebrows arched. "Why did you do that?"

"As you know, Diego had a debt to pay. Now he doesn't, and I have a wife."

"I don't know. I can't think of anything good to say about that man, so you watch yourself." Antonio frowned. "A lot of us would like to know where he came up with the money for his ranch. He doesn't work, he isn't wealthy, yet he could afford land that the rest of us struggled to get. Something doesn't smell right."

"I know. My father used to say the same thing."

"I've met Diego's daughters. Which one did you marry? Teresa? She's the oldest. I seem to remember the others would be too young."

Eduardo explained how Diego tricked him into marrying his other daughter, the one who couldn't speak.

"I've seen this girl before." Antonio stroked his beard, his brow furrowed. "Diego came over here with his family a couple of times when the girls were younger. They called this girl Fealdad. Am I right?"

Eduardo nodded. "I refuse to call her by that name. She can't tell me anything else to call her, so I chose Chiquita because she's so small."

"That's a good name." Antonio nodded. "She was always a tiny thing and very pretty. I don't know why they referred to her as ugly. Diego and Lupe, his wife, used to treat her differently than the others. I asked Diego about it once. He said she was rebellious, and that was the only way to control her. I never saw the rebellion myself. She seemed to be quiet and obedient any time they were here." He smoothed his hair back. "The last time they came as a family, I saw Diego hit her for no reason. I confronted him and told him to stop. We had quite a fight. The poor girl looked terrified. I'm afraid Diego may have taken out his rage on her. The thought makes me sick."

Antonio rubbed his hands down his face. "I've often thought that I should have done something. A father has a right to raise his children as he sees fit, but to beat them for nothing is beyond reason. I didn't know what I could do, though. I planned to keep an eye on the situation, but Diego never brought them back. She was such a young girl then, just a little waif."

"From the way she acts, Diego didn't stop abusing her. She's a brave one. She stands her ground, but I can tell she's afraid," Eduardo said.

Antonio's gaze seemed to bore into Eduardo. "Be gentle with her. I believe she'll be a treasure if you do. She isn't like the rest of that family. Even back then, there was something a little different about her."

Taking another sip of his lemonade, Eduardo pushed thoughts of Chiquita away. He didn't want to remember the way he'd behaved yesterday. He'd been so ashamed, he'd left home earlier than planned so he didn't have to face her. If Diego had mistreated her for so many years, how would she ever manage to be around him with his temper? This morning, before he left, he'd gotten angry with Jorge for a minor mistake that shouldn't have mattered. He sighed. That was another one he would have to apologize to when he returned home. He set the empty glass on the floor beside his feet.

"You asked me over for a reason, Antonio. I know it wasn't to discuss my marriage."

Antonio chuckled. "That's true. I wanted to talk cattle." He leaned forward, a sudden eagerness in his face. "I know you've sold some livestock to the cavalry. Right now, they're the best market in Arizona for our beef. Have you heard the news?"

Eduardo shook his head. "What news?"

"The government is going to start buying cattle from more than one person. So far, James Patterson has had a monopoly on the trade with them. He buys most of the cattle from Henry Hooker." He waved a hand as Eduardo started to protest. "Yes, I know, he's bought a few head of my beef, too, but not enough. Now, though, we have a better chance."

"My friend at the fort, Conlon Sullivan, told me it might be a good idea to begin building up my herd. This must be the reason. I haven't seen him for awhile, or I'm sure he would have given me the news."

"I have something I want you to read and consider." Antonio crossed to a desk and brought Eduardo an eastern newspaper. "This article is about a breed of cattle developed in England. They're not as rangy as ours are. They put on weight easily. According to this article, we could vastly improve our herds by bringing in a few of these bulls."

Eduardo glanced through the article and frowned. "I don't know. Our *criollos* are tough. They're bred for the desert. They forage and can live among the cactus."

"But, Eduardo, the *criollos* are little more than horns and hide. The cavalry wants some meat to feed their troops." Antonio laughed. "I think Herefords are the cows of the future."

Eduardo grinned. "If we bring in some of these fancy bulls, they'll be just like the fancy eastern men that come out here. They won't know how to adjust."

"You could be right, but I'd still like to try it. I think if we can improve our cattle, we'll have a chance to do better in the market. We might even consider shipping some to California. There's always a need for beef there." Antonio glanced at the door. "Ah, here's Maria to tell me lunch is ready. Join us, and then I can show you the changes I've made since you were here last."

After lunch, Antonio gave Eduardo a tour of the small chapel he'd built behind his house. He told of plans to build a schoolhouse someday so that the ranchers in the area would be able to get their children an education. As Eduardo was mounting to leave, Antonio reminded him once again to read the paper about the Hereford bulls.

"I hadn't thought about improving the cattle, but I have thought about the horses. The cavalry doesn't like our smaller mounts. They have so much gear to carry, they want a taller, sturdier horse. When you have the time to visit, I'll show you my new stallion. He's the first in a new line." Eduardo couldn't keep the pride from his voice. He touched the brim of his hat and cantered from the yard. The sun hung low in the west. He would have to hurry to be home by mealtime. The road home was a long one.

⚜

The warm water felt marvelous to Chiquita's aching muscles. She'd done more than a day's work today. She hadn't seen or heard from Eduardo all day. Instead, she'd washed clothes and cleaned the house, which most likely hadn't been cleaned in ages. Out behind the house she'd found a clothesline, so she'd taken the time to beat the rugs before doing the laundry. The whole house smelled fresher.

A pot of beans bubbled on the stove. Fresh tortillas were folded in a towel, keeping warm for Eduardo. Now, all she had to do was make herself more presentable. Her resolve from this morning was wavering. How could someone so ugly ever be presentable?

She found a cake of scented soap among the things Eduardo had laid out for her. The sweet, flowery smell filled the room. Never had she bathed with something so enchanting. The thought of pleasing Eduardo warmed her. She couldn't help but dream that he would like her so much, he never yelled or hit her. She sighed and began to scrub her skin. That was only a fantasy and would never happen.

By the time she climbed from the tub, the water had cooled. The sun outside dipped low, almost behind the mountains. Eduardo would be home soon, and she had to do something about her hair. He'd said he wanted it brushed.

Before bathing, she had done a quick job of taking in the side seams on the yellow dress. Now she slipped it on. The gown fell just right, as if it had been made for her. Crossing to the table, she touched one finger to the inlay on the silver brush. How she wished she had a different one to use! This one might be too fragile. She couldn't bear to ruin Eduardo's mother's special things.

Leaving the mirror alone, Chiquita picked up the brush, careful to wrap her fingers tight around the handle. She left the mirror face down. All these years, Papa told her so many times how fortunate she was to not have to see herself. She believed him and couldn't bear to look.

The mat of tangles resisted her efforts, but she was stubborn. Little by little, they came free. By the time she finished, her hair had dried. It hung to her waist, not as thick as Teresa's, but still full enough. The sides showed a slight wave when they fell forward. Would Eduardo like her hair this way? She felt so vulnerable without the tangles to hide behind.

Outside, a horse whinnied. Chiquita hurried to the window. Eduardo rode up to the barn and dismounted, acting stiff from a long ride. Rico met him, and they spoke for several minutes. She wondered if they talked about the injured man and wished she knew if he was okay. Eduardo led his horse into the barn. He would be inside soon, expecting a meal. After being gone all day, he would be hungry.

Chiquita's hands shook as she put the bowls on the table. Earlier, she'd brought in fresh water for drinking. She ladled some in glasses and put them near the bowls. Peering out the window, she still couldn't see Eduardo coming. Maybe he didn't want to face her. Maybe he was still angry with her for sleeping so late and would come in raging mad.

Her hands shook. She walked back to her room to brush her hair one more time. She glanced at the mirror. Should she look? What if she were as repulsive as her father said? How could she face Eduardo? How could she stand the thought of him being saddled with an ugly wife when he was so handsome?

His lean face swam before her. Dusky brown eyes, the color of the road after a rainstorm, twinkled in her memory. He had hair darker than mesquite bark and a mustache that curved in a graceful arc around his mouth. She felt the burning in her cheeks. When he smiled at her yesterday, he'd been the most handsome man she'd ever seen. She wanted to see him smile some more.

"Chiquita?" The kitchen door slammed shut. Heavy footsteps echoed in the quiet house. Her heart pounded. Would he be angry? She forced her legs to move. The walk down the hallway to the living room felt like miles.

"Chiquita, are you ready to eat? I'm starved. I've been. . ." Eduardo stopped talking as he turned and saw her standing near the hall. His eyes widened. His mouth dropped open. In two quick strides, he crossed the room to stand before her. Chiquita forced herself not to flinch.

Eduardo cupped her cheek and tilted her head until she met his eyes. He stared in silence. She wanted to groan. This meant she was as ugly as Papa said. She stepped back, breaking Eduardo's hold. Tears brimmed in her eyes, threatening to spill over. She turned to run and hide. In midstep, Eduardo gripped her from behind. She was trapped.

Chapter 6

Breathing came hard for Eduardo. He felt like a drowning man, gasping for air, as he stared at the vision across the room from him. When he arrived home, he couldn't believe the change in his house. The air smelled clean and fresh as a spring day. Everything sparkled from the work she'd done. He had no idea how she'd accomplished so much. Then, when he turned and saw her, he became speechless, as tongue-tied as a young boy. He didn't remember moving, but suddenly he stood in front of her, cupping her cheek in his hand.

The yellow dress was perfect for her. Her creamy, tan skin took on the tinge of ripened wheat, and her eyes sparkled with a look of shy pleasure. Her hair hung to her waist. The soft tendrils he touched were the same color as cocoa. For the first time, he could clearly see her face. She had an adorable, slight cleft in her chin and a small mole above her lip on the left side. Her neck was long, straight, and slender; her whole frame, willowy.

He cupped her cheek, needing to touch her. She seemed so fragile, yet with enough spirit to give her an uncommon strength. Tears filled her eyes. She pulled away and took a step back. She wanted to run. Why? Did she believe him to be unhappy with her? He couldn't let her go. Grabbing her arm as she turned, he pulled her to him.

"Chiquita." His voice came out in a husky whisper. "Don't run." He eased her around to face him.

She looked up at him, her eyes sparkling with tears. He could see the doubts there and the underlying fear. "Chiquita, you aren't beautiful." She looked down and tried to pull away before he could finish. "Wait." He put his arms around her to keep her from going. A tremor shook her.

"Let me finish. You aren't beautiful—you're exquisite." He ran his hand through her fine hair. Up close, in the light, he could see golden highlights woven throughout. Soft waves curled along the edges. The scent of lavender soap drifted up to him.

Chiquita's eyes were enormous, the tears shimmering. She had such a look of hope, it broke his heart. Once more, anger at Diego welled up inside him; but he pushed the rage away, lest Chiquita sense his feelings and think they were directed toward her.

"I don't know how your family could have called you that horrid name. I've never seen any girl as pretty as you." He smiled. Her eyelids drifted almost closed, as if she were enjoying the caress of his hand over her hair. Had anyone ever touched her in gentleness? He doubted that.

His stomach let out a loud growl. Chiquita's eyes widened again. He chuckled. "I can smell the beans and tortillas. If I don't get to eat them soon, I'll be too weak to walk to the table."

A ghost of a smile lifted Chiquita's lips. He released her, took her hand, and led her into the kitchen. Eduardo shook his head. He couldn't seem to quit staring at her. Whoever would have thought that tangled mess of hair hid such beauty? He was beginning to believe he'd gotten a gem in this marriage. God had been looking out for him, even though he doubted that yesterday.

After supper, Eduardo went back to search again through his mother's things while Chiquita cleaned up in the kitchen. He thought he remembered his mother packing away the old slate that he used to practice writing the alphabet. Near the bottom of the trunk, he found the things he needed. He grinned. Tonight, he planned to begin teaching Chiquita to read. She seemed to have few blessings in her life, and judging by the look in her eyes yesterday, she would consider learning to read a wondrous gift.

When he came out of the room, Chiquita was seated in the living room with one of his mother's old dresses, preparing to take in the seams. She glanced up as he came into the room.

"Oh, no, you don't." He strode to her chair, took the sewing from her, and pulled her up. She cringed, the look of fear haunting her eyes. Eduardo sighed inwardly. He'd forgotten how fragile she was. The slightest wrong move had her thinking he was like her father. He could see that in the way she reacted.

"Hey, what did I tell you?" He stroked his thumb over her silken cheek. "I won't hurt you. I want you to come over to the desk with me. I'll bring another chair, and we'll start your lessons."

Her eyes widened. She glanced at the things in his hand.

His lips twitched. "Yep, you guessed it. You're going to learn to read. Every evening, we'll spend a little time practicing." He pursed his lips. "Of course, I'm not a teacher, and it will be harder when you can't talk." He gave a slight smile. "But we'll manage. That is, if you want to."

She nodded. Her hair shimmered in the light. Her eyes shone, the closest he'd seen her to happy since she'd arrived. They sat side by side at the desk. He began to show her the letters. She caught on fast, copying them, her head bent forward in concentration.

Eduardo found himself distracted by the perfect curve of her jaw and the slight blush on her cheeks. When she glanced up at a long pause, he felt his face warm. He cleared his throat, trying to recall where they were. Chiquita gave him a puzzled look. She couldn't understand his hesitation. He knew she'd never had anyone admire her before. She probably couldn't fathom why anyone would.

"I think that's enough for tonight." Eduardo almost smiled at the look of disappointment on Chiquita's face. "If we try to do too much at one time, you could get confused. Have you ever heard the Bible read?"

Her brows drew together. She shook her head.

Eduardo rose and stretched. "Why don't you go back to your sewing, and I'll spend some time reading aloud. My father used to read the Bible to us at night and sometimes from other books, too. If you'd like, we can do that."

A look of amazed anticipation made Chiquita's face glow. While he found the place he wanted to read, she hurried to pick up the dress. When she gave him a puzzled glance, he understood and explained why he wasn't starting at the beginning of the book. He turned to the book of John and began to read.

🌵

Smoothing the soil around the seeds she'd planted, Chiquita sat up and stretched her back. She couldn't believe how much her life had changed in the last week, since she'd married Eduardo. For the first time, she was beginning to relax and enjoy living.

She still feared Eduardo. Often during the last week, he'd lost his temper over little things that had gone wrong. On each occasion, she'd been terrified he would begin to hit her. She tried hard not to show her fright because just knowing she was afraid used to give her father satisfaction as he hit her. So far, Eduardo hadn't been violent with her at all, but she didn't trust him to continue that way. Papa had shown her how men treated women.

In the evenings, Eduardo continued to teach her the alphabet. She knew all the letters now. Last night, he taught her a couple of simple words. Then, when he got out the Bible to read, he let her look on the page and find the words she learned. She'd been so excited, she could hardly sit still. Soon she would be able to read by herself.

The ache to be able to read had grown over the past week. Growing up, there had never been any mention of the Bible. Mama had a small niche outside the house. She and her other daughters went there to pray sometimes, but Chiquita had never been allowed to join them. Now, Eduardo read her fascinating stories about a man named Jesus who lived long ago. She'd never heard of Him or the miracles He did. She couldn't wait to hear the end of the story of His life. Eduardo explained that the Bible was about Jesus and His love for all people. Although she couldn't imagine Him loving her, she wanted to find out what happened to Him.

She patted the last of the seeds and dipped water from the bucket to pour over them. Her braid tumbled over her shoulder, and she flipped it back, relieved to finally have her hair in manageable form. Two days earlier, Eduardo had taken her outside to show her the overgrown garden plot his mother once tended. He brought out seeds that were old but should still grow. She'd spent most of the time since then planting and watering. When he found out she wanted to put in the garden, despite the lateness in spring, Eduardo enlisted the aid of his ranch hands, Jorge and Tomas, to turn the earth with shovels. Chiquita loved the feel of the dirt spilling through her hands and the excitement when the sprouts began to grow.

"I see you're done with the planting."

Chiquita jumped and whirled around to face Eduardo. Her breath caught in her throat. Would she always fear his approach? Could she ever learn to trust him?

"Here, let me help with that." Eduardo took the bucket from her and finished watering the newly sown seeds. "There you go." He nodded at the rows. "You've done a fine job. I look forward to the produce. I've depended on Pilar for too long."

Eduardo headed for the house, and Chiquita followed. Glancing at the hills, she couldn't help wondering at the feeling she'd had of being watched. She wondered if Eduardo felt it, too. She wasn't used to him being home this early. He usually spent most of the day on the range with Rico or with one of the hands, checking the cattle or seeing to the horses. The sun was sinking in the sky, but there were still at least three hours of daylight. She hadn't even started to fix dinner. What if he expected his meal early? She fought the panic welling up inside.

"I thought maybe you would like to see the rest of the ranch buildings. You've been here a week and still haven't met any of the hands or Pilar. She's anxious to meet you."

Her heart pounded at the thought of meeting other men. Even getting to know Pilar didn't interest her. After the way her mother and sisters treated her, she had no idea what to expect from this woman. She scrubbed vigorously at the washstand, uncertain how to let Eduardo know she didn't want to meet anyone else. She couldn't hurt his feelings. What if her unwillingness to meet his employees made him angry?

Smoothing the wisps of hair that had pulled free from her braid, Chiquita faced Eduardo, trying her best to smile. As they walked across the yard, Eduardo caught her hand in his. She flinched, wanting to pull away, but she knew that wouldn't be right. Eduardo hadn't hurt her so far. Why couldn't she relax and enjoy his company? He was bright and interesting. He was certainly handsome, yet something held her back. She knew it was his tendency to lose his temper. No matter how hard she tried, she couldn't trust someone who exploded in rage over every little thing that upset him. Papa had done that.

"I want to tell you about the plans I have for this ranch." Eduardo nodded at a pasture with mares and long-legged foals. "My father always raised cattle and had a few horses for use on the ranch. I wanted to spend time to improve our mustangs, and I have. We now supply the cavalry in Tucson with quite a few of its mounts."

Chiquita watched the mares cropping grass while their babies cavorted and raced around the pasture in total abandon. They weren't big horses, but they were well put together. They looked much stronger and sturdier than her father's nags.

"The lieutenant at Fort Lowell in Tucson, who's a friend of mine, spoke with me about what the cavalry needs. These horses, while sturdy and good at working cattle, aren't as good for the men who need to carry enough provisions for two weeks. They need mounts that will carry them and all of their necessities."

He turned toward the barn and tugged on her hand. She followed him into the dim interior. The place smelled strongly of horse, hay, and the leather from the tack.

"This is El Rey." Eduardo stopped beside a stall at the end of the aisle. The horse inside nickered and thrust his head over the wooden partition. "He will be the start of a new line of horses for us." Pride warmed Eduardo's tone. He rubbed the horse's head, running his hand under the dark mane.

"When I bought him a few months ago, I also bought a mare of this same breed. She gave birth to his foal this week. They're out in the pasture to the west. I'll take you to see them after you meet Pilar and the boys."

Chiquita had never seen such a beautiful horse. His liquid brown eyes stared down at her. His muzzle was dark, but the rest of his coat was the color of light copper. The sunlight coming down the passageway made him gleam like fire. His mane and tail were deep brown, and his face had a blaze of white. Although taller than the mares in the pasture, El Rey appeared as graceful as a dancer. Chiquita couldn't help stroking the soft muzzle. His warm breath feathered across her hand while the few whiskers tickled her palm.

She glanced up to find Eduardo watching her. She lowered her hand and stepped back. Maybe he didn't want her to touch such a valuable animal. His grip on her hand became firm. He pulled her back to him.

"You don't have to be afraid—of him or of me."

She could hear the twinge of hurt in his voice and regretted moving away. All her life, she'd wanted to ride, but she hadn't been allowed near her father's horses. Oh, how she wanted to ask Eduardo if he would teach her to ride.

As if he understood her thoughts, Eduardo spoke. "Have you ever ridden?" She shook her head. Her hand crept up once more to touch the stallion's nose.

"Then we'll have to change that. We're pretty busy right now, but by next week, I should be able to take the time to show you how. Once you learn, you can go with me on shorter rides. Would you like that?"

She drew in a sharp breath. This man was full of miracles. First he gave her new clothes, then he taught her to read, and now he offered to teach her how to ride a horse. She wanted to pinch herself and wake up from the dream before she believed it was real.

"Señor! Señor Villegas." A young man galloped up to the barn and jumped from his horse. His breath came in gasps.

"What is it, Tomas?" Eduardo strode down the aisle, still holding Chiquita by the hand. She trotted alongside.

"The foal." Tomas panted, trying to catch his breath "The newest one. You must come."

"What's happened?" Eduardo's grip on her hand grew tight. She could see the anger building and wanted to leave, but couldn't.

"It's dead, Señor. A puma must have found the foal lying down and killed him while the mama was grazing."

"Dead?" Eduardo glared at Tomas as if the death were his fault. He gripped her hand like a vise. She wanted to cry out, but she knew if she did, Eduardo's rage would turn on her. "The cougar came that close to the buildings?"

"Si, Señor." Tomas backed away a few steps. "Rico says you must come to the pasture." He turned and trotted away.

The set of Eduardo's shoulders and the clenching in his jaw spoke louder than words. Now that they were alone, he would unleash his wrath on her. She tensed, fighting the urge to lean as far away from him as his hold allowed.

Chapter 7

Furious, Eduardo watched Tomas gallop back toward the pasture where Rico would be waiting. If he had the puma there, he would wring its neck with his hands. He could almost feel the bones crunching. He heard a moan. The sound seemed to pierce the wall of his wrath, and he turned. Chiquita stood beside him, her face pale, her golden eyes dark with fear.

He glanced down. Remorse washed away some of the anger as he realized he'd been squeezing her hand. "Chiquita." He gasped as he looked at her fingers mashed together in his. He let go, intending to look and see if he'd hurt her, but she leaped away. Backing against a stall, she began to edge down the walkway to the door, her enormous eyes following his every move.

"Chiquita, wait." He stretched out his hand to her. She flinched and moved back another pace. Eduardo let his hand drop to his side. He knew he could reach her before she got too far, but she would believe he was coming to beat her. If he was to ever win her trust, he would have to learn patience. The ache in his heart over the loss of this foal was pushed to the background, replaced by the guilt of what he'd done to his wife.

"I know I hurt you. I'm sorry." Eduardo twisted the tip of his mustache. "I am not a man who causes women pain. In my anger at the puma for killing this colt, I forgot I still held your hand." He stopped. She eased a few more steps toward the door.

"Go on to the house, Chiquita. I'll be in after awhile." He wanted to say they would talk about this and clear the air, but she couldn't talk. How would they ever be able to communicate if all she did was look at him with those doelike eyes? She usually didn't even nod her head; she just watched him.

He waited as his wife slipped out of the barn and hurried across the yard to the house. Striding to his horse he'd hitched outside, Eduardo could feel the rage building. He'd put a lot into these horses. Purchasing the pregnant mare and the stallion was an investment. He needed this foal to build his herd. He couldn't afford to have some hungry cat preying on his livestock.

Rico, Tomas, and Jorge were huddled around the torn carcass when he rode up. Eduardo dismounted, his horse jittery as he caught the smell of puma and death. Holding the reins in a firm grip, Eduardo moved to where Rico stood.

"Tomorrow, we'll plan to spend the day in the saddle. I want to find this cat. I can't afford to lose more stock." His clipped words caused the men to step away from him. He ignored that and continued. "Pilar can watch Lucio, can't she?"

Rico nodded. "He's doing much better. So far, he doesn't have any infection and should be back to work in a few days."

"Leave the foal here. If the cat comes back to feed during the night, we'll get a much fresher trail for the dogs to follow. We'll all meet at first light and begin tracking." Eduardo swung up on his restless horse. The gelding danced sideways, wanting away from the terrifying scents.

Taking a last look at his ruined dreams, Eduardo headed home. He had some work to do around the stable before he went to the house. He also wanted to look in on Lucio and talk to Pilar about going to see Chiquita tomorrow while they were gone. Maybe Pilar could make her understand he wasn't a monster.

Even though rage still coursed through him, he determined to be as gentle as possible with Chiquita. He would teach her as he usually did and read the Bible. Maybe she would begin to see that he hadn't meant to hurt her. She sure didn't want to listen to his apology.

※

The chilly dawn air sent a shiver through Eduardo as he stepped outside the next morning. The lantern swinging at his side threw a ring of light around his feet as he headed to the barn to begin seeing to the gathering of the supplies they would need. He wanted to make sure the horses and dogs were fed and ready by sunrise. Tomas and Jorge were probably already seeing to the chores, but he wanted to make sure. Today, this puma would die. He couldn't have one coming so close to the house. Not only were the foals in danger, but the people could be, as well.

"Mornin'." Eduardo greeted Tomas as he entered the barn. The sleepy-eyed young man was forking hay to the horses. Small wisps of chaff drifted in the air, illuminated by the glow of the lantern. Eduardo hung the bail on a hook and went to check on El Rey. The stallion greeted him with a soft whicker.

Jorge came out of the back of the barn, where they milked the cow. He carried two pails, one two-thirds full of milk, the other about half full. He handed the smaller bucket to Eduardo to take to Chiquita while he took the other to Pilar to use for the men's breakfast.

"I think soon the other cow will drop her calf. Then we will have more milk to share," Jorge informed Eduardo before leaving the barn.

The eastern sky had paled to gray by the time Eduardo got back to the house. He carried the milk inside. The handle thumped as he released it. Chiquita stood at the stove, stirring the eggs. Tortillas warmed at the side. Eduardo's stomach growled. He'd been pleased to find Chiquita was an excellent cook. After the first day, she was always up and fixing his coffee and breakfast when he came back in from doing chores.

"Good morning." He tried to ignore the way she flinched when he came near. Their school lesson hadn't gone well last night. She'd been so afraid of him, that when he finally did get her to sit by him, she trembled the whole time. He'd ended up fighting his anger and frustration at her lack of belief that he wouldn't hurt her. Rather than show more ire, he ended the session early and read to her from the Bible for awhile before going to bed early.

"That smells good." He took a deep breath. "We'll probably be gone all day after the cougar. Stay close to the house until we come home. I don't like the idea of one of these cats coming so close to the buildings. It might be injured and looking for easy prey, so don't go out, all right?"

Chiquita nodded and dished up his breakfast. She began to strain the milk while he ate. He could see the dark circles under her eyes. She hadn't slept well last night. Did she think he would come in the middle of the night and start beating her?

Lord, I have no idea how to make her understand that she isn't the cause or the satisfaction for my anger. Shame swept over him like a wave. He remembered his mama telling him uncontrolled anger was a sin. When he'd thrown fits as a boy, she used to read a verse from the book of Ephesians about anger. Back then, he'd managed to contain his temper, but since the death of his parents, wrath became easier than peace. He'd allowed fury to replace the joy in his life. He didn't smile much at all anymore. He couldn't recall the last time he'd truly laughed.

Finishing his meal, Eduardo could see the pink on the horizon. The sun would be up anytime. He carried his dishes to the washtub, trying to not feel hurt over the way Chiquita moved away from him. "I'm heading out." He lifted his hat from the hook. "I'll see you this evening."

※

Watching Eduardo stride across the yard to where Rico and the two hands waited with the horses and dogs, Chiquita couldn't help rubbing her hand. She hadn't wanted Eduardo to know it still hurt. Maybe it was only the memory that hurt. He hadn't squeezed hard enough to break anything. The fear kept her awake most of the night.

She frowned. She'd planned to go up on the hill today, where she'd seen some yucca cactus. They needed some soap, and the yucca made the best. The men thundered out of the yard, followed by the loping dogs. Surely, if they were chasing the cougar, the cat wouldn't dare come anywhere near the house. It would head for the hills to hide from the baying of the hounds. Gathering the cactus should be safe by this afternoon. Besides, she would be in sight of the house at all times.

In midmorning, a knock sounded on the door. Chiquita froze, the cleaning rag dangling from her hand. Who could be here? Maybe if she were quiet, they would leave. She didn't want to see anyone. The knock came again, followed by a woman's voice calling her name. Chiquita crossed to the door, her heart in her throat.

A middle-aged woman stood outside. Her face, brown and creased from years in the sun, carried a smile that seemed genuine. She appeared pleased to see Chiquita, not at all the way Chiquita's mother and sisters would look at her. "Hello, Chiquita. I'm Pilar Gonzalez, Rico's wife. Eduardo asked me to stop by and see you, since you didn't get to come over yesterday." She held out a covered plate. "I brought some *empanadas*. If you have some coffee, we could spend a little time together."

Chiquita moved back to let Pilar in the house. She gestured to the kitchen. Her hands shook as she filled the empty coffeepot and put it on the stove.

"You are just as pretty as Eduardo said you were." Pilar set the plate on the table and stepped over to Chiquita. Pilar studied her, making Chiquita want to run and hide. Would this woman see how ugly she was and tell Eduardo's men?

Pilar smiled. "I can't see a thing of Diego or Lupe in you. I've seen the other girls. You don't look like them, either. I think you got most of the beauty in the family, but don't tell them I said that."

Pilar continued to talk as the coffee boiled, then perked. Chiquita got out cups for the two of them and poured the aromatic brew. She sank into a chair across from Pilar. As Pilar lifted the cloth from the plate she brought with her, the scent of the pastries made Chiquita's mouth water.

"Eduardo told me you can't talk." Pilar took a small bite, then a sip of coffee. "Have you ever been able to speak?"

Chiquita didn't know what to do. In the recesses of her mind, she could recall a time when she spoke to her sister, Teresa; but the memory was so vague, she always thought it might be a dream. She shrugged.

Pilar gave Chiquita's arm a feathery touch. "I know about Diego. I know he treated you terribly. I think perhaps your mother and sisters did, too." She gave her a sad smile. "I want to be your friend. I want you to know that not all people are like the family you came from. My Rico would never dream of hitting me. He's always kind and loving." She tilted her head. "Sometimes he gets mad at me or at something else, but he would never hurt me. Getting angry is part of being human. What we do with that anger depends on who we are. Do you understand that?"

Chiquita nodded. She couldn't swallow past the lump in her throat. Was Pilar telling her the truth? Could Eduardo be angry and not hurt her? Could she trust him?

"I remember when Rico and I first married and began to work for Eduardo's father and mother. One day, a man named Diego came with his family. They were moving onto some land that bordered the Villegas ranch. They had two little girls with them." She paused, looking past Chiquita, as if seeing the picture of the people. "The oldest girl was just walking. She tried to go everywhere. The younger girl, the prettiest baby I've ever seen, laughed and jabbered at her sister the whole time they were here. Lupe tried to get her to hush, but she wouldn't listen."

Pilar's gaze sought Chiquita's. "I believe you were that baby, Chiquita. I think you have the ability to talk, but you were treated so terribly, you forgot how. Will you let me be your friend and help you? Please?"

A tear dripped on the table. Chiquita hadn't realized she was crying. Was this true? Someday, would she be able to talk? For years, she hadn't wanted to speak, but now she found she did want to. She longed to be able to read aloud like Eduardo did. If she had children, she wanted to read to them. If she could talk, she would say things to Eduardo when he wasn't angry.

She wiped the wetness from her cheeks and looked up at Pilar. She was crying, too. Pilar stood and held out her arms. With a sob, Chiquita stepped into her embrace. She'd never felt anything so sweet.

The afternoon sun felt good on Chiquita's shoulders as she climbed the hill to dig the yucca roots. She carried a large cloth to bundle them in so she wouldn't get dirt all over. She hadn't accomplished much work this morning, but she'd had a marvelous time with Pilar. The foreman's wife told her a lot about Eduardo and the ranch. She talked about Diego and Lupe and how everyone questioned where they got the money for their house. It was an unsolved mystery to many people in the area. Chiquita only shrugged. She had no idea.

A couple of times during the early afternoon, she thought she'd heard the baying of dogs; but the sound had been so faint, she dismissed it as her imagination. She wondered how Eduardo and the men were doing. There was always danger when hunting an animal like a cougar. When cornered, they could be very vicious.

She was wrapping the yucca roots in the cloth when she heard the baying of the dogs. She wondered how they could get this close without her hearing them. The ground shook with the thunder of horses' hooves. Chiquita dropped to the ground, huddled close to the base of the yucca, grateful that this desert plant didn't have the sharp stickers that many others did.

An animal snarled. The barking became frenzied. She began to shake. A gunshot came so close, she started. She curled in a tight ball. The animal's growl was cut off. Rocks rattled down the hillside. Chiquita raised her head a few moments later to see Eduardo and his men standing near her at the crest of the hill, staring down the other side.

Eduardo turned to look back at the house. His gaze locked on Chiquita. His face darkened in anger. "What are you doing? Didn't I tell you not to go outside today?"

She trembled, the kind things Pilar told her about Eduardo almost forgotten.

Chapter 8

This had to be the cagiest cat he'd ever tracked. Eduardo and Rico shook their heads and pushed the horses harder as the trail wound back toward the hacienda. All day, the puma had tried to lose them, but the dogs were too well trained. Although they'd been slowed down a few times, they were closing in now.

Up ahead, the dogs' barking became frenzied and high-pitched. Eduardo urged his tired mount to a gallop. Racing up a hilltop near the house, he could see the cougar stretched out at a dead run. The cat would want to find a place with rocks at its back to face down the enemy. There weren't any places like that close to here. Eduardo pulled his rifle from the scabbard. He wanted to be ready as soon as he could get off a clean shot. This beast wouldn't be allowed to get any closer to his home.

For a moment, his thoughts strayed to Chiquita. Amazing how protective he felt toward her already. He enjoyed having someone there when he came in at night. Although she didn't talk, Chiquita's presence warmed the house. She cooked and cleaned better than any woman he'd ever known. His clothes that were worn or torn were now mended with small, neat stitches that she made while listening to him read the Bible. All he'd seemed to repay her with was his short temper.

All day, he'd been consumed with guilt over the way he'd hurt her last night. During the hours on the hunt, he let Rico take the lead most of the time while he hung back and prayed about his anger. He couldn't bear to see the hurt and fear in Chiquita's eyes again. His parents always had joy. He'd begged God to replace his rage with that same joy. Maybe if he tried hard enough, he could teach Chiquita to be content with him.

The puma spun around at the top of the hill and snarled at the approaching dogs. Eduardo reined his gelding to a halt and raised the rifle. The cat stayed motionless a moment too long. In the middle of his growl, Eduardo's bullet sent the cougar tumbling down the side of the hill, away from the house. All he could feel was relief that the animal hadn't ended up in his backyard, scaring Chiquita.

Swinging down, Eduardo followed Rico to the place where the cat disappeared. Rico held his gun ready in case Eduardo's shot hadn't been enough. The puma lay motionless in a pile of rocks at the bottom of the hill. Eduardo couldn't believe how close this animal had come to his home, his wife.

Turning, he started to look down the other side of the hill at the house below. Something beneath a tall yucca caught his eye. He found himself staring at Chiquita, who huddled in a ball like a terrified child. She'd disobeyed him. She had put herself in danger by coming out here while they were hunting this cougar.

His fists clenched. He could feel the anger begin to course through his veins. As if he were outside himself, he watched as he began to stride toward Chiquita. Her eyes widened, then closed as if she knew a beating was coming. Eduardo didn't slow his pace, but his prayers from earlier that day seemed to brush away the building rage. Instead, he only felt relief that she hadn't been hurt by the puma. In his mind, he could almost picture the horror of finding her injured or killed. Even worse was the thought that one of the bullets, intended for the cougar, might have struck Chiquita by accident since they hadn't known she was there. He didn't think he could live with himself if he'd done that.

Eduardo scooped Chiquita up off the ground. He pulled her against him. She came without resistance, although he could feel the rigidity of her muscles. Wrapping his arms around her, he began to stroke her back, her hair, speaking in a low, soothing tone. He glanced at Rico and motioned with a nod of his head for the foreman to take the horses and dogs and put them up. For a long time, Eduardo held Chiquita. Bit by bit, he felt her relax as she must have realized he wasn't going to hurt her. At last she rested against him, her cheek pressed to his chest. Eduardo thought he could remain like this forever. How had this woman become so important to him so soon? Dare he hope that someday he would come to love her?

"Are you all right?" Eduardo still held Chiquita tight. He picked off some of the plant debris tangled in her long hair. She nodded against his chest. He doubted she'd ever been shown simple affection like this before. "I think we should go back to the house. I'll carry the yucca for you."

He released his hold. She hesitated, then stepped back. For a change, her eyes weren't filled with fear, only uncertainty. She studied him, then her lips lifted a bit, as if she were trying to smile at him but didn't know how. After picking up the cloth bundle, Eduardo held out his hand and waited. Chiquita stared at his outstretched hand. She glanced up at him. He thought she would reject his offer, but very slowly she lifted her hand and let him wrap it in his own. Together they set off down the hill to the house.

⚜

By the time Eduardo finished the evening chores, Chiquita had supper ready. She'd used dried chilies and some early squash Pilar gave her to make a stew. The smell of green chili filled the house, and Chiquita found she was looking forward to spending time with her husband tonight. Always before, she anticipated learning more of her letters and hearing the Bible read aloud. Tonight, she wanted to be with Eduardo.

When he pulled her up off the ground today, she thought for sure he would hit her for disobeying, and she knew she deserved the beating. Instead, he simply held her like a child who needed comforting after a terrifying ordeal. All her life, she'd longed for someone to do that, but Mama had never shown the least bit of affection for her. Papa only showed the opposite. Not once had they touched her without that contact hurting. She'd seen the way they treated the other girls, though. Teresa, Pabla, Sancia, and Zita all were treated as special. Only Chiquita was different. She had no idea why.

Watching out the window, she could see Eduardo stopping to talk to Rico before coming to the house. What had happened to him today? She thought for sure he was angry with her, but then he showed such kindness. After yesterday, she hadn't believed it possible. Puzzled, she tilted her head to one side, studying him. She couldn't define what, but something about him had changed. He stood, talked, and walked a little different, but she couldn't figure exactly how.

He waved at Rico and turned toward the house. Ambling along, he paused to look at the pasture, then up at the sky as if he had all the time in the world. Peace. That was it. He appeared to have a peace within that he hadn't had yesterday. Usually, he strode everywhere he went like he couldn't take the time to be distracted from the work at hand. Tonight, he seemed to not care about distractions. He was taking the time to see the beauty of life around him.

Dishing up the bowls of stew, Chiquita finished the preparations for the meal. The door opened, and Eduardo clomped into the room. He took a deep breath and let it out with a sigh.

"I could smell those chilies all the way across the yard. My stomach almost beat me to the house." He smiled at her, and she felt her face warm. She ducked her head, not sure what to make of the change in him or of the new feelings swirling through her.

During the meal, Eduardo chattered more than her sister, Teresa. He told of the hunt, his dreams for the ranch, and Lucio's amazing recovery. He spoke about his meeting last week with Antonio Soza and their talk of improving the cattle herds. She could barely keep up with the changes in conversation. She longed to be able to join in.

That evening, Eduardo sat closer to her than usual as they worked on learning a few new words. She tried to concentrate, but for some reason, his presence distracted her. Fear wasn't the problem. She found herself wanting to lean closer to him. When his hand touched her shoulder, she jumped as a shock raced through her. She met his gaze, and he smiled. Chiquita couldn't look away. Those dusky brown eyes were filled with emotion. This time, she knew he wasn't angry.

Chiquita stood. Her chair tipped over and clattered to the floor. She held her breath. Eduardo set the chair back in place. He didn't seem at all upset with her. Warmth flooded her. She had the sudden desire to run outside to cool off in the night air. What was happening to her? Was she getting sick?

"I think we've worked on this long enough." Eduardo rose and began to put away the slate and books. "Do you feel up to listening to some more Bible reading?"

She nodded and moved to the safety of the chair where her mending waited. As Eduardo read in his rich, deep voice, she tried to understand this Jesus. At first she'd been awed and afraid when she heard that Jesus was a man. She'd always been so frightened of her father. She didn't know how she could trust a God who became a man. Hearing the stories about Jesus, she came to realize He was different in many ways from Papa. Even when confronted by an adulterous woman, who probably deserved the severe punishment the men wanted to mete out, Jesus had forgiven her. He asked her to sin no more. That had been bothering Chiquita. She wanted to ask someone to explain to her what sin was. She had an idea, but didn't fully understand. Did everyone sin or only certain people? For some reason, she felt an urgency to find out.

"I believe I'll turn in early tonight." Eduardo put away the Bible. "Today was a long one, and I want to take you riding tomorrow, if you'd like to go."

Chiquita's heart leapt. Her hands trembled with excitement as she folded the shirt she'd almost finished mending. Tomorrow she would find out what it felt like to sit on a horse. She used to dream about the wind in her face as she raced away on a horse. Sleep was a long time coming as her whole body tingled with excitement. Her mind kept replaying scenes from the afternoon and evening. She drifted off, thinking about what tomorrow would bring.

Before Eduardo returned with the milk the next morning, Chiquita had breakfast ready to put on the table. The coffee, perked before he left the house to see to the chores, had been kept warm. She couldn't stand still but continued to pick things up, putting them in different places, then moving them back just for the sake of something to do.

The door creaked open. Eduardo clomped inside. "Mornin'." He lifted the pail of milk onto the counter by the sink. "I have a couple of chores to see to before we can go for a ride."

Chiquita turned away to fuss with the forks and plates on the table. She didn't want him to see the disappointment in her eyes. From experience, she knew he had only promised her this treat as another way to hurt her. Her father used to do this all of the time. He would promise something, only to back out later. He always grinned as he watched her misery. She'd learned never to believe him, but after yesterday, she'd thought Eduardo would be different. Now she knew better. She couldn't bear to see his triumph when he knew how much he'd wounded her.

"Hey, wait a minute." Eduardo caught her by her shoulders and turned her around. "I didn't say we wouldn't ride. Rico needs to show me something." He ran his thumb under her eye, catching the tear that trickled out. "Besides, you've got some work to do before you can get on a horse." He grinned at her puzzled look. "It's a surprise. I'll tell you about it after breakfast. I'm starving."

She didn't know whether to trust him or not. This could be another trick. Papa would have done something like this if he'd thought of it. Even though her mind said she couldn't trust Eduardo any more than she could trust Papa,

Chiquita's heart told her different. Eduardo seemed to genuinely care about her and about others.

After taking care of the milk, Chiquita dished up the eggs and fresh tortillas, adding extra chilies to Eduardo's breakfast, as she liked. He smiled as she set the steaming plate in front of him. When she sat down, he reached for her hand. This time, when he prayed, he kept a secure hold on her. She could barely concentrate on his words as the shock of his touch ran up her arm. At the end of the prayer, he let go. Although her hand still remembered the feel of his, she felt bereft and alone.

They ate in silence, Eduardo eating like a man who'd done a full day's work, while she picked at her food. She couldn't get her mind off what he planned to do next. "While you clean up, I have to get something." Eduardo scooted his chair back from the table. "I'll be right back."

Chiquita couldn't finish her breakfast. What would he do now? Was this surprise something nasty, or would it be a wonderful one as she used to dream about? Before she had the dishes washed, Eduardo returned. His contagious grin made him look so young and handsome, her breath caught in her throat. She couldn't look away from his gaze. This was the way the man of her dreams used to look at her. Her heart thudded, feeling like it might beat out of her chest.

"Here you go." Eduardo thrust a bundle of cloth at her. "Why don't you see if you can get this ready by the time I return?"

Tearing her gaze from his, Chiquita saw, for the first time, what he carried. The amber skirt and blouse glowed in the sunlight that streamed through the window. Threads interwoven in a pattern throughout gave the outfit a shiny appearance. She'd never seen anything so rich and beautiful. Her eyes widened as Eduardo held the clothes out for her to take.

"My mother only got to wear this a few times when she went riding. I thought the color would match your eyes." He hesitated and glanced away. "You could get the alterations made while I see what Rico needs. I'll be back in about an hour. Will that be enough time for you to get ready?"

The full skirt dragged at her arms as she let Eduardo drape the material over them. She couldn't possibly wear something so rich. What if she fell and it tore? Would that trigger Eduardo's wrath? Her eyes were drawn to his warm gaze. As she clutched the incredibly beautiful outfit to her, she could see something in his eyes. Was it admiration? For her? He smiled, and she forgot her reservations. She would do anything he asked.

He stepped close. She couldn't breathe. Eduardo brushed a hand over her hair, making her scalp tingle. "I can't wait to see you when you have this on. I'll hurry back, Chiquita."

Chapter 9

Clinging to the saddle with both hands, Chiquita looked like a wooden statue. Eduardo quickly found out that teaching a woman to ride would be a challenge. After he'd lifted Chiquita into the saddle, Pilar came and talked to her about how to keep her feet in the stirrups and how to shift her weight. He could tell Chiquita hadn't realized how far off the ground she would be. Her face had paled at first, even though the gelding she rode was small and stood still. Chiquita couldn't seem to get the hang of going with the gait either. She needed to learn to relax and move with the horse.

"You're doing fine." Eduardo smiled down at her. He rode his stallion, El Rey, knowing the horse needed some exercise. El Rey pranced sideways.

Chiquita's gelding snorted and nodded his head. Chiquita tensed. She gave Eduardo a wide-eyed glance.

"He's just feeling El Rey's excitement." Eduardo patted the big stallion's neck. "They'll calm down soon." He reined El Rey closer to her.

"Here, straighten your back. Let go of the saddle. Hold the reins like this." Eduardo took her hands and turned them, showing her the way to have the most control. "You won't fall. Pilar gave you good advice about how to shift your weight with the movement."

Slowly, Chiquita eased back in the saddle. Her face began to lose the look of uncertainty. She even managed to take her gaze off her mount for a minute and look at him.

"That's the way." He smiled. "See? As you loosen up a little, you begin to feel the movement. Now go with him, not against him." He pointed at the gelding, indicating they should become a team. "You have good balance already."

Chiquita sat even straighter. Eduardo ached for her. The slightest compliment meant so much to her. He could see the same thing when he touched her. Her reaction, although fearful at first, now seemed to be amazement. She couldn't seem to understand that someone could touch her in kindness or love.

Love? Eduardo frowned. Where had that thought come from? He couldn't possibly love Chiquita. He hadn't known her long enough. Yes, he felt protective of her. He could still recall the stab of fear when he saw her lying on the ground yesterday. He thought she'd been hurt. He'd never felt such intense relief before as he did when he found out she was all right. Despite those feelings, he couldn't possibly love her.

El Rey pranced ahead, and the gelding quickened his pace. Chiquita smiled. She looked more relaxed already.

"I think you're going to be a natural rider." Eduardo couldn't quit watching her. Since he'd walked into the house and seen her wearing that riding outfit, he'd been entranced. Even her hair had some of the same color threads woven throughout, and they gleamed in the sunlight. Like a princess in the stories his mother used to tell him, Chiquita now rode proud and erect.

"Would you like to try going a little faster?"

She smiled and nodded. He eased them into a slow canter, not wanting to try the rougher trot. Her mouth rounded in an "O" of surprise. Within moments, she relaxed once more and gave him a tremulous smile. This was the happiest he'd seen her. Even her eyes glowed. He hadn't had this much fun in years.

For the next hour, Eduardo alternated between walking and cantering the horses. He took them in a roundabout circuit, not wanting to stray too far and tire Chiquita on her first ride. She would be sore enough tomorrow without riding too long. As they walked the horses back toward the ranch house, Eduardo veered off the path, motioning to a stand of trees near the bank of the San Pedro River.

Under the shade of the cottonwood trees, he dismounted. Lifting Chiquita down, he held her for a moment to steady her. She started to move her legs, then gave him a surprised look. He chuckled.

"Walking feels funny after you've been on a horse for awhile."

She nodded and took a couple of hesitant steps. Eduardo secured the horses, then took Chiquita's hand. Her troubled gaze told him she didn't understand what they were doing.

"I want to show you something."

She seemed to understand the solemnity of the occasion. Eduardo could feel her hesitancy as she followed him down an overgrown path through the grove of trees. Thick grass, drying now because of the lack of recent rains, tugged at their legs as they passed by. Ahead, a short fence outlined the family burial ground. Chiquita stiffened. She slowed, and when Eduardo glanced back, he could see her reluctance to go in with him.

Pulling her close, Eduardo stood by the fence. He wouldn't push her to go where she didn't feel comfortable.

"I don't know why I brought you here. I haven't come to visit in a long time." Regret filled Eduardo as he recalled how his mother used to come every week to clean the weeds and keep the gravesites nice. She wouldn't like the way things looked now.

Chiquita tugged on his hand. Her forehead wrinkled in a puzzled frown. She gestured at all the small markers and the two bigger ones.

"These are all my family." Pointing to the long row of tiny crosses, Eduardo could feel the old sadness creep over him. "My parents had ten children. I'm the youngest. The first nine didn't live past infancy."

Chiquita's quick intake of breath startled him. She stared up at him, her eyes wide and tear-filled.

"I remember Mama saying that when she found out she was expecting me, she didn't even want another baby. She thought if she lost another one, the pain would kill her right then and there." He paused, trying to swallow around the lump in his throat. "She used to come down here once a week. She'd plant flowers in the spring, then tend them all summer long. I think she liked to talk to her children." He could feel her questioning gaze. "Oh, yes, she loved me. In fact, she probably loved me too much. She and my dad were almost too careful with me. They were so afraid they would lose me." He gave a sad smile. "I'm probably spoiled by all their attention. I sure do miss them."

Chiquita tugged on his hand. Leading him to the gate, she motioned for him to open it. He followed her inside. She went from one small cross to the next, touching each one, as if in greeting. When she came to the two larger markers, she stopped and turned to look at him.

"Those are my parents." He reluctantly followed her to the graves. "They died four years ago. I was off with Rico and the vaqueros, getting some cattle rounded up for sale. Only my parents and Pilar were at the ranch." He turned away, blinking his eyes to clear the moisture.

"When we came back, we found a renegade band of Apaches had attacked. My parents were dead. Pilar had been outside. She heard the commotion and managed to hide. We were all devastated."

He couldn't say more. The silence stretched taut. Even the birds grew quiet. Chiquita's touch was so light that, at first, he thought he'd imagined something. Then he realized she was offering him comfort. Her small hand began to rub light circles on his back. Warmth enveloped him. Eduardo turned.

She stared up at him. Tears pooled in her eyes. She pointed at the largest cross, then at herself.

"Did you know my father?" Eduardo recalled several times when his father had to have dealings with Diego. Perhaps that was what Chiquita was trying to say. She nodded, confirming his thoughts.

Taking his hand, Chiquita brought it to her cheek. Her eyes begged him to understand. Eduardo frowned. He nodded.

"My father was kind to you, wasn't he?" Her eager nod confirmed what he'd said. "That's why you remember him. There weren't many people who were nice. Am I right?"

She nodded again. Turning away from him, she touched the cross at his father's grave. Tears trickled down her cheeks. Eduardo could only imagine the pain she must be feeling if a stranger was the only one she could recall ever treating her with kindness. Anguish, not only for her but also for himself and his lost family, nearly made him groan with pain. He must have made a sound. Chiquita turned. He wasn't sure how it happened, but she was pressed tight against him. Her arms wrapped around his waist in a fierce hug, like she wanted to give him all the comfort and strength she could.

He held her, relishing the peace that flowed over him. "I was so angry when my parents died. Over the years since then, I've grown angrier and harder to be around. I didn't even realize what I was doing." Eduardo's voice rasped in the quiet. "Only when I saw what my rage did to you, did I understand that I had to change. I'm not perfect, Chiquita. I may still get upset sometimes, but I will never hurt you. I want to learn to be happy." He held her away. Her tawny eyes gazed at him full of wonder. "Will you help me? Will you give me time to change?" Her nod of agreement made him want to shout with joy.

❧

Following Eduardo back to the horses, Chiquita didn't know what to think. These feelings were so new. Never in her life had she felt the need to comfort someone. She'd always been the one hurt, and no one ever showed sympathy to her. She wasn't sure how she knew what to do. She'd only done what she thought would be nice. A soft touch in times of distress had been a dream of hers.

This was strange to her. How could she be willing to trust any man? She almost felt like a traitor to herself. After her father's cruel trickery, she knew better than to lower her defenses around Eduardo, but she couldn't seem to help her actions. His admission of his need for help and forgiveness tugged at her heart, breaking the barriers even more. Holding Eduardo felt so right and so good. She hadn't wanted to let go of him. What was she to do?

The one thing she longed to do was talk to Eduardo. Every day, the desire seemed to grow. After her visit with Pilar, Chiquita tried to recall a time when she used to talk. There were vague memories of playing with Teresa. She thought she might have spoken then, but the fuzzy recollection could be just her wanting this so bad. Maybe this was another of her dreams.

When they got to where the horses were cropping grass, Eduardo put his large hands on her waist and lifted her up into the saddle. She could feel his strength. For a moment, she almost reached out to run her hand across his broad shoulders. Catching herself, she worked at arranging her skirt instead. She had to be careful. Maybe this was a trick of his. He acted nice now, but when she became vulnerable by caring for him too much, then he could hurt her even more.

"Are you enjoying the ride?" Eduardo reined El Rey around and started toward home. He glanced back for her answer. She couldn't help but nod. Riding was delightful, and she couldn't wait to do more.

When they emerged from the trees, Eduardo slowed, waiting for her to come alongside him. "I need to talk to you about what Rico told me this morning." He frowned and gazed off at the hills to the east. "We think someone has been watching our house."

He held up a hand at her fearful look. "No, I don't think there's any real danger. It's probably some drifter riding through, although they usually come on down and ask for a meal or work."

A chill trickled down Chiquita's back. Glancing around, she hoped no one was watching them now. The gelding snorted and danced a few steps. Chiquita grabbed the saddle to keep her balance.

"I didn't tell you to scare you." Eduardo reached out to pat her horse. "I only want you to be careful and stay close to the house. Don't gather food alone. If you need to go and I can't go with you, then I'll have one of the vaqueros accompany you." He shrugged. "This is probably nothing, but I want you to be safe."

His smile eased Chiquita's trepidation. She wanted to ask what sign they'd found. Who watched them? How close were they? A sense of unease dimmed the brightness of the day. Although she'd been enjoying the outing, she couldn't wait to get back to the safety of the house.

Closing her eyes, Chiquita forced her tense muscles to relax. For years, she'd done this exercise when her father delighted in frightening her. She refused to let him get pleasure from knowing how terrified she was, so she would put on a brave front. She could do the same now. She didn't want Eduardo to think her a coward. Threats had been a way of life for her for years, and she wouldn't let an unknown peril ruin the life she had now.

She tried to focus once more on her memories. If Pilar was right, and she used to talk, why had she stopped? For the first time in years, she allowed herself to recall her difficult early years. Pictures floated through her mind—bits and pieces of agony: Mama, with her hand raised to strike, her face red with rage; Papa, the sadistic smile on his face as he hurt her. Teresa and, later, her other sisters as they stood wide-eyed, watching her torment.

"Hey, are you all right?" Eduardo's touch made her jump. She almost lost her seat in the saddle. He grabbed her, his concern evident. "I must have kept you out riding too long. You look tired."

Wrapping the reins around the saddle horn, Eduardo reached for her. Her breath came in shallow gasps. The horrible memories were too recent. What did he intend to do? She stiffened, preparing for the worst. Then, looking into Eduardo's eyes, she relaxed. He didn't mean to hurt her. He wasn't like Papa. She had to believe that.

Taking a firm grip on her waist, Eduardo lifted her. His gaze never left hers. Her heart began to pound, this time not from fear. Time slowed. She couldn't take her gaze from his face—his eyes, his mouth. She lifted a hand to caress his cheek. Never before had she felt like this. She wanted his strong arms around her, to lay her head against his chest and hear his strong, steady heartbeat.

Time stood still as Eduardo drew her close. She could feel the warmth emanating from him. Her pulse raced. Eduardo's smile faded, replaced by a look of intensity. He began to lower his face toward hers as he settled her in front of him.

Chiquita's gelding let out a scream. Pain shot through Chiquita. She gasped. El Rey jumped. Eduardo yelled, clutched her close, and kicked El Rey into a full gallop. The pain increased. Her leg was on fire. Dreamlike, Chiquita looked down. The feathered shaft of an arrow protruded from her thigh.

Chapter 10

Panic coursed through Eduardo. He dug his heels into El Rey's sides, urging the big horse to go faster. They flew across the ground toward the ranch house. He tried to ignore the droplets of blood dripping from the hem of Chiquita's skirt. Holding her tight, he prayed she would be okay. Her eyes were squeezed shut, her face pale and beaded with sweat.

Apaches! They'd attacked again. For the last two years, things in Arizona had been fairly quiet. Why were they attacking now? This didn't make sense. The Indians knew the cavalry would be out after them en force. They didn't venture into this area anymore. *Please, God, let her be okay. Help me get her home safely.*

The gelding raced beside him, laboring to keep up with the longer-legged stallion. Blood ran from a wound on his withers. The arrow must have grazed him before striking Chiquita's leg. That was why the gelding had squealed. His eyes were wild with fright as he worked to keep up.

Guilt pricked at Eduardo's soul. He thought of the nights they'd spent together as he read the Bible to Chiquita. He could tell from the intensity of her interest that she'd never heard the Bible before. He'd started reading in the book of John to give her an idea of why the Bible had been written. *Lord, I knew she didn't know You, yet I haven't taken the time to explain the gospel message to her. Oh, God, if she dies, I won't be able to bear it. Please give me the chance to introduce her to You. I know she's interested. Help her understand.*

El Rey seemed to sense the urgency of the moment. He stretched out and ran as if his, not his mistress's, life depended on it. Eduardo knew the longer the arrow stayed in her leg, the more the risk of infection. Even the jarring of the hard run could cause bleeding they would be unable to stop. His arm tensed as he held her close, trying to keep her from being jounced too hard.

He glanced over his shoulder. Were the Indians following? Where were they? He hadn't seen or heard any sign of them. Would they attack the ranch next? Living this isolated always meant running the risk of this type of attack.

The ranch buildings came into view. El Rey's breathing was labored, but Eduardo couldn't let him stop just yet. The gelding had fallen behind. Eduardo began to yell as he raced into the barnyard.

"Rico! Rico, gather the men." He pulled El Rey to a sliding stop. "Pilar, come quick."

Rico ran from the stables, followed by Tomas and Jorge. Pilar appeared in the doorway of her cabin. Seeing him holding Chiquita, she came running as she dried her hands on her apron. Lucio ran out of the bunkhouse, one hand clutching his side. The gelding thundered into the yard, his reins flapping, the whites of his eyes showing. Jorge caught hold of him.

"Rico, Tomas, get your guns. Chiquita's been shot by Indians. I don't know if they're behind me or not, but we have to be ready." Eduardo reined El Rey toward the house. "Pilar, get your medicine. Meet me at the house. We have to get this arrow out."

Pilar wheeled and raced back to her house. The men all went for their guns. Eduardo knew they would do their best to protect the ranch while he saw to Chiquita. At the house, he eased off of El Rey, still holding Chiquita. She moaned as he landed on the ground with a thump. Leaning back against his horse, Eduardo got a better hold on her, careful of her injured leg.

Striding to the door, he heard Pilar coming. She reached his side in time to lift the latch for him. Her breath came in ragged gasps as she waited for him to enter first. He strode through the house to the bedroom where Chiquita had been sleeping, ignoring the questioning glance Pilar gave him.

"I can take care of her if you want to go see to the men." Pilar was all business as she began to examine the way the arrow had pierced the skirt and gone into Chiquita's leg. Eduardo hesitated. She gave a quick nod at the door. "I'll take good care of her."

Stepping outside, Eduardo stayed in the shadow of the house as he scanned the perimeter. No sign of Indians. El Rey stood near the door, his sides still heaving from his heroic run. Sweat matted his red-gold coat. Eduardo grabbed the reins and began to lead El Rey to the barn, where he or one of the men could care for the horse. The stallion deserved an extra measure of feed today.

Rico would be in the barn. He would have either Jorge or Tomas in the loft, watching the surrounding countryside. After the attack that killed his parents, Eduardo had been careful to keep the area close to the buildings brush-free. He didn't want to give anyone a place to hide and sneak up on them. The Apaches wouldn't have an easy time. He and his men were prepared.

He stopped just inside the dim interior of the barn to let his eyes adjust. Lucio was in the first stall with the gelding, sponging down the wound near his mane. Eduardo could see the gelding still trembled from the injury and the terror.

"Tomas and Jorge are both up there, watching. They haven't seen any sign of trouble." Rico strode toward him. "What happened?"

Eduardo began to take the tack off El Rey. "We were ambushed down near the river. We were coming out of the grove of trees where the family's buried. I didn't see or hear anything." Eduardo paused and frowned at Rico. "There's something funny about this attack."

Rico nodded. "If we don't see anything soon, we might try sending Jorge for the Elias brothers. They're the best at finding renegades."

"You're right." Eduardo led El Rey to his stall and began to brush him down.

J. M. Elias knew Indians better than any other man he knew. He would gladly come and help them figure out this ambush.

※

Waves of pain washed over Chiquita. She'd never known this much hurt before. Had her father found some new torture? She moaned and wanted to move away. That wouldn't work. He always liked it when she showed a weakness. Gritting her teeth, she stayed as still as possible, refusing to make a sound.

Once more, Papa stabbed her leg with a hot poker. She cried out. The sound broke free without her permission. Papa would be pleased. Darkness closed in around her. She fought the blackness to no avail.

Later she awoke, coming to in a haze of torment. Pilar leaned over her, deftly winding a strip of cloth around Chiquita's leg. Something hot pressed against the flesh. Pilar glanced up. Seeing Chiquita was watching her, she smiled.

"You'll be fine, I think. The arrow went in the fleshy part of your thigh and didn't make you bleed too much." She frowned. "Of course, when I took the arrow out, you bled quite a bit. I'm sorry that hurt so much." She tied a knot in the cloth and pulled the covers over Chiquita. "You lost some blood coming home. I'm glad you fainted. That saved you from a lot of pain."

Picking up a cloth and dipping it in a bowl of water, she began to wipe Chiquita's face. The coolness felt so good, Chiquita wanted to groan with pleasure. Her face and neck felt gritty with dried sweat and dirt.

"I'll let you rest for awhile with this poultice. When it cools and I have to put a new one on, I'll wash you down, too. I want you to stay still so you don't break open the wound."

Pilar gathered the soiled clothes and carried them from the room. She moved in and out, removing the dirty water and medicines she'd used. Her quick glances at Chiquita spoke aloud how concerned she was. Chiquita knew there was something Pilar hadn't told her. Had Eduardo been hurt, too?

She closed her eyes, trying to recall what happened. She remembered the ride and leaving the grove. A clear vision of Eduardo lifting her from the saddle, a strange look in his eyes came back to her. Once more, her heart reacted. What had Eduardo been trying to say to her with that look? The remembered feeling that had washed through her made her stir in bed. Hot pain jolted through her. She bit her lip, forcing her body to stay still. She still couldn't remember much past the time Eduardo had been lifting her. What had happened? Where was he?

Heavy steps clomped in the hallway outside the room. The man of her thoughts opened the door and peeked in. He smiled. Her heartbeat sped up.

"Pilar told me I couldn't come in if you were sleeping." He crossed the room. Pulling up a chair, he took off his hat and put it on the foot of the bed. "I don't usually listen to Pilar, but when she's caring for someone sick or hurt, she's like a grouchy mother bear."

"I heard that, young man." Pilar swept in, carrying a tray. "If you're going to come in here and disturb my patient, you can make yourself useful. She needs something to eat and drink." Pilar set the tray on a small table near the bed. "Don't stay too long and wear her out. She needs to rest." Giving Eduardo a warning look, Pilar left the room. Chiquita didn't know how she could be so bold and sure of herself.

Eduardo gave Chiquita a sip of water, the cool liquid easing the dryness of her throat. He cradled a small bowl of stew in his hand, acting like feeding her was awkward. She wanted to take the spoon from him and feed herself, but she couldn't get her arms to move. She seemed to have no strength.

"I promise to give you small bites." His mustache lifted as he grinned at her. "I'm sure you're curious about what happened and what we're doing now. Right?"

She nodded, eager to hear whatever he would tell her.

"Well, as long as you eat, I'll talk. When you stop, I'll take it as a sign that you're too tired to hear more." He wiggled his eyebrows, making her want to giggle. "This is my way of making you eat, so you'll put a little meat on those bones."

She obediently took a bite. The stew tasted delicious, although she wasn't hungry. She chewed slowly, hoping this would keep him talking.

"Do you remember being shot?" She shook her head, and he continued. Between giving her small bites, he recounted the story of the attack and the race for the house. He told her the measures they'd taken to see the ranch would be safe. By the time she couldn't eat another bite, he appeared to have finished his story.

"Jorge is getting ready to ride to the Elias ranch. He should be able to return with them by tomorrow. They're the best, and I know they'll help. They were the ones who found the Apaches who killed my folks."

Eduardo stood and stretched. "I think I'd better let you rest. I'll be back in later. Would you like for me to read to you tonight?" He seemed to be especially excited as he asked the question. Chiquita nodded. As he left the room, Eduardo turned and winked at her. Warmth flushed her face. What was this man doing to her?

✤

The next day, Eduardo heard the thunder of hoofbeats as he sat beside Chiquita. That must be Jorge, returning with the Elias brothers. Eduardo smoothed the hair away from Chiquita's forehead. She'd only been sleeping for a short while. She'd lost so much blood yesterday that he was amazed at how well she was doing. She wanted to get out of bed this morning, but he and Pilar insisted that she stay put. By tomorrow, he would have to tie her down to keep her there. He smiled. He'd never known a woman with so much spunk.

Last night, he had hoped to share the gospel message with her, but she'd been so weak, she'd gone to sleep early. He prayed to get the chance soon, but he wasn't sure she understood enough to invite Jesus to be her Savior. Since she couldn't ask any questions, he had to try to guess what she wanted to know. That wasn't easy.

Pilar hurried into the room. "Rico sent me to stay while you go talk with those men. How is she doing?"

Chiquita stirred, then quieted. Eduardo beckoned Pilar to follow him from the room so they wouldn't disturb her further. "She ate well this morning. This is the first time she's fallen asleep."

"Sleeping is good for her." Pilar nodded. "When she wakes up, I'll change the dressing. If she's doing all right, maybe she can get up a little later."

"Don't let her do too much." Eduardo knew he didn't need to caution Pilar, but he couldn't help himself. "That woman works more than three people." He and Pilar shared a chuckle before he trod down the hall and left.

When Eduardo got to the barn, J. M. Elias was examining the arrow Pilar had removed from Chiquita's leg. His brothers, Ramon, Juan, and Cornelio, conversed with him in low tones. The four brothers looked grim as they studied the wood and feathers. Rico and the vaqueros watched from a distance.

Eduardo strode toward the brothers. Dread clenched his gut. He could recall in vivid detail the conversations they'd had when his parents died. They would know how hard this must be for him. All morning, as he sat with Chiquita, he could feel his anger building. He'd tried to pray and give this to the Lord, but his feelings wouldn't go away. His wife had almost died. If the arrow had been a little higher. . . If he hadn't been lifting her from her horse. . . Those ifs had been running through his head since the ambush happened. Rage boiled inside him like a simmering stew.

"I'm sorry to hear this happened. We're glad to know your missus is going to be fine." J. M. spoke for the brothers. His square jaw tensed as if he, too, held anger inside. "Jorge said you haven't had anymore problems, right?"

Eduardo nodded. "Everything's been quiet."

"We took the liberty of having Jorge take us to where your wife was attacked." Señor Elias glanced at his brothers, who were murmuring among themselves as they examined the arrow. "We found the spot where the shooter hid. There was sign of one horse and one man."

Eduardo frowned. "One? Apaches don't fight like that."

"We scoured the area, looking for sign of any others that were hidden elsewhere. Jorge also talked to us about the evidence you've found that someone is watching your ranch house. He took us to that spot, too."

Rico and the vaqueros moved closer. Eduardo could tell by the tense set of their shoulders that they suspected what J. M. was leading up to. He could feel it, too. He tamped down the ire, waiting for the Apache fighter to continue.

"This arrow—" The eldest Elias plucked the weapon from his brother's hand. "This is not an Apache arrow. It isn't even a very good imitation. Someone wants you to think Indians have attacked you. We think the person who's been watching the ranch is the same one who shot your wife. This has nothing to do with renegade Apaches."

Anger burned through Eduardo, making it impossible to think. Who would do such a thing? Who would try to kill him or Chiquita? Which one of them had been the real target of that arrow? A thousand questions raced through his mind—questions for which he had no answers.

Chapter 11

Morning. How's the leg?"

Chiquita sighed. Eduardo had asked her the same question every day for the last week. She still limped, and her leg was sore to touch, but it had healed very fast.

Pilar was amazed with her progress. "I've been treating wounds for years, and I've never seen anyone heal this quickly," she'd told Chiquita.

Chiquita thought the reason had to do more with the God Eduardo talked and read about, but she didn't know how to tell him that.

In the last week, Eduardo not only read to her about this Jesus in the Bible, he also talked about Him afterwards. She'd learned so much and longed to know more. Eduardo seemed to know the questions her heart wanted to ask. Last night, he talked to her about sin. He explained that every person ever born, other than Jesus, who was the Son of God, had sinned. She had trouble going to sleep last night, thinking about how she was a sinner and couldn't get into heaven because of that. Eduardo promised to tell her tonight about the special way God provided so anyone could get into heaven. She wondered what that way would be. Would she have to do some special service? Did this God require money or some sacrifice like they did in the time of the Bible? When she thought about knowing, anticipation made her anxious. She pushed the thoughts from her mind and went to tend the milk, hoping to show Eduardo her leg was fine.

"Jorge saw the Elias brothers yesterday afternoon as they were heading for Tucson. They asked him to let us know there's no sign of any uprising."

Chiquita gave him a puzzled look. Her fingers brushed across the partially healed wound on her leg.

"I didn't tell you before. I didn't want you to worry." Eduardo tugged on the side of his mustache. "The Elias brothers are experts on the Apaches. They're sure the arrow you were shot with isn't an Apache arrow, although someone took pains to see that it looked like one."

Chiquita could feel the blood draining from her face. What was Eduardo saying? If the Indians hadn't shot her, then who did?

Eduardo crossed to her and grasped her shoulders. "I don't want you to worry. I only told you so you would be careful. You can work in the garden and around the house, but I don't want you to go any farther. No more gathering yucca or anything else. If you need something, someone will get it for you."

She could see the tightly controlled anger in his gaze. Did he blame her for this? She wanted to step away, yet she wanted him to hold her and tell her everything would be fine.

"I have to go out with Rico and the boys today. We'll be gone all day. I've asked Pilar to check in on you. If you're outside and you hear the dogs barking, get inside, okay?"

She nodded. Uncertainty made her nervous. The longing to ask questions made her throat tight. Opening her mouth, she tried to make sound come out. Fear that she couldn't succeed kept her quiet. Turning to the stove, she dished up breakfast. Today, while Eduardo was gone, she would spend some time working on her reading and writing. She could read simple words now. If she practiced and worked hard, maybe soon she could talk to him through writing.

A few minutes later, Chiquita watched as Eduardo stalked across the yard to the barn. She wished he had talked to her about what was bothering him. Ever since she'd been shot with the arrow, he'd been distant. He seemed to be holding something back from her. Her inability to express herself and ask what was wrong chafed at her.

⚘

Anger simmered deep inside Eduardo. This was a different kind of anger than he'd had before. This was a helplessness to protect his family and holdings. Frustration at not knowing who was trying to hurt him constantly aggravated him, wearing away all of his defenses. He could feel himself slipping away from the Lord. He needed to turn to prayer to solve the dilemma, but he ignored the small voice nudging him in that direction. Today, he and Rico would take the others and scour the ranch, looking for sign of misdeeds. Whoever wanted to hurt him or Chiquita had to leave some sign somewhere, and he intended to find it.

They were all gathered at the barn, their horses saddled and waiting. Even Lucio had come out to see them off. He'd been disappointed when Eduardo told him he would stay and watch the ranch, but they all knew he still didn't have the strength for a full day of riding. Besides, with the threat hanging over them, someone needed to be here in case of trouble. Lucio should be able to handle most anything. He could be trusted to watch.

Eduardo took the reins of the gelding readied for him. He'd chosen not to take El Rey on this trip. He didn't want to put the stallion in any danger. He was too valuable an animal.

"Jorge, I want you and Tomas to ride across the river and scour the hills over there. Be careful. Watch for any signs of trouble, no matter how insignificant. I don't know for sure what we're looking for or who is behind this." He fixed them with a serious gaze. "Don't take any chances. At the first sign of trouble, get back here. Don't do anything foolish. Is that clear?"

"Si, Señor." Jorge nodded. He and Tomas reined their horses around and loped along the road leading to the river.

Eduardo watched them go, uneasiness stirring inside. Saying a quick prayer for their safety, he turned to Rico. "Let's go. We'll take the hills behind the house. It will take longer, but I think we should stick together."

Rico nodded. "We could cover more territory if we just stay in sight of each other. That way, if something happens, we would be able to help the other one pretty fast."

"Okay." Eduardo kneed his gelding. "Let's start in the east and work our way west. That way, we'll have the sun at our backs this morning." Their horses' hooves thundered across the ground as they left the yard. Eduardo glanced at the house.

Chiquita watched from the kitchen window. Her pale countenance gave him a momentary pang of guilt. He knew she didn't understand his concern, and he hadn't wanted to fully explain. He wanted to keep from scaring her. Deep down he knew, too, that he wanted her to trust him without fear. Maybe he was being unfair, given her circumstances. How he wished she could talk to him!

By noon, they'd found no sign of anything wrong. Eduardo called a halt, swinging out of the saddle, landing on the ground with a thump that jolted his leg. The gelding stepped away, probably too tired to do more. Eduardo knew the horse could sense his mood. The boiling cauldron of rage inside him threatened to explode. He needed to figure out who was attacking him and why.

Rico groaned and arched his back, stretching to relieve the cramped muscles. Eduardo knew the older man had much more trouble spending hours in the saddle, yet he hadn't complained at all during the long morning hours. Rico rummaged in his saddlebags, pulling out the lunch Pilar sent for them. Chiquita would have sent something, too, but she hadn't been told early enough to contribute. Eduardo hadn't wanted her to know what they were doing. She'd faced enough trouble in her life. He didn't want her worrying further.

Taking off a bite of tortilla, Rico indicated the hills spread out before them. They were high enough to have a good view of the hills and valleys leading back to the ranch. The snakelike river wound through the bottom of the valley, weaving in and out of view as the mountains permitted. From up here, the large trees close to the water appeared to be a carved set of child's toys.

"Do you mind me making a suggestion?" Rico glanced at Eduardo.

"I'll take any help you have to offer. I know I'm not thinking straight." Eduardo took a drink from his canteen. "Do you think I'm imagining the threat?"

Rico's eyebrows drew together. "No. Jorge and Tomas have found too many signs that someone is watching us. At first, we didn't mention this to you. They thought it was a drifter passing through."

"You mean this has been going on longer than we thought?" Eduardo clenched his jaw.

"No, not that long. Only a few weeks." Rico waved a hand in the air as if dismissing Eduardo's concern. "The boys often find evidence that someone has spent the night in the hills near the ranch. I think these men want the safety of being near the house, but not the contact. I don't think they're dangerous or responsible for the attack on your wife." He gave Eduardo a steady look.

"So, who do you think is doing this?"

"Someone who wants to hurt you." Rico gazed out across the valley. "You and your father only have one person I know of who might do this. You are very well thought of by everyone else."

"Diego Garcia." Eduardo could feel his stomach knot. That man had been a thorn in his flesh for years. He'd thought that by marrying Diego's daughter, their conflict would be at an end. "I have no way to prove it's him."

"I remember your father saying when you have a rogue animal that needs taking care of, you track him to his lair." Rico raised his eyebrows in a questioning glance. "We aren't all that far from the Garcias' place. We could drop in and see how Diego is doing."

Huffing out a breath, Eduardo nodded. "I guess you're right. Perhaps it's time for Diego's son-in-law to visit." He twisted the strap on the canteen. "After knowing the way he treated Chiquita, I only hope I can keep my temper in check when I see him."

They finished their meal, tightened the cinches, and mounted. Eduardo led the way over the hills to the rutted road that led to the Garcia place. When he thought of confronting Diego, all he could see was Chiquita and the way she feared men because of what had been done to her. Although she had an uncommon strength, anyone who knew her at all could see the terror in her eyes whenever any man showed a force or anger about anything. She seemed to always think the anger was directed at her. Getting rid of her fear might take years.

His roiling emotions calmed as he thought of Chiquita. During the last few nights, she'd seemed so eager to hear the Bible. Last night he'd wanted to explain salvation to her, but he could see her eyelids drooping as he talked. Since she rose so early, she didn't like to stay up late. Still, she refused to go to bed while he was awake. Despite the short time they'd been married, already he couldn't imagine life without Chiquita. If only she would learn to relax around him and trust him. He had to fight this tendency to become angry.

The Garcia home was little more than a shack. The cluttered yard and shabbiness of the house lent an air of abandonment to the place. A dog slunk around the corner of the house. Eduardo could count the pup's ribs without any trouble. The poor thing looked half-starved and cowered as if it had been abused, reminding him of Chiquita. His hands tightened on the reins.

The door creaked open. Teresa sashayed out, lifting a hand to her brow to block the sun. He knew when she recognized him. She smiled, and her swaying walk became even more pronounced.

"Why, if it isn't my favorite brother-in-law." She stopped beside Eduardo's horse and gave him a coquettish look.

"I've come to see your father. Is he home?" Eduardo resisted the urge to move his horse away from Teresa. She made him uncomfortable now, although she hadn't when he met her before.

"He's gone right now. Maybe I can help you." She gave him a smile that made him pull on the reins, causing his horse to dance away from her. "Are you having trouble with Fealdad? Papa can come and give you some lessons on how to get her to do what you want."

For a minute, Eduardo had no idea what she was talking about. Then he recalled Diego using that despicable name for Chiquita. His muscles tensed as he fought down the wrath. How could he have ever thought Teresa would make a good wife?

"Where is your father?"

She took a step closer, reaching out to run a hand down his horse's neck. "I don't know. He likes to go off by himself. Says he's going hunting." She shrugged. "Ever since his cousin stopped by for a visit a few weeks ago, he's been hunting a lot."

Rico snorted. Eduardo glanced at him and could see his foreman's suspicions. Diego must be the one who watched his place and shot Chiquita. But why? Was he there now, watching the place?

Teresa's hand drifted closer to Eduardo's leg. He tugged on the reins, making his horse back away. "When your father gets home, tell him I was here."

"Wait." Teresa raised her hand.

Eduardo wheeled around and raced from the yard. Rico followed close on his heels. The ride home seemed to take forever. They took a shortcut, riding silently, looking for signs.

"Eduardo, stop." Rico's sharp tone halted Eduardo. They were on a hilltop with a clear view of the ranch house, although a very distant one. "Look at this." Rico hopped off his horse and knelt down.

Eduardo joined him. The hard dirt showed the scuffing of hoofprints, as if a horse had been tethered here for a long time.

"Can you smell it?" Rico tilted his head.

Eduardo sniffed lightly, noting the scent of horse, sweat, and something else. "Someone's been smoking here." He followed as Rico edged along the ridge. On the far side of a large boulder, several cigarette butts were squashed into the earth to make them less noticeable.

"Someone's been here recently." Rico poked at one of the cigarettes. "This one is still warm. I'd say he heard us coming and hightailed it."

"Why would they be here watching? You can't see much from here." Eduardo narrowed his eyes, trying to make out any detail in the house below them.

"If you had a spyglass like they use in the cavalry, you could see plenty."

"Let's go." Eduardo surged to his feet and strode to his horse. He couldn't explain the sudden urgency to get back to Chiquita. With every bit of evidence, this was getting more serious.

They made their way to the ranch in grim silence. Desperate thoughts plagued

Eduardo. Did Diego mean to harm him or Chiquita? Was it even Diego doing this? Rage kept rearing its ugly head. As they came over the last ridge, Rico gave a cry and pointed to the yard. In front of the house stood two strange horses. Wrath blurred his vision as Eduardo kicked his mount to a full gallop.

Before the horse could slide to a stop, he jumped from the saddle and sprinted to the house. If anyone had harmed Chiquita, they wouldn't live to tell about it. He ignored Rico's shout as he jerked the door open and raced inside.

Chapter 12

The door hit the wall with a crack like thunder. Chiquita jumped to her feet. Eduardo dashed into the room, rage nearly choking him. All he could see was Chiquita's face turn white. Her mouth thinned, her back stiffened. The fear that shone momentarily in her eyes receded. Eduardo didn't slow until he stood in front of her. She was all right, only terrified of him.

Swinging around, Eduardo saw Pilar seated, holding a glass in her hand. Across the room two men sat with their backs to the sun, their faces in the shadow. One of them wore a gun. They rose. Relief flooded Eduardo, leaving him almost weak from the intensity of his ire.

"Quinn. Conlon. I didn't expect to see you here. Those aren't your normal mounts." He strode across the room and shook hands with his two friends. "What brings you out this way?"

Rico stepped inside, his stance wary. Eduardo could see his friends were puzzled at the reception they were receiving. He nodded to the door. "Perhaps we could go outside and talk."

Glancing over his shoulder, Eduardo could see that Chiquita still stood ramrod stiff, waiting for her punishment for whatever crime she thought she'd committed. "Go on out with Rico. I'll be there in a minute."

Pilar frowned at him, picked up the glasses left behind by the men, and went to the kitchen. Using slow movements, Eduardo approached Chiquita. He knew he'd scared her once again. He hadn't meant to, but he'd been so afraid something had happened to her. The thought of someone hurting her had driven him crazy, yet he didn't know how to tell her that without sounding insincere.

He touched her cheek. There was only the slightest flinching. Her pale skin felt cool. The smell of his mother's lavender soap drifted to him. "I didn't mean to startle you." Running a thumb over her lower lip, he wanted to kiss her. Would she be afraid? Unyielding as she was, he knew he shouldn't push intimacy, although with each day, it grew harder to keep away from her. He longed to take her in his arms, to whisper his love to her.

"I have to go talk with my friends. I'll explain what happened later. Please, don't think I was mad at you. I wasn't." As he spoke, she opened her eyes. Her amber gaze, still a little fearful, made him take a deep breath. He turned away before he lost all reason and forgot that his friends were outside waiting for him.

⚘

The afternoon sun cast long shadows. The squeal of a horse filled the air as some of the foals kicked and raced across the pasture. The wind, coming from the direction of the river, brought the earthy smell of moist ground. Eduardo breathed deeply, trying to rid himself of the last vestiges of anger. Quinn and Conlon waited at the barn. They watched him walk toward them.

"Do you always enter your house like it's getting ready to burn to the ground?" Quinn tried to make the question light, but Eduardo could read the seriousness in his tone. His friends hadn't understood his panic.

"It's been quite a day. Come on in the barn, and we'll sit down." He looked over at Rico. "Are Jorge and Tomas back yet?"

Rico shook his head. "I'll put up the horses." He led their mounts away, giving Eduardo the opportunity to speak with Quinn and Conlon alone.

"I've had some problems here in the last few weeks."

Quinn tensed. Conlon frowned and sat forward. "What kind of problems?"

Eduardo explained losing his new foal to the cougar, the discovery that someone had been watching them, and Chiquita being shot. "We went out today to see if we could find some evidence of who's behind this."

"Did you find anything?" Quinn asked.

"Nothing we can prove." Eduardo smoothed his mustache and told them of his suspicions about Diego Garcia. "On the way home, we found evidence on that ridge. Someone who smokes has been there. Rico thinks they might be watching the house with a spyglass. The problem is, I can't figure out why anyone would do this. Even though Diego is the only one who might be guilty, why would he be interested in us?"

"Maybe he regrets letting you marry his daughter." Quinn frowned. "Although that wouldn't explain his shooting her. Besides, I thought you were marrying Teresa. I've only seen her a couple of times, but your wife didn't look like Teresa."

"That's true," Conlon said. "I remember Teresa talking up a storm, and this girl didn't say a word the whole time we were here. Pilar did all the talking."

Eduardo sighed. "Diego tricked me into marrying his other daughter. I call her Chiquita, because the name he'd given her was so awful."

"If he tricked you, we can take him to court and make him give you the daughter you wanted." Quinn's eyes narrowed.

"No, I don't want Teresa anymore. Besides, I could never send Chiquita back into that family." Eduardo explained what he'd learned of Chiquita's upbringing. By the time he finished, both of his friends were upset.

"That explains why she never said a word." Quinn rubbed at his badge. "I don't understand why a man would do that to his own daughter. He should be put behind bars."

"You're right." Conlon stood and stretched. "Unfortunately, you know as well as I do, there isn't a court that would find him guilty of anything. He would say he was disciplining her. Men can get away with a lot in the name of correction."

"If this doesn't stop, Eduardo, I want you to come and get me. I don't have any jurisdiction out here, but maybe I can put some fear into Diego anyway."

"Thanks." Eduardo warmed at the thought of having friends willing to help out. "You never did say why you came out here."

"I saw Antonio Soza in town the other day. He told me all about some new breed of horse you have here. I came to see for myself." Conlon grinned. "Quinn tagged along because he thought if he stayed home, Kathleen would make him take care of that baby boy of his."

Eduardo chuckled and led the way to El Rey's stall. Pride surged through him as Conlon and Quinn both let out low whistles of admiration. El Rey pranced to the front of the stall. He stretched out his nose, his dark mane falling forward.

"This isn't one of your regular horses." Conlon rubbed El Rey's ears. "What is he?"

"He's an Andalusian." Eduardo grinned as Quinn and Conlon both gave him questioning glances. "The Andalusian breed began in Spain, but some were brought to South America. I read about them but only learned recently that a few had been brought this far north. After some correspondence, I managed to purchase this stallion and one mare."

"What's the advantage to the breed, besides their size?" Conlon asked.

"I wanted a horse that would be bigger because I knew that's what you were looking at for your troops." Eduardo couldn't suppress a surge of excitement. "These horses are incredible. They adapt to their surroundings well, train easily, and they have to be the best-looking horses I've ever seen. They're powerful and agile. As you can see from El Rey, these horses are known for their mild temperament, making them easy to work with. You can teach them to do anything."

Conlon chuckled. "I'm not sure you care for the horse."

Eduardo laughed. "I guess I am a little enthusiastic. The more I learned about Andalusians, the better I liked them. Their history goes back a long ways."

"How soon before you have some foals from him?" Conlon scratched El Rey's ear. The horse leaned against him.

"I bought the mare because she would foal this spring. That's the colt that was killed." Eduardo couldn't keep the anger from his voice. Losing his only purebred foal had been a loss he hadn't anticipated. There were always hazards when raising livestock, but he hadn't counted on a puma coming so close to the house.

"Now I won't have any more foals from him until next year."

"I can't wait to see them." Conlon gave El Rey a final pat. "I have to get back to town. You know, you might consider bringing your wife to Tucson for a few days. Glory and I would be happy to have you visit."

"Thanks." Eduardo walked with them to their horses. "I might do that. I'm getting pretty jumpy with all that's going on here. Besides, I don't know if Chiquita has ever been to town. She might enjoy it."

On her knees, Chiquita worked her way along the row of pepper plants, pulling the young weeds from the ground. The damp earth stuck to her hands and her dress. She loved the smell and feel of the dirt and the plants growing there. She flipped her braid back over her shoulder, wishing she'd taken the time to pin it up before coming out here.

Later, she would take a bath and wash her hair with some of the soap she'd made this morning from the dried yucca roots. After grating the roots, she'd boiled them until the suds began to form. Now, the water was cooling and would be ready to use soon. She almost moaned at the chance to use the fresh soap to get clean after the hard day's work.

Her thoughts drifted. Over a week had passed since Eduardo stormed in the house to find his friends visiting. He must have been mad at her for some reason. Why couldn't she learn to trust him? He wasn't like Papa. He'd proved that over and over, yet every time he got upset about anything, she knew he would hit her. Such a good man didn't deserve a wife like her. Eduardo needed someone who wouldn't be so fearful.

In the past week, Eduardo'd been so busy. Many of the mares were foaling. Every night, he was needed to help with one thing or another. Last night had been their first night together. Eduardo read from the Bible, and she realized how much she'd missed hearing those words. He'd been so gentle as he explained more about Jesus to her. Her fingers continued to pull the weeds as she recalled Eduardo explaining that Jesus, the Son of God, had died for her. Eduardo even read the story of the crucifixion to her. When he read about Jesus being whipped by the soldiers, she couldn't help the tears that burned her eyes. She could feel those lashes. Bending over her work, she tried to hide her distress from Eduardo, but he seemed to know, anyway.

He also seemed to understand all of her unspoken questions. Had he asked the same questions of his parents? When she wondered what she had to do to be accepted by God, Eduardo began to tell her that the only way to heaven was by God's grace. That's why Jesus died, so He would be the sacrifice for her. She only had to admit her sins, which she already had. Then she needed to believe Jesus was the Son of God and ask Him into her heart.

The thing Eduardo didn't understand was that she wasn't worthy of Jesus. He wouldn't want someone as ugly and useless as she. He might have died for people like Eduardo or Pilar—those who were truly good people—but He hadn't died for her. She would have to find another way to get to heaven. The more she learned about heaven, the more she longed to go there. She felt like God was calling to her heart, but it had to be a trick. How many times had Papa told her she was worthless? Would her own father have lied to her? Even her mother and sisters had agreed. Eduardo must be wrong when he said Jesus died for everyone. Her heart broke at the thought.

Swiping at her eyes with the sleeve of her dress, Chiquita continued down the row. She put the weeds in a pile to throw into the horse pasture. If she left them lying on the moist earth, they would only take root again. Papa's words were that way. No matter how many times she tried to convince herself he had lied to her, she always remembered what he said. The roots of those words went so deep inside her, she would never get rid of them. Even in her dreams, she could hear his taunting voice.

At least here, she had a haven of peace. No one yelled at her or called her names. Eduardo paid her such sweet attention. She knew she didn't deserve him. Sitting up, she cocked her head to listen. The dogs were quiet. Birds twittered in the trees near the house. Serenity settled over her, banishing the thoughts of her former life.

Easing up from the ground, she brushed off her knees. She picked up the pile of weeds she'd gathered and carried them to the edge of the garden. She hoped to have the whole garden done in another hour. First, she needed a drink. The sun beating down had warmed her more than she thought, and now her throat was dry.

Returning to the garden a few minutes later, she smiled at her progress. The squash plants were growing fast. In a few weeks, they would have fresh squash. Her mouth watered at the thought. The beans, peppers, and tomatoes would take longer. She always anticipated eating those first fresh vegetables. Nothing tasted better.

Chiquita glanced at the sun as she knelt where she'd left off. She had plenty of time to finish this and take a quick bath before fixing supper. Eduardo had gone to see Señor Soza again today. When he came home, he would be tired. She wanted to have a bath ready for him, along with a good supper.

Seeing a weed on the other side of the pepper row, Chiquita leaned over, stretching out to reach the interloper. A plant on the far side of her exploded. Dirt flew in the air. A sharp crack sounded. She fell forward, confused at what was happening. Had someone shot a gun at her?

Rolling to one side, she struggled to get up. Her dress caught beneath her feet. She fell. A second geyser of dirt erupted. The shot rang out. The dogs went wild. She heard a shout and the sound of pounding feet.

Freeing her dress, she stumbled to her feet. Heart pounding, she raced for the house. She had to get to safety. The adobe brick on the side of the house exploded. Fragments of the dried brick stung her cheek. Racing around the corner, she sobbed in terror. Was she going to die? She wanted to call for help. She opened her mouth, but nothing came out.

Lucio sprinted toward her. He motioned frantically at the house. Didn't he understand she was trying to get inside? Bark exploded from a tree. Sharp pain raced down her arm. Tears ran down her cheeks. She slipped and fell. A sob tore free. Lucio raised his gun. The sharp crack spurred her to action.

Leaping to her feet, she reached the door. The latch refused to work. Maybe she could hide on the other side of the house. She jerked one more time. The latch came loose, and the door flew open. She tumbled inside. Running through the house, she fell to the floor by her bed. Blood dripped from her face. Had he shot her? Was she going to die?

Oh, Jesus, please help me. I don't want to die without knowing You. Help me to know how I can be worthy. She curled in a ball, sobbing. Never would she be good enough for Jesus. Never.

Chapter 13

C hiquita, Sweetheart."
Eduardo's strong arms were lifting her from where she'd curled up on the floor by her bed. She couldn't stop shaking. He cuddled her close.

"Are you hurt?" He carried her from the dim room. She bit her lip to keep from whimpering like a child. She didn't want to go out in the light. What if someone started shooting again? The thought terrified her.

Eduardo sank into the rocking chair. For a long moment, he held her tight. Their breathing melded into one rhythm. She could smell the scent of horses and sunshine on his shirt. He must have just come home. She almost smiled at the way her mind wanted to grasp at normal thoughts when the world was spinning upside down.

"Let me see." His hand was gentle as he lifted her face from his chest. "Oh, Sweetheart, you've been bleeding. Did you get shot?" A hint of panic infused his voice. She tried to shake her head, but her muscles didn't seem capable of responding properly.

The front door banged open. Footsteps clattered across the floor. Chiquita wanted to snuggle into Eduardo again. She'd felt so safe there. Never before had she known that kind of comfort.

Her senses were coming awake. The arm nestled against Eduardo ached. Her cheek stung and felt swollen. Remembering the flying shards of adobe and bark, she repressed a shudder, grateful nothing had pierced her eyes.

"How is she?" Pilar sounded breathless as she reached them.

"She's been bleeding, but I can't see how bad she's hurt."

Hands turned her. Eduardo's large hands lifted her, then Pilar's smaller ones brushed across her face.

"Rico, I'll need some hot water. Jorge, bring me some fresh water for now. I need to clean off the blood and dirt to see how bad this is." Pilar barked the orders like a general. "Bring her over here, Eduardo. I'll have to undress her to make sure she wasn't shot." Pilar leaned close, her face a mask of concern. "Chiquita, can you hear me?"

In a massive effort, Chiquita lifted her head enough to meet Pilar's gaze. She tried to nod, but her body felt heavy, exhausted.

"Okay." Pilar smoothed Chiquita's hair away from her face. Somehow the braid had come undone and the waves tangled around her body. "Eduardo will bring some light, and we'll see how you are."

Biting her lip to keep from moaning at the pain, Chiquita could feel her face drain of blood as Eduardo carried her to her bed. She could tell he tried to be gentle, but every movement sent a jolt of agony through her. Something must be lodged in her arm for it to hurt this much. Had she been shot? She couldn't remember. Everything happened so fast. All she thought of at the time was getting to safety.

Pilar sent Eduardo to get the water and a rag from Jorge. While he was gone, she began to remove Chiquita's clothing. The dress, crusted in dirt, stained with blood, came away reluctantly. When she began to pull the left sleeve off the shoulder, Chiquita cried out.

Eduardo rushed into the room. "What's happening?"

"Look at this." At Pilar's grim tone, Chiquita tried to sit up to see what she'd found. The sight of Eduardo in the room when she wasn't decent made her gasp. Pilar noted the sound and jerked a cover over the top of her.

"Lucio said that the shooter hit the tree as Chiquita ran past. A piece of the wood went clear through her dress and is buried in her arm." Pilar worried her lip with her teeth. "We have to get that fragment out."

Pulling his knife from his pocket, Eduardo began to cut the material from around the wood. Chiquita could tell he wanted to rip the cloth away, but he seemed too concerned about her comfort to do something so rash. When he had the area clear, she could see the flesh puckered where the bark-covered wood had pierced her arm.

"I'll have to get this out." Eduardo sat on the bed beside her, his face serious. His eyes seemed to show a reluctance to cause her pain. Chiquita's heart ached for him. She knew without a doubt that Eduardo was not at all like Papa. Pressing her lips together, she nodded for him to continue.

With a sharp tug, the piece of wood pulled free. She could feel the blood coming out, but she didn't look. Closing her eyes, she tried to stop the tears. She ached all over. She wanted more than anything to be back in Eduardo's arms. Stunned, she realized how much she'd come to care for him. Did she love him? She wasn't sure she even knew what love was.

"Hold this tight on her arm, Eduardo." Pilar pressed a cloth to slow the bleeding. "I think this is the worst. I don't see any bullet wounds. I'll get Jorge to bring some prickly pear pads. We have to get the rest of that dirt out, and the cactus should do it."

As she left the room to give instructions to the others, Eduardo held the rag to Chiquita's arm. She gazed up at him as he touched her cheek where the adobe and splinters of tree had cut her. Anger darkened his eyes. He tensed, as if he wanted to do something about this but didn't know how. For the first time, she wasn't afraid of his anger. This time, she knew he wasn't mad at her. Instead, his gentle touch soothed her. Warmth flushed her cheeks. He'd called her "Sweetheart" earlier. Never, in her wildest dreams, had she thought any man would call her an endearment.

A few minutes later, Pilar bustled back into the room. Behind her, Rico carried a steaming pan. He placed it on a table before leaving again. Chiquita almost sighed with relief. She couldn't bear the thought of someone she didn't know well seeing her like this.

Slipping a hand behind Chiquita's head, Pilar lifted her up a bit. "I want you to drink this tea, Chiquita. This is made with some catclaw leaves. They'll help you relax. Picking out all these stickers could take time. We'll try to be as gentle as we can."

The warm tea had an unusual taste, but Chiquita swallowed obediently. When she finished, Pilar retrieved the pan Rico had carried in earlier. With care, Pilar lifted half of a prickly pear cactus pad from the hot water. She cooled it for a minute, then molded the cut side to Chiquita's arm where the tree fragment pierced her. Taking a long cloth, she wrapped the pad to wedge it tight against the skin. Chiquita gritted her teeth to keep from crying out.

When Pilar finished, Eduardo began to wipe Chiquita's face with a warm cloth. The slow, gentle movement helped her relax. She closed her eyes as he worked to cleanse the area peppered by small splinters. The sedative in the catclaw tea began to spread a heaviness through her limbs. By the time Eduardo finished washing her face, she barely noticed as Pilar removed the shards of brick and bark one by one.

By the time they finished, Chiquita didn't think she could stay awake much longer. The strain of the afternoon, combined with the medicine, made her drift into a healing sleep. Her last memory was of Eduardo pulling a chair beside the bed, telling Pilar to go home, that he would sit with her for awhile.

✿

Cradling Chiquita's small hand in his, Eduardo couldn't help wishing he was still holding her. If she didn't need the rest so badly, he'd be tempted to lift her into his arms once more. He knew if he bumped her arm in the process, he would wake her. Checking the time, he saw he needed to take off the cactus pad, cleanse, and rewrap the wound. Pilar left explicit instructions for him to follow. The problem was, he didn't want to risk waking Chiquita. All he wanted to do was sit here and watch her sleep. His fingers longed to trace the line of her cheeks, down her long, slender neck. He could almost feel the dip of the slight cleft in her chin. The memory of touching her soft skin warmed him.

Protective feelings warred within him. He wanted to stay here to make sure Chiquita rested and recovered. At the same time, he wanted to scour the hills for her attacker. Jorge and Tomas had gone out when they'd arrived home, but they found nothing. They would go out once again, at first light, to renew the search. This time, Lucio and Rico would be with them. As soon as Pilar could come and stay with Chiquita, Eduardo intended to join his men.

God, help me. I want to take vengeance. Help me control my anger, Lord. I can't do this on my own. I want to have joy in my life, but how am I supposed to do that when

all these things are happening? Please, Jesus, help Chiquita. I know she's interested in You,
but I don't know what to say to her. Show her the truth about who You are.

With a sigh, Eduardo kissed Chiquita's fingers. After releasing her hand, he unwound the bandage holding the cactus pad on her arm. She moaned. He frowned. At the time, he hadn't thought much about it, but Chiquita had cried out earlier. He stopped as the memory took hold. Did that mean she could talk? Had something happened to her long ago to make her quit speaking, even though she still had the ability to do so? Knowing how Diego treated her, he knew this must be a possibility. Maybe, given time, Chiquita would be able to talk to him. Hope surged. He would have to go easy on this, but maybe—just maybe—she could.

The prickly pear pad didn't want to pull away from her skin. The juice seemed to adhere to whatever it touched, which made the cactus a worthy drawing agent. As the pad cooled and dried, most of the unwanted particles would be drawn out, and the wound would seal. Eduardo retrieved a warm rag to loosen the edges of the cactus, lifting it free. The place where the wood punctured Chiquita's arm already looked better. After washing her arm with some of the leftover catclaw tea as Pilar had instructed, Eduardo sprinkled powdered catclaw leaves over the cut and wrapped the arm.

Through the whole process, Chiquita slept, moaning only when he removed the cactus. Tucking the covers around her, Eduardo once more sat in the chair by her bed. He picked up her hand. Her fingers were cool to the touch. That was good. Pilar said to watch for fever. As long as Chiquita remained cool, he knew she would be fine.

✤

The smell of tortillas cooking on the stove woke Eduardo. He'd fallen asleep, resting his head on the bed beside Chiquita's hand. He rotated his shoulders, trying to ease out the kinks. His back felt like a herd of horses had trampled across him during the night.

Chiquita's soft breathing whispered in the quiet of the room. She had some color in her cheeks. Last night she'd been so pale, he'd been afraid for her. Touching her forehead, he sighed with relief at the coolness. He and Pilar both knew the dangers of fever.

Chiquita's eyelids fluttered a few times, then opened. She blinked, her honey gaze clouded with sleep. Her cheek, slightly swollen from all of the cuts, looked sore. Eduardo spent a long time last night thanking God that the shards hadn't entered her eye. Several of the cuts were close. She tried to smile. Her dry lips looked painful.

"Let me get you a drink." Eduardo gave her a lopsided grin. "I must look awful. I fell asleep here and haven't even washed up yet."

She started to raise her hand, winced, and shook her head. Her gaze followed him as he moved across the room to wash and bring her a drink. She lowered the cup and tried to smile. He knew from the way her mouth tightened when he moved her how much her arm hurt.

"I think Pilar is here, fixing breakfast. I'll have her come in and help you. Rico is out with the vaqueros, trying to find who shot at you. I'll grab a bite and join them while Pilar stays with you."

Chiquita's eyes widened. The faint flush left her cheeks. Her hand reached for him again, and she grimaced.

Eduardo brushed the hair off her forehead. "Don't worry. You'll be safe. We won't go far. At least one of us will be within sight of the house at all times." She leaned her cheek into his palm. He wanted to stay here forever. "I have to find out who's responsible, Chiquita. We can't live like this, with someone trying to hurt you."

Standing, he jammed his hat on his head. "I want you to rest today and follow Pilar's orders. She'll take good care of you." He winked at her. She relaxed. The corners of her mouth almost tipped up in a smile. Eduardo left the room, lighthearted despite all the troubles plaguing them.

⁂

"What have you found?" Eduardo spoke before his horse came to a complete stop. Rico, Jorge, and Tomas were clustered together, examining something on the ground.

"Look at this." The two younger men moved back while Rico pointed at the dirt. "Someone's been smoking here." Rico nudged the burnt scrap of paper with his finger. "Whoever shot at your wife is the same person who was on the far ridge, watching the house. They put the same twist on their cigarettes."

Eduardo squatted down beside his foreman. His finger traced the print of a boot. "You're right. Look at this boot print. Whoever wears these walks with more of his weight on the outside of his foot, right here. See how the boot's worn?"

Rico nodded. "We think he shot at the house from here, but if so, how did he continue shooting when the señora went around the corner? He wouldn't be able to see her then."

Eduardo stood and looked down on the house. Although a long distance, this spot afforded a perfect view of the garden area, but the angle was all wrong for the far side of the house. Whoever waited here wouldn't have been able to shoot the tree when Chiquita passed it.

"Could he have been moving as she ran?"

"No, Señor. I asked Lucio, and he claims he never saw any movement from the hillside. He would have seen him if the shooter moved."

Studying the ground, Eduardo followed the man's trail to where his horse had been tied out of sight. The deep hoofprints in the hard dirt showed how the horse raced away from this spot. *If only I'd been home, then I could have stopped this madman.*

"I don't understand how he did this. Jorge, you and Tomas follow the trail.

See if you can find where he went, but be careful."

Climbing on their horses, the two young men moved off. Tomas, as the best tracker, bent over his horse's withers, watching the sign. Eduardo turned back to Rico.

"What do you think? At first I thought Diego was responsible, but that doesn't make sense. Why would he allow me to marry his daughter, then try to kill her? I don't know what to think anymore, but I'm scared for Chiquita."

Rico slapped his horse's reins against his leg. He stared across the hilltop. "I have an idea. Come on."

Eduardo followed, wondering what the older man was thinking. A few minutes later, Rico stopped and dismounted. Squatting beside a boulder, he beckoned to Eduardo. There on the ground were more scuffed prints. These footprints were different. The boots were worn in a different area.

Rico glanced up. "There wasn't one man shooting at your wife, Eduardo. There were two of them."

Chapter 14

How's my favorite patient this morning?" Pilar bustled into the house as Eduardo left.

Chiquita suppressed a sigh. For the past few days, Pilar had come every morning to change the bandage on her arm. By the morning of the second day, a slight infection seemed to be setting in, so Pilar made a poultice of malva leaves. She spent the morning putting the hot oatmeallike mixture on Chiquita's arm, waiting an hour, and then repeating the process. The hot poultice wasn't pleasant, but the infection was gone. Now the arm itched. Chiquita knew that was a sure sign of healing.

Pilar set down her basket of herbs. "I've seen caged animals that looked happier than you do. I know you're bored to tears having to stay in the house, but Eduardo knows what's best. Until they find out who's trying to hurt you, you need to stay out of sight."

With a nod, Chiquita moved to sit down and let Pilar begin her examination. She had been bored. She wanted to work in the garden. The weeds would be so thick, she would never catch up. She also wanted to begin watching for the cholla cactus to bud so she could gather some of the buds to dry. They made a delicious vegetable or a good addition to a stew. There was much to be done, yet she was stuck in the house.

"Oh, this is looking good." Pilar probed at the scar. "Is it itching yet?" When Chiquita nodded, Pilar smiled. "As long as it isn't very sore, you'll be fine. If you start having problems, let me know. Otherwise, I think I can leave you in peace."

Panic raced through Chiquita. She'd come to enjoy these visits with Pilar. This was her only contact with anyone, other than Eduardo in the evenings.

"Don't worry. I'll still come every day and see you. Would you like a cup of tea?" Pilar laughed as she looked at Chiquita. "I promise I won't put any foul-tasting medicine in this tea. I'll even add a little honey for you, if you want."

A smile pushed at Chiquita's heart. She'd never had a friend. Pilar always talked as if Chiquita was an equal or better. Quite often she tried to defer to Chiquita since she was the boss's wife, but the lack of verbal communication stood in their way. This past week, Chiquita had tried hard to work on her reading and writing, but she still didn't know enough to converse that way.

So many questions burned inside her—questions about Jesus and how she could become worthy of Him. For years, Mama refused to allow her to pray with her or even come near their small altar. They always said only certain people were good enough, and she wasn't one of them. Doubt had begun to creep in. She needed to ask someone about the truth.

"Here you go." Pilar carried two cups of tea from the kitchen. After handing one to Chiquita, she wrapped her hands around the other and sat down.

The warm tea felt and tasted delicious. The early morning still carried a chill. Later in the day, the sun would warm things up a lot, but for now, the house was cool.

Taking a sip from her cup, Pilar looked up, her gaze serious. "Chiquita, do you have any idea who would be shooting at you or why?"

Chiquita shook her head. She'd already let Eduardo know, but she was afraid he didn't believe her. A lump settled in her throat. How she wanted to reassure everyone here of her innocence in this matter! She hated that she was putting them all in danger. Most of all, she wanted to know why this was happening.

"I've wanted to talk to you about something else." Pilar swirled the liquid in her cup before meeting Chiquita's gaze. "The night we took the fragment of wood from your arm, you cried out in pain. Do you remember that?"

Chiquita shook her head. That day was mostly a blur in her memory. Any attempt to recall what happened resulted in a headache.

"Besides being afraid, you were in a lot of pain. I'm not sure Eduardo noticed you cry out, but he might have. He's very quick to catch things." Pilar leaned forward. "Chiquita, do you want to talk?"

Her breath caught. Did she want to talk? Of course, she did. The problem was, she couldn't. She'd tried the last few days, when she had the house to herself. Not a sound would come out, no matter how hard she tried. Tears blurred her vision as she nodded at Pilar. Pointing to her mouth and then her throat, she shook her head.

"Have you tried to speak?" Pilar set her cup on the floor beside her feet. She took Chiquita's hands in hers. At Chiquita's nod, she gave a gentle squeeze. "Do you remember having a serious disease when you were young or perhaps an accident that would have caused you to lose the ability to talk?"

Chiquita frowned. She had only vague memories of chattering with Teresa when they were very young.

"I know you used to be able to speak." Pilar began to rub Chiquita's hands. "I also have a feeling I know how you were treated by your family. Something must have happened, maybe something that made you afraid to say anything ever again. Is that possible?"

Her heart hammered as Chiquita pondered the question. *Could this be true?*

"Chiquita, if this is right, that you quit talking because of the way you were treated, then perhaps when you feel comfortable here, you'll be able to overcome that fear. Don't give up. Keep trying. It will be worth the effort."

As she worked around the house the rest of the day, Chiquita couldn't get Pilar's words out of her mind. Had she quit talking because of the beatings Papa gave her? The longing that had been in her heart for days now began to swell. She wanted to sit in the evenings with Eduardo and discuss things like she knew Pilar and Rico did. Was she hoping for too much?

Dusting the books, she could almost hear Eduardo's steady voice as he read to her from the Bible. This past week, something had changed between them. It had taken her a couple of days to figure out what the change was. She had begun to trust Eduardo.

After the shooting, he'd become so concerned for her. Waking up to find that he'd slept by her bedside because of his concern had done something to her. No one ever cared about her like that before. The few times she'd been sick, she had still been expected to do work. No matter how bad she felt, she wasn't given a break.

Eduardo, though, seemed to want to pamper her. He thought she should stay in bed or rest rather than do her daily chores. She'd quickly put a stop to that. Other than agreeing to stay indoors for safety's sake, she had continued cleaning and cooking. However, because of the change in him, she'd come to trust him. She could tell when he was thinking about the shooting because anger would darken his eyes, but her fear had disappeared. Eduardo cared about her. She didn't know how she knew it—she just did.

With the chores caught up by midafternoon, an excited shiver of anticipation washed over Chiquita. Eduardo encouraged her to work on her reading and writing. Today, she wanted to take the time to look at some of the books in his room that had the beautiful pictures in them. They fascinated her. She wondered if she could make out any of the words now. She'd made great progress over the last week.

Settling on the floor in front of the bookshelf, Chiquita chose the book she wanted. This one had pictures of birds and animals that she'd never seen. Trying to make out some of the words, she lost track of time. Another world drew her in. She ignored the darkening of the room as the afternoon waned.

A creak of the floorboards in the living room startled her. She glanced at the window, amazed to see the sunlight so far gone. Eduardo must be home already. Stuffing the book back in the shelf, she stumbled up on legs that had gone to sleep. Pins and needles pricked at her as she hurried from the bedroom. She hadn't even started supper.

She rushed into the front room, almost colliding with a man. She gasped and jumped back. Groping for the doorway, she calculated her chances of getting away.

The man gave her a slow, sinister smile, his lips parting to show yellowed teeth. In one hand, he held a pistol. With a flick of his wrist, the barrel of the gun pointed at her.

Fear clutched at her. Chiquita edged a step away.

"Stay right there, Señora." His dark eyes narrowed. His gaze made her want to run and hide. "They said to kill you, but they didn't say how pretty you are. I might just take you with me, instead." He closed the gap between them. Lifting the barrel of the gun, he traced it across her cheek. "I can always kill you later."

Her knees shook. She couldn't think what to do. Who was this man? Who sent him to kill her? Why? The questions made her dizzy. Closing her eyes, she hoped this was only a bad dream. Any minute, she would wake up and everything would be all right.

"Let's go." His painful grip on her arm negated the idea of this being a dream. He dragged her to the door, opened it, and surveyed the yard, his gun ready. Satisfied, he holstered the weapon. Grabbing her wrist, he began to pull her around the side of the house.

Fear gave way to desperation. She'd been mistreated all her life. Most of the time, she took what was dished out. This time, she intended to fight. Chiquita dug in her heels.

The man spun around, his gaze ugly with anger. She yanked his mustache. He yelped. Lifting her arm, she bit his hand, drawing blood. He let go.

She flew across the yard toward Pilar's. She had to get help. His feet thudded behind her. She could almost feel a bullet hitting her back. Her throat burned, her lungs ached for air. He drew closer. His breathing sounded almost in her ear. She didn't have time to get to Pilar's. Darting to one side, she heard him curse.

With a burst of speed, she sprinted into the barn. Racing down the corridor, she hopped up on a bench and fell over the barrier into a stall. Huddling in a corner, she strove to control her gasping breath so he wouldn't hear her.

"I know you're in here. You may as well not hide from me." His grating voice sent a chill through her. "Come on, Honey. You can either go with me now, or I'll have to kill you. I've already been paid for that."

Clutching her knees to her chest, Chiquita wanted to pray. She'd heard Eduardo talk to his God, and with all her heart, she wished she had a God who loved her, too. She didn't want just any God, she wanted the Jesus she'd been learning about.

Jesus, why did I have to be so unworthy of You? If only You would accept me, I would love You with all my heart. She held her breath to stop the sob threatening to come out. *I'm such a sinner, Jesus. I know that's why You'll never want me. Please, if You care for Eduardo, help me, too.*

The crunch of the man's footsteps sounded outside the stall. He paused. The quiet pressed down on her. Her heart pounded, shaking her with the intensity. She held her breath.

"Why, there you are." The stall door creaked as he eased it open.

Chiquita huddled tight in the straw and dirt on the floor, hoping he hadn't seen her. The yank on her hair told her different. Her eyes watered as he jerked her upright. "You didn't think you could escape me, did you?"

In an instant, his countenance went from playful to deadly. He drew her close. The smell of unwashed clothing and man gagged her. Her fists clenched tight as he began to drag her toward the door.

"I'd love to stay and play, Honey, but we have to get out of here before your husband returns."

The sunlight blinded her as they left the barn. She hoped he was blinded as well. Drawing back, she flung the contents in her hand at his face. She turned her head. He cried out. Letting go, he began to claw at his eyes. Bits of straw clung to his mustache. Chiquita darted away. The door to Pilar's house flung open. Pilar stood there, a rifle in her hand. She raised the weapon as Chiquita raced up beside her. Only then did Chiquita turn to look back at the man. He faced them, pistol in hand. Even from this distance, she could see the sheen of moisture on his cheeks and knew his eyes were burning from the dirt in them.

With a snarl of rage, he swiveled around and stalked off. A few minutes later, she heard the rapid clip of hooves as his horse carried him over the hills and away from them.

Pilar dragged Chiquita through the door and set the bar in place. She almost threw the rifle down before taking Chiquita in her embrace. "I saw the gun. I thought he would kill you." The two women clung together, weeping.

❧

Later that night, Chiquita curled up in bed, trying to keep from shaking. Eduardo had been enraged when he'd come home. Through a series of questions, Pilar had already pieced together what happened, and she told Eduardo. She hadn't allowed Chiquita to return to the house until after the men came home. Instead, Pilar gave orders for the two of them to fix supper. She'd taken charge, as if Chiquita were a young child who needed something to occupy her so she wouldn't dwell on the afternoon's terror. Chiquita had been grateful.

Now, however, the earlier events wouldn't be squelched. Her mind went from remembering, once more, the feel of Eduardo's comforting embrace to the horror of the stranger dragging her off. More than ever, she felt a need for Eduardo. That need had been growing, but tonight, she didn't think she could bear being apart from him.

❧

Lying in bed, Eduardo stared out at the moonlit night. He could almost read by the brightness if he'd wanted to, but he knew he couldn't concentrate on reading. Longing and rage warred in his heart. When he'd heard what happened to Chiquita today, he'd been furious. How could any man have the audacity to invade his home and threaten his wife? She had never done anything to anyone. Was this someone he'd offended in the last few years? With the temper he had, he certainly might have insulted someone, but he couldn't imagine anyone he knew wanting to hurt Chiquita.

The longing came from the way his arms could remember the feel of her. Small and soft, she felt wonderful. She smelled of a clean, woman scent. He'd come to the point where he wanted to have her as his wife in all ways. However, he didn't want to scare her. With the rough treatment Diego had meted out, she still feared men. He could see that every time she was around Rico or one of the other men. He had to give her more time. He couldn't force his love on her but had to wait until she was ready.

The door to his room creaked open. Chiquita stepped inside. His breath caught in his throat. In the moonlight, the white nightdress she wore gave her an achingly beautiful appearance. Her hair, flowing free about her shoulders, shimmered with a touch of moonlight. He was afraid to move—afraid she would disappear.

She pushed the door shut. After taking two small steps toward the bed, she halted. She looked like she wanted to run.

Eduardo didn't remember moving, but suddenly he stood before her. He traced the curve of her cheek. She studied him with her wide-eyed gaze. As if in a dream, Eduardo lowered his mouth to hers in a kiss that made him forget about trouble.

Chapter 15

I'm telling you, this is the right thing to do." Eduardo could still see the hesitancy in Chiquita's eyes. "I know you don't remember going to Tucson before, but I have some friends there. You've met Conlon and Quinn. Quinn's the deputy sheriff who was at our wedding. If anyone can help keep you safe, Quinn can." Uncertainty shone in her gaze.

"Oh, Sweetheart." Eduardo pulled Chiquita into his embrace. He knew she didn't want to leave the ranch, but he couldn't keep her here with this threat hanging over them. He kissed her, slow and tender, trying to show her his love. She clung to him. When he ended the kiss, she relaxed against him and sighed. He grinned. He hadn't realized a man could be so content.

"Pilar will be fine, if that's what you're worried about." He stroked her back, wanting to stay like this all day. "Rico can take care of everything until we come home. He knows what needs to be done. Lucio even promised to tend to your garden." That one hadn't been easy, but the young vaquero had agreed.

"Come on. I've got our things already loaded in the wagon." He led her outside, where the others waited.

"Jorge and I'll be riding through the hills on either side of you in case there's trouble." Rico spoke in a low voice. Eduardo and Rico had discussed the need for extra protection at least until they were through the pass. They worried that the gunman would catch them unawares on the road to Tucson.

"Keep a sharp eye out." Eduardo appreciated Rico not saying anything in front of Chiquita. He didn't want her to worry more than she already did. The long trip would be tiring enough without any added tension.

Pilar hurried to them, a basket in her hands. "I've made some lunch for you." Rico lifted the basket into the wagon while Pilar hugged Chiquita. "Don't worry. I'll see that your garden is tended. By the time you get back, you'll have some fresh vegetables waiting for you." She stepped back, blinking rapidly, lifting her hand in farewell as the wagon rattled off.

Clouds gathered on the horizon. There had been a few uncharacteristic showers in the past week. The mountains got most of the moisture. The dust from the road rose up around them. Eduardo hoped the rain would come again, but not until they reached town.

A swarm of bees flew across the road. Pulling the horses to a stop, Eduardo waited for them to pass. Even though swarming bees were usually docile, he didn't want to get in the middle of them. Trying to appear as if he were following the swarm's flight, he scanned the hills. "That sound makes my hair stand on end." He flashed a smile at Chiquita, hoping she couldn't sense his concern. "When we get back home, I'll take one of the boys to see if we can find the hive. We can always use more honey." He couldn't see Rico, but then he'd warned him to stay out of sight as much as possible. Flicking the reins, Eduardo urged the team to start.

The horses plodded up the steep incline. He took Chiquita's hand in his. She gave him a shy smile. He wanted to stop the wagon and kiss her. Instead, he tugged her closer on the seat until they were touching. Somehow, in the last few weeks, she'd become very important to him.

"Would you like me to tell you about the people you'll be meeting?" She nodded, and he couldn't resist giving her a light kiss. She ducked her head. He grinned and gave the countryside a quick scan, knowing she wouldn't notice.

"Conlon is a lieutenant in the cavalry, stationed at Fort Lowell. His wife is Glorianna, and they have twins—a boy and a girl."

Chiquita raised her eyebrows. He chuckled.

"I hope you're not wanting me to tell you their names, because I can't remember." He shrugged. "Conlon mentioned another baby coming, too. I don't know how soon."

"Quinn's wife is Kathleen. They have a baby boy. No, I have no idea what his name is, either." She gave him such a comical look that he laughed. "I'm not good with kids."

Her eyes darkened, turning solemn. He could almost see the thoughts rushing around in her head. Without relaxing his vigilance, he snuggled her closer to his side. "I've never been good with other people's children, but I can't wait to have one of our own." Although he hadn't thought about children, the possibility excited him. A picture of a little girl who looked just like Chiquita warmed his heart. What he'd said to her was true. He couldn't wait to become a father. He pushed the thoughts away. Right now, he needed to keep his wife safe from harm.

"For a long time, I thought I would never want a family."

Chiquita looked up at him, a question in her eyes.

He stared out at the cactus-covered hills, finding it hard to talk about something he'd kept hidden for so long. "You saw the family graves. You know my parents lost nine children. My mother, especially, carried that grief with her until she died." He shrugged. "I didn't want to face the losses they faced."

Her hand touched his cheek. Glancing down, he could see the brightness in her eyes. He forced a smile.

"I know. Most people don't experience death like that." Clasping her hand in his, he caressed her palm with his thumb. He cleared his throat, easing the rawness. "I better pay more attention to the road. The mountain pass can be a bit rough." He still kept her hand in his, but the road wasn't what bore watching. If anyone were to ambush them, the next few miles would be the place. A man with a gun could hide anywhere.

Chiquita leaned against him. Her gaze swept the hills, too. Eduardo regretted alerting her to the danger. For some reason, he wanted to not only protect her, but keep her from any hint of distress. When he thought of what she'd faced the other day, he wavered between rage and a feeling of failure. She was his responsibility. He needed to protect her.

The drive through the mountain pass proved uneventful. Eduardo kept a close eye on their surroundings and the rock-studded hills above them. He prayed continually, unwilling to consider the possibility that something could happen to Chiquita, not when his love for her was growing every day.

Eduardo continued to study the foothills. He caught a glimpse of Rico signaling all was fine. He and Jorge were returning home now. Eduardo could relax his vigil. They should be safe if no one had followed them this far.

✤

A sense of unease had been gnawing at Chiquita all day. She hadn't wanted to leave the ranch. Despite the three attacks on her, she knew Eduardo would be more careful. She felt safe at the ranch. She'd never become comfortable like this at home with her parents. For the first time in her life, she looked forward to each day.

Since she'd gone to Eduardo two nights ago, he'd changed even more. Papa never showed affection for Mama like Eduardo showed her. He seemed to want to touch or kiss her all of the time. Her face warmed as she thought how much she enjoyed his attention. He made her feel beautiful and wanted. He treated her like she was the most precious possession he had. She wanted to accept and bask in his adoration, but she feared one day he would see her as unworthy. No amount of devotion could erase the fact of who, and what, she was. Someday, he would see that.

Eduardo's thumb continued to stroke her palm, pausing at times as he perused the country around them. She knew he wanted to hide his concern from her, but she had already guessed they might be followed and attacked.

Coming down off the pass, Eduardo nodded to a small stand of trees. "There's a little spring there. We'll stop and see what Pilar packed in that basket." He smiled, his eyes sparkling. "I don't know about you, but I'm about ready to cook one of the horses."

She leaned closer, drawn by the warmth in his gaze. He had the strangest effect on her. With just a look, he could make her want to be close to him. His cheeks creased in a grin, as if he understood her roiling emotions. When they stopped for lunch, she didn't know if she wanted him to take her in his arms once more or give her some space to get her feelings under control.

"Here we are." Eduardo jumped down from the wagon, then reached up to help her down. He didn't let go, but pulled her close. His gaze turned darker. Lowering his head, he gave her a lingering kiss that set her pulse pounding.

"I'll water the horses while you set out the lunch." Eduardo's voice had an unusual huskiness to it. Chiquita tried to slow her breathing as she reached for the basket he retrieved from the wagon. Eduardo chuckled when he met her gaze. "If I kiss you anymore, we may not get to town before nightfall."

Her face flaming, Chiquita carried their lunch to a grassy, shaded spot and began to set out the food. Was this the way husbands and wives usually felt about each other? She'd never had anyone look at her or affect her like Eduardo did. Even though she feared it wouldn't last, she didn't want these feelings to ever change.

During lunch, Eduardo glanced at the sky with a concerned frown on his face. Thunder rumbled in the distance. A heavy bank of clouds had settled over the mountains to the northwest of them quite awhile ago. Eduardo stood and stretched.

"We need to get on to town before the storm moves this way. Should the water start running in the mountain streams, we might have some trouble crossing the washes if we wait too long." He strode away. Chiquita began to gather the remainder of their lunch, packing everything back in the basket.

The wagon jolted and creaked as Eduardo set a fast pace. The horses, refreshed from their break, seemed eager to get to town. They snorted occasionally. The scent of rain in the air made them frisky.

The road flattened out, flanked by heavy growths of twisted mesquite and paloverde trees. A coyote trotted into the road a few hundred yards ahead of them and paused to watch them. Like a shadow, the animal disappeared into the brush long before they arrived at the spot where he'd been.

Eduardo relaxed. She knew he thought the danger had lessened once they left the mountain pass behind. Here in the flatter land, with the thick undergrowth, an attack would be harder to commit. Once more, he took her hand, tugging to urge her to come closer to him. So content she thought she might start to purr like a cat, Chiquita leaned her head on his shoulder.

A shot rang out, shattering the tranquillity. A horse squealed. The wagon jerked, throwing Chiquita off balance as the horses stretched out in a full gallop. Another shot split the air. Thunder cracked. Chiquita clutched the seat as Eduardo sawed the reins, trying to slow the runaways, to no avail.

Almost losing her balance, Chiquita caught a glimpse behind them. Her gasp alerted Eduardo. He glanced back. A rider raced after them. Even from a distance, Chiquita could see the rifle he held at the ready. Eduardo leaned forward, not attempting to slow the horses, but urging them on instead.

"Get down." His yell swept away on the wind.

The wagon bounced and jolted, threatening to toss them off at any moment. Chiquita could feel the blood drain from her face. They were going to die. One man on a horse would be faster than the wagon. If this was the man who'd come to their house the other day, she knew, without a doubt, that he would kill them. She had felt the evil in him.

Lightning flashed across the sky, followed by a clap of thunder that urged the horses to run faster. The brush rushed by in a nauseating blur. Chiquita glanced back. The gunman lifted the rifle to his shoulder. She hoped his racing mount would throw off his aim. Eduardo yanked her down so her head was on his lap. She could feel the man behind drawing steadily nearer.

Huge drops of rain began to hit them. Chiquita shivered. How far were they from town? Was there anyone to help them? She had no idea. Glancing at the rifle under the seat, she knew Eduardo couldn't use the gun and handle the team. With a pang of regret, she wished she'd been able to learn one of these skills. That might have saved their lives.

She hazarded a look behind. Something buzzed past. The man was close now. She could almost make out his face. This had to be the same man who tried to take her from her house.

Eduardo shouted something. The man lifted his gun. Chiquita had the feeling she could look directly down the barrel. Would she see the bullet as it came at her? She closed her eyes, unwilling to face the sight.

The wagon tilted, throwing her forward. Eduardo caught her, steadying her. The team, slowing very little, raced into a wide wash. Tiny streams of water ran across the roadway. Eduardo looked grim as he glanced upstream toward the mountains. The peaks had long since disappeared in the dark storm clouds.

Careening wildly, the wagon crossed the wash. The gunman's horse slipped coming down the embankment behind them. His shot went wild. He jerked the reins, managing to keep his mount upright.

Chiquita couldn't stop glancing between the road, Eduardo, and the man following them. At any second, a bullet would find one of them, and everything would be over. The man raised his rifle. Thunder cracked. The rumble seemed to continue. Eduardo flicked the reins on the horses' backs, urging them to go faster. They were surging out of the wash.

The rifle jerked. The man glanced toward the mountains. His eyes widened. Chiquita followed his gaze and gasped at the wall of water rushing at him. Eduardo yelled at the horses. They seemed to sense the danger and put forth a burst of speed. The wagon flew over the edge of the wash.

She caught a glimpse of the first wave of the flood. Brown water churned past. Uprooted trees and undergrowth spun in the rushing waves like chaff in the wind. The rider, still several yards from the bank, couldn't keep his mount upright. A tree trunk, like a mighty hammer, smacked into them. The horse screamed. Both were swept away in the torrent.

The horses, wild with panic, left the roadway. Off center, the wagon careened into a tree. Wood splintered. The world tilted. Chiquita opened her mouth in a silent scream. Thrown free, she tumbled through the brush. Limbs tore at her dress. A fleeting image of Eduardo thudding into a tree nearby faded as darkness overtook her.

Cold drops of rain splatting on her cheeks woke her. She started to sit up. Every muscle in her body ached. She groaned and sank back down. Where was she? Hazy memories and the roar of rushing water brought it all back. She jerked upright. Dizziness blurred her vision for a moment.

Eduardo—she had to find him! The roar of the floodwaters filled her with fear. What if the gunman hadn't been killed? Would he come after them? She heard a groan. Turning on muscles that burned with the effort, she spotted Eduardo a few yards away. Even from this distance, she could see the dark stain running down his face. Unable to stand, she crawled across the wet ground to reach him.

He was still unconscious. The wound on his head wasn't deep but had bled copiously. Blood mixed with the raindrops and ran off into the sand. Pulling up her skirt, Chiquita ripped off a piece of her petticoat. She used a corner of the piece to wipe away the dirt from Eduardo's wound, then bound the cloth around his head. The bandage wasn't pretty but would be serviceable.

The rain came faster. She couldn't get the sight of the man being washed away out of her mind. A shudder raced through her. Thunder rumbled. The storm lumbered east. Rain still pelted down. The roar of the floodwaters captured her attention; the sight mesmerized her. She'd heard of flash floods before but had never seen the power and fury of one.

She reached back for Eduardo's hand, uncertain what to do. How far was Tucson from here? Where were the horses? She didn't want to leave Eduardo to get help, but if he didn't have help soon. . . She refused to think further along that line.

She could hear the sound of hoofbeats in the distance. Someone was coming. Dread coursed through her. Had the gunman survived? Was he searching for them so he could finish the job he'd started?

Chapter 16

The rain slowed. She and Eduardo were both soaked. His teeth began to chatter and his face held an unhealthy pallor. His lips took on a bluish tint. She knew she had to get him warm soon.

Peering through the brush, Chiquita had a good view of the road heading toward Tucson. That seemed to be the direction the horses were coming from. She was sure more than one horse approached. Had the gunman somehow found reinforcements? She crouched over Eduardo, waiting.

Four horses galloped around a bend in the road about a quarter of a mile away. Clumps of sandy mud splattered from the hooves. The riders sat erect in their saddles, not relaxed like Eduardo when he rode.

Panic swept through her. How could she hope to scare off four men? She glanced around, looking for something to help her. Wood from the wagon lay scattered through the brush, but none of the pieces would help. The basket that carried their lunch lay broken on the ground fifty feet from her. The remains of the meal had scattered in the dirt. Near the roadway, a gleam of metal caught her eye. Eduardo's rifle. With a glance at the oncoming riders, she darted for the weapon, then scrambled back to place herself between Eduardo and the men. She lifted the gun, pointing it at them.

The barrel weighed more than she anticipated. Her hands wavered as she tried to hold the gun steady. How did men do this and make it look so easy? Jamming the rifle butt into her shoulder as she'd seen Pilar do, she willed her muscles to tighten and take the weight.

The approaching men slowed. They must have seen her moving to get the rifle. They were all dressed the same, which she found odd. Although she'd spent all of her life away from civilization, she'd still encountered a few drifters who'd stopped by for a meal. None of them wore exactly the same clothing, so why did these men dress that way? They came on at a walk until they were only about a hundred yards away. They stopped, their mounts standing still, as if trained that way.

The man in the lead came forward alone. Something about him seemed familiar, but she wasn't going to let down her guard. He was still too far away to make out his features.

"Hello. We heard gunshots. Then one of my men spotted a team of runaway horses. Is there trouble?"

She centered the gun on his chest. He halted and put his hands up in a gesture of surrender. Only fifty yards separated them. Her palms were sweating, and her arm muscles were beginning to shake with the strain.

"Señora Villegas?" The man leaned forward, squinting at her. He slowly removed his cap. "I'm Conlon Sullivan. We met at your house when I came to see some horses." Without his hat, she could see the shock of black hair. Now she knew why he seemed familiar. A wave of relief swept over her. The rifle wavered, and she almost dropped it into her lap. Tears clouded her vision. These were cavalrymen. That's why they were all dressed alike.

Conlon urged his horse forward until he stopped next to them. His smile faded as he saw Eduardo.

"What happened?" Conlon swung off his horse and bent to examine her unconscious husband. "Were you thrown from the wagon?" She nodded. He stood, waving his men forward. His bright blue gaze met hers. Concern etched his brow.

"We're here to help, Señora. The fort isn't far. I'll send someone for a wagon to take you there."

The wait seemed interminable. Conlon and one of his men checked Eduardo over. She thought they were trying to see if he'd broken anything in the fall. The lieutenant undid the bandage, examined the cut, then rewrapped the wound. By the time a large wagon rattled to a stop, Chiquita was shaking like a leaf in the wind. She tried to force herself to stop shivering, but the chill wouldn't leave.

"My men and I will get Eduardo into the back, and we'll drive you to the fort. We have a good hospital there." Conlon lifted the rifle from the ground beside her and handed it to one of his men.

She refused to sit on the seat with the driver. Instead, she sat in the back with Eduardo's head on her lap. He hadn't come to, but he groaned and gritted his teeth when they moved him. Blood soaked the cloth around his head. She smoothed his hair, traced the lines of his face, hoping her touch would wake him or at least be a comfort.

By the time they reached the fort, Chiquita's teeth were clenched tight to keep them from chattering. She couldn't remember ever being so cold. She barely felt the hands that helped her from the wagon, holding her when her legs refused to support her weight. They escorted her into a building full of unusual smells. Conlon told her this was the hospital. The doctor there would take care of Eduardo.

"Glory, thanks for coming." Conlon smiled at the petite redheaded woman who swept through the doors not long after they arrived. Chiquita, huddled in a blanket someone had thrown around her, tried to smile but failed miserably.

"Hello." The woman plopped into a chair beside Chiquita. "I'm going to take you to our house. It isn't far from here. Alicia, my helper, is heating water for you to bathe in. You need to warm up after the soaking you've gotten. Then, we'll find some clean, dry clothing for you." She glanced up at her husband.

"Señora Villegas." Conlon squatted next to her chair. "I know you didn't speak when Quinn and I were at your house the other day, but if you could tell us what happened, that might help Eduardo. Can you?"

Fear rose up to choke her. Eduardo might die because of her inability to talk. She opened her mouth and tried. No sound issued. She wanted to tell them, but her voice wouldn't work. Tears trickled down her cheeks. She'd failed her husband. Would he be angry with her now? Would all his kindness turn to hate?

"Don't you worry." Glorianna took Chiquita's hands in hers and rubbed them. "The doctor here is very good. He'll fix your husband right up. Now, you come with me."

Chiquita pulled back. She didn't want to leave. She wanted to be here with Eduardo. A wife's place was with her husband. He might need her. She had to see him.

As if she understood, Glorianna gave a gentle squeeze and smiled. "You can't do Eduardo any good if you get sick. After you're warm and dry, I'll bring you back. By then the doctor will be finished, and you can sit with your husband."

She could see the wisdom in this. She would go with Glorianna, but as soon as possible, she would come back to be with Eduardo. Thinking of the man who shot at them, she felt nauseous. Although she didn't want him to die in the flood, she hated the thought that he might still be after them. He wouldn't give up until she was dead, and she had no idea why he wanted to kill her.

※

Chiquita barely noticed the wet earth smell as she hurried back to the hospital. The bath warmed her, but she couldn't relax with the thought of Eduardo lying pale and chilled in the hospital. The fear that he might die made her rush to be back by his side. She pushed the door open and took a moment to get her bearings before setting off for Eduardo's room. When she arrived, he wasn't alone.

"Señora Villegas, I'm Dr. Elliot. Your husband is a lucky man. I didn't find any broken bones from him being wrapped around that tree." The doctor, a portly man who seemed to jiggle with every step he took, patted her on the shoulder. "The problem is the blow to the head."

Chiquita clenched her fingers together. What was this doctor trying to tell her? Would Eduardo die? Her heart ached. She wanted her husband to know that she loved him. She wanted him to hold her again. There were so many things she wanted to do for him.

"We can never tell about injuries to the skull. He still hasn't regained consciousness, but it's possible he will before morning. The longer he stays like he is, the less likely he will recover."

She felt the blood drain from her face.

Dr. Elliot grasped her arm. His face came close to hers. His eyes narrowed as he studied her. "Señora, you have to be strong. I might have a way you can help your husband. Let's sit down and talk." He led her to a chair, making the seat next to her creak in distress as he lowered his bulk onto it.

"I've heard that some doctors have success with head injuries when the patient hears a familiar voice. They say there have been cases where, after recovering their senses, the patient can repeat conversations they overheard while unconscious. I want you to sit with your husband and talk to him. I don't care what you say. That doesn't matter so much as him hearing your voice."

Panic closed her throat with icy fingers. How could she do this? Even if she could talk, Eduardo had never heard her speak and wouldn't recognize her voice. Maybe she could send for Pilar or Rico. He was familiar with them. She didn't know how she could do that, though. Since she couldn't talk, she couldn't tell anyone what she needed. Tears burned her eyes.

"Excuse me, Dr. Elliot." Conlon stood in the open door. "I happened to overhear what you said to Señora Villegas. I'm afraid she won't be able to talk to Eduardo. I don't know the circumstances, but for some reason, she can't speak."

Dr. Elliot gave Chiquita a piercing look. "Is that right, young lady?"

She nodded, giving Conlon a look of gratitude.

"I want you to come with me to my office down the hall." Dr. Elliot put a hand under her elbow. "I want to examine your throat and ask a few questions about why you can't talk."

Relief swept through Chiquita when she finally got to see Eduardo. A young man brought her a chair, placing it beside the head of the bed. Everyone left. She was alone with her husband.

His color, although pale, looked healthier. His lips didn't have the blue tinge anymore. He appeared to be warm and dry, resting peacefully. She put her hand over his chest, then lay her head there, listening to his steady heartbeat. Tears of gratitude traced a path down her cheeks.

She had been with the doctor a long time. Although she'd been nervous and wary of him at first, she soon relaxed because of his professional attitude.

Dr. Elliot seemed to understand what happened to her at home. With only a few questions, he'd found out about Papa beating her and that she had spoken when she was a very young child. He talked to her for a long time, assuring her that this wasn't a physical problem. When she learned to trust other people, she had a very good chance of speaking again.

Reaching under the edge of the blanket, Chiquita twined her fingers with Eduardo's. She ran her thumb over his callused palm, watching his face for any sign of a reaction. He didn't even twitch. Only the steady rising and falling of the sheet as he breathed let her know he lived.

She'd never felt so alone. No one here knew her. She couldn't talk to anyone and tell them she needed help. She couldn't even ask about the man who'd been shooting at them. Why had he been trying to kill her? When he'd come to the ranch the other day, he hadn't said why someone paid him to kill her. He'd only said that they did. She'd never done anything to hurt anyone, yet now her husband, a good man, might die because of her. Resting her forehead on the bed, she wept.

Jesus, I know I'm not worthy to ask anything of You, but I do this for Eduardo. Please, help him. Help me. I can't lose him. I'm so afraid. I don't know what to do. Lord, I've always been unworthy. I'm the worst of the sinners Eduardo told me about. I'm so sorry. Please, forgive me. Please, spare Eduardo.

Peace bathed her in a comforting embrace. An indescribable feeling flowed over her as if she were being washed clean of every wrong thing she'd ever done. She felt like she could float away as the burdens lifted. Her chest warmed, the heat spreading all the way up her throat until even her lips tingled.

She didn't know how long she rested on the edge of the bed. She wasn't even sure what happened to her. If Eduardo were awake and she could talk, she'd ask him. Brushing her fingers across his still face, she felt the need to try speaking once more.

"Ed. . .uar. . .do." The raspiness startled her. She glanced at the closed door, half expecting someone to have come in without her noticing. They were still alone in the room.

Touching her throat, she sat too stunned to do anything. Had that voice been hers? Opening her mouth, she fought back the fear of failure and tried again.

"Ed. . .uardo." This time she knew the voice was hers. Although stronger, the sound still carried a lot of hoarseness from long disuse. "Love. . .you." Delight raced through her to finally be able to say those words to her husband. Suddenly, she couldn't wait to talk more. Her heart felt full to bursting with gratitude for this gift.

⚜

Terror clutched at Eduardo. He could hear the floodwaters racing past, but he couldn't see them. Someone needed his help. Chiquita? Had she fallen back in the wash when the torrent swept down? He didn't think so, yet he couldn't shake the sense of impending doom. He needed to see her. The light was too dim to make out anything. Sometimes voices pierced the mist, but they faded in and out. He couldn't understand any of them.

Pushing upward, he struggled to find a way through the fog surrounding him. Pieces of memory pierced him. The man shooting. The raging waters. Chiquita's terrified face. The horses' screams. Pounding hooves. A crunch of wood. Blackness.

He couldn't fight any longer. His strength faded. Maybe after he rested, he could find a way out of this odd place. The darkness began to close around him once more.

"Eduardo."

Someone called his name. He'd never heard the voice before, yet for some reason, the sound tugged at him. A woman called him. Rising through the fog, he began to fight his way free. He had to respond. She needed him.

"Eduardo, love you. I'm afraid. Please, come back." Her voice ended in a sob.

He blinked. Someone lay with her head on his bed. This couldn't be Chiquita.

She didn't speak. He closed his eyes. Her weeping drew him back. Opening his eyes again, everything looked clearer.

In the dim light, he could still see the pale strands running through the woman's hair. Chiquita's hair looked like that. Could she have spoken to him, or was he only dreaming? He licked at his dry lips. Now he could feel her fingers wrapped around his hand. Using every last bit of energy he possessed, he closed his fist, holding her hand tight.

Chapter 17

Two days later, Conlon and Eduardo headed for Tucson. Eduardo made Chiquita stay with Glorianna. His wife delighted in playing with Glorianna's twins and gave her some much-needed respite. A nagging ache from his wound still plagued Eduardo, the remains of his injury. Dr. Elliot assured him the headaches would pass in a few days.

The hazy memory of the soft voice that pulled him from the blackness still bothered him. He couldn't get over the feeling that he should know who called him. Somewhere inside, he'd had the wild hope that maybe Chiquita had spoken, but she remained silent. She hadn't left his side during his hospital stay. He warmed at the thought. Somehow, she seemed a little different, but he couldn't quite figure out how.

After relating the events of the past few weeks to Conlon, the lieutenant urged him to consult with Quinn. Maybe the deputy would have some helpful advice, even though the Villegas ranch was outside his jurisdiction. Hesitant to leave Chiquita, Eduardo only agreed when Conlon pointed out she would be surrounded by the whole cavalry. Also, he would alert his sergeant to watch for possible trouble.

The first buildings came into sight. Eduardo forced himself to relax. *Lord, You know how upset I am that this is happening. My wife is being threatened. I don't believe this anger is wrong. On the other hand, I don't want it to cloud my reasoning. Give me wisdom to do as You would have me do, Lord.* Peace flowed through him, the comfort that could only come from God. Somehow, he knew this would all work out.

Quinn pushed the door of his house open to let them in. "Good morning." Dark circles around his eyes gave him a haunted look.

"We stopped by the jail, but you weren't there yet." Conlon grinned. "Taking the day off?"

"Naw. Jonathan spent the whole night crying. Kathleen thinks he has colic." He led them into the kitchen and poured some coffee. "I stayed home a little late to see if I could let her get some rest. Right now, they're both asleep."

They all settled down at the table. Quinn took a long sip of coffee before speaking. "So, what brings you to town, Eduardo? Tired of married life already?"

When not even Conlon chuckled at the joke, Quinn turned serious. Eduardo didn't know how or what he wanted to ask his friend. Finally, he started at the beginning, with the discovery that someone on the hillside watched the ranch, to the final attack on the road to Tucson. With the retelling of each event, Quinn's expression looked grimmer.

"We left Chiquita with Glorianna and came here to see if you have any idea why someone is trying to kill my wife. I don't know if this is a grudge against me or my family. I can't imagine how Chiquita could have incurred someone's wrath. She'd never been away from home until we married."

"Do you think the man who chased you on the way to town is the same one who tried to kidnap Chiquita at the ranch?" Quinn asked.

"I never saw the man who tried to take Chiquita." Eduardo cradled the warm cup in his hands. "I did think to ask her if she recognized him. She thinks it was the same man."

"We need to try to find him, then." Quinn drummed his fingers on the table. "If we could talk to him, we could clear up this mystery. I haven't heard anything about someone being after you or your wife. It doesn't make sense to me, either."

Conlon cleared his throat. "As soon as Eduardo told me what happened, I sent some men out looking. Last night, they reported finding the horse several miles downstream from the crossing where Eduardo and Chiquita were attacked. The horse was dead, tangled in brush and drowned. There was a boot still lodged in the stirrup but no sign of the rider."

"If the flood was that bad, he probably didn't survive, either." Quinn frowned. He absently rubbed the badge pinned to his vest.

"I sent them back out again this morning with orders to go farther downstream. They have enough men to search along both sides of the wash. He may have only been injured and crawled into the brush to recover. If so, my men will find him."

Quinn nodded. "That's a good start. I'll ask around town. I have some sources who might help."

They were all silent as Quinn brought the coffeepot and refreshed their cups. Sitting back down, he tilted his head as if listening for something, then relaxed.

"I thought I heard Jonathan." He shrugged. "I think I'll go see Lavette Washington in a bit and ask if she'll help out Kathleen. Otherwise, I might never get any work done.

"Now, Eduardo, I want you to tell me everything you know about the man who's been watching your place. Any little clue you can remember will help. I haven't got any authority where you live, but that doesn't mean I can't help you."

"I know he smokes." Eduardo tried to picture the scenes he and Rico had examined. "His horse wears an unusual shoe on his left hind foot. It isn't curved quite right."

"That's good. I'll talk to Josiah Washington and see if any of the horses he's shod have that kind of shoe. What else?"

"The day they shot at Chiquita in the garden, there were two men."

"Two?" Quinn's eyebrows rose.

"There had to be two, because one couldn't fire the shots from those angles. He would have had to move, and Lucio would have seen him. When the boys trailed them, the riders went into the river. They lost the trail."

"What direction were they heading at that point?" Conlon asked.

"East." Eduardo didn't know if he should say more. Diego's place was east of his, but he hesitated to point a finger at his father-in-law without substantial proof.

"Diego lives east of you." Quinn's flat statement echoed Eduardo's thoughts.

"I have no way of proving he's involved in this. Besides, why would he trick me into marrying Chiquita, then try to kill her? That makes no sense."

"I've found murder rarely makes sense." Quinn's grim words sent a chill of dread through Eduardo.

"Eduardo, I have an idea. Why don't you bring Chiquita here? You can stay with us. She can help Kathleen with the baby while you and I look into this matter. Would she be willing to do that?"

"I think so." Eduardo finished the last of his coffee. "I wanted to take her to the mercantile, anyway, to pick out some material for a couple new dresses. She's having to tailor and wear my mother's old ones."

"Didn't she bring her clothes with her?" Quinn looked puzzled.

Anger crept into Eduardo's tone as he related all that had gone on the day he married Chiquita. "I burned the dress she wore. It wasn't even good enough to tear into rags."

Conlon's jaw tightened. "I have trouble finding a decent Christian thought when it comes to Diego Garcia. That man has a streak of meanness a mile wide."

"By the way, did you know Diego was in town last weekend?" Quinn walked with them to the door. "He was drunk, as usual, and bragging about some relative dying. He claimed he was going to inherit a fortune. He sure had plenty of friends all of a sudden."

❧

Chiquita tried not to cling to Eduardo's arm too tightly as they walked to the mercantile. She'd never imagined there could be so many people. Eduardo told her there were more than seven thousand residents in Tucson. How could so many people stand to be so close together? Just being in town made her long for the quiet of the ranch.

Tucson had to be the noisiest place. Dogs barked. Mules brayed. Men shouted. Sometimes she could even hear a gunshot. Last night, she'd been afraid, but Eduardo assured her the shots were only some men having a little too much to drink. The ground shook as a couple of huge freight wagons lumbered past. They were so tall, she thought she could sit upright beneath them and never have them touch a hair on her head. The driver cracked his whip and let loose with a stream of words that made her want to hide her face.

Eduardo patted her hand and gave her a reassuring smile. Her breath caught. Even with the white bandage on his forehead, he was the handsomest man in all of Tucson. She thought back to the time when he'd been unconscious. She'd spoken to him then and hoped to be able to continue when he awoke. For some reason, she couldn't. Every time she tried, the words stuck in her throat. Fearing to say the wrong thing and make him angry with her, she'd kept quiet. A few times, she caught him looking at her with a strange expression—as if he knew she talked once and wondered why she didn't again.

The door of the mercantile creaked as Eduardo pushed it open. Chiquita stepped inside and halted. Her eyes widened. There were shelves full of different food items, things she'd never thought could be bought in a store. Along one wall were stacks of already-made clothing. Bolts of material in varying colors and patterns caught her eye. In her whole life, she'd never had a dress that no one else wore before her. She'd never imagined there could be so many choices.

Eduardo herded her to one side so other people could use the door. She flushed, embarrassed by her intent scrutiny of the store and her lack of courtesy to other people.

"Don't worry." Eduardo's breath tickled her ear as he spoke. "Take your time and look around. I have to talk to Sam over there about some things we need at the ranch." He motioned toward the man standing behind the counter. "After I'm done there, I want to help you pick out a pair of shoes and at least three lengths of material for new dresses."

Chiquita caught her breath. She stared up at Eduardo. Had he really said she could have new dresses? Her gaze flew to the bolts of material. Excitement made her shaky. She glanced back at Eduardo, and his smiling gaze held her. He made her feel so loved at times. Why couldn't she tell him that?

Eduardo spent a long time going over a list of items with the storeowner. At one point, they even traipsed outside to see something. Eduardo gave her a brief smile before leaving. For awhile, Chiquita wandered past the tables and shelves of goods, puzzling over some items. She had no idea what they were.

At last, she stood before the material, her fingers brushing the different types of cloth. Many were darker colors, good for work clothes, but not very attractive. A few were a shiny material she'd never seen before. Those felt soft and rich to the touch but seemed impractical for everyday use. The more vivid colors caught her eye. One bolt of bright pink with tiny white flowers kept her enthralled. No matter how many others she looked at, her gaze always returned to that one. The material would never do for working in the garden, but the thought of wearing a dress out of that cloth thrilled her. She tried her best to examine only the more practical fabrics, but the pink seemed to draw her back again.

"We'll need a dress length in this pink one for sure." Eduardo's voice at her back startled her. She hadn't heard him or the shopkeeper approaching. Whirling around, she gazed at him wide-eyed and shook her head. He couldn't waste his money on something so frivolous.

"I want you to have something pretty, Chiquita. This one suits you. I can tell how much you like it. Antonio showed me the chapel he built near his house. He plans to have services there on Sundays as soon as he can get a pastor. I want you to have a pretty dress or two to wear then." His warm gaze made her wish they were alone. She thought he wanted to kiss her as much as she wanted to be kissed.

"Which other ones would you like?" Sam tugged the bolt of pink cloth from the pile.

Eduardo gestured at the stack. "Pick out two for everyday, Chiquita. They don't have to be dull, but they should be serviceable."

Trembling, she indicated her choices. This was too much. She didn't know how to react to Eduardo's being so kind and generous. Following the mercantile owner, she picked out the thread she needed and, at Eduardo's insistence, a packet of needles and other necessary notions.

"She also needs some new shoes, Sam. My mother's didn't fit her."

Chiquita longed to hide. She didn't want anyone to see the condition of the slippers she wore. Going barefoot was almost better than this. Her face filled with heat as Eduardo pulled her shoes off and helped her try on a new pair. This would be the first time she'd ever gotten a pair of shoes just for herself, too. She felt like a princess.

Loaded with packages, they left the mercantile. Eduardo carried most of them, but Chiquita insisted on carrying the package with her sewing items. The new shoes were on her feet. Eduardo told Sam to throw out the old ones.

The afternoon sun was sinking behind the mountains as they headed back to Quinn's house. The streets were quieter as people quit work for the evening and went home for supper. Balancing the parcels in one arm, Eduardo kept his other hand on her elbow, guiding her around the various piles of refuse in the streets. She wrinkled her nose at the smell.

Across the street, a door slammed, accompanied by raucous laughter. Two men staggered around horses tied at the hitching post outside the saloon. They spotted Eduardo and Chiquita and halted. Swaying like a gale force wind blew on them, the pair stared openmouthed at them. With the sun setting behind them, Chiquita couldn't make out their faces, but something made her uncomfortable. She edged closer to Eduardo.

"Villegas."

The roar sent chills through Chiquita. In an instant, she was a child again. She wanted to whimper, run, and hide, but her spine stiffened. She faced her father as he wove his way across the street.

"What kind of man are you, Villegas?" Papa's words slurred. His breath stank of alcohol, a smell Chiquita would always hate. "I give you my daughter in marriage, but here you are with another woman, parading her through town."

From the moment her father spoke, Eduardo's grip on her elbow had become almost painful. She could feel the waves of anger rushing through him at the accusations.

"You're not making sense, Diego. This is your daughter."

"Are you saying I don't know my own girl?" Papa stumbled closer, the whites of his eyes red. His companion, a man Chiquita had never seen before, grabbed him by the arm.

"Diego, look at her." He waved a hand at Chiquita. "She looks just like Bella. This is her."

"Who is Bella?" Eduardo spoke the question Chiquita wanted to ask.

"Why, her mother, Bella Garcia de Noriega." The man continued to gaze at Chiquita as he braced her father.

Chiquita barely noticed the package falling from her hands. Her gaze flew to her father's face. He whirled on the man who'd spoken, his eyes blazing. She needed no further proof for the truth of the words. With a sob, she jerked free from Eduardo and raced away.

Chapter 18

"Chiquita, no! Wait!" Eduardo almost raced after her, torn between catching his wife and finding out about this mystery. Chiquita's mother was Lupe Garcia. He'd never heard her called by this Bella name before. Besides, Chiquita looked nothing like her mother. In fact, she looked nothing like any of the others in her family.

Dropping his parcels, he grabbed Diego's shirt, dragging the drunken sot close. "Who is Bella?" Rage simmered inside him.

Diego's eyes rolled back in his head. He crumpled, his heavy weight pulling him from Eduardo's grasp. He sank into the dirt of the road, unconscious.

Before the other man could run, Eduardo caught hold of him. "Oh, no, you don't." He jerked the man back, glad that the street was fairly deserted. The few who were out didn't seem to care about this small altercation.

"Let me make this clear." Eduardo ignored the man's frightened gaze. Twisting the neck of the man's shirt, he gave a little shake. "I want to know who you are and how you know things about my wife that she doesn't seem to know. You have about one minute to start talking."

"Si, Señor." The man's voice shook almost as much as the rest of him. "I am Diego's cousin, Jose. From California." He swallowed. "I bring him news of his family there."

"Who is Bella?"

"She is the daughter of our uncle. I came to tell Diego that our uncle passed away a few months ago."

"Why did you say Bella is Chiquita's mother?"

"Please, Señor, I was mistaken. It is the drinking. I didn't think clearly. Lupe is her mother, and Diego is her father."

"You're lying." Eduardo shook the man again. "I want the truth."

"I'm telling the truth, Señor. Please don't hurt me." Jose tried to pry Eduardo's fingers loose. "You need to go and find your wife."

Glancing down the street where Chiquita had disappeared, Eduardo knew that was true. Where had she gone?

Dragging Jose a step closer, Eduardo gritted his teeth. "Are you and Diego staying in town?" Jose nodded. Eduardo released him, and he stumbled back a few steps. "I'll find you. Even if you leave town, I'll find you. I want some answers, and I can see I'll have to corner Diego to get them. Just remember: You can't run far enough or fast enough to escape me." Picking up all the packages,

Eduardo strode down the street.

He hoped Chiquita had found her way back to Quinn's house, but when he got there, Quinn and Kathleen hadn't seen her.

"I'll help you look." Quinn slapped a hat on his head. "Then, if you want, we'll go see Diego together." He gave Kathleen a quick kiss. "Don't wait to eat. We'll get something when we get back."

Lies, Chiquita thought as she ran, *my whole life has been a lie. No wonder Lupe and Diego hated me. They didn't want me because I wasn't their child.*

She didn't know who the stranger was, but the instant he'd stated that Bella was her mother, Chiquita knew he told the truth. Now she understood the reason she never fit in at the Garcia household. This explained why her sisters were treated differently. She'd always been the outcast, the unworthy one. Even her real mother hadn't wanted her. Her mother thought it would be better to give her to someone like Diego than to be troubled with raising such an unworthy child. Hurt burned inside her.

She didn't know how long she ran. Even the direction didn't matter—she just had to escape. Too exhausted to take another step, Chiquita sank down on the steps of a building. The sun was down now, and the steps were in shadow. No one could see her here. She covered her face with her hands and sobbed. Now, Eduardo would understand how awful and unacceptable she was as a wife. Would he make her leave? She wouldn't blame him if he did.

"Child, are you all right?"

The man's touch startled her. Chiquita gasped and scrambled away. A man in a plain brown robe knelt at the spot where she'd been. He didn't move but gave her a kind smile. Although she usually feared men, this one seemed different. Something in his expression and his eyes told her he wouldn't hurt her.

He held out a hand. "The wind is rising. You have no wrap. Come inside the church so you won't catch a chill."

She glanced up at the façade of the building. She hadn't realized these steps belonged to a chapel. Scrubbing at her cheeks, she tried to wipe away all traces of tears.

"Come, Child." The priest stood and held out his hand.

All fear left her. She allowed him to help her up, then followed him inside the small church. She hadn't realized how harsh the wind was until she walked through the doors. Warmth enveloped her. The priest led her into the wooden pew-lined sanctuary.

"Sit here." She sank down, still tired from her run. "Would you like to talk? I'm a very good listener."

His gentle voice soothed her ragged nerves. Urgency built within her. She needed to talk to someone. Maybe this man knew the Jesus Eduardo knew. Maybe he could tell her what to do to make herself worthy of such a Savior. She ducked her head. *Oh, please, let me be able to talk to him.*

He waited in silence. Without passing judgment, he appeared willing to give her all the time she needed. Once again, she could feel the warmth she'd felt the day she spoke to Eduardo when he'd been unconscious. Her throat relaxed. She knew she could talk again.

"I'm not worthy." Tears burned her eyes. That wasn't what she intended to say, but she couldn't seem to stop. "For Jesus. I want. . .so much. Need a Savior. Don't know how." She looked at the priest through a blur of tears.

"Ah, Child." He leaned back against the pew. "Tell me why you are unworthy."

She struggled for the words. This man of God ought to be able to tell just by looking at her. "They said I'm worthless."

"Who said that?"

"My. . ." She hesitated, not knowing what to call Diego and Lupe. They weren't her parents, but all her life she'd thought they were. "My family."

He frowned, his bushy eyebrows drawing together. She wanted to turn away. He must understand now and would tell her they were right. She would never have a Savior.

"I think there is a misunderstanding." Slipping his hands in his sleeves, the priest straightened. "In the book of Ephesians, the Apostle Paul tells us that salvation is through the grace of God. That way, we won't have anything to boast about." He pursed his lips in a thoughtful expression. "Do you know about Jesus and His death on the cross?"

Chiquita nodded. "My husband. He read the story."

"You see, if there were something we could do to earn our way to heaven, then Jesus died for nothing."

"There's no hope?" Her eyes burned. She blinked hard, trying to stop the tears.

"Oh, there is always hope, my child." He smiled. Kindness shone from his eyes. "You are no different from anyone else. We are all unworthy."

"But. . . my husband. . .he's good."

"According to the Bible, none of us are righteous on our own. In fact, we all have wicked hearts."

"How do people become saved?"

"It's really very simple. You have to admit your worthlessness. Once you do that and you see the truth of who Jesus is, then you simply ask Him to forgive you and be your Savior."

"But, I think I did that." Warmth filled Chiquita as she recalled the night in Eduardo's hospital room and the feeling of peace she experienced. She related the account to the priest, and his smile widened.

"I would say you already have Jesus as your Savior, Child. Trust me, He loves you more than you'll ever believe or understand." He patted her shoulder as he stood. "I'll leave you alone now. Spend some time listening for Him to talk to you."

Tears of joy ran down her cheeks. Chiquita stumbled to the altar and knelt.

With her head on the rail, she stayed quiet. There weren't words for the praise and thankfulness in her heart. Jesus loved her. She didn't have to become worthy on her own. He made her acceptable. Never again would she be a complete outcast. She would always have Jesus.

She didn't know how long she knelt there, basking in the tumultuous emotions pouring over her. The sense of utter joy and peace made her weep until she thought she couldn't cry another tear. When she heard the door open, she thought the priest must be returning to tell her she had to leave. Wiping the moisture from her face, she stood.

Eduardo faced her, his shoulders bowed as if he carried the weight of the world. His face looked haggard and worn. Even from across the room, she could see the despair in his eyes. As his gaze found her, the despair turned to relief, then joy.

"Chiquita, I've looked everywhere for you. I was so worried." In a few steps he held her in his arms, her face pressed to his shoulder. His hand caressed her hair while he murmured of his love.

"Eduardo."

He froze. His hand stilled. She thought he quit breathing.

"Eduardo, I love you." Her whisper filled the quiet chapel.

In a rush of movement, he pushed her back until he could cup her cheeks and gaze into her eyes. "It was you." Wonder filled his voice. "You talked to me in the hospital. I heard someone calling me, but I didn't recognize the voice. That's because I never heard you speak before."

"Forgive me." She brushed her fingers across his brow. "I want to talk, but I'm afraid. At first, I couldn't speak. After the hospital, I thought you would be angry. Maybe think I tricked you." She blinked. "I'm sorry."

"Oh, Sweetheart." He pulled her back into his embrace. "I can't promise to never be angry with you, but I don't want to be. I've prayed about this, and I believe God has helped me overcome my tendency to fly into a rage at the least little thing. I should be the one asking your forgiveness. I didn't mean to scare you."

He kissed her, a long, lingering kiss that made her pulse race. "Why did you run today, Chiquita?" He led her to a pew and snuggled her next to him.

"When the man said Lupe wasn't my mother, I knew the truth. I've always been different, but I didn't understand why." She leaned against Eduardo. "It hurt so much to know even my real mother didn't want me. She let Diego raise me. I felt like the whole world rejected me."

"Oh, my love." He stroked her shoulder, letting her draw comfort from his closeness.

Taking a deep breath, Chiquita began to tell Eduardo about her experience with religion. Starting from her childhood and ending with her discussion with the priest, she told him all that had happened. Through it all, he stayed silent, holding her tight.

"My life is changed. I don't need approval. Jesus loves me. That's enough."

She tilted her head back to gaze up at him. "So glad you love me, too."

He grinned. "I'm glad you love me." He stood and lifted her to her feet. "I hate to end this time together, but we need to get back to Quinn's house. He's been helping me look for you. They're worried." He kissed her nose. "Don't fret. They're not mad at you."

She shivered in the chilly wind as they walked out the door. He wrapped an arm around her, trying to share his warmth.

"Eduardo, please?"

"What, my love?"

"I want to go home." He stopped. She turned to face him, her gaze serious. "I've seen the city. I miss our house and garden. I want to see the horses."

"It may not be safe." His brow furrowed in concern. "We don't know that the gunman who got caught in the flood was working alone."

She traced the strong line of his jaw. "You can protect me."

Eduardo nodded. This afternoon, Conlon sent word to Quinn that the gunman's body had been found. According to Conlon, he was unidentifiable. Whoever he was, Eduardo prayed this was the end of the troubles. "Then let's go home."

The first rays of the sun peeped through the window. Eduardo rolled over and looked at Chiquita, still sleeping. They'd been home from Tucson for three days—three peaceful, marvelous days, full of catching up as she told him about her childhood and all the dreams she had that she hadn't been able to share with anyone. They'd talked for hours. He'd been afraid to leave her alone, although he wanted to find Diego and discover what he and his cousin, Jose, were hiding. He'd tried to find them in Tucson, but they'd already left town. Today, he would ride over to the Garcia place and confront Diego.

Chiquita stirred, rolling toward him. Since she'd lost her fear of him, she'd proved to be very affectionate. She loved to snuggle up next to him at night. Many times during the day she would touch him, as if she couldn't get enough of the connection between them. He smiled. That went both ways. He loved touching her, too.

Her nose twitched. He almost laughed. Her lips pursed, and he resisted the temptation to lean down and kiss her. For a moment, her eyelids quivered. Soon she would open her eyes, and the first thing she would see would be him smiling at her. They'd done this the past few mornings. He loved to see her delight in such little things. She was like a child, discovering a whole new world.

Her eyes opened, shut, then opened again. She gave him a slow, sweet smile. He knew he would never tire of her tawny gaze. The yellow flecks in her eyes were a constant delight. He'd discovered gold, and this gold he could keep for his whole life.

"Good morning, my love." He gave her a tender kiss, wishing he didn't have to get up and do chores. He gave her another kiss before forcing himself to get out of bed.

When he came inside with the milk, she had breakfast ready for him. They held hands as he prayed over the food. He waited until after the meal was over to tell her his plans for the day.

"Chiquita, I'm riding over to visit Diego today." At her stricken expression, he hurried on. "I have to find out what he and his cousin were talking about. You need to know, too. Can you trust me on this?"

She bit her bottom lip and nodded. He wanted this pain to end for her. She deserved to know who her parents were and what Diego was hiding from her.

Chapter 19

The midmorning sun shone bright as Eduardo cantered away from the barn. El Rey, eager to run after being cooped up for the past two weeks, gave a couple of little jumps as he started off. Eduardo patted his copper neck, relishing the feel of the silken coat. As soon as they reached the smoother part of the road, he would let the stallion have his head for a few miles to run off his orneriness.

His gaze roved constantly over the hills as he rode. Since coming home, they hadn't seen any sign of anyone watching the ranch. On the trip back from Tucson, Conlon and Quinn both accompanied them. Nothing out of the ordinary happened. Eduardo did his best to convince Chiquita that the man swept away by the flood had been working alone. He couldn't explain why a stranger would want to kill her, but she seemed to accept his theory.

This morning, Eduardo had Tomas and Lucio work close to home. Rico and Jorge were off checking on some of the cattle, a job that had to be done. The niggling doubts that assailed Eduardo made him keep at least part of the crew where they would be close enough to help Chiquita should she need them.

El Rey snorted and tugged on the reins. During Eduardo's musing, they'd reached the road. The horse was eager to be off. Loosening the reins, Eduardo relaxed, letting his body move with the horse's easy gait. Although El Rey raced like the wind, he still flowed smoothly, rather than in a jerky motion some horses had at a dead run.

Over an hour later, Eduardo pulled El Rey to a stop on the hill overlooking Diego's small house. Although he'd alternated between walking and cantering to keep El Rey from overheating, a light sheen of sweat darkened the stallion's coat. Eduardo could see one of the girls hanging the wash on the line. Another worked in the garden. He couldn't see the other girls, Diego, or Lupe. He didn't know if Diego's cousin was staying with them still.

Nudging El Rey, he headed the horse down the rocky slope. He'd chosen to leave the road a ways back, hoping to surprise Diego. He didn't fully understand why he felt this was necessary, but the feeling was too intense to be ignored. All morning, he'd prayed that he wouldn't lose his temper here. He wanted to act in a godly manner, not according to his human nature.

The girl pinning the clothes on the line glanced up. She shaded her eyes with a hand to her brow, trying to see him. Dropping a clean piece of clothing in the dirt, she raced for the house, shouting for her mother, followed by the sister who'd been in the garden. El Rey snorted a second time, shaking his head as if he were commenting on what might be happening inside the house.

Lupe stepped outside as Eduardo rode into the yard. Chickens scattered through the refuse cluttering the ground. A mangy dog gave a high-pitched sound, halfway between a bark and a yelp, before slinking under the sagging end of the porch. A scrawny cat hissed and batted at the retreating dog. Eduardo reined in El Rey and took his hat off, giving Lupe a nod.

"Is Diego at home, Señora Garcia?"

Lupe folded her arms across her chest and pinned Eduardo with a glare designed to make him uncomfortable. Although she stood less than five feet tall, the woman was formidable. Eduardo could only imagine how difficult a time Chiquita had living with this woman. Most likely, Diego wasn't the only one who abused her.

"My husband has no business with you anymore." Lupe's tone could have frozen boiling water. "He paid our debt to you when you stole our daughter. You aren't welcome here anymore."

"I have some other unfinished business with Diego. I need to see him." Eduardo refused to allow Lupe to intimidate him. "If he isn't home right now, I can wait." He swung down off his horse.

"He's gone." Lupe took a step back. "I'll tell him you were here. He can come to your house."

"That won't do. My wife doesn't need any reminders of what she suffered when she lived here." He took a step forward. "If Diego isn't here, may I speak with Jose?"

Lupe's confidence seemed to melt away. She gave a fearful glance toward the house as she took a couple of shuffling steps back.

"I met Diego's cousin, Jose, in Tucson a few days ago. I'd like to talk to him, too."

"He's not here." She grasped the post at the edge of the porch, causing it to creak as she hauled herself up a step. "Neither one of them is here. Now, go away."

Eduardo stayed where he was as Lupe edged into the house. The woman was lying and scared to death about something. He would almost be willing to bet that Jose, at least, had stayed at home today. Eduardo swung up on El Rey. Staying here didn't make sense. Lupe wouldn't allow him in the house, and he couldn't force his way in. As he left, he deliberately followed the road until he couldn't be seen from the house. Then, he cut up into the hills until he had a perfect view of the place, yet couldn't be seen. Tying the stallion where he would be out of sight, Eduardo picked a good place and hunkered down to watch what Lupe would do.

He didn't have long to wait. Only about ten minutes passed before Jose exited the house in a hurry, Lupe on his heels. Even from this distance, Eduardo could see from her movements and gestures she was giving him orders about something. Jose saddled a horse, mounted, and raced down a path that would take him to the river. Eduardo scrambled back to El Rey. He would follow Jose, who would hopefully lead him to Diego. Maybe then he could get the truth from the two of them.

Lucio had done a good job caring for her garden while they were in Tucson, but Chiquita was glad to be back. She carried water for the plants, moistening the ground where the weeds grew. After they soaked awhile, they would be easier to pull. In the dry ground, the roots merely broke off rather than coming up.

She carefully examined the plants for any bugs or worms that might do damage. The summer squash were already blooming. She touched a yellow blossom with her fingertip. In a few days, there would be enough flowers that she could afford to pull a few to fry for their supper. By tomorrow, one of the baby squash would be big enough to use for their meal. Her mouth watered at the thought.

Humming a wordless tune, Chiquita began to pull the weeds from around her tomatoes. When asked about them, Lucio shrugged and said tomato plants made him sneeze. He'd done well with the rest of the garden, though. Pilar apologized for not helping. She hadn't been feeling well for the past week. Today, Rico said she felt better, but he insisted on her resting most of the time. Chiquita missed spending time with her friend.

Since marrying Eduardo, Chiquita couldn't believe how many friends she had. After spending her growing-up years virtually alone, having Eduardo and all his friends accept her made her happier than she thought possible. When they returned from Tucson, she realized, for the first time, that she belonged here. She had a bond to this place and these people.

A shout came from the direction of the barn. Chiquita sat back on her heels and shaded her brow, wondering what the commotion meant. From here, the big mesquite tree blocked her view, so she couldn't make out much. She heard Lucio shout again and decided to investigate. She needed a drink anyway.

After taking a long sip from the dipper beside the water bucket, Chiquita walked to the front of the house, where she would have an unobstructed view of the barn. Lucio was running across the pasture where the mares and foals were kept. Tomas followed after him. Across the field, the horses stood in a group, facing away from the house. Chiquita couldn't see what they were looking at, but she knew something was wrong.

Picking up her skirt so she wouldn't trip, she trotted across the yard to the fence surrounding the pasture. Lucio and Tomas were pushing the mares to one side. In the center of the group something struggled on the ground. Dread crept through Chiquita. She hurried to the gate and dashed across the field.

Two foals were tangled together in a mass of rope and ocotillo fence. Their white-rimmed eyes reflected their panic. One began to struggle, and the other joined in, causing the thorny cactus to dig deeper into them.

"Hold this one still, Lucio." Tomas held a knife. With his knee and his left arm, he tried to hold the second foal.

"What happened?" Chiquita reached for the filly and tried to soothe her.

"The fence broke." Lucio's expression was grim. "Somehow, these two got caught in the rope when they ran past. The whole thing wrapped around them."

"How could this happen? You just checked this fence." Chiquita knew Eduardo wouldn't allow any of the fences to be in disrepair.

"I walked this line myself, yesterday." Lucio ground out the words. "I'm not sure how this happened, but when I get the chance, I'll do some checking."

Tomas seemed to take forever before he began to cut. Chiquita found herself wanting to yell at him to hurry before the foals bled to death.

Tomas glanced at her. "If I cut the wrong way first, they're likely to struggle more. If the fence digs in too deep, they'll lose too much blood and die."

Chiquita stroked the small head. She thought of all the times she looked out her window and watched these babies buck and gallop around the pasture. Seeing them hurt made her heart ache. She knew Eduardo would feel the pain, too.

"Is there something I can do?"

"In the barn." Tomas motioned with his head. "In the tack room is a jar of salve. When I clip the rope, it will help if we put that on to slow the bleeding."

"I'll be right back." She raced across the field, into the tack area of the barn. Rummaging through the brushes and other equipment, she found a tin of salve. A loud clank echoed at the far end of the barn. She glanced that way but didn't have time to investigate. One of the dogs must be nosing through the stalls back there.

"Is this what you need?" Out of breath, she knelt slowly so she didn't startle the foals.

"That's it. Set the tin down over there, where it won't get trampled." Lucio had his hands full as the filly thrashed, trying to get free.

"Can you go fix a stall?" Tomas wiped the sweat from his forehead. The long ocotillo sticks were hard to work with. "When we get them free, we'll need a clean, dry place for them. If you could put down some straw in one of the empty stalls, that would help."

Chiquita trotted back to the barn. The tension exhausted her. She wished Eduardo would return. He would want to help with this. Midway down the aisle of the barn, she peered into an empty stall. The floor, clean-swept, would be easy to prepare. She only had to spread some fresh straw to have it ready.

"You won't get away this time."

Her breath caught at the voice behind her. Closing her eyes, she prayed for strength and help. Turning, she faced Diego. He stood close to her, an unlit torch in one hand, a cigarette dangling from the corner of his mouth. A tendril of smoke curled up past one eye.

"What do you want?"

His eyes widened. For a moment he stared at her. His eyes narrowed, turning his expression to one of hatred. "All those years, you pretended to be dumb.

Now, you marry someone with a little money, and you think you're better than we are."

"You're the one who that made me marry Eduardo. He thought he was marrying Teresa, but you tricked him with me, remember?"

"Shut up." He slapped her hard enough to knock her back a step. She resisted the urge to touch her stinging cheek.

"I'm here to take care of you, myself. I sent that incompetent fool to get rid of you, and look what happened."

"What are you talking about?" Apprehension clutched at her. Had Diego been the one trying to kill her? Why?

His lips turned up in a sinister smile. "You have to die, you see. I should have gotten rid of you years ago, but you were a hard worker, so we kept you around. That was a mistake."

"I don't understand."

"I guess it doesn't matter if I tell you now. By the time those vaqueros get the foals loose, you'll be dead anyway."

She shuddered. He'd deliberately hurt the horses so he could get her alone. How could she have lived in the same house with this man and never realized how devious he was?

"You were brought to us when you were a little baby. Your mama, my uncle's daughter, wasn't married when she had you. Some drifter passing through caught her out alone and took advantage of her. After you were born, my uncle said she had to get rid of you." He took the cigarette from his mouth.

"Your mama knew she couldn't go against her papa. He was a hard man. She convinced Jose to bring you to us. She paid us to keep you. That's where we got the money for the place we have." He gave a malevolent chuckle. "You bought that for us.

"Everything went along just fine until right after you were married. Jose showed up saying my uncle died. Your mama, Bella, is now a wealthy woman. She's been looking for us since we disappeared years ago. We didn't want her to know how we used the money. I couldn't let you tell her how you've been raised. She wouldn't approve, and that means we wouldn't get any money from her. That's why we hid from her years ago. We were only waiting to hear about her inheritance; then we would let her know where we were."

He touched the end of the cigarette to the torch, then dropped the cigarette in the dirt, grinding it out with the toe of his boot. The cloth smoldered, then caught. Chiquita's heart pounded. She wanted to scream that this couldn't be true.

"Now, you understand. If we get rid of you, we can give her a sob story about how you died of disease a few years back. Jose and I even put in a grave with a marker so she can go there and cry awhile. Part of the bargain was that if we did our best by you, she would reward us handsomely when her father died. Her brother is in charge of the estate, but she received a large share under his authority."

The torch flame burned brighter, dark smoke spiraling upwards. The scent of fire made the few horses in stalls restless. Diego glanced at the door.

"I've talked enough." He took two strides and reached a lantern hanging from a nail in the wall. After twisting off the cap to the oil reservoir, he tossed the lid on the ground and plucked the lantern from the wall. She knew, without asking, what he intended to do as he walked toward her.

"Diego, no." She tried to stand strong against him, but the venomous gleam in his eye sent a tremor of fear through her. The fear of fire that plagued her since childhood overwhelmed her.

Chapter 20

Her senses heightened. She took in every detail—the dirt under Diego's fingernails, the faint crackling of the flames, the crunch of the straw littering the aisle as Diego walked toward her, the all-too-familiar smell of cigarettes that clung to him, the acrid taste of fear in her mouth. Faint thunder rumbled outside.

Catching the bottom of the lantern in his right hand, Diego lifted it high. Chiquita's skin began to prickle as terror shot through her. Unexpected energy washed over her. She jumped to the side as Diego began the downward motion intended to douse her with oil. Her hand jerked up, knocking his arm aside.

The thunder grew louder. Three horses raced up to the barn, their hooves sending a shower of dirt into the air as they slid to a stop. She heard Eduardo yell. She tried to turn and run to him. Her foot slipped. The fall knocked the air from her lungs. She could almost feel the heat from the torch. The stench of oil and smoke filled her nostrils as she finally drew in a breath. She rolled, trying to get away from Diego, praying for Jesus to help. Someone screamed, a horrible, fear-laden sound. The stench of burning flesh made her gag.

✤

Eduardo leaned over El Rey's neck, urging the stallion to run faster. Rico and Jorge followed behind him, their grim and determined expressions matching his own. The horses' hooves thundered on the road leading back to the ranch house.

When he left the Garcia place, following Diego's cousin, Jose, Eduardo hadn't gone far before he realized Jose was taking the back way to the Villegas ranch. Taking a shortcut, Eduardo came around in front of Jose and stopped him. The man tried to put up a front, but Eduardo had little trouble convincing him to tell the truth about Diego. While he was getting the answers he needed, Rico and Jorge rode up to see if he needed help. He couldn't have been more grateful to them, especially when he found out that Diego had gone to find Chiquita in order to make sure she was out of the way.

Leaving Jose behind, the three rode hard and fast to the ranch. Eduardo couldn't remember when he'd prayed so hard. He knew Chiquita would be outside working in the garden or doing other chores. Diego would have little trouble getting to her. Even with Tomas and Lucio watching, any little distraction would keep them busy elsewhere long enough for Diego to harm Chiquita.

For the first time in years, Eduardo realized he wasn't filled with anger. He did feel concern and determination, but this had nothing to do with the unhealthy rage he would have felt a few weeks ago.

As they raced from the river road toward the barn, Eduardo could see Lucio and Tomas in the field with the horses. He wanted to shout at them. What were they doing there rather than watching over his wife? Lucio glanced up, saw the riders, and motioned wildly at Eduardo to join them. He knew he couldn't possibly see what Lucio wanted until he found Chiquita and made sure she was all right.

The rumble of hoofbeats echoed as they hit the hard-packed ground of the barnyard. Hauling in on the reins, Eduardo's gaze was drawn to the open barn doors. In an instant, he took in the scene. Chiquita stood with her back to a stall, facing Diego. Diego held a lantern over his head with one hand and a burning torch in the other. Eduardo's heart thudded. Even someone as cruel as Diego wouldn't do something this evil.

"No!" He hit the ground running almost before El Rey slid to a stop.

He saw Chiquita fall. Diego's arm, knocked aside by Chiquita, flew up. At the same time, Diego must have heard Eduardo's yell. He pivoted. The oil from the lantern splashed across his shirt and his face, then ran down his chest and back.

Squinting his eyes closed to keep the oil out, Diego began to wipe the liquid away. The torch, brushing by his face, flared. The flames touched the oil, igniting and spreading rapidly, following the trail across his body. Diego screamed. Dropping the torch and lantern, he ran from the barn. Eduardo tried to intercept him, but Diego moved too fast.

As Diego raced across the barnyard, the flames leapt higher, fueled on by the fresh air and wind. Rico and Jorge both ran after him. Eduardo turned back to the barn. The discarded torch had caught the straw-littered floor on fire. Snatching up a saddle blanket, Eduardo began to beat at the flames. The need to get to Chiquita urged him on. He had to get the fire out first before he checked to see if she was hurt. Finally, he knelt beside his wife. She lay curled in a ball on the ground.

"Chiquita." He touched her. She flinched. "It's me, my love."

Her tear-streaked face turned to him. "Eduardo?" She almost flung herself at him. He pulled her close, sitting down on the floor to rock her as she sobbed. An unbelievable peace stole over him. Despite all that had happened, he knew everything would work out just fine.

❧

"Come on, keep your eyes closed a minute longer." Eduardo led Chiquita by the hand, his pulse racing in excited anticipation. One of the things he recalled about his parents was their ability to have fun together. After all that had happened to him and Chiquita since they married, he knew they needed to find a way to laugh.

Chiquita had difficulty sleeping some nights. The image of Diego's burned body haunted her. She often struggled with guilt over not being the right kind of daughter that he could love, even though he wasn't her natural father. After Diego's death, Lupe insisted on returning to California with Jose, choosing to go home to relatives there. Eduardo made Lupe tell them the whole story. He wanted Chiquita to realize her mother had to do what she'd done, and the deception and cruelty were Diego and Lupe's fault. Lupe admitted that Bella had been a virtual prisoner in her own home. Although Lupe said Chiquita could have the land and house she grew up in since they'd used her money to purchase the place, Eduardo still insisted on paying her something. He couldn't see leaving her destitute when she still had four daughters to raise.

"Can I open my eyes yet?"

"In one minute." Eduardo positioned her so she would have the best view when he let her look. He ignored the drops of sweat trickling down his back. Placing the bundle he carried in the soft grass, he stood to one side of his wife. He wanted to see her reaction to this place. She'd never been here before.

"Okay, you can look."

Her eyes flew open. She blinked. Her mouth dropped open, her eyes wide. A slow smile lit her face.

He glanced to the side, looking at the view she saw. This small, natural spring had been one of his parents' favorite places. Surrounded by cottonwood trees, the oval pond formed by the stream looked cool and inviting. Sunlight rippled in sparkling waves across the half of the water that wasn't shaded. Grass grew in abundance here, the blades reaching almost to his knees in spots.

"It's beautiful." Chiquita's voice held a note of awe. "I didn't know this was here."

He put an arm around her shoulders and tugged her close. "My parents used to come here quite a bit during the summer. This was their special place. I thought maybe we could make this our place now."

She looked up, her eyes shining. "I just can't believe a place like this exists here."

"Take off your shoes. The grass feels wonderful on your feet." Eduardo sat down and tugged his boots off. Chiquita giggled and removed her slippers. He could see her toes wiggling through the soft, green blades.

He clambered to his feet. "Now, I want to show you what my parents used to do here." She smiled up at him, totally unprepared for what he was about to do. He swept her into his arms and stepped to the edge of the water. Her eyes widened in shock as he swung her in the air and let go. The splash as she hit the water almost drowned out her gasp.

Spluttering, she floundered for a moment before discovering she could stand. He knew the water only came to her shoulders at the deepest part.

"Why did you do that? My clothes are soaked." She started for the bank.

"Don't you dare come out here, or I'll throw you back in again."

She glared at him. Tossing his hat on the ground, Eduardo jumped. Landing in the pond close to Chiquita, his resulting splash soaked her again. The shock of the cool water faded, replaced by sheer enjoyment. He laughed. Eduardo couldn't remember the last time he'd laughed like this.

Chiquita stared at him. Her braid had come partially undone. Strands of drenched hair streamed across her face and shoulders. Her eyes began to twinkle. He couldn't seem to stop laughing.

Drawing her hand back, she brought the palm forward through the water, lifting at the last minute to send a huge splash directly into his mouth. He sputtered.

"War it is, my love." He sent a splash back at her, making her squeal and stumble away.

In minutes, she was using both hands to get him as wet as he was getting her. Her melodic laugh startled him. He realized he'd never heard her laugh before. Diving for her, he pinned her arms to her body as she squealed and fought him. Catching both of her hands in one of his, he caught her face with his other hand. She quit laughing as he gave her a long, lingering kiss.

"This is what I want for us, Chiquita." His voice was husky with emotion. "We'll have a lot of hard work, but I want us to laugh and enjoy one another. Do you think we can do that?"

She tugged one hand free and caressed his cheek. "Yes. I love you so much, even when you try to drown me." She chuckled. "What if I couldn't swim?"

"I would have been your handsome prince and jumped in to save you."

She giggled. "I thought the prince always had his servant do the dangerous work."

"Then I'll be the servant who rescues you, my lady." They both dissolved in gales of laughter.

The afternoon sun was waning as they strolled, hand in hand, back to the house. Eduardo had brought a change of clothes for each of them so they didn't have to wear their wet things home. They waved to Lucio and Tomas, seeing the pair exercising the foals that'd been hurt. The babies would be fine after a few more days of pampering.

A buggy stood outside the house. Chiquita glanced up. "Were you expecting company?" Her hand lifted to her damp, loose hair.

He frowned in thought. "No, not that I know of. Whoever it is, Rico or Pilar must have let them inside."

The door creaked shut behind them. As they entered the living room, an older woman rose. Her well-made gown suggested money. She looked familiar, but it took a moment before Eduardo knew where he'd seen her before. She was an older, darker version of Chiquita. This must be Bella, her mother.

"Estrella?" The woman took a hesitant step forward. "I'm sorry. I hear you are called Chiquita now. I've always thought of you as Estrella."

Chiquita's eyes widened in understanding. She glanced at Eduardo. He smiled and nudged her forward.

"My name is Bella. I've waited so many years to see you." The woman's voice broke. She stretched out a slender, gloved hand to Chiquita. "I wanted you to know—I loved you so much. I'm so sorry your birth had to be kept a secret for so long." Tears glittered in her eyes.

Chiquita hesitated only a moment longer. With a cry, she flew across the room into her mother's arms. Eduardo left them to get acquainted. He would have time to join them later.

That evening, after supper, they sat together in the living room. Eduardo held his wife's hand as she snuggled next to him. After her mother retired, they sat for awhile, enjoying the quiet and each other's company.

"I've tried to get used to calling you Estrella, but I can't." Eduardo spoke softly near her ear. "That's such a beautiful name for a beautiful woman. You do remind me of a shining star, but somehow you'll always be my Chiquita. Do you mind if I call you that?"

She shook her head. "I will always love you calling me Chiquita."

He kissed her. "Can you tell me what you and your mother talked about?"

Chiquita gazed up at him, her expression more peaceful than he could ever recall. "She's so beautiful, isn't she?"

Eduardo caressed her cheek. "You look just like her."

Chiquita lowered her gaze. "I don't know how I could. For so long I've thought of myself as ugly, it's hard to think otherwise." She gave a sad smile. "My mother felt so bad. She already talked to Jose and found out how Lupe and Diego treated me. It's nice to know she thought of me and wanted me all these years. Her father was a tyrant—almost as bad as Diego."

"I'm glad you're not angry at her." Eduardo couldn't seem to quit touching her.

"I think this is all such a shock. Maybe if I'd thought I had a choice, I might have been bitter. Although Jesus could take that bitterness away, I'm so glad that all I feel is love for her."

"Come here. I want to show you something." Eduardo pulled her up from the couch and led her to the mirror hanging on the wall. "Look." His hands on her shoulders, he made her face the looking glass.

She stared at the floor. "I can't. You know that."

"Please, for me." He brushed a strand of hair from her cheek.

Reluctantly, she glanced up. She'd never had the courage to look in a mirror. The young woman looking back caught her eye. She stared. The face was her mother's, only much younger. She had lighter hair and eyes, but her features resembled Bella's.

"You see." Eduardo's whispered words sent a shiver through her. "You are beautiful, just like your mother."

They were quiet a few minutes before Chiquita spoke again. "She told me about my father and what happened. She had been visiting a friend. While she was returning home, this man tricked her into thinking he was injured. She got off her horse to help him, and he attacked her." A tear slid down her cheek. "Even after all these years, she still carries the hurt from what he did."

"You mustn't think of him, though, my love. Consider the gift God's given you of such a great mother." He turned her to face him and put his arms around her.

She smiled up at him, her hand stroking his cheek. "And, what a gift I have in you."

He smiled. "All I wanted was someone to be here in the lonely evenings, and God blessed me with you. I love you so much."

Her eyes shone with love as she returned the kiss he gave her. "I love you, too."

A Letter to Our Readers

Dear Readers:

In order that we might better contribute to your reading enjoyment, we would appreciate you taking a few minutes to respond to the following questions. When completed, please return to the following: Fiction Editor, Barbour Publishing, Inc., P.O. Box 719, Uhrichsville, OH 44683.

1. Did you enjoy reading *Tucson?*
   - ❑ Very much—I would like to see more books like this.
   - ❑ Moderately—I would have enjoyed it more if _____
   _____

   _____

2. What influenced your decision to purchase this book? (Check those that apply.)
   - ❑ Cover
   - ❑ Back cover copy
   - ❑ Title
   - ❑ Price
   - ❑ Friends
   - ❑ Publicity
   - ❑ Other

3. Which story was your favorite?
   - ❑ *Sonoran Sunrise*
   - ❑ *Sonoran Sweetheart*
   - ❑ *Sonoran Star*
   - ❑ *Sonoran Secret*

4. Please check your age range:
   - ❑ Under 18
   - ❑ 18–24
   - ❑ 25–34
   - ❑ 35–45
   - ❑ 46–55
   - ❑ Over 55

5. How many hours per week do you read? _____

Name _____

Occupation _____

Address _____

City _____ State _____ Zip _____

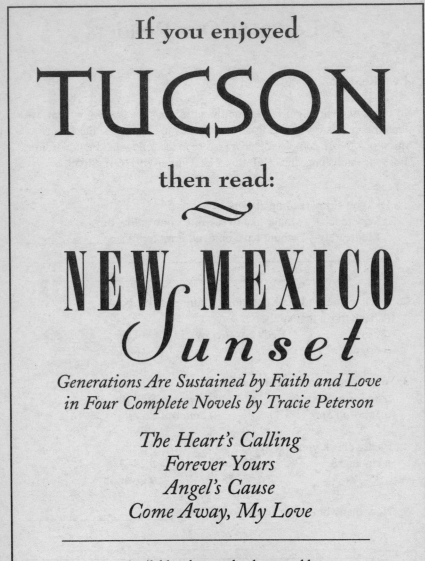

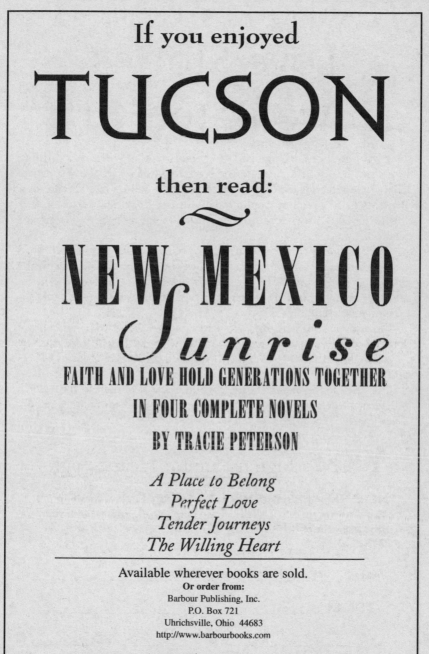